GARDEN OF SORROW
KNOCK KNOCK...
RARE FIND

Books #4–6 of Psychic Visions

Dale Mayer

PSYCHIC VISIONS SET 4–6
Beverly Dale Mayer
Valley Publishing Ltd.

ISBN: 978-1-988315-73-7
Print Edition

About This Boxed Set

Garden of Sorrow

After spend a brutal year trying to cope after the loss of her sister, Alexis Gordon knows she needs to get on with her life. Only, instead of the normal work day she'd anticipated as the means to begin her journey back to the land of the living, reality as she knows it disappears…

Kevin Sutherland is a detective and a psychic. Recognizing Alexis's gift and aware she has no idea what's happening to her, he calls his friend and frequent case consultant, Stefan Kronos, an artist with psychic gifts. Stefan leads a community of psychics able to help Alexis understand and develop her unique skills.

Alexis has unwittingly become involved in a case unlike anything Kevin has ever seen before. The killer seems to have a personal vendetta against Alexis herself. He intends to eliminate her before she uses her psychic gift to discover not only his identity but the garden of sorrow he's buried his long-dead victims.

Only Alexis can stop this madman who fully intends to survive…even after death.

Knock Knock…

Revenge has no best-by date. On the contrary, it's ideally served cold…

Wealthy and beautiful Shay Lassiter runs a prestigious foundation that she built with her considerable connections and resources. Both amounted to less than nothing the day her fiancé tried to murder her. Who to trust? Shay guards her heart…while using her knack for reading people's intentions, whether they're good or evil, to guide her through the dark, unfathomable maze that's become her normal life. Inexplicably, foundation clients start dying. Shay turns to the new man she's been seeing – computer specialist and ex-cop Roman Chandler – needing his protection.

Roman has been giving her mixed signals in order to keep a secret that involves Shay and could easily ruin the fragile relationship he wants to build with her. Damningly, he can't tell her the truth, so he somehow has to convince her to trust him instead.

Whoever's behind the troubles plaguing Shay's world is about to turn his need for revenge on the source of his rage. When vengeance comes knocking, the results are sure to be deadly…

Rare Find

Injured people in need of aid call out to friends and family or even strangers for help. Who can animals turn to who would not only hear them but understand their cry for help? Such a creature would truly be a rare find.

Determined to bury her aching heart in service of her animals at Exotic Landscape, Tabitha is caught unaware when she's yanked out of her cozy little retreat by the appeal of someone needing rescue. Responding to that call gets her more trouble than she bargained for.

Understanding secrets isn't difficult for someone with quite a few of his own, but Detective Ronin Chandler learns that the mysteries of the universe can take on a whole new level of meaning. With the woman he loves in jeopardy, Ronin struggles to comprehend what's happening, what Tabitha needs, and how to even help her…before he loses her, maybe forever.

Danger escalates at every turn. Determining who to trust – and who not to – becomes as much of a challenge as figuring out who wants them dead.

Sign up to be notified of all Dale's releases here!
https://geni.us/DaleNews

Books in This Series:

Tuesday's Child
Hide 'n Go Seek
Maddy's Floor
Garden of Sorrow
Knock Knock…
Rare Find
Eyes to the Soul
Now You See Her
Shattered
Into the Abyss
Seeds of Malice
Eye of the Falcon
Itsy-Bitsy Spider
Unmasked
Deep Beneath
From the Ashes
Stroke of Death
Ice Maiden
Snap, Crackle…
What If…
Talking Bones
String of Tears
Inked Forever
Psychic Visions Books 1–3
Psychic Visions Books 4–6
Psychic Visions Books 7–9

USA *Today* Bestselling Author

DALE MAYER

A Psychic Visions Novel

GARDEN OF SORROW

Dedication

This book is dedicated to my four children, who always believed in me and my storytelling abilities.

Thank you!

Acknowledgments

Garden of Sorrow wouldn't have been possible without the support of my friends and family. Many hands helped with proofreading, editing, and beta reading to make this book come together. Special thanks to my editor Pat Thomas.

I thank you all.

PROLOGUE

*I*F ONLY HE *could turn back time, … be there when he'd been needed.*
The night was bright and clear. The moon full, happy. The opposite of what he wanted, what he felt. There should be thunder and lightning destroying the world, … just as his world had just been destroyed.

He sat in the borrowed truck and studied the funeral home. Inside the stone building lay that beautiful little one, cold and alone. He couldn't stand it—that she was dead, that he'd never hold her again, never play with her or bring her gifts or watch the sunshine break free with her smile. It broke his heart … and damn-near crippled his soul. To think of her inside that box, … alone for all eternity, … was too much to bear. For all its fancy brass and plush interior that coffin would seal her up and would keep them apart forever.

He couldn't lose her. He loved her too much. That said everything … and nothing. The term *love* was overused, misunderstood, and didn't begin to explain this ache so strong it had turned the pit of his stomach to a cavern of emptiness. How could one adequately describe the light of your life? The reason you got up each day? She'd been his savior in this dark existence. His reason for being.

She couldn't go into that grave. So dark. So far away. So alone.

It couldn't happen.

He wouldn't let it.

Irrational blind rage boiled inside him. She was a child, but she'd been the only light in his world. That she'd died *not* in an accident was just another wrong he couldn't prevent. It happened when he hadn't been there to look after her. He'd been away. He hadn't wanted to go. But he'd had no choice.

He couldn't fight everyone all the time. He and she had both had a shitty life, her and him. At least *her* suffering was over.

Now his was just beginning. He had to go on. With his new purpose—to make them pay.

But he couldn't do it alone. He had to have her at his side.

Somehow. Somewhere. Someone would help him make that happen.

CHAPTER 1

Many Years Later

SHE SHOULD HAVE stayed in bed.

"Un-freaking-believable." Alexis Gordon stood, hands on her hips, at the edge of chaos. Cops, kids, dignitaries, and everything in-between wandered through the green spaces of the park. She sniffed the aroma of hot buttered popcorn and hot dogs permeating the air.

Smaller communities, like theirs, got fanatical about local events—like today's groundbreaking ceremony for the new gardens. A ceremony to celebrate the completion of the gardens made sense to her. Too bad the politicians in the small community of Bradford, Oregon, used events like this to garner votes. Not just at the beginning of the ceremony but at the end too. Bradford was smaller than Portland but independent, like neighboring Gresham. And Bradford politics were a complicated issue.

Alexis blew out a gust of breath and ran her fingers through her long superfine hair. Why hadn't she stayed home? She was a gardener, not a politician, and it was Sunday, after all. At least she didn't have to wear her work boots today. But her presence, apparently, was mandatory, since she was employed by the city.

Tucking her yellow cotton shirt into her faded jeans, she headed away from the crowd and behind the cordoned-off construction area. Her crew had set up a makeshift bridge to cross the huge culvert, where the city was installing new sewer pipes. That ditch clearly resembled a wading pool after last night's rain. Scott McIver, her immediate boss and best friend and father figure and big brother, approached from the other side.

"Hey, Alexis, be careful! Without work boots, that thing's a bitch."

Alexis nodded at Scott's warning, refusing to let her lightweight sneakers keep her from crossing the bridge. She kept her eyes firmly glued to the slick surface in front of her. Once at the other end, she grinned in triumph, reached for his outstretched hand, and jumped the last foot. "See? No probl—"

The soft dirt edge fell away from under her foot, as she landed on the left one, and her fingers slipped from his grasp. "Shit!"

"Jesus, Alex!" Scott made a grab for her ... and missed.

His voice rolled over her, as she tumbled in a mad downward scramble, clawing against the dirt wall for something solid to grab, but still in a slow muddy slide. A fresh puddle of muck waited for her at the bottom.

"Oh, hell!" The oath slipped out, as she pulled herself up on her hands and knees, grimacing, as slime oozed between her fingers. "I don't need this today." The smell of wet earth and minerals assailed her senses. It might be a new ditch, but it already smelled like a sewer.

Everything ached, but nothing appeared damaged. She was more pissed at herself than anything. Alexis glanced up to see Scott staring down at her, a worried frown deepening his heavily wrinkled face. "I'm okay. Just give me a minute."

Feeling more or less normal—if disgusting were normal—she attempted to stand. As she pushed against the ground to get up, something sharp dug into the palm of her hand. Her fingers automatically closed over it, only it squished out the top of her fist and back into the mud.

"Ouch." A thin stream of red oozed from her mud-covered fingers. Whatever that thing was, it had scratched her palm. She stared at the surrounding puddle. Where had it gone? There, beside her right foot. Alexis leaned over for a closer look.

It couldn't be.

Several voices called down to her. She ignored them and tugged the muddy piece free. Blowing away several strands of hair blocking her view, she swished the item around in the rainwater and cleaned off most of the dirt.

Small, white, and with a distinctive shape, it resembled a bone. More like several tiny bones barely connected by stiff mud. And, oh God. ... It looked like ... *a finger!*

Ice settled into her spine. She held a finger.

A tiny finger.

A child's finger, still wearing a toy ring.

Her fingers tightened around the fragile piece. Her insides warred to keep the precious item safe, while another part of her wanted to throw it far away from her.

Then something changed.

Dizziness and nausea fought for supremacy, as her vision blurred. Disoriented, she wavered, as the ditch before her suddenly lengthened and narrowed, morphing into an interior hallway.

Alexis froze, her horrified gaze locked on the changing scene.

Dear God, what was going on? Her mind raced to sort out the change. How had the dirt bank turned to gray paint? And the sewer smell now smothered by heavy cooking odors? Fried chicken?

Where was she?

Alexis stared down the hallway. A young child, caught inside this peculiar scenario, stumbled toward her, with both hands clasped over her ears. Tears streamed down her young face, and her T-shirt was inches above the dirty shorts. Bruises decorated her lower legs, and, well, … dirt covered the rest of her. As if she'd recently been playing in a dirt pile. Alexis tried to run to her, to hug her tight, to protect her, … only to find she couldn't move. Her feet were paralyzed in place. Terror filled her heart.

She opened her mouth to scream. No sound came out.

Run. The scream seared through her mind.

Dimly in the background, loud crashes and yelling could be heard, as if someone gave chase. Fear of retribution accented every step the distraught child took. The sound and tone distorted.

Alexis shuddered. Tears clogged her throat, and pain choked her heart.

"Alexis. Alex? Alex!"

Scott's alarmed voice pulled at her from outside the vision that held her transfixed. Caught between two realities, Alexis jerked toward Scott, the object dropping from her fingers.

Instantly the hallway disappeared, as if a vacuum had sucked the dirt walls back into place, with a rush so powerful it forced Alexis to lean forward. Then, as if caught in a giant rubber band, the force suddenly released, throwing her into reverse. She flew backward and landed, once again, on her butt in the middle of the large puddle.

Her gut screamed, and bile tried to escape her throat. She shuddered. What the hell had just happened? She swallowed convulsively, willing her breakfast to stay down. Tremors started at her toes and rattled up her spine.

"Alexis, damn it. Answer me!" Scott demanded.

"I—I'm fine." Was that croaking *her* voice? The finger. … Where was it? More than a little daunted by the prospect of touching it again, she remained seated and eyed the surrounding mud.

There.

It rested on the muddy surface, … waiting for her.

Eerie. She hated to touch it again, the last experience too horrific to repeat. She reached for it, but her fingers shook so badly that she stopped. Yet she couldn't force herself to leave it behind. Compromising, she pulled a tissue from her shirt pocket and gingerly picked up the finger.

The size bothered her. The vague image of the running child from a few moments ago slammed back. Ruthlessly she pushed the vision from her mind. She couldn't even begin to analyze what had happened. It had been way too weird. Alexis focused on what was important right this moment. *Where there is one finger …*

She studied the high expanse of dirt wall. She dimly remembered digging her fingers into the bank on her downward tumble. But how high up had she been? The ditch stood eight to ten feet deep.

"Here's the ladder, Alexis," Scott said, as Mike, another coworker, arrived with the ladder. Scott held the long metal structure several feet off to the side.

"No!" she motioned. "Please, bring it over here. Where I fell in."

Scott shrugged, and the two moved the ladder to the right spot.

Alexis struggled to position it the best she could, near her original flight path. Once the ladder was secured, she moved upward, one rung at a time. At each new level, she stopped and searched. The bone must have come from somewhere.

"Oh, for the love of God. Alexis, what are you doing?" Scott peered over the ladder at her.

Alexis didn't answer. What could she say? Three, maybe four feet from the top, a speck of white caught her eye. Reaching between the ladder rungs, she gently brushed some of the dirt away. Another bone, possibly another finger. Vomit lined her throat. She rested her forehead against the steel frame of the ladder for a long moment. "Scott?" Her hands squeezed the ladder tight. She kept her voice low.

"Yes, beautiful. What's going on?" He crouched down for a better look, but he was at the wrong angle.

"Are any police close by?" She cleared her throat, tears suddenly clogging her throat. Willing him to not ask her any questions. "If not, go get one—*now.*"

Startled, Scott stared at her for a brief moment, before disappearing from sight, his heavy footsteps fading rapidly. Mike held the ladder steady. Alexis let her head remain on the rung and waited, her arm wrapped around one side of the ladder. The steel dug into her forehead, as she realized something important.

This wasn't just a ditch. This was a grave.

DETECTIVE KEVIN SUTHERLAND chose a spot off to one side, where he could watch the proceedings. He tugged at his collar and unbuttoned his one good suit jacket. If it weren't for his boss, he wouldn't be here.

This was so not his scene. The warm sun already sent sweat down the small of his back, and he had more hours to go. Irritation pulled at him. He had no time or patience for this. Up half the night on a domestic violence call, he should be catching a few hours of much-needed rest. Instead he'd been badgered into coming here to support his elected officials and to ensure everything went smoothly.

He snorted. Support, his ass. When would they support his request for extra manpower to keep the community safe?

"Kevin, it's good to see you." Mayor John Prescott approached, his hand out to shake. With a wary glance around, John asked in a low voice, "Everything okay?"

Kevin narrowed his gaze on the mingling crowd. "Everything appears fine." He paused. Except for one thing. The hairs on the back of his neck stood on end, a sure sign that something was wrong somewhere.

The mayor nodded. "Great. Let's keep it that way." He sharpened his gaze, locking it on Kevin's face. "Keep that other issue in mind today too."

With a curt nod, Kevin said, "I'm on it."

The mayor returned to the crowd, his politician smile firmly in place.

Kevin slipped farther back from the noise to the large stand of evergreens. He had his own special way of finding out where the trouble came from. Alone, he opened his mind, allowing his senses free rein. From this new perspective, he opened a special portal and reached out mentally, like a trouble-seeking probe, searching.

The music blaring over the loudspeaker mixed with the shrieks of children on the playground. Normal. Widening his perimeter, he checked the parking lot and side streets. That area seemed fine too. Turning slightly, he half-closed his eyes, sending energy behind him.

There.

Cold tendrils of fear crept toward him from the back of the construction area. He did another quick mental check. The energy was calm but insistent. Not static and flaming, which meant the problem wasn't violent or an emergency. But someone needed help.

After a quick survey of the crowd, he took off to answer the silent call.

ALEXIS SHIFTED HER sore butt, as she stood on the ladder. Fatigue like she'd rarely experienced had slid inside her bones. As much as she wanted to distance herself from what she'd found, she felt oddly protective of it too. She could have easily stood guard from above but couldn't leave that little bit of skeleton alone and exposed. It had been part of a person once. To be so lost all this time made Alexis's heart ache.

Rotating her tense shoulders, she waited. Her muddy jeans clung to her calves, and her shoes were a write-off. She shivered in the sunlight. Grief pulled at her for this lost child … and for her own sister. Memories slammed into her. Alexis slammed them back out. This wasn't the time or the place. Still, the trigger refused to be ignored. After all, she'd just found a child's grave, one year to the day when she'd placed her kid sister in one.

"What's the problem here?"

Startled, Alexis tilted her head and squinted up through the morning sun's rays to find a man at odds with his voice. The suit fit the tall muscled frame a little too well for her peace of mind. The angular face and tone of voice said business all the way. She couldn't take her eyes off him. He had to be media.

Better to get rid of him fast. "The media booth is on the other side," she replied, eyeing his suit, the perfect contrast to her fashion statement in mud.

"I'm a cop." He rested his hands on his hips, gazing down at her.

A cop? She reassessed him. Deep-set gray eyes. High cheekbones supported by a square jaw. This man had little patience for fools, regardless of what he wore. Damn, was that a silk shirt? Alexis shook her head. No way he was a cop. "Look. I'm not an idiot. My morning wasn't going well before I got here. Now it's pissed itself right down the drain."

"How appropriate, considering where you're sitting." He reached into his inside jacket pocket and pulled out his badge. "I repeat. What's the problem?" Exasperation sharpened his voice.

Alexis clambered up the last two rungs of the ladder. Seconds later, she stood before him, covered in drying slime. "Let me see that, please."

He held his badge before her face.

"Detective Kevin Sutherland." Okay, maybe he was telling the truth. She held out her hand. With her free hand, she gently unfolded the tissue.

His back stiffened, and his angular face sharpened as he studied the bone. "Where did you get this?"

"When I fell in, I must have dislodged it from the wall. I think more is down there." Alexis pointed in the general direction of the ditch.

"Show me." He was all business now. He stripped off his jacket and tie, discarding both on a spot of clean grass.

Alexis stared, as he started down the ladder. You had to appreciate a man who had his priorities right. She moved to the side of the ladder and pointed. "Search through the third and fourth rungs, off to the left."

A moment later, his heartfelt whisper floated up to her.

"Shit."

CHAPTER 2

HOURS LATER, YELLOW police tape cordoned off the entire park area. Uniforms worked alongside the coroner. A forensic anthropologist had just arrived from Portland, and investigators were collecting trace evidence. In general, it seemed too many authorities were here, but everyone was doing something. The gathered crowd showed no signs of dispersing, the police guarding the area a draw instead of a deterrent. She had to love the curious mind-set of today's society.

Alexis grabbed her work coat from her red Toyota truck, but shivers still racked her body. A hot shower would be perfect right about now, but she couldn't leave.

Somber silence greeted the appearance of the tiny outline in an oversize body bag.

"It isn't right. It just isn't." Scott's Irish accent thickened with sadness.

Alexis tucked her arm through his, appreciating his support and happy to give some in return. She'd become a loner over the years, first from necessity, as the disease had slowly decimated her sister, then out of preference in the aftermath. But this barrel-chested Irishman hadn't let her hide in her darkness. He'd pushed, prodded, and propelled her back to life. She'd hated him for it then. Now he epitomized the father figure she'd never had, the older brother she'd always wanted, and the best friend she'd ever known. "Life isn't fair. Better to learn that now and save yourself some heartache," she murmured.

His disgusted snort washed over her. "You don't believe that drivel. Better to feel and to know you're alive than to walk through life as if you've never lived." His muscled arm wrapped around her shoulders in a clumsy, but caring, hug. "I know you're thinking of your sister. Be hard not to, with all this going on." He swept his other arm wide to encompass the hub of police activity. "Don't hold all that pain inside. Lissa is gone. Time to rejoice in her living. Don't focus so much on her passing." He squeezed gently before letting Alexis go.

Caught on an inward spiral of pain, Alexis barely noticed his intense gaze. Horrified understanding overtook her confusion. Was he right? Had she focused so much on her sister's death that she'd forgotten to honor her life?

Please, let it not be true.

One tear formed at the corner of her eye, hung for a brief moment, then slid down her face.

"Miss, … uh, sorry. I need to get some information from you."

A fresh-faced policeman interrupted Alexis's painful musings. She made no attempt to wipe the tear from her cheek.

"I need to take your statement," he said. "If we could start with your name and address, please."

Scott gently prodded her. "Alexis."

A sidelong glance at Scott's concerned face prompted her to speak. "Alex, … Alexis Gordon."

"What's your full address and phone number?"

Startled, she stared at the cop. He looked like he should be selling raffle tickets for a Boy Scout trip. "Why?"

"You found the body. We need your statement."

Shaken, she quickly supplied the required information, as Scott stood silent at her side. Just as they finished, her irritating district supervisor strode toward them.

"Do you do things like this on purpose? Show up late, sneak in through the back, and wreak havoc on everyone's plans?" *Rick the Dick,* as the rest of them not-so-affectionately called him, glared at the mess of the opening-day ceremony. He too sported a full three-piece suit, although his was more designer than business.

Alexis scowled at the stinging unfairness of Rick's words.

"What a disaster!" her boss snapped.

"That's one way of putting it, Rick." The detective, now with his jacket back on and looking very much the worse for wear, joined their little group. "Hey, Scott. Haven't seen you for a while. Sad day for a reunion." He glanced down at his mud-encrusted clothes, flicking off small clumps still clinging to the material. "These pants are history."

She turned her back on Rick to speak to Scott, trying to ignore the unsettling knowledge that everyone knew each other but her. "Nothing for me to do here, so I'll go home and get cleaned up." She ignored Rick and had done so since he'd refused her time off for her sister's palliative care. She'd gotten it eventually, … after going through the higher-ups. At a price—her relationship with her boss. That Lissa had lasted much longer than the doctors had expected hadn't helped Rick's attitude toward the situation. For Alexis, every additional day had been a gift.

Alexis watched as Scott snuck a sideways glance at their fuming boss. "I'll walk her to her car. Back in a minute."

Scott ushered her toward the parking lot for their first chance to speak privately. He waited until they'd reached the relative quiet of the area before the words exploded from him. "Now that we're alone, what the hell happened to you?"

Alexis stilled, almost convinced that the incident after her fall had gone unnoticed. "I don't know," she admitted. "Maybe I was just a little shaky from the fall."

"Well, you scared the bejeezus out of me." He clasped her face in his big mitts and studied the look in her eyes. "You've been in a fog all morning. If you hadn't let the paramedics check you out, you wouldn't be going home now either." His hands dropped away.

"I'm fine," she retorted. Taking a deep breath, she tried to make light of his concern. "At least *I'm* normally awake." She grinned at the heavily wrinkled man, who loved to nap at every opportunity.

His smile flashed and disappeared just as quickly. "You could've been badly hurt, falling like that." He glanced behind her and frowned.

Alexis pivoted. The coroner's vehicle had made its way through the parking lot to the exit, where it stopped before heading out onto the road. She shivered, tugging her work coat tighter around her.

Should she mention the vision? No. If she couldn't explain it to herself, how could she explain it to him? "Go home and rest." Scott nudged her toward her truck. "I'll go back and sort things out with Rick."

Alexis had an uncanny ability to piss off Rick within seconds of them being together. Scott had warned her several times to button her lip, and, for the most part, she had managed pretty well. This morning's lapse only proved how badly she'd been affected by what she'd found in the culvert.

Scott glanced behind him, probably to make sure she was really leaving. Something odd *had* happened down in the ditch, something besides finding a body, which was enough to rattle anyone. He'd have to wait until she recovered before quizzing her more closely.

But he would.

KEVIN AND RICK stood outside the perimeter of the crime scene tape, when Scott joined them. Rick glared at him, the words, obviously barely held in check, finally burst free. "Damn it, Scott. What the hell is her problem?"

Scott narrowed his eyes. Slurs against his friends were never allowed. Damaged and hurting, gentle Alexis needed his support. Her life had been hell for a long time. She deserved a champion. It didn't matter if she hid her hurt so well that others were fooled by her apparently caustic comments. Behind all that, Alexis had heart. Besides, she never turned on anyone who didn't deserve it.

He held up his hand, forestalling Rick's next outburst. "Her problem is that she just found the grave of a dead child. Come on, Rick. You know about her kid sister. Is it too hard to see that today might trigger some tough stuff for her? Hell, I won't sleep well tonight after this, and I didn't lose anyone."

"What happened to her sister?" Kevin stood off to one side, his gaze going from one to the other.

"She died of cancer a year ago." Scott stopped and frowned. He glanced down at his watch. "Shit. She was buried one year ago today." He glanced up at Kevin. "Such a shame. Just seventeen years old."

Kevin nodded. "Today will trigger all sorts of issues for her. You might consider seeing that she gets some help."

"No room in the budget for stupidity." Rick stared ahead, a muscle in his jaw twitching.

Both men stared at him in surprise.

He glared at them both. "What? She didn't have to walk on that damn bridge. She knows the safety rules as well as anyone." Rick shoved his hands in his pockets. "Shit, I don't need this now. I'm heading home. See you both later."

Scott watched Rick storm off.

"Is he really that cold to her plight? Or is she really a loose screw?" Kevin asked Scott.

How to answer that? Scott didn't know. Was Kevin asking as a cop or as a buddy he'd shared a couple beers with every month? Was there a difference?

"Alexis and Rick have a feud going on. For myself, I side with Alexis, but Rick's my boss, and I don't want to lose my job. I'm not sure Alexis cares about that aspect anymore." He shrugged and glanced at Kevin. "I can tell you this. Their issue has nothing to do with the body part Alexis found."

Scott waited, as Kevin studied his face before he nodded once. "Good enough. If she's earned your loyalty, she must have something going for her."

Someone called Kevin's name.

"Excuse me, Scott. I have to go."

"No problem. Let me know what you find out."

Nothing was good about finding the remains of a child. But to find the child's family? … Now that would help.

ALEXIS MADE HER way to her vehicle. "Rest, he says. After this morning? He's got to be joking."

The crowd was breaking up and filtering through the parking lot, making it difficult to drive. Alexis watched a young mother hug her child tightly to her chest. A grim heavyset man passed them. She sensed these people had experienced a paradigm shift today, one that could set in motion a complete reevaluation, of their lives. Alexis didn't need that shift. Her world had been jolted years ago, when cancer had moved into her home.

Before Lissa's death, Alexis had lived for every moment. She'd savored every remaining hour she'd had with her sister, and still, the precious time had slipped away too fast. At seventeen, cancer had been a painful wasting away of someone so bright, so vibrant, and so full of life. It wasn't fair.

Lissa would laugh, saying, "That's why it's okay for me to leave. I find joy in every second and beauty in all things. Life goes on for both of us. You'll see. I'll find a way to come back and see you." Alexis had always hoped that Lissa had been right, and Alexis had to admit that she'd been looking for a sign from her sister ever since.

Alexis shook off the heavy memory, determined not to focus on any more death, as she rattled her red Toyota truck onto the main road. She just wanted to go home.

Long moments later, she pulled into her parking spot at her apartment building. Serenity Haven. What a joke. The cement building looked more like a juvenile correction center. She hated living here, but she'd sold the family home after Lissa's funeral, unable to deal with the memories. That aside, this place had no soul.

Maybe she'd rented it for just that reason, as a punishment. In what way, she didn't know or understand. Yet it felt like a punishment to drive home to this cold concrete box every day. Maybe it was time to leave.

The idea had merit. Maybe she could find another little house, one with a huge garden, where she could start her hanging-basket business again. She'd built it up, with Lissa's help, as an add-on to her full-time job. The long-term plan was to expand and to eventually make it full-time work. When her sister had gotten sick, Alexis had given it up.

With fresh eyes, Alexis examined her surroundings. The walls leading to the entrance were chipped, peeling, the elevator decorated with graffiti. Even the gray hall leading to her dismal apartment was dingy and showed a lack of care. It was essentially clean, but a sense of desolation permeated the place.

Alexis stopped as she reached her apartment door, casually glancing back down the way she'd come.

And froze.

Horrified recognition washed over her. Terror gripped her throat, before escaping in a gasp of shock. Uncontrollable trembling racked her lean frame. Her fingers lost their grip, and her keys tumbled to the threadbare carpet below.

The hallway. Dear God, it looked to be the same as the one she'd experienced in the ditch.

CHAPTER 3

IT COULDN'T BE!

Alexis bent slowly to retrieve her keys, keeping a wary eye on the hallway. She desperately wanted inside the safety of her apartment but didn't dare turn her back on the creepy space.

Her fingers trembled so much that she couldn't get the damn key to work. Finally the lock clicked. She flung open the door and raced inside, slammed and locked the door behind her. Alexis leaned against the door, shaking and sobbing. Her heart hammered in her chest. What the hell was happening to her? She rubbed away her tears. Her life had been normal up until today—sad in many ways but normal.

It took several long minutes before her legs could function. It took several more before her breathing calmed. Still shaky but no longer panicked, Alexis slowly moved to the bathroom.

"God, I'm cold," she muttered, turning on the water for a hot shower. And so tired. Steam filled the room, as she stripped off her clothes. Alexis scrambled under the hot water, where she tipped her head back and let the full force of the water pour down. The steam soothed her senses, the heat easing her aching muscles. Only when the water ran cold did she turn off the taps. Her legs trembled slightly, as the rough towel whisked off the moisture.

The images wouldn't leave her alone.

That poor child, lost and forgotten in the garden, discarded, ... like garbage. Alexis dressed quickly, pulling on a heavy sweater and tugging her wet hair free of the wool. Shivers rattled her teeth. "Why can't I get warm?" Grabbing a spare towel, she twisted her hair inside it and headed for the kitchen.

She put the kettle on for a hot cup of tea.

While waiting for the water to boil, she gazed out at a world that appeared so calm and normal on the surface. Was she the only one who'd dipped beneath the facade? Had the years of enforced calm—holding it together at all costs, in a world so beyond her control—

damaged her psyche?

Alexis.

The fragile voice broke into her musings. So clear, so sharp, yet so … whispery. Prickles rose on the back of her neck, goose bumps across her skin. *It couldn't be!*

Afraid to look—but more terrified not to—Alexis twisted with agonizing slowness.

Lissa!

A beloved and so familiar wispy vision of her sister sat at the table, as if waiting—like she had for so many years—for her cup of tea.

"Lissa," Alexis whispered, her voice aching with tenderness …

Alexis was petrified that the sound of her own voice would break the spell, … and the miracle of her sister's presence would disappear. She'd hoped for, prayed for, such a visit. Her heart swelled with joy … and awe … and fear. "Lissa, is that you?"

The apparition flickered, then slowly began to fade.

"No, don't go, Lissa!" Alexis cried out. "Please," she begged. "Please don't go!" Her voice faded, as the vision dissipated into the air.

It was too much.

Alexis crumpled at the table, her head in her arms, and sobbed out the last year of grief and loss. Pain, held in too long, burst free. Her shoulders shook uncontrollably, as her body weathered the storm.

Eventually the tempest expended itself, leaving a heavier exhaustion and an emotional devastation behind. Alexis laid her cheek against the cheap Formica tabletop, staring at the spot where she'd thought she'd seen her sister. The occasional hot tear still welled up to slide down her cheeks.

What was happening to her? Was she having a breakdown? That would make sense. She'd endured a horrific amount of stress and loss in her world. … But why now? On the anniversary date? The time to break down would have been the day she'd buried her sister. But for it to happen a year later? … That didn't make sense.

The teakettle whistled on cue. That was normal. After all, she'd put that teakettle on. She could accept that—unlike the rest of her day. Feeling as if she'd aged fifty years, she poured water over the teabag and watched the tea stain the liquid. Wafting her hand over the top, the steam warmed her fingers—as it should. This was the normal, the usual, and the right.

She'd survived Lissa's death because she'd depended on that normalcy. She expected it. She counted on it.

And today her whole world had been blown apart by—dare she say it—a vision, a body, and … a ghost.

THE WIND BLEW hard outside the double glass doors. Branches swiped the edge of the railing, making a faint scratching sound, … like a ghost asking to come into the private nursing home room.

The older man chuckled. No such thing as a ghost. If there were, he'd have been haunted years ago. Still, the concept had given him pause over the years, … for a moment or two.

He shifted closer to the prone man on the bed. He studied the man's slack features, as he twirled his balloon glass slowly. The rich aroma of his Glenfiddich whisky swirled in an ever-rising circle, bursting forth to assail his senses. His brother's favorite. He closed his eyes and breathed deep. He kept a bottle here in the room for evenings like these. He sank his thin frame deeper into his armchair, facing the glass doors to the gardens beyond. Heavy rain bounced off the patio, flattening the delicate rose petals.

Odd how that rain could be a blessing for grass, yet signal the end of the blooms on a rose. Such delicate plants. It was the same for people. What was a disaster to one was a gift to another. Some people were hardy and could withstand the harsh elements of life, and then the others, the delicate ones, needed protecting. He was good at that—the protecting part. Of course people didn't always understand or appreciate his protective method or didn't know what was good for them.

Stretching out his arm, he grabbed the remote and turned on the television. Maybe his brother would like the distraction. Had to be something to break up the monotony of lying there day after day. Personally this was his favorite time of day. A little peace and quiet, a little time alone, where he didn't have to pretend to be something he wasn't—with his brother.

The evening news came on, the announcer bubbling about some large contribution to a local charity. A moment later, he brought up today's headlines.

The man straightened in shock. *What the hell?*

THE NEXT MORNING started clear and warm, with one insistent message rattling around inside Alexis's head—she needed help and soon. She didn't know who to ask or even what kind of help she needed. Still, just admitting she had the problem could be thought of as a big step forward.

Regardless, at the moment she needed to get to work. Her soul needed the comfort of the gardens. Only nothing was likely to be peaceful about them today. The damage from the excavation yesterday could be extensive.

Arriving at work twenty minutes later, Alexis cast a wide glance across the park. From the looks of them, the gardens needed her too.

They'd been trashed. She wanted to howl at the damage. Damn.

One officer stood off to the side. She nodded at him but stayed away. Some of the police tape had been removed, though most still sagged in place. Several long strands of it cordoned off the grave and the surrounding area. A few forlorn pieces blew aimlessly across the park. Heavy vehicles had left muddy ruts in the grass. Litter decorated muddy footprints. The carelessly discarded disposable cups and cigarette butts really burned her.

The park definitely had a morning-after appearance.

She exhaled hard, rolled up her sleeves, and tucked her shirt into her jeans. She pulled several garbage bags from her truck. After putting on her work boots, she stomped her feet a couple of times to settle in, then locked her truck and stormed around the site on her clean-up mission. Every area of the park came under her scrutiny, as she searched for offending human trash—every area but one.

When she finally realized what she'd been unconsciously avoiding, Alexis forced herself to walk toward the tiny open grave. The police officer stood to one side, his narrowed eyes watching her.

The grave remained achingly difficult to gaze upon.

Alexis couldn't stand the lonely uncared-for look of it. She had to do something.

She couldn't enter the area, but she stacked several rocks just inside the cordoned-off perimeter, where the ground held deep ruts from the vehicles. Maybe this location for her construction would reduce vandalism. Stepping back, she studied her handiwork.

As a memorial, it left much to be desired.

Plants. It needed the healing energy of plants. Chewing the inside of her lip, she surveyed her gardens. Her understanding of Mother Nature had been well-honed over the years. Her coworkers called her spooky because of the way the plants responded to her. According to them, she could bring any dead plant back to life almost immediately and could even make flowers appear out of season. That wasn't true of course. Not totally.

She couldn't save them all.

As for the plants flowering off-season, who said plants could only flower at specific times? Alexis couldn't explain why her methods worked. She only knew they did.

Alexis gave them the same loving attention she gave to animals and kids. Walking through the flowers, she called out softly to them. "How are you guys doing today? Yesterday was tough on all of us, wasn't it?" She stopped here and there, once to smooth a bent leaf, another time to stroke a particularly bright petal. "It's okay. It's all over. Everything is back to normal now."

She continued to speak to her babies, murmuring soft words of comfort, as she checked out each one. Her senses picked up on the energy levels of the plants around her. One small daisy plant with multiple white petals had a dark dull color to it. Alexis walked closer.

The leaves drooped miserably. It cried out for help. She couldn't resist. Gently her hands hovered over it. Years ago, she'd read several books on tricks to improve plant health, and she had to admit, with practice, it seemed to work better all the time. The more caring and attention she devoted to her plants, the better they did. Nothing magical about that. Common sense really. One of the books also mentioned something about playing music and using soft lights. She grinned. Like her boss would let her do that.

Within a few intense seconds, the plant brightened ever-so-slightly, almost appearing happy to have the company. Alexis laughed at that whimsical thought. She did have a good imagination.

That thought wiped the smile off her face. Had Lissa's ghost been a figment of her imagination? God, she hoped not.

Using another technique from the book, she focused a loving green—for health and healing—light around a different listless daisy plant.

"What else can I do for you, little one?" She chuckled at her words, for, in truth, it was a decent size. She glanced over at the grave and, without giving herself a chance to reconsider, she dug up the plant, making sure she kept a large root ball attached.

"Yep, they'll really think I'm nuts for this one." Alexis checked the surrounding area. Outside of the silent ever-watchful police presence, she was still alone. "I can always move you again, if you're not happy there," she murmured.

It would be the public that showed its displeasure. A lone flowering plant wouldn't be considered an artistic improvement. Yet, as a memorial, it was a start.

Using her hands, she carefully loaded up as much of the rich black dirt around the ball as she could then carried it over to the rock pile. After planting it deep, she rearranged the rocks in an artistic pattern, creating a backdrop for the daisy.

Scott found her almost an hour later.

"Alex?"

Bent over her tools, Alexis raked the footprints from the flower beds. She straightened and smiled up at him. "Hi, Scott. About time you showed up."

"Don't you be worrying about me. The real question is, how are you?" He studied her face.

Alexis grimaced and looked off in the distance to avoid his piercing blue eyes. He had a way of seeing things a little too clearly. "I'm better. It helps being in the gardens." She motioned to the mess around them. "We have a lot of work ahead of us."

"There's time. I don't know if the police are done yet." He studied the daisy flower memorial. "Did you do that?"

"What? Oh, yeah, I did." She searched his expression. "I had to do something," she added warily, hoping for, but not quite expecting, understanding. She needn't have worried. Scott was already nodding his acceptance.

"You're different this morning. What's the matter?" he asked.

Startled, she hid her expression behind the fall of her hair.

"Come on. What's going on?" Concern thickened his tone, making him harder to understand.

She didn't know how to answer him, so she said nothing, just looked quietly into his eyes. What could she say that he'd believe—that wouldn't make her sound on the edge of a breakdown? Accepting the visions seemed too far-fetched, even for her.

The intensity of his gaze changed. "Oh, wow," he muttered softly. "You've always had a touch of the Sight, but something's changed." He studied her face. "But what?"

She missed the last part, too startled by his first comment. "I don't have the Sight, whatever that is."

"Like hell you don't. Don't be trying to hide it. You've always had magical speakings with them little plants of yours." He did a sweep with his arm to encompass the whole of the gardens. "That's how you make this so glowing. Only someone with the Sight could accomplish all this."

Alexis flushed with warmth, followed immediately by an icy fear that he might know more than she'd intended him to know. "No, you don't understand. I just practice some exercises I read in a couple books.

Anyone can do it."

"No way. I can't." He grinned. "But my gram sure could. That … and more. You probably see all their colors too, don't you? My gram could tell all kinds of things about her plants just by the colors she saw."

He was so matter-of-fact she could only stare at him in shock. She shook her head violently. "That's nuts!" She plunked down on the ground, her hand on her forehead. His words had shaken her very foundation.

A loud snort answered her. "That's your modern thinking interfering. Me? … I have a healthy respect for the Sight."

That she had the Sight, or whatever he referred to, so didn't make sense. She was a gifted gardener. *That* she saw and accepted. More than that? *Uh-uh.* Over the years, she'd had some indications that her abilities were out of the ordinary, but she really hadn't given it much thought. Her *skills* were a natural part of her world, so why question them? Besides, the Sight meant psychic stuff, premonitions, visions. Ghosts? Her world slowed. *The child in the ditch. Lissa.*

Oh, dear God.

She stared at the sky above, her mind blank, her heart pounding— but not in shock—more like after a revelation.

"What would make these skills suddenly change?" she asked, not really sure she wanted to hear the answer.

His clear gaze seared through her.

She shuddered at the sense of exposure. As if he saw what she could not.

"That's what yesterday was all about, wasn't it?" he asked.

Slightly afraid, she nodded—a tiny, barely perceptible movement—then said, in a small voice, "Maybe."

"Ah, lassie. … Scared yourself right and proper, didn't you?"

His words startled a crooked smile from her. "I don't understand any of this. Life was pretty normal, until I fell into the ditch. But now? … The things I'm seeing? … That's scary." She was confused and more than a little relieved to talk about it with someone.

"What did you see?" Curious, Scott sat down on the grass beside her, close enough to be supportive and far enough away not to crowd her.

"I saw a little girl in a hallway. I think. I mean, I saw a little girl. Or I thought I saw a girl, … but she wasn't real. … It's like she was mist or something and in a hallway. … in the ditch." She stopped, confused.

Scott nodded. Keeping his voice low and calm, he said, "Start at the beginning and tell me what happened. Step by step."

Alexis checked around to make sure they were still alone. The sun was almost directly overhead. A few people walked around or sat on benches, but she and Scott were at the other end of the park.

She took a deep breath and began to explain. She left nothing out. Her voice wobbled, as she finished by telling him about her sister's visit. "I thought I was having a breakdown, Scott. My God, Lissa was so clear. She was right there in front of me. She said my name." Shock and disbelief colored her voice.

"Ah, lassie." Scott pulled her into his comforting embrace, squeezing her tight, before releasing her. "You should be joyous, not afeared."

What could she say to that? She studied his compassionate gaze. "Really? It's that simple to you?"

"Is *what* that simple?" A strong voice reached across the flowers to them.

Alexis pivoted. *Detective Sutherland.*

What was it about this man that made her back straighten and her knees weaken at the same time?

"Hi, Scott. Alexis. I need to speak with the two of you. But first, who put that memorial together? It's within the crime scene." The detective's stern face towered above her.

"Oh." Alexis snapped to her feet, brushing the dirt of her pants. "I did. I'm sorry. I'd hoped it would be far enough out of the way for you but deter vandalism because it was inside the tape."

His chiseled features eased. "The tape is there for a reason. We aren't done with the scene yet."

Alexis twisted around to look at the memorial in the distance. "I can move it outside, if you need me to."

Casting a quick glance at Scott, who now stood beside Alexis, the detective continued in a calmer voice. "Should you even be at work today? Most people would understand the need to take off a day or two after yesterday."

Alexis shook her head. "I'm fine. I'm better off doing something constructive." She hesitated. "Have you identified her yet? I can't imagine what her family has gone through all these years." Alexis stuffed her hands into her pants pockets, as she waited. Her insides trembled. She didn't know why his answer mattered so much, but it did.

Suspicion shone in his eyes, as he stared her, his jaw firmly locked in place.

His instant shift from casual stance to hardened investigator had Alexis asking, "What?"

"You called the skeleton a 'she.' What makes you so sure it is a little girl?"

Confusion clouded her mind. Good question. How had she known it was a little girl? Because she'd assumed it was the same child that she'd seen running in the ditch.

The men waited for her answer.

"I guessed," she answered lamely, not ready to share her bizarre vision with this man.

Skepticism washed over the detective's face, but thankfully he left it at that, at least for the moment.

Scott was a different story. He quirked his eyebrow at her, but she shook her head.

Detective Sutherland watched the silent exchange. Alexis could almost feel his mind cataloging her and Scott. Figuring who they were, what was their relationship, and if they were hiding anything. It was obvious this man missed little.

His body stance relaxed, in total opposition to the sharpness of his attention, and damned if her contrary hormones didn't find that attractive. What the hell was with that?

"Do I need to move the memorial? I just felt that the grave needed to be respected and marked." Her fists clenched deep inside her denim pockets. She wanted to wipe them dry on her jeans but didn't want to arouse his suspicions any more than they already were.

"I'll see. A crew will be here later today to map out the gardens to compare to aerial photographs." He glanced at Scott and gestured to the spot above the ditch. "Scott, you've been here a while. … How long has this garden bed been here? Do you know?"

"Since forever, it seems. I can't give you an exact year, but I've been working on it for over twenty years."

The detective nodded. "Right. And, in that time, has any major work been done? Work that would have brought the skeleton to light, if one had been here then?"

Both Alexis and Scott turned to study the bed. A beautiful blue spruce stood close to twelve feet tall in the center, with weeping maples and begonias filling in the bulk of the area beneath. Bulbs flowered and went with the seasons, and annuals were planted each spring for bright cheerful color.

"Even if we dug it over, like we do in the fall, we wouldn't go that deep," Alexis said.

"Aye, that's true enough, but this city park was upgraded with this spruce and new perennials around twelve to fifteen years ago. I'll have to check the records." He paused, a frown twisting his face. "But that spot where the body was found was part of this big bed here." He motioned to the spruce bed. "We moved all the smaller plants at this end of the bed last year, when we were notified about this job with the pipes. There weren't many big plants, so we didn't go very deep. It wasn't a big area and was fairly easy to shorten up to make way for the construction." He walked around the garden bed, studying the plants flourishing in the rich mulch. He pointed to the end where the grave sat. "And that spot had originally been put in about a decade ago, ... maybe even fifteen years or so."

"Pictures and plans are on file," Alexis offered.

Detective Sutherland smiled. "Pictures and plans would help a lot. Help establish a time line. Scott, send over anything you have, and I'll add it to the file." He glanced at the large silver watch on his wrist. "I'm short on time. Make sure nothing else is disturbed in the crime scene. Don't be surprised if you come in one day to find your memorial has been moved. We need full access to the entire surface." He nodded to both of them and headed back over to the grave.

Alexis watched as he stood in front of the memorial for a long moment. *Don't touch the plant*, she pleaded in her heart. Instead, he pulled on thin rubber gloves and moved over to the open grave, where he sifted through the lightly packed dirt close to the surface. He filled several small vials and then repeated the process from lower, inside the ditch. Back on top again, he pulled out a notepad and started writing.

"Now what the hell is he doing?" she muttered. It shouldn't matter, but everything to do with this case affected her. She needed him to do his job and to find out who this little girl was. It was important. Alexis just didn't know why she felt it so strongly.

Finally he must have finished because he tucked his notebook back into his pocket.

With each sign that he'd soon be leaving, Alexis felt her tension drain away. It had been years since any male had rattled her cage, like this one did.

The detective walked toward the parking lot, but, instead of going to his car, he strode down a path that looped through the trees.

She relaxed. In the distance dark clouds gathered. Rain threatened.

"What's going on now?" Scott asked.

"I hardly know how to explain it." How could she? "It's like the little girl is real. Trying to say something to me, ... through me. Only I don't know what she wants me to say." She cast a glance his way. "Scott, what if I'm losing my mind?"

"Why? Because the dead are speaking to you? They only do that when they have something important to say. They won't leave you alone, until you give them a voice." He shrugged, helpless to offer more comfort. "Maybe you should go study up on it?"

Alexis nodded. "I can do that easily enough. The internet is full of information." She silently wondered if she should do more, … like book an appointment with her doctor.

"Internet, now that's bad stuff. How can all that information float around in the air?" The huge man looked around uncertainly, as if words and pictures from the internet would jump out of thin air and attack him. "That can't be good for you."

Alexis snorted. "Listen to you. It's okay for dead people to be speaking inside my head, but it's not okay to send data through cables or fiber optics. Yeah, that makes sense."

"Don't you go being disrespectful of the Sight. It'll get you, if you do," he warned.

"Get me how?" This new worry stopped her cold. She rubbed her arms, brushing the first summer raindrops off her bare skin. She always carried rain gear in her truck but didn't bother to go after it. The horizon shone bright blue. This could just be a short squall.

"No way to know. Mostly it's demanding that you listen—or else." Scott studied her face.

"Like I need more to worry about." She changed the subject. "What do you think about the detective?"

He looked sideways at her. "In what way?"

At his teasing tone, her face warmed. "Do you think he's a good cop? You obviously know him. So what's he like?" she asked, exasperated.

"Oh, is that what you mean?" he drawled. He nodded, as if he believed her, but his cheeky grin said otherwise. She rolled her eyes at him. He shook his head. "He's a good man. Driven. Stands for the victims and their families and bulldogs through to see they get justice. Doesn't think much of politics, politicians, or any superior for that matter. Made himself a few enemies because of that. A loner too, just like you. He doesn't talk much about his past." Scott thought about it for a moment. "Come to think of it, rumors have it that he's a bit odd himself."

"Odd how?"

"He gets things done. No one questions him too much because they like the results."

That could mean anything. Not that it mattered to her. She didn't want to know the detective's methods—or his secrets for that matter.

He meant nothing to her, and that was how she wanted to keep it.

"The energy around you two fair crackles. Be a shame to waste it fighting."

"What?" She rounded on Scott, caught his grin, and smacked him on his shoulder. She held her hand up to stave off any more comments. "Don't even go there. I've got enough problems to deal with, thank you."

"Can't ignore it though. Almost made me want to offer me van for a couple hours."

He couldn't go unpunished for that one. She raised her hand and smacked him lightly on his shoulder again.

A great shout of laughter was her reward.

"You damn well better be joking," she muttered.

"About the van? Maybe. About the crackling of energy going on around you two? No way."

Alexis shot him a dirty look. "He pisses me off."

"That's passion too."

"Not the kind that matters." She definitely needed to change this subject. Once Scott got going on her nonexistent love life, there'd be no stopping him.

"There's only one kind. How you use it is what matters."

Alexis turned and strode back to the gardens, her face warming in irritation. "Don't hold your breath. It won't happen."

"Never say never, Alexis." Scott's voice floated behind her.

"Like hell," she muttered to herself. "Not in a million years."

"NOT IN A million years, huh?" Kevin didn't know if he was amused or miffed at her offhand rejection. He'd taken a circular path and had ended up close enough to hear their conversation. Standing under a huge spruce tree, he'd stopped to watch Scott and Alexis. They were an odd pair. Yet an obviously strong bond held the two together. *Interesting.* Bonds like that usually developed over a seriously long time—or through shared hardship. According to his records, Alexis had worked for the city for just under five years. Scott, on the other hand, had been here for close to twenty.

Alexis intrigued him. Strong cheekbones, pert nose, slim to the point of being thin, with an abrasive personality that would turn off most men. And that hair. ... Long, flyaway, and blond. Yet according to a couple people he'd spoken to, she was a softie inside.

Now her boss, ... he had a different tale to tell. Rick didn't appear to be a fan in any way. Some hidden story there.

Suddenly Kevin's mind filled with erotic images of Alexis. Heat, pounding hearts, skin slicked with sweat, and … satisfaction. He couldn't breathe, his heart blasting away against his ribs.

Just as quickly the movie trailer was gone. Leaving him stunned and more than a little aroused. Visions were a rare occurrence for him, but he knew better than to dismiss them. They'd never been wrong before. He grinned and headed to his car. Who knew the twists and turns life could take?

CHAPTER 4

WORK DOMINATED THE next day for Alexis, even though rain continued to pour. The wet weather had eased some, but, just when the sun started to poke through, the skies opened up and soaked everything all over again. The soggy weather didn't stop the work on the sewer line, although it commenced farther away from the grave.

By quitting time, Alexis's energy had crashed. She'd worked hard these last few days, finding it easier to exhaust herself with weeding and plant care, rather than leave any energy available for worrying. Her muscles screamed as she loaded the last of the shovels into the back of Scott's truck. She stripped off her raincoat and carried it over her arm. She hated wearing the damn thing. All coats—raincoats, evening coats, it didn't matter—suffocated her.

Alexis rubbed her sore back and yawned. She walked toward her truck. A vehicle drove in and parked beside hers. Detective Sutherland, in an unmarked police car. She stopped and frowned. What was he doing here?

"Where are you off to?" Detective Sutherland slammed his car door closed, before striding around her truck.

"Home." Tired, she turned her back on him and unlocked her truck. She didn't want to care what he did. Not wanting to care didn't stop the curiosity though. Resolutely she tossed her raincoat into the back seat and tried to ignore him.

Scott came up behind the two of them, carrying several large shovels. "Hey, Kevin. How's it going? Back to the scene of the crime, eh?"

The two men greeted each other with such a friendly rapport that Alexis turned to watch. She shook her head. She'd forgotten to ask Scott how he knew Kevin.

"Just walking around some." Kevin motioned to the gardens. "Get the lay of the land, as it were."

"Have fun. Right. I'm off. Alexis, I'll see you in the morning." Scott turned his bright blue eyes on her. "You're okay, right?"

Alexis smiled. "I'm fine. Looking forward to a hot shower, food, and a good night's rest."

Her friend nodded. "Sounds like a plan." His truck door creaked open. He hopped in, backed out, and took off, gravel spitting out behind him.

Alexis turned to get into her truck, but Detective Sutherland stood at the front of the grill, motioning for her to join him. She frowned at him.

He pointed to the right side of her truck. "You have a flat tire."

"What?" She slammed her door shut and walked around the front end. "Shit." He was right. She didn't need this right now. A few large drops hit her head. Alexis looked up at the sky, ready to explode again. "Lousy timing."

"Do you have a spare?" He squatted down to take a look. "It's not totally flat yet, but it's too low to drive on."

"Yes, but I have a can of inflating stuff, which should get me to the closest garage." She checked her toolbox in the pickup bed. She'd bought the stuff just a couple months ago. "Aha, here it is." She pulled it out, a big grin on her face.

The detective bent down and unscrewed the cap on the tire valve. "Here. Pass it to me."

Within minutes, the tire started to reinflate.

Alexis laughed. "Just like magic. I love that stuff."

"I've never used it before. Good idea for emergencies." They stood watching the tire return to normal. Once it was fully inflated, he popped off the can and replaced the valve.

"I'll head to the garage now, while the tire's still holding air." Alexis accepted the empty can, hopped into the driver's seat, and shut the door. "Thanks, Detective."

"Kevin."

"Pardon?"

He walked to the driver's side. "Call me Kevin."

Alexis nodded, tongue-tied. What the hell was she supposed to say now?

"You're Alexis, aren't you?"

Alexis flushed. Stupid. She couldn't even engage in a normal conversation with him. "Yes."

"So, Alexis, what are you hiding about those bones?"

Her eyes widened. Alarm whipped through her. "What? Nothing." This couldn't be good. She turned slightly away, so she didn't have to look him in the eye.

He lowered his head to the open window. His gaze pierced her to the core. Slowly he said, "I notice things. Sense things." He narrowed his eyes. "And one of those things is that you're not telling me everything."

Heat washed across her neck and face.

Kevin's gaze deepened, as if searching her thoughts. "Unfortunately I don't know what you could be holding back."

Thank God for small miracles. Alexis planted her hands on the steering wheel, tossing back her long ponytail. With a confidence she didn't feel, she snapped, "How nice for you. Make a lot of friends that way, do you?" She looked through the windows at the deserted park. How did she get out of this conversation?

Then it happened.

Something brushed the back of her neck. A gentle caress, a stroke of smooth fingers. Alexis twisted her head. "What … was that?" she asked. Her hand crept up to cover her nape.

She hadn't imagined it. She couldn't have. The sensation still burned. Could a touch of her hair feel that way? She shook her ponytail experimentally. No. Not even close.

Twisting, she confirmed that the back of her truck was empty; so was the front of the cab. She searched through the windshield. Everything appeared normal. She glanced carefully at Kevin. If the sensation hadn't been so creepy, it might have felt soothing.

"What's wrong?" Kevin asked. He straightened, shooting her a curious look. "What happened?"

"Something touched me. I swear it. Did you see anything?" She looked over at Kevin, more than a little unnerved. He stared at her—an odd look on his face.

Unconsciously she rubbed the back of her neck. The weird feeling was gone, leaving uncertainty and more than a little fear behind.

"*What?* I'm not crazy. I really did feel something." The defensive tone rang loudly in her own ears.

"You're just tired. I'm sure it's nothing."

Goose bumps rose on her arms in the warm evening air. Alexis rubbed the chill from her arms. "I need to get to the garage and get my tire fixed." *And get the hell away from him.* But she kept that thought to herself. "Thank you for your help. It's late, and I've got to run," she babbled, feeling like a fool. She started the engine, then gently reversed out of the spot.

Kevin called out, "You can run, but you can't hide."

He looked so eerily sure of himself, her nerves couldn't take any more. She slammed her gearshift into Drive and raced off.

LONG SHADOWS FELL on the empty parking lot, as Alexis escaped.

"Well, well, well," he whispered to the empty parking lot. That was a first. Occasionally a probe made someone feel odd, uncertain even, but that was after he'd had a good chance to check out their energy. Alexis was unique. He'd barely opened his senses, barely sent out a smidge of his consciousness before she'd noticed the shift in energy. *As a physical touch.*

Then she'd panicked.

Kevin considered some of the things he'd heard about her. Scott had said she was well-liked but a loner with a spitfire temper. That she wasn't afraid to call a spade a spade, a great friend to have on your side …

Whereas her boss said the exact opposite. Rick's comments had been caustic, and he basically said, "Alexis is walking trouble, with an attitude."

Mostly she was an enigma. One he had no intention of walking away from and for more than one reason. Psychic intuition had supplied the knowledge of an upcoming relationship—an intuition that had yet to fail him—and his imagination had filled in the rest. Images so vivid, they'd driven him half-mad last night. Which, considering she wasn't even close to enjoying a night in his bed, had frustrated him beyond sleep.

Thank God, she couldn't hide her response to him. He'd take some solace in that.

He grinned. He could expect one hell of a fight getting her into his bed.

That was all right. It would make the victory all the sweeter.

For both of them.

ALEXIS SHUDDERED IN relief, when she finally turned off the truck's engine at her apartment. Not the most pleasant trip to the garage and then home. She couldn't explain the continued sense of unease. It lived under her skin these days. She ran to the front entrance.

"Hey, Alexis."

She raced past her neighbor with a fast wave and headed for the stairs, knowing she still had to navigate the hallway. Afraid her nerves would overtake her if she slowed down, she ran up the three flights to her floor. The door to her hallway stood on her right, but her fear of a repeat of yesterday's hallway vision made her hand hesitate, hover over the handle …

Irritated by her lack of control, she forced herself to pull open the stairway door.

So far, so good. The hall looked normal. With a confidence she didn't feel, she strode down the length to her apartment. Just as she unlocked the door, a faint voice reached out to her.

Hello.

Alexis pivoted in surprise. "Who's there?"

A small rippling mirage wavered in front of her. Transparent and wispy, the outline of a child slowly appeared. Alexis reared back. It was the child from the ditch.

Help me, the voice intoned. *Please. … Help free me …*

Trembling and weak, Alexis shook her head in denial. Her mind screamed, even as she reached for a semblance of control.

"Who are you?" she whispered to the miniature apparition, so clear and yet so transparent. "What do you want?" She wiped her hands on her jeans.

Huge expressive eyes beckoned to Alex, drawing her closer. She noticed the odd brownish tint first, only to realize it was a dingy carpet showing through. The child's eyes were empty windows to an old soul.

"Dai … sy. Help me …" The voice trailed off as the image rippled, then faded into nothingness in front of her.

"Oh God, oh God, oh God." Alexis couldn't stop her frantic litany of a prayer any more than she could control the mad trembling that prevented her fingers from opening her door …

Finally she made it inside. Alexis leaned against the locked and chained door, taking in deep gulps of air.

Talk about déjà vu. Adapting to ghosts was so not on her agenda. And helping them? … She shuddered at the thought.

When she finally peeled herself off the door, she couldn't stop pacing. Nervous energy sent her storming around the tiny apartment. Her nerves couldn't take much more. Chills iced their way down her spine, sending her in search of a heavy sweater. She pulled it tightly around her. A cup of tea would be wonderful right now, but she was too scared to go into the kitchen, in case Lissa was there. Alexis didn't think she could stand to see her sister's ghost too. She'd loved her sister dearly, but seeing Lissa in ghostly form hadn't exactly been the warm bonding experience she'd so foolishly dreamed it would be.

But it could be.

"Who said that?" Alexis spun around, as panic coursed through her. She was alone—wasn't she? "Help. Please, someone help me," Alexis called out. Tears coursed down her cheeks. She brushed them away.

She had to talk to a doctor, before she lost it altogether.

The phone rang, startling her with its piercing demand. Alexis crossed the room to stare down at it warily. She picked it up. "Hello?"

"What's wrong?"

"Huh?" Heavy traffic noises filled her ear.

"Damn it, answer me, Alexis! What's wrong?"

"Kevin?" God, she was so rattled she'd actually called him by his first name.

"Who the hell were you expecting?" he snapped. "You've been calling for help out on the ethers for the last ten minutes."

She was? On the ethers? Oh God. Alexis closed her eyes in disbelief. What was he talking about?

"I'm less than two minutes away. Stay calm, and I'll be right there."

The phone went dead.

How did he know where she lived? *Duh.* She'd given her statement to the police after the garden incident. Of course they had it on file now.

His heavy pounding broke through her musings.

She unlocked the door but never had a chance to open it.

Kevin barged in. "Why the hell did you unbolt the door when you didn't know who was on the other side?" he roared, storming past her.

The raging maniac in her living room was a little hard to understand, but his meaning was clear. Her back bristled. "And to think I actually let you in," she snapped at him, only to back up at his hard look.

"You couldn't have kept me out. Now what the hell is going on?"

Cold and deadly, this was a new cop persona she hadn't met. She'd only seen him a few times, and, each time, he'd seemed different. His changeability had stopped her from finding a level of comfort with him. "What makes you think something is going on?" She moved around the living room, straightening up magazines that didn't need it. She wrapped her arms tight about her chest.

"No more games."

Startled, she turned to face him. "I'm not playing games."

"Like hell you're not. I'd almost made it home when you started crying out in my head." He glared at her.

She blinked. This conversation was beyond bizarre. "Let me get this straight. You came here because you thought I *might* be in trouble," she said slowly, watching him. He straightened as if preparing for something. And it had damn well better be to provide an explanation. She had no clue what was going on. And she needed to understand.

"Sometimes I hear things." He shrugged. "I've learned to listen." He studied her carefully. "That means something *was* going on." He looked around at the tiny apartment. "Although what, I can't imagine." His gaze swept her from head to toe and back up again.

"You appear to be fine physically and no one ..." He swept his arm around the tiny space. "No one appears to be attacking you, so ..." Again his irritated voice trailed off. He ran his fingers through his hair instead. "I can't explain how I know, but you were afraid. I felt it."

That he understood she'd been afraid was comforting in a way. It disturbed her to think that he could pick up her thoughts—and from miles away. The silence stretched between them, as she considered his admission. "I was upset."

He sighed in disgust.

She shrugged. Okay, so he already knew *that*. She chewed on her bottom lip, as she considered what to tell him. Given what he'd just said, maybe he would understand. It was either that or book in with the doctor. And maybe both. "I don't know what's happening to me."

"Explain." His voice was curt, clipped, and all cop.

Alexis paced the small dingy room. She couldn't bear to see the look of disapproval on his face, nor could she get out the words. Alexis changed direction and marched into the kitchen, not caring if he followed or not. She bustled around, making a pot of coffee. She needed a clear head for what was coming.

When she surreptitiously checked on him, she found him sitting at the old kitchen table, looking around at his surroundings with interest.

"Have you lived here long?"

"Just under a year. Although I've been thinking about moving lately. Why do you ask?" she asked.

He nodded noncommittally, still looking around. "Where did you live before here?"

What was he noticing, and what was going on in his mind? She looked at her grimy walls. The walls were bare; she hadn't gotten around to putting up any personal mementos. The same dingy color covered the walls as when she'd moved in, which was probably the same color as the decade of tenants kept it before. Dull, boring, bland, ... and, in truth, downright ugly.

"I lived in a little house with a big heated greenhouse in the backyard." Her face softened.

"With your sister?" he probed, searching her face and eyes for the truth. At her wide-eyed look, he added, "Scott told me."

She put two cups on the table and said, her voice now tinged with sadness, "Yes, with Lissa. She was a fighter. Lived much longer than anyone expected her too, but …"

"I don't mean to intrude …" He paused, a wry look on his face. "And I realize it must seem like I'm doing just that." After a moment, he added, "Try understanding my position. You're the strongest transmitter I've ever connected with. If I could understand the source of the pain you feel, then I might differentiate it from a different transmission. It would also help me if you'd apply a level of control."

Alexis kept her gaze on her cup of coffee, wishing it had something stronger in it. She could use the boost right about now. This whole conversation was too crazy. She studied Kevin over the rim of her mug. He seemed serious. Almost too afraid to ask, but needing to know, she asked, "Transmitter?"

His stunned gaze pinned her in place. Disbelief oozed from his voice, as he asked, "You didn't know?"

Alexis got up and walked over to the sink, where she turned around and leaned against the counter to face him. Putting distance between them didn't help. Confused and a little apprehensive, she had to ask, "Didn't know what?"

Bemused, Kevin could only gape at her. "You're one of the strongest psychics I've ever come across. And the only one, to date, who had no idea they were." At her look of total incomprehension, he added, "Look. I don't know *why* this is happening, but the *what* of it I *can* explain. When you feel strongly negative about something, you're actually sending out a distress signal to any receivers—psychics who can receive your signal—who are in range. That's why I called you a transmitter. You're transmitting or broadcasting emotions."

CHAPTER 5

TIME STOPPED.

A transmitter? Is that what she was?

She rolled the idea around in her head, trying it on. Did it fit? Maybe, … in some ways. But there was so much more to it than just that. Like seeing the vision of the little girl, seeing the hallway shift, and even hearing the voices.

And, if she were transmitting, like Kevin said, how come no one else heard her but him?

Another thought struck—what about her plants? She'd thought she just talked to them. Was she transmitting when she talked to them? Yes, that made more sense. But what about her understanding of their needs, their colors, and even their sounds. Didn't that make her a receiver too?

Was there such a thing?

"Does everyone have this ability?" she asked cautiously. "Lying latent until something brings it to their awareness?"

"Researchers say we do, but only a small fraction of the population uses it or even knows those abilities are there to be used. It can also get more confusing because all receivers are transmitters but not all transmitters are receivers." He leaned forward, locking his hands together in front of him. "This whole idea *is* new for you, right?"

"Absolutely." And with the word came a question. Should she tell him everything or wait?

He cocked an eyebrow in surprise at her answer, but he continued. "Chances are something triggered this. Something like finding the body, maybe?"

"The finger," she added softly, needing to tell someone. Maybe he would understand. "Something happened when I picked up the bones and realized they belonged to a child's finger." The horrific memory made her wince. God, she didn't want to revisit this.

"Tell me," he urged. "Exactly *what* started with the finger?" He rose, neared her.

Slowly, haltingly, she related the weird series of events from the ditch. He let her get it all out, and somehow, in the process, her hand ended up cradled in his.

Mesmerized, she watched his strong, sinewy thumb stroke and slide over her palm, warming and comforting on a level she hadn't felt in many years. It moved over the rounded pad, sliding down the valley between her fingers, sensuous, sexy, and definitely seductive.

She ordered her hand to withdraw. But her long fingers had a mind of their own and refused to obey. They chose instead to nestle against his much larger and stronger ones. As if they belonged there …

Enough. Alexis broke the trance and snatched her hand free, tucking it into her pants pocket.

"What else?"

She glanced at him.

"Is there anything else?" His question prodded gently for more.

Alexis wavered, but no point in keeping the rest from him. As clearly and as succinctly as she could, she described her visions of the hallway, of little Daisy—and of Lissa.

"When you heard the little girl calling you, did it come from outside your head or inside?"

She smiled without humor. "Believe it or not, I'd wondered that myself. I don't have a definitive answer."

Kevin seemed to consider her words. "Is that everything?" he asked.

She flushed.

"It would help if I knew it all," he suggested quietly, his gaze never leaving hers.

She wanted to believe in the understanding, the compassion, and the acceptance he offered. Taking a chance, she shared the last bit about her gardens and the need to transplant the suffering plant to the child's grave.

"You planted a daisy on her grave, and you're saying the ghost child said the same word was her name? That's odd and too much of a coincidence to ignore."

"I know. I'm presuming it's her body we found."

"Anything's possible." He pulled his sleeve back to check the time. "I need to leave. Let me know if anything else like this happens." He paused, gave her a wry look, and added, "Or else I'll find out the same way I did last time."

Alexis almost laughed, but, now that he spoke of leaving, Alexis found the thought of being alone disconcerting. How stupid. She hadn't wanted him here in the first place. Still, he'd gone a long way toward helping her tonight.

"Will you be okay here?"

"Of course. This is home." Even though she hadn't put much effort into making it hers. She cast an unhappy glance around the cold place.

"We need to talk some more about your abilities and how you can learn to control them. I have a friend, Stefan, who might help. I'll talk to him." He walked to the doorway, jacket in hand. She'd trailed behind him, helpless to abate the sense of loss already threatening.

Slowly she closed the door behind him and turned to look around the empty room. An odd thought struck. Outside of Scott, Kevin was her first real visitor in a year.

How pathetic.

When her sister's cancer had first been diagnosed, priorities had to be set. Everything had been about Lissa. Afterward, Alexis had remained secluded, inside a wall of pain that refused to ease.

When had that changed? When had the pain reduced her to the point that she'd just been hiding?

KEVIN WALKED OUT to his car. Given Alexis's skills and lack of control, he had one more thing to do tonight. He headed to Stefan's house.

Stefan lived in a huge cedar post-and-beam home on a couple acres just out of town. Evergreens lined the long driveway and ringed the property. But that was nothing to the damn plants surrounding the house that looked like they lived on steroids.

His psychic skills, many of them still developing and expanding, were extraordinary. Stefan had worked alongside most major police departments throughout the country. He had often quipped that he'd been forced to learn more and faster just to stay one step ahead of the criminals.

The door opened to a yawning Stefan, rubbing his fingers through his rumpled hair. He snorted at the sight of Kevin. "Did anyone ever tell you that your timing stinks?"

"Were you sleeping already? Sorry, but sleep is reserved for those not on guard duty, Stefan. You know that. You can go back to bed in a minute. I'm not coming in." He gave his friend another minute to wake up further.

Stefan was an artist who used his creativity to release the images and visions that haunted him. His art gave a deep insight into the extreme sides of his personality. His work hung in private collections all over the world. He painted when he required release from his emotional hell. Rare were the privileged few welcomed into his inner sanctum. Intensely private and eerily accurate, Stefan walked a path forged with his own boundaries.

"So what's going on?" murmured Stefan. "Oh …" An intuitive pause was followed with "You have girl trouble. How very funny." He really looked amused as he propped himself against the doorway. "So there *are* ladies in your world." After a heavy pause, his face leaned out, deepening with pain. "One of them is dead, the little one."

Kevin waited for his longtime friend to sort through the onslaught of impressions. That's what happened when you had an extreme psychic as part of your circle of friends. Nothing was private.

Stefan rubbed his eyes. "What do you need from me?"

Kevin knew Stefan had seen too much of this world and the next to be surprised by anything much these days. "If you have anything that can help on the child's case, I'd appreciate it. But it's the other female I really need help with."

Stefan grinned. "Is that so?" he drawled. "I never thought I'd see the day."

"I'm not sure you're seeing clearly now," Kevin said wryly, crossing his arms over his chest. "Take another look."

Silence stretched between them.

"Right." Stefan was all business now. "What's her phone number, and have you told her about me?"

"Yes." Kevin pulled out a piece of paper with Alexis's number on it. Like many psychics, Stefan had no luck remembering numbers. Occasionally he could come up with dates, but, more often, he couldn't recall numerals of any kind. He said it had frustrated him to no end at the beginning. Now he acknowledged that as a weakness.

"I'll call her in the morning."

Kevin grimaced. "Or you could call her tonight."

Stefan frowned, his eyes focusing inward. "Not everyone keeps your hours."

"Except I just left her, and she wasn't in any shape to sleep."

Stefan's long-suffering sigh brought a grin to Kevin's face. "Thanks, Stefan. Let me know what happens." He headed toward his car. "Also, if you learn anything about the little one …"

Stefan waved him off. "As always. I'll let you know if I pick up anything."

Kevin honked once and drove away.

LATER THAT SAME evening, exhaustion caught Alexis by surprise and startled a yawn from deep down. She closed her book, placed it on the paisley bedspread covering her and snuggled deeper into her bedding.

Hi.

Alexis bolted upright. She searched the empty room. What the hell was that?

My name is Stefan Kronos. I'm a friend of Kevin's.

Damn it. Alexis bolted from the bed and ran to the living room.

Alexis stared at the room, absolutely freaked. She spun around in a circle. How did you run or hide from voices in your head? Shivers slipped down her body, and she wrapped her arms tightly around her chest. Her pounding heart had no place to escape and continued to knock against her ribs.

The voice in her head sighed. *Fine, we'll do it your way.*

The phone rang, scaring the bejeezus out of her again. She stared at her cell, like it was a bomb about to go off.

Cautiously she picked up the phone. "Hello?"

"I'm Stefan," said the voice on the other end.

Shit. Her knees knocked so badly she might collapse. Unintentionally she blurted out the first words in her mind. "Was that you?"

"Me?"

"In my head a minute ago?" Oh God, she shouldn't have said that. Alexis ran her shaky fingers over her face. She sounded like a lunatic.

"Yes."

"Yes," she shrieked. "Yes, you were inside my head? Why? How?" Alexis sat down on her couch with a *thump.*

"Kevin asked me to call."

"Kevin? You know him?" Alexis latched on to the one sane thing he'd said.

"Yes. We need to meet. Tomorrow would be good. Cardinal Park around six-thirty p.m. We'll talk then." He hung up.

Alexis gaped at the phone still cradled in her hand. "My God."

How had her life gotten so crazy?

Still troubled, Alexis knew any sleep would be a long time coming.

THE NEXT MORNING, Alexis pulled into the lot at the garden, tires squealing and ten minutes late. Striding over to Scott, she handed him one of the two coffees she'd picked up on the way in, hoping it would work as an excuse in case her boss, Rick, beat her to work.

Scott accepted the cup and flashed her a grin, before he quickly sobered, nodding toward something behind her. "Good morning, Rick. How're you doing?"

Rick? Alexis stiffened at Scott's address but then forced herself to relax. Rick was irritating but harmless.

"The mayor is very unhappy over the regrettable end to the ceremonies." Rick's voice washed over Alexis like lighter fluid.

Ever-so-slowly she swiveled to face him. "What did you say?" she demanded.

Rick took a defensive step back.

"Did you just say the *mayor* was upset at all this unpleasantness?" she questioned caustically. "How about the parents who, even now, are looking for their missing child? A child was murdered. Don't you people understand that?"

Alexis was warming up to rip into her boss again, when Scott placed a heavy hand on her shoulder—a gentle but indomitable warning. "Take it easy, Alexis."

Scott's intervention barely allowed her to regain an appropriate level of restraint, only it wasn't enough to still her piercing anger or the grief she felt welling up inside. She spun away from the men and walked off a short distance to be alone. She looked toward the makeshift memorial and gasped in surprise.

The grave was heaped with flowers, candles, and balloons. Teddy bears smiled out at the world, among the glorious blooms and ribbons festively adorning the jumble. She couldn't resist walking over to stand in awe at the testimony to a much warmer humanity than she'd seen in a while. Tears formed in the corners of her eyes. Toys, cards, and notes spoke of a community mourning the sad resting place for the lost little girl.

In a small way, Alexis was proud of her contribution to the beautiful gardens. If the child had been tossed away so casually, at least she'd had one of the prettiest resting places while she endured the long wait for discovery.

Alexis could only hope it wouldn't be an equally long wait to find the girl's killer.

"Alexis, if you want to work on the south bed today, we'll go over some of the other work to be done later. I've got to go downtown with Rick for a meeting." Scott had walked up behind her. "Will you be okay?"

She knew what he was asking. "I'll be fine. Go on. Just make sure you take him with you."

"Go a little easy on him. He's the mayor's confidant. What affects the mayor affects him." Scott shrugged.

"I know. I know. But he's an arrogant, cold, brown-nosing ass-hole." Now she felt better.

Scott patted her back, before joining Rick and driving away.

When the dust settled, Alexis put her cup down and spread her arms wide. Time alone. Finally.

Her spirits lifted, as she did something she'd always done naturally, but only now understood for the intricate communication process it truly was. She sent out a wide belt of joyous green energy to her plants. Their glorious energy bounced back. Her heart embraced the bright colors and cheerful sounds exploding in her mind.

So that's what being a transmitter meant. She just hadn't known what it was called.

CHAPTER 6

A T THE END of her workday Alexis had stopped for a quick meal and then hummed contentedly as she drove to Cardinal Park. She was early for her meeting with Stefan, and, not knowing what else to do, Alexis wandered around the garden, admiring the plants. Their colors were slightly different than those she normally worked with, but they had a serenity she hadn't seen before.

While enjoying one particular arrangement, the flower petals brightened, almost as if a light had come on from within. How curious. Alexis compared them to the petals on other flowers. Now they all appeared to be lit up. What the hell?

That's the result of both our energies combined.

Alexis froze. That voice spoke inside her head. Again.

It's me. Turn around.

Ever-so-slowly, Alexis turned to look behind her.

That's right. I'm the one talking to you.

Alexis's mouth dropped open.

That brought a knowing smile to the man in front of her. Did she say a man? What an understatement. *Man* implied ordinary. … This guy could pass for a GQ model. He was stunning!

Thanks for the compliment.

Alexis flushed. Not only was she hearing him in her mind, but he was also reading hers! Oh, God. She closed her eyes in mortification. How embarrassing.

Proving her assumption, he spoke telepathically once again. *Don't be embarrassed, please. I wouldn't normally do this, but it seems like you are the type to need proof. I'll get out now.*

Instantly her mind felt empty—bereft even. She was mystified. How could she miss what she'd only just noticed?

He smiled at her. "It's the loss of a connection that you hadn't experienced until now, one that you'd always longed for, because, on some level, part of you knew you were incomplete."

Her gaze widened at the hypnotic-sounding voice. As he obviously could read her every thought, it would be best to be totally honest. … But wow! "It's not fair. You're too gorgeous for *any* woman to ignore," she complained, startling a surprised laugh from him. "Could we start again?" she asked drily. Quickly recovering her composure, she held out a hand. "Hi, I'm Alexis."

When his chuckles calmed down, he shook her hand. "I'm Stefan. Kevin told me a little about you, but he didn't say that you would be a breath of fresh air to my jaded soul."

"If you can read my mind, I might as well speak it. I don't think I can communicate telepathically like you do."

"Wrong. If you can understand me as easily as you do, you are certainly capable of speaking your thoughts in the same way. And I heard yours. Remember? You just have to learn how to focus them, then send them." He tucked her arm into the crook of his elbow. "Let's walk."

They meandered through the twisting pathways. There was so much color that it distracted Alexis from her purpose.

"You love the plant world, don't you?"

She nodded at his question.

"Why?" he asked.

"I have no easy answer." She took a minute to gather her thoughts. "I feel better when I work with plants. They've helped me to heal, to grieve for my sister."

She stopped to smile down at a particularly valiant pansy, trying to bloom between the flagstones. "I admire the wild ones, like this little guy. In the face of all odds, he makes a tremendous effort to live his life the best that he can."

"Isn't that what you're doing?"

Startled, she stared at him. He was very intuitive, regardless of any psychic abilities. "My struggle hasn't been all that difficult."

He allowed that one to pass, for the moment. "Where do you see yourself going from here?"

She snorted. "It's all I can do to get through each day right now." Her fear and frustration bubbled over. She *had* to tell him. "All of a sudden, ghosts, voices, even weird visions have taken over my life without warning." She searched his face closely. She didn't know what she'd do if he laughed at her.

Stefan only nodded.

A weight in her chest eased. "I've talked to plants for years, but I hadn't seen that as odd. Many people have a green thumb. But, after finding those bones, well, I don't know if a green thumb explains it anymore."

Stefan motioned her in the direction of a large stone bench. "Now, start where you found those bones." He remained silent, as her words poured out …

"Then you called me," she finished lamely, feeling a bit foolish at the end of her emotional spiel.

Stefan looked at her with admiration. "Kevin is an old friend, from a difficult time in my life when I didn't want friends. In truth, I didn't want anything—especially life."

Alexis turned to face him at his surprising confession. "*You* were suicidal?"

Her shocked disbelief brought a wry smile to his face. "Yes, I was. The reason, however, is all you've just said … and so much more. I saw dead people all the time. I answered questions in people's heads, under the assumption that they'd spoken to me. I knew things would happen before they did. The worst part was …" He paused for a moment. "Nothing I did stopped events from happening. I couldn't *do* anything to keep the bad things from coming to pass. I was helpless. That made me a victim myself." He fell silent.

Alexis watched his face darken, with the shadows of memories. He'd turned inward, as if staring off into a horrendous past.

"How did you get through it? My God, I've only been dealing with this for such a short time, and I didn't think I'd make it through *that*." Alexis cringed at what he must have endured. His childhood must have been one long, lonely nightmare.

"I met someone, a parapsychologist, who recognized the mess I was in. After that, I studied, practiced, and learned to mentally control my abilities. At least to a certain extent. That helped me regain perspective." He smiled. "I was no longer a victim, and that made all the difference."

"What makes these abilities start up? No prior warning, just, all of a sudden, ghosts walk toward me? I don't get it." And she didn't. It was just too odd to think that, one day, she'd fallen into a ditch and had woken up like this.

Stefan patted her hand. "There are still so few answers. Your abilities with the plant world left a door open, which triggered the next stage of development. There seems to be no limit to how far these abilities can progress." He stood and pulled his jacket closer together in the front, before burying his fists deep into his pockets. "In my case, they are in constant flux. I never quite know what's next."

"So *just get used to it*, is that it?" The thought of the intrusion left a bitter taste in her mouth.

"You can learn to accept your gifts and eventually develop them, or you can fight them and slowly go crazy." He smiled a little grimly down at her. "The choice is yours." He started to walk away, leaving her sitting there alone.

"Wait."

He stopped but didn't turn around.

"I'm scared. This is pretty freaky stuff." She chased after him to stand next to him. "How do I learn to control all this? Please understand. I didn't ask for this." That brought a disgusted look to his face, rushing her back into speech. "I can't live with my life always being out of control. I need to know how to direct it."

"It won't happen overnight. But you can do some things to minimize the impact and to speed up your recovery afterward." He hesitated, his expression undecided.

"Please," she pleaded. "I need your help."

Finally a single decisive nod came. "We'll try to meet twice a week. But you have to work with it every day between. If you can't make that commitment, then neither will I."

"Agreed."

He considered her for a moment, then spoke slowly, "As time appears to be an issue, we'll start tonight." He pulled out his card and handed it to her. "Meet me at my place at seven-thirty. We'll cover some basics this evening."

Startled, Alexis took the card that read Stefan Kronos. Consultant. Psychic Investigator. When she lifted her head to ask him what kind of investigation could one do in that field, she found he'd walked off, leaving her to stare after him.

KEVIN SAT DOWN at his desk, determined to find some proof to support Alexis's vision. An eight- or nine-year-old girl and the name Daisy was all he had to go on. He logged on to his computer and set up a search.

Within minutes, he'd traveled deep inside the national data banks. He started locally, then branched out county by county, researching missing person files.

A grim realization settled quickly on his shoulders. He found so many cases of missing children, so many destroyed families who existed in an endless state of waiting and hoping.

By the time he'd run through all the searches he could, the name Daisy still had no hits. Kevin slumped in his chair. Fatigue screamed through his muscles as he stretched his arms overhead.

"Damn." He hadn't expected to solve this mystery in the first five minutes, but it would've been nice to score a little information. From his desk, he saw the black shadows cast by the old clock tower above the square. He found no comfort in the familiarity of the scene tonight, not when a different kind of darkness gathered in the deep silence.

His intuition screamed that this heinous crime related to a child buried in the park was just the tip of an iceberg. He had no idea what lurked beneath the surface. He'd find out though. This was what he was born to do. It defined who he was.

A hunter.

Every instinct flashed on red alert now.

Why that location? What drew a killer to that spot? A garden? Had it been the softest spot to dig up at the time? Or perhaps the prettiest spot to lay the child to rest? Did the place seem like a memorial to the perp? Surely burying a body, no matter how small, would have been noticed by the gardeners who worked there at the time. Or dogs in the ensuing years. Then again, if the gardeners used heavy chemical weed sprays or fertilizers, that could have kept the dogs unaware.

Wouldn't Alexis, with her abilities, have sensed something was wrong there, when she gardened close by? Although it's possible she might not have known or understood, on an energy level, what she'd received. She was a beginner in energy work.

Kevin was well past frustration. He'd walked straight into disgust. What had made him consider, for even one minute, that Daisy was the name of the child they'd found? It sounded more like a nickname than a proper name.

He shoved back his chair, stretching out his arms to rotate his shoulders. He needed a break. Glancing at his watch, he swore, stood, and raced from his office. He would be late for his meeting with the mayor—a very perturbed mayor, who'd just received another threat this morning, according to the early phone call.

The mayor's favorite café around the corner had become a steady lunchtime gathering place. Two blocks away, it catered to a varied clientele. The food was good and always came hot. Kevin didn't care about much else. This was their third such meeting at the same place. So far, the mayor had proven to be a creature of habit.

John Prescott stood, talking on his cell phone, outside the restaurant. Seeing Kevin, he finished his call and smiled at him. "Good to see you. Life is busy these days, isn't it?"

They walked in and were immediately seated in one of the far corners. At the exact same table as last time. "It's too damn busy. Our town is growing, and it's hard to stay ahead."

Kevin couldn't resist passing on a reminder that the town needed more law enforcement officers to keep everyone safe. "Could use more staff."

"Noted." John moved into the corner and took the far side of the table, his back to the wall, where he could watch the rest of the restaurant. He didn't look at the menu, choosing instead to order his regular hot sandwich and salad from the waitress.

Kevin waited his turn, then ordered the special, a hot roast beef sandwich and mashed potatoes. One good meal today would hold him for a long time. Who knew when he'd get home tonight? Besides, if their lunch meeting followed their regular pattern, they'd eat quickly and then go walk in the park, while they discussed personal stuff.

Sure enough, today was no different.

Once outside, John led the way into the large park in front of Bradford's Central Hall. Once away from the crowds, he wasted no time. "Any news?"

"Nothing, John. Absolutely nothing."

This whole blackmail mess felt wrong. There had to be more to it. Kevin felt it. To this point, the mayor had received threats but no demands, except to say that the mayor had better step up and tell the truth—*or else*. It was the last part that bothered Kevin. He hadn't spent all these years on the force without gaining a deeper, darker understanding of humanity. In this case, blackmailers usually had something to use as a bargaining chip. Only the mayor denied such a thing existed.

The mayor lowered his voice, his body almost vibrating with tension. "Kevin, this is unacceptable. I need answers. Hell. I need more than that. I need solutions, damn it." He clenched his fists, glaring at the bright sunny gardens surrounding them. "This asshole will ruin my life," he spluttered to a stop, then started up again. "I can't sleep for worrying. What the hell is going on here?"

John, as a politician, had faced criticism and verbal abuse before, but he told Kevin it was never like this. For the last ten years, he'd served the citizens of Bradford well. The public record showed he'd been a businessman in Redding, California, before that. The timing had been perfect for his move here, as the locals were more than ready to get rid of their corrupt politician. Through the years, John remained a popular figure, easily being reelected.

"I'm looking, but I haven't found the answers yet," Kevin stated.

"Then you'd damn well better find them fast," the mayor grumbled. "Before this asshole makes good his threat."

Kevin got the message. But he couldn't help wondering what the mayor might be hiding. He'd once probed gently to see if he could find out but had hit a wall immediately. It happened that way sometimes.

As he walked back to the office, Kevin's mind once again turned to Alexis. Had Stefan called her? Instincts said he had. A twinge of unease settled in his stomach. Stefan's looks often stopped women in their tracks. It wasn't Stefan's doing and in no way did it affect their friendship, but Kevin found himself hoping that Alexis wouldn't react like all the rest.

Stefan kept his love interests private, but generally the relationships were short and intense. Stefan had said once that his potential partner wouldn't show up for another few years, and that would happen only if she found him. When Kevin had asked for an explanation, the answer had been even more confusing.

"Energy, like colors or musical notes, have to combine to make the right kind of music, or I don't go there, no matter how willing or how gorgeous the woman is. Especially for a long-term relationship."

Colors? What did that have to do with anything? It boggled Kevin's mind.

As did the thought that he wanted Alexis for himself.

He couldn't help but wonder if Alexis blended with his colors, creating the potential to make the right kind of music.

And, if they did, how long before they could start to sing their colorful song together?

ALEXIS DROVE CAREFULLY to the address Stefan had given her on his business card. The driveway, lined by tall trees, appeared well-kept and normal. She wasn't sure what she expected, but considering what this man could apparently do, it wouldn't be an ordinary home. She followed the curve of the road and hit the brakes.

What the hell?

The gardener in her was stunned. Both the transmitter and the receiver in her were overwhelmed … with joy. Gently she parked her truck to the side and got out. She took several steps forward, tears in her eyes.

It was apparent in this setting that she was but a newbie student to a master when it came to gardening or plant health. All the bushes, flowers, even the trees looked like they were on steroids. The house itself twinkled through the greenery that both hid and guarded it from prying eyes. One side of Stefan's house was all glass that reflected the setting sun. The rest was crafted from logs. Some of them so huge she'd wished she'd seen the trees before they'd been felled. Evergreens bordered the property, and they glowed with some otherworldly shimmer.

Everything was alive in a way she had never seen before. Birds twittered and sang in the garden as she stood in awe.

"Were you planning to come in or to just stand there?"

Stefan. She didn't bother to glance at him. Her gaze was desperately trying to delve deeper into the miracle in front of her.

"Earth to Alexis."

"I'm here. I'm just … overwhelmed." She'd never seen roses with blooms so big. And the colors. Everything practically radiated joy. Wood carvings peeked out from parts of the garden, catching and holding her attention. Such craftsmanship.

"Don't be. You're very talented with plants as well."

That caught her attention. "No," she said. "I'm skilled." She waved her arms around her and added, "This … is talent. I don't even recognize some of these plants."

"I'm a bit of a collector. Have plants from all over the world." He grinned.

She stared for a moment, then grinned back. "And you are too damn good-looking as well."

This time he chuckled. "But only temporarily. Once you get to know me, I won't look that way at all."

She frowned and walked closer. "Why? Does the troll in you shine brighter the better I get to know you?"

He stepped inside and motioned her to enter, but she couldn't. She stalled at the open front door. Made of wood, it was as if she saw Tolkien's tree Ents coming to life. Faces had been carved, making unique use of the wood grains. She shook her head and walked in. "You didn't answer my question."

She followed him through the house, loving the unique space, the bright lights, … and, oh my God, the stained-glass windows. She spun around, trying to take everything in, and realized she couldn't. The walls were covered with paintings that drew her in and wouldn't let go.

"I don't need to."

Had she insulted him? She hoped not. Damn her unruly tongue. She studied Stefan's features carefully. He didn't appear to be upset.

He motioned her to a chair. "We'll start right now. And we'll keep it short. I want to show you how to protect your space and how to run the energy you need for your system. I'll show you several techniques to help you meditate. From there, all kinds of skills can be worked on."

"Like?" Alexis sat where he pointed.

"Talking safely with ghosts, for starters."

She flushed. Dare she ask about the *safely* part? But he was already giving her instructions to sit comfortably and to take several deep breaths. She tried to let the questions go and followed along.

And hoped she could trust where he led.

Forty minutes later, she was still hoping.

"Okay, we'll try to put all this into practice right now, then call it a night. Close your eyes. Focus on deep breathing. One breath in. ... Let it out slowly. And again. As each thought flits into your mind, acknowledge the thought exists, then let it slide away. Let it go. Let them all go. Let the thoughts drift in and then drift out. Just like your breath. Deeper breaths, longer exhales. Feel the tension drain away.

"Now think of a favorite place where you'd like to be. A waterfall, a beautiful meadow. One of your favorite gardens perhaps. See yourself there. Be there. Smell the fresh air. ... Feel a breeze on your skin."

Alexis walked forward toward a waterfall she'd loved as a child. She was on the path through an open meadow. The grass was high, the sun hot. The sound of the water beckoned. She felt so alive. Strong. Vibrant. She tilted her face to the sun and smiled.

Feels good, doesn't it?

She turned to answer Stefan, somehow not surprised to see him in her meditation. *Yes, it does.*

Good. Now let's work on your energy pathways.

She followed his instructions and saw the energy in her body glow, as he pointed out how to move it up the meridians that crisscrossed her body. He showed her how the little hiccups in the meridians could be smoothed out and how to increase the energy as the two of them moved about.

She lost track of time in this alternate world, as if just the two of them were in a whole new world.

Actually it is a new world. It's a different facet of the old world—but in a whole new way. For you. For me and many others, this is a place we come to often.

She could believe it.

Someone else is here as well. Someone hoping to say hi.

She turned to look at him. Lord, he looked different. Surreal, glowing even. At the beginning of this exercise, he'd looked like he had when she'd arrived at his house. Now he looked, ... well, ... ghostly.

He laughed. *That's because we crossed into a new dimension. We're on the dead side of life, so to speak. The other side. An alternate plane of existence. And, because we are here, at least this much inside the energy field, someone wants to see you. Someone who has stuck around instead of traveling into the light. Someone who has waited a full year for this moment.*

A glowing purple-gold light stepped out from behind him.

Alexis stared. The form became more distinct. Clearer. More easily identified.

Her heart stopped. Then raced forward. Her feet unknowingly did the same. She ran into the wide-open arms ready to receive her.

Lissa!

CHAPTER 7

ALEXIS'S WEEK DISAPPEARED under a heavy load of work and practice sessions. She went to work each day, impatient to end her workday in time for her sessions with Stefan or to work on her lessons at home. And to have more visits with her sister.

Focusing on her day job, she raked, weeded, and hoed her way down the rows and the beds. The plants were reaping the benefits of her developing skills. The colors of her flower beds no longer erratically jumped and zinged around. As she practiced being calm, loving, and centered, the plants followed in kind. The colors of some were less exuberant perhaps, but all were healthier looking.

Who'd believe that stilling her mind and opening her chakras, a concept Stefan had shared with her, could happen in the first place? Or that, when the chakras were open, the energy moved through the body in a healing way that automatically spread outward to others?

If only she could learn to calm her thoughts. After just two sessions with Stefan, she'd already learned so much, but mastery of that knowledge was a long way off.

"Hey, Alex!"

Alexis turned to see Scott striding toward her.

"What's going on, Alex? Lately you're taking off like you've got a hot lover stashed somewhere. It's not like you." Scott's long shaggy hair flipped in the wind, with his shaking head. He stopped to take a closer look at her. "You don't, do you? You'd tell your good buddy, Scott, wouldn't you?" he teased.

"Are you nuts? You'd post it in the newspapers, if I told you. I'm not quite that naive." Her heart warmed at the sight of him. "No, I've found someone to help me with the Sight."

His laughter stilled as he grew serious. "That's good, that is. Just don't be believing everyone out there. Plenty of charlatans in this world."

"This one isn't." She was dead certain of that. Stefan had such incredible abilities, and she knew he hadn't even found his own limits yet. Currently her practical psychic work centered on controlling her energy, so she could respond to Stefan's telepathy in the same way—with mixed success. She still didn't know if her telepathy would work with anyone else, although she suspected she might communicate that way with Kevin eventually. According to Stefan, Kevin had far more than just basic psychic abilities. Stefan had refused to elaborate, insisting instead that she ask Kevin herself.

Unfortunately she hadn't seen the irritatingly sexy detective in days.

LATER THAT DAY she arrived at Stefan's for their prearranged training session. She pulled up beside a truck and parked, a little nervous but excited to see him. She knocked on the front door and took a step inside, calling out, "Stefan?"

"We're in the solarium." His voice came from deep in the house.

Figured. Stefan appeared to live in that room. She headed to the room where she'd gone for most of their practice sessions. "Hi."

Stefan sat in his big corner chair and beamed at her. She glanced around for Kevin but found no sign of him. She raised an eyebrow. "Is that Kevin's truck out front?"

Stefan nodded toward the large deck beyond the open doors.

Her gaze searched, slipped past, then locked on the silent man, leaning over the railing. She didn't need to be psychic to know that something was wrong in Kevin's world. Quietly she asked, "Do you want me leave? We can do this another night."

"No, you might be good for him tonight."

Startled, she stared at him. "I doubt that."

A secretive smile played around the corner of his lips. She eyed him suspiciously, "Go say hi to him," he urged. "Or better yet, sit here and try to read him telepathically. Figure out what is bothering him."

Soberly she took up her meditative position. She distanced herself from the outside world and let her mind open, like she'd been taught. Thinking of a beautiful waterfall, she imagined herself floating gently in the warm pool of water beneath, and she relaxed. She let her mind empty of all thoughts, accepted when something popped in, then gently released it again. Hesitantly her consciousness stretched outward, past the walls and beyond. She floated lightly in Kevin's direction.

Keeping her concentration focused on Kevin, she said, *Hi, Kevin.*

As if she'd opened a door, strong colors surged into her mind, stretching her ability to see them, as the maelstrom filled her. The same reds, blacks, and whites swirled around Kevin in an angry vortex. The force of the colors stunned her. She didn't need to open her emotional center to understand his feelings. They swamped her.

Fear! Pain. Anger. Frustration. Something was wrong, and he didn't know what. *Police, children, death, torture,* the words poured through Alexis's mind in an endless, horrific stream of ghastly movie clips that she couldn't turn off. She slammed that door shut immediately. The withdrawal jolted her painfully back to Stefan's living room.

Her hands trembled, as she shifted her position. She tucked them under her thighs to calm down the tremors, and her heart raced, even as she gasped for breath. Elated yet shaky, she evaluated her success. She'd done it, but what had it gotten her? A glimpse into Kevin's nightmares? That she didn't need. She had enough of her own to deal with.

"Satisfied?"

Startled, she looked over to see a disgruntled Kevin, leaning against the doorjamb, staring at her.

Worried, she asked in a small voice, "Did I overstep some unspoken boundary?"

The darkness on his features lightened. He shook his head. "No, I would have bumped you out if you had. What did you find out?"

Slowly she concentrated on formulating an answer. "That you don't know what's wrong yourself. You feel like something bad will happen, only you don't know what. Even if you did know, you couldn't change it, and *that's* what you really hate."

Cool gray eyes surveyed her. "Not bad, not bad at all."

She shrugged dismissively. "Those were the feelings that I could read. The words were much harder."

"What words?" he demanded sharply.

"*Death, children, pain, torment, blackness, torture ...*" She recited the litany blindly, ignoring the look of utter astonishment on his face. She tried to stay detached, but the utter bleakness of the memory and of the words themselves got to her. She fell silent, as her throat clogged with emotions.

She closed her eyes and shuddered, wanting to ease his nightmare but not knowing how. It took several minutes to regain her balance. When the heavy emotions finally receded, she opened her tear-rinsed eyes to find Kevin crouching before her.

Not able to help herself, she reached for his hand and held it up against her chest. She wished she could take his soul inside her own and chase away his darkness. She stroked his fingers, his arm. Wanting, wishing she could help him … ease his pain, alleviate his sorrow …

"You have to grow a tough shell in this business, or it will destroy you." He spoke simply but with conviction. "So much pain and suffering is in the world, you must find a way to detach, or the knowledge of it *will* kill you."

"Have you? Found a way, I mean?" she asked shakily, staring into eyes that were windows to a world she'd never known existed. And now that she knew what his job put him through, part of her wished she could return to ignorance.

"Sometimes. And sometimes man's brutality is just too much for any of us to handle."

"How can you bear it?" she cried out. "What outlet is there for all this poison?" Her heart ached with his pain. "How can you do this job? Live through these conditions?" Alexis closed her eyes, as emotions poured through her. Her fingers clenched, then soothed his fingers with soft strokes.

"Don't do that. You're not strong enough." Kevin's sharp voice cut through her.

She tilted her head and frowned at him. She wasn't *doing* anything. "Do what?"

"You were absorbing his pain," Stefan said from the doorway.

Shock coursed through her. She turned to face Stefan, now standing behind her. "I'm what?" *Was that possible?*

Both men's voices slammed into her mind. *Yes!*

Startled, she looked from one to the other. Had they both spoken in her mind?

They both nodded.

This so didn't make sense.

Stefan, his gaze on hers, crossed the room to squat in front of her. "You mentioned to Kevin how the doctors were surprised your sister held death at bay for so long. The seriousness of her condition would have put anyone else into their grave much, much sooner." Stefan sat down on the floor beside her, laying a gentle hand on her knee.

Alexis could only stare at him in distress. She lowered her trembling fingers to her lap, clenching them together. "She was always strong, even as a little girl," she whispered.

Kevin placed a soothing hand on her shoulder, as Stefan continued, "She did so well, … and you didn't," he said, then added pointedly, "because you took her pain away. She held off death for those extra months because of *your* abilities. You activated the receiver in you. You received her pain, took it from her." He waited a moment for her to absorb his words. "But you suffered every day. You didn't know how to dump her pain from your aura or how to protect yourself."

"No, that's not possible!" Shock hit her. She shook her head violently. "No way." Except, along with the wonderment and the disbelief was a faint touch of understanding coloring her voice. He had to be wrong.

Still, a flame of hope that she might have helped her sister brightened inside. Lissa had suffered terribly. If Alexis had helped ease that for her—even a tiny bit—she was grateful.

"Not only possible but, in this case, definitely. You've probably been developing your abilities for years, first with the plants, then with your sister." Kevin dropped his hand and stepped back. "Only now are you aware that this is something not everyone can do to the extent you can."

"This is too much." The overwhelming concept besieged her. Memories, thoughts, and confusion crowded in, saturating her already overloaded emotions. She wrapped her arms around her chest, rocking in place.

"No, it's not. It's just new. You can do this." Stefan smiled down at her. "You *are* doing this."

"Come on, you need a break. Let's forget your session with Stefan tonight and get you some fresh air." Kevin pulled her to her feet, half tugging and half pushing her toward Stefan's front door.

Stefan watched with a paternal benevolence on his face. "He's right. That's enough for now. Go home and rest. Give it a few days before we move on to other techniques." He stepped forward, as if to return to his solarium, but stopped and turned back. "Because your senses are open, you must protect yourself at the times when you can't consciously deal with them. Before bed every night, you need to meditate and to follow this ritual. It will allow you to sleep undisturbed."

She gave him a tired nod. "I'll remember."

"The only reason it hasn't happened yet is because no one has tried," he warned. "Some of these people are desperate for help, and some are just plain evil. A door has been opened. From now on, you must take care."

Kevin tugged her outside. "Come on." Nudging her in the direction of his truck, he said, "I know a nice little café down the road a mile or so. I'll drive you back here later to pick up your truck."

Alexis nodded, too numb to talk. Her bones ached like never before. Fatigue lived inside her. Information overload had set in. She sat, silent, as he maneuvered his truck down Stefan's long driveway, then onto the main road. A few moments later, after the countryside had blurred into a collage of images and colors, he pulled up in front of a small building with several large patios.

"Come on. You'll feel better in a little while." He guided her into a small cozy restaurant and on through to an open-air patio, where he tucked her in behind a table located by a cheery outdoor fire. Even though summer air blasted around her, she welcomed the comfort of the flames.

Two frothy coffee concoctions arrived quickly. She hugged the mug, while warmth slowly returned to her cheeks. Eventually a deep sigh escaped, bringing with it a lessening of her tension.

"Don't think about it."

She didn't bother replying. How many people had to deal with this psychic stuff?

Lots.

"So you can speak in my mind too?" At his nod, she added peevish-ly, "When do I get to speak in your mind? It's not fair that you get to do all the fun stuff." She winced. She sounded like a two-year-old.

He obviously agreed, if his deadly grin was anything to go by. God, she was tired.

"Did you eat?"

His question caught her unaware. She had to stop and think. "No, I don't think I did."

He shot her a disgusted look, before getting up to grab a menu from the front counter. He tossed it down in front of her. "Pick out something."

"I'm not really hungry."

"It doesn't matter. You need food. Choose something."

It was easier to order than argue. Afterward, she sat mesmerized by the fire, as he returned to the counter to place their order. There was an ironic element to this mess. As a child, she'd always wanted to be a witch with magical powers. As an adult, she knew better. Fairy tales were kids' dreams. Now she'd learned that the old adage was right—be careful what you wish for; you just might get it!

Anybody else would be excited to learn about these talents, wouldn't they? What was wrong with her? She should be happy that she'd helped her sister. Instead, this bothered her. *Why?*

"What are you thinking?" Kevin studied her face. "And, no, I won't read your mind without your permission."

She couldn't help but snort. "These abilities terrify me." She slumped back, as horrible fears filled her heart. "What if I screwed up?"

"You loved your sister very much. You were driven by your need to help, to ease her pain. Motive is everything here. If you came from a position of love, then love is what you transmitted and received." He studied her features. "And you loved her, didn't you?"

"Absolutely." The answer burst free. She smiled, as relief blossomed inside. "Thank you. There is so much to consider. To deal with. It's overpowering."

He grinned. A carefree motion that let her know his earlier unrest had eased. That he could live with all the stuff, said a lot about his temperament.

"That's understandable. All your beliefs have been challenged. This isn't a comfortable sit-back-and-enjoy-yourself type of ride. This is an intense, painful, and downright unnerving process."

"Were you scared? You know? When you first found out?"

A twinkle shone from his gaze. "Terrified."

His honesty disarmed her. "Really?" She searched his features intently for any attempt on his part just to make her feel better. He radiated only sincerity.

"Any normal person would be alarmed if ghosts suddenly showed up in their world. In my case, the ghosts were all connected to my work."

She hesitated to ask, then couldn't help herself. "You didn't have these talents as a child?"

"No, like you, I came into them after a major shock. In my case, I was shot. I died on the operating table. Luckily I didn't stay that way." His face pinched.

She grimaced. "Yeah, I can see how that might do it." She needed to know more. "Tell me."

His finger traced the scalloped pattern on the iron table, as he sighed and lifted his gaze to hers. "It was years ago. I was at the scene of a bank robbery. There'd been a standoff, before the two perps gave up. On their way out of the bank to surrender to the police, one of them pulled out a hidden gun and fired off several rounds before being shot dead. Two of his bullets found targets—in me."

Silence fell over them. Alexis stared down at the table. Without knowing it, she'd cradled his hands within both of hers. Subconsciously she'd reached out to remove his pain. Her hands froze.

Stefan and Kevin had been right.

She didn't know exactly what she was, a transmitter or a receiver—or both, as apparently they went together for some people—or whether she was something else again. But she did know she'd mentally been siphoning off his troubled energy. Easing his aura. His soul.

She sat back, disturbed by a reality she could no longer ignore. This was no quirky gift that she could play around with for fun. It was a part of her identity that she hadn't known, hadn't understood even existed. A part of who she was.

During the lengthening somber silence, the waitress arrived with their food.

Alexis stared at her meal. She needed her strength, her health. With that new understanding, she ate ravenously. He sat back and watched. She barely looked up.

"Change of heart?"

"Maybe."

He watched as she polished off her sandwich and salad. When she eyed his remaining food, he quickly finished it.

"Just joking." She grinned hugely. That grin widened cheekily, as she watched his lips quirk with an answering grin.

God, he was sexy. After years of celibacy, the awakening of her hormones was excruciatingly intense. Like everything else happening in her world right now. It was like nothing fit anymore. Or after a long winter, summer clothes felt odd, leaving her more exposed than she was used to. She suspected Stefan would explain that the awakening of her other senses had awakened these ones too.

She turned to look around the room, afraid he'd read her thoughts. Stefan had tried to show her how to put up a wall to block her thoughts from being read, but she'd not yet succeeded.

And Kevin wasn't relationship material, not with a job like his. She'd loved and lost too many times to ever contemplate going there again. At least that had been her position up to now.

Besides, could she trust her emotions right when they were in chaos? With her desire escalating every time she was around Kevin, did she have a choice?

"Alexis?" Kevin called out, his voice darkly sensual.

Slowly she turned and gazed at him. His eyes, like charcoal magnets, pulled her deep into their depths. She was drowning in sexual awareness and didn't even care in that moment.

They might have been the only two people on the patio for all the notice they took of their surroundings. Pure streaming energy flowed between them.

"Alexis?" he repeated, his voice velvety smooth and full of secrets. Secrets he invited her to share.

Oh boy. Alexis closed her eyes briefly and drew herself back, shudders sliding over her skin in withdrawal from his unspoken promise.

"Damn," his voice cracked in agonizing acceptance. His shoulders sagged. He turned to look out into the darkness. He swallowed convulsively, looking everywhere but at her.

She whispered into the agonizing silence, "I'm not ready."

He dropped his gaze, a pained grin showing. "I know, but I'd hoped."

Her lips curled knowingly, spiking the energy once more. "Thanks. And ... I'm sorry."

The evening ended soon afterward. She was careful not to physically touch him, in case she risked starting something she wasn't ready for. The trip back to Stefan's was fast and silent.

After a quick goodbye, Alexis got in her truck and headed home, comfortable in her skin for the first time in days. If there would be ghosts in her life, then she wanted a say in when and where they appeared to her.

Lissa. Her name floated painlessly on the air—for the first time in over a year. Feeling lighter, sweeter, and so full of love, Alexis swore she heard Lissa's laughter tinkling around her. It had to be her imagination, but the memory of it brought tears to Alexis's eyes. She knew in her heart that Lissa was okay.

Alexis could finally move on.

"So what do we know at this point? Caucasian female?" Captain Mark Gosling dropped the report on his desk, continuing to read aloud. "According to the initial report, the probable cause of death is a broken neck. Age ..." He flicked a couple pages. "Approximately eight to ten years old, based on mixed dentition. Buried in a yellow dress and an *M* ... is embroidered on the collar." The captain frowned. "Maybe the start of her name?"

Kevin stood quietly, his copy of the coroner's initial report in hand, waiting for his friend and boss to go over the more salient points. He shrugged. "Maybe. Anything helps at this point."

"I don't like the next bit though." Blustery, loud, yet infinitely capable, the captain had no problem showing his displeasure. "X-rays show the kid had multiple fractures ... on left arm, right wrist, and badly broken left tibia. Not to mention broken and badly healed index finger on the left hand and two cracked ribs."

Damn. Kevin knew the chances of those manifold injuries being accidental were slim. "All those had healed. So the assumption is that the child was possibly abused over a long time period. *Damn*."

Kevin sat down in the armchair opposite the desk. "We're waiting on the lab results, possibly collecting DNA from the teeth. We also determined that the grave was not the primary crime scene."

"Which isn't unusual. But no proof that this is a murder case."

"No," Kevin spoke slowly, organizing his thoughts. "We're still waiting for more test results to come back to understand how long the skeleton was there." Kevin pulled out his notebook to check his notes. "According to Scott, those particular gardens have been there, basically undisturbed at that level, for fourteen years. Around that time, backhoes were brought in, and major work done."

"Therefore," the captain said, "the body has been there less than fourteen years, presuming the work went as deep as the bones we found. Identification is top priority. Do what you need to do. Keep me posted. A child's skeleton in our city gardens. What next?" The captain turned back to the tall stack of files, sitting on the corner of his desk.

What next, indeed?

CHAPTER 8

THE VOICE STARTLED her.

Alexis had spent a few happy days with no strange phenomena; she had almost convinced herself that the anomaly was over.

So focused was she on transplanting fresh color into the huge beds, she never paid any attention to the multitude of noises around her. The colors of the young plants were not as vivid as they should have been. They badly needed nutrients. Alexis mentally calculated the amount of nitrogen they'd need.

Help. Help me, please.

Alexis spun around, still on her knees. No one was there. Far off on the other side she saw another colleague working hard. But the voice had been too soft, sad even, to be him—and way too close to Alexis.

Something—or someone—was here. Another spirit? She took a deep breath and made a quick decision. Rather than just let things happen, she'd try to control how it happened.

Hiding in the shadow of a large bush, she sat down and closed her eyes, as Stefan had taught her to do. Slowly she took several deep breaths, letting the stiffness slide from her spine and drain into the ground beneath her. Feeling the stress and the nervousness ease, she visualized walking through a beautiful meadow, every step freeing her from the physical reality of her existence. She reached a waterfall, and a beautiful glistening pool waited for her there. She couldn't resist; she sat on one of the rocks surrounding the water. She dipped her toes in and felt more relaxed than she had in a long time. From this position of peacefulness she widened her consciousness ever-so-slightly.

Instantly sensations forced their way in—fear, pain, loss, grief, and sadness. Alexis slammed the door shut, gulping for air. It was one thing to practice, but quite another when reality kicked you in the stomach. Briefly opening her eyes, she was relieved to find herself still alone. Inhaling deeply, she closed her eyes and tried again. This time she opened the door just a smidgen.

The rush of emotions was still there but not quite so demanding.

Alexis opened her eyes and gasped. The world had a completely different look to it—surreal colors, with less definition but with a brighter, eerily translucent color blending.

A young girl stood in front of her—the same little girl Alexis had seen in the ditch. Alexis sighed softly. The cherub was tiny, blond, and beautiful. She appeared to be dressed in a yellow party dress, matching ribbons in her hair, except the grass from the park lawn showed through her dress, giving it an oddly alive look.

"Hello," Alexis whispered softly.

The angel smiled, creating a golden light that warmed Alexis's heart.

Hello, Alexis.

Alexis studied the waif intently. She was spectacular. No way Alexis wouldn't have remembered her if they had ever met. "You know my name?"

You're the garden lady who makes the plants laugh.

Alexis leaned back in astonishment. "Do I?" She loved the sound of that. "Do you hear them?"

I listen sometimes and watch, the child said.

A wistful longing crept from her voice, breaking Alexis's heart. "Do you have a place to go? You know, like a home?"

No, the little girl whispered in Alexis's mind forlornly. *I can't go home. Ever.*

Alexis struggled with that last single word. *Ever.*

Then the child spoke again telepathically. *I have to stay here, so he won't do it again.*

"Do what?"

He says, if I stay with him, he won't have to hurt any more little kids.

"Who? Who is hurting kids?" Alexis tried to keep her voice calm, peaceful. But damn it was hard. She hated to think someone was hurting children. And what would this little girl have to do with stopping him?

The translucent angel stared back, solemn but silent.

Alexis tried again. "Doesn't he like little girls?"

Oh, yes. He loves little girls ... and boys.

That didn't make sense. Alexis didn't want to scare her off but needed clarification. Slowly she asked, "Then why does he hurt them?" The sunlight slid into something else, stormy, cloudy, and a little eerie. Shadows rippled in the background.

The little girl's form hitched and wavered, before rippling away in a fast fade-out.

"No, wait. Don't go."

The shadows shifted. Other little pale faces formed before dissipating in the fog.

I'll come back, … if I can get away, echoed the ghostly whisper in Alexis's mind.

She was gone.

The blackness was absolute.

Alexis closed her eyes, trying to shift realities, and slowly returned to her surroundings. Icy chills filled her. Stefan had warned her that she might never feel warm again, as long as ghosts were among her closest confidants. Each person experienced a different reaction. Hers seemed to be freezing and tiredness.

Shivers raced down her spine. As much as she didn't want to, she also felt obligated to tell Kevin about her experience. Surely every bit of information counted. Not that she had much to offer. Still, the station was only one block away.

From a coffee shop situated beside the police station, she stopped to pick up two of the largest coffees they had. Walking inside the police station, sipping her coffee, she moaned softly as the warm cream-laced brew slid all the way down, curling her chilled insides with delight.

"May I help you?"

She took one more sip, before answering the police officer at the front desk. "Yes. Is Detective Sutherland in, please?"

"Just a moment. Who's inquiring, please?"

Alexis gave the female officer her name and sat down to wait. Maybe he'd be too busy to talk to her.

"Alexis, nice to see you." Kevin stood smiling in front of her. "Are one of those for me?"

She handed him the second cup. "I hope you like it black." She took a sip of hers, collecting her thoughts. "May I talk to you for a moment?"

He instantly became businesslike. "Sure. Do you want to come into my office or take a walk over to the park?"

She perked up. "The park's a great idea."

Kevin held the door open for her.

They walked companionably for a few moments. When they reached the park, almost at the same spot where she'd seen the little girl, Alexis's words blurted out, "I saw her again."

"Who?"

"The little girl, Daisy."

He searched her face, as if to read what she *hadn't* said. "What happened?"

A sigh gusted out heavily. "I followed Stefan's instructions on opening the door consciously but just a little bit at a time. That made it easier." She rubbed her arms. "Except, after this time, the cold's much worse. I'm not as tired maybe, but definitely colder."

"Hence the hot coffee?"

She nodded at his astuteness. "Daisy said she couldn't leave. She couldn't leave until he stopped hurting little girls." Alexis paused, thinking. "No, that isn't quite right." She concentrated on the little girl's words. "She said, she has to stay, so he won't hurt any more little kids." She finished in a rush, relieved to have remembered.

She paused a moment, staring morosely at the beaded drops on the surface of her take-out lid before continuing, "She also said that he doesn't hate little girls and boys. He loves them." Alexis sipped at her drink, as despair wafted through her already muddled emotions. She'd never get warm at this rate. The child's odd words had sent another chill directly to her very soul. Maybe it wasn't the vision giving her the chills but more likely the concept of a child abuser. Like how wrong was that?

"Could be a serial killer, or could be something else altogether. Not sure if that fits what little we know—if that's her body we found."

"What did you find out?" Alexis gazed at him warily.

"The child had been embalmed. As far as we can figure, she was stolen from her grave right after burial—or from the funeral home before her burial—and then was buried here."

"What? Why?" Alexis froze in shock. Why would anyone do such a horrible thing? She sat down on the closest bench. This new information rocked her to the core. She shook her head in disbelief.

He shrugged. "I don't know why."

"So she might not have been murdered either, right?" The rest of the conversation came back in a rush. "She said, I'm the lady who makes the plants laugh. What are the chances that the gardens—and me, the gardener—are a connection between the children?"

Heaviness settled in the blossom-laden air.

"It seems a stretch, but it could be. Then again, it's probably too early to make a connection." He shrugged. "We've run a DNA sample through the database, in case her death was a criminal case. I'll check to see if any missing bodies are mentioned in the case files or if this has happened somewhere else. Another possibility is facial reconstruction. If we can get a picture of her face, created from her skull, then we can send that to the media, hopefully to identify her that way. But that is expensive."

Alexis hated to think the child had been there all these years, and yet no one knew. From what she'd seen in her visions, the child hadn't had a great life, and to think she might have been buried, dug up, and then reburied was just too much. This child had been through enough.

They had to help free her.

IT WAS LATE when Alexis headed to bed that night. She dropped into dream sleep immediately.

In her dream state, she walked through a beautiful wildflower meadow, with sunshine and yellow finches. Lissa walked beside her. It felt wonderful. The two of them were full of bubbling girl talk. Alexis couldn't tell her dream from her memories. They seemed the same.

She loved it.

Alexis ignored the subtle changes going on around her. The joy at spending time with her sister overrode any other worries. Then Lissa froze, staring into the growing blackness moving over them.

Where had that dark wall come from? The sun had been shining only seconds ago. *Lissa? What's wrong?*

Alexis spun around, looking for answers. She found nothing. Literally nothing. Only a smoky black fog surrounding the two of them. Lissa never answered. Alexis swiveled, searching Lissa's starkly pale face. Alexis placed her hands on her sister's shoulders and shook gently. *Talk to me. What's going on.*

Go! Get back. Lissa pushed away Alexis's hands and tried to turn Alexis around, shoving her forward. *You have to go back.'*

Go back where? What are you talking about?

The sun went out, as if on a switch, leaving the two of them in total darkness. A terrible sense of foreboding washed through Alexis. *Lissa, what's going on?*

He's here. Alexis, wake up. You're not safe. Wake up. Wake up!

Alexis woke up.

Her heart raced, trying to escape her rib cage. Her lungs gasped for air, while her mind pleaded to know what had just happened.

Only her nightmare wasn't over.

Someone was in her room.

Fear and sweat poured off her skin. Huddled under her covers, she shivered. Excruciatingly quiet, terrified of moving and attracting attention, Alexis desperately tried to calm her ragged breathing.

He hadn't moved. *Why? What was he doing? Who was he?* Fear shut down her ability to think.

Macabre laughter filled the tiny room—or was that in her mind?

You can't fool me. I know you're awake. I can smell your fear. That's very smart of you. Be afraid. But you're not so wise to talk with my Daisy. She's mine and don't you dare forget it.

The disembodied voice faded, taking with it the horrific sense of an intimate brush with evil.

Alexis waited several long minutes. When she was sure he wasn't coming back, she tried to sit up and turn on her light.

Only to find out she couldn't.

She wrestled uselessly inside her body, trying to force it to shift. Alarms sounded, until she relaxed back, gasping at the nasty twist. She could breathe and blink, but she couldn't move her arms or legs. Panic ripped through her.

Dear God. She was paralyzed.

She screamed—soundlessly.

Into the chaos of her mind came a voice.

Alexis. Try to stay calm. Stefan's voice brought an instantly comforting realization. She wasn't alone. Stefan had come to help her—at least telepathically.

That's better. Focus. Now. What's the matter?

I'm paralyzed.

In another part of her mind, she heard and felt the overwhelming emotions screaming to whoever heard. But it was disconnected from her, as if it were someone else. How odd. Then someone found her volume switch and turned it down. Whoever it was, adjusted it downward yet again.

Explain.

Calmer, with her mental functions allowing her to think, she tried to answer Stefan's question. Talking to Stefan with her baby telepathy skills demanded all her focus. Shakily at first, then with building strength, she gave him the details. She was forced to relive the horrible memories that were now permanently etched in her mind. And to feel them again.

You're not physically paralyzed. You're paralyzed by your fear.

"Feels the same," she muttered aloud. It took a minute for it to register. She'd spoken out loud.

See? The fear is easing. That's why you could speak that time. Continue to work on relaxing your mind and to know that you are safe. I'm here in your mind with you. Your muscles will slowly unwind, as you calm down.

It took another ten long, painful minutes before she could move her hands.

Good. It's improving.

She continued to calm her mind, relaxing her muscles. With the worst of her fright under control, she took one deep, ragged breath and released it slowly—only to freeze again at the powerful banging on her front door.

"Alex! Alexis, open this door. Damn it, open up."

Kevin.

"I can't," she whispered, knowing her voice couldn't reach the front door. She hadn't recovered to that extent. *Stefan?*

I'll tell him.

Emptiness filled her mind as Stefan withdrew. Terror resurged to the surface as she realized she was alone again. Shudders raced down her body. She grappled with the horrible sense of aloneness.

No, she could do this. She had to be strong—to control this. She was almost there.

The pounding on her door ceased.

"Alexis, I'm coming in."

Kevin could do what he wanted. She couldn't stop him. Within seconds, she heard the sounds of her door opening and Kevin rushing toward her. She lie here, waiting for his reaction.

What she received both stunned and touched her and brought hot tears to her eyes.

Kevin dropped to the floor at her bedside. In an incredibly tender movement, he lowered his head until his warm cheek rested on her cool one. "It's okay. You're not alone anymore," he whispered against her ear.

He shifted to sit beside her, before wiping the tears from her eyes. Pulling back slightly, he picked up her hand and stroked her arm in a calm, soothing motion. "You'll be fine. I'm here now. Everything will be all right. Just relax."

His comforting presence helped ease her rigidity. Her paralysis faded, leaving behind a coldness and a bone-weary exhaustion.

She'd never felt heaviness like this before, like her bones were made of concrete. She seemed to be part of the bed, sinking through the mattress to become one with the floor—a rather disconcerting sensation.

"I think I'm okay." She shivered.

She attempted to sit up, but Kevin placed his hands on her shoulders to keep her down.

"Don't move yet. Even though it feels better, you'll experience a numbness, a time lag between your mind and muscles for a while."

The conviction in his voice explained his understanding. He'd been through this himself.

"This is no fun," she said peevishly. As she began to feel more like herself, irritation quickly replaced the trailing splinters of fear.

He grinned down at her. "No, it isn't, is it? With any luck, now that you've been through it once, that won't happen again."

Alexis couldn't quite understand how or what had happened in the first place. Thankfully he seemed to understand her confusion. He picked up her hand, holding it gently in his. His thumb stroked across the back of her hand in a slow, comforting movement.

"There are possible variations on how to explain what happened. The first is that you left your body, and you jumped back in too fast. The shock of that can paralyze you. The other is that fear snapped your consciousness awake too fast and created a state of temporary paralysis."

At his explanation, Alexis's attention shifted away from the odd feeling of having her hand cradled in his. "Out of body, … returning to the body. I don't think I like the sound of either of those."

"For many scientists, it's an accepted theory that you leave the body every night to astral travel."

A hard quiver rocked her body. Now she really didn't like what he was saying.

"Stefan just hadn't gotten that far along in your education." Kevin shrugged. "Easy to understand. After all, no one expected your psychic development to move along so quickly." He patted her hand and stood. "You can try to sit up now. Expect your muscles to feel like rubber. I'll make you a cup of sweet tea. Back in a minute."

She watched him walk out of her room. Damn, he looked good. Casually in charge, he wore power like other men wore suits. A rush of sexual energy flowed through her, slowly reawakening her body. *Holy crap.* The sensations caught her unaware, leaving her open and unguarded, as erotic images whispered through her mind. Her body shifted restlessly on its own. Silk sheets smoothing over her bare skin. Sensitizing the nerve endings.

Dear God, if Kevin jumped in her mind now …

Breathe. Control. Detach. This was *so* unfair.

She sat up on the side of the bed again and consciously emptied her mind, which was easier to say than do. Focus. … *Shit!* She groaned at the constant stream of sensual images firing through her mind.

"Is something wrong?" Kevin's concerned voice carried from the other room.

"No," she yelped. She had to get up.

Moving as fast as her rubbery muscles would allow, she tugged an old terry cloth robe over her silk cami set, before wobbling from the bedroom. The living room clock read two in the morning. So much for getting some sleep tonight.

"The tea's almost ready. Are you moving around okay?"

She grimaced. "Did you feel like you'd been hit by a cement truck when it happened to you?" She walked slowly into the living room.

"A whole convoy of them." He nodded in sympathy but that grin of his? … Lethal. "It takes a while to get your balance back. You'll feel even worse tomorrow."

This time, his grin was pure mischief. She didn't know if she should believe him or not. The way she felt now, it couldn't get much worse. The exhausted feeling was a direct contradiction to the liquid lust, and both were battling for supremacy. She didn't dare look at him, afraid he'd read everything she was trying so hard to keep hidden. There had to be something to distract her unruly hormones.

"What were you dreaming about?"

That did it.

Her horrific nightmare surged back to the forefront. Ice raced down her spine, as she remembered Lissa's terror and her conviction that danger closed in. Even now, Lissa's screams for Alexis to wake up before it was too late echoed in her mind.

Yet waking up to that scary apparition in her room had been even worse.

The phone rang.

Its harsh sound startled Alexis, while grounding her back to this physical reality. Unconsciously she looked at Kevin.

He nodded. "It's Stefan."

She needed a pipeline like these two had. They were irritating.

She picked up the receiver. "Hello, Stefan."

"How do you feel now?" Concern tinged his voice, and she shuddered quietly in embarrassment. What if he'd been in her mind again, had seen the vivid sexual images playing through? She didn't think she could discuss those right now either. She looked again at Kevin, hoping he wasn't picking up on the vibes.

Stefan's velvet voice whispered in her ear. "Later. We'll discuss it later."

She closed her eyes. He *had* seen them. *Damn.* Regardless of the awkwardness, she knew she needed his help. Even more now. "Fine. Some weird crap's going on here." She took a deep breath. "Someone was in my room tonight."

"I know. He won't return tonight. I promise. We'll discuss that tomorrow too. You need to get some rest."

She snorted in disgust, the sound spinning Kevin around to face her. "And just how do you suggest I do that? I was asleep when it happened. Remember? I may never sleep again," she said bitterly. "I've never seen evil before."

"It's taken me a long time to understand the people out there. Some of them are twisted. Very twisted. I no longer see evil as an ungodly spirit but more as a person who does ungodly things."

"So these people are just the opposite of us?"

"Exactly." As always, Stefan knew what she needed. His soothing tones melted over her.

"It will be all right. You have to remember to follow the steps that I showed you before going to sleep now. Instead of it merely being important, after tonight, it's mandatory. It will prevent you from being tracked and located. Someone has picked up your signature." The soothing tones disappeared, and his voice returned to normal, then hardened. "I won't explain it all now, but you no longer have that option—not if you want to stay safe."

She replied in a very small voice, "I will."

"Good, now let me speak to Kevin."

Silently she handed Kevin the phone.

He searched her face as he answered. "Hello, Stefan."

Alexis tuned out the conversation, as she drank her warm tea. She could still hear Kevin's voice. Oddly enough she could also hear a faint echo of Stefan's voice still in her head. This psychic communication stuff would take some getting used to.

God, she was so tired. She slumped down at one end of the couch, fatigue sinking her deeper into the cushions. Filling her mouth with warm tea, she leaned her head back and let her eyelids droop. Mentally she followed Stefan's instructions.

Minutes later, in a feat she'd never have thought possible, she was asleep.

STILL IN THE kitchen, Kevin continued to talk with Stefan, while keeping an eye on Alexis's movements. "I think she's out."

"Good. I did some energy work, easing her chakras. Glad it helped." Stefan paused for a weighty moment. "Will you stay the night?"

"Yes." Kevin volunteered nothing else. He didn't need to; Stefan already knew.

"Without taking advantage, right?"

Kevin let him wait, pissed he'd even been asked.

"Right?" Stefan's voice was no longer amiable.

It wasn't prudent to push Stefan's buttons too far. "You know I wouldn't do anything when she's this vulnerable. But ..." This time Kevin was the one pausing. "I give no promises for what happens tomorrow."

"Tomorrow she's a big girl again. She can make her own choices."

Kevin chuckled. "As long as she makes it through the night, I'll be happy."

"You're also in danger of losing your heart."

"Like hell," Kevin answered amiably, as he walked into the living room to check on her.

"I know what I see and feel. I'll mention it to you again in a month, and we'll reevaluate. Have a peaceful night." With that, Stefan hung up.

Kevin wanted to move Alexis to her bed but satisfied himself with gently rearranging her into a more comfortable position on the couch. The apartment was cooling off. He walked quietly into her bedroom for a blanket.

Her real personality showed here. The sheets were emerald silk, the duvet sporting a matching embossed pattern. At least a dozen pillows were probably initially on her bed, before her nightmares had tossed them wildly to the floor. Her closet was open, showing myriad colorful fabrics he'd never seen her wear. Wistfully he wondered what it would be like to see her all dressed up for a night on the town. He nudged the closet door wider with his feet. His heart leaped with joy at the sight of bright red spike-heeled shoes.

At heart, she was still *that* girl. Life had boxed her into the caregiver persona, quickly followed by the loner and the lonely existence. ... He could help her find this part of herself again. What he wouldn't do to see her in those shoes.

With another quick glance around, he took in the dresser, an old-fashioned mirror covering the back, and tiny perfume bottles laid out like soldiers, untouched. Yet ready. They spoke volumes about who Alexis had been and who she could be again. She just needed a gentle nudge, ... a reason to live again.

Feeling a little like an intruder, he snagged the duvet and returned to Alexis and covered her. She hadn't moved. In the huge armchair across from the couch, he made himself as comfortable as possible and waited for her to wake up.

CHAPTER 9

A LEXIS STRUGGLED INTO awareness. "Ouch," she murmured, shifting painfully on the couch. Rubbing the sleep from her eyes, she started and then bolted upright. Kevin sprawled out of her oversize chair, head tilted to the side, fast asleep. She winced at his position. His poor spine should be screaming right now.

What a gentle giant. He was a sweetheart to have stayed and watched over her.

Moving quietly, she slid off the couch and bundled up her duvet, returning it to her bed. Yawning again, she stepped into a hot shower. The heavy spray pounding over her tired body was painfully refreshing. Ten minutes later, she almost felt prepared to face the day.

Coffee would help. She tiptoed back through the living room and into the kitchen. Kevin still hadn't moved. While the coffee dripped, she rummaged through her cupboards. Between one thing and another, she hadn't taken time to shop. Now she regretted it. She had a sleeping guardian angel in the living room, who was liable to wake with a ravaging appetite.

Alexis grinned. Shivers rode up and down her spine, as another appetite stirred to life. While a weekend fling would be amazing, she didn't think she'd dip her big toe in, test the waters, and then walk away. Their weird psychic connection had the huge potential for delight ... or disaster.

The latter might not be enough to stop her though.

Denial wasn't something she was good at.

As a child, she'd had a bubbly enthusiasm and a glowing optimism that matched Lissa's. The death of their parents had wiped it all away for the then-eighteen-year-old Alexis. She'd worked hard to build a warm protective cocoon to keep the two of them safe. That had worked fine until Lissa's diagnosis.

Alexis stared out the window, when a deep, growly voice disturbed her reverie. Alexis turned to face him.

"Good morning." Kevin stood hesitantly in the kitchen doorway.

Bare-chested, top button of his jeans undone, and the material clinging lovingly to heavily muscled thighs, he ran his hand casually over the heavy morning shadow on his face. His utter maleness swamped her senses. Intense desire unfurled deep in her belly. Alexis swallowed thickly. He was devastating to her senses.

"Good morning," she finally answered, speaking carefully. She was afraid the wrong words would rush out. "How are you feeling?"

He smiled. "Isn't that my line?"

Her lips twitched. "I'm fine. At least I got some sleep. I'm sorry I don't have an electric shaver to offer up. You're welcome to use a disposable one if you wish." She shrugged. "That's all I have."

"Not to worry. I'll go home and clean up before going anywhere." He walked toward the coffeepot. "Besides, I find the lack of a man's razor encouraging. May I have a cup of coffee, please?"

She flushed at the comment and her lack of manners. "Sorry. Sit down, and I'll pour." She waved him toward the tiny table. She filled two mugs and retrieved the milk from the fridge. "The sugar is over there." She pointed to the plain clear bowl at the end of the table. "No razor is encouraging?" she questioned cautiously, not sure she wanted to know what he meant.

"Yes. You aren't accustomed to having men sleep over. *That's* encouraging."

Her face burned hotter. She didn't know what to say. For some reason, she felt he deserved the truth. Maybe it was because he'd cared enough to stay and to watch over her. "I haven't had a relationship since my sister got sick," she said quietly.

He slowly lowered his cup, staring deep into her eyes.

He's making me nuts.

Then Kevin reached across and tilted her chin up, until she was forced to look at him. His eyes twinkled. "Very encouraging."

Dear God. Her heart flip-flopped, before racing on again. She pulled back to a safe distance, rushing into speech to cover her reaction, hating the telltale heat washing over her cheeks. "Sorry, I only have toast for breakfast. I haven't gotten around to shopping."

"Just coffee's fine."

His intense gaze was unnerving. She glanced quickly at him and away again. "Thank you for coming to my rescue. Stefan too," she added, as a sincere afterthought.

Kevin nodded. "Stefan said we were to meet at his house this morning. Does that work for you? I didn't think you worked Saturdays."

Alexis nodded, slightly daunted at the prospect. "That's fine. We can grab something to eat on the way."

"That works. Maybe I will borrow your razor before we leave after all."

THE LATE MODEL truck was parked in the shade under the drooping willow tree, waiting.

"You're late."

The young man slid into the cab. "I came as soon as I could get away." He shifted nervously on the posh leather seat, his hand resting on the door handle, hoping, planning to make an early escape.

The automatic locks snapped down. He jerked involuntarily. Damn it.

A disgusted snort was his only answer.

"Look. I don't really know anything. I'm just a rookie. No one tells me nothing."

The older man's cold gaze cut through the excuses. "I have something to tell you. Make a bigger effort. You're only of use to me if you can supply valuable information." He paused a moment. "What can you tell me about this body from the garden?"

"That one's bizarre." Relaxing slightly, as if realizing he might have something to offer after all, the rookie answered, "The whole office is buzzing about this case. As far as they can figure, the little girl had been embalmed and may have even been buried, before being brought here and reburied."

"What?" The figure behind the wheel pursed his lips in a soundless whistle. He stared out the truck's window for a long moment, then turned his black gaze on his hapless young victim. "I need more," he snapped. "Call me tonight." He turned the key and started his truck. The sharp *click* of the locks being released echoed through the air.

Not having much in the way of options, the rookie officer nodded. He'd been in trouble before and had gotten out of it. But this time? ... He had to find an answer to this mess and fast, or he'd lose everything he'd worked so hard for, and he'd be back where he started—on the streets.

STEFAN SETTLED INTO his easy chair in the solarium. He needed a few minutes to unwind before Kevin and Alexis arrived.

She needs help.

Bold, concise, and irrefutable. That the warning came from someone no longer in this world in no way mitigated its truth. Stefan sighed. Rotating his neck and shoulders, he eased some of the tension building in his muscles. *I know.*

What will you do about it? The energy wafted through the room, its female voice imperious—impossible to ignore.

Stefan tilted his lips into a small smile. As much as he enjoyed his abilities and this female ghost who refused to leave him alone since he'd started working with Alexis, he wouldn't be dictated to. *Don't be pushy. They're on their way. We'll sort it out when they get here.* Stefan removed the lids from several of the small ceramic pots in front of him, creating just the right blend. *You might want to hang around and join in the session.*

Like she's ready for that.

Stefan grinned, knowing she was right, but also knowing that there was little anyone could do to make Alexis ready.

Let me help her. I know him. I know what he's like. I can warn her if it gets bad. The energy settled in front of him. *I love her. I need to help her, like she helped me.*

Stefan sighed. *It's not a good idea.*

Maybe not, but I have to. She needs me.

NO EXPENSE HAD been spared in creating a healing, soothing space for Stefan. So talented, yet tormented with overwhelming sensitivities, Alexis saw the small touches that had been added for his comfort—extensive use of soft pastels, overstuffed cushions, stereo system piping music into every room. A soft instrumental in the background.

"Alexis, when you're ready."

Alexis grimaced, putting her tea on the table. It was time, like it or not. No more trying to focus on anything but the matter at hand. Stefan and Kevin had waited patiently, while she'd attempted to settle herself. But fifteen minutes had gone by, along with their patience. "I'll tell you what I remember."

It didn't take long to recite her short crystalline memories of the night before. "Because the nightmare had been so vivid, so powerful, it took several minutes for me to realize I was awake and safe in my room." She stopped, swallowed convulsively several times, before continuing in a low voice. "Only I wasn't safe. The same evil presence from my nightmare was in my bedroom, waiting for me."

"Could you see it?" Kevin asked, his face alive with curiosity.

"No. The room was dark, full of shadows." She paused again, closing her eyes for a moment. "But I heard him. I don't know if he spoke in my head or aloud in the room." She clenched her trembling fingers tightly in her lap, trying to hold it all together. "He said I was wise to be afraid and to stay away from his Daisy."

"Daisy?" Kevin bolted to his feet, quickly coming to her side and bending close to her. "He actually said her name?"

Alexis nodded. "Yes, he did, and, from her voice, Lissa must have known of him, of his presence on her side." She stared at Kevin and Stefan in growing horror, as she realized what that meant. "Surely Lissa can't be in danger? She's dead." Her voice rose. Alexis couldn't do anything about it. Irrational fear for her sister chilled her skin to an iciness that quickly worked its way deep inside. "Oh, dear God," she whispered. "Is her soul in danger?"

Kevin wrapped his forearm around her shoulders, tugging her close in a protective hug. Alexis leaned gratefully into his warmth, craving security. How long had it been since she'd allowed herself to be held and comforted?

"*Shh.* … Your sister is fine. Her soul is fine." He squeezed Alexis gently before releasing her.

"God, I hope so." Relief washed through her. Then a slow burn of realization hit her. "You know what makes me so mad?" She glared at both men. "I was almost comfortable with these weird events happening and the psychic-ability thing goin' on, you know? Almost okay with it all, and then this happened." She hopped to her feet and paced around Stefan's living room. How plainly the space spoke of Stefan's personality. Sparse and clean, yet soothing.

"This is all happening too fast. I can't get a handle on it." Alexis stopped in front of Stefan, her hands fisted on her jean-covered hips. "You mentioned a signature. Just what is that?"

He took a sip of tea, while he collected his thoughts. "Everyone has an individual energy pattern. Like DNA, there can be no two energy patterns the same. These are signatures of your soul. Once recognized, they can be used to track someone on both sides of existence."

Alexis stared at him, appalled. "You mean, follow?"

He gazed back at her solemnly. "Follow." He paused again, obviously considering something. "This person read your signature on the other side and returned with you."

"So now he knows who I am and how to find me?" That was too

much. She slumped back down to her chair in defeat.

"Possibly, and possibly not."

"What does that mean? Why is everything so cryptic?" she cried out. Pain and confusion battled together in her mind. "A madman ghost out there knows me, but I don't know him or what he intends to do."

"Yes, you do." Both Kevin and Stefan jumped in together.

Alexis looked at them in bewilderment. "I do? How? I didn't see him. I don't know how to read his signature. What can I possibly know about him?"

"Tell me. If you were ever in the same room with him, would you sense that same evil again?" Stefan asked.

"Definitely." The answer flew out. "But that doesn't mean I would know where it was coming from."

"With time, you will. Just as I can," Kevin reassured her.

Kevin had never mentioned his skills before. She was curious. "Is that why you showed up at the park the first day we met?"

He nodded. "I knew someone needed help. I opened my mind and let this same 'knowing' find you." He grinned. "Of course what I found was a little unexpected."

She grimaced, remembering the mud-spattered mess she'd been. "Does that technique always work?"

"Here's the trick. These skills will work for you if you work with them. You need to be centered before you start, or it's much harder to understand what you're seeing and perceiving."

Alexis winced. "It sounds like a bad sci-fi movie to me."

"Just like this 'evil' presence is your imagination?" Stefan laughed. A large cushion hit his shoulder before landing on the floor beside him. "Thanks, I appreciate a second one." Calmly he added the pillow she'd tossed to the one he was already using. Alexis glared at him in frustration.

The two men waited for her with understanding and compassion written on their faces.

The main question burned away deep inside. "Why would he warn me to stay away from Daisy? What is he doing to her?"

Stefan said, in a determined voice, "That's what we'll find out."

"I'D LIKE TO state, for the record, I think trying to contact Daisy about why this guy is holding her is a bad idea. Even if Lissa can help Alexis, I still say it's a *really* bad idea." Kevin stood before Stefan and Alexis. His hands clenched on his hips, he radiated disapproval.

Alexis had come to see this stalwart stance as his policeman mode. When she recognized it, she could almost see him in action against the worst of the criminal elements—and winning. A formidable foe.

Damn, not only was she attracted to this man but she also respected him. Not good. Up until now, she'd viewed police officers in the same way as she had hospitals. She'd feared them.

"It won't be easy either." Kevin's frown deepened. "I might help, but this could go south in a really bad way."

Stefan walked the couple steps to stand in front of Alexis, reaching out to hold her hands. "Do you want to go ahead?"

Alexis closed her eyes, abruptly shutting out their conversation. Did she want to take this step? More to the point, was there a choice?

Kevin's harsh voice broke through her musings. "You don't have to try this. It doesn't have to be this extreme."

"Have you ever tried doing it in a different way?" she challenged him.

"Yes. I've been forced to search for victims of a killer on the other side," he answered shortly, his chin locked into position. "I survived, but the whole thing was a bad deal."

"Ouch," she murmured, at the tortured look on his face. "What other options are there? We need to contact Daisy. Find out what hold he has on her. I also want to find a way to loosen his hold on me. I have to try."

Kevin looked at Stefan. "Are there any ways to do that?"

Stefan let out a tired sigh. "I don't know," he admitted. "You know as well as anyone, damn it. There are no certainties in this business."

Kevin slammed his fist in the heavy cedar beam at the entrance to the living room. "Do what you want. It's not like you'll listen to my warning. Unfortunately."

"Does that mean you're leaving?" Alexis struggled to keep her voice calm and steady, but, inside, her stomach sank. It was important for Kevin to stay, though she couldn't explain why.

Kevin snorted in disgust. "No, I'm staying. This way, I can watch every stupid step."

She threw him a hurt look, before turning to look wistfully at the unlit fireplace. There was a chill to the summer afternoon that even a fire couldn't warm, but she'd have loved the welcoming comfort the dancing flames could bring. She rubbed her arms unconsciously.

Kevin grasped her by the shoulders, turning her away. "Go sit down. I'll light the damn thing for you."

"And I'll get the wine. We'll need something stronger than tea."

Stefan walked into his kitchen, leaving the pair alone.

Kevin stacked kindling in the blackened fireplace. Smoke residue blanketed the brick mantel, giving it a cozy, well-loved look. Alexis tried to ignore him, as she settled on the cotton cushions of the futon and closed her eyes. Her stomach flip-flopped with nerves, ignoring her command to calm down.

"I don't want you to get hurt." Kevin's brusque tone accented his words. "And this course of action is likely to do just that."

Fear wobbled through her voice. "Thanks for being concerned … and the warning. I'm aware it's dangerous. I think the spirit I met last night is out to get me—to kill me even."

"And you think meeting him on the ethers will stop him? What lunacy is that? Besides, Daisy may not know anything helpful. Spirits often don't. This could be a wasted trip." Kevin's voice rose.

Alexis shrugged. How could she explain such a feeling? "Maybe. But I want to try. I felt like his prey. And I hated that."

"That he knows about your connection to Daisy is disturbing in the first place. But this makes your evening jaunt insane. I know you want to understand. To control this so you're not a victim, but last night should have shown you how hard this craziness can be."

"Precisely why I want to go back there." She swallowed painfully. "Maybe it will be easier now that I do know."

He lit the paper with the burning match. After a second's hesitation, the flames fired up, consuming everything in their path. Kevin watched the fire, still crouched in front of the hearth. "You're a rank beginner compared to him," Kevin said, his aggravation and fear spiking his voice up to a dull roar. "Stefan walks on both sides when he has to, but he never takes a casual stroll." He spun around to face her.

Stefan reappeared, bearing a wine bottle and three glasses. He poured the wine. "Take it easy, Kevin. You didn't listen back then either."

Kevin stood aggressively before them, a muscle in his tight jaw twitching, as if to some inner debate, until finally he lowered his head, acceptance written on his face. He stayed still and silent, before reaching up to rub his forehead. "Fine, let's get it over with, … meaning, talk to Daisy and then get out before you're recognized."

Damn him for his wording. This entity had felt distant and not quite real up until now. Kevin's words brought the entity into the present, big-time. Several soul-searching moments later, Alexis realized she didn't have a choice. She had to do this. *Something* wouldn't let her do otherwise. Instinct? Intuition? Or just the hope that Daisy would know *something* useful? Now if only Alexis could get at what that was.

Within minutes, the lights were dimmed, the fire roared, and, in true Stefan style, they all sat comfortably on the floor. Lit candles completed the warm, intimate look of the space, as did the half-drunk glasses of wine.

Stefan calmly and quietly directed Alexis's mind.

"Visualize the same path that you follow in your meditations. Take a walk through the door to the beautiful, calm, sunny meadow. Feel the sun on your face, the breeze in your hair. Smell the flowers blooming around you. See Lissa waiting for you on the other side. Walk toward her, happy and full of joy at seeing her again." Stefan's smooth velvet voice spoke calmly, pausing at times to allow her to slip deeper and deeper. "Now that you're relaxed and happy, open the door and set your mind free."

Alexis appreciated the two men's presence. She'd been this far in a few times during practice but had never allowed herself to go farther while alone. Until she'd followed the path into her dreams last night.

Stefan's calm voice guided her. "See yourself in the same meadow full of wildflowers. Use the light as your guide. Know I am at your side. See the path you've traveled and know Kevin stands at your back."

Alexis smiled, tilting her face upward, as she enjoyed the freshness of being free. She knew few people would understand this sensation— no words truly described it. She found herself trying to store memories for later. The fresh smell of air, taken in through nostrils that weren't there, colors that brightened and blended at will, no longer regulated by the physical constraints of vision and reality. Heat or coolness, it all depended on where she allowed her thoughts to flow. It was unique and incredibly addictive. She realized her earlier meditations, where she'd thought she walked freely, had been simple explorations. Unlike this time.

Focus.

Trust Stefan to keep her on track. Almost instantly, she found herself in Lissa's meadow, as she'd come to think of it. Happily she called for her sister.

Alex! I'm over here.

The two sisters hugged and laughed for joy. Alexis knew she was only in her meditative state, but her sister seemed so real. According to Stefan, she was real, just not in the same reality as Alexis.

Hello, Stefan. Lissa glowed with an incandescent light, as she recognized the presence with Alexis. *Thanks for helping my sister.*

It's not as if I had a choice, he said humorously.

Lissa's laughter tinkled lightly. *When you're on this side of the physical plane, it's a pleasure to find someone like Stefan to talk with.*

Is that all you were doing? Up to now, I thought you were nagging me to take care of Alexis. Stefan materialized as a luminous glow, his dry sense of humor unmistakable.

Alexis found it difficult to accept the totality of the experience. A whole other world was out there. All she was missing was Kevin. … Otherwise this reality seemed perfect. Alexis started. Could Stefan and Lissa read her mind here?

Lissa's laughter rang free. *All your thoughts are totally open here. What you think, I hear. It's simple.*

Stefan's voice cut in. *Not only your words but every thought is visualized and transmitted.*

As her mind hooked on to that new information, the images surrounding her wavered—the edges started to dissipate.

Keep your focus! Stefan ordered.

Alexis snapped to attention. *Sorry.* She immediately recognized her returning clarity was the result of her improved concentration.

You're doing good, sis. Lissa's warm smile wrapped her in a translucent hug. Alexis couldn't help but shiver in pure delight. Visits with her sister were priceless. Her focus blurred.

Focus, Stefan snapped. *You can visit with her later. She damn-near haunts my place.*

Lissa's laughter filled the air.

Alexis grinned.

Are you ready to get to work? Stefan once again cut in.

Yes, but can't we stay and visit for a bit longer? Alexis felt she'd only been there a second or two. How long had it been?

But suddenly she felt it. The air was changing, becoming thicker, cloying. On cue with the air's changes, the sun slid behind a large gray cloud that suddenly appeared. A shadowy darkness moved toward them.

No time.

Lissa turned from Alexis to Stefan. *He knows you're here. Make sure she's protected, Stefan.*

Alexis. Stefan's voice sharpened. *Stay in the light of love and stay focused. You can do this. Your abilities are strong, just untried. Keep your focus.*

The sunlight went out. Alexis spun around, searching the area. When she turned back, Lissa had disappeared.

Where is she? Alexis spun around, anxiousness crawling over her skin.

She's gone. Now are you ready to contact Daisy?

No sooner had her name floated out on the ethers than the child's tiny frame, dressed in the same party dress, solidified in front of them, as if by magic. Fear contorted her face. *He's coming. He doesn't like it when I visit with you.*

Stefan's calm voice controlled the conversation. *Why?*

He wants me all to himself.

Daisy ... Alexis hesitated. The child turned those huge blue eyes her way.

What? The child's high-pitched voice was sweet, ghostly, and extremely unnerving. Which, considering where and what Alexis was doing, seemed exactly as it should be.

Focus!

Shit, she'd done it again. Alexis concentrated harder. *Daisy, you said you stayed, so he wouldn't hurt other little kids.*

Yes.

Stefan's question than floated through the air. *How long have you been with him?*

Forever, Daisy answered, looking around the meadow nervously.

Alexis had to ask, *Did he kill you?*

I don't know.

Daisy! The peremptory order, from nowhere and everywhere, shocked them all.

Daisy vanished. She just poofed into the air. Alexis spun around, looking for her to reappear.

Stefan? Alexis called out. She could no longer sense his presence.

She felt a moment of lonely silence, before his faded whisper broke through her doubts. *I'm here. Give me a moment.*

Alexis waited restlessly. This was no longer a comfortable experiment.

Loneliness enveloped her. Nervousness dodged her heels. On the heels of that thought, the air around them went smoky gray. Alexis couldn't see her hand in front of her face.

Stefan whispered harshly, *Stay calm. He's here.*

She already knew that. Her skin screamed, as a million spiders crawled over her nerves. Everything evil materialized in one deep black oozing fog.

Hellooo there, my dear. You don't listen well, do you?

Alexis shoved down the fear and steadied her spine, taking a deep breath. She refused to be intimidated. *Apparently not,* she answered calmly.

Unholy chuckles wafted around her. *Fine with me.* Deep blackness reached for her.

Alexis took a step back, but the ooze kept coming. Her fear rose, threatening to overwhelm her. Her throat clogged, choking her, as if he controlled the very air she breathed. The intensity of the situation increased with her thoughts. She fought against it, struggling to stay calm and aware. She couldn't allow him the upper hand.

Focus! Stefan shouted.

Her spine snapped ramrod straight. Right. She could handle this.

Instantly, before she could do anything, the overpowering essence of evil lessened. She could breathe again. With each passing second, the air was lighter and less intense.

Horrible laughter greeted her thoughts. *Don't think you can stop me. Your fear is my joy. You misjudged your skills and mine. You won't make that mistake again. Neither will I.*

Horrific pain reached out and clawed at her, reaching inside her mind, twisting and churning through her brain.

Focus! Stefan yelled to her through the black whirling mist.

Macabre laughter drowned him out. *She can't. She's not strong enough.*

Yes, Alexis, you are. Stefan's disembodied voice supported her in the blackness. *Don't let him do this. Don't fight. Trust in me and think yourself to the other side of this.*

Alexis heard their comments in the distance, but it was so hard to make sense of them. There was so much pain. It crippled her. Oh God, he was in her head. … She couldn't do it. She couldn't fight him. He was too strong for her.

No, he's not. You can do this!

She screamed, a horrific tearing sound that brought the man sitting beside her in Stefan's living room to his feet. She couldn't make herself stop. All the fear and agony kept pouring from her, until the air was filled with her never-ending wail.

CHAPTER 10

"**A**LEXIS!" KEVIN CRIED out. "Come back. Come back to me."

Hoping she heard him, Kevin repeatedly relayed instructions. "Damn it, Stefan—help her!"

"I need a moment." Stefan's thin reedy voice came from his prone body, where it had collapsed during the last part of the journey. "Keep calling her."

"She's not responding." Kevin's heart pounded away inside his chest. God, what could he do? He had to help her. Touching her physically was out of the question; he had only one option.

He jumped into her mind—and fell headlong into the long stifling black night of her fear.

Alexis?

Kevin, she whispered in agony. *My God, this hurts. You didn't tell me it would be this bad.*

He's blocking you. It only hurts if you let him. Damn it, Alexis. Don't give in. Surround yourself with white light. Boot him out.

Off in the cold smothering blackness, Kevin could sense the other shifting presence. The asshole. *Alexis, sense my anger. Feel how pissed off I am.* Kevin waited a moment to sense her probe. When it wasn't forthcoming, he snapped out, *Do it now.*

He waited anxiously for the first magical touch that would show him that she was there and listening. Faint and trembling, a whisper of her energy moved toward him. He waited until it touched him. *Now feel our connection. Really feel it.*

I'm trying, … she whispered.

Damn it, don't try—do it! And I mean now, he ordered.

Got it. You don't have to shout, she snapped weakly.

Damn straight I do, he answered, slightly mollified. *Now use that anger to clear a path through the blackness.*

I'm pushing at it.

Again he cut in. *Don't bother. Use the anger to understand what he's doing. Your fear is crippling you. Once you understand what he's doing to manipulate you, your fear will ease, and he'll have no power over you.*

Almost instantly the black fog started to dissipate. Alexis's disbelieving laughter broke through. *Oh, wow. Now I see.* The strength of her conviction matched the pace of the disappearing fog.

Do you see what he was doing? He was using your own fear to build that fog.

She sent him a warm hug. Her thanks hung gently in the air all around the two of them.

Home now.

KEVIN WATCHED ALEXIS slowly return to the present. She would be damn sore tomorrow.

He reached out to stroke her arm. "Are you okay?"

She tried to reassure him, them. "I'm fine. Really I am. I'm very tired though, and almost feel a disconnect with my body. And you're right. I had to experience that to believe it." Alexis looked at Stefan curiously. "Just what *did* happen to you?"

Disgusted, he answered, "My own fault, really. I split off, used one part of my consciousness to help you and another to track him. Unfortunately he's good—ancient-with-years-of-experience good. While he was using your inexperience to his advantage, he went after me and kicked me out. Something he could only do because I was functioning in two levels at once, and, therefore, each piece of me was only half as strong."

Alexis stared at him. "You can do that?"

Kevin couldn't believe it. Stefan had some mad skills, but this? This seemed too far out to be real.

"I've been working on it." Stefan reached for the wine bottle to top up their glasses. He waited several moments, before adding, "And not very successfully apparently. It was a little disconcerting to be kicked out of the ethers so easily." He shook his head, muttering under his breath. "I'll have to work on strengthening the energy to each piece. At least in this instance, trying this technique was the right thing to do."

A dual snort escaped both Kevin and Alexis. They looked at each other in surprise; Kevin winked at her before turning to stare at Stefan.

"How do you figure that?" asked Alexis.

"Because of what I learned." He waited, a bright-eyed look on his face. He tapped away at the armrest. Waiting.

Lifting the wineglass for a sip, Kevin eyed him over the rim. "Okay,

I'll bite. What did you find out?"

"He's earthbound."

Kevin leaned forward, roaring, "What?" His voice dropped to a shocked whisper. "That's not possible."

Alexis glanced from one man to the other. "I don't understand. Many souls are earthbound, aren't they?"

Stefan stated simply. "He's not dead, Alexis. This asshole is as alive as you and me."

THE THREE EXHAUSTED people quietly sipped their wine. Fatigue hung heavily in the air.

"I don't get it. What does this mean?" Alexis's befuddled mind couldn't understand what Stefan's findings meant. "What difference does it make if he's alive or dead?"

Kevin, in full detective mode, answered, "It's possible he murdered little Daisy and has kept her spirit captive. She can't escape him, even in death." He winced, frowning into the bloodred liquid swirling in his glass.

She cried out, "Oh, my God! Is it even possible to keep a spirit captive?" Alexis's voice rose in horror. "That poor child. How could things like this happen?" Alexis felt another of those solid foundational beliefs of life and death, that she'd always counted on, now rocked unsteadily. Abruptly she said, "We have to help free her."

Both men looked at her, their faces stern but unsurprised. Stefan spoke first. "I wondered how long it would take you."

"We have to."

"We will. Don't worry, Alexis. We'll help her," Kevin said, his voice soothing and calm. "But we need to do it properly. This isn't something we can just jump into."

"Maybe, but it feels like we need to move quickly." Tension gripped her. A sense of pressure built. From where? From the asshole? Or was she still experiencing that weird sense of disconnect from her body, from reality?

Everything had shifted. Changed. The rules she'd lived by had been wiped out in a single slash. This was a whole new game—again.

"The more you develop in this area, the more you'll see and experience what you'd believed was the impossible." Stefan looked over at Kevin. "That might explain Daisy's body."

Kevin studied him. "Meaning?"

"What if he did murder her, then following the burial proceedings, he stole her again for his own purposes? Perhaps he needs that physical connection or proximity to lock her down here with him? And, no, I have no idea how. It shouldn't be possible, but ..." Stefan held up his hand to forestall their exclamations. "I know it sounds 'out there.' But this case is beyond weird."

Twisting his head to the side, Kevin studied his friend. He nodded slowly. "I don't know how he's keeping Daisy under his control, but, *if* he needed her body to do so, then what you suggest might be possible. It's also possible he just *thought* he needed her body. We have to consider there might be other victims. Or that, as we now have her body, he might go after new victims."

A heavy silence filled the room.

"So he had to murder her to do this? Or could she have died accidentally?" Alexis hated the idea of the child suffering.

Stefan pondered the concept. "Could be either. He must have been close to her both physically and emotionally, I'd think, in order to have the connection he needed at her time of death. But I don't know for sure. This is a new one for me."

"If hers was an accidental death," Kevin said, "it would explain why there's no file."

"Right, but there could be other reasons that you haven't found her in the files. For example, she may have been dead for much longer than ten years." Stefan continued, "That's just one possibility. What if she was murdered in Florida before being moved here? You'd have to contact every county in every state across the country."

"But that's not likely though, is it? Why or how, for that matter, would anyone move a dead body across the country?" Alexis stared first at one man and then at the other. "Surely he wouldn't move it more than a short distance?"

"You forget that she's been embalmed, meaning, she could travel for a longer time without the same level of decomposition that a newly deceased body would have. He could have frozen her for a time. Even long enough to complete the move. After all this time, it would be hard to prove that action either way."

The last vestiges of warmth left Alexis's face, leaving her chilled deep inside. Alexis's stomach heaved. How could someone be so evil? At least with death, a person's suffering was thought to be over. Should be over. She closed her eyes.

"Alexis." Kevin placed a comforting hand on her knee.

"I'm fine," she whispered, after a moment. Opening her eyes, she found both men studying her, concern creasing their faces.

"I can't let him do this!" The words exploded from her unintentionally, but she meant them. She would *not* leave Daisy in the clutches of this maniac.

"Stopping him won't be easy," Kevin snapped. "You have no idea what we could be facing—how difficult this can be."

"Did you?" challenged Alexis. "Back when you first got into this stuff, did you really know what the hell you were in for?"

"More than you do. I'd already spent years in hell on the force. This only showed another dimension of the horror I'd seen many times before," he shot back. "You're an innocent. You don't have to let monsters into your world. Get out while you can."

"Can Daisy?"

Kevin glared at her. Alexis knew she'd brought up the one point that Kevin couldn't argue. If they didn't help this child, who would? Quite possibly no one else out there could even understand …

"Damn it." Kevin's quiet acceptance whispered through the room.

A heavy sigh slipped from Stefan's chest. He straightened. "Then we have a lot of work to do."

IT WOULD BE Kevin's pleasure to nail this bastard. But what if Stefan was right, and Daisy hadn't died in the state of Oregon? A nationwide search could turn up thousands of cases. Kevin flung his pen down in frustration.

"Problems?" John Prescott, the mayor, stood in front of him—looking for all the world like a casual visitor, except for his white-knuckled grip on his briefcase.

"John. How are you?" Kevin half stood, reaching to shake his hand. Then he motioned to the empty chair in front of him. "What can I do for you?"

John fell into a defeated slump on the chair. "I'm glad you're here. Damn it, Kevin, I received another note today."

"What?" At John's worried nod, Kevin held out his hand. "Where is it?"

The briefcase clicked open to reveal a Ziploc bag with the offending paper secured inside. It was small, printed on loose-leaf paper, written in block caps, very simple.

"*Confess,*" Kevin read the single word aloud, in confusion. "That's it?" He looked over at John in disgust. "Whoever he is, he's not very imaginative."

"I couldn't care less about his creative writing ability. I just want him stopped!"

John's fear and outrage was palpable. Kevin felt the waves reaching across the desk, engulfing him. He found himself, not for the first time, studying John's face for signs of guilt or, at the very least, hidden knowledge. He saw nothing. Stumped, he stretched back and propped his feet on the desk. *What the hell was going on here?*

"I need you to put an end to this. Sandra doesn't know about these notes, and I don't want her to find out. You know she doesn't handle life well at the best of times. Damn it, we just straightened out her medications again." John's frustration dwindled down to fatigue. "Hell."

As he ran his hand over his face, it was evident the months of never-ending worry had worn him down. And his fragile wife was another big concern. John sat quietly, staring out the window for a few long minutes.

Kevin waited patiently, quietly observing the changing emotions on his friend's face.

"My son Charles turns thirty this weekend. The last thing we need is to have something go wrong at the huge gala event Sandra has spent months planning. It sounds like the whole damn town has been invited. It's been too much for her, but she insisted on doing this. I wonder if Charles even appreciates it?"

John got up and paced around the small office. His short steps clipped along in military style. "I was on my way to visit my brother, Glen, when I found this damn thing. Now I don't dare drive until I calm down. I'd probably get road rage and snap at some innocent," he said with a half laugh.

Kevin watched calmly, though his senses piqued with curiosity. A little whisper of intuition spoke, telling him he should be noticing something more than the obvious. *But what?* A disgruntled-father issue? A victim-of-blackmail issue? Or just a frustrated-man-with-too-much-on-his-plate issue? Kevin looked up, ever watchful. "How is Glen doing?"

"Glen?" John shrugged. "He never changes. How can he, hooked to life support as he is? I should sign the damn papers to let him go, but I just can't, even if it's been almost twenty years. If there's any chance he's in there still, I have to give him that chance. He's my brother, and I love him. God, that was a tough time in my life."

Kevin couldn't imagine how devastating that car accident must have been for the whole family. John's brother, Glen, had been a vegetable ever since. John continued to visit faithfully, finding a measure of comfort in the contact. Who could blame him for keeping that relationship with his brother alive, if he found comfort in it?

"At least you have him in a great home, where he receives round-the-clock care."

"True enough. He'd lived in Bradford for years. He never liked California. When we lucked out and found him this bed, there was no question it was what he'd want."

There was a moment of silence, then John faced Kevin, this time with a real smile. "Come to the party. You'll enjoy it. Besides, I'd feel better having you keep an eye on the proceedings, just in case ..." He strode to the door. "Saturday afternoon. We'll see you then."

Kevin stared at the empty doorway. Something was wrong with this picture. But what?

Hell. The answer continued to elude him. With the note still in its plastic protector, he headed to the lab.

ALEXIS SLUMPED AGAINST the large rock garden, too tired to get up. Content, she surveyed the last flower bed. She'd been practicing her plant-growing skills every day and saw the difference now. The flowers hummed with joy. Several people had stopped by recently to comment on the glorious colors of the blooms.

Scott walked up to her. "Glad to see the plants are reaping the benefits, lass." He turned his electric blue eyes on her and grinned. "Let me know when you're going to move into the healing arts. Your work is a fine recommendation." Pure mischief gleamed down at her.

"What type of healing do you need, you big oaf?"

"Why, to heal my broken heart, of course, lassie. It's fair hurting with unrequited love."

She chuckled. "I doubt it. More like the legion of broken-hearted women you've left behind needs healing," she teased. Her colleague's attractiveness to women was legendary.

"What can a man do? So many women in want of a good loving. I'm helpless before their needs." His grin deepened, as if caught in the memories of too many hot loving nights.

Amazed, Alexis savored the rare glimpse into the devastating attractiveness of her longtime friend. She shook her head to clear her mind, with a new understanding as to why so many women willingly and easily took the walk into the night with Scott. It took away her breath. "Whew. Scott, I feel like I barely escaped unscathed."

"And don't you be forgettin' it." He nodded sagely, his grin never dimming.

"Go on with you. Your ego needs no more stroking."

"True. I came to see if you were wanting to go for a pint?" He looked slyly at her from the corner of his eye, watching for her reaction.

Alexis looked up. He positively glowed with leprechaun anticipation.

"Right." She punched him lightly. "What's the matter? Are you between women right now? Has someone not succumbed to your legendary charm? You need me to keep you company? I know. You've met someone …"

Scott's face turned beet red.

Alexis stared at him in astonishment, before collapsing on her back into the rich green grass. She howled with joy.

Scott glared down at her. "That's enough, that is."

"Not nearly!" Alexis tried to stop, but a few more chuckles slipped out. "How perfect. Even better, your reaction tells me that she matters to you. So who is she?"

"What reaction?"

"Normally you'd be laughing with me." Alexis smiled up at the big teddy bear. "Instead, you're embarrassed and uncomfortable. You care." Her lips twitched into a fat smile. "You're falling in love."

"I am *naw!*" He snapped out the words, horror in his eyes.

That did it, Alexis rolled around on the grass in delight.

"Stop that." His big mitt swatted at her playfully. "I'm not falling in love. I'm too old for such nonsense."

"You're never too old to fall in love. And it's bloody well time."

From her prone position on the grass, she watched a strange look of comprehension slide over his face. He hadn't known. He was beautiful, smart, and the best friend a girl could have, yet he hadn't known what falling in love was like.

Truly he deserved to find someone, and Alexis would get a lot of mileage from it. She grinned. "So," she said nonchalantly, "who is she?"

The clouded confusion disappeared instantly. "Oh no, you don't. I won't tell you." He turned away from her and looked around, as if just returning to his senses. "I need to think on this." He strode over to his truck and drove off.

Alexis sat up, staring at his dust in shock. "Hey, what about our beer?" But he was long gone. Alexis got to her feet and brushed herself off, looking down the road at the dusty cloud from his truck.

Damn. She'd have enjoyed going for a pint tonight. It was past time to go home. Late and gloomy, the rain that had been threatening for several days now started with light droplets. She still needed a good ten minutes to finish up. Would the skies be kind enough to wait before dumping on her? She noticed several other workers heading home, after shutting down the heavy equipment for the day.

"See you tomorrow, Alex," one of the operators yelled from his pickup, as he pulled away.

She tossed him a goodbye wave. By the time she was ready to leave, the black clouds rumbled menacingly, making her look around nervously. For the first time, she realized she was alone. *Odd.*

Normally that never bothered her, but today the strange electric feel to the air sharpened her uneasiness.

A brilliant flash lit the sky, followed quickly by a resounding clap of thunder. The skies opened, sending down sheets of rain, as she raced to collect her tools.

"Shit." Alexis raced to her truck and threw her tools into the toolbox. The black sheet of rain washed out her vision, as she tried to stab her key into the door lock. Guiding the key with her other hand, she finally made it inside and pulled the door shut.

"I don't believe it." A river covered her windshield. She grabbed her sweater from the passenger seat and vigorously rubbed her sopping hair with it. A couple tissues left in the glove box were enough to wipe down her face. "Where did that come from?" she muttered to herself. She turned on the engine. Thankfully it purred to life. Now, if she could only see, she might get home.

The headlights shone eerily silver on the wall of rain. Her red truck picked its way carefully through the parking lot to the exit. "Damn it, I could've been home by now," Alexis muttered in disgust, hunching over her steering wheel to peer closer. What was on the road ahead? Alexis slowed her truck to a crawl.

Quicker than she'd thought possible, the object loomed directly in front of her. A huge rock? A person? She couldn't tell. She squinted and leaned closer, her nose almost touching the glass when it happened.

The object smashed into her windshield.

Alexis cried out, slammed on the brakes, throwing her arms up protectively against the impending collision.

Only it never came.

Alexis peeked out apprehensively, her ragged breathing almost covering up the heavy pounding of her heart.

And it had waited for just that lull and immediately smashed through the windshield.

Alexis screamed.

Only the glass never broke.

There was nothing. Except for the horrible sounds that slipped out the back of her throat. She choked her whimper back, until the silence was deafening.

Alexis opened one tightly squeezed eye. Whatever it was had sealed itself against the glass. Shocked, Alexis reared back as a doorway appeared in her windshield. She swallowed several times, as her mind tried to wrap itself around this new development. Shivers rippled through her.

Alexis's breath caught, as the strange doorway morphed into an old black-and-white movie in front of her. She didn't think she wanted to see what was to come, but she couldn't close her eyes, paralyzed to do anything but watch the movie roll on.

Her windshield opened into a hallway with another dingy carpet and gray walls, but the paint chips and cracks on these walls were bigger. The sounds started up suddenly, startling Alexis, as she was assaulted with yells and cries of fear. She clapped her hands over her ears, but she couldn't look away.

Her training with Stefan allowed her, in a small way, to detach. Not enough though. A horrible inner knowing told her something ugly was about to occur …

Focus, damn it. Remember your breathing. If there ever was a time to practice her lesson in detachment, this was it. The cries of fear turned to a child's screams of pain, and the yells became angry bellows. Someone was beating a child. Could this be Daisy? Or a vision of another child?

Uncertainty helped her distance herself even more. She pulled back mentally and changed to a wide-screen view. Instantly she stood in a ratty bedroom, as someone left the room. All she saw was a scuffed black shoe as the person walked out. The child sobbed uncontrollably on the bed.

A little boy.

Alexis's heart wept. Crumpled into the mussed blankets, the child wrapped his arms tightly around a pillow. Sobs racked his slight frame.

Alexis's eyes shut, as his sorrow and pain overwhelmed her. This vision was the oldest yet. But for Alexis—the pain was fresh. When she could finally bring herself to open her eyes again, hot tears clung to the corner of her eyelashes.

The vision was gone.

CHAPTER 11

"WHAT HAPPENED?"

Alexis wasn't surprised to hear Kevin's voice at the end of the phone. In truth, she'd half-expected it. She tucked her slipper-covered feet up on the couch beside her. She'd barely made it home before the numbing cold and tiredness had hit.

"I had another vision." Quietly and as emotionlessly as she could, she told him what she'd seen. "I think this has to be related, but I don't know in what way. All I can tell you is this one seemed to happen a long time ago."

Kevin listened intently, seeming to hear and to understand all she hadn't expressed. "You're receiving more visions, so there could be more victims involved. Are you okay now?"

"Yes," she whispered, needing and appreciating his understanding and the explanation. "Why are the visions so painful? Why can't they show me happy times?"

"That's the whole point of these visits. These people are in pain and need help to finish business here, so they can truly pass on." Kevin's soothing voice went on to explain some of the research that had been done in this area.

Alexis listened with only half an ear. She could only imagine what a lifetime of feeling other people's pain would do to her.

"They will either destroy you, or you will learn to deal with them."

It took her a minute to realize she hadn't voiced the question, but he'd answered it anyway. She closed her eyes. "That might become irritating one day," she said.

"By then, you'll set boundaries, telling me what I can or can't do. Not to worry. For the moment, this transparency is a good thing."

"By the way, when I had the vision, did you know?"

"I knew you were experiencing something emotionally painful. My sense told me it was happening. But it also told me the vision wasn't dangerous, so I didn't come to look."

"Right." She shook her head at his words. "You make it seem so simple."

She shifted on the uncomfortable couch. Dressed in her night-clothes and bundled under her heavy robe, she was almost warm. Almost. It might be time to invest in thermal underwear if this continued. At least until she learned to cope better.

"WELL?" ASKED THE man impatiently. "I haven't got all day. What did you find out?"

"Sutherland's got nothing." The younger man almost bubbled over with his news. Finally he had something to offer. Maybe it would make this guy happy enough to leave him alone. He straightened his shirt collar.

"And?"

The young man leaned forward conspiratorially. "He's searching the databases for unsolved cases involving murdered children."

"All children?" the man asked, his searing gaze making the other man nervous.

"No, he's focusing on little girls called or nicknamed Daisy." He snickered. "What kind of a name is that?"

"Daisy!" An odd look transformed his slick features, as the man silently contemplated the news. A heavy pent-up breath gusted out, and he whispered, "At last."

He said nothing more, but a curious light filled his eyes.

STEFAN PULLED INTO a small spot so far off to one side it was almost on the grass. He gave her a sidelong glance. "Ready?"

She stared at the massive estate's grounds, jammed with vehicles and people. As she stared at the mess, she started to understand just how much she hated crowds. "Why are we here again?"

"Because Kevin called, asking for our help. It's the mayor's son's birthday, and the family is throwing him this massive party. I told him that I didn't want to attend, but he's looking for something that could be wrong on this psychic plane. So ..."

"For the mayor's son's birthday party?" She took a deep breath. "I guess, if Kevin asked us to check out something, then we need to help out if we can."

"Look at it as practical experience."

"Right." With a sigh, she opened the door to Stefan's jet-black BMW and stepped out.

People filled the landscape in all directions. She wouldn't have minded joining the group of young boys playing basketball in the monster-size parking lot.

Stefan's lethal male grin perked up her spirits. She couldn't help but smile back.

"Much better. It doesn't do my ego any good to have an unhappy woman on my arm."

She tossed him a disbelieving look. "You're too damn gorgeous for that."

"True," he answered smugly, startling a laugh out of her.

He placed his hand on the small of her back and guided her through the crowd. "At least this conversation distracted you enough to get you in here."

Alexis looked around in disbelief. She was already in the middle of the damn crowd. This man was dangerous.

Stefan moved slightly in front of her, magically clearing a path for them. She couldn't see what he was doing, but the warmth of energy flowing outward from his body said he'd done something. *Damn.* She so needed to learn that trick.

"Alex," boomed a thick Irish voice from across the room. "I didn't think you'd be here." Her barrel-chested friend rolled toward her, parting the crowd, before planting himself directly in front of her, arms open wide.

Alexis laughed and walked in for her hug. "Hello, Scott. How are you?"

"Bloody fine, lass. How are you? I couldn't believe my eyes when I saw you." Scott studied the man at her side. "What's this? Did you bring a date?" he drawled, his eyes wide, as he assessed Stefan. "Well, now. I wouldn't have thought you were into models."

Alexis snorted. "Not likely. Scott, this is my friend and mentor, Stefan. Stefan, this is my boss and friend, Scott."

At the word mentor, Scott narrowed his eyes and reassessed her companion. Slowly the huge shaggy head nodded, as he recognized what he was looking for. "Good. It's nice to meet you. For helping out my Alex"—Scott held out his hand to shake Stefan's—"I thank you."

The two men seemed to come to a silent but instant understanding. Alexis could only shake her head at that whole male-protectiveness thing.

"Come on. The food is over here. Let's get you some lunch."

Scott's burr rumbled through her ears, his words blending and merging with the crowd around her.

God, she hated social scenes like this.

KEVIN WATCHED ALEXIS and Stefan meander through the crowds, an apparent twosome. He frowned. *Damn it.* They looked entirely too comfortable together.

Jealousy didn't sit well with him. He didn't have much experience with heavy emotions. All his relationships, to date, had been light and easy. Like the one he'd had years ago with Mandy. He glanced over at the petite redhead, who had turned to speak with someone else. No spark existed between them anymore, but it was nice to see her again. He often ran into her and her son, Kyle, around town, but he hadn't spent any real time with them in years. He'd intended to stop by more often, but ...

Sandra, the hostess, stepped forward. "Kevin, how are you? We so rarely get to see you these days." Sandra smiled her little girl's smile, making her appear years younger than her mayor husband. She tugged Kevin to the back of the house and into the full library, where many political friends surrounded John. Some would have said attending this function was politically correct. Others would have said it was simple networking. Regardless, far too many were in attendance to try to sniff out dirt.

Kevin accepted the offered beer. "So, John, where's the birthday boy?"

Several other heads nodded at the question, looking around for Charles. Though, at thirty, one couldn't really call him a *boy* any longer.

"He's here, probably surrounded by women. You know how it is when you're young and single." John smiled with fatherly pride.

The men grinned. At that point, someone tossed out the topic of single-child syndrome, starting up a whole new discussion.

"They are usually more assertive, taking what they want in the world."

"You mean, more spoiled, expecting everything from the world to be handed to them."

"Here, here. And on a silver spoon, no less." The good-natured wrangling went on around him.

Kevin tuned most of it out. His senses, both natural and supernatural, searched the group, trying to find signs of unease. When his gaze landed on John again, he felt the wave of pain, even before it reflected itself on his friend's face. John looked distinctly uncomfortable with the conversation and was hedging away. Who could blame him? It was obviously too close to home.

"John, it's too bad about your daughter," said one older man. "It does my heart good to see you and your family getting on in the world so well. The wife and I are awaiting our first grandchild." The speaker beamed, as his news caused a flurry of well-wishes and other personal stories.

John winced at the mention of his daughter, a ghost of a reaction that slipped past fast.

Kevin kept his eye on John, while filing away the news that John had had a daughter. *Had*, because John had told him that his son was an only child. John's expression was quickly masked after one baleful look at the beaming man, who basked in those compliments.

Surviving another ten minutes with the discussion, Kevin then escaped to the other side of the house to the buffet luncheon and the coffee service. He bet Alexis was more than ready for a cup.

"Did you get yourself something to eat, Kevin?" Sandra popped up at his side again, ever the good hostess, making sure that everyone was taken care of.

At his smile and nod, she murmured, "Good, good," and moved on. Some older ladies were gossiping on the far side of the buffet, and Kevin watched as Sandra headed for them. He heard snippets of their conversation.

"Daughter would be an adult now, wouldn't she?"

"Yes, I think so. Wasn't there something suspicious about her death?"

"Ruled accidental, if I remember correctly," chimed in another of the main society leaders.

Eager murmurs of condolences contradicted themselves, as everyone waited with baited breath for more gossip.

"*Shh*. She's coming." The frantic whisper silenced them all.

Amazed, Kevin noted how the whole group simultaneously donned cheerful smiles before facing their hostess. Sandra appeared to not have heard, although how that was possible, he didn't know. Maybe she just didn't want to hear.

The ladies on the other side surrounded Sandra, bubbling away with compliments over the social gathering.

Right, as if they cared. While Kevin didn't have much use for gossips, he knew enough to pay attention. You never knew where the next lead would come from.

He struggled with the bits that he'd learned. He himself had only been in town for seven years. He wouldn't have heard about the child's death if it had happened decades ago. It must have been incredibly painful. Not to mention Glen's accident happening in there somewhere. A lot of hurt for one family.

Still, something bugged him about both issues. He made a mental note to take a closer look.

THANK HEAVENS BEAUTIFUL gardens were here. Alexis desperately needed out of the packed house and into the world she understood and loved. Any events with crowds were stifling, but this one more than most. An air of covetousness by many of the guests made her want to gag. It wasn't about the structure of the estate but more about the living energy of the place. Stefan could explain the feeling much better, but, for her, the place had the smell of hidden secrets.

Not her style at all.

When Charles introduced himself to her, she'd felt like a fool. She hadn't even known who the birthday boy was. And, from the snippets she'd heard, she had thought Charles to be a child, not a tall, slim, fully grown man a couple years older than her. With the mad crush of people inside the house, she'd jumped at Charles's offer to show her the grounds.

Yet the farther they moved from the house, the more she realized she'd made a mistake. Charles was … too smarmy, … too intimate, … and way too pushy. Every time she put distance between them, he quickly regained his lost ground.

It was ludicrous. He was so opposite from her taste, … and his persistence almost made her cringe.

And, if he didn't get his frickin' fingers off her, she would cause some serious damage. She'd never been one to tolerate being mauled.

Several times she looked around the garden for someone she knew, but the two of them were slowly drifting away from everyone. Great. If this jerk tried to kiss her, she was liable to belt him one, birthday boy or not.

"Let's head back," she said nicely but firmly. "I never did get my coffee and a piece of your delicious birthday cake." She swiveled back the way they'd come, only to find he'd slipped around to stand in front of her, and he was much too close.

The hot sun poured down on them. Alexis hated it today, feeling overheated and a tad angry. His next comment made her even more so.

"I never got my birthday kiss." His words oozed, his smile made her skin crawl.

Masculine charm aside, he was as attractive as a wet bullfrog in slime. Not that she had anything against actual frogs.

"Sorry," she snapped. "I don't do birthday kisses."

"Oh, I think you will. Do you like our new home? This estate is basically all mine. There's no other family member who counts." He wafted a leisurely wave across the impressive grounds. "Most women would be delighted to spend an afternoon with me."

That did it.

"But I'm not most women. This …" She wafted her own arm sarcastically around. "This doesn't impress me. I wouldn't spend an afternoon with you ever. If you don't move out of my way, I'm liable to puke all over you. *You. Make. Me. Sick!*"

She shoved past him. Arrogant asshole. *Who the hell did he think he was?*

She quickly returned to the back garden. With her head down and her thoughts still in a fury, she didn't see who was waiting for her at the end of the path.

Kevin stood, holding two coffees, a whole gambit of emotions running across his face. He'd obviously heard her. Alexis watched him quickly mask his gleeful amusement. He held out her cup of coffee. "Shall we?"

Silently she accepted the cup and strode forward, happy to have him beside her and even happier to put more distance between her and the degenerate she'd left behind.

As they walked closer to the house, sounds of yelling and shouting rushed toward them.

Kevin sped up, almost running by the time they'd reached the house. Alexis heard him mutter, "Damn it, now what?"

A sentiment she echoed.

He entered the house, but she waited outside the glass porch doors. From her position, she saw several men crowd around Kevin, all talking over each other in an effort to be heard. Scott seemed to be in the middle of them. Thankfully the glass kept the words out of her hearing. She really didn't want to know what was going on.

"Yes, you do."

Alexis pivoted to find Stefan standing slightly behind her. She hadn't heard him approach. "How do you do that?" she asked irritably. "You're almost a phantom."

A ghostly smile appeared, exasperating her even more. Sudden thuds, and even louder yelling, turned her attention back toward the house. It sounded like the argument had jumped to a whole new level.

"Why do I want to know what this is all about?" She nodded at the chaos going on inside. Kevin actually held an irate Scott, keeping him separate and apart, while several other men held two other men away from him. Of course a fight was an open invitation to an Irishman.

And Kevin seemed to think he had Scott under control. What a joke. Scott must be calmed down or Kevin would be flying through the air, detective or not.

Alexis grinned at the image in her mind. "They almost look like they're having a good time in there."

"Not all of them." Stefan joined her at the glass doors.

"So what's going on that I need to know about?"

"Threats and blackmail, suspicions and fears." Stefan continued to stare into the room. His voice thinned and lengthened in a weird parody of a tape suddenly being reduced to half speed.

It sounded beyond weird. Alexis looked at him curiously, recognizing the change in energy patterns around him. He was lost in a vision of his own.

He'd told her that sometimes he had no control over them. The realization had startled her. Knowing it was the same for her made her protective of Stefan in this defenseless state. Alexis shifted closer. Dropping her voice, she asked, "What do you see?"

"Pain, betrayal, loss, grief, … murder." His voice trailed off, leaving the last word as an eerie hook.

"Murder?" she demanded. "*Who? When?* Talk to me."

And, just like that, Stefan was back to normal. "I would if I could, but I have no idea what that was all about."

Alexis studied him, checking deep in his eyes to see if he really was back. The lopsided grin he gave her as he recognized what she was doing convinced her to believe him, as nothing else could have.

"Alexis!" came the yell from the other side of the glass.

The two looked, Kevin motioning both of them inside.

"These two need to go to the hospital to get checked over." Kevin pointed out two middle-aged men, both sporting bloody noses. Kevin's voice was clipped and irritated. "And Scott needs to get his head checked out."

"*Achh,* there's nuttin' wrong with me head." Being upset, Scott had slipped back into a heavy burr.

"No, just with what's in it," Alexis snapped, eyeing the blood drying on his temple.

"I'd call this in, but they don't want the police involved. What a surprise," Kevin added drily, giving the two older men the once-over. She sensed that Kevin didn't know either of them well. Both of them had the grace to blush in embarrassment. When Kevin pinned Scott in place, now that had been comical. Scott actually shuffled his feet like a shamefaced child.

As if just noticing the crowd still hanging around, Kevin called out over their heads, "Show's over, folks. Go back to what you were doing and forget about it. They were just fighting over their golf scores."

That elicited a wave of laughter. In a town like this, golfing tournaments were a way of life. If there was one fight the populace would believe in, that was it.

Alexis watched, wondering what his announcement had to do with her.

"I'll take them to the emergency room. I won't be back." He pulled Alexis off to one side. "Why don't you come along?"

"To the hospital?" At his nod, she pulled away. "I don't think so. I don't like those places."

"I didn't mean for it to be for fun. I meant to help me with these two and Scott. He might be more manageable with you along. He's still pretty riled."

"Not bloody likely," she retorted, amazed at his assumption. Scott, in fighting mode, was a scary sight, indeed.

Still, a few minutes later, she somehow found herself in the middle of the back seat of Kevin's truck between the two older men. Scott sat in the front seat, half turned to face her.

"If he hadna 'cused me, then I wouldna thrown the punch." Scott's accent had thickened again, making him next to impossible to understand. "But I didna do it."

"Do what?" Alexis looked to the two men beside her for an explanation. With none forthcoming, she pinned Scott again. "Scott?"

"He 'cused me of writing a word on the mum's writing board."

"A word?" she asked cautiously. *All of this over a word.* She caught Kevin looking at her in amusement through the rearview mirror. She rolled her eyes in disgust. "What kind of word?"

The kindly gentleman on her right, sporting a bleeding cut to his nose and what would eventually become a beauty of a black eye, answered, "We saw him by the board, and mistakenly thought he'd been the one to write 'confess' on it."

"Confess?" Bewildered, she could only look around the vehicle full of men. *Who'd fight over that?*

"There have been some weird notes left for the mayor. The main message in all of them has been for John to confess something. When we saw Scott here at the board, we thought we'd found the bastard who'd been sending all these notes."

"I told you. I didna see the word. I dunno who wrote it, ye daft mon."

"And I accept your word now." One of the older men gingerly reached up a hand and explored the mess of his face.

Alexis couldn't believe it. "What? He pounds your face into the ground, so now you'll listen to him?"

They all looked at her in surprise. "Of course," was their collective answer.

They were all nuts.

The emergency room was quiet for once. A welcomed relief, as that meant there'd be no wait. The two older gentlemen were examined first. Both had minor injuries and, after being cleaned up a bit, were released.

Alexis sat beside Scott in the waiting room, thinking on the strange afternoon. So much for practice sessions at the party. With the fight, that had brought everything to a halt before she'd even had a chance to ask Stefan about his plans. She certainly hadn't picked up anything odd. Other than the arrogant SOB birthday boy.

A tall woman in scrubs approached. She stood in front of Scott, her hands on her hips, as if she were about to deliver a lecture. "Well?" she demanded.

Alexis was surprised at her attitude. Not the usual bedside manner of nurses. The attractive woman openly studied Scott. It was obvious he recognized her. His face changed from a man to that of a boy in the midst of a scolding. Amused at the revelation, Alexis kept watching.

Now Scott was actually blushing—even mumbling incoherently.

It took her a minute to catch on, but, when she did, Alexis couldn't stop giggling. Scott sent her a disgusted look, silently telling her to be done with it.

"I'm sorry for laughing. I'm Alexis." She hopped off her waiting room chair and held out her hand to the nurse.

The nurse smiled a classy, enduring smile. Alexis was impressed. Scott had found himself a lady this time.

"I'm Moira," she said, with a lilting Celtic accent.

Ahh. That explained it. She was from his home country.

Moira turned to the grumbling Irishman with a heavy sigh. "Let's go, ya big lug. We needs ta take a look at your head."

"Now, Moira. Isn't anytin' wrong with me head. I just took a wee blow, and look." He tilted his head to show her. "Almost no blood."

Moira wasn't having any of that. She ignored his pleas and steadfastly tugged him into a small cubicle.

Alexis, watching the two of them wrangle and spar as they moved off, was surprised and overjoyed for her friend. If anybody deserved a good woman, it was Scott. For the last couple years he'd been stalwart in his role as Alexis's friend, protector, and, if need be, ass kicker. He'd been heartbroken over the news of Lissa's disease, visiting often during her illness, bringing laughter and light to a family who had too little at the time.

At the funeral, he'd cried—because Alexis couldn't.

Now it looked like he'd found the mate to his heart.

Anticipating their happiness made Alexis feel alone in a way she hadn't felt for a long time. Stupid really. Scott was a friend, not her own life partner. By rights, she could gain another good friend in Moira. But this development was another change in her life, and she had enough of that to deal with already.

Funny how she'd used the term *life partner*. That had been Lissa's phrase. 'One day you'll find your life partner and realize that you will never be alone again.'

Did she believe it? Patiently Alexis sat in the long hallway, where sounds of the hospital moved quietly around her. Yes, she did believe it. She wanted someone to share her thoughts, to hold her at night, to wake up to in the morning, ... maybe even, down the road, to have children with.

What would Lissa have thought of Kevin?

THAT NIGHT ALEXIS prepared for bed as usual. Although more moody than normal, she dropped off easily.

Her dreams started out cheerfully enough. Then without warning, *his* voice drove through her happy thoughts, bringing with it a darkness and a smothering sensation. She twisted on her bed, agonizing in her struggle for breath. The smell of death, rotten with desolation and fear, permeated her mind. Her fight continued, as if she fought for her very life.

Somewhere in the middle of the fog and the horror, words mixed and interspersed with her pain and fear. A child's disembodied wail followed her journey through the black of night. *He's hunting again.*

As Alexis raced back to the safety of her room in her dream, his cold hollow voice drove through her senses and left her soul quaking with his words.

It's not your turn yet, ... but soon, oh, very soon.

CHAPTER 12

S TEFAN SAT IN his solarium, enjoying a few minutes of peace. A necessary interlude after all he'd been through. He picked up his cup of chai tea from the small Japanese table.

Boo!

"Jesus!" he roared, as hot tea streamed over his leg. He sprang to his feet, dancing and shaking his legs free of the hot liquid. Glaring at Lissa, he said, "Did you have to do that?"

She grinned. *Yes.*

"I thought you weren't into haunting people," he muttered in disgust, as he pulled the still-warm cloth away from his skin. "This definitely falls into that category." He settled back down and wished, not for the first time, that he wasn't an open communication system for those on the other side.

She's having nightmares every night.

"Many people have nightmares. Alexis will need to deal with this, as she has all the other issues." He glared at Lissa, wishing for a return to the peace and quiet he'd enjoyed a few moments ago.

It won't happen.

Stefan knew better, but he didn't need to boot this spirit out of his space. She was hurting. The same as Alexis was hurting. And he couldn't seem to help himself from helping.

It's him.

"Until he does something more than torment her, our options are limited." He sighed heavily, running his long fingers through his blond hair. "In the meantime, she's getting stronger every day, and that makes each additional day a gift." His words hung there, before slowly fading on the summer evening air.

Her voice dropped to just above a whisper. *I know. I just wish there was another way.*

In a gentle voice, he said quietly, "So do I. So do I."

IT HAD BEEN days since Stefan had told them that he was certain that this asshole was earthbound, yet, since then, they'd learned nothing new. Alexis had searched the ethereal plane, with what little skill she had, and had left the detective work to Kevin. They still hadn't identified the skeleton she'd found.

But she was hoping to change that. She wanted to check schools, birth and medical records, whatever it took, to see how many children who'd resided in the community of Bradford over the last thirty years, or in Portland for that matter, had the name of Daisy. It was such an unusual name, she couldn't imagine there being many, if any at all.

Kevin had his police database, but she wanted to double-check that against vital records. Yet she had to do it manually. No complete online record had been created to date. The county officials had online records on the more recent births/deaths/marriages, etc. It took time to input all that.

At the end of the day, Alexis headed to the public library. She'd gone in early to work in the gardens, given the high temperature forecast for the day. She also appreciated the early end to the day's work. It was barely one p.m. She thought the peaceful atmosphere of the library would be a good place for her to do her research. At least that was her hope.

Instead she kept looking behind her, as she roamed the stacks, searching for information. She had the horrible sensation that something was stirring on another plane—in the world that both fascinated and terrified her. It was bad enough she always had to worry about two-legged predators, but now she knew ones could walk around outside their bodies. And, if that thought didn't get her nominated for the freak award, nothing would.

That she could communicate with her sister on any level was a joy and … unnerving. She loved the closeness, that whole reconnection—particularly when it was something she'd believed could never be.

But the rest of what she'd learned was pretty horrific.

And it was happening now again. Shudders and cold sweat trickled down her chest. Tension built, her palms sweaty. She turned to search behind her. Something was getting ready to blow, only she didn't know what.

Or when.

But it would be nasty.

Like someone would die.

Die?

Since when had the vague impression crystallized into a single word? This bastard continued to torment her, stalk her even, … as if he were ready to pounce. The anticipation created a sick kind of darkness that had taken over her days. She couldn't explain it very well. But it was as if he were taunting her, telling her that he could do what he wanted, and she'd be helpless to stop him.

It was hard to concentrate. To think. This energy, this person had taken over her life.

She glanced around. What if that had been his plan from the beginning? Making it impossible for her to think this through. Could he be doing something to her? Like putting blocks in her mind to stop her from going down a certain pathway? And how terrifying would that be? And why would he? To keep her from discovering something? From seeing something? From understanding something?

And again she looped back. What could it be that he didn't want her to discover?

What could this person really want? A rich businessman always went after more money. A real estate mogul always went after more properties. A serial killer always went after more victims …

And the cry the other night had said the person was hunting.

Hunting what? The obvious answer was *more victims.*

Was that what this was all about? While Alexis was distracted, he was choosing his next target. So that she couldn't see the victim? Communicate with his victim? She didn't know how or why she knew that, but suddenly she did. And she couldn't get that thought out of her mind.

The same vague uneasiness filtered through her again. Somehow she was inviting trouble, if she didn't back off. Again, nothing specific, just gray impressions of dire consequences. His haunting words, *Your turn will come,* still tormented her sleep.

Several hours later, in the public archive section of the library, she slammed down her pen on the notepad, letting her head drop to her forearms in defeat. She was getting nowhere. She closed her tired eyes for just a minute.

Evil swept past her.

Fear slid up her spine, rooting her in place. Oh, dear God! *He is here.*

With her heart pounding, Alexis sprang to her feet, attracting curious looks from several other people. She gave them only a cursory look, enough to know they weren't who she searched for. At least she didn't think so.

Instinctively leaving her computer and books in place, she circled the main floor of the large library, searching to find the energy she hoped she'd recognize. It was the busiest time of day. With nothing more than intuition and a driving urgency, she moved from right to left, feeling the evil ahead of her, rapidly moving farther away.

She headed down the hallway toward the washrooms and a series of other doors. Alexis stood indecisively in front of the multiple choices. Just then the door to the men's room opened, and two men, deep in conversation, exited. Her breath exhaled in a gush. She sucked in another one. Deeper, harsher, louder. She cast a quick look around. She was alone.

Flushing sounds echoed deep within the same room, indicating more occupants. As she stood there uncertainly, she sensed lightness, a lessening of the heavy energy. The energy was dissipating. He'd gone. She rubbed the goose bumps on her arms. How could he just disappear like that? A choked laugh escaped. Who knew what this asshole could do?

Quickly she retraced her steps, trying to understand. Had he felt her following him? Did he know who she was?

Or was his presence here a coincidence?

And coincidence wasn't something she was real strong on.

She returned to her spot at the table and collected her laptop and papers before escaping to her truck.

Once in the driver's seat, she leaned back and tried to relax. Uneasiness continued to niggle at her senses, weaving in under her chest, causing her breath to catch on frissons of fear.

She closed her eyes in an effort to regain her center of balance. Instantly the inside of her truck disappeared, and she found herself in a tiny dark enclosed space. She opened her eyes, thinking she was still inside her truck. She was wrong.

Trying to talk the bile back down into her stomach, she slowly explored her surroundings. Claustrophobia dragged at her consciousness, as her arm gradually slid up the wall in front of her. Her eyes grew accustomed to the lack of light.

Her hand? Tiny fingers wiggled at the end of a fragile hand.

Oh my God. It was tiny, the hand of a child. She was caught inside a child's body. The vision had an antique look to it, making her think this scene happened a long time ago. Not that it mattered. It was as fresh to her today as it had been to the child. She closed her tiny teary eyes and wept. Emotionally it was brutally different. This poor child was terrified. A whole different child. Curled against the pain and terror, she'd wedged herself in a corner. Alexis felt dampness between her legs. The tiny waif had wet herself.

Pity welled from deep inside Alexis. The poor thing. Tremors racked the thin frame. The odd sob broke free.

Stefan had tried to teach her to back off emotionally, so she could regain mental control. She sent the little girl comforting thoughts, wrapping her in a warm hug, as Alexis surveyed the small dark space. Above her head, the shadows slowly formed into the underside of multiple hangers full of clothes.

She was in a closet.

The door stood to her right. In truth, the child's body was wedged against the hinges. She knew, without looking, that the door would be locked. But what was on the other side?

On the heels of that thought, Alexis found herself on the other side of the door.

Free from the little girl's body, Alexis felt her mind wanting to stretch and to shake off the human confines. She felt neither human nor dead, just caught somewhere in-between. An incredible experience—one that, given different circumstances, she'd love to explore.

Glancing around, the room appeared to be a bedroom, the walls a dull purple. The bed was too painfully neat. Tucked under the top cover slept a raggedy teddy bear, waiting for its owner's return.

The child's return.

In its sparse state, nothing about the room could bring joy to anyone.

Alexis pivoted to look to the closet. Not only was the door locked but a block of wood had been jammed under the door handle. The child couldn't leave until she was released.

If she were released.

The bile fought to reach the top of her throat. Alexis was slammed back to present time and the interior of her overheated truck.

What an idiot. She'd parked in the sun, and the windows were closed. She'd been out a long time. Too long. She squinted through the hot glare of her windshield and shrieked.

Kevin's distorted features stared at her through the glass.

He pulled open the driver's door, yelling at her. "What fool stunt are you up to now? Are you looking to get heatstroke?" All the while he tugged her arm, half pulling her from the vehicle. "Of all the idiotic things to do! God, you need a keeper."

Leaning against the side door with the cooler air washing over her, Alexis realized just how hot and oxygen-starved she'd become. Everything blurred, even his words, as they ran over her in rapid abrasive tones. And he wasn't about to give her time to rest or adjust either. He dragged her, none-too-gently, down the street to a sidewalk café, and shoved her roughly into a white wrought iron chair.

"Stay here. I'll find something cool for you to drink." He stalked into the dark interior of the building, reappearing quickly with several bottles of juice. "Here. Drink this." A cold bottle of orange juice smacked into her still numb hands. "I said, drink," he growled, still pissed.

She stared at him, then at the bottle. He was right; she needed this. The icy zest hit her numb taste buds, snapping them back to awareness, as the cold juice flowed down her throat. Alexis shuddered.

"Much better." Kevin watched, eagle-eyed, as she finished the bottle. "Isn't it?" he barked. At her nod, he relaxed into his chair.

"Thanks." She took another long drink and had to admit it did feel better. Curiously she asked, "How did you happen to see me?"

He shot her a disgusted look. "You were transmitting again." He gave her all of another minute to rest and recuperate, before continuing, "Now, just what the hell were you doing?"

She studied his grim face. She could count on him saving the day, whether she liked his methods or not. Her problem lay in what to tell him.

"Don't even think about it!"

Startled, she widened her gaze. "What?"

"Don't even think about lying to me."

She glowered. "I wouldn't."

He snorted. "Like hell you weren't. I can see your brain checking out its options right now." Kevin leaned forward, his ire snapping to the forefront. "Spill. What the hell were you doing?"

"Research!" she snapped. "I was doing research at the library, when I thought I felt him close by." Alexis wrapped her arms around her middle, as the remembered sensation rushed back through her.

"Him?" He leaned forward, his eyes narrowing. "Where? Here?" Intent and cold, his voice sliced through her silence, as his eyes skimmed the parking area.

She waved down the street in the direction they'd come. "In the library," she whispered, suddenly so tired she couldn't think. Hating the fatigue and the shock threading her voice, she straightened and infused a confidence and a strength that she didn't feel into her voice. "He was in the library. I was focused on my research, when this horrible sensation *wafted* past. It took me a moment, then ..." She winced against what she knew was to come. "I went after him."

"What!" he roared. Several other customers looked over in concern. He looked around, quickly lowering his voice. "What do you mean, you went after him?" he asked in an ominous voice. "Are you nuts?"

"We've already established your opinion of my mental health, thank you." She reached for the second bottle of juice and took a long drink, the sharp citrus firing straight into her brain. "Okay, so it wasn't the most sensible thing I've ever done. But I don't know who this guy is, and it's only recently come home to me that this *asshole*"—she paused— "is alive and well here in Bradford."

He glared at her.

She tried again. "I believe he's on the hunt for his next victim. At least that's what I'm feeling." She took a deep breath against his next reaction. "Then he'll come after me."

She didn't get the bellowing she expected. Instead, his face paled to a stark white, throwing the planes and angles of his face into harsh relief.

Kevin slumped into his chair. "He's coming after you? When did he say that? Since when have you been communicating with him?" He studied her weary face, then added quietly, "Start at the beginning, and leave nothing out."

She did, slowly and carefully, gradually bringing him up to date on the latest odd developments in her life.

"That's when I came back to the present, hearing you pounding on the truck window," she concluded.

"Are you sure about him hunting another victim?"

Alexis shuddered. "Maybe because I'm speaking with Daisy, he feels he's losing her. Maybe he's hunting for a replacement. I don't know." She took another long sip of the cold liquid. "There was an aged quality to the vision, like it happened a long time ago. I don't have any evidence of that, just a feeling. I think this killer has been operating for a very long time."

Shifting in his seat, Kevin studied the crowd walking by. After a long silence, he finally said, "We don't *know* if there were other victims."

Rubbing her temples, she snorted in disgust. "Like hell we don't. Daisy is one, and I think I've seen three other children. *At least* three others," she amended, thinking of all the shadowy faces in her visions.

"But that's all supposition," he said. "And I need something concrete to go on. Like a body."

"You have one child's body," she cried out. "Why can't you find out about her? Hasn't she paid enough? Haven't they all?"

"Easy." Kevin reached over and captured her hands gently, compassion and caring written on his concerned face. "We're working on it. It takes time."

Alexis clenched her fingers, unintentionally squeezing Kevin's hands. "I can't stand that she has no home."

"I know that, honey."

Honey? Rough skin rasped across her soft palms. Tingling, arousing, yet comforting at the same time. Alexis stared, mesmerized as his strong fingers evoked sensations she hadn't felt before. Who was this man who moved her so? Why had he come into her life now?

"Let's go. I'll take you to one of my favorite places for a couple hours. You need to get out of town for a bit." He held up his hand to forestall her arguments. "I'm not asking you to come. I'm telling you." He stood, holding out his hand.

Alexis glanced up at him, more than a little surprised at this sudden development. "I just want to go home and rest."

"I know. But this is a special place and just what the doctor ordered." He smiled smugly.

"Now you practice medicine, I suppose?" Her sarcasm had no effect on him.

He pulled her to her feet and tugged her in the direction of his truck. "Part of the job description. Let's go."

Scant minutes later, they were in his truck, heading out of town. The miles of suburbia gave way to miles of green forest. Alexis couldn't remember the last time she'd gone in this direction. Maybe never.

Listlessly she watched the rapidly disappearing miles. They'd turned onto a well-traveled dirt road, heading into a deeply wooded area, with second-growth trees and long meadows. She'd heard a chain of small lakes were in the area but hadn't taken the time to check them out.

The truck bounced over a rise, and the whole vista changed. Alexis gasped, as sparkling blue water opened up in front of her. "*This* is gorgeous."

Kevin smiled at her. "You haven't seen anything yet."

And he was right.

A large stream flowed down the mountain behind them through a series of small glistening pools. It resembled a blue sunlit necklace, winding down to feed the incandescent jewel in the valley.

"Oh, my God." Alexis exited the truck and raced to the water's edge. The musical laugh of the moving water refreshed her soul. Fresh air refueled her senses as nothing else could have. "What is this place?"

"It's private property." Kevin came to stand beside her. "I'm building a house back here in a grove of trees."

It took a moment for his words to sink in. "You mean, you own this piece of heaven?" At his complacent grin, she shook her head in disbelief. "I didn't even know that something like this existed." Alexis turned slowly, trying to take it all in.

"This has been in my family for generations. Everyone enjoyed coming here, but I'm the first to want to live here." They walked upstream a few hundred yards. Kevin showed her rock steps, leading into one of the pools. "I have many happy memories from here."

"I believe you. It's spectacular." In fact, she was deeply shocked that someone could own this and yet not find a way to be here every available minute.

"Construction has gotten much easier with the times. I'll be bringing power down here. The foundation is complete, as is the well. Do you want to see?"

"Do I ever!"

They walked over to the deserted site.

"Have you got a contractor building this for you?" She saw signs that someone had been working. Tools were neatly stacked off to one side. Yards of lumber for framing sat ready under the trees, the much-needed generator in plain view but tucked farther underneath the branches.

"Yes, but it's a buddy of mine, so he works on this when he doesn't have other work. He's putting up a double garage for someone else today."

Good. Alexis was glad to not have noises marring the silent beauty of this place.

"Do you want to go for a swim?" he asked, smiling broadly.

Crestfallen, she looked over at him. "I didn't bring a suit."

Despite the words, the water drew her back to its side. She wanted to immerse herself in the cool crisp ripples. Did she dare?

"I'm going in. You make up your own mind."

Startled by his words, she turned to face him, only to stop in shock at the sight of his beautifully muscled behind. Dear God, Mother Nature at her best. A moan of delighted surprise escaped—the sound brought his head around sharply.

He grinned. "Like what you see, do you?"

Raw heat washed over her face, but she refused to look away. Keeping her eyes on him, she admitted softly, "Oh yes."

"Enjoy," he tossed back cheerfully, taking care as he stepped on the stone stairs and descended into the rippling water. "But wouldn't you prefer to come in yourself?"

"I'm thinking about it." In this setting, with just the two of them, alone in nature, it seemed natural to be nude. As it was, she felt overdressed, hot and decidedly uncomfortable. Without allowing herself to think of the consequences, she stripped off her clothing. The cool air instantly soothed her overheated skin. She sighed in relief. She glanced over at Kevin, but he rested against a large flat rock, his eyes closed.

Inexplicably she was miffed. To hell with it. She strode, with a confidence she didn't feel, to the water's edge, gasping in shock at the temperature of the water as she slipped in. Cool waves lapped at her skin, as she sank down to settle against a smooth rock, grateful to close her eyes and to relax.

CHAPTER 13

H E WAS NO angel, for heaven's sake, and she'd test the strength of a saint. Although he'd hoped she'd follow his lead and loosen up enough to join him in the water, Kevin hadn't dared to believe it would happen. For all her wholesome, natural look, she held herself in tight control, as if fearful of letting go.

He couldn't resist sneaking a quick glance.

God, she was beautiful! Long and lean from many hours of physical work, tan marks highlighted the secret areas of her body she kept hidden from public view. Gentle waves reached up to caress her heated skin as she slowly sank, inch by inch into the water. But her nipples, oh God. His eyes slammed shut, and he focused on controlling his breathing.

No force on earth could stop him from opening his eyes for a quick second look.

Damn him for looking in the first place, and damn him for not looking sooner. The water already lapped at her breasts, lifting their delicate weight to float on the gentle waves. Kevin shuddered, grateful for the swift current that would at least distort her view of his arousal. His eyes slid closed once again, taking with him the incredible erotic memory of her expression, when she'd first felt the cool water enveloping, caressing, and cooling her skin. That look would feed his fantasies for a long time.

He'd love to have Alexis be more at ease with him. She needed to relax more, to smooth away the constant pinched look she always carried—a look he presumed had been there since her sister's death, if not before. She'd isolated herself inside a tower of pain, refusing to rejoin the world.

Now that she was taking her first tentative steps, he really wanted her to enjoy her life ... and he wanted to be in it in some capacity. He didn't know in what capacity or where he wanted this relationship to go, just that he wanted a chance for them to move forward together.

ALEXIS STRETCHED OUT. The gentle current washed away the many layers of stress that had built up slowly over the last few weeks. With the blue sky, hot sunlight, and incredible water vistas surrounding her, nothing resembling ghosts or evil was allowed.

She was thankful for the respite.

She was also getting cold.

They'd been resting in companionable silence for several minutes, maybe even longer, but, without any movement to warm her up, the chill had started to settle in.

"Had enough?" Kevin called to her.

"I think maybe. I'm almost numb," she answered, not opening her eyes. Splashing sounds warned her of his approach. Casually she shifted, allowing the water to hide most of her. She was no prude, but the energy between them already hovered at a flashpoint. It didn't need any starter fluid.

"Can't have that." He stood in front of her, concern written on his face. "Let's warm up in the sun."

He held out his hand.

Alexis looked at his outstretched hand carefully. It was such an innocent gesture but fraught with hidden implications. Shivers raced down her spine.

He waited, his palm still outstretched.

Why was she making such a big deal out of this? Because it was a big deal—at least it was for her. Her hand moved on its own accord, sliding into his much bigger one, mocking her indecisiveness. She watched, shocked, as her fingers nestled contentedly into his. *How dare they?*

Easy. They'd bypassed her mind and had followed her heart.

Shit!

He tugged her gently to her feet and into his arms.

Ice met fire. Heat seared her cool body, igniting flames of scorching passion. Kevin held her snug against him from chest to thigh, wet skin to wet skin, causing heat to smolder inside. Her breath caught, as her nipples shifted against his lightly haired chest.

"Are you all right?" he whispered against her hair.

"I think so, but I'm getting cold," she answered, slightly out of breath.

"Impossible. I'm burning up." He laughed lightly only it slid quickly into a groan.

Startled, she searched his face. Color flushed his high cheekbones, tension pulled at his very skin. But his eyes, oh, dear God. Deep, metallic, and mesmerizing, she felt them reach inside her soul, searching, seeking, asking something of her.

Kevin lowered his head, sealing her mouth with his. Flames ignited her, warmed her from the inside out. A moan escaped on a breathless sigh, when he lifted his head ever-so-slightly, before dropping once more to take her mouth in a blazingly passionate kiss.

Steam should be rising around them, Alexis thought, as her mind floated in a daze. He turned her fully against him, sealing her from breast to hip, before sliding his tongue deep within the sweetness of her mouth.

She ceased to think at all.

His erection prodded insistently against her belly, unfurling a deep throbbing in hot rolling waves. She moaned again. Dear God, his hands! They slid from shoulder to hip, then back again, pressing her closer, each wet slide bringing more shudders.

"We shouldn't be doing this," she protested faintly, when she finally could.

"Like hell, we've been heading here since you climbed out of that ditch."

"No," she protested weakly, as his hand slid around her shoulders to her chest, sliding downward to rest on the rounded top curve of her breast. Her eyelids closed, as continuous tremors turned her spine to jelly.

"No?" he questioned in disbelief.

"That's not what I meant. Hell, I don't know what I meant."

He resumed his assault on her senses, trailing tiny kisses across her cheeks and up over her eyelids. His touch was tender and comforting. "*Shh,* you think too much." His tongue traced the delicate lines of her flushed lips. "Just feel. Anything this good can't be wrong. We need this," he added fiercely, using hot kisses to accent his words.

She leaned against him, unable to formulate a coherent sentence when her thoughts could only center on one thing—his hand was too high. Rising on tiptoe, she shifted so his fingers lovingly cupped her aching breast. She moaned in relief, tilting her head back in acquiescence as sensations overwhelmed her.

Kevin took advantage of the soft skin presented, sliding delicate kisses down her smooth throat. Her moans changed to soft gasps.

"What?" he whispered in her ear. Delicately he traced the shell shape with his tongue, slowly, sensuously reawakening nerve cells that had lain dormant for years.

Snuggled tightly against his chest, Alexis was treated to a symphony of sounds as Kevin's heartbeat boomed through her, his own ragged breathing inexplicably reassuring her. She laughed in sheer joy, a tinkling lightness that echoed over the waves lapping at their bodies. "Nothing, nothing at all."

He lifted his head to look at her. Then he grinned, revealing pure male satisfaction. "I'll have you know this is considered to be a whole lot more than nothing, my dear," he teased her.

A startled laugh burbled out. "That is not what I meant!" she protested with a giggle.

He smirked. "Good, my manhood is a delicate issue, and this is cold water."

His grin was pure dynamite and, as such, blew any remaining resistance right out of the water.

While he watched, she stretched upward in a feline movement, sinuously rubbing her belly and soft curls against his eager, welcoming body. "There doesn't appear to be anything delicate about this at all."

His shoulders shook, as chuckles rumbled through his large muscled frame. In pure delight, the two of them smiled, enjoying the moment.

Until their eyes caught and held—in a promise of much, much more.

Instantly laughter died, and passion rose between them.

This time when he took her mouth, nothing was tentative about it … or in Alexis's eager response.

Lost in her passion, Alexis was only minimally aware of being propelled up against a cold barrier. They stood flush together while water swirled and rippled around them. Kevin pulled back slightly.

"No," she whimpered, searching for him with her fingers.

"*Shhh,* it's all right. I'm just moving you up and out of the water."

True to his word, he lifted her onto a large flat sun-warmed rock. Before she'd realized what had happened, she was stretched out under the hot sun. Gracefully she arched upward, enjoying the sun's warm kiss on her chilled skin.

"Sex kitten," Kevin whispered, as he splashed up beside her on their warm bed, receiving a smug feline smile for his efforts. "Damn, but you're gorgeous."

That startled her. Alexis knew she was okay to look at but had never put any stock in her looks. That he was enchanted inordinately pleased her.

"Thank you," she responded shyly.

His infectious grin caught her sideways, breaking her own smile free.

As her lips curved upward, Kevin's eyes dropped to follow their slow tilting movement. His eyes deepened to a smoky gray, and his face flushed, highlighting the planes and angles of his features.

Alexis's stomach tightened and twisted in anticipation. This man overwhelmed her senses as none had before. There was no room for anything else but him.

Time stilled. Receded …

Alexis reached up and tugged him down to her.

His lips branded her with his heat. Hot and cold contrasted and blended, covering her mouth in a molten heat that moved and caressed, before pressing deep, forcing her lips open. Lava washed through her, as his tongue stroked and explored the inner recesses.

No, there were no fireworks or horns blowing in the background. But there was an incredible undertow in the sexual current that grabbed hold and dragged her under.

His hands stroked, cupped, and caressed, as they journeyed over the sun-warmed valleys of her tingling body. It was a delight to be touched with such caring. Alexis lost herself in the enchanting sensations. For years, she'd been the caregiver, the one dishing out the comfort and love—so much so that she'd forgotten the joy of being on the receiving end. She reveled in it now. Arching and twisting, she moved under his ministrations, turning up the heat between them with her unbridled pleasure.

"You love this, don't you?" he murmured against her cheek, as he nuzzled her. "You're more sex goddess than you realize." His hands continued to stroke and to pet her, moving from one sensitive spot to the next.

"It feels wonderful," she admitted softly, an unaccountable shyness washing over her, as if she'd let him in on a great secret. But, as tensions twisted tighter and higher inside her, coherent thought was no longer possible. She explored his body with the same abandon. Soon his gasps blended with hers, as the two forgot about words and communicated with the more intimate language of lovers.

This was no short intense coupling, but a joyous taking of time to get to know and to learn each other's secrets. A time of caresses given and accepted, as the two lost themselves in the joy of soul-touching intimacy.

Time had no meaning, and, indeed, with the sun beaming down on their overheated bodies, it seemed to stand still. But eventually they could hold off no longer, and Kevin took control. Holding her soft, warm gaze with his own, he shifted, until he was between her spread legs, propped on his elbows. He waited, … silent.

As if he waited for permission, but, at this late stage, that seemed unnecessary. Puzzlement and confusion had her drawing back from the passionate edge, where she'd precariously balanced.

His large hands cupped the sides of her head, holding her, so he could gaze into her passion-soaked eyes. "I want you with me," he whispered.

That brought a hiccup of a laugh, followed by a groan, as her sensitized nipples nestled deeper into his curly chest hair. "I couldn't possibly be any more with you than I am now."

"Not true," he whispered.

Confused, she looked him. *What did he mean?*

"Open your mind and let me in."

Understanding lit tiny flames in the dark depths of her eyes. "You mean, you're actually asking this time?" she teased.

He pressed his hips teasingly against her pelvis, and the feel of him made her eyelids droop. She tilted her own hips helplessly upward.

"Open up, and let me in."

That suggestion of a duality was her undoing. Needing the physical completion that his body could bring and curious to know what new experiences the blending of their minds could add, she visualized a door in her mind and consciously opened it.

Sensations tossed her high into a sexual reality that overwhelmed, while, at the same time, it drove her right back to passion's edge. She read his thoughts, knew it was his sexual passion that she felt—all of it mixing and blending with hers to push both of them even higher. Colors and heat exploded around them.

Their bodies blended into one and so did their distinctive colors—both becoming something else again, something better, brighter, and far more powerful.

Alexis, poised on the cliff's edge, cried out, as her mind overloaded. Her body twisted frantically beneath his.

"Don't think. Just feel." Kevin's comforting voice was a lifeline through the turbulence of her inner world.

Trusting in him, she clung to his energy, as she let herself fall from the cliff. Dimly she heard his cry, as he dove after her.

For a long moment, she sensed nothing but his voice, his energy … and, dear God, his body. Possessed in all ways, she wouldn't and couldn't have asked for anything different.

"Now you're mine," he whispered, his voice full of masculine satisfaction. How could she argue? He was right. She was his.

The overwhelming possessiveness made her smile. Allowing that to go unchallenged had to be the result of complete satiation. She couldn't see any other circumstance in which she'd have allowed it. Right now she was too happy to care.

Her eyes drifted slowly shut, and she slept. Her spirit smiled, when he slid over to lie protectively beside her on the hard rock surface in the sun.

"TIME TO WAKE up, sleepyhead," murmured the insistent voice.

Alexis murmured her displeasure and tried to roll away from the disturbance—but nothing doing. Something warm and smooth stopped her. The bright sunshine made opening her eyes difficult. But, as a shadow moved over, she opened her eyes to find Kevin smiling down at her.

"How long was I out?" Alexis wished she could think, but it was difficult when she felt so lethargic.

"Just under an hour. I wanted to let you sleep longer, but I don't want you getting sunburned. Some very tender parts are exposed right now."

That reminder had her sitting up in embarrassed surprise. She flushed as she realized what she must have looked like. Totally replete, she'd brazenly slept like a child of nature. Surreptitiously she glanced at Kevin, unnerved to find him watching her intently.

"None of that," he said firmly. He stood and held out a hand. "Let's go for a quick swim, then head back into town. I think you've had enough sun for today."

And other things, his voice implied. But she really didn't want to think about that. Tonight, when she was alone, she could revisit all the uncertainty whirling through her head.

She eyed his outstretched hand. This was a little too reminiscent of his earlier invitation. To have concerns now would definitely be a case of too little, too late.

Reaching up, she accepted his help, and they walked silently into the cool water. He was right, she realized with surprise. The cool water had a bite, as it reached for her sun-kissed skin. Seconds later it became a soothing tonic. She might need to put on some aloe vera cream at home.

As she floated, she realized that other parts of her were in dire need of some attention too. Her back was scraped from lying on the rock, and her tender inner muscles were aching from the unusual activity. She'd be sore in the morning.

"Are you all right?" Kevin's concerned voice broke through her reverie.

She smiled self-consciously. "I'm just realizing what parts of me will be uncomfortable tomorrow."

A startled laugh erupted from him. "Not too sore, I hope. Next time we'll find something other than hard ground to lie on." He dunked his head, breaking through to flip water droplets everywhere.

She felt inordinately pleased by his words. So there would be a next time, would there? That was good. *Wasn't it?*

Half an hour later, they were dried off and dressed. Kevin had found an old towel tossed to dry over the bushes. Alexis didn't really want to think about who might have used it before her, but neither could she put jeans on over wet skin.

She hated the drive back to town. They drove back in silence. Every mile felt like ten. Like the return to reality from their fantasy world, it left her feeling insecure. This was all new for her. She didn't know how to act. She didn't know what to say, so she said nothing. Alexis felt Kevin's gaze on her several times but avoided looking at him.

They pulled up beside her truck, still parked outside the library. Kevin keyed off the engine and turned to face her. "Take it easy for the rest of the day. You've been through a lot lately. Today was special for both of us." He stroked her hand gently. "I'll call you tomorrow, okay?"

Alexis nodded mutely. Where the hell was her cool casual attitude when she needed it? Then where was her understanding of this relationship when she needed it either?

But, in the heat of the afternoon, no reassurances had been handed out. No discussion of a future mentioned. And she didn't think she could do short-term with him. Not successfully.

Not without getting badly hurt. And she was afraid she'd just opened herself for that anyway.

CHAPTER 14

K EVIN WATCHED ALEXIS flee. There was no other word for it. She was swiftly putting as much distance between them as she could. He wondered if she realized it. Instincts had taken over, and she'd bolted. On the drive home, she'd started out sitting in the middle of the bench seat, but, by the end of the trip, she'd almost wedged herself up against the door. He didn't think she was aware she'd done so. He'd restrained himself from going into her mind, although the temptation to delve for the answers had been hard to resist.

With a heavy sigh, he watched her truck race from the library lot and disappear into the traffic.

Damn it. His fist pounded the steering wheel in frustration. He shouldn't have let her sleep. He should have woken her up like he'd wanted to and made love to her again. But he knew she'd be sore from their earlier lovemaking. Instead, he woke her because he didn't want her to be sunburned.

Damn him for that decision. When she'd woken up, everything had been different. She'd immediately started rebuilding her walls, and then he hadn't known how to get back to their earlier closeness.

He shouldn't have let her leave like that either.

Decision made. He slammed the truck into Reverse and backed up. Just then his phone went off. "What's up?" he growled.

"A six-year-old girl didn't make it home from school."

"Shit!"

Two hours later, he switched to much stronger words. A full-scale search had been organized, an Amber Alert had been sent out, and, so far, they'd found nothing.

Several times he'd tried to contact Stefan, but he wasn't answering his phone. Telepathically he wasn't home either. That usually meant that Stefan had holed up with his paintbrush. When he finished a session like that, he usually contacted Kevin on his own.

Usually.

A sick feeling told Kevin this was a kidnapping—or worse. That before the night was out, it could be a murder. He'd driven around town, opening his senses to search on all levels but with no luck.

His cell phone rang.

"Stefan," he said, as soon as he heard the tired voice on the other end of the phone. "I need help."

AT DINNERTIME, ALEXIS puttered around in her apartment. She wasn't scheduled for a practice session with Stefan that evening, and it was a good thing. She didn't know what was wrong. Her energy had fallen below low. She felt like she'd left it behind or had had it siphoned off. She collapsed on the couch and closed her eyes.

As soon as she did, faces and noises swamped her in a mad chaotic vision. The sheer volume deluged her, drowning out any hope of making sense of the images. She couldn't sort out the voices either. Pissed and tired, her beleaguered mind finally had enough. She yelled to the empty apartment, "Stop!"

Dead silence overcame the room, now thick with tension.

Just what the hell was going on?

A frantic child's cry cut through the air. *He broke his promise. You have to help her.*

Alex spun to the left. Daisy stood a few feet away, her form thin and wavering. Bright sparks surrounded her, making her look more nightmarish than ever. Several other small shadows collected at her side. Pale faces, almost recognizable but not quite. One was the boy she thought she'd seen in an earlier vision.

"Daisy, help who?" Alexis cut to the point.

The little girl. He has her. Daisy zapped out of the room. Her companions disappeared with her, leaving a very scared and confused Alexis.

Instinctively she picked up the phone and called Kevin. It was busy. After several failed attempts, she called the police station but couldn't get through there either. What was going on? She turned on the television to catch the evening news.

And heard that a child had gone missing.

Terror swept through her. The madman had a new victim.

Alexis huddled in the corner of the couch, her knees tucked to her chin, and tried to bury her head. So much evil was in the world. She didn't think she could stand it.

Like you've got a choice. Damn it, Alexis, get yourself under control. You're transmitting in Technicolor, and we're trying to work! Stefan's voice slashed through her pity party.

Alexis's tears vanished. She wasn't alone in this—even if it took an occasional boot from Stefan to remind her.

She leaned forward, realizing what they must be doing. She snatched her phone and dialed Stefan. When he picked up, she didn't even give him a chance to speak. The question rushed out of her mouth. "Stefan, can I help? Tell me what to do."

Just moments ago, she didn't think she could handle even living in this world; now she understood it was the inability—the helplessness—to do anything that had bothered her. But, if she could help stop this asshole, well, that was a completely different story.

"Kevin?" Stefan asked. He'd put the phone on Speaker, lending a tinny hollowness to his voice.

"She's not ready for this."

Kevin's words pissed her off and instantly made them combatants again. "Shut up, Kevin. You don't know what the hell I might be ready for."

"Neither do you."

"Really? Well, Daisy just told me that the same asshole who is holding her has this little girl and that I need to help her."

A fraction of a second of silence passed, before both men exploded. "What? When? What did she say?"

"Damn it, Alexis. You should have contacted us immediately."

"I tried," she mumbled. "Your phone was busy. It was only a few minutes ago, and she didn't say anything else."

"But she did confirm that it was the same asshole?" That was the detective in him speaking again, needing to nail down the facts.

"Yes."

"Shit."

A soul-weariness to Stefan's voice worried Alexis. "Can you find her, Stefan?"

"I've been looking but, so far, … nothing."

"Is he blocking you?"

"Yes, I'd say so—or, if not blocking, at least putting up a different energy to hide behind."

"Same thing," cut in Kevin.

"Can Daisy help with that?" Alexis asked.

"She might be able to," Stefan said. "Can you connect to her again?"

Alexis didn't know half the time if she was speaking aloud or thinking in her mind. Their conversations had become so complex, so strange, yet so intimate on these different levels. Their thoughts and hers blended to become one. Weird. And she held the phone in her hand to complicate matters even further. "I can try."

Kevin broke in hurriedly. *Not alone. Go to Stefan's house and let him help. I have to continue with the search. Let me know if you learn anything.*

Alexis's mind instantly lightened, becoming empty and feeling lonely in a way. To know that someone was with you so intimately was something she was starting to enjoy. It gave her a sense of belonging that she had never experienced before.

Do you want to come here, or shall I come to you? Stefan's words were neutral, but Alexis could sense the fatigue flowing off him in waves.

"No, don't come here. I'll be at your place in a few minutes. Put on the coffee."

With that, she grabbed her keys and headed back to her truck.

STEFAN'S DOOR WAS wide open when Alexis arrived. Nothing suggested foul play, but she found herself approaching cautiously. She couldn't resist a sigh of relief that Kevin was at work. She couldn't deal with her own confusion over him at the moment, much less explain it to him. And he'd want an explanation sooner or later.

"Hello? Stefan?" She took a couple steps inside, even though she got no answer. The room looked, as always, sparse and clean, everything in its place. Where could he be?

"Stefan!" she called out louder. "Are you home?"

"Back here," he called from the rear of his house.

She walked through to find him comfortably seated on the bench in the center of his back garden. "Stefan? Are you okay?"

He grimaced. The early evening light cast long shadows in his face. It was hard to see details, but his face glowed in the weird light, solemn and intense. "I will be."

"That doesn't make it any easier though, does it?" Alexis sat down beside him, concerned at the melancholy look to him. "You think she's dead, don't you?"

He looked at her in surprise. "Not at all. It's just that I've seen this so many times before, and they usually end badly."

"It's not like you to be so negative."

"I call it realistic." Stefan suddenly stood and motioned her back to the house. "Let's go see if we can make a difference."

They settled into the living room. Stefan immediately started to follow what Alexis now recognized as his work ritual. Once tea was poured, they each relaxed for a few minutes. "Where do we start?" she asked.

Stefan looked at her, his head tilted in consideration. "Why don't you tell me?"

She looked at him questioningly. Where should they start? With Daisy? Or with this asshole to see if they could find out something on their own? She closed her eyes to turn inward.

And found Lissa standing inside her mind.

"*Aacck!*" Startled, she opened her eyes. Lissa sat cross-legged beside Stefan. How did one get used to that?

"Maybe we should ask my sister?" Alexis suggested drily. "She might know what we can do."

Stefan grinned at Lissa. "Her? Now what could she know that we don't?"

Ghostly laughter lit up the room. Alexis's heart lightened proportionally. It was so good to see her sister again. Lissa looked over at her knowingly. Alexis grinned. She couldn't help being delighted at these meetings. Lissa had stayed for her. It couldn't last forever, but, for now, … their time together was a joy. And, of course, being on the other side of the veil meant Alexis could go visit Lissa. "Let's get down to business."

She's alive. But that's all I know. Lissa's voice was faint and reedy.

"Is it the same man?" Stefan asked.

Lissa's faint form nodded weakly. *Yes.*

"Why this child?" Alexis asked.

There is a connection. I just can't tell what kind.

That made sense, but it wasn't enough to go on.

"Anything more specific?" Stefan asked. "Can you see her? Can you see where she's being held?"

Only that he's stashed her in a dark place, and she's scared. I can't see her. I get the odd spike, as her overwhelming fear bleeds onto my plane.

Stefan nodded. "Good enough to start. Do you want to begin, Alexis? I'll watch your back."

Alexis agreed. Getting comfortable, she followed the rituals Stefan had drilled into her. Within moments, she'd escaped the physical world to walk through her favorite meadows. Lissa now walked beside her.

The meadow slowly changed, moving into a stark, desolate landscape. Alexis consciously worked on her thoughts to manipulate the scenery back to something more pleasant, but nothing would shift.

It took a moment to understand. This wasn't her world. It was his. Had he noticed her presence already? How could he not?

I don't think he has seen you. I think you've picked up on him intuitively. Lissa looked around as if it all made sense now. *That's why we're here. This is his place.*

Alexis froze, as the first tendrils of remembered fear snaked up her spine. From a long distance away, Alexis heard Stefan's calm, steady voice talking to her.

Focus, Alexis. This is a good sign.

Says you, she muttered. The air around them deepened, thickened, and filled with a rank odor. Her nose wrinkled against the smell. He must know they were here.

No, I don't think so. Just as affected, Lissa had lowered her voice to a whisper.

Then what's with the scenery? Alexis asked. They continued to move cautiously forward. It was hard to breathe and even harder to see.

Stefan's voice rang clear and succinct in her head. *Did you hear what you just thought? You aren't breathing or seeing in any physical sense to begin with. In this dimension, you can clear your surroundings with your mind. That's his projection, but that doesn't have to be your perception.*

Oh, hell, you're right. Instantly the air cleared and began to smell bright and fresh again.

With her new understanding of her personal control, she formulated a beautiful rock to sit on. Sitting comfortably, Alexis brought up the image of the missing girl she'd seen on television. With Lissa at her side, Alex focused at a deeper level than she'd ever tried before. Deeper and deeper she went, searching for a connection that would take her to the child.

She whistled through long tunnels and around corners. She floated, flew, and raced through different scenes in a mad search that took on a life of its own. Without warning, she found herself falling into a black hole. The only viable sense left to her was sound.

What she heard was heart-wrenching sobbing.

Alexis reached deep for control, detaching as completely as she could, in order to bring her other senses back into use, and found a frail child awkwardly crumpled in a corner. Her poor face, half covered in straggly blond hair, was buried in a moldy blanket. Alexis searched the gloom for details, anything helpful to indicate her location.

An odd hum echoed from somewhere, and the room oozed a stale mustiness. She couldn't tell if it were an actual room or some other containment. She needed to find something soon. No telling when *he'd* show up.

Alexis gently brushed the child's forehead. She didn't want to scare her, but the child needed comforting. Outside of a simple flinch, the girl didn't recognize the motion for what it was. No surprise there. Taking an extra second, Alexis consciously pulled some of the fear from the little girl's energy. Alexis's own heart rate picked up, as she absorbed the pain and fear into her own space. Shuddering slightly at the ripples of nastiness, she dumped it from her system as quickly as possible. She ran a light sweep over her own aura and swept out the negative energy, as Stefan had explained to her. A simple-enough mental process now that she knew about it.

Pulling back slightly, Alexis shifted to the other side of whatever barrier was hiding the child. The interior space disappeared. She now floated above an unrecognizable highway, looking down on evening traffic. A van drove steadily below her, an ancient white van with smoked windows. Was that it?

Alexis felt her energy fade. Wasn't much more she could draw on. Desperate to have something concrete to take back, she gathered the last of her energy, zooming in on the back of the speeding van. The distance widened rapidly. She strained to the limits of her abilities. It took every bit of effort, but, with one final burst of speed, Alexis surged down, barely catching several letters in the license plate.

Got it!

She hit the end of her spiritual rope. A huge vacuum sucked her backward through an endless tunnel. This time her journey was much faster, spinning her helplessly in a rotating tunnel, accompanied by endless blinding noise for too long of a time.

Until she was slammed back, once again, into Stefan's living room.

"ALEXIS?" STEFAN'S SOFT, caring voice called to her over and over. "Take a moment to bring yourself back. Slowly return to this plane." It took several long minutes for her to recognize he was stroking her shoulder gently.

"I'm back." Her voice cracked, grating against the serenity of the room. Nausea rose, then calmed in a big ocean wave. Her vocal cords seemed awkward and rusty. "*That* was a rough trip."

"Is there any other kind?" He waited a minute before asking, his voice barely hiding the hint of anxiousness, "Did you learn anything?"

That brought her quickly around. Sitting up too quickly, she collapsed back down again. "Oh, my head," she groaned.

"I said, take it easy for a bit. It's always worse after a bad trip."

"You need to contact Kevin." She took a deep breath against the pain battering away inside her head and then quickly related what had happened.

Even as she winced, she recognized Stefan's inner shift. He'd already opened communication with Kevin. Almost immediately Kevin was in her head, confirming the parts of the license number that she saw and the type of van being driven.

You're sure you didn't get a description of the driver? Kevin's impatient voice demanded.

"No," she whispered painfully. Her head was killing her, the tempo beating between the lobes of her brain. Kevin's questions weren't helping. God, she wished he'd disappear, at least until she felt better.

Stefan pivoted sharply to look at her.

"What?" she asked, confused by the strange look on his face.

"Did you do that on purpose?" At her look of incomprehension, he added, "You just shoved Kevin out of your mind and slammed the door." He grinned, winking at her. "You should hear him now."

Her head did feel better. How odd. She smiled wanly, hoping Kevin wouldn't hold it against her. "Maybe I did, but I didn't know that's what I was doing. My head's been killing me since I came back from that astro trip. His telepathy was making it worse." She shrugged in bewilderment, adding, "I couldn't stand it." She hadn't meant to shove him out though. In fact, she didn't even know that was something she could do.

"So you gave him the boot? Congratulations, you just took your next step. From now on, we'll require your permission to enter. Keep that in mind, any time you're in trouble."

That gave her pause. Several times she'd welcomed their unexpected presence in her mind, reassuring her that she was never truly alone. Now what would it mean? "Will it be difficult to open the door?"

"Like now, no real way to teach it to you. It will open, or it won't."

"Lovely," she muttered. It had better not refuse to open when she was in trouble. Of course she could always scream at them. That had worked so far. Stefan's wry look told her that he understood her thoughts regardless. "You can read my mind but can no longer talk to me in my mind, until I learn to open that door? How does that work?"

"It doesn't take a telepath to read your mind right now. There is also a big difference between reading your mind and speaking in your mind. Think receiving versus transmitting."

Alexis raised her hands in disgust. "Whatever. When does this ever get easier?"

"Never!" His final word was succinct and to the point, with the added implication of *get used to it.*

IN ANOTHER PART of town, an old beat-up car pulled into a very popular watering spot. Unfortunately this town sported several bars that stayed open well into the night. The young man, casually dressed in jeans and a T-shirt, quickly walked through each, searching for the asshole, before heading back to his car and driving on to the next bar. Grim satisfaction settled on his young features, each time he failed to find his suspect. It was possible that he'd missed him, but he didn't think so.

He didn't know quite what to do about the information when he found it. He needed proof of this man's activities first. If he could find this asshole first, it could give him an edge. Maybe enough to get his life back. Grimly the young man continued his search.

He had to find him before anyone else got hurt.

ALEXIS LIE QUIETLY on Stefan's couch. She'd recovered, only to find herself in an odd melancholy mood, feeling tired and chilled, the remnants of recovery mode. Today had been traumatic, to say the least. A long hot soak in her bath would help, but she couldn't leave Stefan's until she knew they'd found the little girl.

Fatigue weighed heavily upon her, and she closed her eyes. Had it only been this afternoon that she'd had such an incredible interlude with Kevin? Unbelievable. It already seemed like days ago. She sighed.

So far, they'd heard nothing.

Stefan returned to the living room, this time bearing a platter of fruit and cheese.

"You don't need to take such good care of me, Stefan. I'm not helpless."

"I'm enjoying it. Besides, after the day you've had, this should help." He carefully placed the full platter down on his low table—missing the odd look that came across her face.

"My day? What kind of day have I had?" she asked in confusion.

He snorted at her forgetfulness. "Don't forget that hiding something from a psychic is difficult at the best of times—and impossible when you're an open book anyway."

Her face burned.

He grinned at her.

"I didn't want to think about it at all," she mumbled sheepishly, too embarrassed to look him in the eye.

"So don't. Deal with it instead. Not to worry. I won't probe for details. That's private."

He spoke so nonchalantly that it gave her pause. She hurriedly reached for a bunch of grapes, uneasily aware of just how much information he could have accessed, if he'd so chosen. "Thank you for that."

"Anytime. I might tease Kevin about your wild afternoon but not you, never you."

She rolled her eyes at him. Heat still warmed her cheeks. She couldn't imagine how Kevin would react to Stefan's teasing. But then he'd been dealing with Stefan for much longer.

"But he hasn't had very many relationships during this time either."

"I thought you had to have permission to read my mind now," she asked, irritated.

"No, just to enter it. A small difference."

Alexis shook her head at the hairsplitting. She popped a grape into her mouth and tried to sort through the difference Stefan talked about.

"The van has been spotted at the mall, just on the outskirts of town. What is that place, Cottonwood Mall or some such thing?" Stefan's distant voice interrupted her musings.

He looked off in the distance as if receiving more information. As she watched him, Alexis could almost see the silent communication going on.

"Cottonwood Mall?" Alexis chewed on her bottom lip, anxiously watching Stefan's face.

"Kevin's en route and will call later." Stefan blinked several times and returned calmly to the food in front of him. "Eat up. You need to rebuild your strength."

They enjoyed their simple meal and chatted quietly.

"Stefan, what type of side effects do you have after your psychic trips?" He didn't answer. She looked up at him. "Stefan?"

Stefan stood frozen, his hand hanging in midair, a chunk of cheese halfway to his mouth, a glassy look in his eyes, giving him a vacant, not-at-home look.

Jesus, he looked scary. Alexis swallowed hard several times, all the while watching him. "Stefan?" she whispered cautiously. "What is it? What do you see?"

Unexpectedly he answered her. "They've found the van. And the child."

"Oh, thank God." Alexis was elated. It was a far better outcome than she'd feared might come of this night. "Is she okay?"

Stefan continued slowly, almost hypnotically. "The child was drugged but appears to be unhurt. An ambulance is on the scene."

"What about the kidnapper? Did they catch him?" She urged him to provide more.

Stefan went deeper inward. "No," he whispered dejectedly. "They didn't get him. He wasn't in the van." He paused for a moment, his eyes rolling upward. A moment later, they rolled back down. He slowly continued, "I'm searching for him."

Alexis held her breath against the pain knifing through her. The bastard was still loose.

"He's nowhere." Stefan slowly opened his eyes. "For just a moment, I caught a whiff of his energy. Incredible anger, madness even. Then he was gone."

"But, if he's losing control, wouldn't it have been easier to find him?"

"Theoretically, yes. But, in this case, he *isn't* losing control. He's coldly, terrifyingly, and dangerously *in* control."

"More treacherous than ever, you mean?"

Stefan stilled, staring at her somberly. "There'll be a horrific backlash from this night."

Alexis stared at him, as painful understanding came crashing in.

The asshole would find a way to retaliate.

CHAPTER 15

KEVIN CLIMBED WEARILY from his truck and trudged toward Stefan's front door. He could have called, but, this way, he saw Alexis at the same time. And he needed that contact tonight. She might prefer space, but he was scared to give her too much. So, here he was, incapable of walking away.

"Good evening, Kevin."

Kevin startled at the sound of his name. "Sorry, Stefan. I must be half asleep."

"Half something, yes. But I'm not sure it's asleep."

Kevin flushed, shooting his friend a dirty look. He got a cheeky grin in return. Kevin pushed past him, calling back, "Where is she?"

"Who?" asked Stefan, a little too innocently as he followed casually behind.

"Alexis!" Kevin called out.

"*Shh*, she might be asleep," Stefan cautioned.

"Now you tell me," Kevin said in a much softer voice, as he walked quickly through the hallway and into the living room—where he suddenly stopped.

Alexis slept, curled up like a kitten on the couch, with a soft mohair blanket tossed casually over her legs. He winced at the deep shadows under her closed eyes.

Hopefully finding the child unharmed tonight would go a long way to helping her recover. "How was she earlier?"

"Pretty wiped out," Stefan answered, nodding toward the kitchen, so Kevin would follow him. Once there, he put on water for a cup of tea.

"Skip the tea. Do you have any beer?" At Stefan's nod, Kevin pulled open the fridge and grabbed himself a cold one. He removed the cap and took a long pull, before turning back to face Stefan again. "We lost him."

Stefan was compassionate in his silence. He gazed steadily back at

Kevin, waiting.

Damn. Kevin wished he could be so calm. He wanted to pound something. "Did you pick up anything on him?"

Stefan shook his head. "Not really. I caught just the faintest scent of him in the mall." He paused and then forced himself to continue, "He's almost insane in his fury."

"That's to be expected."

"But not like this. He's after revenge."

Kevin looked at him sharply. "What do you mean?"

"I picked up some bits. It's almost as if he believes you stole something from him, and now he'll look for something of yours to take in revenge."

"But does he know it's me?" Kevin looked out the window thoughtfully. He hadn't expected this twist. If Stefan was correct, it seemed incredibly personal. Adding weight to the idea that he probably knew the killer.

"My impression is that he does. Besides, your name has been all over the media. It would be hard not to know you're handling the investigation."

"Interesting."

"What's interesting?" Alexis's voice broke through the intense silence.

The two men pivoted. Kevin walked over and pulled her into a warm, comforting embrace. "How are you feeling?"

"Better." She looked up at him solemnly. "Or at least I will be when you confirm the little girl is okay."

"She is." Kevin smiled with satisfaction. "She's in her mother's arms as we speak."

Alexis closed her eyes in relief, letting her head drop onto his chest. Grateful, Kevin held her close, allowing his cheek to rest on her hair. After a few minutes, she disentangled herself and moved over to give Stefan a quick hug. "At least something good came out of tonight."

Stefan led the way back into the living room. "Kevin, any idea why he chose this girl?"

"Not yet. But neither the mother nor the little one are in any shape to talk. Tomorrow I'll speak with them again." Kevin sat down beside Alexis. "Are you working tomorrow?"

She looked over at him in surprise. "I'd planned to. Why?"

"I wondered if you wanted to come with me to meet the mom and little girl."

Alexis was shocked. "Why? I'm not the police. That's your job."

She was so surprised at his question that she missed the grin on Stefan's face.

"News flash, Alexis. Remember all the headlines? 'Psychic Helps Police Find Abducted Child'? Guess what? That's you."

Alexis stared at the two men, as comprehension hit. Dear God, they were right. She'd just assisted in her first police case. A groan erupted, loud enough to be heard over the men's laughter, as she collapsed against her chair. "Shit! I don't want people to know."

"Calm down, Alexis. It's not the end of the world. No one will really know it's you—this time," Kevin said.

That horrified her even more. "And they had better not find out!" she cried out. "Yes, we found the little girl in time but ..." She slapped her hands flat against her thighs. "But the asshole is still free. He'll just go after someone else. What if we can't save them?" Thoughts tumbled through her mind. Just the thought of meeting the little girl scared Alexis. No way she wanted to be involved to that extent.

Except she already was.

Kevin broke in, his voice soothing and stabilizing. "Which is why it would be a good idea for you to go away and to visit a relative for a while instead. If this guy finds out that you helped us, he could decide to come after you."

"I don't think he's too worried about waiting. He already said he would." Anger washed through her. Alexis glared at the far wall, trying to contain her temper. She should be afraid at the idea. Instead it just pissed her off. How dare he make her a victim? Stefan had an odd impressionist painting hanging on the wall. She concentrated on that. She'd noticed it before, but today it seemed more vibrant, alive almost. In trying to block out Kevin's words, the picture drew her in. How odd.

"Alexis?"

The colors twisted and shifted, mixing rapidly, even as she watched. Bloodred and stark white—blood flowed over jagged bone. The image struck home. Someone would die. Pain, intense white lightning, struck her in the abdomen, the agony of it doubling her over.

"What is it, Alexis?" Both men rushed to her side. Kevin crouched anxiously in front of her. "Alexis, what's the matter?"

"The picture," she gasped. "On the wall."

They both looked at the painting in question. Stefan got up and walked over to it. Everything appeared normal now.

"What about the picture?" Kevin asked. His gaze roved over her face.

Alexis tried to reassure him with a smile, but it was difficult. "It looked like bones and blood. An image. Maybe of something to come. But it's gone now. I had the feeling someone would die."

The pain had eased but not her understanding. Her ability constantly forced her to adjust now. A few cautious breaths later, the pain had reduced to a mild ache.

Had that pain been from the image? She gently rubbed her stomach. When would her life return to normal? Could a normal life ever exist for her again?

"Not likely," said Kevin, his eyes full of understanding.

"You're reading my mind again."

"You're transmitting again," came his sharp retort.

"Was not," she responded childishly. It certainly felt like he'd been in her mind. Still was. She concentrated for a quick second and mentally booted him out.

"Thanks, at least now I know the last time was no accident," he said bitterly, pulling away from her, hurt etched on his face. He snagged his beer and walked back into the kitchen. The door slammed behind him, announcing his departure to the garden.

Alexis looked over at Stefan in concern. "I didn't mean to hurt his feelings."

"I know, which doesn't change the fact that you did." Stefan sat down beside her. "It's difficult to learn boundaries in this field. You have to decide what you're comfortable with and stick with it. You and Kevin share a special bond now. He just wants to keep you safe."

Alexis latched onto the main issue. "Bond?" she asked tentatively.

"From the first time the two of you met, an intuitive bond existed, which has strengthened with time. There is one between the two of us, only different. Now, because he could, he used that link to make sure everything was okay in your world. He knew that, when you finally had some control, you *could* kick him out, but, until then, he wanted to keep tabs on you. Keep you protected." Stefan held up his hand to forestall her indignant outburst. "Before you blow, you knew, on a subconscious level, what he was doing. He couldn't have forged that link without your permission."

"What happened to the link after our love, ... ah ..." She stopped, flustered. "What happened to the link now?"

"A physical joining strengthens the mental or spiritual link. It's up to you two, but it can become almost permanent."

Alexis didn't know what to think. "Almost permanent?" What a mind-blowing concept.

"Right."

"Does that mean, like, we're 'special' together? As in 'forever' to-gether?" Alexis couldn't get her mind wrapped around this. What she could understand damn-near blew her mind—and her heart. "The thing is, I'm not sure that's what I want. That I'm ready for that." And maybe not with Kevin. And his job. She'd lost so many loved ones already. She didn't know if she could live with the fear of him heading off into danger every day.

Did she even have a choice any longer?

Kevin's caustic voice cut through her speech. "I suppose you just wanted to scratch an itch, huh? Gee, thanks. ... Nice to know I was of some use."

Heat flushed over Alexis's features before draining away, leaving her chilled and wan. "That's not fair."

Stefan's calm voice stepped in, easing some of the tension in the air. "Be nice to the lady, Kevin. This is between the two of you."

"She's the one who brought it up with you."

"I was trying to understand why you were hurt when I closed the door in my mind. That's all." Alexis's voice lowered to a soft, vulnerable pitch. "Now I'm wondering just how the afternoon even happened. It was so unlike me. Did you ...?" She broke off, not sure what she wanted to ask.

But Kevin knew.

Angry disbelief blasted back at her. "What?" he roared. "So now I'm an unscrupulous seducer of young women. I get them under my power, and they're helpless to resist! Do you really think I used some kind of hypnotic suggestion on you?"

His obvious disgust and sense of betrayal shamed her. She didn't think she'd meant that ... Although she didn't think he was to blame, a part of her still felt uneasy. Never would she have seen herself doing what she'd done so casually. That it could be something incredibly powerful, like fate, destiny, or even—God help her—love, wasn't something she could look at right now. It was much easier to hide behind her anger than look at the rest.

She knew the two men were watching the emotions flicker across her face. She kept her mind closed off. She had to sort this out without prying eyes, no matter how well intending they might be.

Kevin snorted in disgust, grabbed his coat, and stormed to the front door. "Thanks for the beer, Stefan. I'm gone. Maybe I can still grab some sleep tonight."

The door slammed behind him.

Stupidly she felt hurt that he didn't say goodbye. What an idiot.

He was pissed at her and maybe rightly so. That still didn't change the fact she'd have liked a goodbye hug and kiss after what they'd shared earlier today. Even though she had second-guessed—out loud— whether, for her, it was right or wrong.

She sighed and looked at Stefan, who watched her with one eyebrow raised.

"You could have said goodbye too, you know?" Stefan said quietly to her.

Once again she flushed. "I didn't think of that in time," she said quietly. She stood to gather her things. "Kevin's right. We should both be trying to follow his example and get some sleep. Morning will be here soon." She glanced at the living room clock and grimaced. "Very soon."

With a quick hug goodbye, Alexis walked slowly to her truck.

Way too late, she remembered the *almost* in Stefan's shocking revelation on being bonded. Just as shocking was the realization that such a bond was too precious to lose.

What had she just done?

THE SPORTS CAR ripped up the long drive, screeching to a dead stop, as if a drunken driver had slammed on a brake. Charles smiled. The lights were out. The good mayor and his wife were already in bed. They'd never notice his return, the recalcitrant son. Slamming the car door shut, he sauntered casually toward the sprawling mansion. Glancing around, he thought he saw another vehicle hiding under the trees at the fence. He laughed. Not bloody likely. No one would dare trespass on his daddy's all-important property.

Too bad.

He'd been tempted several times to smash his car into the front of the stone-cold building, but knew it wasn't worth the reproach and the reminders that would continue forever.

Almost walking straight, he made it inside the front door.

"Hello. Anyone still up?" He hoped not. He wasn't in the mood for more tears and lectures about his lack of career or his heavy drinking—especially not today. He closed his eyes against the pounding headache. God damn them anyway.

There never seemed to be a reason for these headaches, but they'd been killing him for years now, since he was a teen, in fact. Early on his mom had taken him to doctors and had tried hard to help him, but then, when nothing seemed to work, she had given up.

"Hello," he called out a little less quietly. Still no answer. Good.

"Keep it down, Charles," his dad called from the library, his voice boozy. "Your mother is asleep. Will you join me for a nightcap?" His father stood in the doorway to his study, drink in hand.

Asshole. Jesus, his old man was a royal bastard. One of these days, the mayor wouldn't be so cocky. Still, Charles had to maintain the status quo. He accepted the proffered scotch, before sitting down beside the fire. "Any news from around town?" he asked, smiling.

John stilled. "About what?"

Charles shrugged, tugging his tie loose to dangle down his shirt. "I heard something earlier on the news. Something about a missing child."

"Oh, that. The child's been found safe and sound." John lifted his glass of scotch in salute and took a healthy pull. "Don't know what we'd do without Detective Kevin Sutherland. He found the vehicle where the child was being held. Unfortunately the kidnapper is still at large." He shook his head sadly. "Terrible story."

"But the little girl will be okay, won't she?"

"Yes," John reassured him. "They found her in time." He looked over at his son curiously. "By the way, where were you earlier?"

"What? Oh, I was just driving around," Charles mumbled into his glass.

His father looked at him closely. "Did you go to the mall tonight? That's where the child was found."

Charles stared at his father. *Why the hell had he asked that?* "You don't think I had anything to do with her disappearance, do you?"

"No! No, of course not." But John focused on the swirling amber liquid in his glass, refusing to meet his son's gaze.

Sourly Charles looked at the hint of suspicion on the other man's face. "What about you? Did you go out earlier tonight?"

The other man's face paled, then flushed in fury. "What? My behavior has never been in question."

"But then your constituents don't know everything about your world, do they, Father?"

Horror and pain flowed from the liquid haze in John's eyes. "Why do you hate me so?"

No answer was forthcoming. Charles felt a grim satisfaction for putting his father firmly in his place again. But he knew his father would get his revenge soon—he always did.

He was big on that.

CHAPTER 16

S CREAMS OF TERROR woke Alexis in the middle of the night.
They were hers.

In bed, sweat soaked her silk camisole, and her heart pounded inside her chest. Oh God. What the hell was that? She was in her room but not. She was awake but not.

She was caught somewhere in-between.

The difficult day had roller-coastered her heart and mind into one endless tumultuous ride. Exhaustion had finally married the two into an uneasy truce for the night. Trembling in a crossover between psychic journey and sleepy wakefulness, Alexis didn't know where she was—or why.

Bitch!

Recognition and terror shuddered through her small frame. He was here, in her room. She curled up against the headboard, frantically searching the dark corners of her room.

Damn right, it's me! Thought you'd spoil my fun, did you? A macabre laughter floated through her gray world. *Well, guess what? I found something to entertain me anyway.* More haunting laughter echoed in the darkness. *Or should I say, ... someone?*

Alexis woke fully chilled to her soul. She'd never understood the phrase "in a cold sweat." Now she did and wished she didn't. Her throat rasped painfully with every breath. She didn't know what had just happened but knew it was important.

Automatically her mind reached for Kevin. Her mind zeroed in with perfect aim. It took several scary moments before the phone beside her rang.

"What?" growled back his disgruntled voice. "Why the hell did you wake me in the middle of the night?"

"He was just here."

"Who?"

His question alone explained his lack of wakefulness. Alexis waited patiently for it to kick in. It didn't take long.

"Him? The suspect? Was … He's gone? Are you okay? What did he say?"

Quickly she reassured him and related the asshole's words, emphasizing the tone of voice. "He sounded so satisfied, exultant even. I'm scared, Kevin. I think he's killed someone."

The long silence on the other end revealed Kevin was digesting her words. "That's not a total surprise. We saved the girl. It made him angry. But, if he's killing for revenge, then his behavior is escalating."

Alexis's hand tightened around the phone. She took a deep breath and expressed what really bothered her. "Maybe. I think he's picked someone you or I know, trying to make it personal."

Sudden silence filled the room. "I hope not, but no way to know until the call comes in. Get some rest. You'll need it."

Rest? Not likely. No way she would close her eyes again. That asshole could be waiting for her.

KEVIN FOUND IT impossible to go back to sleep. The initial heat at the sound of Alexis's voice had dissipated into anger. It was easier than dealing with the hurt inflicted last night. He still wanted to kiss her mindless—or at least until she had no doubts about the two of them. He'd never been much of a talker and knew he was reaping the reward of letting her run away yesterday. He'd seen her barriers go up, had sensed her insecurity, and didn't know how to return to the closeness they'd shared earlier. He'd let her run. If the call about the child hadn't come in then, … well, … at least she was talking to him this morning.

Immediately his mind returned to her message. His mind flitted through everyone this killer could target. There were too many of them. After an hour of going in circles, he finally got up and made coffee. It was just after four in the morning. Too early to start the day but too late to grab more sleep.

While sitting with his first coffee, his neck started itching. He opened his consciousness slightly. Awareness slammed into his senses with incredible intensity, letting him know the problem had been there a while, but he'd just tuned in.

Quietly he closed his eyes and opened his mind wider. He wasn't as good as Stefan yet, but he could usually search the scope of his county to pinpoint the area of trouble.

Next he went high and broad, looking for the black cloud, only to zoom back down into a corner of town he knew only too well. The question was, how did the killer know it too?

He hovered about the familiar two-story brick house. His breath whooshed out of him. His heart squeezed painfully before clamping down tight. He couldn't catch another breath. Mandy, the beautiful young lady friend, his former lover and Kyle's mother, lived there. One of the best people Kevin knew.

Now death had moved in.

Kevin returned to his living room, exhausted. He buried his face in his hands. Tears, hot and painful, welled up. Pain sat on the edge of his soul. God, he didn't want to go forward with this day.

Are you okay? Stefan's sleepy voice wove through Kevin's fatigue.

"No," he answered sadly. Too tired to use telepathy, and knowing the coming day would ask more from him than any day in his life, he'd spoken out loud and let Stefan do the work.

What's the matter? The sleepy voice was compassionate but not worried. Already he understood the emotion flowing through Kevin's mind, even if he didn't know the circumstances.

"The killer got personal last night. Very personal."

Waves of sadness vibrated between them as he allowed Stefan to watch the movie on continuous replay in Kevin's mind.

I'm sorry, Stefan murmured gently. *If it makes you feel better, I think that finished the killer's fury.*

"I agree, or I'd be standing watch over Alexis right now."

He waited no longer.

His fellow officers had all the sleep they would get this night.

He drove to where Mandy lived, at the end of a quiet residential block. Everything looked normal on the street. Years ago, when their relationship was going nowhere, they had decided to be good friends. Kevin had seen Mandy and her son many times over the years, the last time at Charles's birthday party. He'd always enjoyed seeing how Kyle had changed as he grew older. Now he just wished he would find the little boy alive.

He already knew Mandy wasn't.

Shit!

He walked up to the front door and knocked.

A crushing sense of evil permeated the air.

"Hello? Anybody home?" The front door was locked. He pounded loudly, hoping for Kyle's sleepy voice. Walking around to the back of the older house, Kevin looked carefully for any sign of forced entry. Mandy's car was parked in the back alley and was cold to the touch. She'd been home all night.

He rapped loudly on the back door. Nothing. The pit in his stomach solidified. He knocked once again, before calling out, "Hello? It's me, Kevin."

No answer. After pulling on gloves from his pocket, he tested the kitchen door. It opened easily. He pushed the door open wider. With his first step, the metallic smell filled his nostrils, and expectancy of the pain to come overwhelmed his soul. He knew he shouldn't enter. But he couldn't help himself. What if he'd been wrong? If there were the slightest chance that one of them was still alive, he had to help them. Several carefully placed steps led him into the kitchen and then to the small hallway. Kyle's room was empty.

And destroyed.

It was slow to come, but his police training kicked in, allowing him to peruse the room again. The killer had been pissed.

Kevin searched quickly, but he found no sign of the boy. Relief warred with hope and terror as he glanced down the hallway.

What were the chances Kyle hadn't been home last night? If he'd been the killer's target, the man would be pissed to not find him. That would explain why the child's room was smashed. And why the killer had gone after Mandy, why his victim hadn't been a child. The child hadn't been available.

Kevin didn't want to walk in any farther but knew he needed to check on Mandy. All the wind escaped from his lungs as he looked on the battered and bloodied body of his friend.

"Christ!" More prayer than invective, his heart cried for her.

She hadn't died easily or quickly.

Kevin ran back outside for fresh air, his stomach heaving. He did finally regain control, but with it came a blinding red haze of fury. This was an insane act of revenge.

The killer had declared war.

Kevin wouldn't rest until the animal was put down—one way or another.

But first, where was Kyle?

ALEXIS CHECKED HER watch several times during the day, while working at the main park. Kevin hadn't called with news. She'd expected a call.

But no such report came.

Alexis tried to phone Kevin at work on her lunch break, only to reach his voicemail. She didn't bother to leave a message. Neither did she attempt to contact him, as she had in the middle of the night. The door to enter his mind was closed. She'd used her baby skills to check. And maybe she deserved that, after blocking him yesterday.

Alexis lost herself in her gardens for the rest of the afternoon. She wallowed in the healing comfort of her plants. Several people wandered around, enjoying the beautiful sunny day. Mothers sat on benches, watching as children scampered about happily.

Alexis watched one group arrive in a dark sedan. A warmly dressed mother-daughter pair exited. A tall suited male stayed by the car, watching. The females must have been boiling hot. The little pixie of a girl tugged on the collar of her coat trying to loosen it up. But her mother held such a tight grip to her hand, Alexis saw there'd be no loosening in any direction.

"We only have a few minutes to visit, honey, before we have to leave. This is just a quick goodbye stop."

"I know, Mommy. I wanted to see the pretty flowers once more before we leave."

The mother smiled lovingly down on the pretty girl. "Say goodbye then, so we can go." She turned, in a nervous manner, to peruse the open spaces surrounding the park and took a step closer to her daughter.

Alexis watched, trying to understand. Her heart was touched, as the little girl bent to smell the flowers and to caress the petals of a bright, perky daisy. This was why Alexis did what she did—so the people could take the beauty and the healing spirit of plants into their own hearts. The little girl looked slightly familiar, but Alexis couldn't place her.

"You do love those daisies, don't you, sweetheart?

The little girl nodded. "They're special."

Alexis's heart hitched.

The young woman smiled lovingly down at the blond cherub. "Absolutely. I'm sorry. It's time to go."

The child beamed up at her mother. "That's okay."

As the child turned to walk away, her profile shone clearly. Alexis gulped. In her heart she knew this was the kidnapped child from the van. The one she'd been hesitant to meet. She slumped to the grass, watching as the two strolled through the winding flagstone paths toward the man and the waiting car. The bond of love shone from them both.

And yet their auras had a ragged edge, and Alexis felt a tight, locked-in connection that could stifle. Hoping to help, Alexis swept over both auras of mother and child, pulling the pain and fear into her own space. Instantly the energy around the two lightened, the edges smoothing out, and a slight glow began to weave joy around them. The mother's smile brightened a little, and she stood more relaxed.

Alexis did a swift cleanup of her own aura, dumping the negative energy, before it could affect her.

Warmth slid through her as she watched the child she'd helped rescue last night leave with her mother. Both happier and more at peace with the world. This answered one question. Alexis now knew why she'd continue to do psychic work. She'd do what she could, when she could, … and maybe help save others, … like this child.

Were the gardens the connection between the kids? Did they share the same love of the flowers? She didn't know how these psychos thought—perhaps he'd noticed this tenuous connection all his victims had to the flowers. Deep in thought, she tugged at the fingertips of her gloves and pulled them off to reach for her cell phone. Damn. Hers was at home on the charger. She had to let Kevin know.

Scott was wielding a shovel on the far side of the park. Alexis wandered in his direction, hoping to use his cell phone.

"Hey there, beauty. How've ya been?" His booming voice reached out for her before she'd made it halfway there.

She was helpless to stop the silly grin. Damn, she liked that man. "I'm good. How's the local lothario?"

A cheeky grin beamed at her. "Oh no, I'm not answering that question."

"What's the matter? Did she break up with you?"

"I'm not talking." Burly arms crossed resolutely over his huge expansion of chest, accentuating his words. But his chin jutting defiantly in the air caused her to break out laughing.

"I'm just teasing you, sweetie. Keep your lovely lady to yourself for a while. I can always go to the hospital and invite her out to tea."

He spun around quickly, his huge blue eyes bulging in alarm. "Ya wouldna, … would you?"

"Maybe. Of course, if you let me use your cell phone right now, I might reconsider."

The item in question appeared lightning quick in her hand, causing another round of giggles.

She punched in the numbers and waited. "Detective Sutherland, please." Scott waggled his raised eyebrows at her. Alexis rolled her eyes and walked a few steps away.

"Alexis, I can't talk right now."

She rushed into speech. "Kevin, I just saw a mother and little girl here in the gardens. She looked like the little girl from the van. Could it be them?" Alexis listened to Kevin's confirmation of what she already knew. "She really loves the gardens. I think there has to be some connection."

"Thanks, I have to go." He hung up.

"Damn it all. Anyway." She glared at the silent phone in her hand.

"I don't think he's listening to you, darling," Scott teased, motioning to the dead phone clutched uselessly in her hand, while she continued her one-sided conversation with empty air. "Or are you so good now that you no longer need any technology?"

If he only knew.

CHAPTER 17

S TEFAN SEEMED STRANGELY preoccupied that evening. He didn't mention a reason, so she didn't ask either. She kept an eye on him though, as they enjoyed the first few sips of Stefan's traditional tea. An odd look settled on his face. Alexis eyed him curiously. "What is it? Did you come up with something?" She couldn't stop the dread from sneaking into her voice. "Stefan, what aren't you telling me?"

"Did you listen to the news?" Stefan's voice held a sadness to it.

Alexis looked at him sharply. "What news?" But inside, she already knew. It was just the details that had to be filled in. "Who died?"

Their eyes met and held. Stefan broke away to bow his head. "An ex-girlfriend of Kevin's. Her son wasn't home at the time. He'd had a sleepover at the neighbor's."

Alexis sank slowly down beside him. *Oh no.* Her stomach clenched and heaved. Dear God, what kind of monster was this?

"A thwarted one."

Alexis gulped several times, before whispering, "I suppose that makes as much sense as anything. Poor Kevin."

Stefan picked up his teacup and took a sip. "He found her."

Shards of agony pierced her heart. How terrible for him. Kevin must have gone through hell. That had to top the list of things she never wanted to experience. Finally Alexis became aware of Stefan's careful scrutiny. She moved to break the silence. "Have you learned anything about the killer?"

"Some. I know I'm up against something unique. He's stronger, more cunning, and has years of experience remaining undetected. I have one advantage though. He's not used to being hunted on the other side."

"Good. At least that gives us something."

"We'll need much more than that."

At the same moment, they heard a car pull up out front.

"Kevin?" She raised an eyebrow at Stefan. He nodded.

They waited, listening for the approaching footsteps, then for the door to open.

"Good evening, you two." Kevin leaned against the archway to the solarium. Dark shadows sagged below his bloodshot eyes.

Alexis wanted to run over to hug him. Something held her back, but she couldn't explain what. "I'm sorry." She eyed him carefully. A black mantle of depression had settled on his shoulders, with a white-lipped, pinched fury just below the surface. She eyed him warily.

His head nodded in a sharp jerk. "Thanks. I gather Stefan told you?"

"A little." It was as if they were strangers, exchanging polite banter. "What's happening now?"

"Everything!" Kevin's expression chilled. "We're doing everything we can, thank you."

"I know that. I didn't mean to imply that you weren't." She stopped one second before confessing, "I'm sorry. Maybe I did, but only because I'm scared and worried." Alexis shrugged defensively. "People are dying. Always before, I've put my trust in the police to find a speedy solution." She looked between the two men, nervous, uncertain, and ashamed of her feelings. "The thing is, this time I feel like I'm supposed to be part of the solution, and I feel like I'm failing everyone."

"No one knows about you or your abilities. There's no expectation that you'll—"

"Except me." She twisted her bracelet nervously. Her insecurities had no boundaries tonight.

Kevin clamped his large hand down hard on her fingers.

Startled, she realized that her fingers were twisted and snarled in her bracelet. "Sorry, I'm not myself. I think it's time I went home. Maybe I can get some sleep tonight."

Before she reached the front door, Kevin joined her. "I'll take you home."

"No, it's okay. You're tired. Besides, I'll be fine."

He turned her by the shoulders until she faced him. "Maybe, but I don't like the idea of you going home alone."

She couldn't resist. "Okay, but I don't want to leave my truck here. If you want, you can follow me home. Make sure I get there safe." Opening the door, Alexis walked to her truck.

"Fine," he said shortly.

As Alexis drove home, she worried about what to do with him, when they arrived at her place.

Minutes later, she exited her truck and waited, while he parked beside her. On their way to her apartment door, she pointed out the hallway where the odd psychic incidents happened.

"This hallway looks a lot like the one I saw in the vision in the ditch, but I don't know. Maybe the whole world is filled with long dingy gray hallways."

He walked into the dark living room behind her, shutting the door with a resounding *click*. "I checked out past tenants. Nothing popped."

Alexis walked over to the lamp, wondering why there was no light answering all her attempts. "The lights aren't working." She tried the wall lamp against the window. "Odd."

This time, she headed for the kitchen and flipped the wall switch. "Oh, great. Like I need this."

"What?"

"A power outage." She slung her purse to the kitchen table. Damn, she wanted a hot bath.

"How can that be? The elevators worked and the hallway lights were on." Kevin moved carefully around the darkened apartment. "Was everything okay earlier?"

"Yes. I made dinner and had tea. There were no issues then."

Kevin unclipped his gun, surprising her. He motioned her to get behind him. Only she didn't understand, causing his motions to become more frantic.

"Kevin, what's the matter?" she whispered.

He held up his hand, as if to keep her quiet.

"Surely this is a simple utility issue. Isn't it?" she whispered again.

Kevin never said a word, but he grabbed her arm with one hand and her purse with the other. She snatched up her cell phone still in the charger on her counter.

"*Shhh*," he whispered, tugging her to the front door, then shutting it quietly behind them. He lost no time hustling her straight back out to their vehicles.

"We're taking mine. Get in."

She scrambled into the front of Kevin's truck without protest. She sat quietly, while he called the station. By the time he'd finished the conversation, a cruiser pulled up with two uniformed men inside.

Kevin waved to them and pulled out onto the road.

Alexis waited a moment. "What was that all about?"

"I didn't tell you before, but Mandy ..." He choked up slightly, then continued, "Mandy, the woman who was murdered yesterday? ... When I arrived at her house, the house had no power either. Yet all the neighbors' houses were fine."

He shifted the truck one gear higher. He glanced over at her. "Alexis, there's a good chance he was coming after you tonight."

Alexis swallowed hard. Wouldn't she know if the killer hunted her? And, if she didn't, what good were her psychic abilities? When she'd finally calmed enough to speak, what she said surprised them both. "Why didn't you search more thoroughly then?" she said indignantly. "We could have caught him."

Kevin looked over at her in astonishment. "It's the 'we' part that's a concern. I deemed it more important to get you out safely first. Those officers will check it out."

By the time she'd processed the concept of cops going into her apartment, they'd reached Kevin's house.

"I'll make some calls, once I get you settled in." He followed her to the front door of his small cozy house, tucked behind an evergreen hedge.

Alexis barely noticed where they were. She was still reeling at the implications of the killer seeking her now.

"Alexis?" Kevin reached out and snagged her into a close hug. "Hey, it'll be all right."

"How can you say that?" Nothing would ever be right again, ... until this asshole was caught.

"This is just a precaution," he reminded her. "Maybe I overreacted, but I'm not taking any chances. I saw firsthand what this asshole is capable of. You won't be his victim—ever." He squeezed her tight before stepping back. His voice grim, he promised, "I won't let that happen."

That made for a sobering shift back to reality. "I'm really sorry about Mandy." She watched sorrow deepen the lines of his face.

"Thanks. ... So am I. I'm also grateful the bastard didn't get his hands on Kyle. That's why I'm not taking any chances."

"Fine." She followed him into the hallway and stopped in her tracks. "Oh, wow!"

His house startled her. Huge flower pots held an overwhelming array of tropical plants in all sizes, textures, and every shade of green. Every windowsill was laden with an assortment of cuttings and flowering houseplants. The pièce de résistance was ivy that crawled halfway across the living room ceiling, wandering down to a huge dining room. Waves of welcoming energy surrounded Alexis as she walked through the main floor.

"They're beautiful," she whispered reverently. Her smile broadened, as the warm energy visibly strengthened in response to her appreciation.

"I thought you might like them. I hadn't realized you could communicate with them quite so effectively." He looked at the plants he'd lavished with so much care. "Unbelievable! They already look happier." He walked into his kitchen, checking out his plants in bemusement.

"You've done a wonderful job. I'm sure you know that already." Alexis trailed behind him, a little confused by his reaction. "I didn't mean to barge in on your territory. Plants just react whenever I'm around."

He spun around, surprise lighting his face. "I'm not upset with you. I'm in awe. I've never seen so much raw power in someone so unaware." He walked over to the fridge. "Do you want a beer?"

"No, thank you. I'm so tired that would finish me."

"Will you sleep?"

Alexis felt the intensity of his gaze, knowing he was gauging her on all levels. "Stop that!"

"Yep, definitely need sleep. Follow me." He led the way to the set of stairs they'd passed on their way into the kitchen. "Up here are the bedrooms." The top of the stairs opened into a cozy nook and several doors. He pushed open the closest one. "This is the one and only guest room."

Alexis walked into a simple but comfortable-looking room. She looked around. It seemed generic, almost had a hotel look to it.

"I don't get many visitors. At least not many who sleep in here."

She shot him a dry look. How was she to take that comment? But he'd already moved toward a second door. "Your own bathroom is in there. Do you need anything else?"

You.

No, she didn't dare. She would not be the one who opened that discussion. "I'll be fine, thank you."

"Great. We'll sort everything out in the morning. For now, you're safe." He walked back to the hallway. "Get a good night's sleep. I'll see you in the morning."

Then he was gone.

Alexis gazed at the empty doorway. She really would sleep alone tonight. She'd wondered, anticipated, and worried over the night to come. Now she felt inexplicably disappointed.

Without any nightclothes or toiletries, her evening ritual took mere seconds, allowing her to crawl into bed before her energy fled completely. She remembered to follow Stefan's evening preparations and dropped off into a deep sleep.

DOWNSTAIRS, KEVIN REACHED for a beer. It would be a long night. But he had to stay focused. If the bastard knew about Mandy, then locating Kevin's home was an easy next step.

Alexis hadn't seemed interested in spending the night in his arms, and he'd been looking for any sign of encouragement. But then he hadn't exactly shown any interest either. She'd have to make that next gesture herself.

But it was too early for her. Damn and double damn. She'd gotten that stupid idea in her head about him using some hidden advantage against her. He snorted. Yeah, right. All he'd had was his overwhelming need. Every time he saw the damn woman, he was hungry for what they could have together. His constant state of arousal made it difficult to think clearly around her.

He'd tested the door to her mind once, but it had been firmly closed against him. For her safety, he needed it open. With her guard up against him like this, he couldn't even talk to her about it.

Once this was settled, then …

His watch beeped, reminding him of the time.

He quickly dialed his office. There'd been no word on Alexis's apartment yet. Kevin sat down for the long evening ahead.

It left plenty of time to think about Mandy and about what would never be again. Most of all, it left plenty of time to think about the bastard who'd destroyed her son's world. Kevin took a drink of his beer and raised the bottle briefly in homage to Mandy. That this asshole had chosen an ex-girlfriend of Kevin's likely meant the killer was someone who knew Kevin, and possibly someone Kevin knew. Sure, a stranger could have asked around. … Mandy's name could have come up in conversation. But, in a town this size, it was just as likely that Kevin knew Mandy's killer. He'd seen her last at John's party. His stomach soured. Had someone seen them together?

Kevin closed his mind to the images that tumbled through his heart. Pain welled up. Kevin brutally slammed aside the images and took a hefty drink. The beer soured on its way down his throat. Kevin wouldn't let anyone else get hurt, especially not Alexis—if he could help it.

A scream ripped through his house.

ALEXIS, DID YOU enjoy my sweet revenge? I thought you'd like to see what I

can do. Shall I show you more?

No! Alexis stood in the middle of a black tornado. She was lost in time and space. She had no idea how she'd arrived in this hellhole or how to leave it. Horrific images swirled around her. Faces appearing, then disappearing, as others took their place. Other victims, other deaths. The force of the furor blinded her to all else. *No! Stop! No more victims, please. I beg you.*

Her wail of agony ripped through the energy vortex, making her tormentor laugh with joy. *They aren't victims. They are my guests. For all of eternity.*

Not all of them. Surely not. He'd only killed Mandy for revenge— hadn't he? Was she now one of his guests?

Yes, all of them. I've enjoyed this little hobby of mine for decades. Since I was a young man actually. I was never caught. Never even a suspect in all those child murder cases. I took a break in there, but now I'm back, ... and your turn is coming.

The images circling her increased, the wails and cries of his victims drowning out her hearing. The crescendo of pain and agony built until she couldn't stand it. Her horrified scream slashed through the house and woke her up.

Sobbing for breath, she trembled in shock under the twisted covers. She recognized Kevin's wary approach to the bed. Her teeth were chattering so uncontrollably that she didn't think they'd ever stop.

Kevin sat down on the edge of the bed, looking her over carefully. "I didn't want to approach you too quickly. That can be dangerous. Remember?" A large palm cupped her cheek tenderly.

Alexis leaned into it, gratefully accepting the comfort. "I'm so cold," she whispered. Her fingertips were a curiosity, bluish-gray in color, probably a perfect match for her lips. The chattering showed no sign of slowing either.

"Move over," he whispered huskily. "I'm coming in." He pulled back the warm blankets and slid under to lie beside her. Without giving her a chance to argue, he snuggled her tightly against his chest. "Just concentrate on getting warm."

He felt so good and so right.

She lie still, accepting his comfort, until his body heat finally started to chase away the chills. "He spoke with me. He said my turn was coming," she whispered against his chest.

Kevin's arm tightened around her.

"All his victims were screaming and crying out for mercy. A mercy they never found. So many victims over so many years." As the horrible shrieks echoed in her mind, the tears started to fall. Knowing she had to get it all out now, she quickly repeated the conversation. Her voice dropped to a whisper, before choking into sobs.

Kevin let her cry, but she couldn't seem to stop them.

"*Shh.* ... Stop now. That's enough. You'll make yourself sick." His hands stroked her back and shoulders, over the T-shirt she'd worn to bed. "*Shh,* it's okay, honey. Please stop."

When his words had no effect, he shifted her and dropped comforting kisses on her cheeks and eyelids. "Please, Alexis, stop."

She opened her eyes and solemnly gazed up at him. Somehow she'd ended up stretched out beneath him. The intimacy of the situation struck her.

He was right where she wanted him.

Something in her eyes must have shown her thoughts for his gaze warmed in response.

"Are you feeling better?"

She didn't trust her voice, choosing to nod instead. He dropped yet another kiss on the corner of her lips. "Are you sure? I could kiss you better here." He dropped a kiss on the other side of her mouth. "Or here." Another kiss landed on her nose. "Or even here." This time, a kiss closed her eyes with his sweet touch. "Anything to make you feel better."

"You're missing the one place which needs it the most."

He hesitated, then dropped to angle a soft kiss on her nose. "Are you sure? I don't want any doubts later."

She smiled warmly. "No doubts in the morning." She'd have to explain her feelings, her confusion ... tomorrow. Tonight they needed this. They needed each other.

"Good." Holding her gaze, he lowered his head and laid a burning, explosive kiss on her lips.

Oh God, she'd missed him. Only as her heart melted under his loving touch did she recognize this as a homecoming—something to think about later. Right now, her brain was turning to mush.

"Is this better?" His lips continued to travel, distracting her from his words, as she followed his pathways with intensive interest. Nerve endings were once again alive, igniting sensations, warming her with their heat.

"Almost."

"Am I getting closer?" His lips whispered down to the nape of her neck.

"Definitely."

"How about here?" He descended farther, catching the loose neck of her T-shirt with his teeth and pulling it down to get better access.

She murmured in anticipation, her body twisting and turning with a will of its own. "Almost ..." she whispered achingly. "You're almost there."

Kevin shifted onto his knees, letting the bedding fall down his back. Large warm hands slid under her shirt, moving the offending material up to her chin. As he exposed her full breasts, he ducked his head and took one plump nipple deep into his mouth.

She arched off the bed in response. "That's the spot."

He murmured, satisfied, and proceeded to feast on the bounty spread before him.

Alexis slid quickly under his magical spell, forgetting all else. Only one thing existed for her—him.

She didn't know when her T-shirt joined the scrambled bedding on the floor or when his clothing flew haphazardly to join the rest. She only knew that, for those few seconds, she was lost without him.

"*Shh*, I'm here. It's okay, baby." His warm hands took her back under in a sexual haze that had no beginning and no end. It had only him.

In the dark of night, they burned with a light of their own, which sustained them throughout the long hours until morning.

CHAPTER 18

"I'M AWAKE," SHE murmured, her eyes still closed against the coming morning.

"The day is upon us, whether you're ready to face it or not."

"*Not* is my choice." But her luscious lips smiled. She snuggled closer, loath to answer her body's call for the bathroom. "I'm trying to ignore my bladder already."

"I know the feeling. Somehow I don't think that works for long." He hugged her, then loosened his arms and slowly stood, stretching the kinks out of his spine.

She peeked up at him, only to have her eyes pop open wide. "Are you sure you don't want to come back to bed? It'd be a shame to waste that."

After last night, not even those words popping from her mouth of their own volition could embarrass her. Kevin was strikingly beautiful to her at any time. In his early morning aroused state, he was dynamite.

"I wish. You do realize it is almost nine. Are you supposed to work today?"

At her nod, he sighed. "Unfortunately so do I." With those words, he walked into the bathroom and a cold shower.

Watching his rear walk away did nothing to slow down her heartbeat. But he was right. Today was not a holiday or a weekend, and she was now officially very late. Searching for her cell phone in the chaos of her room, she called Scott.

"'Bout time, you called. Rick's been asking where you were. I told him that you'd gone to see the doctor, being still upset over the murders and such. He didn't like that much."

"Thanks, Scott." She tried to cover her huge yawn, but he heard it.

"Did you have another bad night then?"

Alexis smiled at the concern in his voice. How to excuse her night without letting everything slip? "I had a few bad moments. I'll explain when I get there in half an hour or so."

After ringing off, she made a beeline for the bathroom and her solo shower.

When she finally raced down to the kitchen, dressed in yesterday's clothes, and ready for work, she was grateful to accept a travel mug full of rich coffee. "Oh, thank God. You're a lifesaver."

"Do you want me to drive you to your truck or directly to work?"

She checked her watch. Her half hour was past gone. "Straight to work, thanks." Maybe she'd be lucky and could slip in unnoticed. If there were guardian angels, she hoped one was watching out for her and would keep Kevin's presence undetected.

If such angels existed, they were on their early lunch break when she arrived at work.

Several of the men stood around, drinking coffee, when they arrived—including Scott.

"Good morning, Detective." Respectful greetings flew in his direction. No one said anything to her.

"Thanks for the ride, Kevin." Alexis waved casually, studiously refusing to look at the men. She rolled her eyes at Kevin, sparking his huge grin.

She headed for the garden on the farthest corner of her area, knowing Scott would be on her heels. She wanted to separate him from his cronies. Shyness had definitely taken over.

Whatever. She could only hope he'd let it slide.

Yeah, as if.

"Good morning. So you had a bad night, did you?" Scott's gruff voice half teased.

"Yes, you could say that." She looked over at him casually, catching the curious look on his face. She smiled. "And, yes," she drawled slowly, "Kevin made the night much better."

"Well now." Scott rubbed his hands together gleefully. "It's about time."

Alexis couldn't help it. She broke out laughing. He'd been pushing her in this direction for a long time. He should be happy. "And you're right. It was time."

His booming laugh reached across the gardens. "Good for you." His face closed down with a sudden worry. Alexis watched in amusement.

"You won't jump into this too quickly, will you? You're a little off balance, vulnerable even, right now. I wouldn't want anyone to be taking advantage." Scott latched on to this new concern and wouldn't let go.

Alexis walked closer to reassure her gentle giant of a friend. "I am taking it easy. I know things haven't exactly been normal. As far as the Sight goes, well, the detective has several abilities of his own. Actually," she added, with a resigned look, "he's far more skilled than I am."

"That might be good. He could help you." Scott spoke cautiously, as if wording his thoughts carefully. "He wouldn't be having any special power over you, now would he?" He narrowed his eyes in concern.

"No," she answered slowly. "Though, when you can go into each other's minds, an element of helplessness or vulnerability is involved." She shrugged. "What do I know about relationships and what men will do to get into a woman's bed?" She looked at Scott teasingly. "That's your specialty, isn't it?"

Scott's eyes narrowed even farther, as a detached inward look washed over his face.

Alexis got a little alarmed. "Hey, I'm teasing, Scott. I didn't mean to imply anything." She stretched out to rub his shoulder reassuringly.

"No, but I do know what men might do, being one *meself*." He snagged her into a big bear hug. "And now I'm more than a little concerned about what a man with extra senses and insider knowledge might do."

"Nothing. He'd do nothing. Don't worry."

"Sure." Scott brushed it off, but the look in his eyes left her with lingering doubt.

"Don't you do anything stupid, do you hear me?" Alexis asked.

"Me?" he asked too innocently.

Not feeling reassured by his tone of voice, Alexis dropped the pleading for now. "Shall we get some work done? I have to do something to justify my pay."

"Especially because Rick was here earlier."

"Right I forgot." Alexis tucked her hair behind her head, more than a little bothered at being found lacking at work once again. "What did he say?"

"He wants to see us in his office at the end of the day."

THAT STATEMENT LINGERED heavily on Alexis's mind. By the time she had completed her day's work, it was later than normal.

"Alex? Are you ready for your meeting with Rick? I was asked to attend too."

"Sure, why not. If I'll get chewed out, it might as well be now."

"Don't go there, chippy. It won't help, you know?"

"Nothing will help," she grumbled, as she brushed off her clothes, resolutely determined to get the meeting over with, her temper intact.

When they arrived at the office, they found something entirely different than expected.

The mayor and Kevin—in full detective mode—were already in Rick's office. Their raised voices were too loud to be ignored.

"Sounds like fun," Alexis grimaced. She didn't need a full-blown confrontation.

As they approached, snippets of conversation were easily heard.

Rick's voice was the clearest. "She's the one who might pose a problem, damn it."

"She won't. We'll see to that," Kevin said easily. "We need your cooperation."

"What difference will that make?" A loud snort echoed down the hallway, followed by Rick's disgusted voice. "*She's* the one who won't cooperate."

Alexis looked over at Scott in concern. She had no doubt the female they'd mentioned was her. Scott raised his eyebrows, motioning her to the door first. "Shall we?"

With a comical look in his direction, she rapped loudly, interrupting the ongoing discourse on the other side.

"Who is it?" Rick's imperious boss voice made Alexis's hackles rise.

"It is 'she.'"

A moment of dead silence ensued, while Scott rolled his eyes at her inappropriate humor.

The door opened abruptly. Kevin stood there.

"A job promotion? ... Detective to usher perhaps?" she murmured for his ears alone.

"Maybe you should take a lesson in subservience. It would be good for you." He motioned her inside.

"That'd be a waste of time," Scott quickly interjected, pushing Alexis none-too-gently farther into the room and past Kevin. He turned to face his boss and said, "Hey, Rick. Are we disturbing you? I didn't know the mayor was in here with you two. We can come back tomorrow, if that's a better time."

Rick glared at Alexis. "What's the point? She'd disturb me just as much tomorrow."

"Nice to know I leave such a lasting impression." Alexis couldn't stop the snappiness in her voice. Rick always brought out the worst in her.

Kevin said, "Enough. This is official business."

"Then it doesn't involve us. I thought Rick wanted to see me." She quickly stood again, anxious to leave the men alone. "We can do this another time."

"Sit down." Kevin's voice brooked no argument.

Startled, Alexis obeyed, turning to face him.

But it was Rick who spoke. "Alexis, Detective Sutherland wants you to leave town."

Alexis froze. She narrowed her green eyes at Kevin, who stood there with his arms folded across his chest. He was waiting for her explosion. Well, she'd be damned if she'd give it to him.

"Why?" There. That was simple and adultlike.

"The power loss that you experienced last night was isolated to just your apartment."

"And …?"

"There's evidence to show that whoever staged that power outage was the same person involved in yesterday's homicide."

Scott's indrawn breath had her reaching out to him. She offered him a tentative smile. "I said I'd had a bad night."

"But you weren't telling all, were you, lass?"

She rubbed his shoulder. "It would have upset you."

"That be the truth." Scott turned to Kevin. "You must think she's been targeted, if you want her to leave town."

"But I can't leave town. I have a job and a paycheck to collect," she snapped. Those weren't the real reasons, but she'd be damned if she'd explain in front of Rick. Besides, they would *not* gang up on her.

"Which is why we're here." Kevin looked over at Rick and then the mayor. "Would you like to take it from here?"

"You are to go on 50 percent paid leave, until this is over." Rick didn't want to continue, but, at the sharp look from the mayor, he sighed in disgust and added, "Under duress, I promise your job with the city will be here, waiting for you."

The look on his face was almost worth being in this position. He'd been forced to play this hand, and he didn't like it one bit. He'd like her gone for good. "Thanks for the generous offer, but I'm afraid I'll have to refuse."

A tiny minute of shocked silence ensued before everyone jumped on her.

"Like hell!" roared Kevin.

"Don't do anything foolish here." Scott squeezed her shoulder.

Rick smirked. "I told you. She's the one who won't cooperate. She never does."

Alexis knew she had to stay. She hadn't had time to sort out how or why. And maybe she didn't want to look that deep. In ways she didn't know or understand, she had to be here. She had no other option.

"This would only be for a few days," the mayor said, speaking up for the first time. Alexis hadn't even seen him standing slightly behind Kevin. "I have every confidence in our police force. Detective Sutherland has always come through for us before. No reason to doubt that he won't this time either."

Was he for real? Alexis couldn't believe the politically correct drivel that sprouted from his mouth. It's not that she didn't believe Kevin would do his best. But this murderer was something else.

Kevin spoke again. "Thanks for the vote of confidence, John." He smiled winningly at her. "Alexis, you must see how imperative it is that you remain safe and that we can focus on the investigation without the distraction of watching you every moment."

Her look of innocence fooled no one. "I have the utmost confidence in your abilities. I'm sure you can find a way to make that happen without sending me out of town." She nodded at the mayor. "I agree wholeheartedly that our city is safe under the watchful eye of Bradford's Police Force, especially Detective Sutherland."

"Shit!" Kevin looked at her, disgust on his face. "You won't cooperate, will you?"

Alexis took an inventory of the men's faces—only one gloated happily. Rick had been right about how she'd take the news, and he loved being right.

"Nope. I *need* to be here."

Both Kevin and Scott narrowed their eyes at her. It wasn't the time or place to ask questions.

To that end, Scott half lifted her from her chair. "I'll take her to the pub and talk some sense into her."

Before Alexis realized it, she'd been ushered back out to Scott's truck. He never said a word, until they were seated in their usual corner of the smoky room and held big frothy mugs. "Now what the hell is going on?"

Taking her time, Alexis explained the series of odd events that had precipitated staying at Kevin's last night.

"Not good news. Something's gone bad in this town, Alexis. I wish you'd listen to them and leave." Heavy wrinkles lined the burly Irishman's face. Scott cared sincerely about the people in his world. Alexis was one of those. "Please get out of town, Alexis."

"Scott, it isn't that bad yet." Alexis didn't quite get the reaction she'd been hoping for.

He leaned closer, until he was almost in her face. "Were you planning on waiting until it got right bad then?" Sarcasm glinted in his eyes. His voice rose in a crescendo until he was almost shouting. "And how were you gonna know when that is? When you're dead perhaps?"

"All right. *Shhh.* You're attracting attention. Calm down, Scott." Gently she stroked his shoulder. It took a few moments before the giant settled back down again.

"The thing is …" Alexis paused to collect her thoughts into a coherent pattern. "I don't know what to tell you, except … I *have* to stay." She studied his face. "Something's been bad here for a while, and it's just now rising to the surface. When it goes to hell, I'm supposed to be here."

"This be the Sight again?" Scott shook his head, stumped. "You can't be alone anymore. I can stay with you during working hours, but what about the rest of the day and night?"

"I could ask Kevin." Alexis looked into her beer, wrinkling her nose. "But I don't want to depend on him to that extent."

"And I'm thinking it's too late to worry about that now," Scott teased. "You've already made a choice. All that's left is to see how it works out for you."

Alexis frowned. What a great way to put it. And what would Kevin think of her decision?

BACK AT THE office, Kevin spoke with two younger officers.

"I need you two to dig up everything we have on a serial killer who may have operated in this area close to thirty years ago. We suspect he targeted children who spent a lot of time in the city's gardens. The cases were never solved, the murders stopped after a decade, and the killer never resurfaced. I want names of the victims, a list of suspects at the time, pictures, … especially pictures of the victims, if we can gather those. They would be in the cold case files." He shifted. "A few people are still left on the force who might remember added details. Pick their brains. I need everything and everything now. Before you go, what did you two find on Mandy and Kyle leading up to the murder?"

The senior of the two started. "We've compiled the information from the interviews of the neighbors yesterday. Apparently nothing noticeable happened during the day, but neither had been seen after dinner. Kyle attended school, then went to his friend's house afterward. He stayed for dinner and then called his mom around seven p.m. and convinced her to let him stay for a sleepover. The victim had put in a full day's work and apparently went home and stayed there. Her coworkers had nothing useful to add." As he finished, he looked over at his partner.

The younger man, Allen, picked up the story. "We did pick up several full and partial prints. We might get lucky."

Kevin grimaced. Not likely but they could hope.

"The coroner's report isn't in yet, and, so far, there's no news on the forensic material. We found several hair samples that might lead to something useful, but those will take time and will still require something to match them to." Allen shrugged, as if to say, *What can you do?*

The three men discussed their next steps, before going their separate ways.

Alone again, Kevin watched the late afternoon sun wash his town in orange. His neck itched. That scared the hell out of him. Several minutes of searching the ethers still gave no explanation as to the source of the itch, … but he was sure the vibe came from the same killer they were trying to track down. Kevin recognized the energy pattern. Closing his eyes again, he freed his mind to search. This time he sensed nothing.

He returned to the stack of paperwork on his desk. Nothing else to do but wait.

CHAPTER 19

A LEXIS SPENT A weird evening with Kevin last night, as her guard. Not as her lover. She sighed deeply, as she took a short break the next morning, wishing she had coffee to go with it. Instead, she sat down under a maple tree and worked on Stefan's lessons. First off was to see if she could reach out and touch Stefan. With little effort she saw him in her mind. She grinned. Then stopped and her smile fell away. She focused harder. His energy was pale, almost translucent. She didn't like it. *Stefan?*

She got no answer. More worrisome was the absolute lack of movement in his form.

She pulled out her phone and located the number she needed. "Hi, Kevin," Alexis couldn't believe the relief she felt at hearing his voice. She glanced around the park. Scott stood a short distance away, speaking with another gardener. She lowered her voice. "Something's wrong with Stefan. I can't reach him, and I can barely feel him. His energy is weird. Off somehow." She quickly explained, adding, "I'm heading out there now."

"I'll meet you there."

By the time she'd explained the situation to Scott and had made the drive to Stefan's house, Kevin already stood on the front step, knocking.

"Why don't you break in or something?" She waved her arms toward the windows.

He shot her a disgusted look. "Just because *you're* impatient doesn't give *me* the right to break in."

That did it. "Look. We know something is wrong. If the police don't have the right, how about caring friends?" Her hands rested on her hips defiantly.

"Calm down. I just got here. Stefan hasn't even had a chance to answer the bell." He watched as she headed around to the back of the house. "Hey, where are you going?" He followed quickly behind her.

"Alexis, what are you doing? *Alexis?*"

"I'll knock on the back door of course. You stay there."

"Like hell."

Alexis ignored him. Several knocks on the back door produced no results. She peered through the darkened windows, searching for any sign of life within.

Then she tried the doorknob. It wasn't locked. Knowing she didn't have the right, she pushed it open anyway. "Stefan!" She stepped into the silent house. "Stefan, it's Alexis. Are you home?"

Kevin came up behind her.

"*Shit.*" Alexis spun around in fright. "You scared the crap out of me."

"Calm down. You're terrorizing yourself. Stand back." He stepped in front of her and entered the kitchen.

Alexis studied his movements as he stopped and surveyed the area. He sniffed the air cautiously, before moving on. She followed slowly.

In the living room, Stefan laid on his hardwood floor, wrapped in his favorite wool blanket. He looked to be sleeping, except for his utter stillness. Was he even breathing? She reached toward him …

"Don't. Remember? We can't touch him."

She looked at him, puzzled. "He needs help. How can we help if we can't touch him?" She watched, even more puzzled, as Kevin approached slowly, wafting his hands in an odd manner, almost stroking the space around Stefan.

"What are you doing?" she whispered.

"Checking out his energy. Stefan is off in the ethers."

"But he's okay, isn't he?" Alexis approached from the side, yet stayed behind Kevin. She sank slowly to her knees beside Stefan. His energy seemed odd. "He's surrounded by pure white light," she whispered in reverence.

"He's incredibly powerful." Kevin looked back at her. "He's been practicing that new technique of his but didn't give me many details. Now I wish he had."

"What can we do?"

"Watch over him." Kevin got up and took a step back. "At least that's all for now."

Alexis didn't like the sound of that. She preferred action to inaction any day. Besides, this didn't feel right. Using her inner eye, as she'd been taught, she looked over Stefan's prone body. His energy, although white, was faint and pale. It did not brim with a vital life force. "Something's wrong. His energy is very low. His silver cord is pale and thin, almost nonexistent."

"You can see that?" Astonished, Kevin crouched down to take another look.

"Yes. He's not loose in the ethers. He's lost, period." Alexis followed the wispy trail as far as she saw it, but it dissipated a few feet away from Stefan's body. She laid on the floor beside Stefan. Apart, but close enough to touch him, if she needed to. "How and why, I have no clue."

"What are you doing?" asked Kevin warily.

"I'm going after him," Alexis said simply and closed her eyes.

"Do you know what you're doing?"

"I think so."

Her comment received only a snort and a caution. "Be careful."

That made her smile. "Always."

This time, she had a trail to follow. Blocking out everything else, she zeroed in on Stefan's faint signature. It went on forever, traveling through a permanent light fog. She continued moving faster and faster, until she could no longer tell how far she'd gone.

Had she become as lost as Stefan?

Finally the thread thickened ever-so-slightly. With that concrete improvement, she increased her speed. The miles whipped past. There had to be another way to do this. This passage seemed endless.

On the heels of that thought, she reached a huge solid wall. *Solid? Here? How could anything be solid, yet cold to the touch?* Alexis carefully explored the obstacle. She still had much to learn. But this just didn't make sense. Could it be a blind to confuse her?

It vanished. Just as quickly another took its place. Stefan had to be on the other side, but was he the one putting up the barriers—to keep her out? Or could there be someone else trying to keep Stefan in there? Either way, it wouldn't work.

What could she do? Stefan's energy! She needed to focus on him. Wrapping Stefan's lifeline in love, she warmed his energy with her own. Using the same methods she'd perfected over the years with her plants, Alexis surrounded his cord with bright green energy.

She could sense the difference immediately—again she was surprised by the ease of that accomplishment. Nothing in this area worked the way she thought it would. As the surrounding energy continued to warm, so too did the air. The fog lightened and slowly lifted, allowing Alexis to see where she was.

Stefan stood in front of her. Pale, tired, and too insubstantial to be considered healthy, but he was smiling. Alexis grinned back in relief.

"Can we go home now?" she asked.

"Almost."

"Almost?" she asked, astonished.

"Yes, I came here for a reason, and I'm not quite done. *You* have to go home." He looked behind her. "Now."

At that, a heavy shove snapped a surprised Alexis backward and pushed her right out of the psychic field. And into her physical body.

Alexis sat up in Stefan's living room, moaning, as the room spun around her. *This could take some getting used to.*

"Alexis?" Kevin squatted beside her. "Are you okay?"

She was dazed but looked up at him, nodding slowly. "I think so. I just need a minute."

"Take your time."

Alexis heard the relief in his voice. Poor Kevin. She hadn't exactly considered him when she'd plunged in after Stefan.

Kevin's large hand cupped her elbow to support her, as she attempted to rise. "Easy, easy." He led her over to the couch.

"I'm okay." She collapsed onto the forest-green leather. "I found Stefan."

"And?" Kevin asked sharply. "What's he doing?"

"He didn't explain. He said, he wasn't finished. He shoved me back, saying I had to leave." Alexis looked around Stefan's living room. "So here I am."

"Good." Kevin walked out of the room.

"What are you doing?" Alexis called after him.

"Making tea."

Of course they'd all picked up the habit. It made sense, in a way. She had to admit a cup of tea would be welcome. They needed to stay up and wait for Stefan to return.

Alexis crashed on the couch, after the second pot of tea.

She woke several times in the night to check on Stefan. But found only minimal change. When Alexis woke early in the morning, cold had seeped into her bones. She opened her gritty eyes slowly, trying to place her surroundings. As memories flooded back, she leaped up to check on Stefan.

He seemed the same, only he wasn't. *What was the difference?* Alexis walked around his body that still laid in the same position. Not even a hair was different. But something had definitely changed.

"What's the matter?" A tired Kevin joined her, still rubbing the sleep from his eyes. He stopped suddenly and narrowed them in concentration. "He's back."

"What?" Stunned, Alexis looked from one to the other. "How can you tell?"

"Can you see his cord?" For the first time, Kevin reached out and touched Stefan. There was no reaction. He checked Stefan's pulse. "He's barely alive."

Kevin reached for his cell phone, starting a process that left Alexis stunned by its speed. Less than an hour later, she sat waiting, once again, in the place she hated most. The hospital.

The waiting room was full. Feeling wrinkled and badly in need of a shower, Alexis sat squished between a screaming child and a family who looked like their world had just collapsed. Alexis could sympathize. She'd spent many long hours in this place, trying to hold it together, hoping against hope for a miracle that never came.

Only on Lissa's last day had Alexis finally accepted the reality of what was happening—finally acknowledging she could do nothing to stop disaster from destroying her world once again. Four hours later, Lissa was gone.

"Alexis!"

Caught up in her memories, Alexis jumped up and raced toward Kevin. "How's Stefan?"

Kevin stilled her hands, making her aware for the first time that she'd latched onto his shirt with a death grip, almost shaking him. She took a deep breath and prayed for the return of some of her famous detached control.

"He's in a coma." At her horrified gasp, he quickly added, "The doctors say he'll be fine. Stefan's specialist is on his way. When he's assessed him, we'll know more."

"Specialist?" Alexis's breath caught in her throat. "What specialist?"

Kevin shrugged noncommittally but didn't explain.

She sighed. It didn't really matter, ... except she hated waiting for answers.

"Come on. Let's get something to eat."

Minutes later, Alexis stood outside the hospital, staring up at the early morning sky. It seemed a long time since she'd had a normal peaceful day to enjoy the sun and the blue sky. She wanted this horror to end.

THE NEXT DAY was crap. By the end of it, Alexis was ready to kill her wonderful daytime bodyguard, Scott.

Kevin shook his head as he unlocked her passenger door with the click of a button. "What is your problem?"

"Today, everything," she snapped, as she sat in Kevin's truck. How to explain the torture of having Scott hanging at her elbow for the entire day, too concerned to let her out of his sight. She loved the man dearly, but his constant presence had become downright irritating.

"Let's go see Stefan." Kevin smiled at her. "Maybe that will help switch your mood."

After being shadowed all day, she'd love some time alone. But Stefan came first.

"Come on." Kevin herded her through the front door of the hospital. Alexis walked past the reception area and headed straight down the left hallway.

"Uh, Alexis. Where are you going?"

Alexis turned around to find him stopped at the reception area. She stood, confused. "I thought we would see Stefan. What's the matter?"

"Alexis?" He pointed to the opposite hallway. "Stefan is down here."

Alexis flushed, unwelcome heat warming her cheeks, as she realized that, from habit, she'd headed toward Lissa's old room, ... even after a whole year. "Damn it," she muttered, as she approached him. "Sorry."

"Don't be. Habits die hard. You spent a lot of time at Lissa's bedside, didn't you?"

She smiled sadly at him. "That seems a long time ago."

The two approached Stefan's private room. As she did, she realized Stefan had become a close friend, though, when she thought about it, she realized she really hadn't seen much of Stefan's world outside of his kitchen, living room, and solarium. She'd never been invited to view his studio or his finished works, other than the one piece. Someday she hoped to be welcomed into his inner world.

"When he's ready, he'll show you."

She shot Kevin a dirty look. "Quit reading my mind."

"I didn't have to," he replied smugly. "Lately your face is an open book."

"Then quit reading my face."

The two approached Stefan's bedside cautiously. He looked the same, except for the various machines surrounding him and the IV in his arm.

Her heart sank. Her hand automatically moved to her throat.

"Look beneath the surface."

With a startled glance at Kevin, Alexis complied. A blue haze surrounded Stefan's prone body. A shifting, almost shimmering energy that moved around him, over him ... Her gaze widened. *And through him.*

"How is that possible?" she whispered.

"A very powerful healer is working on him. Her name is Maddy. She runs a special program, not all that far from here." He smiled. "I'll assume, now that he's in her hands, Stefan will be just fine."

Alexis reached out, hesitated for a moment, and then covered Stefan's hand. "He's cold," she said quietly.

"He's fine." The voice from the door surprised them both. A doctor walked in, holding out his hand to Kevin. "Detective Sutherland, nice to see you again."

"Hello, Dr. Radnor. What can you tell us about Stefan?"

"I'm happy to say his condition is essentially a deep exhaustion. Whatever he was doing wore down his life force completely."

"He'll be okay though, won't he?" Alexis hadn't realized anyone could get as ill as Stefan from simple exhaustion.

"Oh, he's in a coma," Dr. Radnor said. "It's his body's defense mechanism, which allows him to recover and to heal." The doctor walked closer. "He's just taking a very long and a very deep nap. I suspect he'll stay like this for another day or two, then slowly come out of it."

The doctor took a closer look at the two of them. "You two look almost as bad. Go home and take care of yourselves. I don't want you to end up in here with him."

Kevin smiled his thanks, and, after confirming they'd head to Alexis's place to pick up a few things, he ushered her out ahead of him.

The old apartment building was not welcoming or warm. She unlocked the door and entered with Kevin. As she walked into her living room, Alexis became aware of her exhaustion and wished she could go straight to bed. She was relieved Stefan would be fine, but, at the same time, her emotions were all over the place.

A few steps inside her apartment, she froze.

The energy was all wrong.

Or maybe it was her whacked-out emotions? Right now she didn't think so.

Someone or something had intruded her space.

Police or the asshole? Not that it mattered. She felt violated. All she wanted was to get out of here. She grabbed a few of her clothes and walked out.

CHAPTER 20

A FTER STOWING HER clothes in Kevin's spare room, Alexis returned to the living room, feeling a little lost.

"I'll sit on the porch and have a beer. Do you want one or would you prefer something stronger?" Kevin offered, as he walked over to a cupboard. "There's scotch, rum, and even a little bit of brandy left."

"Brandy would be nice, thank you." She didn't like the uncomfortable tension she'd felt since they'd returned to his house. They were involved in a relationship of some kind. She just didn't know what she had to give, nor did she know what she wanted from it.

He handed her a large balloon glass with the amber liquid. "Do you want to join me outside or take it up to your room?"

Alexis hesitated. The beautiful evening would soothe her soul better than hiding away in her room. "Sure, I'll come out for a few minutes."

The stars were bright on a deep velvet sky. They more than sparkled, they put on a beautiful jeweled display.

The longer she sat and watched and sipped, the more Alexis felt her tension drain away, leaving her mellow and relaxed. A heavy sigh escaped.

"That came from way down deep."

"It did." Calm seeped into her body. "Why haven't you married?" She hadn't meant to ask that, but, once the question was out, she was glad she did. Had he never wanted to? Had his job been a mitigating factor? How did women do it? Watch their man leave for work each day, never knowing if they'd see him again?

Despair welled up at that thought ... No, being involved with a police detective, ... that wasn't a life Alexis wanted.

"I don't know. I guess, so far, it just never worked out. I've gotten close a couple times, but not quite that far." He spoke easily.

She smiled in relief. His lighthearted tone convinced her that his heart had yet to be touched.

"What about you?"

Alexis shrugged dismissively. "Like you, I never reached that point."

The evening silence lengthened and deepened comfortably around them. After the highly charged sexual encounters between them, and the panic and the horror of recent experiences—both psychic and grounded in the real world—she felt this time of peace was a joy. It made her realize how abnormal their relationship had been to date.

"Are you ready for bed?" Kevin asked gently.

"*Uhm ...*"

A few minutes of comfortable relaxing silence passed; then Kevin broke the silence. "Can you make it back up to your room?" Kevin teased.

Only this time she didn't respond. Alexis, too relaxed to speak, fell asleep under the stars.

Kevin smiled, as he lifted her and brought her to her room.

THE NEXT DAY, Kevin stood in the doorway to Stefan's hospital room. His friend's waxy looks weren't encouraging. Instincts had brought him here. He'd called earlier, only to be told that there'd been no change. Kevin couldn't ignore his inner direction and had come to see for himself.

Come in. Don't just stand there.

Kevin smiled, relief and pleasure lighting his face. Damn, it was good to hear his friend's voice, even if only in his head. "How are you doing? Can't say you look too good from where I'm standing."

Then you'd better sit. I'm fine, or I will be, when I get some energy back. That's the closest I ever want to come to total burnout.

Kevin grabbed the visitor's chair and sat down close to the bed. "That's because the next step is death. As you, better than anyone else, know."

True. Stefan's voice was faint, making it hard to understand. Even so, the determination came through clearly.

"What the hell happened to you?" The words burst out with such force, they even surprised Kevin. "Did you go hunting him? Did you see him?"

No, but I saw some of the things as he saw them. When he let me.

"When he let you? Are you saying he knew you were there? I don't like the sound of that." Kevin leaned closer, checking out his friend's color.

Once in a while, he would pick up on me. His energy is erratic. A lot of old energy is around him. He's been doing this for a long time, but he's still learning. Or learning new tricks. Stefan's internal voice stuttered to a stop. The communication obviously required tremendous energy.

"Do you know who he is?" Kevin's voice was sharper than he intended. He looked around to see if anyone might have come in. He'd sound like a nutcase talking to himself.

They were still alone.

No, but a cop is helping him.

"What? Who?" It couldn't be. He didn't know all the men at the station as well as he'd like, but it curdled his stomach to think of a deception like this.

A young one. Check it out. Stefan's voice was getting fainter and fainter. *Today.*

"I will." Kevin hesitated, hating to ask more of his friend. But they were out of time. "Did you learn anything else?"

His pattern is old, decades old. Yet a long period of inactivity for some reason. His victims were always children, … until Mandy. Something odd about that energy, something new. A renewed excitement, like he's coming back to a favorite sport. Find him. Stefan paused painfully, gathering the needed strength. *Before he finds someone else.*

With those last words, the telecommunication trailed off into a faint echo of Stefan's former energy.

Kevin walked back to the door, with one last look at the still form on the hospital bed. "I'll come back tonight."

Bring her. Faint but decisive, Stefan's voice brooked no argument. Neither did Stefan need to clarify who he was talking about. Kevin already knew.

"I will." With that, he walked out and headed back to the office. At the office, the captain waited for him. "My office. Now."

Kevin frowned. He waited until the captain shut his door and took his seat at the desk.

"What the hell is going on?" Captain Gosling glared at him. "I received an anonymous phone tip today about someone in the office leaking information about a recent homicide."

Kevin whistled softly. A homicide could only mean Mandy. Speaking slowly, he said, "It's hard to believe anyone here would do that."

"I know," came the somber answer. "If one of our men had anything to do with this leak, I want *him* caught."

So did Kevin.

The captain watched for Kevin's reaction, then nodded. "Precisely, and that leads to the next problem. I don't know why the tip was offered, how accurate it is, or whether it's just an attempt to discredit the office, but we need this checked out and fast, before Internal Affairs hears about it."

No argument there.

In the privacy of his office, and armed with Stefan's tip, Kevin made a list of all the rookie officers on staff, including the two who were no longer attached to their division. The experienced officers didn't come under the heading of young—as far as Kevin was concerned—so he bypassed those.

That left eight names in all. The two who no longer worked in his office, he tentatively crossed out. One worked out of New York now, and the other had transferred home to Alaska. He'd focus on the other six. He'd known two of them for years. Both young men had grown up here. They both came from working families. Neither had excelled at school, but both had done a reasonable job. One was particularly athletic, and the other enjoyed sports at the community level. Overall, nothing about them raised warning flags.

There were four more. The first was a particularly enterprising young man, who could go far with the right connections. The second, with a so-so average personality, could go either way. The other two he didn't feel he knew at all. The third one spent most of his free time working with Kevin's former partner. The fourth he knew only by sight.

Which one of these betrayed the force, and why? What would cause a young man, starting out in his career, to risk it all and to quite likely end up in jail? Had this person done this willingly? Kevin hated to think so. But otherwise, what pressure could be applied to make someone do something like this? Blackmail? Extortion of a police officer was not a new thing. But what could the leverage be?

Kevin pondered the scenarios, before picking up the phone and calling the captain. Quickly he explained about Stefan's news, rapidly running through his points and the research to date. "Any suggestions, Captain? Do you know anything about these guys that would suggest where to look?"

"Not really." The older man pondered the news thoughtfully. "But I hope you're right about leverage being used. It would be easier to accept. He could even be protecting a family member."

Kevin stared off toward the far wall, then said, "I think I'll bring them in and see what shows up."

"Do it fast. We're running out of time."

Only two of the young rookies were at the office. Kevin called them in, one at a time. With each, he asked for a rundown of the cases they were currently working on. As it was no secret that Kevin had a hand in suggesting promotions and shifting personnel within departments, both men quickly complied.

Kevin listened attentively, while he probed their energy fields, looking for anything that made them appear culpable. They both were innocents, as far as he could tell. Their minds and energy were wide open. He didn't think they were capable of deceit at this level—but he'd been wrong before.

He thanked them both and let them go with words of appreciation for the jobs they were doing.

His notebook was rapidly filling with rough information on the possible suspects, when a package arrived on his desk. Nancy, the longtime clerk from the front office, smiled down at him. "Directly to you. No stops and no other eyes. Those were your instructions, weren't they?" She grinned at him, watching as he ripped open the heavy padded envelope.

Finally.

"Thanks, Nancy." In midrip, he stopped and looked at her pointedly. She raised her eyebrows but obediently left the room, shutting the door with an exaggerated movement.

This was the information he'd requested on John's family. He couldn't believe the difficulty he'd had to get this material.

He opened it, pulled out the copied material he'd requested, and started reading.

"What the hell?" he whispered.

Moments later, he put down the sheet of paper in shock.

A heaviness settled in his stomach, as he tried to digest the details. There had been many different accusations of child abuse concerning their daughter, and neighbors complained of screaming and fighting— all over the last four years they'd lived in Redding, California—even a statement from the little girl's physician.

Intuitively Kevin knew John had paid to hush up any suspicions of foul play. Money might have saved John decades ago, but today he held a position in public office. If this leaked out, they'd crucify him. It wouldn't matter if John hadn't been the bastard who'd dished out the child beatings, the suspicions alone would finish him. No wonder he'd left town.

Was this what the blackmailer wanted John to confess to? Or was it for something worse?

A paragraph caught his eye. According to the case file, the child had fallen from a tree in the front yard, suffered a broken neck, and died several days later. Everyone in the family had been questioned, but the death had been declared accidental, and the case closed. The little girl had been eight years old.

He shuffled through the documents, looking for the start of the problems. There it was. Four years before her death. That was the first time where suspicion of abuse was noted in the file. She'd died thirteen years ago.

That fit the time line too.

This then is where the whole mess started—years ago.

ALEXIS FELT THE mounting pressure. Nothing specific—but the heavy atmosphere and the constant tension drained her. It was the same for the townspeople. Everywhere she went, people looked suspiciously at each other, seldom maintaining eye contact or stopping to talk.

After finishing lunch with Scott, they returned to the gardens. Alexis heaved a sigh when she saw Rick waiting for her. What could he want now?

"As you refuse to leave town, I have the perfect job for you. It will keep you safe and out of sight. I want you to clean up last year's paperwork." Rick smiled at her evilly.

Alexis spluttered. She couldn't even form a protest because her mind had frozen. *Paperwork.* A year's worth! He knew she hated that type of work.

Scott's lips twitched. When he finally grinned at her, Alexis shot him a look of disgust. He could at least help her out of this mess.

"I know you'd like to stay here and have Scott as your babysitter, but, believe it or not, he has other jobs to do. And one of them is a meeting now with the city planners for the new building to start next month."

"*Ach*, hell, I forgot." Scott groaned. "Sorry, Alexis. It's not something I should miss."

"Why can't I go with you?" She'd enjoy being in on some of the planning decisions for the new section. Actually that idea perked her up.

"No need. You'll be totally safe in the office. No one could find you under all that filing." Rick was savage with his satisfaction. Turning back to Scott, he said, "Take her down and leave her there. Call the detective and let him know."

Filing? Oh, hell no.

IT WAS AN unbelievably long afternoon. No one had filed the time cards, supply lists, or myriad other papers in months. By the end of the day, she was ready to scream. *"Arrgh!"* Alexis threw her pen across the room. Dry laughter hit her ears from the doorway. She looked up to see Kevin, leaning casually against the doorframe.

"Have you come to rescue me?" she demanded. "Otherwise I might just have to hurt you."

"I think this job suits you." Kevin took a seat on the one chair that wasn't fully covered in reams of papers. "A desk job."

"Like hell."

He sat across from her, with a cheeky grin, but heavy lines creased his face. He opened an envelope he'd brought and slid out several photocopied pictures. "Can you look at these and tell me if any of them look familiar?"

Alexis frowned. Pictures of children. A good half dozen but the quality was poor. She shuffled them apart, so she saw them better … and froze. Tapping the picture of one young boy, her heart ached as she whispered, "Him. I saw him in one vision."

Kevin nodded, his face grim. "Any others?"

She studied the others, before singling out the photo of a young curly haired girl. "Her, I think. But I am not as sure of her as I am of the little boy. She looks different in the picture."

"How about the rest?"

"I haven't seen all that many clearly. Several are always hanging around Daisy in the background, but I haven't gotten a good look at them." She separated out three more photos. "I think these ones as well. But," she cautioned, "I can't be sure."

Kevin smiled. "Don't worry about it. These children all disappeared over twenty years ago. Their cases were never solved. A serial killer was suspected to be in the area, but the information back then didn't travel as quickly as it does now. The killer was never caught. Instead, he just went quiet."

"And he never resurfaced?" How odd. She watched, as Kevin collected the pictures—the first tangible evidence of her visions. Until now, the children in them had faces but no names. That kept them in the realm of being almost imaginary, as if she hadn't really seen them. Now there was no refuting the facts. She pointed at the one. "What's his name?" she asked, suddenly needing to know.

He narrowed his gaze, considering what he'd been asked. "Eric. Eric Mason."

That fit, sort of. "These kids I see, were they all murdered?"

He shook his head. "Not necessarily. Spirits can stay here for many reasons. It's possible you are connected to any child who is lost."

That made her feel better.

A sudden smile brightened Kevin's face. "One good thing happened this morning."

At her sudden interest, he nodded smugly and said, "Yep, I talked to Stefan."

"He's awake?" she asked, jumping out of her chair and reaching for her purse. "Let's go!"

But Kevin didn't move. "No, he's not awake."

Confused, she moved to stand in front of him. "But you spoke to him?"

"Yes, but only telepathically." Kevin slowly stood and stretched, the envelope in hand.

"How is he?" She studied the fleeting nuances on his face.

"He's fine. Very tired and he'll need several more days of rest—but, considering what he's been through, he sounded okay. He wants to speak with you." He walked to the office door, before glancing over at her. "Aren't you coming?"

She preceded him from the building.

"Don't you have to lock up or something?"

"I hope someone steals it all," she snapped. "It would serve Rick right."

ONCE INSIDE THE hospital, they came face-to-face with Scott's beautiful Moira.

"Hello, Moira." Alexis walked up to her and held out her hand. "We haven't been introduced but I'm—"

"Alexis. Scott's *bin* telling me about ye." The Scottish woman smiled a friendly greeting. The two women shook hands. Moira turned to Kevin. "Good day to ye again, Detective Sutherland."

"Hello, Moira. How's our patient?"

"He's the same. No change as far as I know. You're welcome to visit." She waved them in the direction of the room, then grabbed her charts and headed down a hall.

Stefan remained in the same position as when Alexis had last seen him.

"He looks better." A wealth of satisfaction wove through Kevin's voice.

"Does he?" Alexis studied the prone body curiously. "He doesn't look any different to me."

Kevin glanced at her in amusement. "That's because you're looking with your eyes."

Embarrassed to be reminded, Alexis checked out Stefan's energy. It was much stronger, a smooth, calm whiteness that spoke of peace and gentleness. It wasn't back to its full vibrancy, but, if he continued to improve, he wouldn't need to be here too much longer. "He's pretty vulnerable like this, isn't he?"

Her wording caught his attention. "He wasn't attacked or anything. I doubt he's in danger here. Are you picking up something?"

"No. Not really. He just looks so vulnerable." She walked closer to the bed, taking up Stefan's fine artistic hand. His skin was warm and smooth, with a healthy pink color. She curled the long fingers around hers, as if he were grasping her hand on his own.

You don't need touch to know that we're together.

Alexis laughed aloud. "Now that's where you're wrong. I do. It's you who doesn't need to touch."

Nonsense. If you'd wanted to, you could have spoken to me anytime. You just need more confidence in your abilities.

Alexis listened to Stefan's warm, teasing voice in her head. She lifted his hand and dropped a kiss on the knuckles. "It's good to hear your voice again."

Not half as good as it is to hear yours. Are you okay, after your trip in to find me?

Alexis smiled at what already seemed like a week-old memory. "I am, and thanks for showing me some of your much more advanced skills."

No problem. I thought I could accomplish something over there. But I overestimated my abilities.

"Or you just burned up faster than normal because it was new and more difficult to attempt than anything else you'd done." Alexis backed up a bit. "At least, *I* find things go better on the second attempt."

I needed you here to warn you. This bastard checks in on you all the time.

What! Kevin's voice ripped through Alexis's mental space, making her wince at the tone and volume. Damn, that hurt.

You heard me.

"In what way is he watching?" Alexis asked curiously. Just what was this asshole capable of? "And why?"

He likes to know where you are, what you're doing. Not only on an energy level. He's often out physically keeping an eye on you.

That sent shivers down her spine. A stalker. That added a whole new dimension of creepy to this mess. "But why? Why me?"

He's scared of you, of what you can do to hurt him.

Alexis was stunned. "I can hardly do anything compared to you. Even Kevin's abilities exceed mine."

"I'm not so sure about that," Kevin said quietly. "You don't realize how far you've come and just how many areas you've just barely touched on, … so far."

It had never occurred to her that her abilities might worry a predator. It wasn't something she even wanted to think about. Stefan overrode her worries with a completely different observation.

It's your ability to communicate with his victims that disturbs him. He's afraid of what they could tell you. Stefan's voice became even fainter. *Information that will give him away.*

"Why? It's not like they've told me anything useful. Why would he start worrying now?"

"Actually you've helped quite a lot," Kevin said. "You're the one who pinpointed the license plate that allowed us to rescue the child. And it was you who recognized that Stefan was in trouble."

He knows he was careless in the beginning, before he learned to hide his tracks. He's scared you might find something from back then that could give him away.

Alexis didn't know what to think.

For whatever reason, those who passed at his hand are contacting you. Stefan's voice weakened, became thin and reedy. His ability to converse was almost gone.

Kevin stepped in to take control of the conversation. *Stefan, is this why you asked to see Alexis, or is there something else?*

She … She needs to meet the rookies. With that, Stefan's voice faded into the distance, leaving a blank emptiness in the room.

CHAPTER 21

"ROOKIES?" ALEXIS WAS puzzled. She looked to Kevin for understanding. "What did he mean?"

"Come on. Let's go. I'll explain on the way." He gently untangled Stefan's hand from hers, tugging her toward the hallway. Outside, they headed for the parking lot, almost running.

Kevin slid into the driver's side and started up the engine while Alexis settled in the passenger seat. Without saying anything, he pulled out of the lot and drove through the main part of town. The sun shone heavy in the late afternoon sky, giving everything a wavy, surreal look, as glimpses of it flashed by. Suspicious, Alexis studied Kevin's sassy grin. He was up to something.

While she contemplated just what that could be, Kevin pulled up to a Chinese restaurant. Alexis started to get out, but he stopped her.

"I'll go in and pick it up."

Surprised at that, she watched him exit the truck, then came back a few minutes later with the food. Takeout worked. They needed to talk, and he'd said it was easier to do that at home. This probably meant his home, given the circumstances. But he continued to surprise her as he drove through town and headed on out again. With rising delight, Alexis realized where they were headed.

Relief, greater than she could have imagined, settled inside her as Kevin turned onto the well-worn dirt road leading to his lakefront property. She needed this, had craved it even. The natural surroundings filled her with peace and not only because of the memories of their passionate interlude. Simply said, the beauty of the place suited her soul.

Once there, they parked and got out. The layers of tension dropped off, as they made their way to the water's edge. Alexis sighed happily, as she dropped down onto a flat rock and divested herself of shoes and socks.

"*Brrr.*" The water chilled her hot, sore feet. She couldn't ignore the impulse to roll up her jeans and to let her toes dangle in the water.

Dropping her jacket on the rock behind her, she proceeded to use it as a pillow.

"Oh, this feels so good." Alexis moaned in delight. She even went so far as to pull her tank top up to her ribs and loosen the button on her jeans.

"Don't let me stop you from stripping down to the skin. Have a swim if you want."

"Nope, don't want to, but neither do I feel like moving again for a while. Do you mind bringing dinner over here?" Alexis never even opened her eyes as she spoke, but seconds later she heard him approach with the rustle of the paper bags. The rich aroma of Chinese food caused her stomach to growl, loudly announcing its neglected state to a very amused Kevin.

"Dinner is served, m'lady."

"*Uhmmm*," she murmured sleepily, refusing to move.

"Eat first, nap later." Kevin opened the various tubs and boxes.

She rolled over and reached for the plate he held out. It was the perfect picnic.

Working through her dinner, she realized that Stefan's continued improvement had given her peace of mind. She couldn't imagine moving forward with this psychic stuff without him. Besides, he'd claimed a spot in her heart too.

How quickly she'd adjusted to this new reality. She munched on her dinner thoughtfully. She hadn't given much thought to her future, since Lissa's passing. At the time, she felt her continuous existence was a punishment, not a gift.

For the first time in a year, she understood just how many gifts she'd been given. It was sobering to realize how long she'd walked around in a fog of grief. Lissa's death may have been the reason, but it was no excuse to continue.

"Heavy thoughts again, huh? You're the darnedest one for those."

She eyed him wryly. "It's that time of life for me."

"You're too young to have a midlife crisis. So what's the issue here?" Kevin's voice took on a coaxing tone. "Come on. Spill the beans."

"I've already lived a lifetime in many ways. If I want a *mid*-midlife crisis, I will have one," she said in a light voice. "Actually, I've decided it's time to move."

Kevin straightened at her unexpected announcement. "You mentioned something like that before. But where?" he asked cautiously.

"I don't know yet, but I know I need a change," she mused. "Being here makes me realize how a space can improve or dampen my state of mind. My apartment's doing nothing for me. I need a welcoming space again. Maybe I'll start my business back up or start a different one. I need to think on it a bit more. Do I keep my job, go to part-time, or find something different altogether?" She watched him fill his plate for the second time. "Suggestions?"

"Don't make a major change until this mess is cleared up," he advised. "Everything is out of whack for you right now."

"These changes aren't new ideas." She gazed over the sparkling pools of water, glistening in front of them. The cooler evening, combined with the slight breeze off the water, dampened any desire she might have had to swim. Even so, the amazing view soothed her aching soul. It was such a spectacular view that healing energy literally surged through her, leaving peace and contentment in its wake.

"I need something like this. So much pain and sorrow has been in my life to date. This"—she motioned with her arms—"or something like this would help me heal, when I come home." She could tell from his face that he understood what she was trying to say. "My heart needs a place to rest and to rejuvenate."

"That's partly why I'm building here. Some days, because of my job, I feel like I have nothing more to give." He stared down at his half-eaten food. "The things I've seen ..." He shook his head. "Many evenings I've driven out here to just sit and forget." He smiled with deep understanding. "It makes the rest of what I do easier to deal with."

Alexis stood suddenly and brushed off her pants. "I thought about contacting a real estate agent to see if something comparable is out there. Preferably with a house already standing on it." She surveyed the area. "Are any trails to walk out here?" She slid a teasing sidelong glance at him. "You never did show me around the last time we were here."

He got up, grinning at her lighthearted reminder. "We had more pressing issues then. Let's go this way, and I'll show you my world."

THE HOSPITAL VISITING hours were winding down. Slowly groups of people made their way to exits all over the vast building. It had been an ordinary evening for most people. It was a welcome chance to say hi to loved ones and to bring them something to brighten their stay.

Dressed casually, the tall, slim man walked through the hallways. He knew how the system worked here. The nurses tended to ignore the comings and goings at this hour, for they knew that visitors could be the bright spot in the day for the people forced to stay behind. If one or two laggards came in during the evenings, anyone with half a heart turned a blind eye for a little bit longer. Their rounds would start soon enough, and then they could chase the last stragglers out the door. So finding someone walking around the halls past visiting hour wasn't exactly a suspicious event.

Which was fortunate.

He strode down the halls with purpose. As he passed the nurses' station, he didn't even receive a questioning glance. Perfect.

A large set of metal shelves were at the far end of the hall. Both clean laundry and dirty laundry sat heaped in their respective places. As he approached, he saw a white lab coat tossed over the edge of the dirty bin. Without a thought, he snagged it and quickly put it on.

Look at that. It wasn't even a bad fit. If not knowing who'd worn it, or where, made his skin crawl, he ignored that. It was necessary, and he'd be damned if he'd turn down the unexpected gift.

When he reached the correct door, he glanced about surreptitiously and saw the hallway was empty. He pushed open the door and stepped inside.

The room was empty but for the single occupant. It appeared to be the right man. Tonight's visit was all about removing what could be a potential problem. It didn't matter so much if he killed the wrong man, but, if he left the right man alive because of uncertainty, that would be a serious error in judgment.

But, from where he stood, he recognized the man's energy. It seemed frail, almost nonexistent. Maybe he'd die anyway. No, that wasn't likely. This asshole was too tenacious to die.

On his own.

He shoved his hand into his pocket. Now, should it be the needle or the pillow?

ALEXIS LOVED THE scent of pine trees. The rich aroma wafted up with every step.

"We used to come here every day in the summertime," Kevin reminisced. "My cousins and I ran around out here for hours ..." He turned toward her, his face lighting up, as if to say something, when suddenly the color drained from his face, and he fell to his knees, gasping in shock.

"Kevin!" Alexis reached for him, dropping to her knees to support his weight. "What's the matter? Kevin? Talk to me, damn it." She'd never seen him like this, and she didn't like it. He'd always seemed so strong.

"Stefan," he whispered, digging his fingers into her arms.

She leaned closer to hear. "What about Stefan? Is he okay? Kevin, talk to me." She helped him to the ground, as the shadows deepened around them. "Is Stefan in trouble?"

Kevin nodded, now gasping for breath. "I have to help him." His eyes rolled up in his head, and he was gone.

"Kevin!" There was no answer. "Oh God! Now what the hell do I do?"

Call the hospital!

Alexis barely deciphered Kevin's faint telepathic message. She was galvanized into action. Her fingers grappled for a cell phone. She punched in the numbers still permanently emblazed in her mind.

She couldn't believe her luck. "Hello, Moira, is that you? This is an emergency. Please run and check on Stefan. If there's ... Moira? Moira, are you there?"

Alexis looked down at the cell phone. There'd been a *clunk*, followed by faint hospital sounds, leaving her to assume that Moira had literally dropped the receiver and run.

Odd, you'd think she'd have questioned Alexis. But then, as Alexis's mind worked through the oddity, she realized Scott had probably told Moira about Alexis's odd abilities.

Abilities? Could she use them now? She closed her eyes and thought of Stefan. She tried to reach out, but all she saw was a maelstrom of energy contained in such a way that she didn't know how to penetrate it. He'd said she could reach out to him anytime. She just needed more self-confidence.

She tried again to reach Stefan. Nothing. She saw movement. Action of some kind but she wasn't a part of it. She had to trust in Kevin. And Stefan.

With the shadows deepening and darkening by the minute, Alexis didn't know what else to do. Hang up the phone and call back or wait? There was no decision to make regarding Kevin. She couldn't possibly move him on her own. She disconnected the hospital call. She eyed the phone in her hand and then dismissed it. Kevin wouldn't thank her for letting others know. As he'd watched over her, she could stand guard for him.

She sat down on the cooling ground to wait. Damn, she hated that corpselike look on his face.

After a few minutes, she redialed. "Hello, is Moira there? ... No. Do you know where she's gone? ... Okay. I just phoned in an emergency in room 207 but was cut off. Could you please check on them?" She tried hard to keep her voice cool and controlled. Inside, panic ruled. What could have happened to Moira? "Fine. Yes, I'll ring back in a minute."

Now she had to wait again.

Gloom no longer gently enveloped them. Chilly darkness had settled in instead. There was no change in Kevin. She didn't dare join him; there'd be no one to protect the two of them. She had to trust that the two men could handle whatever hell they were in.

The wait seemed interminable.

Several times, she called the hospital. Then someone picked up, "Bradford General Hospital. How can I help you?"

At least someone had answered. "I need to speak with Moira, please."

"I'm sorry. She is unavailable at this time."

"What? I just spoke to her less than ten minutes ago. She went to check on a patient for me."

"I'm sorry. I only know that she is unavailable."

"Has she been hurt? You don't understand. I sent her to check on a patient who might have been in danger."

"I'm sorry, ma'am. Maybe you need to contact the police."

Alexis snorted. "The police are already on it, you idiot," she snarled into the night, as she ended the call. She glared at the man still prone beside her. "Well, Kevin, isn't it time to come back?"

Silence. She tried to look into his mind. And came up against his walls. No entrance for her there. Damn.

"Now what?" She spoke aloud, finding comfort in the sound of her own voice. The answer came in a flash. Scott.

"Hey, it's me, Alexis." Quickly she explained what had transpired. "They just said she's unavailable. Scott, I'm scared something's happened to both of them."

"I'm already in the truck and heading down the road. I'll be at the hospital in a couple minutes."

"Call me." She gave him the number.

Again she waited. The underbrush rustled off to her left. The night creatures were foraging for food. She shivered in the cooling air. By now, the two of them were in total darkness. Why couldn't Kevin have collapsed by his truck? She had no idea how far up the trail they'd traveled.

Long minutes later, Kevin's cell phone beeped, scaring the bejeezus out of her. "Alexis, it's Scott."

"What did you find?"

"Moira apparently fell and hit her head. She's still unconscious."

"What!" Alexis was stunned. That didn't feel right. Intuitively she knew something had happened, but falling and hitting her head didn't fit. "Where did it happen?"

"In the hallway outside of your friend's room."

"Damn." She hesitated to ask but knew she had to. "Scott, has anyone checked on Stefan? That's why Moira went there in the first place."

"He's the same. There's been no change."

A huge sigh of relief escaped. "Thank God. I'm thinking Moira might have interrupted an attack on Stefan."

"And she was assaulted instead?" Scott roared, his burr thickening with his anger. "That's naw good, that isna."

"I'm hoping he's gone." A horrible thought occurred to her. "Or else he's waiting for a second chance at Stefan."

Shocked silence came through clearly.

"That's it. I'll be staying right here for the night."

Alexis nodded. "That's probably a good idea. If you can, would you mind checking in on Stefan as well?" She looked down at the still male beside her. "We'll get to the hospital as soon as we can."

If and when Kevin woke up.

Is this how he'd felt when she'd tried to track Stefan into the ethers? She hated this being-left-behind stuff. It was damn scary. The waning moon flitted through the treetops, adding a surreal, eerie tone to the evening. She sensed Kevin out there, working in the ethers. She saw his energy busy doing something. And how weird … and wonderful was that. How quickly she'd become used to him there. That connectedness.

She hadn't expected him to take up residence in her heart, but, so far, he showed no sign of making a quick exit. She still couldn't believe the speed in which everything had happened. Her heart might be comfortable with it, but her mind was troubled. Males were such foreign animals in her world.

Damn, what could Kevin be doing?

"I'm here." The masculine growl lifted her heart. Relieved, she bent over his beloved face and dropped a kiss on his nose. "Hey, how are you doing?" She smiled tenderly. Even in the dim glow of moonlight, she saw his weary grin.

"I'm okay. Just tired." He struggled into a sitting position, rested a moment, then lunged upright.

"Hey." Startled, Alexis fell back in surprise. "Aren't you the one who always says to take it slow and easy when you come back?"

"Yeah, but that's when it's you." He reached down to help her up.

"And what the hell happened to you just now? It freaked me out when you collapsed."

"Stefan called for help." Kevin held on to her hand and strode off toward his truck, pulling her with him. "We have to go."

Alexis practically ran to keep up. Her heart pounded, while her mind still grappled with the rapid shift in events. His behavior scared her. "Why? What's the matter? Is something wrong with Stefan?" His long legs ate up the miles. He didn't waste any of his precious energy on speech.

"We're heading there now. He should be fine, but I'll put a guard on him overnight."

"Oh, good."

Every once in a while, the moon popped up between the treetops to give them a glimpse of the world around them. It was enough.

During the trip back to Kevin's truck, Alexis listened as he made several calls—none of them eased Alexis's anxiety. By the time they'd reached his truck, they were almost running.

Once at the truck, he hopped in and barely waited for her to buckle up before he hit the gas. Gravel spit out behind them as he spun the truck around and gunned it. Once on the main road, it actually felt like the problems were rushing toward them, pulling them faster and faster into the crisis awaiting them. A police cruiser was parked directly across from the Emergency entrance. Not an alarming sight in itself, but, with a multitude of officers milling about, her alarm bells rang a notch louder.

Once they parked, several of the police officers walked over to Kevin.

"Sir, we've been waiting for you. No sign of an intruder. Mr. Kronos appears to be stable."

Kevin nodded, never slowing his stride as he covered the length of the hallway in record time. Alexis ran to keep up.

At Stefan's door, yet another officer stood guard. "Kevin, the doctors just went in. I don't think you're supposed to …"

Kevin cut him off with a look and walked in. Alexis followed. Two doctors were deep in discussion. An officer stood at the wall behind them.

"Hi, glad you finally got here," the officer said, with a smile.

Both doctors looked on as Kevin nodded curtly and walked straight to the bed to stare down at his friend.

"Kevin, he's fine. Whoever tried to do this didn't succeed."

Alexis looked over at the one doctor who'd spoken. "What do you mean? What did they try?"

Dr. Magill, according to his name tag, held up an evidence bag containing an almost full syringe. He handed it over to the officer behind him. "This was found on the floor."

"What is it?" Kevin eyed the amount left in the syringe with a practiced eye. "Is there any chance he received some of it?"

"We've taken blood samples, but the results won't be back for a bit. With no change in his vital signs at this point, we assume not." Dr. Magill looked at their patient. "He's being closely monitored. He's a very lucky man." The doctor studied Kevin, adding, "He had a very capable friend." At Kevin's sharp look, he nodded, as if confirming something. "Now it's up to the police. Maybe you can sort this out."

"Don't worry. I'll get to the bottom of this."

No one in the room doubted that for a minute.

Alexis stepped closer to Stefan and gently stroked his hand. Kevin wrapped an arm around her.

"His skin has a waxy, undead appearance," she whispered.

"He's fine. Come on. Let's check on Moira."

They didn't have to go far. Scott had heard the commotion of their arrival.

"How is he?" The big Irishman stood protectively in Moira's doorway. Concern and worry blended with the flames of his ire.

Alexis understood. Someone he cared about had been attacked. Alexis silently dared that bastard to return. Alexis walked up and hugged him. "They think he'll be fine. The consensus is that the intruder was interrupted before he could carry out what he came to do."

"Aye. Chances are, Moira took the brunt of it."

"Has she woken up yet?" Alexis was sorry for sending the poor nurse into what had obviously been a dangerous situation. Her concern had been for Stefan.

"Don't you be worrying none. You did the right thing."

Scott's rough pats on her back had her smiling—the bloody big ox. "Still, I didn't want her hurt."

"Yet, it could have been so much worse," Kevin reminded her bleakly. "They've both been lucky." Scott still barred the doorway with his bulk. Kevin raised an eyebrow and nodded to the interior. "May we come in?" he asked sardonically.

Scott flushed. Kevin was still a law officer. The bigger man moved aside and led the way to her bedside. Moira was sitting up, waiting for them.

"Good evening, Detective. Is my patient okay?"

"He appears to be," Kevin quickly reassured her. "Thanks for checking on him."

"No problem." Moira shifted in bed, wincing in pain. "I don't think I did much good though." She waved Scott away as he moved to help her. "I'm fine. It's just a wee bit of a headache."

"Do you remember what happened?" Alexis asked, steering the conversation to the main issue. She walked to the other side of the bed and sat down on the visitor's chair.

"Not really. I remember what you said, then racing down the hallway, wondering who was visiting Mr. Kronos …"

Alexis interrupted. "He had visitors?"

"Well, I thought I heard a noise, so I figured he must have had someone in there. I walked in, but I must have slipped and hit my head when I went down. I don't remember more than entering the doorway. I never even saw who was in the room."

Scott's voice sounded black as hell. "I think someone hit your head for you."

Moira looked startled. From watching her face, Alexis saw that, the more she considered it, the more reasonable that possibility appeared to her. "It's possible, I suppose. I've never slipped at work before. I thought a spill of some kind made it happen."

Kevin shook his head. "No evidence of anything like that." He stepped closer, checking out her color. "Has the doctor checked your head?"

"Yes, I'm fine, and I want to go home." She glared at Scott. "Scott won't let me."

"Yes, I will but not alone."

The stalwart Irishman wouldn't budge and with two such stubborn characters, they were at an impasse. Alexis hid her smile. These two were good together—or would be, if they ever got a chance.

To that end, Alexis suggested, "Moira, it's probably a good idea to let Scott stay on your couch overnight. The extra protection wouldn't hurt, and you shouldn't be alone after a head injury." Alexis saw Scott nodding his head, emphatically agreeing with her.

But Moira's next comment wiped his smile right off. "Except he wouldn't stay on the couch."

"Aye, I would," he protested in hurt tones. "I won't be going where I'm not invited."

Moira shot him a look of disgust.

He looked so innocent, but even Alexis saw the leprechaun peeping out, fooling none of them. "He'll stay there," Alexis stated emphatically, looking over at the Irishman, now standing defensively with his burly arms across his chest. "Scott's an honorable man." Alexis's tone left no doubt about what she'd do if it didn't turn out that way.

Kevin burst out laughing, garnering looks from them all. "Welcome to having your days numbered, my friend."

Scott blushed and mumbled under his breath, "Danged women."

"What?" asked both Alexis and Moira.

"Nuttin'," the Irishman snapped back and glared at the three of them. "She's going home. You two can leave anytime."

"Actually, you two men can leave. Alexis, would you mind giving me a hand to get dressed? I'm not sure I can bend to put on me shoes."

"Sure." Alexis glared at both males. "Out!"

The two men left, both grinning like mad monkeys.

"You do that well," murmured Moira, as she sat on the side of the bed, catching her breath.

"Practice." Alexis grinned at the woman she knew instinctively she would come to know and to love quite well. She bustled around the room, collecting Moira's things. "Seriously, if you *were* attacked, the intruder might worry that you did see him. I think it's unlikely, but let's play it safe." She brought over her shoes and squatted to slip them on the unsteady woman. "Let Scott be protective."

"I don't much like the thought of someone coming after me," Moira admitted.

"Nobody does. But we have a murderer in this town. We're getting closer to him every day, and he knows that, and he's starting to make mistakes. So don't *you* make any before we get a chance to catch him."

The women stared somberly at each other.

Alexis smiled at the raised brow and the stern look from the other woman. "No, I won't."

CHAPTER 22

B ACK IN THE truck, Alexis yawned widely. "I'm tired but not enough to sleep yet."

"It's the adrenaline rush. Afterward, you're fatigued but not sleepy. Which is a good thing right now." Alexis's color was good, so Kevin didn't worry too much. He probably looked worse.

He pulled into the police station and parked. Turning to face her, he said, "A couple rookies are on tonight. Stefan suggested you come meet them."

That woke her up. "Any idea why Stefan wanted me to meet them?"

In truth, he wasn't sure what to tell her. "I'm not sure." They exited the truck and headed inside. He needed caffeine. The trip to the other side had exhausted his energy reserves.

Several officers called out greetings as they passed. Kevin stopped to talk to a couple of them, catching up on anything he might have missed. At the same time, he was handed a large stack of messages—more than a few from John. Kevin felt the shadows in his world deepen. Fatigue pulled at him. This was getting to be a bit too much.

"Problems?" Alexis broke his reverie gently.

Kevin looked at the woman who'd become a beacon in his world. He hadn't planned it. He hadn't really wanted it. But here she was, and he knew he couldn't walk away from such a precious gift. He needed her.

He wrapped an arm around her shoulders and tucked her close against him. She needed him too. If she'd just accept what they could have together … She was close to that point; he felt it, but, at the same time, he sensed a part of her wanted to hold back. She still didn't recognize and accept how essential they both were to the fabric of each other's lives.

SITTING IN THE chair across from Kevin's desk, Alexis sipped her coffee. She couldn't stay focused. Her mind was exhausted and slow thinking, … coasting. It made her process information slower. Along with that, her emotions were running high.

Kevin appeared to be struggling. Given the mess with Stefan, the murder of his former girlfriend, and this asshole killer, that came as no surprise. If he'd been a woman, she'd have suggested a good cry. This new insight into his crazy life was both a gift and a responsibility that Alexis recognized and now honored.

Compassion swelled her tender heart that felt more open and touched than she could remember being in a long time. She knew it was because of the recent changes in her life … and because of Kevin. He had yet to grieve for Mandy, and, therefore, the pain had built up inside. No tears were allowed to escape, so she wept for him.

Alexis tugged Kevin's grief inside her heart, to ease his pain, then released the energy to the universe. Fat tears welled up at the corners of her eyes, before slowly starting their descent down her cheeks.

"Alexis?" he asked in confusion.

She couldn't answer. The emotional edge cut too deep. All she could do was let the tears roll and hope it helped to heal them both. Slowly she rose, walked around the edge of the desk, and waited. He moved, as if to stand, worry creasing his face.

She shook her head and crawled into his lap. Tenderly she covered his heart with the palm of her hand, tucking her head into the crook of his neck. Kevin wrapped his arms around her tightly, holding her close.

They stayed motionless for long minutes.

Alexis didn't know why she did this. She only knew she couldn't ignore her instincts. Stefan had been right. She was driven to help. She just didn't know what skills she could offer otherwise. She didn't know the difference in energy terms between receiving, transmitting, and healing. Maybe they were all different methods to achieve the same thing.

Sinking deeper into his psyche, she sent the energy to circulate along his meridian pathways, allowing the soothing energy to enter his system. To stroke and to calm as it traveled throughout. Kevin had showed her maps of these energy lines on the body. She didn't have all of them memorized yet, but she'd learned the main ones. On the return path, Alexis drained away Kevin's depression and pain, absorbing and then releasing them, as Stefan had taught her.

Many long minutes later, Kevin sighed, a heavy, heartfelt release of pain and tension. He squeezed her tight once, then released her. Only then did Alexis allow herself to smile. Now she knew he felt better. She had made a difference, and any words to the contrary she'd dismiss as male ego talking. This is what she needed to do with her life. She wasn't sure how or in what way, but it had to include making people feel better.

And you can.

Alexis tilted her head back to smile up at the tough, capable features above her. "Really?"

A knock on the door interrupted their privacy. Alexis shifted over to the chair by the window and watched as Detective Kevin Sutherland collected himself and went into action.

And what action it was.

Alexis could have been a ghost for all the attention he paid her over the next hour. Rookie after rookie came through the door. They were asked a few terse questions, their answers cataloged, further questioned as needed, then the officer dismissed.

What the officers couldn't see, and what totally amazed Alexis, was the efficiency of the energy search Kevin did of each man within the first minute after entering the office. Not one of the men noticed when their energy fields were searched—a quick dip in and out, then on to read their energy patterns. Within seconds, Kevin had a rounded view of each individual's world and insight as to whether Kevin needed to do a much closer interview.

"Where's Arnie?" Kevin asked the young officer, sitting in the hot seat in front of him.

"I don't know, sir." The officer wiped his brow nervously.

Alexis felt sorry for the uneasy young man. She'd already determined that Kevin had found nothing to be suspicious of with him. She waited for Kevin to speak.

"He's here somewhere. I need you to find him and to send him in." Kevin looked up from the papers in front of him and pierced the hapless young officer with his questioning gaze. "Understood?"

"Ah, yes, sir." The young man exited in a rush, banging into the chair in his effort to escape, but he soon left them alone.

"Ouch," Alexis murmured, trying to be quiet.

Kevin still heard her. "What?"

"You're the very devil to them, aren't you?" Alexis made the comment casually, never expecting the response she got.

"What are you talking about? They aren't afraid of me."

She couldn't believe what she heard. "Like hell they're not. Every one of these guys was incredibly edgy in here."

"Oh, that." Kevin casually dismissed the base reactions from the men. "It's the situation, not me."

"I see." But she didn't. "If I were one of them, I'd be terrified."

He glanced over at her in surprise. "Why?"

"I don't know. But they sensed something. They all ran out, as if Satan himself were after them."

Kevin stared off into space, considering her words. "Maybe it is the scan. It's not something I would normally do, but the circumstances are anything but normal." Soberly he looked back at Alexis's understanding face. "A murderer is out there. I have to stop him before he kills anyone else."

Alexis stood and stretched. "Don't you think you're being a little hard on yourself? You've already stopped two attacks."

"It's still definitely a concern." Kevin picked up the phone and used an outside line. "Good evening, John. Yes, I know it's late. I need to go over some information that I have. No, not tonight. In the morning—say, nine? Good. Thanks, and have a good night."

When Kevin hung up, the phone almost dropped from his grasp.

Alexis watched curiously but couldn't understand all the undercurrents. She'd just decided to ask him when the door opened to admit yet another young police officer.

She couldn't say why, but her spine stiffened, and every sense went on alert. Alexis slipped back to her place by the window, watching the man intently.

He appeared to be a bit older than the others.

Rough justice and street wisdom were written all over him. This young rookie had survived a difficult childhood. But he hadn't come out unscathed. He'd built one hell of a no-holds-barred shell to hide his scars.

But could he be hiding something else?

DAMN IT TO hell anyway.

That stupid bitch of a nurse! He hoped she had a hell of a headache. Had she seen him? He didn't think so, but it could be a huge mistake if he were wrong. He'd have taken care of her later, but that bloody Irishman had sat on guard until she'd been ready to leave.

He didn't know what to do now.

Turmoil circulated through his mind in a never-ending spin cycle, bringing on a hell of a throbbing pain at his temple. This was piss-poor timing. He hadn't wanted to move up his timetable just yet. His damn rookie hadn't provided enough information. And then the asshole hadn't answered his phone all evening.

The longer he sat and thought on the problem, the madder he got. If they wanted to force his timetable forward, fine. And, if that damn ghost whisperer wanted to be next, then that worked for him too.

KEVIN MOTIONED THE young man farther into the room. "Hi, Arnie. Thanks for coming in. Take a seat." He waited for the rookie to comply before adding, "This is Alexis Gordon. Alexis, this is Arnie Morrissey." Kevin watched the two nod politely at each other. If Alexis was on the stiff side, he let it pass.

Within seconds, Kevin's energy reached out, only to be instantly rebuffed. Kevin sat back and perused the tight-lipped face in front of him. "Arnie, is something bothering you?"

"No, sir."

His whole persona came across as too cold and hard for one so young. Kevin found it incredibly painful to watch. "You've been a good cop here for the last …" Kevin picked up the file in front of him. "It's been almost nine months now, hasn't it?" He eyed Arnie over the top of the folder.

Arnie only nodded.

Kevin wondered what it would take to break such intense self-control. Though brittle and edgy, he suspected it would shatter under gentle pressure. Kevin looked at Alexis. She looked ready to burst. He nodded.

Alexis blurted out, "Arnie, does the word *blackmail* mean anything to you?"

Arnie paled to an ashen gray. Fear made his eyes look like black marbles. His clenched fingers turned white at the knuckles.

Kevin barely hid his surprise. He'd have to remember to ask where that word had popped out from … and why. But first, he turned his stern gaze on the young man. "Arnie, tell me about it."

The poor man swallowed several times, tried to speak, but gave up before the words could make their way out. His downcast gaze dropped to the floor.

"You can take a few minutes to collect your thoughts but realize no one is leaving until we understand just what is going on here." Once again, Stefan had been right.

Arnie visibly swallowed hard several more times before giving up the ghost. He slumped against his chair in defeat. "I didn't know how to tell you," he whispered painfully.

Both Alexis and Kevin leaned forward to catch his barely discernible words.

"Tell me what?" Kevin let his voice soften. Experience guided him. It would be so easy to have everything go wrong right now. He could only hope Alexis would stay quiet. "Arnie? Tell us what?" he coaxed. "Are you in trouble?"

Arnie looked at him, a world of despair in his eyes. "I tried so hard. Honest I did."

"I believe you," Kevin said.

ALEXIS BELIEVED HIM too, although she couldn't explain why. Sincerity and dismal realization permeated the air. Arnie had meant what he'd said, and somehow he'd still failed to avoid what was happening. Her heart went out to him.

"I thought, if I could fix it, I wouldn't have to lose my job. I love being on the police force. It feels so good to be doing something positive after all those years of being on the wrong side of the law. But someone found out." The troubled young man paused. Frustration and anger boiled over. His fist slammed against the arm of the chair. "Damn it, it's just not fair. Everything was going so well."

"What's not fair?" asked Alexis quietly. "Just as important, what did someone find out?"

He looked at her briefly before turning away. "I have a record. Someone found out." He shrugged, as if the rest of the story was obvious.

It took a minute to sink in.

Kevin sat back. "You're being blackmailed?"

Arnie nodded, refusing to meet his gaze.

"You're right," Kevin said. "You should have found a way to tell the captain or me. Someone who could help." He leaned across the desk. "Arnie, despite whatever mistakes you have made, you have to tell me the whole truth now." He stared at the face across from him. "Do you understand?"

"I understand." Arnie straightened up in the chair. He leaned forward earnestly. "That's part of the problem. I don't know his name."

"Can you identify him in any way?"

Alexis wouldn't believe otherwise. She knew his answer would tell her a lot about this rookie's character. To deny this would mark him a liar and would give them a completely different set of problems to deal with.

"Yes." He looked up at his superior in resignation. "I know what he looks like, where we've met and …" He hesitated.

"And?" snapped Kevin.

"I've tried following him but haven't had much luck."

Alexis could appreciate that he'd tried to do that. She might even have done the same.

"What information did you give him?" Kevin asked, curt and to the point.

"Originally he just wanted little stuff, like how many staff worked here, how many senior officers, that kind of thing. I thought it all quite odd, but none of it was high-level security stuff, so I didn't worry about it." The young man shifted uncomfortably on the hot seat.

"And then?" prodded Kevin.

"He started asking questions about different cases. When the little girl's remains were found at the city park, he really started bugging me for information. I had to report in almost daily about anything connected to that case. For a while, I thought he might have been a reporter. But he isn't. I checked the local rags." Arnie stopped again, then continued, "He seemed eager, almost anticipating the news. If I didn't have anything, he'd be furious. Once, he found something new out on the evening news. I'd been so busy that it never occurred to me to call him. He was furious about that and wanted to know about the autopsy report of the child."

"Did he offer anything about himself?" Kevin asked.

Alexis sifted through the odd bits of information. Was this blackmailer just a busybody or someone eviler?

Arnie started to shake his head, only to stop and consider. Then he spoke, as if thinking aloud. "There was one funny thing. He lit up when I mentioned the name Daisy. But I didn't know what that meant." Resignedly the young man looked at Kevin. "Does this mean I've lost my job?"

"I can't say yet. It's not up to me." Kevin's expression closed down, giving no indication of his thoughts.

"Something very positive *could* come out of this," Alexis interjected. She knew it might not be her place, but Arnie was young. Maybe they could turn this around.

"In what way?" Kevin asked.

Arnie's hopeful gaze locked on hers.

"Can't we use Arnie's connection to this person to set a trap?"

Both men considered her point with a dawning realization.

"Sir?" interrupted Arnie hesitantly. "I think he's involved in much more than blackmailing me."

"Like?" Kevin spun back to face the hapless young man.

Alexis watched Kevin zoom in on Arnie, putting the poor man back on the spot.

Arnie shifted uncomfortably. He wiped his damp palms on his pants. "The night the little girl was kidnapped, I went looking for him. I had a gut feeling he might be involved."

"What!" Kevin's lethal voice split the air. "Why didn't you say something then?"

"I didn't have any proof," Arnie explained. "I still don't. But his reaction to the name was over the edge. I put two and two together ..." Arnie, seeing Kevin's stance wasn't softening any, tried again. "He seemed to know so much about it already. Later it occurred to me that the news report wasn't that detailed."

"Right." Kevin stood. "You are to meet the police artist now. I want a composite sketch within two hours." Kevin walked to his door before turning back. "Are you sure there's nothing else you can tell us?"

Arnie hesitated. "Once I saw his car parked outside the mayor's house."

Kevin slammed his door shut again and stormed back to his desk. "Is this man young or old?"

"Early thirties maybe. Five foot eleven, slim, well dressed."

"You do know what the mayor looks like?" At Arnie's immediate nod, Kevin eased back a bit but not much.

"It wasn't him. I'm sure of that."

The description Arnie gave twigged something else. Kevin cocked his head as he studied the young policeman. "What about his son? Would you recognize him?"

Arnie shook his head.

"That's the first photo we need to show you. Where else have you seen this guy? What's the license plate, and what kind of vehicle does he drive?" The next words burst out in a half bellow. "And why the hell did you not come to me with this information before?"

The rookie sank deeper into his unforgiving chair. "I thought, if I could solve it, then I wouldn't be kicked off the force."

"Did you ever suspect that the man you gave information to was involved in the recent murder of a young mother?" A muscle twitched in Kevin's cheek as he pinned the younger man to the spot.

"No, never!" Arnie appeared sincerely horrified at that idea.

Alexis believed him. And, in her mind, it changed his culpability.

Arnie continued with his protestations. "I wouldn't do something like that, honest. You have to believe me. I just didn't know what to do."

"Idiot!"

Alexis winced at the one word guaranteed to get her back up. "It makes sense, Kevin. Not for you, and maybe not for me, but for someone who feels they've done something wrong. They want to fix it before anyone finds out."

"Who asked you?" Kevin snapped.

"I did," she said cheerfully, fully aware of the shocked fascination coming from Arnie as he watched their exchange. "Maybe Arnie was right to be afraid. And right about the other … As long as he didn't give out something major, maybe this can be fixed." She smiled reassuringly at Arnie, presenting a confidence and an authority she didn't feel. There would be repercussions from Arnie's actions, but she had no idea how severe they'd be. From the look on his face, Arnie'd already assumed the worse.

"This *is* in your hands right now, Kevin." Alexis smiled gently. "What you do from here on in affects everything."

Kevin glared at her, his eyes laser hard. "Damn it, Alexis. You can't fix everything."

She smiled. "But *you* can fix some things."

Arnie gawked at her, as she continued.

"I know *I* can't fix everything. But you have authority to minimize the damage, Kevin. Talk to the captain about Arnie first, before anything else." She nodded at the still figure in the chair. "This young man's future doesn't have to be destroyed." At the look of hope on Arnie's face, she held up her hand. "But reparations do have to be made. Otherwise this can never be left in the past."

Alexis looked at the still-pissed Kevin. "Did the department know about Arnie's past, when he was picked, trained, and then put on the job within this force?"

At Kevin's grudging nod, Alexis turned to face Arnie. "Did you hide something else from the department when you made this career step?"

"No, nothing. I was shocked they accepted my application. Thought maybe my file hadn't been looked at closely enough or something. I had worked hard to clean up my act but figured my past would go against me. I thought that maybe they didn't know all of it, when they let me into the training." He shrugged at Kevin.

"Drugs, alcohol abuse, grand theft auto, prostitution all before twelve. You did three years in juvenile hall, then lived in a halfway house for a year, with rehabilitation and retraining for another year after that." Kevin's cold recital made them both stare in stunned amazement. Kevin shuffled some papers on his desk. "We decided that you'd had enough time and had chosen another way. *Our way.* We put our faith in you. A small department like ours has the ability to make these kinds of choices, ones that a big city police department can't."

The look on Arnie's face was as painful to look at as the recital he had just heard.

"Arnie, what went on in your early family life to send you on this path?" Alexis knew something had happened back there. And it needed to come out. Now. How she knew, she couldn't say.

The young man spoke dismissively. "The usual. Broken home, abuse, parents both alcoholics, mother a prostitute. What's to say? It was hell."

"No, there's something else," she prodded. Pain oozed from a hidden cavity in Arnie's soul. Alexis couldn't stand it. "Something hurt you badly and eventually sent you on this pathway to become a cop. Something inside you needed to pay retribution or maybe ..." Alexis paused, feeling her way, yet knowing the storm inside Arnie could break with her next words. "Or maybe because you needed revenge?"

Kevin looked at her in shock. "What are you getting at, Alexis?"

Needing to see something, anything else but the torment being released from his soul, she turned toward the window, overlooking the sleepy street outside. Behind her, she heard the young officer's gulps and sobs of a long-held agony.

"Jesus." Kevin's ire had quickly been replaced with understanding.

Alexis had sensed when Arnie dropped the barrier, hiding a lifetime of betrayal and pain, leaving his past wide open, exposed. She didn't want to look, and Kevin could easily see the details for himself. Hell, psychics anywhere in the world could have accessed the information with Arnie transmitting so loudly.

Then he told them in words. Arnie said he had a younger brother he'd doted on, until he'd died. Arnie explained he had been looking after him. They'd gone into a large mall. Arnie wanted to pilfer some candy and left his little brother to sit on a bench just inside the store. When he came out, the younger boy was gone. He'd gone through the automatic doors to pet a puppy waiting outside. When the puppy had run, he'd followed, directly into the path of the oncoming car.

"Oh hell." Weariness marred Kevin's features as he slumped in his chair. He walked over to Alexis. The two stood, not touching physically but wrapped in the comforting energy of the other, while giving the other man time to adjust to his disclosure.

"Sorry." Humiliation and embarrassment colored Arnie's voice.

Alexis sighed at the sad story. "Don't apologize. We each have had times when the pain is so bad that we can do nothing else but let it pour out."

"But you need to tell us the details." Kevin's voice was still cold but now had a thread of compassion running through it.

Broken, but still willing, Arnie explained again, in detail.

Alexis waited a few minutes after he fell silent to allow him to recover a stronger grip on his self-control. "I suppose you thought, if this came out, no one would let you stay here?"

"I was supposed to look after him. Keep him safe. It's all my fault."

His confession confirmed her guess. That was the problem with old abiding guilt; it ruled your actions forever. "Well, it won't. We all have demons, Arnie. Yours are more difficult than some, but no one here would judge you for it."

"*He* did."

Kevin spun away from the window to glare at him. "*He* knew?" Two quick steps took him to the front of his desk. "How could he know? Did you tell him?"

Arnie reared back, away from Kevin's intensity. "Uh, no. I didn't tell him. He already knew. He scared the hell out of me."

Alexis smiled at the past tense usage. The young man still looked terrified, only now Kevin was the looming danger.

Kevin picked up his phone, barking an order to have an officer report to his office pronto. Waiting for the knock on his door, Kevin stood, opened the door, and spoke to both officers now. "Okay, Arnie, I want you to start from the beginning and go over every word from every meeting." To the senior officer, Kevin said, "I want full descriptions with sketches of the perp's face, details about vehicles and locations where Arnie met him. This guy has a pattern, and I want to know what it is." Standing with his hands on his hips, he added, "And I need someone to find a picture of Charles for Arnie to see. Fast."

The senior officer nodded and led Arnie into a private room to take his statement. The police artist was on standby, but hopefully she wouldn't be needed.

Kevin called the captain and filled him in. Finally something had shifted.

As Alexis waited, she almost nodded off. God, she was tired. She wondered when they'd be heading home.

"I know you're tired, Alexis." He pondered the problem for a moment. "I can send an officer with you to my place, or you can grab a couple hours sleep here. We have two rooms with cots in them." He grinned at her. "Actually, we have a whole jail full of them."

"Thanks, but no thanks." Alexis considered the not-so-great options.

"Or I could have a cot brought into my office," he suggested with a raised brow.

Right on cue, Alexis yawned again. "Did we eat tonight?"

"Yeah." He reminded her. "Chinese at the lake. Remember?"

She grimaced. How could she have forgotten? This day had been brutally long. "Maybe I could crash here. Are you sure I won't be in the way?" Even as she said the words, fatigue washed over her.

"Not at all."

Kevin quickly ordered a cot brought in and grabbed his stuff to take to another desk.

"You don't have to leave." Alexis hated to move into his space, if it meant moving him out.

"Honey, I have to talk with Arnie anyway. I need to find out everything I can before I meet with John in the morning." He walked over and tugged her gently into his warm embrace. "Lie down and sleep. This could be an all-nighter. We might need your special skills. Rest while you can."

She sent him a look of disbelief that made him laugh. "Like I can help."

"I mean it."

Even as he spoke, the door opened to admit two men carrying a small folding cot.

After the men left, she moved over to the makeshift bed and stretched out on it. There were no blankets or pillows, but she didn't care.

"I'll rustle up a blanket or two for you. Go ahead and get some rest." He left the room.

Alexis did the exercises Stefan had taught her, though she was tempted to just fall asleep. It felt so damn good to shut off her mind. To know that, for now, she could leave everything in Kevin's capable hands.

Within minutes, she'd fallen asleep.

CHAPTER 23

A LEXIS SLEPT SOUNDLY. She didn't wake up until the light crept through the blinds on the windows. Had she closed those? She couldn't remember. Another few minutes went by. She didn't want to get up, but Kevin had to be around somewhere.

"Good morning, sleepyhead. How are you feeling now?"

Kevin sat quietly at his desk. From the look of him, he'd been there all night.

"Did you get any rest last night?" Alexis rubbed her eyes, noticing she now had a blanket and a pillow. Interesting. A shower would be wonderful, … but coffee would be better.

"I caught a few minutes of shut-eye in my chair somewhere between three and four. Not enough, but it will have to do for now."

Alexis shook her head. He couldn't function efficiently this way.

"Don't say it. I already know. But there have been a lot of surprises overnight, and things are starting to move very quickly."

Startled, she could only look at him. "Coffee," she pleaded in a croaking voice. "First coffee, then information."

After several slugs of dark-and-deadly harsh cop coffee, she smiled. The caffeine hadn't had a chance to hit her bloodstream, but just knowing it was on the way made her mental faculties cooperate enough to ask, "Now, what did you find out?"

"Charles is the blackmailer." He waited for her reaction.

"What? That slimy-toad-of-a-birthday-boy blackmailed Arnie?" She couldn't get her mind wrapped around the idea. "It's not that I don't believe you. It's just hard to imagine. Does he really have the brains to pull off something like this?"

Kevin watched her, a big smirk on his face. "I thought you'd say something along those lines. You really didn't like him, did you?"

Alexis looked at him and shuddered. "What's to like?"

"Most ladies don't have a problem with him."

She thought about it. "I'm not so sure about that. He mentioned something when I walked with him. He made it sound like the house, the money, and the prestige all belonged to him, and, if I was nice to him, he might share."

Alexis became the target of Kevin's narrowed-eyed glare. "He said *what?*"

From the overriding disbelief in his voice, she couldn't tell if she should feel insulted or complimented. "He said something else that was odd. Something about no other family that counts." She looked at Kevin.

"His uncle is in a long-term care facility on life support. John keeps paying the bills because he can't stand the thought of letting his brother die." Kevin looked down at the stack of papers on his desk. "Although, from what he's said lately, he's getting ready to sign the papers to pull the plug. Something about it being time to let his brother go."

"How sad. But like I said, Charles is a toad." Imagine feeling that way about a family member? "Would Charles get any money then?" Alexis visibly shuddered at the next thought. "If he is the blackmailer, does it change the direction of your meeting with John this morning?"

He looked startled.

"Sorry." She blushed. "I didn't try to listen in on your phone conversations, but I *was* here in the office."

"I'd forgotten. There's a good chance Charles has been leaving the threatening notes for his own father."

She sat back and stared at Kevin. "Does he hate his father so much?" Alexis couldn't imagine a family willingly doing such damage to each other.

"That's something I need to discuss with John this morning." At her look of interest, he quickly interjected, "In private."

That was only fair, even if she didn't like it.

He grinned.

She shrugged dismissively. What could she say? "What's happening with Arnie now?"

That wiped the smile off Kevin's face. "He's in with the captain now. They're questioning his every move since he started here. His future is up in the air."

"That will be tough on him." Alexis stood stalwart in her defense of the young man. She knew he deserved another chance. But would he get it?

"It's not up to us any longer, so let's concentrate on what we can do something about." He stood with a large stack of papers in his hand. "John should be here any minute."

She glanced at the watch on Kevin's wrist. "Is there a computer that I could use for a few minutes before I go to work?"

A few minutes later, she looked up in time to see John being ushered into Kevin's office. The door shut firmly behind the two of them.

Damn, she wished she were in there.

"GOOD MORNING, JOHN." Kevin motioned his visitor to take the chair across from the desk. He couldn't help but look at his friend differently now.

"I presume you have something for me, as you called this early morning meeting?" John replied, somewhat testily.

"I think so. That doesn't mean you will agree with me." Kevin hadn't looked forward to this meeting. But some skeletons had to be taken out of the closet for another look. "John, I'm sure you felt you had a good reason for withholding this information. But, since reading this old file, I wonder seriously if this information doesn't all tie in with the current blackmail mess." Kevin looked directly into John's bleached-white face.

"Old file?" John asked faintly. All of a sudden, all the pomposity sagged out of him, and he fell back against the chair. "What old file?"

"The old file on your deceased daughter. The accidental death that reads more like a manslaughter case." He watched the expressions flit across John's face, … shock, fear, horror, and pain. The whole gambit raced by. Some Kevin expected, yet some he hadn't, like fear. If John were innocent, he had no reason to be afraid. Kevin waited for John to speak.

"What does that file have to do with my blackmailer?" John's reedy voice slowly regained its former strength, obviously boosted by years of denial.

Kevin found it difficult to stare into those blank eyes. "Maybe everything," he suggested cautiously. "Someone wants you to confess something. Maybe they know about your past and suspect you to be the villain."

"I loved my daughter." He was calm, cold, and unequivocal in this statement of fact.

"Be that as it may, your tormentor may have a different spin on things." He shuffled through the various papers in the open file before him. This would be more difficult than he'd first anticipated.

Silence.

"John?"

The two men studied each other, the breach between them widening perceptibly. It was uncomfortable, this shift from friend to interrogator, but not entirely unexpected. It didn't make the rest of the meeting easier.

"I had another reason for asking you to come in. Someone else was being blackmailed in town."

John leaned forward. "Who?"

"I can't say." Kevin hesitated. "This other person has identified his extortionist as Charles."

For the second time, the color leached from John's face. "What? This can't be. He's a good boy."

Kevin let that one pass. "We bring him in for questioning today." Kevin checked John over, looking for any sign that these shocks had been too much. "Is there any chance Charles is also blackmailing you?"

John looked at him blindly, obviously having difficulty processing the information and what the question implied. Kevin had heard of people seeming to age upon receiving bad news, but he'd never seen it himself, until now. It was incredibly painful, for both the person in question and for the observer. Kevin stood and walked over to the window, remembering Alexis slipping over here for exactly the same reason. It hurt to see such human suffering.

"Could he hate me so much?"

The frailty of his voice made Kevin wince. He turned back to face him. "Would he blame you for his sister's death?"

John shrugged in defeat. "How do I know? The subject hasn't been brought up since we lost her. I tried to make it seem like it had never happened. Otherwise I couldn't stand it." The painful memories obviously overwhelmed the man, making it hard for him to speak. "Charles couldn't think that. I loved her—we both did."

"Was Charles close to her?"

John smiled. "Very. The difference in their ages added to that maybe. She was his special baby sister. They played together all the time, especially in the garden. They loved the flowers. He even had his own nickname for her. Charles went to pieces when she died. He'd already lost his uncle, four years earlier. ... It was a lot for him to deal with. I should have gotten more help for him," John said. "But then we were all a mess at the time. Charles seemed to straighten out after a while." John shuffled in his chair. "Then Sandra collapsed. My marriage almost didn't make it, for the second time, and I know I lost the close bond with Charles." He brushed a shaky hand over his hair. "But for Charles to do this to me?" His head shook sadly. "I just don't believe it."

"Maybe it wasn't him, but he had the access, the hidden knowledge, and the motive."

"What motive?" John turned to Kevin in surprise. "What possible motive could there be?"

"Any number of possibilities. He might want you to suffer for what he believes you did." Kevin waited a moment before plowing ruthlessly on. "There is no statute of limitations on murder."

That finished John. Kevin saw the walls of John's foundation crumble to the ground around him.

"I swear on my mother's Bible that I did not kill my little girl." Tears welled up and slowly rolled down his face. "I loved her. She was everything to me."

John appeared to be telling the truth, but Kevin didn't know what to believe. He'd seen too much in his career as a cop to be surprised by anything. Besides, what did he really know about John?

Kevin opened the file and studied the contents, while John composed himself.

There had been an investigation at the time of the child's death. Her death had been ruled accidental, and the case closed. Kevin checked a couple sheets, looking for the officer in charge at the time. This deserved a follow-up call.

"John, is there any chance, with the understanding that, *if* her death wasn't accidental, and you weren't responsible for your daughter's death, then ... could it have been Charles? Is he capable of something like this?"

John didn't look surprised at the question. In fact, he appeared resigned. "He changed when Glen had his accident. My brother didn't die, but he might as well have, as he's been nonresponsive ever since. Charles took that hard. So ... I don't know. For almost twenty years, I've wondered. I don't want to believe it. Mental illness runs in the family, and, at one point, Charles needed serious help. We thought he'd improved. Then he would just stop taking his meds. It was a roller coaster ride for all of us. We had to keep a close eye on him for many months, until the doctors could straighten him out again." John stared off into the distance sadly, as if looking down the long tunnel of his own past. "I don't know anymore. The boy I knew couldn't have done it, but then he wouldn't have blackmailed anyone either."

"We have an odd case open right now. Believe me when I say that I wouldn't be asking without good reason, but can you tell me what clothing your daughter was buried in?"

"Daisy? But she's buried in Redding, California." John stared at him in shock.

Kevin's heart hitched. He leaned forward to pin the hapless man in place. "Daisy? I thought her name was Marie Leanne?"

"Yes, yes, it was, but Charles nicknamed her Daisy when she was just an itty-bitty toddler. The name stuck. I think the dress she had on had her name on it."

"Which name?"

"Marie. She was buried in her favorite yellow sundress, with white stockings and black shoes. I had to help pick out the clothes. Sandra was inconsolable at the time. She hadn't been herself for a long time already, but that …"

Hearing confirmation that the body Alexis found was likely that of John's daughter, although necessary for the files, hurt. The next question would devastate John.

Keeping a sharp eye on John's face, Kevin continued, "There is a strong possibility that the body we found in the city gardens could be your daughter. We'll need DNA tests to confirm."

"What?" John lurched forward, before falling back into his chair. The color drained from his face. "That's not possible. I told you that she was buried in the family plot in California. We actually gave her Glen's burial plot because he was here."

"And now she's probably here." Kevin studied John's face. No way John could have faked this response. He hadn't known. The man was shocked and devastated.

"I can't believe it. No one even knew about her. Who could possibly have dragged her from her resting place to dump her alone in the city gardens?" He raised a trembling hand to his forehead. "I can't believe it. I just can't believe it."

"I need to ask for a DNA sample in order to confirm her identity as your daughter. She was found wearing the remnants of a yellow dress with the letter *M* embroidered on the collar."

John shuddered. "Yes, of course. Anything you need."

"We'll also need to talk to everyone in your family, particularly Charles." Kevin studied the older man. "We're picking him up now." He doubted that Charles had the wherewithal to be a killer. He wasn't the kind to get his hands dirty. Blackmail, yes. Murder, no. But then how well did anyone know Charles these days?

A grave robber? Who knew?

John nodded. He opened his mouth to speak, then hesitated. In an almost pleading voice, he said, "I would like to keep Sandra out of this. She's not been very well lately."

"Sorry, John. That's no longer possible."

ALEXIS HOPED KEVIN and the mayor wouldn't be much longer. Even as the thoughts whirled around in her head, the door opened, and John shuffled out. Dear God, what had happened in there? John looked like he'd aged fifty years. And Kevin?—Well, he looked like the cold detached detective she'd first met at the park.

Alexis waited until Kevin looked around for her, before getting up and walking over. "Are you okay?" she asked in concern.

"Yeah, I'm fine. This morning is shaping up to be hell. Are you sure you want to stay?"

"I called Scott. He's rescuing me from Rick's accounting office for the morning. We'll head to one of the parks."

"As long as you stay with him." Kevin then returned to his desk to collect some papers.

Alexis quietly withdrew. He needed space, and she needed freedom.

Ten minutes later, she stood inside the station entrance, waiting for Scott to pick her up. She hoped to be gone before the officers returned with Charles. The thought of seeing him made her skin crawl. Luckily she spotted Scott's vehicle and stepped outside.

Scott's cheery grin poked through the passenger window, as he pulled up beside her. "Hallo, beauty. Waiting for a ride, are ya? Well, git in."

Thank goodness for friends. Alexis hopped in. Within minutes, they were heading to his favorite coffee shop and then on to their gardens. "How was Moira when you left?"

"*Ach*, she was fine. Said she'd check in on your friend, as soon as she arrived at work."

"Good." Kevin had called the hospital that morning, but there was no change. Alexis couldn't help but wonder if more was going on there than anyone knew. Determinedly she shrugged off the negative thinking. Stefan would be fine. She refused to contemplate any other option.

For the next couple hours, Alexis and Scott lost themselves in the gardens. The place was deserted, and a nice light breeze combated the sultry heat. Alexis worked tirelessly, enjoying the return to a normal day.

Scott's phone rang. He checked the number and handed it over to her.

"I've been trying to reach you but only get your voicemail," Kevin said. Alexis detected a fine tremor of tension threading through his voice. At his words, she dug into her pocket and pulled out her phone. Shit. She'd accidentally shut it off. Probably while it was in her pocket. "Sorry. My phone was turned off. What's going on? Did Charles come in for questioning?"

"Hell, yes. He's definitely the blackmailer, but he's adamant about his father's guilt over his sister's death. This will get pretty ugly."

"Could he have had anything to do with Daisy's death?" Alexis waited for Kevin's answer, uncertain about the odd energy she sensed surrounding him.

"Not likely. He'd have been pretty young. We've confirmed Charles' whereabouts at the most crucial times in regard to the kidnapped girl found in the van and to Mandy's murder. But we have more to look into."

Alexis winced. She wouldn't want that job. At the prolonged silence on the other end, she felt the bottom of her stomach drop. She asked, "Do you think, intuitively, that Charles is the murderer?"

"I don't know." Kevin spoke slowly and thoughtfully. "I can't read him. I get a black wall that seems impenetrable."

Alexis had just about rung off, when a thought occurred. "Kevin, I need to ask. What was Daisy's real name?" In the background, she heard papers being moved, as if he were searching.

"It's here somewhere." Another pause came, then he read quickly, "Marie Leanne Prescott."

"Marie. Interesting."

"But also quite common," Kevin pointed out. "I have to go."

"Wait. I know this isn't a question you want to hear, but I wondered if it is possible to contact Mandy?" She bit her lip, wondering if she'd gone too far.

Kevin spoke with great difficulty. "As far as we know, a person who has recently crossed over can't communicate right away. A period of adjustment is required."

That made sense, sort of. "Could Lissa communicate with her?"

"There's a slim possibility, but apparently they can't direct their focus over there, like we do here."

Alexis didn't know what else to say. They were playing a waiting game. Only it was a game in which one person seemed to make up all the rules.

CHARLES WALKED OUT of the police station, smiling, Daddy's pet lawyer at his side. He'd given his statement. His father had, of course, refused to press blackmail charges in order to keep his only child out of jail and out of the news. Charles had also freely admitted to pressuring Arnie to give up any information to help convict his father. Of course the district attorney said they'd be filing charges for blackmailing a police officer. Charles would let the lawyers battle that out.

The police were idiots. What would it take for them to focus on his father? His dad didn't deserve to live after what he'd done to Daisy. It had taken a long time, but Charles believed punishment day had finally come.

His mom wouldn't understand. She didn't seem to be all there, even with the latest round of drugs—something else he could blame his father for. Rather than outright murdering her, his father had chosen to kill her slowly with medications.

At his car, Charles opened the front door and sat inside for a moment, before starting the engine. Even as he smiled grimly in the rearview mirror, a shadow crossed his face.

He frowned. That shadow had been there for as long as he could remember. He didn't know when he had first noticed it. Not that it mattered. The shadow wasn't separate and apart. It was part of him.

Maybe it was the weight of finding justice for his beloved sister all these years. Or maybe it was just another of his many drugs kicking in. Whatever. He didn't mind the shadow showing.

Shadows had dominated his life for the last decade on the inside. Longer even. Why not let everyone else see them too?

Enough hiding had been going on.

It was time for the truth.

CHAPTER 24

I T WAS LATE. Almost everyone would be asleep, lost to dreamland at this hour. Until evil slid in their back door.

Evil didn't rip through, announcing its presence. It slithered in. He should know—he'd perfected the process.

He circled the outside of the house first, keeping to the shadows. Then he approached the back door.

But he was particularly careful now. This was a cop's house, after all. For a cop, his alarm system left much to be desired. Still, a crappy system made his job easier. Faster.

Moving stealthily, the intruder slid through the main floor, taking note of everything he'd need to finish this scenario. Like many plans hatched out of revenge, this one had taken on a life of its own. This meddling trio had shown more talent for causing trouble than he'd thought possible. Good thing they didn't know everything.

And he intended to keep it that way.

ALEXIS HAD BEEN fully prepared to spend another night at the station, but Kevin had been adamant. He'd already worked through one night—he couldn't go for a second. As soon as he'd been able to, he hauled her out for a quick dinner, and then they'd headed home for an early night.

This time he hadn't even shown her to the spare bedroom. He'd excused himself, gone for a shower, and had tumbled exhausted onto his own bed. She'd taken the initiative and climbed in beside him, following him into a deep slumber.

Until something woke her up. Something wrong.

A cold, clammy sweat covered her slim body. She looked over at the other side of the bed. She was alone.

"*Shh*, Alexis. I'm right here." His voice was pitched low and urgent.

Kevin stood next to the closed bedroom door, his bare chest gleaming in the pale moonlight, every muscle tensed against an unseen foe. He'd pulled on jeans and held his handgun at his side.

She slid out from the crumpled blankets, pulling on underwear, pants, and a T-shirt, tugging that down for some measure of warmth against the massive chill shaking her body. "What is it?" she whispered.

"Use your other senses," Kevin whispered back.

The minute she understood what he meant, she felt *him*.

The bastard was close by.

"He's here," she said. Kevin already knew, she realized. She opened her mind yet another sliver. She could almost feel the evil clawing at her throat. She swallowed convulsively. He was so strong.

A soft *thud* from downstairs had Alexis staring fearfully at an equally grim Kevin. Their intruder had entered the kitchen.

"*Shh*. Stay calm." Keeping Alexis an arm's length behind him, he opened the bedroom door to creep into the hallway. Alexis stayed close. She had no intention of being left behind.

Cautiously they moved down the stairs. Alexis feared her ragged breathing could be heard from the next room. Another step caught a creaking stair. The loud sound pierced the silence, freezing them in place.

Alexis could sense the evil blackness swirling in place below her. Seconds later, she heard the slam of the back door and the fainter echoing sounds of running footsteps.

Kevin jumped the last few risers and raced out into the night after him.

Alexis made her way to the couch and collapsed.

Never before had she felt such malevolence. She needed to put a face to it. In her heart, she knew Kevin wouldn't catch him, although he'd give it his all. She glanced at the clock; it was almost three in the morning. She closed her eyes, resting against the back of the couch.

Then that she felt it.

Stefan's signature.

She couldn't explain it. It seemed like he'd popped in and quickly left again, leaving a straggling trail. Though he was recovering, he'd tried to come to their assistance. But he hadn't quite succeeded—for reasons she didn't want to contemplate.

The impulse to call the hospital couldn't be ignored.

Several times the phone rang, before someone with a harried voice answered.

"Hello, is Moira there?" Alexis asked.

"No. Can I help you?"

"I'm wondering how Stefan Kronos in room 207 is doing? I know it's an odd thing to call at this hour, but I woke up with him on my mind."

"His vitals were checked not quite an hour ago. There's still no change."

"Oh, uh, thank you." Alexis quickly hung up the phone. She didn't know if that was good news or bad.

"Who did you call?" Kevin walked through from the kitchen, breathing heavily from the exertion of the chase.

"The hospital." She looked around the room with her inner senses. The faint energy had dissipated. "I couldn't shake the idea that Stefan had been here or had tried to come." She shrugged in exasperation. "So I called the hospital. The nurse said there'd been no change."

Kevin closed his eyes and reached out mentally. Alexis watched, knowing exactly what he was doing. In this skill, he was more advanced than she was.

"And?" she asked with raised eyebrows. "Could you feel him?"

"Yes," he answered quietly. "And no." She raised an eyebrow.

He explained further. "I found a mirror image of his energy, but not his energy, as if it's only part of him." Kevin grimaced. "That's the only explanation I can think of for his energy pattern at this time."

"Didn't he say that to split his energy up like that would make each strand weaker than if he'd stayed whole? And he's so weak as it is …" God, just listen to her. Sometimes this whole business was just too bizarre.

"Theoretically, yes." Kevin gazed in the direction of the moonbeams, as they landed on the couch where Alexis sat. "Stefan seems to think that this is not only possible but necessary in some difficult cases, especially where we have to keep track of many problems at once. But it's taken a lot for him to develop the necessary skills."

Alexis heaved a sigh. "I can't even keep track of one thread." She studied Kevin. Damn, he looked good. An effervescent glow surrounded him. Instead of angering him, the nocturnal visitor had energized him. It made no sense. An intruder coming into his house should have pissed him off—only he looked grimly satisfied at this turn of events.

"Do you know how he got in?" Odd that she felt so calm. The sense of evil had passed, leaving no lingering fear it would return. Instead, a sense of peace surrounded them. Definitely odd. "Why am I not more disturbed? Shouldn't I be scared, terrified even?" Her reaction bothered her a lot.

Kevin smiled down at her.

"What?"

"Look around you." His relaxed manner seemed almost amused. What did she not know?

"What?" Confused, she looked around carefully.

"Look again. This time, look with your inner eye." Now there was no mistaking his humor.

Immediately the colorful energy slid into her view—warm, protective, comforting, *safe* energy. Every window had been outlined in this protective alarm. All possible entrances had received the same treatment, with one exception—the rear kitchen door.

"You did that on purpose." She turned to him in stunned understanding. "You left him an open door." Alexis couldn't believe what her mind slowly realized. "You expected him. Not only that ..." She eyed the growing smile on his face. "You were waiting for him to show up!" By the end of her statement, she was almost shouting.

"*Shhh.*" Kevin ran his hands soothingly up and down her bare arms, as if trying to calm her.

She didn't feel like being appeased. Instead, she snapped to her feet and paced around the room. Kevin took her place on the couch.

"How dare you set this up and not tell me!" she snapped, as she stormed around. "Why couldn't you have told me?" He opened his mouth to answer her, but she spoke right over his attempt. "I don't get it. If you were expecting him, why weren't you waiting for him?" She spun around and stalked back to stand by the window, hands on her hips. She was royally pissed off.

Kevin once again opened his mouth to speak, only to shake his head, his face lighting with laughter as she walked right over to him. "You had the perfect opportunity, and you slipped up. I just don't get it." Alexis collapsed on the couch beside him and suspiciously glared at his grinning face. "What are you grinning at?"

"You. You're priceless. You won't even give me a chance to speak." He reached over and pulled her onto his lap. "Now listen." His large hand slipped around to coax her head against his chest. Gently he caressed her hair. "Let's see if I can explain. First off, you were never in any danger."

He ignored the half-buried snort of disgust and continued, "Our bedrooms had a similar alarm. So he couldn't have snuck anywhere without waking us. Next, if I could have caught him tonight, I would have. I did try," he reminded her. "But that isn't the reason why I left the kitchen door accessible. Obviously it gave him a way in. 'But into what?' you may well ask." He waggled his eyebrows in a hilarious Groucho Marx imitation, startling a surprised giggle from her. He explained further. "Into a video camera, which, with any luck, took his picture."

God, she must be tired because it took her a minute to realize what he said.

"Oh my God! You set *him* up! Oh my God." Alexis couldn't contain herself. She bounced up and tugged him into the kitchen.

Kevin went to work immediately. Standing on a chair, he attempted to retrieve the camera. Alexis waited anxiously, feeling positively wired.

"Can we check it now?" Alexis hopped from one foot to the next in excitement.

"No." The camera proved to be difficult to extract, tucked away as it was, inside the glass panel at the top of the cupboard. It took several intricate maneuvers to release it from its hidey-hole. Once safely down, Kevin looked from the camera to Alexis. "How do you feel about spending the rest of the night at the station?"

"Let's go."

A little later, Alexis looked seriously at Kevin, as they whipped through the deserted streets. "Will I ever have a normal life again?"

Kevin smiled at her. "Nope, never."

Minutes later, they walked into the quiet precinct office. Several officers looked up in surprise. A couple made light comments. Alexis tolerated their well-meaning teasing—apparently it went along with the job. Besides, the group seemed to be a fun-loving bunch. If this kind of teasing helped relieve the depression and the tension that plagued their jobs, so be it.

Once inside his office, Kevin turned on his computer and downloaded the images, while Alexis watched. He fast-forwarded to the time frame they wanted.

Alexis waited breathlessly.

Kevin slowed the film down to when they should have arrived home. It would get interesting fast. They'd gone to bed soon afterward.

There.

Someone was coming in the back door. Not much light shone in the room, and that made it hard to see anything but shadows.

"Got him!"

Alexis couldn't see what though. Impatiently she waited and watched as Kevin cut and cropped, lightened, then darkened the background, as he brought the figure forward. Once again he cropped and enlarged just the head this time.

"Oh my God. It's Charles!"

Or was it? she thought with a frown.

She'd have trouble recognizing this Charles in daylight, as well as in the darkness of night. He was positively horrifying. His features seemed distorted by dark grooves and hollows.

Alexis sat back in shock.

Kevin stayed equally quiet beside her.

Still staring at the picture, she nudged his shoulder. "What's wrong with this picture?"

"Everything and nothing. It's Charles, but not the one I know. It's like his evil twin."

"Or is it just a side he doesn't show in public? Does he have a split personality?" Both were possible. Medical science dealt with these questions all the time, … although their answers were still inconclusive. "It would explain a lot."

"True, but I'm not sure if that's what's going on."

Alexis sat down beside him, focusing on him and his words, instead of the disturbing picture in front of him. "What are you talking about?"

"Look here." He pointed his finger to the cloudy haze around the image's head. "This is odd." He leaned closer, using the mouse to point it out on the screen. "A weird outline is surrounding his head."

"Couldn't that just be an effect from all the cropping and enlargements though?" Alexis studied the haze uneasily. She hoped it was. Anything else would be bad.

"No, I don't think so." Kevin studied it intently, before adding, "But I'll have to check with our specialists."

"What difference does a cloudy area make?"

Kevin stood as he answered, "All the difference in the world." With the disk in hand, he walked out of his office, leaving Alexis behind to wonder what had just happened.

ALEXIS SAT ACROSS from the three policemen, ready to scream. They were having such a good time teasing her. Unfortunately they hadn't brought her enough coffee yet, so she wasn't handling it well. In truth, she wasn't handling it at all. She'd woken up from her nap sore, stiff, grumpy, craving caffeine—and alone.

Only she wasn't alone any longer. Kevin had left strict orders that the remaining men were to keep an eye on her.

Damn, she wanted to hiss and spit.

It didn't help that they'd filled her in on what had transpired while she slept. Kevin, accompanied by several officers, had gone to pick up Charles for a second time. Only he was nowhere to be found. A specialist had taken a look at the security file from Kevin's kitchen and had said that the weird lighting had nothing to do with the film or what Kevin had done to it.

"Drink up! Kevin said you need at least *three* cups, before you're safe to talk to."

Alexis glared at the speaker but took another healthy slug. "Any new word on Charles?"

"Nothing new. They're still looking."

Alexis nodded. "Do I get to go to the ladies' room without you guys?" At their comical faces, she reminded them drily, "And I will be sure to let Kevin know if I'm not."

"Sure, you can go on your own," said the officer sitting on her left.

One grinned at her from the right. "After all, how dangerous can that be?"

"This *is* the police station," joked the one on her left.

Alexis finished off her coffee, reached for her purse, and excused herself. The bathroom was a definite necessity now. She looked for a clock to tell her the time but couldn't see one on her way. It felt like five in the morning. Her eyes still had grit caked in the corners.

She pushed open the door to the ladies' room and walked through to the large mirrors. Those were definitely bags under her eyes, a sure sign of stress and lack of sleep. She needed this chaos to end before it was the end of her. She yawned. Damn, she was tired.

Then she remembered. Stefan's instructions to safeguard her energy before falling asleep! Had that made her vulnerable again? Dear God, she'd forgotten to follow them last night. She'd collapsed on the cot again in Kevin's office and had closed her eyes.

Unease settled deep in her bones.

She hurriedly used the toilet, washed up as well as she could, and then brushed her hair. Another hit of coffee would go down nicely now. Then she might just survive the day after all. Humor softened her face. Maybe two cups of coffee would make her sociable today and not three, like they'd been warned. Just this once. It wouldn't do to spoil the guys too much.

Alexis headed back into the deserted hallway.

She hadn't taken two steps, when blinding pain ripped through her skull, and she collapsed to the floor.

CHAPTER 25

K EVIN STALKED INTO his office, pissed. He regretted that Charles, the damned weasel, had been allowed to walk out of the station after the last time they'd questioned him. But that was lawyers for you. So far, Charles had yet to be located again. Had he run? If so, why? No way he could have known about the camera. Kevin had set it up himself.

He eyed the empty cot. At least it looked like Alexis had gotten some sleep. He sure as hell hadn't. Long ago he'd become used to working through the night when on a case. He'd tried to close his eyes last night for a few hours, with limited success.

One of the guys walked in behind him. "She's just gone to the washroom. Give her a couple minutes. You don't want to disturb her. She hasn't had her three cups of coffee yet." Kevin glared at Peter, a fellow officer he'd worked with for years. Peter placed a full cup of the same hot heady brew in front of Kevin. "You two have so much in common."

He didn't deserve an answer.

Kevin wrestled with his temper, catching up on what he had missed, finally managing a reluctant smile. "What the hell is she doing in there? I've been back for ten minutes already."

"Don't know." The other man shrugged.

"Who does?" Kevin got up and strode impatiently down the hallway to the washrooms. Using the men's room first, he returned to knock on the women's door. No one answered.

Belatedly his neck itched.

Shit!

Guilt screamed through his fatigued brain. He should have picked up on the sense something was wrong earlier. He had to find Alexis.

"Did you find her?" called a voice behind him.

Kevin turned to find several concerned fellow officers crowding around.

"No, she's gone."

The entire station ripped into action. It took mere seconds of frantic organization to search the building. When that produced no sign of her, everyone went into overdrive. All officers on duty and a few who weren't joined in. Alarms went out to mobile units, and alerts went out to all surrounding counties.

Alexis was nowhere.

ALEXIS STRUGGLED AGAINST the wave of nausea and pain. She knew she had to fight. It was important. Only she couldn't remember why. For long moments, she worked desperately to reach this seemingly impossible goal. To fight what held her in the fog. The effort burned up her frail energy reserves. Yet the deeply buried instinct to survive couldn't be ignored. She struggled onward, upward, searching for an anchor to pin her energy on. She couldn't see anything, ... as if in a vacuum with no senses of any kind—except pain.

She slumped against the cold hard surface, as her urge to fight waned. The goal of wakefulness that had seemed so attainable a few minutes ago now became impossible. With walls of excruciating darkness pressing down on her, she collapsed into the pit of unconsciousness, only too happy to forget what it was she'd been trying so hard to achieve and why.

UNCONSCIOUS, ALEXIS NEVER roused when the vehicle she was in finally came to a rolling stop.

Good. Charles smiled.

Not that anyone would care. No one cared about anyone or anything other than themselves. At least not for long. People deluded themselves into thinking others cared about them. That lasted for a month or two or maybe even a year or two, ... but that's all it was, a facade that everyone saw through eventually.

He preferred to live out of the limelight, unlike his father. God, he hated that man.

It had been too easy to snatch Alexis. After running out of the cop's house last night, he'd parked around the corner and followed the two of them back to the station. At that hour of the night, the place was close to empty. He'd waited until dawn broke. Going in the back entrance in coveralls, as if he were part of the cleaning crew, had been a no-brainer. Besides, the guy he'd replaced wouldn't be telling on him ... or anyone again.

Making himself wait until the opportune moment to grab her? ... Now that had been hard.

He didn't bother checking up on her in the back seat. Either she'd survive or she wouldn't. It was too late to worry and way too late to care.

Charles drove carefully, not wanting to attract attention. Damn, there was that headache again. He never felt like himself when this happened. He grimaced and reached for the bottle of pills in his pocket. The fucking things didn't work anymore. Why were the headaches so bad these days? Sometimes it scared the hell out of him. He didn't care about dying, but he sure as hell wasn't into suffering through cancer or something equally nasty.

He rubbed his forehead, as the pounding tempo increased. Shitty pills. When would they kick in? He peered outside. The house looked the same. It always did. After all, it was the perfect house for the perfect couple—to hell with the fucked-up son.

Charles chuckled, the sound closer to a cackle. He parked near the garage's side door and entered. The garage was dark but spotless. When had it been anything but? He opened up the back seat, tugging the blanket off his captive.

Still unconscious, Alexis had curled up in a fetal position, her arms tucked in close to her sides. He laid his hand on her neck, checking her pulse. Slow, deep, and steady. One surreptitious glance around, then he tugged her up and over his shoulder. He grunted as he took the full brunt of her weight. Damn good thing she wasn't any bigger.

On the way to the huge storage closet, he grinned savagely, kicking the work table that held spotless tools. The clatter screamed through the cavernous room. Instead of making him happy, he winced as the beat in his temple increased.

None too gently, he lowered Alexis to the cement floor of the closet, the spotlessly clean cement.

God, everything pissed him off today. The freedom to finally act out his plans brought out the submerged feelings he'd spent half a lifetime hiding—even from himself.

Alexis laid crumpled and still on the cold floor. He couldn't waste any time or emotion on her. He had nothing left to give anyone. For years, he'd been a shell on automatic pilot, waiting for someone to throw a switch. Finally someone had.

Arnie.

Quickly Charles finished setting things in order. His final act was to close and to lock the closet door.

Nonchalantly he walked through into the main part of the house. "Hello! Is anyone home?"

The house appeared silent. He knew better. She'd be here, hiding in her bottle. He walked through to the solarium. There she sat, just as he'd expected, all dressed up for company. Company that would never come. She was the epitome of the perfect lady, except for the heavy lacing of Glenfiddich whisky in her coffee, her favorite choice of wake-up drinks.

He'd been close to her—once. He didn't know whether the drugs had sent her off or the booze, but she wasn't often the mother he remembered.

"Good morning, Mother. How are you this morning?"

A faint tremor washed through the older woman. Visibly regaining control, she couldn't quite hide the shudder of revulsion in her eyes as she looked at him.

He smiled nastily. "What's the matter, Mom?" He stressed the title, knowing how much she hated it. "Are you not having a good morning?"

"It's fine." She refused to add more, choosing instead to take a hefty fortifying drink from her cup.

Sitting there, she looked almost perfect. Not a hair out of place. Appearances for her were everything. He almost felt sorry for her—her world was about to bust apart.

On the heels of that thought, his headache lashed out, catching him above the temple. He winced, as agony speared through him.

"I told you to get those headaches checked," she lectured in her patronizing voice.

God, he hated that tone. "And I told you that I'm fine. I won't see any more damn doctors."

"Well, maybe your medication needs to be changed. You are taking it, aren't you?" she asked fearfully. "Remember what happened the last time you forgot?"

Irritated, Charles sat down across from his mother. She flinched. "And, if I don't, what the hell could you do about it? You're nothing but a useless washed-out alcoholic whore."

Pain mixed with faint tendrils of fear filled her gaze. "Are you taking your medication?" she demanded sharply. "Are you?" At his sneering look, she reiterated, "Charles, you have to take it. Do you hear me? Bad things happen when you don't. You're not yourself without them."

Her voice mocked deep into his weak soul. "Don't you mention that again, you bitch." He shoved away from the table, standing threateningly over her. "This time, I've made sure it will be *him* who gets locked up. Not me!"

Sandra's face bleached white. "Dear God, what have you done?" Frail hands clutched her antique gold necklace.

"You'll find out." He gave her a salute of mock respect and turned his back on her, then walked out. "When it's too damn late to change it."

He left.

SANDRA'S HEART POUNDED, as terror, never far from the surface in recent years, slammed into her head.

Dear God, what had her son done now? He was a good boy really. But there'd always been something a little ... off ... but only sometimes. She loved him so much but was so afraid something was terribly wrong.

She'd always wondered if Charles had had anything to do with her beloved Marie's death. They'd tried so hard to keep him stable. Like Sandra, Charles was ... delicate. Not always himself.

And, when he wasn't himself, ... she was terrified. Of what he'd do. Of what he'd done.

She gasped in pain. A decades-long torment rose once again to the surface. She had tried to stuff it back down. Down where her other fears lived. The constant bruises, the small accidents befalling her little girl. That horrible intuitive feeling a mother has ... that something, ... someone was hurting Marie.

And the fear of finding out who. Sandra had drowned those horrible fears in her whisky, hating the suspicion always inside, eating away at her family, poisoning everything around her.

It had been easier to forget it all. To block it out. To black it out.

She clutched her hand to her heart.

It had been so hard to survive all these years after losing her only daughter.

Too hard. But she'd tried. Tried to salvage her marriage, tried to be a mother to her son.

Now her frail, worn-out shell of a woman who'd seen too much, who had been dealt so many lethal blows, gasped and fought for air. The faint gasps finally gave out to a crushing, squeezing compression of her weak heart.

She couldn't think, as a gray fog filled her brain. Blue color slowly overtook the blank whiteness, as she fought for air and against the pain. Stumbling off her chair, she collapsed to the hardwood floor, struggling to reach the phone on the side buffet. She crawled partway, a bit more—was almost to the phone—when a voice reached out to her.

"Oh my God, ma'am. Wait. Hold on. I'm getting help."

The frantically struggling woman never heard the sounds of help arriving. Blackness choked her in an unending constricting torment, until she slipped into blessed unconsciousness.

KEVIN WAS BESIDE himself. He found no sign of Alexis on the physical or ethereal planes. Cruisers were out looking for both Alexis and Charles. With Stefan practicing his new technique, Kevin found it impossible to talk to him telepathically.

He desperately needed his friend's help.

Kevin strode through the double doors of the hospital entrance, heading for Stefan's room. Never in his life had he needed his friend like he did today. "Stefan?" He called out as he entered the peaceful room. "That's enough. I need you. You have to come back. Alexis is in danger or, … or worse," he said.

"I know," whispered Stefan, his voice faint. "What makes you think I can help more on this side than on the other?"

"I don't give a damn where you help, just so long as you do!" Kevin said forcefully, approaching the bed with quick steps. "I can't feel her. Something bad has happened."

"She's there."

"Where?" Relief sharpened Kevin's voice to steel. "You can feel her? Where is she?"

"She's unconscious, caught in the fog between here and there."

"Can you contact her?" Kevin wouldn't give up. "Find out where she is!"

"Take it easy. You aren't helping any."

Kevin forcibly pulled back. Stefan was right—going to pieces now wouldn't get her back. Stefan needed his assistance, not his distraction. "Fine. And, when you can, tell her to open the damn door to me," he said shortly. "What can I do to help?"

"Walk me through what you do know." Stefan's voice trembled with the physical effort. He stirred restlessly on the bed. "I'm not back to full strength yet."

"It's a damn good thing you did wake up, or I'd be tempted to crawl inside your head and force you back." He was only half joking and saw by Stefan's faint smile that he understood. Kevin relented. "Sorry, Stefan. I can't think because I'm worried."

"So quit wasting time and fill me in."

It took a few minutes to give him the scant details. Painful silence followed. Stefan said briskly, "All right then. I'll go look for her, as she did for me."

Kevin had to be content with that.

STEFAN, USING THE closely developed bond with Alexis, finally picked up her faint trail. It wove through dark fog and gloom, as a glowing silvery thread. From his perspective, he could tell she had no idea where she was. There were no visuals.

Odd. If anyone else were involved, Stefan found no indication, no imprint. He pondered this as he zeroed in on her. Minutes later, he felt her warm, comforting spirit. But he couldn't see or hear her.

Using methods he'd fine-tuned over the years, he slipped into her mind.

It was empty.

Shards of icy terror slammed through his consciousness. What the hell was going on? Slowly he pivoted in the brilliant crystal cave of her consciousness. Nothing to see but ice. Sounds were muted, deadened by the vast denseness of the frozen wasteland. Eerie echoes bounced in his head. Fear for Alexis clouded his mind, and he struggled for control. She was in incredible danger. He had to help her. But first, he had to find her in this bizarre space of her mind.

Expectant numbing silence prevailed, a waiting stillness, ... for something or someone. Stefan pivoted in disbelief. Dead in front of him stood a specter. He thought he was past being shocked by anything. He still didn't understand how this could be possible. *Who are you?*

Your nemesis.

Yeah, right. Stefan almost thanked the bastard, as his comment returned a sense of realism. This asshole was, and always had been, just one clever son of a bitch. But Stefan wasn't fighting for himself. He was fighting for Alexis and for all those earlier victims. His thoughts, easily heard, echoed through the cavern of Alexis's mind.

Why worry about them? What are they to you? The specter opened his arms wide.

Pardon? Who could not care? Stefan didn't get it.

I used to believe in people, a long time ago. Now I use people just as they used me.

Depths of unrelenting bitterness stretched out toward Stefan. He saw fragments of a huge unresolved history swelling up. Cautiously he asked, *So you blame someone for your rotten life, and now hold all of humanity responsible?*

Don't psychoanalyze me. I know what I'm doing and why. The why is easy—because I can. And because they deserve it. John deserves it.

Macabre laughter echoed hollowly in the odd chamber. Alexis's mind! God, how could he forget! He glanced around. Bizarre stalagmites stretched forever upward around him. He felt as if he stood in the deep ice caves of Norway.

Don't bother.

Stefan pivoted back to full attention. *Don't bother what?*

Don't bother looking for her. She's frozen in her own world. A little parlor trick I've perfected. What passed for a face grinned evilly.

Stefan's stomach revolted. *Frozen?* What the hell did that mean? *Is she dead?*

Hell, no. But now I can do what I want. Use her as I wish and let her go. Of course she'll probably die then. They usually do. He shrugged dismissively. *That's not my concern.*

How did you learn to do all this? Stefan waved futilely around his bizarre surroundings. *It's incredible.*

Thank you.

The specter actually preened—talk about an ego.

I tripped into this accidentally, but, once I realized I could have a life, and a secret life that most of the real world would never know about, I was hooked. Such power. Such control.

He laughed again, making Stefan wince at its mocking resonance.

You still don't understand, do you? I'm whole here in spirit, but in the physical world, my body is useless. Useless! he shrieked. *Do you know who's fucking responsible? For me being hooked up for life? Existing in a world with no control? A victim to his every whim? My goddamned asshole of a brother, that's who.*

Stefan's mind rapidly filled in the pieces of what he knew. Dear God, this had to be Glen, the comatose brother of John Prescott, Mayor of Bradford—in Alexis's mind.

The madman's face twisted. *Now you're starting to understand. Can you comprehend the extent of my relief when I realized I could be free from that rotting vegetable in the hospital bed? My brother must have loved sitting there, drinking my favorite whisky, watching spit slide from my lips, knowing I was locked in a prison of his making. Did I tell you that he caused my accident in the first place? He rammed my car and ran me off the road.*

Angry sparks flew in all directions with his rage. *Asshole. My fucking brother couldn't go out and make his own way in the world. No. He had to take what was mine, so he tried to kill me. And fucked that up too. While I'm here in a coma, he took my house, my cars, even my business. Would he let me go then? Would he let the doctors pull the plug and release me? No!*

Stefan fought for control as the poisonous tirade lashed out at him. The pain, the anguish of betrayal without physical control, had become a hurricane of human emotions. Stefan struggled to avoid the maelstrom. He needed clarity to find the advantage hidden in this man's loss of control.

I've had decades to watch, to learn, and especially to control other people.

The energy force turned violently black and purple with his feelings.

Do you really think John's wimpy useless son, Charles, is responsible for any of this? He's so weak he has no idea what he's done versus what I've done through him.

More laughter came, calmer this time and all the more eerie when matched with his words.

He was a perfect tool. Easy to manipulate. Easy to make him hate his father. John deserved to lose everything, … like he arranged for me to lose everything.

Stefan was staggered. How much damage had this embittered soul done? The scope of this diseased mind was too horrific to contemplate.

You'll never know all that I've done. No one will.

WITH GREAT DIFFICULTY, Kevin stayed quiet, as he hovered in the background of Stefan's mind. The truths were too many, delivering more shocks than he could absorb all at once. It was totally incomprehensible. They'd come up against some devious and twisted minds before, but he'd never known someone could physically live confined in a deep coma for decades, yet live freely on the ethereal plane and take over, at will, the physical bodies of others who were weaker.

He hadn't exactly asked Stefan's permission when he'd hitched a ride on Stefan's energy trip. He hoped Stefan would understand. When Kevin hadn't been booted out immediately, he'd assumed all was well, and he'd stayed quiet. This was too crazy. How could they help Alexis now?

The asshole continued to speak.

You see, if you and the nosey cop hadn't butted into my business, then this game could have gone on for another decade or two. But knowing how weak Charles is, I started putting a contingency plan in place, just in case I lose my host.

Host? Stefan asked.

Stefan's surprise matched Kevin's horror. Dear God, is that all these people were to him?

Yeah. You know that I use their bodies to achieve what I want to achieve. If I'm forced to be here in this world, then I'll damn well live it the way I want to.

His demeanor was that of someone casually discussing a piece of paper that, once used, had no value and was discarded like garbage.

Only these people weren't litter.

Finally Stefan asked the question burning inside of Kevin. *Why Alexis?*

That did it.

The blackness deepened to billows of hollow smoke, as Glen struggled to hold his dark image together. *That bitch!* The edges blurred, shifted, and then reformed again. He paused before continuing in a slightly calmer voice. *She's the only one who seemed to find out about the real me. My history. My actions. My motivations. She could actually talk with some of the children. She could sense when I was around. I'd never experienced anything like it before.* He snickered at Stefan. *You could have, if you'd looked, but you're so locked down that I operated under your nose for years, and you never knew.* He positively beamed as he considered his own craftiness.

Kevin felt like vomiting. He swallowed heavily, forcing the bile back down.

Stefan asked cautiously, *Have you been doing this for long?*

Glen laughed. *God, I snatched little children when I was in my twenties and thirties, when I was healthy and whole. I used to keep them for a while before I killed them.*

Stefan hated the thought of a serial killer getting away with these crimes for so long. Kevin's thoughts mirrored the same disgust.

You couldn't have killed very many then, Stefan prodded. *Not if you were never caught.*

Bullshit. I won't give anything away, but you can bet there were over a dozen back then, until my asshole big brother stepped in and decided to steal what was mine. Now that I've learned to live again, I think Charles will develop the traits of a pedophile.

Kevin shuddered.

Where is Alexis now? asked Stefan humbly, as if bowing gracefully to a talent bigger and stronger than his.

Kevin laughed humorlessly. *As if!*

The ripples of mirth slid through Stefan's mind, only to be quickly stomped on, in warning.

She's locked in a closet, the asshole explained comfortably.

Kevin almost lost it. A fucking closet! He barely heeded Stefan's silent warning to stay in control. He closed his eyes, forcing away the horrific image of Alexis's suffering. He had to remain strong, or he'd be of no help.

A closet, that's smart. Presumably she can't get out?

Stefan's friendly conversational tone surprised Kevin. While his stomach churned, and bloodlust blinded his vision, Kevin knew Stefan was calm, cool, and collected. Kevin had never admired him more. Was he still probing the ethers for Alexis's physical location?

Yeah, I left her in an incriminating place, at least for John. His statement seemed to amuse him to no end, as gales of laughter overwhelmed him.

That must have been difficult.

For you maybe, not for me. I've been using Charles and several others to do my dirty work for years. Glen shrugged dismissively. *They made it almost too easy.*

If everything is working for you, why take out John now? asked Stefan.

Maximum destructiveness. I want him to suffer. He's responsible for destroying my life. I'll destroy him. His useless wimp of a son should get the same. I've perfected my next step, which will allow me to enjoy their confusion and pain from the most advantageous place.

Gloating satisfaction oozed from the madman's energy, as his projection shone with pride. His mocking commentary almost drove Kevin to his knees. How many people out there were acting under this maniac's commands? Kevin would have to consider this carefully.

But don't you want them to pull the plug on your physical body, so you can finally find peace?

Stefan continued to talk calmly, almost reverently of the other man's exceptional talent. An ego-stroking that nauseated Kevin, even as he understood the need for it.

It no longer matters what they do to my body. Once my dear brother is taken care of, I will move on to my next host. From my new vantage point, I can do what I want. They probably will pull the plug on their own, if he's not there to continue paying my exorbitant medical bills. And he'll be gone soon. Everything's almost in place.

The words rolled over Kevin in mass confusion. Surely Glen couldn't continue to control these people without a physical presence?

Somehow this madman had found a way to make dead no longer mean totally *dead.*

The asshole was still talking, and Kevin had to forcibly refocus. Only Alexis mattered now.

I'm confident that I'll carry on my existence in the same manner. After all, I've had years to work out a solution to this problem. I don't need my body to be alive anymore. I can control more now than I ever could alive. Keen intelligence gleamed through the blackness. *In the beginning, it was a different story of course. But, with endless time for practice, I think I've perfected the transfer. I believe I can make it permanent. Through lifetimes even. Over and over.*

His seeping malevolence wavered, appeared to dissipate, before solidifying once again in front of them. Kevin watched and listened in horrified fascination, as the maniac continued his gloating.

And don't think I'm stupid enough to let you know where I'm going, or how I'm doing this. He smirked at his own superior knowledge. *You'd like to know though, wouldn't you? Too fucking bad.*

I don't understand what you could have done with Alexis. After all, it's her mind we're in now. Stefan kept awe and confusion in his voice.

Kevin waited, breathless.

Of course you don't because you're thinking from the human perspective, not the soul perspective. You have to work on that! he admonished. *Like they say on TV, you have to think outside the box.*

Sorry, it's difficult while grounded in physical life.

True.

The asshole seemed somewhat mollified by Stefan's admission of a lesser status and talent. Yeah, right.

Kevin waited and watched. At the same time, he tried to observe the frozen stalagmites forming the visual of Alexis's mind. He didn't understand—how could this be? Everything about this case could have come from a horror show. Were these surroundings hers or the asshole's? Not that it mattered, but Kevin had to locate her and to help her free herself.

He scanned the space he saw. There! Off on the far wall, back slightly out of view, stood something frozen in the ice. *Alexis.* Excited, Kevin started to tell Stefan, only to be cut off immediately.

I know. You need to get over to her but don't let this maniac know. Stefan's faint whisper came as an impression felt rather than clear words.

Go to her? How?

The ice is Alexis's vision, only she doesn't know it. Become one with it, and you'll become one with her.

Shit. He'd never tried anything like this. It didn't matter. He had to succeed. He had no other option. He didn't know about becoming one with the ice, but he could definitely relate to water. Could he warm the surface of the ice enough to melt it to a film of water?

It was easier than he'd thought. Almost instantaneously, he found himself slithering across the frozen surface, inside the slightly warmer film connecting him to the icy particles that made up the chamber of Alexis's mind. A small part of his brain watched the proceedings in awe. How was such a thing even possible?

He had no time for amazement or shock. That would surely follow, but, for now, he raced through the cold watery flow to help the woman he loved.

CHAPTER 26

ALEXIS FOUGHT THE rising tide of panic. None of this made any sense. Disjointed images flooded her subconscious, washing her in sounds and impressions that refused to fit together. She shuddered under the chaotic onslaught. Pain and confusion blinded her. Inundated on all sides, she fought for clarity.

When clarity finally came, amazement beset her. She existed simultaneously in two planes. Always before, she'd been focused in one energy field, blocking out any vivid awareness of the other. Not this time. That juxtaposition merging in itself seemed as horrifying as it was exhilarating. The panoramic vistas of both realities overwhelmed her with their sharpness.

This lucidity she didn't appreciate, once she realized she was a prisoner in both worlds.

In the physical plane, ropes strangled the circulation in both her ankles and her wrists, and a tight cloth gagged her mouth. Worse than that had to be the awkward position she'd been twisted into. It felt like she was the last item shoved into an already-full closet, before the door was slammed shut quickly to prevent her from falling out.

Right now, falling out would be a welcomed relief.

Tears welled up, as she tried to shift her body. Muscles screamed for relief but could only move scant inches in any direction. The gag pulled the skin on her cheeks, and worse were the few loose hairs caught in the tape over her gag that ripped her scalp with each tiny movement. Defeated, she collapsed to her original position.

She was going nowhere here.

Simultaneously she was transported to the other world. She drifted in and out of sleep and wakefulness. Icy cold surrounded her in this place, where pain and fear inundated her.

This reality was no better.

Imprisoned and suspended in an icicle, she appeared to be in the middle of a huge stalagmite that dominated an icy cavern. Peripherally she registered the presence of others.

Yet something was familiar. What? No, not what—who? *Kevin!* Was Kevin here? She concentrated harder, searching for his tangible thread. *Yes.* She felt his comforting presence. And Stefan's too! Joy pulsed through her. They were both here.

Then she sensed a third presence. *The asshole.*

Numbing coldness encroached on her emotions, fighting with gripping fear. Her captor was here. This last realization, oddly enough, was what grounded her firmly in this reality and made things clear.

He had to be stopped.

Now, through the surrounding frozen wasteland, she felt and, even to a certain extent, saw, the vague outlines of both the asshole's and Stefan's energies.

Stefan's energy looked distinctly odd—tight, controlled, yet wispy. Alexis focused next on his adversary. A malevolent force she recognized straight away—evil oozed from the center of his black heart.

Where could Kevin be in all this? Carefully she closed her eyes and opened her senses. She felt him but did not see him. She smiled. There he was. He was ... everywhere. Kevin existed in the ice that surrounded and supported her, that covered and held her.

Alex? His soft voice rippled through her consciousness. His words slid in at the DNA level. Without sound, without form, only a distinctive knowing that allowed her to understand. And to respond in kind.

So relieved to hear you. Maybe you could explain what is going on? Alexis whispered. Her mind opened wider, as the words slipped out on fragile snowflakes—the link between the two of them made words unnecessary.

True to thought, images played through her mind. Became a movie of what had happened and how they all came to be here at the same place.

That place being inside *her* mind.

Dear God.

Alexis slumped, understanding what her reality had become.

Don't, Kevin admonished.

Don't what? Be depressed? Be afraid? I think I'm entitled to feel a little alarmed over a science fiction war currently being fought inside my head, she said, fear sharpening her voice to that of a razor's edge.

True, but you're not alone, Kevin said. *We won't let anything happen to you.*

His soothing tones washed through her, but she knew better. *Too late!* she lashed out.

It is not. We're trying to find the physical you. Can you help us? Do you know where you are?

In a padded cell? If not now, I probably will be soon, she muttered.

Stop! You are not crazy. Help us.

Excuse me, she snapped. A fraught minute later, she pulled back. He was right. They all needed to keep their wits about them, or she'd never survive. There'd be time for a full-scale breakdown later.

It won't happen, so don't even think about it.

Harsh crystal tones jarred her senses. *What do I need to do?*

Do you have any idea where you are? Did you see anything? Glen mentioned a locked closet.

That sounds about right. I'm jammed behind some kind of wooden door. It could be a closet or a storage locker. That's all I know. I only just woke up. She felt like apologizing for her predicament. Alexis hesitated as his words sank in. *Glen?*

I'll explain later. Are you hurt? Do you need an ambulance? Can you tell us anything else? he prodded.

No, it's too dark to see.

What about smells, sounds—anything distinctive?

Smells … She paused to consider the odd scents that assailed her nostrils. *Car smells, gas, oil. Maybe a garage or a mechanic's shop. Not overwhelming, possibly someone's garage.*

Good, keep thinking. Did you hear anything? Did you feel anything unusual? Think.

Alexis remained silent for a moment, letting the words sink deep into her consciousness. *Movement. I remember traveling, maybe being carried, but the memories are slippery, inconsistent,* she protested. *We can't rely on them.*

Wrong. Even though you were out cold, these sensations were emblazoned on your consciousness. You can tap into them.

If I were to guess, I'd say I was brought here to someone's garage in the trunk of a car.

Good, excellent!

Alexis didn't understand his sudden excitement. *It's not as if I told you anything new.*

But you put things together in a different way, and that made all the difference. I think you're inside John Prescott's garage.

What? Why there?

I think Charles has stashed you there to implicate John. Glen said something about "maximum destructiveness."

Alexis found her focus wavering. It was getting harder to concentrate.

Alex?

His sharp tone forced her attention back to him. *Sorry,* she whispered, *I'm losing focus.*

Alexis, stay awake! Do you hear me?

Barely. Her voice faded away for a moment, before rallying once again. *I think I'm hurt.*

Then she was gone.

"DON'T PANIC. DON'T panic." Kevin raced through the hospital corridors, dodging people and carts, heading for his car and fresh air and his cell phone. "Just because she faded out doesn't mean she's badly hurt," he muttered to himself, ignoring the many fascinated looks from people walking the same corridors.

"Detective Sutherland," Scott called out in a thick Irish burr.

Kevin whirled to see Scott, striding quickly behind him.

"I called out several times, but you must be doing some very hefty thinking to not hear me." He smiled, but thick worry lines showed on his face. "Sorry to bother you, but I can't locate Alexis." He paused for a mere second. "Have you seen her?"

Kevin motioned for Scott to follow him out of the huge building. "She was kidnapped from the police station this morning. I'm on my way to check out a potential lead now."

"I'm coming." Scott barreled beside him, anxious to hear the details. "Don't you be thinking I'm not."

"I wouldn't dare." Kevin rolled his eyes at the huge man. "Get in."

After throwing lights on the top of his roof, Kevin ripped out of the hospital parking lot and cut the corner too close, bouncing over the curb. Kevin felt Scott's sidelong glance, but he chose to ignore it. He used his cell to call Dispatch for backup and an ambulance.

The nightmarish trip continued through town, until Kevin's truck came to a screeching halt, just ahead of the black-and-white backup car. The ambulance also waited for them.

As the two men raced to the front entrance of the house, the door opened, and a stretcher was wheeled out. Kevin stopped, transfixed.

It was Sandra, John's wife.

"What the hell happened?" he asked, his voice sharp with worry. His gaze darted in all directions, as he searched for signs of Alexis.

"Looks like a heart attack. We're taking her in now." The two ambulance attendants maneuvered the trolley carefully down to the waiting vehicle.

"Is she stable?"

"For now, but she needs to get to Emergency."

Kevin nodded. "I need you to wait another moment. We have reason to believe another injured person is on the premises."

Both paramedics looked at each other, before nodding. "Only long enough to get her loaded, or we'll have to come back."

"Done." Kevin didn't waste any more time, he headed into the front foyer, Scott following closely behind. The other policemen were directed around back. Kevin knew the layout of the house, and he headed for the door leading to the garage.

He entered at the same time as the other officers entered through the outside door. Carefully he looked around. The space appeared deserted. A large closet occupied most of the far wall. Kevin couldn't recall ever seeing it open.

A large bolt secured the wooden doors.

"Useless things, these are." Scott reached out a meaty fist and wrenched the whole door off, taking the latch and bits of cheap pressboard with it.

Alexis, unconscious and bleeding from her head, slumped to the floor at their feet. One of the two backup officers raced out, calling for the paramedics, while the other three people bent over her prone body.

"Is she alive?" asked Scott anxiously.

"Yes, she's breathing." Kevin grimly sliced through the tight bindings that pinned her poor arms back. As he did so, a low groan escaped from her slack mouth. Quickly the others took care of the remaining bindings, as a paramedic arrived.

The medic checked her over thoroughly. "She has a head injury, almost certainly a concussion, but I don't see any breaks or major bleeding. Let's get her to the hospital, where they can check her out."

The second stretcher arrived, and, within minutes, they were on their way to the hospital, an anxious Scott holding Alexis's hand.

Kevin had to stay behind and finish his job.

For long moments, he contemplated the empty driveway and the plume of dust, as the ambulance peeled off. Charles was physically responsible, but was he mentally responsible? Who would pay the penalty for these crimes? More aptly, who should pay for the murder and mayhem? Glen had mentioned finding a new host. ... Could he even be stopped?

Would anyone believe this tale, let alone convict a coma patient of being a serial killer? Shaking his head at the vagaries of fate and the other side of reality he found himself policing, he headed back inside to take care of business.

Charles drove up an hour later and parked in the driveway. Calm and cool, he walked into his father's house, using the front door, calling out, "Hello! Is anyone home?"

Kevin walked out to meet him. "Charles, we need to ask you some questions involving the kidnapping of Alexis Gordon."

The younger man looked at him in astonishment. "What are you doing inside my house? And what are you talking about? I had nothing to do with any kidnapping."

"Eyewitness accounts tell it differently." Not quite the truth, but Kevin hoped to prod him into revealing more than he would have otherwise. So far, Charles's surprise appeared genuine.

"Bullshit! I've been at work all morning. Go ahead and talk to the construction crew about it."

Kevin stopped to consider that. "Someone will corroborate your story? In the meantime, what makes you think she was kidnapped *this morning?*"

Charles looked at him in confusion. Stunned and bewildered, he didn't appear to know what to say. "I don't know. I guess I just assumed it."

Could Charles be ignorant of Glen's actions when being used as a host? It was often that way with multiple personality cases. Kevin nodded noncommittally. "Like I said, we need to ask you a few questions. Shall we sit for a few minutes?"

"I don't want to bother my mother with all this," Charles replied stiffly.

Kevin grimaced at what this young man didn't know. Kevin made it brief and succinct.

Charles didn't adjust well to the news. Bitterly protesting, Charles took a seat in the kitchen. One of the officers stood quietly off to one side and slightly behind him.

Kevin phoned the hospital to get an update on their latest patients. Hearing that all was as well as could be expected, with Alexis still unconscious and his mother still undergoing tests, Kevin updated Charles. Giving the man a moment to deal with the news, Kevin then worked on getting the answers they needed. "Let's start with where you've been since last night."

Charles willingly complied, giving a full and detailed account. If Charles's statement heavily implied that his father had been somehow involved, Kevin ignored that.

"Charles, I need to ask about your little sister's death. What can you tell me about that?"

"The only important thing to know is that my father killed her." He seemed almost relieved, even delighted to say the words aloud.

The door behind them opened wide, and his father entered the room abruptly.

"I certainly did not kill my daughter!" The shock of betrayal laced John Prescott's voice.

This didn't sound good. On the other hand, maybe now they could get to the truth.

"John, I didn't know you'd arrived home." Kevin studied John's ravaged face. "Have you heard about Sandra?"

A shudder rippled down John's back. "Yes. I'd hoped to find Charles here, so we could go to her at the hospital together." He motioned to Charles. "Let's go, son."

Charles sneered at him and stayed seated. "Like you care."

Deliberately staying between the two men, Kevin gave John the update he'd gotten a few minutes ago. "I'm sorry. We need to clear up a few things first." He motioned to another empty chair. "Please take a seat."

John sat down slowly, his outrage at his son slowly replaced by grief. He asked Charles, "How could you think I don't care? Is that why you've hated me all these years? Do you really believe I killed your sister? I loved her, Charles, just as I've loved you all these years." The expression on John's pale face wilted further.

Kevin studied John's features, then scanned his mind. No sign of deception. John appeared genuinely devastated by the accusations of his son and by the news of his wife.

"Like hell. You were always jealous of the bond between Daisy and me." Charles slouched against his chair, turning away from his father.

"Listen carefully." John leaned forward earnestly, trying to make his son understand. "I didn't kill Daisy. She was the light of *my* life!"

Kevin straightened. Maybe now they could find the truth. The evil root. "Do you have any idea who did?" Kevin asked his friend.

John, shamefaced, turned to look at Kevin. "Sandra was supposed to be looking after her. She'd been drinking heavily those days. She'd have blackouts and wouldn't know what she'd been doing, sometimes hours would be unaccounted for. Or so she said. On top of that we couldn't get Sandra's medications straight. I got home from work that day, too late to save my little girl from Sandra's neglect." He hung his head in pain.

"I know what you're thinking. But there was no proof. And she didn't do it on purpose. She wasn't herself. Wasn't responsible for her actions. Please try to understand—I was devastated." He swallowed hard. "Sandra said she didn't see Marie's fall that broke her neck, that she had turned her back for a second. That it was an accident. … At the time, I couldn't think straight and …" He stopped, tears hanging in the corners of his reddened eyes. "And punishing her wouldn't have helped. There's no way to know the truth of what happened that day. And no amount of blame would have brought my Marie back."

Shocked silence hung heavily over the table.

"Sandra's harmless when she isn't drinking, and she's even better when her medications are under control." He glanced between Kevin and Charles, blatantly pleading for understanding. "And I know it's no excuse, but, between Glen's care, my business, a teenage son, and Sandra, … I just couldn't deal with it all." He locked his fingers together, staring down at them. "So I took the easy way out."

Charles sat forward. "What?" Shock and horror shone from his young face. "No! You're lying! No," he said, shaking his head frantically. "You have to be lying!"

"Why?" prodded Kevin, needing to push Charles as far as possible.

"It's just not possible." Charles stood, gripping the edge of the table in a white-knuckled grip. "It just can't be how it happened."

"Because then everything you've done since your sister's death was done for the wrong reasons?" suggested Kevin matter-of-factly.

"Exactly," murmured Charles, lost in his own world. He glared at the father he'd spent a lifetime hating. "You have to be wrong. Daisy was being abused. I saw the bruises, heard her cry at night. I knew it. It had to be you. You never took care of her. And you let that bitch keep neglecting her."

John shook his head frantically. "Don't call your mother that. Still, I can't hide your mother's problems anymore. It wasn't abuse. It was neglect. Sure she might have hit her once in a while but never badly. It was always the booze talking."

Kevin hated the denial on John's face. How often had Kevin heard the same thing from other families? Too often.

When Charles turned, face-to-face with his father, shame, even acceptance covered John's features. There was a sense of waiting for judgment to be passed …

Suddenly John realized what Kevin had said. "What do you mean, Charles did things for the wrong reasons? I don't understand." He turned to his son and asked, "Do you mean those threatening notes? You expected me to say I killed Marie? But I can't confess to something I didn't do."

"It doesn't matter right now." Kevin bypassed John's question, wanting more of his own answered first. "What precipitated your move to this place, so long ago, John?"

He shuddered. "That was a horrible time. The police investigated Daisy's death and finally determined it was accidental." He stopped speaking, visibly holding back tears. "Even with that ruling, it seemed like the public persecuted us. So I moved everyone here. And, after losing Daisy, I wanted to be closer to my brother."

"I spoke to the police years ago. Tried to get them to take another look at you. But they weren't interested," Charles said.

Kevin sensed there was more to the story. "And Daisy?" he asked John.

"It was so hard to leave her behind, but we needed a fresh start. And Glen needed us too. I felt I could be of more use to the living." John slid a surreptitious glance his son's way. Charles glared at him, obviously not quite ready to give up all his long-held beliefs.

Kevin thought about that. It wasn't uncommon to leave an area for a fresh start. Moving a loved one from cemetery to cemetery was much more difficult. After a moment, he continued, "But that's not every-thing, is it? The problem goes back further, doesn't it?"

John looked at him in confusion. "I don't understand."

"Tell me about your brother's accident."

"What's to say? He ran his car off the road years ago. He was in his early thirties at the time and has been in a coma ever since. He had an affair with Sandra. Wanted to take her away, but she stayed with me. Though I disliked what he tried to do with my marriage, I haven't pulled the plug. Instead, I funneled tens of thousands of dollars into his care, hoping he might one day recover."

"More half-truths!" Charles interrupted, his fingers drumming the tabletop. "You inherited all the family businesses, Glen's house, his cars, in fact, his whole fortune. What did you have before his accident? Nothing—that's what." He turned his back on his father. "Accident, my ass."

Kevin watched their interaction with interest.

John held out his hands. "No, that's not true. What have I done to make you want to crucify me like this?"

Sarcastically Charles answered, "Nothing apparently, except let my sister be abused at the hands of a raving drunk."

There was no doubting Charles's sincerity. This man truly believed the worst about his father and wanted to see him hang. As Kevin turned to study John's face, an odd black shadow caught in his peripheral vision. Another presence hung around John. *Shit!* It had to be Glen, trying to control the scene. *And damn it.* This was a little out of Kevin's league. Where the hell was Stefan when you needed him?

Right here!

"Thank you!" whispered Kevin under his breath.

Get rid of the other cop.

Kevin called the other policeman over, for a moment of private conversation. Quickly the other man left. Kevin's actions received strange looks from both father and son.

"I have something a little odd to discuss with both of you." Kevin sat down, motioning for Charles to retake his seat, opposite him. "Very weird psychic occurrences are going on here that you both may or may not be aware of."

John stared at Kevin in astonishment.

Charles's face changed, almost a mockery of his former features, and he grinned malevolently. Obvious signs of possession—for those who knew what to look for—became more apparent by the second. As he spoke, there was no longer any doubt. The voice was hard, raspy, and mature, ... well beyond Charles's normal voice.

"Finally you'll give me an opportunity to speak. *Hallelujah.*" The macabre laughter both fascinated and horrified Kevin. John's face twisted in confused horror, as he stared at his son. He obviously didn't understand.

"What's the matter, brother? Don't you recognize me?" Charles's face seemed to even elongate, shaping itself into a travesty of the more mature man.

"What? Charles, what's wrong?"

The laughter seared John. This time, even Kevin winced at the sound.

"You still don't understand, do you? You simpleton. I'm Glen, right now, ... inside Charles. Using your precious weak son for my own purposes. He barely exists in here any longer. But this isn't about him. It's about you. Have you enjoyed my life, brother? The life you stole from me."

John went from disbelief to shock. "This ... isn't possible. Is it?" Fearfully he looked from his son to Kevin. "Kevin, please tell me this isn't happening."

"Sorry, it's happening all right." Kevin didn't dare take his eyes off the malevolent manifestation in front of him. He'd never seen anything like it before.

And hopefully you won't ever again, murmured Stefan.

Kevin had forgotten Stefan's presence, faced with this new development. He wasn't sure what either of them could do at this point, except watch the scene play itself out.

"Are you really Glen?" John spoke faintly, obviously not believing what he'd witnessed so far.

"Of course. You never would pull that damn plug, would you?" Bitterness rolled as easily as the laughter had. "For years, I lie there, helpless, while you enjoyed my wealth, my hard work, my favorite whisky. God, I hated you, until I learned how to do this. Just look at what I've accomplished." Again the disembodied laughter chilled the air. "No way you'd have attained even a fraction of my success."

Kevin watched the awareness on John's face change from incredulity to shocked certainty.

John hastened to explain. "Dear God, I always hoped you'd wake up to enjoy a normal life."

"Sure you did. That's why you sold my car collection and disbanded my businesses. What kind of life would I have now? Do you even have *any* of my money left?"

John started to explain. "Well, I have some, but, with the economy and your care, … a lot of it is gone."

"Like hell. You gambled it in high-risk investments and lost most of it."

John tried to protest but to no avail.

"You should be a fucking millionaire many times over by now." Charles—rather Glen—grinned. "Now it's too late. You'll spend the rest of your life as a prisoner, just like you forced me to be!" His voice gained in volume, until, in the end, he was almost shouting at his hapless brother.

"For what? Why should I be punished?" John raised both hands. "I loved you. I spent hours at your bedside. I couldn't bear to let you go."

"For trying to kill me, you jealous, greedy, worthless son of a bitch."

"No, you can't know about that!" John whispered.

Kevin could only stare. Would the shocks never end? He'd never seen a family so full of pain, betrayal, and murderous intent.

"*I* know." Bitterness oozed from Glen. "You ran me off the road, hoping to kill me. When that failed to complete the deed, you felt guilty and refused to let me go. Bastard. Do you have any idea what you sentenced me to? To hear and understand everything but to have no way to communicate? No. You don't."

"You learned to do this"—John gestured at his son—"for revenge?" It was clearly all too much for John to take in. He leaned forward, hiding his face in his hands. His shoulders sagged against the weight of the evidence facing him. "Dear God, what have I done?"

"That's a good question. Just what did you do?" Kevin queried forcefully.

"He's right. I was so jealous," John admitted, guilt and pain dominating in his face. "He had, well, … everything. Both of our parents doted on him. Even Marie may have been his …" John stopped at the snort erupting from Charles's mouth.

"It's true. Everyone loved you, Glen," he snapped. Then, just as suddenly, all the air seemed to *whoosh* out, to deflate him, and he sagged forward. "I didn't mean to hurt you. We were both heading home from a dinner out. A rarity for us. But you'd bragged the whole time about all you had. Including Sandra. On the way home, you were in your fancy car ahead of me." He looked sorrowfully at the other two men. "What can I say? I gave in to a fit of jealous madness and ran him off the road." If possible, John sank even farther. "I'm so sorry, Glen."

"A little too late, brother." Glen snickered.

Enough was enough. Kevin stood and said, "John, let's get you downtown for a statement."

John, beaten, nodded. "What about Glen? We don't even know all he's done."

"That's something we may never know." And it bothered Kevin terribly. How could he stop someone like Glen?

John must have had the same thought. He pulled out his cell phone and automatically dialed a number. "Yes, this is John Prescott. I need you to fulfill the requirements on the signed request form you've been holding for me. … Yes, that's the one. Thank you. No, I won't be in to say goodbye."

"What? You think you can pull the plug now, you asshole! I need a little more time first. Damn you." Charles raced out of the room, the surprise move giving him a head start.

Kevin raced after him, the officers and John at his heels, but Charles ran into his father's study, and opened the drawer on the right-hand side. He scrambled to pull out the loaded gun, as John walked in behind Kevin.

"Charles, don't do this!" John said. "Things are bad enough. Put the gun down. Please, we'll get you some help. Please!"

Charles laughed. This time it *almost* sounded like Charles. "You idiot. Do you really think Glen can take over my mind without my permission? We've been working on this for years. I like what we do when we're together. I didn't at the beginning, but I grew to like the sense of power and control I felt when he was with me."

Kevin knew things had gone south in a big hurry. He had no idea how to stop what would happen next. But his muscles tensed, awaiting an opportunity.

"You know Glen doted on Marie when she was born." Charles shrugged indifferently. "Her death came so close to his new awareness and abilities that, at first, he didn't understand what had happened. She'd come to him in confusion over her own death. It didn't take him long to figure out a way to keep her with him, at least temporarily, while he worked on a long-term solution. Once he figured that out, there was no stopping him." Charles nodded mockingly to Kevin, then continued to explain.

"When I heard we were moving right after Daisy's funeral, Glen panicked. He was sure the connection would be broken, without Daisy's body close by. He couldn't take the chance. And I, … I couldn't leave her behind. So I broke into the funeral home after the staff left and stole her remains that night before the ceremony. With a quick burial and a small private ceremony, no one noticed. Or should I say, no one gave a damn. Except Glen and I."

Charles glared at his father. "Then I wrapped her up in my hockey bag and moved her here at the same time the family moved. You say you wanted a fresh start, but you moved within days of her funeral. That was too fast for Glen to find a way to stay connected, so we couldn't leave her behind. And we had no time to find a better solution." He wrinkled his nose. "Of course that new city garden bed had just been planted, and it made for an easy place to keep her safe, while Glen continued to practice." Charles laughed at his dumbfounded father. "You still don't understand all he's done, do you? He was molesting and killing kids before his accident. You actually did society a big favor by running him off the road back then."

Kevin's stomach heaved, as he remembered hearing that Glen had been a long-time resident of the area.

"Dear God, that's not possible. Not Glen," John prayed aloud at the monstrosity of that belief. "How could he hurt those children? They didn't do anything to him. They were so young."

"He liked them young or old. He wasn't all that fussy, Father." Charles's face deepened, darkened, and he took on the look of Glen.

"I did many things that you have no idea about," Glen said, Charles's personality submerged. "I kept Daisy with me on this side. I used her love for her precious brother, your Charles, to keep her with me. Even she doesn't know all I did before her time."

"The cold cases on my desk." Kevin shook his head. "Wow, what a family."

Charles pointed the gun at his father. "You never did know Glen, … or me, for that matter. I know him so much better than you ever could. I can't have you changing our system. Glen empowers me. Without Glen, what am I? Nothing."

The gun fired without warning. John fell backward.

Kevin crouched, his own gun in hand. The second police officer who had been hiding behind the door, launched into the room, his gun up and ready. "Charles, put down the gun."

Charles laughed and turned the gun on Kevin. "You can't beat me."

Kevin fired.

Twin pools of spurting red sprang from Charles's chest. Stunned horror filled his face. "No!" he cried out in disbelief, even as his body collapsed to the floor.

John had fallen face upward, one neat round hole in the center of his forehead. Dead. Kevin crouched beside him, futilely checking for a pulse.

"He's gone, Sutherland. No one could have survived that shot." The other cop stood up again.

"I know." Kevin sighed heavily as he walked over to where Charles laid. His eyes were still open but pain-filled and slightly glazed over. Yet, for the first time, his face looked normal—younger and innocent, as if Glen's influence had finally left.

"Kevin, I didn't want to kill him," Charles gasped. "It was my uncle. All my life I watched myself doing things." He panted heavily, his chest gushing more blood. "But I could never stop myself. Daisy, everything I did was for … Daisy. I let him do terrible things, in order to keep her soul safe from him. He told me …" Charles gasped.

"Take it easy, Charles. It's not a concern right now. Help is on the way." Kevin tried to soothe the fatally shot man.

"Like hell." He coughed, bloody foam ringing his lips. "Take it easy on Mom. We won't ever know the truth about my sister now. Mom was drunk so much of the time. … Please let Daisy be free … and safe from him … now." His fingers clenched spastically in Kevin's hand, before falling back, limp, to the carpet.

Charles was dead.

"Sir, I've called the station. Another ambulance is on its way."

Kevin nodded, staring grimly at the sad remains of what had once been a family.

CHAPTER 27

"WHY WON'T SHE wake up?" The pain and uncertainty from the last five days tore at Kevin. The regular doctors had more or less warned him that Alexis might never wake up. Stefan's specialist was out of town until tomorrow.

Kevin couldn't live with that. To think Glen might have succeeded in ruining more lives was unacceptable.

In the last few days, he'd hardly left Alexis's side.

Sleeping in the chair had been an uncomfortable experience. He'd long since taken over the small hospital room, using the hooks for his jackets, spare clothing, even his holster, which hung within easy reach.

He'd spent the long hours talking to Alexis too. Speaking of anything that might tweak her interest—like Arnie being offered a second chance, if he met certain conditions. Kevin spoke of the sad funerals for both John and Charles. He'd even told her that Daisy's remains had been placed in a small plot just outside of town, with daisies decorating the grave.

All to no avail. Alexis never moved an eyelash.

"She can't. I keep telling you that." Stefan sat comfortably on the single visitor's chair at Alexis's bedside.

Perched on the window ledge was Lissa, standing watch as always.

"Damn it." Frustrated, Kevin glared at his friend and mentor. It was always the same irritating conversation. According to Stefan, Kevin had to go in after her. Only Kevin didn't know how. Which always precipitated the second ongoing conversation.

"Damn it, Stefan." Kevin was ready to tear his hair out. Instead, he satisfied himself with running his fingers through his hair in aggravation. "I don't know what to do."

"Yes, you do." Stefan was adamant.

Defeated, Kevin slumped on the side of Alexis's bed, opposite Stefan. "Okay, let's go over this one more time."

"There's nothing to go over. You have to go in there after her."

Kevin shot him a disgusted look. "Do you really think that I haven't tried?"

"Try again. That's the vision blocking you. This time, come from a position of love and not fear. Go ahead. The bed is big enough."

Kevin eyed the potential space in disbelief. Deciding that he'd have to trust Stefan, he sat down carefully on the bed, turning on his side to wrap his arms around her. She seemed so defenseless and lost. His heart hurt, if he thought about it for any length of time. He closed his eyes and slipped into her mind.

ALEXIS SMILED IN her frozen world. There was really nothing else to do. She'd been here forever, or at least it seemed that way. Day and night had melded and blended into one long stasis state. In truth, reality as she'd known it had long since faded away past the ice and cold. This condition had seeped into her consciousness. Caught and imprisoned, she just existed, happily unaware of ever being anything else, loving the beauty of the fragile wonderland of snowflakes and ice patterns.

Alexis?

Alexis hummed happily as she turned toward the sound. *Hello, Daisy! How are you?*

I'm fine. … The little girl hesitated, watching Alexis curiously. *How are you doing?*

I'm doing good. I'm happy you came to visit me.

The child worried her bottom lip. *Uh, Alexis? How can you be so happy here?*

Why wouldn't I be? Alexis didn't understand what the child meant—and didn't care either.

Because now you're his prisoner.

I'm what? She laughed. *Nonsense. I'm no one's prisoner.*

Slowly Daisy dipped her head. *Yes, you are.*

At first, Alexis let foggy confusion cloud her comprehension, but the longer she gazed at the slowly nodding child, fragments of Alexis's old world seeped in. Recognition and comprehension slowly slid back into her reality. *Is this … what happened to you?* she asked Daisy.

Daisy nodded, her curls bouncing, even as her eyes reflected windows of sadness.

Alexis couldn't believe what she'd so easily forgotten.

That's him. He keeps you in a fog for a while. It helps you to detach from those you left.

Fear spiked through Alexis, stopping her cold. *Am I dead?*

Daisy's eyes commiserated with Alexis's plight. But she didn't answer.

I can't be. No, she added more definitively. *I'm not dead. Dying maybe but not dead. At least not yet.*

Daisy made a tiny, almost imperceptible shrug but remained silent. The truth would be shown soon enough.

Alexis tried to focus. Visions of her other world had been dipping in and out of her mind for a while, but they'd gradually faded off into the distance. Now she deliberately searched for those fragments, drawing them to the forefront.

Focused, she visualized those she loved, as brightly and intensely as she could.

Kevin.

Kevin. … He was worth fighting for.

Damn right!

Alexis smiled. Her visualization was so strong, she could even hear his voice.

What the hell have you been doing? We've been calling for you for days. You never answered.

It was him! Dear heavens, but it was good to hear Kevin's voice.

You scared the shit out of me, he said.

Kevin's gravelly tones shrank the emptiness in her world and lit up her heart. *Damn, I thought I'd never hear your beloved voice again.*

Beloved? I like the sound of that.

But I'll only be happy when you're back, back where you belong. So come home, sweetheart, please!

Show me the way, and I'd love to, Alexis muttered sarcastically.

That gave him pause. *Can't you get home?*

I can't see where home is.

Why not? Kevin pressed her.

He's blocking me. I'm trying, but I only get vague sensations of my past. I can feel you, but it's different than everything else in my world here.

I should bloody well hope so. Kevin snorted. *I hate to tell you, sweetheart, but that's your fear talking. He is dead.*

Dead? He is not! His wasted body might be but not that evil soul. Alexis knew that for truth, at a deep, elemental level. She could still feel his pulsing evil presence. No way this was leftover energy from his earthly sojourn.

Kevin rushed to reassure her. *He is. They pulled the plug on his life support system days ago. In fact, I think Glen's funeral was yesterday.*

But she'd have none of it. Instead fear clawed at her throat. She had to make Kevin believe. *He's got you fooled into thinking he's dead, but he's still here,* she enunciated forcibly. *Feel him yourself.*

Kevin's energy flared in disbelief. *It can't be.*

Well, he is. Alexis felt agitation wiping out her calm. The pervasive sense of evil smothered her newfound focus. Not good.

Wait. Kevin's energy distorted, as he went deeper into his own consciousness.

Dread filled the yawning silence. She needed Kevin to believe her. They couldn't lose track of the asshole at this point. If Glen could go underground to such an extent, no telling the damage he could inflict on the unsuspecting world.

He did say something about having a plan to continue his existence. But I didn't believe him because he said he needed a little more time. As Kevin spoke, his voice oddly thinned out. *I never really thought about it, with so much else happening.*

Alexis thought on it furiously. What choices were available to a madman without a body? *He must have found another host, an even weaker one this time—one that would allow him complete control. One he could overwhelm so inclusively that the person only existed to function on a physical level. And to do his bidding.*

Hell.

I'm right. I know it. I think he tried it with me, or ... he's planning to later.

Who else would he have chosen? Who was close enough to him to accept this hooks into that strongly? *For just a while. We have to stop him. Alexis, come back home.*

You have to help me. I'm not strong enough to get free and to fight him alone. Once again, apprehension built. Only now there was the added dread of being left alone once again. Maybe forever.

Yes, you are strong enough. I've never seen anyone shine like you have. You are strong enough. You just have to beli—

His energy blinked out.

Kevin? Kevin, come back. What's wrong?

But he was gone.

She didn't know how, but she knew something bad had happened to him. His energy hadn't faded—it had vanished. Just winked out.

Or been vanquished.

Panic set in. The icy cage, instead of being a winter wonderland, instantly reverted to being a prison of isolation and cold. She had to get out. Kevin was in desperate trouble.

She had to help him.

Using everything she'd learned, she reconnected with the reality of the physical world. Stronger and faster, the puzzle pieces finally floated into place with her renewed purpose. But, with every step of visible progress, she had to struggle harder and harder. She had to get to Kevin. Each second she could move forward brought her closer.

Until she came up against a blank wall of deep, thick, impenetrable ice.

No matter what she tried, she couldn't get through it.

Daisy's forlorn face peered at her from the other side. Before, when Alexis had been less aware of her imprisonment, she hadn't seen the density of the ice. Now she knew it was as impossible a barrier to cross as the Atlantic Ocean in a hurricane.

Aggravated and depressed, she slumped back to regroup. Fear kept her nerves firing with continuous panic messages. Her heartbeats thrummed through her soul. She had to get to Kevin.

How, damn it?

Silence greeted her.

It couldn't end like this. The bastard couldn't win. Alexis railed at her world. *Not this time*, she vowed fiercely. *Not this time!*

She directed her fury against the frozen vastness, blasting at her stalagmite barriers.

Again nothing happened.

Her heart wept. She hadn't really expected that to work. It wasn't her style. Her back stiffened; then she laughed for sheer joy. Of course it wasn't her style. She wasn't a fighter. She was a healer. She could receive and transmit energy. And, with that memory, it clicked.

On her new path, she opened her heart and sent out warm loving energy, just as she would for an ailing plant. Thinking it might help, she transmitted a thick broadband of power toward Kevin. Even as the love flowed from her psyche, thick fat droplets of water dripped down the icy prison walls. She turned up the heat, firing warm colors and powerful energy outward at the ice, already cracking under the curing power of her love.

Long seconds later, she was free.

And back in her body.

An almost soundless groan escaped, as she assimilated her mind into her physical world.

No one noticed, so locked were they in the frozen tableau playing out in her hospital room.

Alexis opened her eyes a faint crack, trying to decipher the strange feel to the atmosphere.

Relief swelled in her heart, as she recognized that the heavy weight over her waist was Kevin's arm. Her relief quickly turned to horror. His arm was limp and lifeless. What was wrong? She cracked her eyes open a little more.

Only to slam them closed.

Shit!

Carefully she peeked again. Sandra, wearing a hospital gown, held a handgun in her weak fingers. It looked like Kevin's gun.

Stefan stood mere steps from the smoking firearm. "Easy, Sandra, take it easy. Please, we need to get help for Kevin."

Quiet, Alex!

Alexis started at Lissa's caution.

Kevin's hurt. Help him, but don't let anyone know that you're back. Stefan will take care of Glen.

What? She was still groggy and disoriented. Her mind struggled to adapt. Something about Kevin being in danger? Right. That's what had snapped her back.

Then she sensed what was wrong. Alexis plunged into Kevin's mind and into his body. Dear God, he'd been shot! His searing pain stabbed through her.

Alexis ceased to be in that moment.

She gave of herself and liberated the loving energy of her own body and transmitted it to him. With that, she opened the door between them. Not just the door between their minds but the door between their souls.

Waves of her loving energy poured through him, becoming one with him. Blood seeped through the wound in his side, dripping relentlessly onto her hospital bed. Her energy received the pain, even as she transmitted her healthy energy into him. Mending. Rebuilding. Healing.

Hot energy flashed and sparked, as it encompassed the injury, warming and communicating with the damaged cells. She understood something momentous was happening. A bonding that could only be broken by death ... and maybe not even by that.

She transmitted every healing thing she could pull from her energy, his energy, and that from those around her. *Heal. Be strong. Help is on its way. Be one and be whole—join with me. Together we can finish this. Together we are stronger. Undefeatable.*

The lights in the room flickered, as she pulled in even more power to transmit to Kevin.

She shifted slightly, snuggling against his unconscious body.

Groggy whispers echoed through her mind. *Alexis, in case I don't make it …*

Shh! None of that. You'll be fine. Feel the healing, it's unmistakable.

You're in my mind! And my body? Amazement poured off him. *See? I told you. You're phenomenal.*

Her warm energy radiated, laughing in triumph—even ringed as it was with fatigue. *And I will celebrate, when this is over.* She widened the energy pathways, pulling healing energy from the world around her into her space and transmitting the life force for his body to use. She poured all that she was into him. Why the sheets weren't burning with the heat, she didn't know. She turned it up a notch, feeling the drain on her resources at the new demands.

Stop! You're exhausting yourself. I'm fine now. Stop it, Kevin added sharply.

Instinctively she toned down her actions and checked her own energy levels. *I'm okay. I'm trying to read Sandra's energy at the same time.*

What?

Check out what's going on in the room. Her voice wavered. She wasn't strong enough to do this for long.

STEFAN WATCHED THE continuing tussle on both levels as it played out in front of him.

It appeared that the ultimate act of firing the gun had brought Sandra back to the forefront, and she was now caught in the horrifying battle for life, … with Glen trying to control her every move.

Sandra, who'd hidden from most of the unpleasant issues of her life, couldn't seem to bring herself to fire the weapon a second time. The war in her head seemed to be more than she could deal with. She no longer knew who she was, … only who she wasn't.

The struggle was mirrored in the wild expression in her eyes and in her tortuous, snarling features, as the fight continued for control of her physical body.

Stefan and Lissa could only watch, helpless to do anything.

SANDRA, WHISPERED ALEXIS urgently, inside the older woman's confused mind. *Fight, Sandra. You can't let Glen win. He's taken everyone you love from you. Fight, Sandra.*

I can't, whimpered the tired woman. *I loved him once. He's too strong, and he knows me too well.*

Yes, you can. If you let him win, you will be no more. Fight! Alexis ordered harshly. Sandra had curled up, defenseless, in a tiny corner of her own mind, helpless to continue the unfair battle that Glen was winning.

Forget about her. She's weak, Glen said, and then his harsh laughter amplified ten times over in the small space.

Alexis's fury knew no bounds. This man couldn't be allowed to continue. *Sandra, he killed John. He killed Charles. Don't let him continue.*

What would get the woman's attention? Alexis didn't know the truth, and, knowing that Sandra wouldn't know at this point either, Alexis pulled out all the stops. *Glen killed Marie. He had been abusing her for years before. And he made you carry the guilt for that because you chose John over him.*

That caught Sandra's attention. Her quavering voice asked, *Do you really think he killed my baby girl?*

Pity welled in Alexis's heart. This poor woman. *Yes, Sandra, I really do. Worse, Sandra, he abused Marie before she died by controlling you. He hurt her through you. Over and over again. He enjoyed it. Making her suffer. Making many other children suffer. … Making you suffer. Don't let him live to hurt more children. Sandra, fight! Please!* Alexis pleaded anxiously. Sandra had to stand up for her right to her own life.

But in her mind, Sandra squeezed into the tightest ball that she could be. It was a feeble attempt to protect herself against the villain living in her soul.

Glen mocked her. *What the hell will you do, Sandra? I am in control, not you. Stupid bitch!*

Sandra was flung back against the wall by an unseen power that came out of nowhere, dominating and controlling her, as he would a cringing pet.

But everyone has a breaking point, and Sandra had finally reached hers. Alexis watched the painful video of horrid thoughts pouring through Sandra's damaged mind. How many times had this man controlled her like this, making her do things she didn't remember? Would anyone ever know the extent of the damage inflicted by this madman?

Alexis held her breath and watched anxiously, as Sandra gathered her failing strength for one last battle.

Dismissing Sandra as already lost, Glen redirected his energy toward Alexis, casually flicking her out of Sandra's mind and slamming her back into her own.

There was no time to adjust. Alexis opened her eyes to watch the scene unfold in slow motion.

Sandra lifted the handgun, pointing it first at the couple entwined on the bed, zeroing in on Glen's choice of target, before lifting it in an agonizingly stilted motion to her own head. She held it there, fighting for supremacy, for what seemed like an eternity.

No! came the eerie echo reverberating inside Alexis's mind. At the same time noises filled the room, as Glen fought desperately in his losing battle for dominance against Sandra's will.

In breathless horror, the audience could only watch.

Sandra pulled the trigger.

Blood and brain splattered across the room.

Sandra had won ... and lost.

Traumatized silence reigned.

Then the air was filled with sounds of yelling and running, footsteps rushing toward them.

Alexis closed her eyes. What a waste ...

Relief, sadness, and thankfulness filled her. It was over.

Exhaustion washed over her, pulling her under. And she let it, happy to sink back into the sea of semiconsciousness, connected as one with Kevin, barely aware and wholly uncaring of the chaos going on around her.

CHAPTER 28

Three Weeks Later

"ALEXIS, ARE YOU sure you're ready for this?" The group gathered comfortably in a circle on Stefan's living room floor. The ritual of drinks had already been observed, and they were now ready for the evening's work.

Alexis smiled at Stefan. "I'm definitely ready. Besides, I'm not the one who got shot," she teased the quiet man, sitting close to her.

Kevin smiled at her, reaching out to tousle her hair. "I'm fine. I'll get a lot of mileage out of my injury, won't I?"

"Maybe," she agreed cheekily. "At least until the next time."

He snorted. "As it won't happen again, don't hold your breath. Besides, I'm not the one who tangled with a serial killer's twisted mind."

A sobering reminder. "True. That's why it's important we finish tonight's work. Only then will this be over. For what Glen did to Daisy and all those other children, he deserved to be in a coma all those years. But those children need to be freed."

"The children have been there for a long time. If they have to wait a little longer, it won't make that much difference. He can't hurt them now."

They still didn't know how many early victims of Glen's were caught in-between. Alexis hoped they would eventually, but ... "No." Alexis was resolute. "Tonight we rescue them and show them the way home."

Some of the victims' bodies might never be found, but, at least this way, she could rest easy, knowing that their souls were free to go on. She hadn't seen the little boy, Eric, since the first time, but she knew he still wandered, lost.

Kevin was following up on several of the other leads, if only to find closure for his sake and for the sake of the children's families. Maybe more victims would surface and maybe not. This was enough for now.

She smiled at the two friends who had shown her so much. Lissa sat with them, her form just visible enough for Alexis to see.

She didn't want sadness to destroy their efforts tonight, but she couldn't resist asking, *Lissa, you do know that I'll be okay now, right? ... If it's time for you to leave, I'll understand, and I'll be happy for you.*

Alexis dreaded her sister's answer. But, after seeing those children locked in-between life and death and beyond, Alexis knew that, no matter how much she missed her sister's presence, she wouldn't wish that on any soul.

Lissa's tinkling laughter whispered through the room, with the softness of a warm wind. *I'll be here for a little while longer. I'm sure other people could use my loving assistance with their lives.* She looked pointedly at Stefan.

Alexis grinned. Was it her imagination, or did Stefan look decided-ly uncomfortable at Lissa's suggested inference? "Then let's begin." Closing her eyes, Alexis opened the door in her mind, then released loving energy waves to create a path forward.

She opened her eyes to see Daisy laughing, running down the path, a string of children following her.

DALE MAYER

A Psychic Visions Novel

KNOCK, KNOCK...

Dedication

This book is dedicated to my four children who always believed in me and my storytelling abilities.

Thank you!

Acknowledgments

Knock Knock… wouldn't have been possible without the support of my friends and family. Many hands helped with proofreading, editing, and beta reading to make this book come together. Special thanks to my editor Pat Thomas.

I thank you all.

CHAPTER 1

There is no revenge so complete as forgiveness.
...Josh Billings

ICE HIT HER first. Inside and out.

Shay Lassiter woke to find goosebumps marching across her cold skin in the early morning. She tugged up the chocolate brown duvet she'd thrown off sometime in the night but even that didn't account for the cold filtering slowly through her waking consciousness. The rest of her brain screamed at her to wake up all the way. *Something was off.*

Morris, the ever-present ghost of her beloved childhood pet, snuggled up close. She didn't understand the miracle of his existence, but she rejoiced in it every day. The deep purr rumbled at her shoulder making her smile. She was thankful his gentle blue ball of energy sat on her bed most days. She rarely saw him in physical form, but he was always there in spirit – offering immeasurable comfort. Most times, the sound of his engine powered through the small room. That oversized orange tabby had been the size of a small car, but had a diesel truck motor for an engine.

The purr shut off.

Shit.

Her internal alarm finally kicked in as the bedding pressed down on her, confining, where moments before it had been comforting. She threw the duvet back, springing from bed, her heart pounding. A clammy film coated her skin. *What the hell was wrong?*

She spun around, searching her darkened bedroom for the cause of the unease settling deep in her soul.

There was no one there with her.

Last night, she'd gone to sleep without a problem. That was surprising because she'd had an argument with her fiancé, Darren, before going to sleep. And it had been a bad one, making her doubt their relationship...again. But still, she knew that discord hadn't created this type of response. Her psyche often chose the wee hours of the morning to wake her up and chew away at her, but she'd never woken up quite like this. Shivering, she looked down at her cami and boy shorts to see the hairs rising on her smooth skin. Her teeth chattered as she ran to check the thermostat in her room. It was normal.

Of course it was. It *should* be warm; it was summertime.

She ran back to bed and huddled against her headboard with her duvet high up on her chest.

Shay?

Stefan Kronos spoke, his familiar voice swept through her mind, calming her. He must have heard her silent distress in the night. *Stefan? Something's wrong. Only I can't see what it is.*

I'll check it out.

The emptiness in her mind told her Stefan had left. God, she didn't know what she'd do without him. He didn't always respond this quickly, but her psychic friend always knew when something was wrong.

Then she heard *it…*

The click of her front door opening…then closing. Something moved across her living room floor.

She had an intruder.

Alarm swept through her. *Oh no.* The door had been locked. She'd double-checked it before going to bed. There's no way anyone could get in.

Unless they had a key.

Shay? Get out of the apartment. Stefan's sharp voice sliced through her frozen state. *There's a rogue energy heading toward you.*

Too late, she whispered in her mind. *It's too late. He's inside already. Call for help, Stefan. Hurry!*

Hide. I'm getting help.

"Shay? Oh, hi, honey. I hadn't expected you to be awake." Her fiancé stood at her bedroom doorway, a crooked smile on his face. Darren held up a key in his hand. It gleamed in the slice of moonlight creeping through her drapes. Dressed all in black, he cut an elegant figure. His handsome good looks and confidence had been part of what attracted her to him in the first place.

Relief swamped her. "Oh thank God," she murmured and closed her eyes. Her rigid spine relaxed. There was nothing to worry about after all. Feeling much better and slightly foolish, she opened her eyes and smiled warmly at him. So happy to see him after their fight and her initial panic.

It's just Darren, Stefan.

Silence in her mind.

Darren? he asked in a flat voice. *Your fiancé?*

Yes. She gave a small deprecating laugh.

Shay? Then…why the fear?

Her eyes widened. Good question. "Darren, why are you here at this hour?" She glanced at the clock. "It's two in the morning." She stared at him, confused, as something else registered – finally. "And where did you get the key?"

He shifted away from the door, his smile widening. But there was something off about that twist to his lips. A little too tight, and an odd glow added to the toothy shine. "When you wouldn't give me a key, I decided to have one made up on my own."

She blinked. That didn't make any sense. Did it? No. It was wrong. She tossed back her long brown hair, trying to clear her head. And wished her roiling stomach would calm. She couldn't seem to think straight.

"Why? I don't understand."

His lips quirked. He tossed the key on the bed. "I know. But I figured that I had to do something. After all, we're fighting more lately. Not making up the same. It's as if we're on the verge of a break up."

"Oh, I don't think–"

"Stop." He held up his hands. "You know you don't look at our relationship quite the same anymore. Neither do I." His hands dropped and he shook his head. "You also know you've been spending more time on that damn Children's Hospital project than ever. Even when I said I didn't like it."

Oh shit. He was breaking up with her. But then why get a key made? And of course she spent a lot of time on that project. It was special. The kids were special. He knew that.

Didn't he?

Why was nothing making any sense right now?

Stefan whispered through her mind. *Shay, something's wrong. What's happening?*

She stared at Darren. *I don't know.*

To her fiancé, she said, "I don't understand."

"I know you don't. That's okay. I can explain." He walked over and sat down at the edge of her bed. "It's too bad, though. You're a beautiful lady. Inside and out."

"Thank you, I think?" Shay might be confused, but some truths were making their way inside. He'd had a key to her home made without her permission and he had let himself into her apartment in the middle of the night. Like Stefan had said, something was wrong.

And now she was starting to feel more than a little nauseous. And, she felt...slower. Her mind sluggish. As if she were in shock. Or hurt... But she wasn't. She gazed down at her arms and the rest of her body. She felt weak, faint even, but not like she was injured in any way.

"You don't get it, do you, Shay?"

She stared up at him, puzzled. "No. And I'd appreciate it if you'd explain. This isn't very funny."

"No, it isn't. You ruined all my plans."

She tilted her head and tried to focus. "Plans?"

"Yes, plans." Looking relaxed and at ease, he crossed one leg over the other and then clasped his hands over his knees. "See. I need money. Lots of money."

Feeling foolish and spaced out, she asked, "Why?"

He smiled, a knowing smile. "For lots of things." He tilted his head and looked at her steadily. "Are you feeling okay?"

She tried to swallow, her tongue thick, unwieldy. "I don't know. I feel a bit...weird, actually."

"That's all quite normal. I'm making it easy on you."

Normal. What was *normal* about any of this? "I...I don't understand."

He gave an exaggerated sigh. "No, I don't suppose you do. So let me make this simple." He stood and walked over to the window. "I need money. You have money. And, if we were together, that wouldn't be a problem. On top of your personal fortune, you control an amount that's unbelievably large. See, that's really attractive. Plus, taking you to bed isn't exactly a hardship." He leered at her. "In fact, that part has been sheer fun. I figured I was in clover. We were engaged—"

"Still are, I thought."

His smile didn't quite reach his eyes. "So you say. See, I understand the female mind. I know that you aren't as happy as you were. And once that thread of discontent starts, it only gets worse. Our fight tonight was about moving up the wedding day. But you didn't want that. You're hesitating. And that means you have doubts. And doubts are dangerous because they could mean the end of my plans – and make me very unhappy." He moved the blinds slightly. "I can't have that."

He sighed. "I thought I could save you... I have to admit that even now I'm having doubts..." He cocked his head and stared at her. She could barely see a softening in his features. A pondering. A weighing of options.

Then he straightened, stuck out his chin and shook his head. "No. It has to be this way." The moonlight shone in through the crack between the blinds. "Too bad though; you showed such promise."

Shay closed her eyes as his words and tones filtered through the growing fog in her brain.

Stefan, Dear God, I need help.

It's coming. Stay with me.

I don't know if I can. I don't know what's happening.

Nothing good! Damn it, I told you there was someone better out there for you.

She'd have laughed if she could. Instead a strange lassitude had filled her veins, mixed into her bloodstream. *I can't think.*

The buzz of Stefan's thoughts disturbed the clouds fogging her mind.

Shay, read his energy. Shay? Shay! Damn it, stay with me. You need to read his energy.

She didn't want to. It was difficult. She could barely understand Stefan's instructions. Something about Darren's energy. Her head lolled to the side. "What did you do to me?"

"Well, I'm punishing you, of course. Actually it's not that much of a punishment. If I thought I could control you, I'd keep you around, but I can't. The decision has been made." He paused and tilted his head. "You're strong, you know. Not as strong as me, of course, but still strong."

He hesitated; his gaze turned inward as if listening to an inner voice. Then sighed and shook his head. "No. I can't change my plans. If you ever found out what you could do with all that strength… If you could be trained to use it properly… But no. You aren't trainable. I've seen that already." He walked around the bed, studying her. "It's almost over. See? This is a nice way to go. Just fall asleep and you'll be gone. But of course, everyone resists it. Too bad. So sad. Everyone keeps clinging to their pathetic little lives even when that point is long gone."

Then she got it. *Oh God.*

"You're going to kill me?" The fog deepened. She struggled to push it back. To find clarity. To find answers. To find a way out of this hell.

Stefan had said, 'Read his energy.' Not an easy task. The fog thinned slightly, a small victory, and she tried to shift her vision to see Darren's energy.

As she'd done when things became serious between them. It was almost instinctive self-preservation to do so. She'd discovered he had a few anger issues, a few regrets, some energy heading into his past. A few walls saying he had a few secrets, but nothing to make her feel like she should delve deeper into the core of the man.

And now she realized her mistake. When it was too late to do anything about it.

She'd believed what she'd seen. The façade he'd presented. And had missed seeing him for who he really was. On the inside.

He was talking again, preening. "You live out your days worrying about what to do with all that lovely money. Oh poor you. You were so focused you never even saw who came knocking on your door. Didn't really see me. Not as I am inside. Only as I wanted you to see me."

She closed her eyes and opened her senses. With her fading strength, it was easier to function entirely on a soul energy level. The physical form was so much harder to sustain and control as it failed around her.

Clouds of dark black, sickly green energy surrounded him. Like a hard shell, it protected him on the inside, while he... *While he what?*

She couldn't see clearly enough. Fog rolled in. She blinked several times, trying hard to understand. There was a long cord from his root chakra to...the bed. And then to her. *He'd connected a cord to her.*

That connection, in itself wasn't the issue. Most people had hooks or cords into others, but not like this one.

Stefan's voice murmured deep in her psyche. *Stay with me, Shay. The cops will be there within minutes.*

Too late, she whispered. *His energy... It's sick. Deep, dark, diseased. Dying. Stefan, see it for yourself. I can see him. The real him. He's been hiding all this time. Somehow masking who he really was.*

And that betrayal hurt. So much. She'd loved Darren. Had planned to marry him and bear his children. She had planned to link her life with this man, who now stood so separate from her, watching her die by his own intent. Dear God. How had this happened? How had she not seen the man for who he was?

Because he could hide himself. And his personality is what's sick. He's not dying. You are!

Her thoughts drifted, scattered. *How is he doing this? I feel so weak. It's as if he's draining my very soul.* She couldn't hold a focus. She understood in theory what Stefan had said...but reality felt distant. Like this was happening to someone else.

He's opened your heart chakra. Draining your energy in a torrential wash. He's going to syphon you dry.

She pondered that bit of information. She should be upset about it. Should probably care. But it was hard to connect the information to its logical outcome – to use it.

You have to do something, urged Stefan. *Don't fight it. Embrace him with love. Start from that power position. Remember, energy is everywhere. You cannot be drained if you remember that universal energy flows through you at all times.*

She blinked at the tidbits of understanding as they filtered in.

Know that I am here. Part of you. As he drains you, I'm refilling you with love.

She couldn't move, she couldn't do anything but exist, caught in a war between life and death.

How?

Open your crown chakra to the universal energy. Create a spinning loop between your chakras to build power. But protect yourself; don't let him see you turn the tide of the energy flow. I will start it for you, but you have to help yourself.

His words penetrated slower than the energy. By the time she understood what Stefan meant, she was working on her crown chakra, opening it. She already felt the effects and, bolstered by the rise in her own energy, she immediately picked up the pace, refilling her body, enlivening her soul.

Don't feed the anger. Feed the love. Feel the power in the loving energy. Feel it strengthen you on all levels. You don't have to be his victim.

I can make him my victim. She had to admit, a part of her loved that idea.

Don't. It will change you. It will be something you will never forget. We need to find another way.

There isn't one. We can't hold him off forever, she whispered. *And how else can anyone stop him? Or others like him?*

Stefan's silence gave her the answer. She could stay in this unlimited loop, or she could do something about it. Something lethal. What choice was there? She had to do something before Darren realized what was happening. Shay focused on funneling more and more universal energy though her body, creating a swirling vortex within her. Gaining strength. Gaining purpose. Gaining determination for what was to come.

"How many have you killed?" she whispered, letting her eyes close weakly. He needed to believe she was dying. That he'd won. And she needed to know the extent of the damage he'd inflicted on those around him. To know she was doing the right thing in destroying him.

Darren stepped closer to hear her question. "How many? Is that what you asked?"

"Yes." She kept her eyes closed, focused on the energy pouring through her, gathering, waiting for the right time.

He laughed. "So many. It's really easy once you understand how. The biggest trick is hiding what I'm doing until I'm ready for people to know. Like you. You're very intuitive. Very astute. I had to be especially alert, in your case. It was good for a while. Kept me on my toes. But tonight I deposited a nice fat check you were kind enough to write out for me." He laughed. "Oh, you don't remember writing me a check, do you? That's okay. I'm great at forging signatures, too. I stole the checks awhile ago… It's not like you'll need them after today."

"How many?" Her voice gained a desperate strength. She needed to know. Even one death was too many. If he'd killed other people, she'd have no problem doing what needed to be done. She'd have to. He had to be stopped before he went on to kill again.

In the far distance, she heard sirens.

"Isn't that nice? You're curious. You can't stop the process now, you know. I chose Friday on purpose. No one will find you until Monday. When you don't show up for work, they will come looking." He glanced around the bedroom. "It's really too bad. I'd so hoped that this would be my forever home." He chuckled. "Odd to think I'm still using that childhood phrase. So few would understand it."

"How many?" she insisted, her voice stronger as anger stirred dangerously close to the surface. She had to keep herself in check. Had to keep her anger reined in. She had to take him out the right way. Or her actions would be impossible to live with.

He laughed. "Dozens, over the years."

Dozens. And with that, she knew there was no one else, no other way to stop him. He had ways of killing people that no one would ever know. That no one would ever understand. That no one would be able to prove. He had to be stopped. And there were so few people capable to do that.

She was one of them. Stefan was another.

Stefan. I need all you can channel my way.

I'm open and pouring. Do it. We can't hang on like this for much longer.

She opened her eyes and stared at the man she'd once loved. Now, her heart was filled with loathing for what he'd done – she hated him with a passion that fed her actions like she'd never felt before. But she had to find a way past that to the core of love from one human being to another. She had to come from a soul level.

She could do that.

"Darren."

He looked up at her, a sarcastic smile on his face. "What's the matter, Shay? Aren't you going to plead for your life?" he said mockingly.

She made it look agonizingly difficult to raise her arm and motion him closer. And to make that arm drop down weakly to the bed. He thought he'd almost drained her dry and had no idea what she could do. Good. She just needed him a little closer.

He sat down on the bed with his hip pushing up again her thigh. Now, if she could only reach... Her arm trembled with effort as she stretched it out and placed her hand on his chest. Right over his heart.

Barely holding the building energy force back, she asked, *Stefan, Are you ready?*

"What did you want to say, dearest Shay?" Darren's mocking voice floated through the room, surrounding her. Filling her. Firing her actions.

She opened up her swirling vortex. In her mind, she said to Stefan, *Now.*

She looked Darren in the eyes and whispered, "Go to hell."

She channeled the vortex to jettison the stream of loving soul energy forward to his heart – the actual organ – with all the energy that she could manage. With all the caring she could find.

He gasped once, his eyes going wide.

Shock and disbelief flashed livid on his face. Understanding lit the deep depths of his gaze. But it was too late for him to act. His opportunity was gone before he ever saw it.

Or, maybe, it wasn't.

Even as his eyes darkened, a firestorm of energy ricocheted through his heart chakra and back into her, burning though her palm as some type of fireball lit the room.

Something else – *someone else* – had joined the fray. And combined, they were stronger, more powerful and...desperate...to survive.

Shay poured energy, opening herself up to the universe and channeling everything she could access into the fight.

Stefan. What's happening?

I don't know. Another element has been added. Possibly another person...

Then we can't win, she cried out in pain and frustration. *That's two against two. And they have the advantage. How do we save this?*

Look out!

A small blue fireball leapt from her bed and flew into the energy torrenting through her hand.

No! Shay cried out.

It was too late. Morris, her ghostly feline, had joined the fight – and turned the tide as his loving, protective energy joined hers. There was a momentary pause, as if both sides were re-evaluating the balance of power, and then a deep purr sounded from the center of the maelstrom.

The space beneath her hand exploded.

Shay was thrown back against the headboard.

Darren was flung to the floor.

Regaining her wits, Shay scrambled to her feet to look over the edge of the bed.

Darren's features had frozen, his mouth open in a horrible rictus of terror, and like a tidal wave after it has lashed a beach and receded back out to the ocean, the color had slipped from his skin – leaving a gray wasteland behind.

But he was still alive.

Her heart squeezed tighter. Pain and shock rippled through her.

His eyes dimmed.

And that's when she saw it. A second light inside. A second awareness? A second person? A different part of Darren? How? Was he manipulated? Possessed? Or was this the other 'something' that had joined the fray?

She cried out, *Stefan, look!*

But it was too late to stop the process.

A deep sigh whispered from Darren's chest one last time, and his eyelids dropped closed.

He was dead.

CHAPTER 2

Almost one year later...on a Saturday evening...

SHAY WALKED INTO the packed ballroom, a fixed smile on her face. Her heart beating nervously in her chest. This was their big day.

She'd been waiting a long time to meet Roman Chandler. They had become acquaintances via email years ago, initially connecting over their grandfathers' mutual friendship, and then they became friends...close friends. And now...? She didn't know what they were. But, despite her last bad experience, she hoped.

If she had doubts about whether she was ready for a relationship again, she shoved them down and out of sight. She wanted to be ready. She could be ready. She had to be ready. Roman wasn't likely to wait. Her stomach somersaulted at the thought.

I haven't gone there since Darren...

She dismissed that thought. She'd take it slowly this time. Make sure she knew exactly what she was getting into before diving in too deep.

Still, no matter the confused and wounded state in her heart, she was totally excited to meet Roman in person. She already knew his twin brother Ronin, a detective with the Portland Police Department, but on a more professional basis. Of course, their grandfathers were best friends so it only made sense that their families would rub up well against each other.

Only Roman hadn't lived in Portland for years. He'd just recently moved back.

She didn't think he knew she was coming to the reception tonight. Then she couldn't put it past Bernice to have told him in confidence – she'd been trying to match the two of them for a long time. This charity event was Bernice's baby.

The ballroom was stuffed with people – mostly couples.

Who said being tall was a disadvantage? At almost 5' 9" without heels, Shay appreciated the view all the time, but in her toe-crushing stilettos, she was really enjoying being able to see over the heads of the others gathered here. With subdued classical music in the background, the many crystal chandeliers and ornate draperies and exquisite paintings provided a perfect backdrop to tonight's event.

Bernice Folgrent, of Folgrent's Foundation, never did anything small.

The noise and ambiance had the urgent tempo of schmoozing, smooching and the what-the-hell, the-booze-is-free atmosphere. A typical high-powered business reception for a big name charity foundation with hush-hush conversations, secretive smiles, handshakes and private deals. Millions of dollars would cross hands tonight and she, for one, was glad of it. There were so many in need.

Still, this function was so not her choice. But as the trustee for her family's foundation, she had to attend all sorts of these events, and she was as comfortable here as in the animal shelter where she helped out. One just had to remember the animals *here* were more dangerous. Plus, she could be proud of herself – she was neither a boardroom broad nor a high roller's arm candy. Thank God for that.

But no matter her personal preferences, tonight was a necessity and a delight. She'd come at Bernice's request. At eighty plus – and the number in that plus was a well-guarded secret – Bernice was a force to be reckoned with. When she wanted two people to meet, you had to either follow along or leave the continent. And even *that* might not save you.

Besides it was Roman who Bernice wanted Shay to meet... She didn't know that the two of them had been corresponding for a long time already...

"Shay!"

Shay pivoted smoothly to see a beautifully dressed older woman bearing down on her. Shay grinned. Bernice, dressed in gold brocade and evening gloves, only needed a cigarette holder to complete the old-time elegant picture. Still, despite her glamorous packaging, she was not to be misunderstood or underestimated, particularly when, like Shay, she also controlled millions of dollars.

For most people, it was a case of be nice to Bernice or face the dragon. Thankfully, Shay had known Bernice since she was a little girl and Shay had no need of Bernice's money because she controlled millions of her own. Besides, Shay loved the grande dame but that didn't make her blind to the old woman's machinations.

Bernice wrapped her in a smothering hug, her thickly made-up face passing discretely close to Shay's cheek as she kissed the air. "Darling, you look simply fabulous."

Shay smiled. "Thanks, Bernice. You're looking pretty stylish yourself."

"Of course, my dear," Bernice said comfortably. "The only difference between us is that I need hours to look like this – you do it naturally." She smirked. "And of course, I know what to *do* with my looks." She winked outrageously.

Shay laughed. Bernice wasn't going to change at this stage of her life. One either accepted her or avoided her. And Shay always had a soft spot for her.

"Come along now. There is this stunning man you have to meet."

"Oh, but–"

"No buts. You have to get out on the scene again. No more hiding away. Roman is the perfect person to catch your interest. You need to balance business with pleasure…and you need to spend more time with the *right* animals." Bernice nudged Shay, nodding her head in the direction of two men conversing off to the side.

"You're incorrigible."

"And you're too reclusive. Come on. Life is for living. Men are for loving." She motioned toward the two men. "I'd take those two any day." Bernice gave her a smug smile. "In fact, I took on a pair like them not all that long ago."

"Whoa." Shay held up her hand. "I so don't need to know. No more extolling your escapades, please. I still haven't recovered from your last titillating story."

"Now if only they'd do you some good. You have to forget about that dweeb fiancé of yours that died so tragically. He was never the man for you. You changed, and not for the better, when you were with him. Such a terrible thing to watch."

Shay turned to Bernice in shock. Inside, she was still struggling with Bernice calling Darren a dweeb. Bernice prided herself on keeping up with the younger set, but it still sounded so wrong to hear that word come out of the older woman's mouth. Or maybe it just sounded wrong when used in connection with her ex-fiancé? The man had been a lot of things, but he was not inept and geeky. Too much the opposite in fact. But he *had* died tragically.

Thankfully.

"What do you mean, *I changed?*"

"Oh my Lord, you became this dishrag, ready to wipe his nose and fetch his coffee. Don't you realize how much better you are than that?"

"I did *not* act like that." She couldn't stop the outrage that whipped through her. "Bernice, that's not fair. I loved him."

"Of course you did, my dear. That's the only reason anyone tolerated him in the first place." She barreled through the crowd. A crowd that parted magically as people understood it was *Bernice* that wanted to get past. Several times Shay murmured a polite 'thank you' as people stepped out of the way. Bernice had no such inclination.

She walked a path, accepting the magical bowing out of the way as her due.

"The man was a user," Bernice tossed back. "You need someone to light your fires, not squash them before they get a chance to catch. You're such a firecracker in every area but your damn love life. And we're going to fix that."

Shay put on the brakes. "No way. Bernice. Stop."

Not only did Bernice not listen, she doubled back to Shay, snagged her arm and tugged her forward – nicely of course. Everything Bernice did was nice, but there was also enough steel behind her actions to make her a formidable opponent.

Damn.

Shay plastered a laughing smile on her face while catching up to Bernice. "Stop pulling me," she whispered to Bernice.

"Then stop dragging your heels!" Bernice sent her an admonishing look. "I know you're here for other reasons, but you'll have to make time for this. I won't be around forever, you know. Soon, I'll be cha-chaing my way downstairs."

"Ha, even the devil doesn't want you down there with him. You'd order him around for all eternity."

Bernice spun on her heels, her eyes suddenly desperate, frail. She lowered her voice. "Don't joke about the devil. And don't ever, ever make a deal with him. You never know who he has working for him. Some people are just evil."

Whoa! What had gotten into Bernice?

Casting Shay a warning glance, Bernice glanced around furtively. Then she whispered, "I'm serious. You, more than anyone, should understand what I mean." Bernice turned and dragged Shay forward again.

Shay groaned. What was Bernice talking about? Had she gotten another nasty email? She'd been plagued by several lately. Typical Bernice had tossed them off as unimportant. As just expressions of discontent by those who wanted money and weren't going to be getting any. But that brushing off, itself, was unusual for Bernice. She had a tendency to bring in lawyers and scare off potential lawsuits.

Running foundations was big business, and drumming up new money was a constant challenge. These receptions were cornerstones of that process.

Shay was part of the same world. Dealt with the same driven – and sometimes desperate – people. She had her own methodology for finding the shysters and removing them from the honest applicants for her own foundation. And because they shared similar challenges and experiences, Bernice and Shay often compared notes and worked closely on joint projects. Their assistants also stepped in to help resolve problems on each other's projects. It helped to have that type of close working relationship. They watched each other's backs.

"Roman, darling. Here is the young woman I adore as if she were my own." Bernice reached out, latching onto the arm of a tall, suited gentlemen. She tugged him around and pointed to Shay. "Isn't she gorgeous? Just like I promised."

Oh lord. Shay groaned inside. Bernice really hadn't needed to make a public spectacle of this meeting. But why was she surprised? This was typical Bernice.

"Shay, this is Roman Chandler, the grandson of my dearest friend, Gerard Chandler."

Heads had turned at Bernice's loud introduction and color stroked up Shay's neck as she fought back her embarrassment. She should be used to it. But wasn't.

Still, she faced Roman, kept her plastered-on smile in place and lifted her gaze to his.

And sucked in her breath.

The look in his eyes. It was so…intimate. So knowing…as if he knew her…all of her, inside and out. And as if he liked what he knew.

They'd emailed. Chatted. Though they'd corresponded for a few years, over the last year they had built a friendly almost… intimate… relationship over the Internet and phone. And they had talked – like really talked. Theirs was a relationship she hoped would grow. But she'd never *met* him before. Hadn't shared everything with him. She didn't know him – not in the way he seemed to know her.

The heated look in his eyes unnerved her…and yes…intrigued her.

And she had to admit…sparked an answering awareness.

Shay had no illusions about her looks, regardless of Bernice's constant matchmaking attempts. She was too tall for many men, was slim, with milk chocolate brown shoulder-length hair and a largish mouth, and instead of symmetry, her nose was slightly crooked and one eyebrow was slightly off line. All minor in the scheme of things but those same flaws had given her terrible, angst-ridden moments through her teenage years. Now she could brush off the negative thoughts as they came and even though she could get her nose fixed, it no longer mattered to her.

According to the look in Roman's eyes, her flaws didn't matter to him now either. Of course he'd seen pictures of her. But that wasn't the same thing as this. She secretly had high hopes about Roman, but she'd never expected this level of appreciation from him right off.

When he spoke, his voice held both promise and familiarity. "Hello, Shay. I'm delighted to finally meet you." He glanced at Bernice, standing beside them both with a smug, knowing look on her face.

"Hello, Roman." *Did he look at all women as if they shared special memories?* She so badly wanted to ask. Instead, she said, "How nice to meet *you*." She paused then added, "Finally."

His gaze deepened to midnight blue, and he smiled. That wide movement of his lips released her from the intensity of his gaze. She could breathe easy again.

"This is so much better than email," he murmured, "and you are so much better looking in person than in photos."

Under Roman's midnight blue gaze, Shay's stomach churned with unanswered questions and delight. She wanted to take a more in-depth look at his energy, but thought she'd better save her strength for when a deeper reading might be needed.

A strange sound had her turning to face Bernice, her hostess and mentor.

Bernice opened her mouth to speak when she suddenly stopped, an odd look on her face. Her breath sucked in so loudly, Shay leaned closer in concern. "Bernice? Are you all right? What's the matter?"

Silence.

Shay studied her old friend, but Bernice's face had turned ashen, her eyes locked on something behind Shay's back. Shay twisted around to look, but the only thing behind her was a wall. A blank wall.

Turning back around, and seeing no change in her friend, she said, "Bernice, talk to me. You're scaring me."

Bernice's breathing turned ragged, stuttered then almost appeared to stop. Her features locked in place yet her chest rose and fell in a natural movement.

The hairs on the back of Shay's neck rose.

Jesus, she must be having an attack of some kind. "We'll get you some help. Can you talk to me? Can you tell me what's wrong?"

Roman bent to study Bernice's face. "I'll get a doctor." He took off.

Bernice's mouth worked. Still, no sound came out.

Silently, Shay willed Roman to hurry. But from the looks of it, he wasn't going to be fast enough. She raised her hand to call for help when her arm was grabbed. She stared, surprised to see Bernice's bronzed nails cutting into her soft skin.

"Bernice?" Shay rubbed the papery skin on the back of Bernice's fingers with gentle soothing strokes. "Hang on. Help is coming."

From a distance, she could hear rapidly approaching footsteps. *Thank God. Please let her friend be all right.*

Worried, Shay stared into Bernice's eyes, and Bernice stared back. Her gaze dark. Bottomless. Blind. Shay's heart squeezed in fear. "Bernice. Damn it, stay with me. Please talk to me if you can."

Shay willed Bernice's eyes to return to normal. Willed them to blink. To move. To do *something*.

Then *something* else happened. Inside, deep inside, Bernice blinked. A clear movement that Shay could see and understand.

Except for one thing.

On the surface, Bernice's eyelids never moved.

ROMAN CHANDLER STOOD off to one side of the ballroom entrance as the paramedics moved the stretcher out through the foyer and into the ambulance. It was certainly a different world out here than the expensive event going on behind him.

Damn. He'd found Bernice was a good friend and benefactress to the people. 'My people,' as she'd say. To see the old fighter brought low by age and sudden change in health was a blow most people here would struggle with – one that would make them look at their own health and wellbeing. She was formidable. Creating stress and tension and love and affection with a few words, a flick of her hand and the flash of her smile.

He hoped whatever was wrong would turn out to be minor but given Bernice's age – well…she hadn't looked good. He'd already called his grandfather and given him the news. His grandfather would no doubt make it to the hospital before the ambulance did. He'd been there for Bernice for over thirty years. That wasn't going to change now.

His thoughts drifted back to the woman who stood beside him, the woman Bernice had just introduced him to…the woman who had intrigued him since their first email. Now he knew his gut reaction was right about Shay.

Shay was…dynamite. Everything he'd hoped for. Hell, he couldn't have hoped for this… He hadn't even known this kind of connection could exist, let alone was something to *hope* for. She'd entered the ballroom with an attitude that caught every man's attention. He knew because he'd watched them all turn to mark her progress.

She had to be almost as tall as him, in heels. And every inch was smoothly muscled and as delectable as any woman he'd seen. And he'd seen plenty. And learned that the inside rarely matched the package.

That he'd *recognized* the delicate line of her neck, the smooth curve of her shoulder, the delicate bones of her wrist, had shocked him. The level of familiarity and desire he felt for her, terrified him. And delighted him. The recognition could *not* be explained away by the plethora of email conversations and a few pictures.

He'd been painting her for years. A delight that had him open to making that initial contact. Since then…well, she'd worked her way into his life, his psyche…even his dreams. Some days she was all he could think about. He'd been looking forward to this meeting for months.

Still his reaction to finally meeting her shook him to the core. From the moment he laid eyes on her this evening he'd wanted her. He'd known that already on an intellectual level. She was so damn interesting. But to have the physical person match his fantasies…well, that's when he'd been deluged by an overwhelming sense of recognition. Not just a superficial knowing, but an understanding of her at a deep, visceral level. It was as if he knew her for who she was, really was. Without the trappings of society, the painful past, the solitary existence he knew she lived. He just knew Shay.

And she wouldn't be happy that he knew as much as he did about her life. She liked her privacy. She would likely blame Bernice and their grandparents… And it's true, they'd started his interest in Shay – at least initially. After that. Well, he was no fool…

He'd almost frozen with shock when she spoke to him. Her voice had been a surprise. Light, cool. Whatever else she was, life, vibrant life, swirled inside. She presented as calm and poised, but that calm exterior in no way hid the richness of the woman on the inside. When she spoke, the artist in him wished he knew how to capture that rich throaty fullness and knew his medium would be lacking if he tried. The sensual promise of her voice sent shivers down his spine and straight to his loins.

And that's the woman he wanted to get to know better. Needed to get to know more.

His paintings didn't do her justice.

The artist in him tried to memorize her details. Like a video camera snapping off stills, he tried to capture the special essence that made up this remarkable woman. He could only hope that later, much later, he'd remember some of what he'd seen and recorded in his mind.

His grandfather had warned him about Bernice's matchmaking surprise tonight. And Roman was grateful. Bernice didn't have a good history as a matchmaker, but she was hell on wheels when she had an agenda.

She'd thrown Callie at him years ago, hadn't she? Look how well that had turned out. *Not.* Still he'd been young and infatuated with his young wife. He couldn't blame Bernice for his own lack of judgment. Callie had been too free-spirited to stick faithfully to one man – even her husband. The divorce had been painful with the list of her flings including names of several of his friends.

Callie was part of *his* history. A part he didn't want to revisit. A mistake he didn't want to repeat. Along with the bullet that had ended his police work. Now he specialized in Internet security. Even had his own company.

This time he knew better.

And he knew Shay had her own history to get over.

Besides, without that painful breakup and change of career, he'd never have returned to the passion of his youth – painting. And he couldn't imagine how empty his life would be now without that constant creative need and drive washing through him.

Moreover, his emotional breakup with Callie had endowed his work with a new edge. But those post-breakup pieces were nothing compared to the work he churned out now. Somewhere along the line, he'd become fixated on his current series and hadn't managed to paint it out of his system. Though he'd tried.

Maybe now, he understood why.

"Excuse me." A man walked around him, making Roman aware that he stood in the middle of the elaborate front entrance, holding back the crowd as he stared down the curved driveway.

He hoped Bernice was all right, if only for his grandfather's sake. He'd be devastated to lose her. His grandfather was getting on in years and wasn't as resilient as he once was.

Another reason for his return to his hometown. To be closer to his family.

It had been time.

IN THE TOO-SILENT silence, Shay and the rest of the hushed crowd watched the paramedics efficiently load Bernice into the ambulance and drive away with siren blaring and lights flashing.

Bernice had been a larger-than-life presence for so long; Shay couldn't imagine the void she'd have in her life if Bernice died. She shouldn't think so negatively, but it was hard not to. Shay *knew* what lively, life-giving energy looked like. Their last conversation had been so strange. And Shay knew what at-the-edge-of-death energy looked like. Bernice's energy now indicated that she'd lived well past the best-by date.

And it hurt to think that Bernice might not bounce out of bed and give Shay royal hell for sleeping alone – again. Shay looked for the man Bernice had all but pushed in her direction.

Roman had stood off to one side, casual, concerned and competently keeping the crowd back. Many of those who had gathered had disappeared inside by now.

Shay appreciated that.

Still, whatever she'd seen deep in Bernice's eyes during the episode made her suspicious. She needed to find out just what that double set of eyes had meant…if anything.

She had to do what she could to find out. She stepped back into the ballroom. Despite the thinning masses there were still too many people around for her to do much by way of finding answers. Regardless, she opened her senses and studied the sea of colors swirling through the crowd. Emotions rippled outward as everyone absorbed details and dealt with the crisis in their midst.

She couldn't avoid hearing the words whispering outward as each person's thoughts swirled around them, carried on their energy. Even though she normally saw more images than words, right now, in this crisis, these thoughts damn near screamed in the ether.

Is that Bernice?

The old dame is finally coming to the end of the road.

Oh dear, I hope she'll be okay.

The world won't be the same without her.

About time that old bat bit it.

The last thought had Shay spinning around and pinning a look on a young, rakish-looking man standing off to one side. She studied him, half recognizing him. Still there wasn't any real negativity rolling off him. His energy was more like that of a disgruntled nephew who was hoping he'd be getting something from the will…but wouldn't be, and he *so* knew it.

Shay dismissed him as unimportant, and let her gaze continue to roam, still hearing the whispered thoughts like dull noise in the background. Studying those standing around her, she let her gaze zip past Roman and came to a sudden stop. She slowly retraced the short distance to Roman's aura and studied it.

Her heart slammed into her chest, and she gasped.

He was a man of power. Psychic power.

Like Darren.

But she didn't know what kind of power. It could be anything. And she didn't know if he knew. Many didn't.

Roman turned to look at her, as if just becoming aware of her interest, and raised an eyebrow in concern. He took a half step toward her. She gave a tiny panicked shake of her head and averted her gaze. It was only her strength of will that stopped her from backing away from him. She desperately tried to control her breathing. When she could, she stole another glance at Roman's energy.

And her heart stalled.

Part of him was shielded. Behind a protective wall. She couldn't read him. He could be anyone in there. He could be a good guy...or another bad one.

And for all she knew he could be just like Darren, her dead fiancé who'd tried to kill her.

Knock, knock...?

Hi Shay. There you are. Too bad you can't hear me. Standing in the middle of the chaos as usual. Did you enjoy the show? I made sure you got a front row seat.

And you have no idea I even exist. Just the way I like it.

See, or don't see me...it doesn't matter. I'm still special. I can get inside people's auras and sneak into the part of their consciousness they don't like to see. That they hide or bury. The parts that exist but that can't be acknowledged — even from themselves. I can make my hosts do things. Not too much yet. And not for very long, but I'm getting better. Stronger.

You might ask, what's the difference between me and a serial killer? The serial killer gets his hands dirty.

I don't.

And the difference between me and the guy I'm stepping into is...nothing. Because under our skin we all want the same thing. Even you, Shay.

I'm just one of the few that found out how to do it. It's taken time, and a lot of effort, but I'm getting better all the time. Now I don't have to be beside the person; I don't even have to be in the same building. Actually, at this point in my evolution, soon I won't even have to be in the same fucking city. I'll have mastered this technique and can live anywhere. Any way I want.

It's not about money. I can get all I want. It's not about prestige. I could have that too if I so choose. No. This is about the essential building block of our lives. The piece that makes or breaks a person. The piece that says who they really are. What's that piece, you might ask?

It's called power.

Power is all I want and I have lots, but now…now I have the capability to take your power, too. And add to mine. Why would I do that to you?

Easy. You took something very special from me.

And for that, Shay, you will pay.

But not to worry. There are a few other people I plan to meet with first.

We'll see each other around.

Oh, my mistake.

No, you won't!

But I'll see you.

CHAPTER 3

ONCE IN THE elevator, on the way up to her apartment, Shay phoned the hospital for an update on Bernice, only to be told there was no improvement and the doctors were still with her. It didn't look good. She'd immediately called her grandfather to update him on Beatrice's condition. She'd learned he was already at the hospital. Shay offered to join him.

He'd been almost incoherent and inconsolable but ultimately wanting to be alone with his beloved. Bernice was a huge part of their lives.

Shay hoped Bernice would pull through, but given her age… Still it was shock. She'd been indomitable for years with a spine of steel and a body meant for lusty horizontal dancing. Of course, she'd relied on frequent surgeries to keep her in as decent shape as modern medicine allowed. The what and how of all that was a secret between Bernice and her doctor.

Speaking of secrets, Shay remembered Bernice's comment about making a deal with the devil. She wished she understood what she meant by that.

There was no mythical devil in Shay's world. All people were capable of doing evil things, but few thrived on it. Those that did were…the worst. She had experiences with a different reality, giving her insights that well and truly locked her mind to a whole different belief system. One where evil was an all-too-common occurrence. And where dead wasn't necessarily dead.

Shay walked into her Portland apartment later and kicked off her shoes. The waterfront view called to her troubled soul, promising to ease and sooth her tattered nerves. But first she wanted to be comfortable. She changed out of her evening wear into cami and pants, then walked back into her kitchen where she popped the cork on an open bottle of wine. She poured herself a glass and with that in hand, she walked out to the small garden deck to sit under the stars. She needed this space.

It had been a long day.

The stars shone bright in the clear sky, easing the pain slightly. Her life would be forever changed. Bernice had been a huge influence and would be dearly missed.

When her tattered nerves calmed, Shay checked in with Stefan – her friend, her mentor, her apprentice. Who'd have thought she'd have anything to teach the incredibly gifted psychic? Not her.

But he'd convinced her she had something to offer.

She could do some energy tricks and he told her those had value.

And you *do,* he said in her mind, interrupting her musing. *Stop second-guessing yourself.*

Too tired to bother, she answered back readily. *I'm going to call you on the phone. Hang on.* She picked up the phone and dialed his number. "Hey. Bernice had an attack of some kind. A stroke, maybe. I don't know. It was weird the way it happened. She's at the hospital right now, but I don't know how she is."

"You do, but you don't want to look that close."

That was true. She didn't. Some things she didn't want to know.

"Yes." Shay hesitated. Stefan, like her, had seen too much of the world. "Something else happened at the same time. I want to shrug it off, but—"

"But you can't. So tell me."

Haltingly, she refocused her thoughts and explained the weird sense that someone else had stared – no, blinked – out at her from Bernice's gaze.

"And this wasn't a possession?"

"No. There was no sensation that anyone took her body, took her over in any way. At least that I could sense at the time. Except that damn gaze, as if someone else was looking out at the world from within her head. It was beyond freaky." She took a deep breath. "It was almost like what I saw *that night.*"

"*That* night?" he asked.

"Yes. When Darren died." A half-choking laugh escaped. "No, it couldn't be anything to do with him… That's crazy."

"Hmmm."

"What do you think is happening?" She knew he was going to ask her to check and, damn it, she didn't want to. She didn't want to delve into the dark and see the boogeyman tonight.

"I'm not sure. I'll have to ponder it." His voice faded slightly. She smiled and settled back, realizing Stefan was off in his psychic realm, disappearing into the mist like only he could.

Having a psychic in your life meant adjusting to new privacy rules.

She shivered. Being psychic made you who you were. Every aspect of your life was affected. You just didn't always like *how*. None of her 'regular' friends knew of her abilities. And she preferred it that way.

It was hard to find anyone who could understand. For that reason, she didn't see her friendship with Stefan ever lessening. Changing, perhaps, as each grew and developed, but their connection would never stop. They couldn't sever it if they wanted to. And they didn't. Connected on the ethers as they were, it felt as if they were psychic twins. And if that concept didn't blow a person's mind, then nothing would.

Now she was used to the connection, and she appreciated the closeness of someone's life mirroring hers. Thankfully, they were not exactly the same, but enough alike so she didn't feel alone – anymore.

And she knew it was the same for Stefan.

Stefan was a special friend. He was not her lover, but they had a friendship in the deepest sense. Something most men would say was impossible. But most women would be envious of such a relationship. And Stefan wasn't gay.

She'd asked the stunningly handsome man early on in their relationship and his answering look of horror had kept her laughing for days. Even now the memory made her grin.

Another time he'd told her his partner was living her life, unaware that he was there waiting. And that Shay herself was doing the same thing. He told her if she'd look harder, she'd find the truth of his words.

The thing is, she saw too damn much as it was. Why would she want to look any closer?

"Stefan?" she said cautiously, not wanting to pull him free if he wasn't ready to return to this reality.

"I'm here. Just trying to see what's going on with Bernice."

Shay straightened. "What do you see?"

"Not sure. Her body is almost gone. Lots of energy filling the room right now. Her soul is free and wandering the room. It just doesn't feel...right, though."

"That's hardly scientific." She almost laughed. The two of them used their senses the way other people used facts and logic. "You know how the rest of the world would react to your statement?"

"Good thing they don't know about it then, isn't it? There are several people in Bernice's room."

"Is my grandfather there?" In her heart, she hoped so. Pappy had been holding a lost-love candle for Bernice for decades. He'd loved her and lost her, according to him, and Bernice was a once-around type of gal. So far no male had managed to hang onto her. Pappy was just one in a long line of discarded lovers. She wondered if Bernice had any idea how many broken hearts she'd left behind.

"Maybe you should go to the hospital. She's fading quickly."

"I'm not sure I want to be there when she passes."

"She wants *you* there."

Damn. Shay really didn't want to go. Not just because of the whole hospital thing, but there was the death thing. And then there was also the whole Pappy thing.

"She's calling for you."

Shay stood up, asking sharply, "She's awake?"

"No."

"She's calling on the ethers for you," Stefan murmured.

"What?" Shay gasped. "How is that possible? I never heard her."

"She's struggling to be heard. She is new to this. But she knows. She's always known about you."

SHAY, NOW IN jeans and t-shirt, walked across the hospital parking lot, all her psychic guards solidly locked in place. Like most people gifted with psychic abilities, she hated these institutions. The veil between life and death was thin here. Those overly affected by liminal places had to strengthen their walls to stop the emotions from creeping into their own psyches. Then, of course, there were the walking, talking, living ghosts in every hallway.

The new wing on the children's hospital that Shay's foundation was funding was different. The energy lighter, brighter. Livelier. Innocent. And ghost-free – so far.

Other psychics saw the ghosts themselves, whereas Shay saw the ghost of the person's energy. A slight but important difference.

She read, saw, understood energy.

The auric energy. Someone's chakra energy. The way a person used that energy. The way their body used its energy to function and to heal. Not a very useful skill to most people, but to some people, who wanted the information she could provide, she could be a little *too* useful. And had learned to keep her mouth shut.

If anyone needed to know what a person did with their money, for example, she could find out. Or if someone needed to know if someone else was trustworthy. Or how stable someone was mentally... These were things she could tell with a degree of certainty. She knew, to her own regret, that she wasn't infallible. That when it had counted most, she'd been fooled the same as everyone else.

Hence the need to ensure the secrecy regarding her talents and her joy in the relationship she had with Stefan. He knew and he cared...for her. Not about what she could do for him. Or what information she could supply. Or how she could use that information to his advantage.

He told her there was a group of similar-minded people, all with...abilities like hers. She'd met a few. And probably would enjoy meeting the ones she hadn't. When Stefan said that day would come, she'd smiled.

She entered the hospital entrance and took the right turn down the empty hallways. It had been a tough day already and she didn't think she'd like the way the night would end. Bernice's attack had sent all thought of Roman from her head – at the time. Now however...

The thought of his wall made her cringe.

Shay also knew that having a protective wall didn't make him a sociopath. It made him someone with something to hide. The *what* of the something was what concerned her.

He'd made his interest in her clear, and prior to walking into that room, she'd been crystal clear about him too. Now...she had to ask some hard questions. And she had to reconcile the overwhelming attraction she'd felt between them, that inner knowing that said he was worth it, with the fear that a relationship with him could end badly.

She didn't want to go down that road again.

Her abilities should have shown her who the real Darren was – at least enough to have sent her running in the opposite direction.

Only she'd seen *nothing* wrong in his energy.

Instead she'd let herself be lulled into a false sense of security, sucked into the new love relationship and all the giddiness that state offered. Sure, they'd had problems. Truthfully, there had been times she'd had her doubts about the major step she agreed to take – marriage wasn't for the faint of heart. But she'd put her doubts down to first-time wedding jitters.

Until that night when he'd entered her home unannounced and she'd realized it was too late.

After the mess had finally ended, she'd gone into a full-blown crisis over her ability to accurately see the energy of those closest to her. Always looking for what she might have missed. She'd locked down her feelings and that had created huge trust issues for herself and others.

But was that fair to Roman?

No. But trust, once crushed, was hard to offer again.

In Darren's case, she'd tried to read him and had seen only what he wanted her to see. In Roman's case, she'd read him and had seen the damn wall. And had nearly bolted. What was he hiding? And did it matter?

The long hospital hallway finally ended. She turned the corner and entered Bernice's private room.

"Shay, I'm so glad you made it in time." Her grandfather stood at Bernice's bedside, cradling her pale, limp hand in his. Even after all this time, his love, open and hurting, shone from deep inside his puppy-dog eyes. "She's failing, my dear. I fear she won't last long." Pappy's rheumy gaze zeroed in on Shay sorrowfully. "I'd hoped she'd wake up, at least one more time, but it appears she'll go off gently in the night."

"And maybe that's the best way, Pappy." Shay wrapped an arm around her beloved grandfather's frail shoulders and squeezed. "We don't want her to suffer."

He shook his bowed head, the corner of his lips trembling. "No. We don't."

"Well, Charles. Has there been any change?" Gerard Chandler walked into the private hospital room, disrupting their moment. He and her grandfather were old friends, and both were Bernice's lovelorn suitors. Shay smiled at Gerard and saw the same ravaging grief as on Pappy's face.

"No. She hasn't moved a muscle, unfortunately." Pappy patted Bernice's hand. "Shay just arrived in time to say good-bye."

"Good. Now she can tell us herself what happened last night." Gerard took up the matching position to Pappy's on the far side of Bernice's bed, glaring at her as if Bernice's condition was all Shay's fault. "Roman explained, but we need to hear it from you."

Knowing that both elderly men needed to hear every scrap of information she had, she went over the evening's events. "That's all I know," she lied. "Dr. Fitzpatrick, who was on hand at the gathering, looked after her, and the paramedics arrived very quickly."

She waited a beat, swallowing to moisten her dry throat. "There was nothing I could do to help her," she said, her voice thick with emotion. She said this more for herself than for them. "There was nothing anyone could do."

There was no point telling them what she'd seen in Bernice's eyes at the end. They wouldn't understand. Hell, she didn't understand.

Pappy nodded, reached out one hand and patted her shoulder. "Of course, my dear. I know you did everything you could. It's just her time.

And soon, it will be ours."

"Speak for yourself," Gerard grumped. "I'm not ready to kick off."

"I don't think Bernice was either." Shay smiled at the memory. "Just moments before she collapsed, she urged me to start living again. She looked and acted normal. Was our typical, vibrant, life-loving Bernice."

Both men nodded.

Pappy said, "She was unique. Everyone knew and loved her."

The way he spoke, using the past tense, showed an acceptance of what was coming. She opened her psychic vision to see how Bernice's energy was doing and barely stifled a gasp. There was a skin of energy lying heavy and pale on top of her body…as if Bernice's astral body lay on top of her physical body. Shay tracked the pale energy upward to Bernice's face. It lay in peaceful repose as if asleep. That was all good. The end would be soon.

Also good was that the silver cord that connected her astral body to her physical body was thin and weak. Almost ready to be severed. Except a tiny thread wafted around the room. She tried to trace it and found a mass of light gently shimmering energy by the window ledge.

Bernice.

Or what was left of Bernice – her astral soul might be a better way to put it. It was more ghostlike than an astral projection. More ghostlike than those walking on the ethers. This was Bernice as she was ready to depart. And there was still a sparkle to her. A luminescence she'd appreciate. Shay had to smile. Even in transition, Bernice would shine.

And Shay could just imagine Bernice trying to raise a little hell on the other side.

She let her gaze wander the room, looking for a way to interact with Bernice's energy without being noticed. She couldn't guarantee that Bernice would respond; she might not be cognizant in this state – most weren't.

If only she could get the two men to leave the room.

As if on cue, Gerard's phone rang. Pappy snapped at him for disturbing Bernice's solitude.

"It's Roman," Charles said. "He's just arrived. Come out in the hallway. We need to discuss Bernice's arrangements."

Pappy stiffened. "She's not gone yet!"

But Pappy trundled toward the door. The two men stood in the doorway, their heads bent together.

And the cell phone call gave Shay a wonderful idea. She pulled hers out and held it to her ear. She walked over to the window as if to make a call. Bernice's energy wobbled as Shay approached.

As if speaking into the phone, Shay asked in a quiet voice, "Bernice, are you there?"

The glowing mass smiled as if lit from inside. With more of an impression than actual gestures, Shay heard Bernice's voice. *I wanted to tell you something.* She paused. *But I've forgotten what it was.*

"Is this related to what you were trying to say last night?"

Could an astral person pale any more? Shay watched in fascination as Bernice's form wavered before her.

"Bernice?" she whispered. "What's the matter?"

In a horrible repeat of the night before, Bernice froze. She stared at Shay and her mouth opened as if to speak, only no sounds were heard – physically or psychically.

Shay leaned closer, afraid Bernice would disappear before she could get the information she needed. "Bernice, please. Tell me what's going on."

Bernice seemed to make an effort to pull herself together; her form firmed and then wavered. *I love them both, you know. Don't let them suffer more than necessary when you sort this out, my dear.*

"Sort what out? Bernice, I don't understand." Shay tried to keep her voice down but her hushed whisper resounded through the room.

"Shay, are you okay?" Pappy called out behind her.

Shay turned to smile reassuringly at Pappy.

Concerned, he made as if to walk toward her.

She waved him back. "I'm fine, Pappy." She held up her phone as if to say she was still in a conversation. He nodded and turned back to Gerard then stepped out into the hallway to talk to someone else.

Relieved, Shay turned back to Bernice to find her…gone.

She spun around.

Bernice lay still, her skin even more gray and transparent than before. And the pale mist that had hung over her head was no longer there. Blue veins pulsed slowly up her hand and arm. Bernice had gone back into her body, but judging by the sounds of the raspy breathing she didn't rest easy. Shay doubted Bernice would last the hour.

"Bernice?" she whispered, leaning over the old woman. "Please, can't you tell me anything more?"

There was no answer, only the rasping that sounded overly loud in the silence.

Pappy walked over, his hand gently going to Shay's shoulder. "It's almost over."

Gerard walked to the far side of Bernice's bed. He picked up Bernice's right hand, holding it gently. He whispered lovingly, "Go, my dear. Stay safe. Until we meet again."

Indeed, as if she'd heard him, Bernice's chest rose once more, stretching to the extent her rib cage would allow and then sagged downward for the last time.

Then there was only silence.

Pappy choked, his hand patting the back of Bernice's faster than before. His shoulders hunched. He whispered so softly Shay almost missed his words. "Good-bye, my love. Good-bye."

Shay had to wonder about a woman who kept these two men so in love with her that they'd never resented being alone for all these years.

And they didn't resent it. They'd always felt blessed to spend time with her. Even though they were no longer lovers. Even now as she lay dying.

Poor Bernice... And poor Shay. Tears welled at the corner of her eyes. She'd loved Bernice – a larger-than-life presence that no one could ignore. She'd been a lovely friend, a trusted confidant and an exceptional woman. Her legacy would live on for decades. Bernice had done such good works.

A huge hole was opening in Shay's heart. She'd known this day would come. But she wasn't ready to let her surrogate mother go.

She'd always been there for Shay. And Shay's life would be so much emptier now.

A commotion at the door had Shay turning around. Roman walked in, and his suit did not hide the beautiful animal beneath. He attracted her like no other, though she knew better than to respond.

She deliberately turned her attention back to Bernice to give herself a few moments to compose herself. The attraction for Roman scared her even as he intrigued her. And Bernice, who'd been trying to set them up, would probably scold her for being afraid. Bernice would tell her wake up and live a life full of joy and experience. And she'd already said Roman was worth the chance.

And if Shay was wrong about his wall, and what could be hidden behind it, he could be the other half of her heart. And she'd have missed her chance.

Stefan had tried to explain energy and love to her. He had a leading theory about energy blends and music with color combinations. Not having been interested at the time, and having sworn off relationships, she hadn't delved any deeper, but damn if Roman didn't have her dredging her brain for little bits and pieces of Stefan's sage advice. And she'd come up empty. She'd have to ask Stefan later. And take his gentle ribbing as payment.

"I'm glad you're here, Roman. Bernice has just passed on." Gerard spoke quietly from the other side of the bed.

Shay stayed at Pappy's side, waiting for him to regain control of himself and finish his good-byes.

"Hard to believe she's gone." Roman's voice was respectful, calm. She studied him under her lashes feeling the same familiar tug. He was awfully collected. As if he had more insight into the daily life and death in a hospital than she'd first suspected. But then he had been a cop.

"She's been such a big part of my life." Gerard's voice trembled ever so slightly.

"Let me know when you're ready to go home." Roman's dark chocolate voice slid down Shay's spine, seeming to linger on every bone before stroking lower.

Christ. She closed her eyes and mentally zipped up her chakras to keep him from going deeper. He could be lethal.

Thank God he didn't know what he was doing to her libido. *Or did he?* She snuck a glance at him, and found him staring directly at her.

"Shay? How are you doing?" Once again, that smooth, caring voice stroked her blood.

She swallowed hard, gave him a polite smile. "I'm fine. Thanks. It's Pappy who's just lost one of his best friends."

Roman cocked his head, that intense gaze locking hers in place. "Wasn't Bernice a friend of yours too?"

She smiled wryly. "Bernice was a force of her own. She was a very good friend. But she was one of Pappy's best friends." She sniffled. "And she will be dearly missed by all of us."

Roman's deep golden brown eyes warmed, smiled. "Isn't that the truth? There aren't many Bernices left in the world."

"There won't ever be another Bernice." Pappy spoke for the first time. He glanced over at Shay. "Give me a moment, will you?"

Happy to give him the time he needed, Shay nodded and walked to the door, motioning the other two men to leave in front of her. "Let's give him privacy."

Gerard shook his head, saying, "I'll stay with him. We both have things to say to her."

With a last glance at Pappy, who nodded, Shay and Roman turned and walked out.

"Hard to believe those two are good friends," Roman said, glancing back to the two men huddled together at Bernice's side.

"Especially when they've loved the same woman for as long as they have."

Roman gaze zipped back to her. "Sounds like you don't approve."

"I'm not sure I do," she answered coolly. "Pappy has been at her side for decades, waiting and hoping for her to change her mind. Almost like a favorite puppy dog, hoping for a pat on his head."

"And, from my understanding, she made it clear she wouldn't change her mind."

"True enough." Shay turned to study the two older men and whispered, "It feels like the passing of an era right now."

The two older men hugged each other while Roman and Shay looked on. Then, first the one, and then the other, bent to kiss Bernice's cheeks.

Using the moment of silence, Shay switched her vision to search the room, on the off chance that Bernice was still there. It happened sometimes. That people stayed close to their bodies after death. Close to what they knew. She searched carefully. And there was no sign of Bernice – in any form.

"What are you looking for?" Roman asked, his voice reeking with curiosity.

She started. "I don't know, just looking at the private rooms." God, that was lame. She raised an eyebrow at him.

A smile played at the corner of his mouth. His gaze, direct and determined, held hers. "And now that we have a few moments of privacy, I have another question for you."

"Oh." Shay stared are him, waiting.

That gaze, that could be so warm and caring, deepened to one that was dark and penetrating. "Why are you afraid of me?"

Oh shit.

ROMAN WALKED INTO his loft drained. The evening at the hospital had been emotionally charged with Bernice's passing. Gerard and Charles had loved that woman, with a deep abiding love that Roman had never dreamed existed.

Grateful for this piece of calm and serenity within the city, Roman walked out onto his large waterfront deck and breathed deeply of the fresh evening air.

He'd just come home from dropping off his grandfather. He'd hated to leave him alone, but the older man insisted he wanted to grieve on his own. In truth, Roman also wanted the time to think. To think about Shay.

She'd been so caring, so loving with her grandfather. He respected that. Actually he loved that about her. The work she did, the people she chose to help. He had known about that, and who she was, before they met. But he hadn't *known* her – not like this. In fact, he was liking everything he was learning.

Needing the connection, Roman walked into his studio and stared at the latest sketch. He glanced at an earlier one on the wall. Not good enough for showing, but something about the colors made the hanging one special. Like many of the early pictures, he had been compelled to add pale blue in the picture. Like gentle smoke.

He'd fought against adding it, but it seemed the pictures weren't complete until he'd added a blue swirl. For that reason, he often incorporated the blue into the flowing design of the draping material or gown.

Then about a year ago, that insistence had eased, the blue was still there, but it was no longer as prominent.

For a long time he'd wondered about that compulsion to add blue, then decided it had to be part of his artistic growth. As he looked at his current picture, he realized that there was a thin blue film over the figure in the painting, like the brush had whispered a faint blush of blue. It created only the slightest of shimmers.

Done in midnight black, Shay's long, elegant back faced him with her hair drifting across the canvas. The picture stopped at the chin line. His own preference. He wanted to do a full body with her beautiful facial features but so far had resisted. Something had stopped him. He didn't know what or why. While the pictures remained only of her form, then he could fool himself to believe she was *only* his model.

If he did break down and add her face – something he knew he couldn't do yet – he'd be telling the world who she was…and how important she was to him. By creating her full image for all eternity, he would be acknowledging Shay was his muse.

And that would change things.

His muse was a living, breathing thing to him. A relationship he lived with daily.

And if he acknowledged she was his muse, he'd be acknowledging that she was not only necessary in his world but she was his passion.

He swallowed hard. *Could that be?*

And if she was his passion…it was a short hop to considering… acknowledging he wanted her to become his partner, his other half…his one true love.

Still that was a step he hadn't taken. Yet.

The next morning on the other side of town…

WHY WAS HIS neighbor coming down his walk? David Cummings lowered the gas can nozzle into the small tank of his lawnmower when Melanie Sergeant called out his name. She tugged her poodle toward him.

David swore under his breath. His wife often teased him that he mowed his lawn every Sunday morning from April to October, like clockwork, as particular about his lawn as the teeth of the patients in his dental practice.

And that meant his neighbors knew where and when to find him. Most of the time that was fine.

Just not today. Today was special. And he didn't have time to chit-chat. He hoped Melanie wasn't selling any more chocolate bars for the school she taught at. He just didn't have time today.

He planned to take Angela to brunch and surprise her with a cruise to Scotland. Five kids and she deserved it. Hell, he deserved it, too. She'd likely cry when she found out. Hell, he might too. Thirty-five years together and still going strong. Damn he was a lucky man.

And he could survive a chat with his neighbor for a few minutes.

"'Morning, Melanie. How are you doing this beautiful weekend?"

As Melanie walked closer, he realized there was something different about her. She looked normal, but… His throat tightened and instinctively he wanted to back away from her. He swallowed hard and resisted. That was foolish. He pasted a smile on his face.

"I'm doing great. It's a lovely day, isn't it?" She gave him a bright smile then a frown appeared on her forehead, and her eyes darkened.

Like really dark.

"Are you okay?" He stepped toward her, and as he did, her eyes sharpened, and went almost black. That was wrong.

He forced himself closer, if she needed help… He wasn't a physician, but he knew enough to give basic CPR. Though his skin was creeping, and his head…

What was wrong with his head?

He blinked. Then blinked again. What was wrong with her eyes?

The light was off. Surely that must be this sudden headache. And the pain stabbing through his chest. Stabbing and stabbing. He could hardly breathe. He opened his mouth to speak, but the only sound that came out of his mouth was a name.

"Angela."

His wife. The love of his life. Angela. He held onto the thought and the image of her as the pain accelerated. He dropped to his knees, then slid sideways to the grass. Damn. Please let this not be a heart attack. The doctors had warned him, but…

Melanie was leaning over him, a look of horror on her face. And her eyes, wide, brown… normal again. How? What?

Then she was screaming and running with her dog to the house, and he was staring at the sky. The pain lower now. In his chest. And he knew he was going to die and would not make it to Scotland.

Suddenly Angela was bending over him, tears running down her beloved face. "Hang on, David, don't you dare die. Damn it, I love you. I need you."

He opened his mouth. It hurt to breathe, much less talk. But if he didn't say it now… "Love you." he choked out. His chin trembled as he fought against the pain, as if it were a live thing inside him—not like any death that he'd ever imagined—and he managed one smile and one more word. "Yes."

Then the pain took him and he cried out. She squeezed his hand and cried out, "David I love you."

I love you back.

And then the pain stopped, and there was nothing.

CHAPTER 4

Monday morning…

MONDAY MORNING DAWNED bright and clear. But Shay was still tired and confused and chose to take refuge from the crazy weekend by checking out the large animal sanctuary, Exotic Landscape. This was one of her pet projects funded by her foundation. These animals, all kinds and sizes, needed help…and Shay was a sucker for kids and animals. Interestingly enough, Tabitha, who ran the operation, was like Shay…psychic.

Shay'd always loved going there, but this last year she'd damned near lived there. It was a place she could rest, drop her barriers and relax.

And there was another reason to go to the sanctuary – she could use the healing calm for herself right now. And it was Shay's way to get her animal fix. Something she'd needed since Morris's disappearance a year ago.

The animals, of course, required a whole different level and kind of energy care. They didn't hide, manipulate or deceive. Each animal had a happiness or health level that was easy to see. Shay always walked through to make sure they were doing okay. Of course, Tabitha did that regularly. And under her care, the animals thrived here.

Tabitha worked Tuesday to Saturday. Once the two women, of similar age, found each other, and discovered what the other had been hiding from the world, they had become fast friends.

After all, they could communicate on the same level.

They couldn't hide anything from the other – for that same reason. It had taken years to solidify the trust, but once they'd found a comfort level, the relationship gave them immeasurable peace.

Tabitha barreled into her office and plunked down on the single visitor's chair. "Okay, give."

Shay rolled her eyes. "I thought this was your day off?"

Tabitha grinned. "It is. So? No trying to change the subject.

What's with you and the hunk?"

"Hunk?" Shay asked dryly, trying to marshal her thoughts, knowing it was hard to hide anything from her friend.

"That's how you think of him so that's what I know." The heat climbed Shay's face, and Tabitha chuckled. "And I am delighted for you."

"Hey, it's nothing."

Tabitha tilted her head and let out a heavy sigh of disgust. "It's me, remember. You wanted to meet this guy."

"Yeah, well… It's not so simple." Leaning back, she shared what had been going on and what she knew. "Besides, there's lots of weird stuff going on in my life right now."

"Have you looked at him closer?"

"Only briefly. He's got a big wall up. But I don't get the impression he's like that with other people, just me. There's something he doesn't want me to know. And that scares me." Shay stared at her old friend. "And because I know there's something there—"

"You're scared to have anything to do with him." Tabitha nodded. "But that reaction is just common sense. Still you can't compare everyone you meet to the asshole, Darren. And even if there is something else there…it doesn't have to mean that he's out to harm you. It could mean anything."

"I know, but—"

"But you're avoiding going any deeper just in case," Tabitha finished for her. "There's that fear factor again.

Shay dropped her gaze to study the stack of papers on her desk.

"It's difficult."

"And yet, don't you want to know for sure?" Tabitha prodded.

Shay stared at her in astonishment. "But that's the problem. I won't ever truly *know*. I'll look, assume what I see is what's there, and wonder ever after if he is camouflaging what he's doing, like Darren did. Darren could make his energy look *so* normal on the outside, yet he was something *so* different on the inside. He could change his energy so I'd never suspect." She shrugged. "So why bother trying with Roman? Why torment myself wondering if what I'm seeing is real or not?"

"That doesn't make sense, you know that? You'll torment yourself if you never take the chance to find out." Tabitha shook her head. "You're going to wonder anyway."

"I know." Shay sighed. That's what Stefan said."

SHAY STRODE INTO her office Monday morning and sat down in her leather executive chair. She'd come in early enough to be alone – or so she'd hoped. There was something about having the space to herself before the day officially began…

But today that wasn't to be.

Jordan, her assistant, raced in behind her, discarding her coat and purse on the way. When she had Shay's attention, she said, "Oh my God! Did you hear the news?"

Oh no.

Dread coiled inside. *Was this about Bernice's death? Or something else?* Hadn't she had enough bad news already? "I don't know. There's been a lot happening. What news are *you* talking about?" she countered, flipping through the stack of folders on her desk.

"It's about David Cummings. He's dead." Jordan brought today's mail to Shay's desk and sorted it in front of her.

Shay looked at Jordan and blinked. Her gaze latched onto the silver, cascading rings lining Jordan's ear. Surely that much weight, if not the incessant clanging as the rings banged against each other, had to give Jordan a headache? With difficulty Shay focused on what Jordan had been trying to tell her. *"Who?"*

"You know. The guy with the application you just approved. We were about to send him a check. For the dental center on 46th Street, Westside Dental… The one that does dental surgery for the kids?"

Shay struggled to put that proposal to the name. She remembered the dental shelter. They'd been funding it for a couple of years. "Sorry, I don't remember that name. That's tough on his family and colleagues."

"We were dealing with Max Charter, and then he moved to the Eastside, and Dr. David Cummings took over the management of this one." Jordan raised an eyebrow. *"He's* the guy that died."

Ah. Now that wasn't good for the dentist or for the Center. Still things like this happened, and they had to deal with it. "That's sad. I presume there is someone stepping in to take over from David?"

"Oh sure. We'll make sure that the new manager is briefed before the money is sent over," said Jordan as she started making notes on a pad of paper she produced out of nowhere – an ability that continually amazed Shay.

Jordan was always organized. She could put her fingers on the files Shay wanted within minutes and usually knew what Shay needed on a day-to-day basis as well. Shay had another older woman, Rose, working in the general office handling the phones and clerical duties but she couldn't begin to compete with Jordan's super organization. On the other hand, Rose handled people with a finesse that smoothed much of Jordan's abruptness.

"Briefing the new manager is a good idea." Shay thought about the amount of funding, winced and forced herself to ask, "Do we know how David Cummings died?"

"Collapsed while mowing his lawn," Jordan said with relish. "They are probably doing an autopsy right now."

Shay rolled her eyes. "They don't do autopsies for every case."

"No?" Jordan looked crestfallen. "That's too bad."

"How do you figure?" Shay stared at her assistant curiously.

"Well, they might make a mistake without it." Jordan shrugged. "Everyone deserves an autopsy to find out the truth."

What? Shay stared at her young assistant in surprise. Rose walked in just then, her subdued navy skirt and blouse a peaceful contrast to Jordan's bright colors. Then her unruffled middle-age personality was hugely calming beside Jordan's youthful bubbliness.

"You know…" Jordan said helpfully. "What if people murder other people and leave no trace? It would be easy to make a murder look like an accident or heart attack."

"It would *not* be easy to do that," Rose said as she brought a stack of folders to Shay's desk. "In fact, I'd imagine a certain amount of skill would be required to dupe the police and medical profession."

With a tinkling headshake, Jordan said, "It happens all the time."

"I don't even want to know how you know that." Shay shook her head.

Jordan laughed. "TV, of course. There are awesome crime shows these days. And even more awesome websites. They show everything."

Rose groaned and disappeared into the outer office.

"And that's so helpful for the budding criminal element, I'm sure," Shay said. "Bring me the Westside Dental file will you? I want to make sure that the situation is monitored carefully before the payment is sent."

"Sure." Jordan bustled off. Her energy bustled about in a smart, attentive manner, just like her personality. Shay shook her head. She'd done her research before hiring Jordan, and there hadn't been any surprises in the last year. She was hard working, honest and reliable. Friendly puppy material, with dynamite organization skills. Those qualities alone, made her valuable. Jordan's energy was always alert and sharp as she went through her day, assessing what needed to be done and deciding when to do it.

If Shay could, she'd hire another dozen like her. Because she'd proven to be so competent, Shay had given Jordan more and more responsibility, and so far her assistant handled it well.

Workers like Jordan were hard to find.

Projects to fund, were not. Unfortunately.

There was never enough money to help everyone, so Shay focused on helping as many children and animals as she could through her foundation. She hated to turn down good causes, but she did when they were run by rotten people. Her psychic skills allowed her to read people's energy to see that much. The good-hearted but totally inept. The liars and the cons. And those with the know-how, plus the skills, to do what needed to be done.

But this death didn't ring her 'happy trigger.' That had nothing to do with her own compassion and caring, but because she knew people and what they were capable of doing to each other – and that made her naturally suspicious.

There was a lot of money at stake. The Lassiter Foundation – and by extension, Shay – controlled millions of dollars. It was up to her to make sure the funds were used properly. She left energy markers with each application she personally approved, and then once a month, she went through and checked out how the money was used.

It took time. The more applications, the more time was required. Occasionally, the news hadn't been good. She'd used a private investigator several times and had a couple of detectives on speed dial to prove what she could sense energetically. She ensured the system worked.

This case raised all kinds of alarms. But apparently this man had died at home. Was this significant?

Time to hit redial and find out.

Just as she pulled out her cell phone, Jordan raced back in. Her wide-eyed look had Shay stalling on the call. "What's the matter?"

"There's a man here to see you. His name is Roman Chandler." She gave an appreciative motion with her hands. "He says he has an appointment, but I don't have him in the books. He also said to ask you."

Shay sighed. "He doesn't have an appointment. But he's the kind that thinks he doesn't need one. Send him in; he knows you're talking to me."

Jordan's expressive face flushed bright red. "Oh. Sorry, I never thought of that."

"It doesn't matter. I spoke with him last night."

A big smirk wreathed her assistant's face. "Oh, last night, huh? That's awesome. He's hot. What a great pair you'll make."

Shay groaned. "Jordan, stop. We didn't go out on a date. We were at the hospital. Bernice passed away last night."

Jordan gasped in horror.

Shay nodded. "Exactly. Now just send him in, please."

"Sure. I am so sorry about Bernice." Jordan went as if to leave, but not before winking at her. "You should still go for it. It's about time, you know."

"About time for what?" Roman stood in the open doorway.

Jordan gasped, her face flushing bright pink again. She shot Shay an apologetic look and raced out.

"Nothing that pertains to you," Shay said smoothly as she stood up to face him. *Drat.* This man's appearance could make the earth move, and she hadn't even noticed because even from a distance, he'd already rocked her foundation.

Sneaking a quick glance, she checked out his energy. Dark greens strode up and down over his body in a calm, controlled manner. That figured. The healer, the moneymaker and the cop.

Gerard ran a huge company dealing with prosthetics and hospital equipment, things along that line, but he was getting old and needed help now. Roman told her he'd created Internet Security Corp after leaving law enforcement. *Could he do both?* Or would he sell his own company to help his grandfather?

That Roman came wrapped up in the best damn package she'd seen in a long time was a bonus.

Now if she could just reconcile that wall of his…

"Take a seat." She motioned for him to step in further. "What can I do for you?" She sat back down and crossed her hands serenely in front of her and waited.

"We didn't finish our discussion last night."

She gaped at him. "Really? You came to my office to ask me why I'm nervous around you? Scared of you?"

"I don't want you to feel that way." He tilted his head, his gaze intent. "I'd like to ask you out to dinner and if you're nervous…"

Oh boy. She hadn't expected that. Yet she should have. It was a natural step for the two of them to take, but…

"I've surprised you." He grinned, a boyish smile that revealed the charmer. "Sorry."

"Yes, you did surprise me," she hedged, not knowing what to say.

"So just say yes." He paused. "Please. I've been looking forward to deepening our relationship from the moment I moved here. Saturday hardly counted."

Flustered, she willed the heat wave to stop its climb up her throat. The intense silence grew thick as she felt Roman's scrutiny. It took more will than she'd had to use in a long time, but she kept her smile firmly in place. Inside…was another story.

She took another peek at this energy. *Wow.* His aura was contained. The energy circulated in a soothing manner.

Then he smiled, and she was almost ready to forget about his shields. And that made him very dangerous. But she watched, fascinated as a slow dawning awareness of her on a whole different level took over his whole face. Shivers of delight whispered through her.

"So what is your answer?"

She stared at him, trying to figure out what to say. Did she want to go out with him? Yes. Should she? She totally should not. She opened her mouth to refuse, only to hear herself say, "Yes."

"Good." He stood up. "Friday night?"

She tossed her hair back and sighed. What had she done? "I don't know when Bernice's funeral is scheduled. It could be earlier than Friday, but if not—"

"Let's make it Saturday evening so we're sure." He walked to the door. "I'll get back to you about the funeral arrangements."

And just like that he was gone.

"OMG. You're going on a date with him." Jordan practically danced through the room like a teenager. "He's gorgeous. Oh my. Where are you going and what are you going to wear?"

Wear? She had no idea. Five days was a long time away. Anything could happen.

ROMAN WALKED OUT of Shay's building and down the block toward his own office – or rather, his grandfather's office. The traffic beeped by in a confusion of noise. The sidewalks were full. He stepped into the fast morning crowd and a typical business day in the downtown core. And so not where he wanted to be. He wanted to be working his own business and doing his art.

If only the dynamite CEO for Chandler Inc hadn't quit. And it could take a long time to replace him. Roman's help was supposed to be temporary, but…

On the upside, it would keep him here. Give him time to get to know Shay better. But he could do that without coming to his grandfather's company on a daily basis. It hurt to think about his grandfather getting older. That one day he might not be here.

Roman's mind shifted gears. Bernice, Charles and Gerard had been inseparable for as long as he could remember. And over the last year, each had filled him in on Shay's life in bits and pieces. He knew about her lousy fiancé, his death, her isolation.

Bernice had said Shay was 'different.' Had some unusual skills. He'd pressed her for more information, but she'd clammed up. He'd often wondered what those skills could be. Maybe she was a belly dancer? A magician…? He had asked Ronin about Shay, but not even his twin was willing to share – said Roman would find out, in due time. And he'd told Roman to keep an open mind.

Whatever the hell that meant.

Then again, Ronin knew some interesting people, Dr. Maddy for one. Roman had re-evaluated some of his beliefs after meeting her through a fundraiser. Dr. Maddy had introduced him to a whole new world of paranormal theories, and he had to admit, he supported her children's project when he could.

There were so many people in need.

Did Shay have skills similar to Maddy's? Ronin had just smiled when asked. He had a cop's brain and strong intuition. And knew when to keep his mouth shut.

And Ronin also knew Stefan Kronos. Someone Roman would love to get to know. Not for his apparent otherworldly abilities – Roman wasn't at all sure about those – but for his art. Stefan's work was talked about…everywhere, and yet, somehow he remained a mystery.

That whole psychic thing was unbelievable to many people. There was enough proof – measurable results, like Dr. Maddy's – to keep Roman's doubts at bay. He thought most of what people talked about was garbage, but something about her and the results she'd achieved, just couldn't be explained away. There was media talk, too, about psychics working with the police to solve missing persons and serial killer cases. If psychics could help catch assholes like that, Roman was all for them.

As soon as he entered his grandfather's reception room, Celia, his grandfather's office manager, spoke from behind her monitor. "Roman, your grandfather has been calling you constantly since you left. You forgot your cell phone again, didn't you?"

"Sometimes, I just like to be without it for a while." In fact, the more he painted, the less he wanted to be connected to the world twenty-four-seven.

"If you say so." She shook her head. "Please call him. It will save my stress levels."

He walked into his office, sat down and reached for the phone. "Hello, Grandfather. Yes, the arrangements are being made. Yes, everything will be ready for Bernice's funeral on Friday."

Silence, then his grandfather gave his two cents worth. "Harumph. If you already knew what I was going to say, why did you call me back?"

Rolling his eyes, Roman sat back and stared up at the ceiling. "So that you would know that I know. Stop worrying. Bernice will go to rest in fine style."

"So long as Charles doesn't go changing anything. Damn, that man has been calling me constantly."

Roman grinned. "You two have talked a half-dozen times a day for decades. Today isn't going to be any different."

"I know." A tired sigh wove through the line. "We're sure going to miss her."

"And yet, you still have each other."

"And you have no one. Why aren't you married with a family of your own?"

Roman groaned silently. Since he'd returned to Portland, his grandfather hadn't quit harping on Roman's single status. "I was married, remember?"

"That was a childhood romance. It lasted what...two years? Then divorce. Bet you don't even remember her name," barked his grandfather. "Young kids these days... You don't know what marriage is anymore."

There wasn't much Roman could say to that. Not anything that he hadn't said a dozen times before. "When I find the right woman, I'll get married again. Until then, I'll just enjoy my single status."

"Ha. When was the last time you went on a date? You're always working."

Finally he had something new to add. "That's not true. I'm going on a date on Saturday night. I'm taking a young woman out for dinner."

"Do I know her?" Grandfather asked suspiciously.

"Yes, you do. It's Shay."

"Ah." His grandfather chuckled. "That would make Bernice happy. She always thought the two of your should meet. She spoke highly of Shay's business acumen — and for Bernice that was something. But a couple of times, I sensed she wanted to say more about her but she always stopped herself before saying what was on her mind."

That fit. Bernice wouldn't likely have said too much to his grandfather. Grandfather's comments were nothing if not pointed. He said at his age, he shouldn't have to hold back for fear of offending anyone. Still this behavior hadn't just started. He'd been very vocal all his life.

"Where are you taking her?"

"Not sure yet. I haven't had a chance to try out too many places here."

"Take her to the Sandors. Great seafood."

"Maybe." Except all the patrons there were Grandfather's age. Roman had actually hoped to take her dancing. He didn't know if she danced or not, but with that body she was probably a natural. And he sure wouldn't mind holding her in his arms for a little while.

And he didn't know what she was hiding, but she was hiding something.

And he wanted to find out exactly what.

FINALLY SOME ACTION. After the old bat died. Not much yet. Not enough for Shay to understand. But she would figure it out. And the police would, too. Eventually. But by then they wouldn't be able to do anything about it.

And damn, if Shay didn't look to have another hunk at her heels. At least the type of man she favored — he'd hovered by her side at the Foundation reception. Roman Chandler. Wealthy businessman and budding artist. The Chandlers are a well-known family.

He looked good too. Damn good. In many ways, the two suited each other. And Roman Chandler had walls, too. Getting around them was possible, but it would take time — time that wasn't available.

There was a deadline to meet. A death to honor. Justice to be served. It was long past due. But it will be done… Then I can move on.

CHAPTER 5

Monday mid-morning...

AFTER ROMAN LEFT the office, Shay pulled in her scattered thoughts and hit the first speed dial number on her phone, trying for a second time to make this call. She leaned back in her comfortable chair, hoping Roman's brother was available. She couldn't ignore the niggling unease in her belly. Something wasn't right.

Ronin must have recognized her on caller ID. "Hi Shay. How are you doing?"

The calm, warm voice on the other end made her smile. How anyone could do the job Ronin did and still have such a lighthearted personality amazed her. Though she didn't know Roman's brother all that well, Ronin'd been there for her every time she needed him. He was a good man to have on her side. As he'd proved when Darren died. She could only hope his brother was a good man, too.

She laughed lightly. "I'm fine. As always."

"Not if you're calling me, you aren't." He paused. "I heard about Bernice. I am sorry." His tone turned serious. "So what's the problem?"

And that was the best part about dealing with the same people over time, the relationship was already in place, and you could go directly to the heart of the matter without the small talk. She passed over Bernice's death and got to the point.

"Dr. David Cummings, the man behind the Westside Dental Center, has passed away. Our foundation funds the center. I'm wondering if you have any details, and if this is something I need to be concerned about."

"I haven't heard anything about this." His tone was brusque. "Is there a lot of money being funneled into that project?"

She heard the tapping on his keyboard as he searched for information.

"Over a million at this point. It's a dental practice for kids in need.

It's constantly busy. I think there are four dentists working full time and all the support staff. It's totally charity funded."

"Hmmm. From your end, is there any reason to suspect that there's a problem?"

"Not sure. The application had been received as per the annual deadline, but there were a couple of issues that were flagged so it was brought to my attention. They aren't big. It was more like someone else filled out the paperwork this time instead of the regular person. Someone who didn't know the ins and outs of the Center's paperwork."

"Hmm." Ronin's voice was thoughtful, distant. His keyboard clicked a few more times. "David Cummings keeled over at his home, apparently while talking to a neighbor. According to the eyewitness, he'd been alone for maybe a half hour before he died. Apparent heart attack. No signs of a fight.

"Because he had no history of a heart condition and was only fifty-two, it raises some questions, so an autopsy…" His voice trailed off as he clicked through a few more screens. "It's scheduled for later tomorrow. Depending on case load."

"Understood." This gave her nothing new to go by. "If you hear of anything odd, let me know, and if anything pops up on my end, I'll give you a ring."

"Thanks. And hey, go easy on my brother. He's been waiting to meet you since forever."

Ronin rang off, leaving Shay spluttering, staring down at the phone in her hand, her mind full of Roman – again. *Damn.* She tried to refocus on the problem at hand.

She couldn't run any scans on David's body, as he was already gone, but every action and reaction required energy. And the first law of the conservation of energy said that energy cannot be created nor destroyed. It can only change form. Therefore, the energy involved in this business had either left behind a trail, transformed that trail to something else, or hadn't existed in the first place.

Meaning he'd died by natural causes.

That happened.

The energy from a paranormal being could have physically touched him in such a way as to cause a heart attack. If that were the case, in theory, then its energy would still be on David's body, but it would be dissipating rapidly. It would be difficult for that energy to change form on a corpse. Not an easy medium to work with.

Not that it wasn't possible. The more she understood, the more she realized she didn't understand anything…

There were assholes out there; some were psychics who had skills far beyond anything she'd ever been able to imagine. And it was so not easy to catch up to them.

Stefan might know who and how, though.

She tuned in and sent him a message. It bounced off the door to his mind. She sighed. He was likely painting.

He'd get the message when he stopped and opened his psyche up to the rest of the world again. In the meantime, was there anything she could find out on her own?

She pondered that. Shay knew Dr. Maddy could scan a body remotely. Shay hadn't had much luck with distance scanning.

But there was a technique whereby Shay could retrace her path to take another look at places, people and events that she'd already experienced. In rare cases, she could go back to certain situations that loved ones had experienced by hitching a ride on their memories.

It was great for remembering details. Not great for determining murder or murderers. Still, she couldn't quite let it go. It would at least tell her if anyone in the office held any serious animosity toward David – something worthy of a second look.

So should she try at home, or from here?

Making a sudden decision, Shay stood up, walked out into the main office and saw that both of her office staff had left to take their lunch breaks. *Good.* She returned to her office and locked the door. Setting the phones so incoming calls all went straight to voicemail, she settled into her chair.

She closed her eyes and pictured the center where David Cummings had worked, as it was on her last visit. That's how her skills worked. Because she'd been to a place once, she could visualize it and access it from her mind.

The front door of the center loomed and she pushed it open mentally and walked in. Shay smiled at the office staff, busy on the phone and talking to customers. Just as it had been last time. She hooked into her energy's memory and retraced her steps through the last visit.

David, looking happy, saw her and smiled. He excused himself from the discussion with the office manager and walked over, hand out to greet her – as he had that day.

"Nice to see you."

Her body reached out to shake his hand while Shay's astral body watched the interaction from outside the physical plane. Separated from the physical reality, Shay was free to observe the interactions involving others around her.

Moving forward, David led her to his office.

Shay studied the room and the energy trails of the people who'd entered and left – their energy, wispy and dispersing. Nothing seemed out of the ordinary.

But if there'd been anything obvious, she'd have noticed it on the day she'd actually been there. At least she hoped she would have.

Now that she wasn't grounded in the physical experience, she could take the necessary time to look around. See what else might be going on. She couldn't separate from the memory to wander on her own, but she could turn around and see the main office, the dashes and flares of energy as people communicated with one another.

Every word spoken required energy. Every facial expression required energy and as it manifested, it gave off energy that went to the other person in the exchange. She could see the exchanges. The energy also blended and blurred, shared and moved through the room as people said one thing and meant another. Or if someone spoke to one person but wanted to speak with another. The first person would receive the energy as it was directed to them, but some energy snuck around that person and snaked over to the person that they really wanted to speak with.

Trails and lingering blankets of energy spoke of lots of interactions at many levels.

The staff had their interactions with each other, with the customers and with their bosses, and then there were messages, spoken and unspoken, about their private lives – the stuff people shared with each other and the stuff they kept hidden. And then there were the lies. She hated seeing the details of some people's personal lives.

Some of it was incredibly private and she tried to move on quickly.

And for every action there was always an equal reaction. The energy pushing the message was going to be buffered by the person perceiving or receiving the message. The bottom line was this: everyone left vestiges of themselves behind, and connected to others, and only a few special people understood that some people could see it all.

Some people – like her.

At least when she dropped her walls she could see it all – unless the person protected themselves like Darren had. She refused to drop her walls in public because she'd be inundated with the onslaught. Right now, having stepped back into a memory as she had, it was easier to deal with others' energy than if she were in real time. Like watching a movie instead of participating in a play. She could also apply a filter of sorts and focus acutely on what caught her attention.

What people didn't realize was that energy didn't tell lies, whereas words could. But the energy behind lies was obvious – to her.

One woman was speaking about her coworker's new hairstyle. Shay could hear the disembodied words when she spoke. "I love it. It makes you look so much younger." Those were the words. Nicely delivered. Just the right tone of warm appreciation. Yet the energy, on which the words were delivered, was ragged, shaky, vibrating with something else. Jealousy, maybe even anger. The energy that moved from the first woman to the second was spiteful, and the sentiment was reflected in sickening gray to black energy waves.

The first woman hated the second. But the work environment demanded that they get along in a manner that was acceptable to all. But did any of this have anything to do with David's death? She searched the colors, the smoky clouds and the heavier and lighter energy to sort through recent layers then moved down to the older ones.

To sort through the nastiness to find truly authentic emotions, she had to look deeper.

Not an easy thing to do. She spun away from the multiple people working in the busy office and focused on David. His aura resonated with goodwill and a pleaser personality. A definite media type. But what was underneath it?

Shay moved around him and studied David from the different angles. He couldn't be this happy and friendly all the time. No one was. He stood up to get a file from the table across the room and she saw it.

There was a black circle, small and almost hidden under his good cheer. It wasn't at the heart chakra; it was centered on his third chakra. She studied it, a frown coming to her face. It could portend a health issue, but, it was almost too perfect. Too round.

She had no doubt the circle was man-made.

Planted. It was a marker. Someone who understood energy work had planted it there.

Shit. And once she understood that, her mind spun endlessly. *Why? Who? How?*

"Shay?"

A pounding on her own office door broke her altered state of consciousness, snagging her attention away from the scene playing out before her.

Damn. Rotten timing.

"Shay, are you in there? Your light is on but I can't get through on your phones." After a moment, Jordan's voice came again, higher and louder. "Shay, you're scaring me."

Time to return to her normal reality.

Shay closed her eyes and forcibly disconnected from the memory. Her consciousness slammed back to her office chair, with bile climbing the back of her throat. *Shit.* She hated coming back from a trip so suddenly. The hard landings always made her stomach revolt.

"I'm here," she croaked. She cleared her throat several times, and then managed to get up off her chair. She let the changing energy ripple through her, letting it settle and ground her.

Making her way slowly to the door, she struggled with fingers still not feeling quite normal, to unlock and open it. For Jordan's sake, she put on a sleepy smile and rubbed her eyes. "Sorry. I locked the door to have a nap."

"You scared me shitless. At least leave me a note." Jordan stormed into her office, turned around as if to satisfy herself that all was well, and then came to stand in front of Shay. Her gaze narrowed. "You need coffee."

Shay rubbed her eyes. "Thanks. I could really use a cup."

"So could I. This time, I'm going to lace it with something much stronger."

Shay had to smile. "Feel free. I'll take mine black, thanks." She watched Jordan walk over the side counter and set up a fresh pot of coffee. The whole time the young woman muttered under her breath.

But her energy only showed relief and concern. Caring. That made all the difference in the world. And because they were friends, and Jordan had been scared, Shay said, "I'm sorry. I'll leave a note on your desk next time I decide to have a nap at work."

"Do that."

Shay returned to her desk and sat down. She dropped the smile.

She'd love to take a return trip to David's office for a closer look. But every time she returned to the same place, the energy would have dissipated a little more. And it took a lot of her energy to make these trips happen. She needed to recharge as it were.

Instead, she could only guess at what really happened. And what the black marker meant. And that didn't make her happy.

ROMAN LEFT THE office early. He needed to be in his own space for a bit. Even if he was only going to his studio for an extended lunch – it all helped.

He shut the door and strode across the expanse of studio floor to the windows on the far side. Unbuckling the latches, he propped the large glass window wide, giving thanks that he had a place to breathe so deeply. Creativity required space, and as a messy painter, he needed more space than most. Still, he cleaned his studio himself, not trusting his housecleaning service to do it properly in this room.

He rolled up his sleeves as he surveyed the gray Portland sky around him. He had just enough time to pack up a couple paintings for the new show and see if Roger, the gallery owner, had a preference in style. Normally Roman was very private about his art, and this showing was going to push him out of his comfort zone like nothing else. He handled big business and employees easily, but his painting was…private, personal. He didn't have the same hard edge for that part of his life that he did for business.

In the beginning, he'd never signed his creations. Then, after gaining some experience, he started using a different name. Now, after some modest success, he signed the pieces with his own name. Progress came with appreciation. Only no one here on the West Coast really knew about him – except his family. Back East his art was better known.

He knew that would change soon. Not that he expected to be an overnight success. He just hoped his show didn't bomb.

And he hoped to hell that no one recognized his model.

Still, he couldn't help but wonder what Shay would think of his latest works. He hadn't planned on this collection, but after Bernice had sent those headshots of Shay, he hadn't been able to help himself. He called the collection, *Complicated*.

Like she was.

And she'd been the inspiration that fired up his imagination.

Thankfully he'd not painted her face on the nudes.

But he'd used her body.

"Stefan. I could use some help."

"Always. What's up?" For all the willingness in his voice, Shay could never really forget that Stefan pushed himself too hard and for too long, too often. Whether it was helping someone, offering his services to someone in law enforcement, or creating his artwork. And right now, it was obvious that fatigue held his voice up, giving his words form.

"You need a keeper," she said abruptly.

That surprised a laugh out of him.

"I'm serious." And she was. But that had nothing to do with what she wanted to talk to him about.

"Are you volunteering for the job?" Amusement slid through the phone. "Although Alex's ghostly sister, Lissa, hangs around enough, certainly filling in that position."

"Good. Someone needs to. Especially if your so-called future partner has any of your abilities and knows about them. She's liable to kick my ass down the road for not doing a better job."

This time he laughed aloud. "I'm glad you called, Shay. I needed the laugh. My particular future partner doesn't have any idea about me, and that's probably a good thing."

"I don't know. It's going to take time for a woman to figure you out. Then there's that whole needing-to-accept-you stage," she admonished. "You're not an easy person to get along with."

"Really?" He added in a slow thoughtful tone, "And here, I thought I was a model friend."

"You are, but..." She bit her lip, then sighed heavily. "Actually I'm wondering if you can tell me something." She explained about David's death. "There aren't any signs of foul play. An autopsy is scheduled, but should the results come back with nothing definitive, the police aren't going to think it was anything but a simple heart attack."

"But you're not sure?"

"Right. There was this one black spot on one chakra. It was abnormal – perfectly round. It felt like a marker planted there for some purpose." She sighed. "The thing is, I don't know what that means."

"Or if it means anything. Could be just his wife's subconscious way of checking on her husband's health."

She frowned. "I hadn't thought of that."

"Sometimes appearances can be deceptive," Stefan reminded her. "What else did you see?"

"Not much," she admitted. "The energy in the building is extensive, as the place swarms with customers all day long. There are kids, parents, staff – and that's just for starters. You know how confusing it gets when these people add in all their stuff."

"Love how you use that term – stuff."

"It's true. You know that. Everyone has garbage they haul around with them throughout their day. For me to work through all of that is distracting and tiring."

"And you care about this, why?"

She sighed. "That's the crux of the matter. I just want to make sure this incident has nothing to do with the money we've funneled into the Center. Another payment is due to go out next week. If there's any sign of this being more than a heart attack, I don't want to send the check. And..." She paused, then continued painfully. "I want to make sure that I didn't miss something."

"Ah." He left that last bit alone for the moment. "How big a payment?"

"It's big." Happy to focus on the business aspect, she added, "They're planning to purchase a building and renovate it to make a larger facility so they can do more. The purchase price is the bulk of the payout."

"Hmmm. So if this person did die of natural causes, what would happen to the plans and the payout?"

"If they have a chain of command in place, and the business manager continues following the same proposal and building purchase plan, then we'd send the funds. However, if they change things, there would be a hold on the money until we were sure the Center, under new administration, is managed properly."

"So killing this person would actually hurt the Center. It could cause the Center to close. Is that what you're saying?" Stefan's voice sharpened. "I'm looking for motivation to help me figure out if foul play is involved."

"Money? Maybe? It's a large check I'm cutting for them. Someone might want to step up and take control of receiving the funds and the project to have access to the money for another purpose – or to steal them. Or someone within the Center could have a personal grudge against the Center and want to close it." Shay knew there were other possibilities – if David had been murdered – but at this point those possibilities were all moot. No one had declared it a murder.

"Hmmm. We've seen murders done for a lot less." His voice cooled. "And you didn't see any other pathways, darkness, anything in the auras of the other people?"

"No."

"And did you look?"

She winced. "I tried to. Look, I know I'm having trust issues that come into play when I interpret people's energy. But if something had popped, I like to think I'd have taken a second look."

"Yes, you would have. You just need to regain your self-confidence. Don't let Darren's deception make you doubt everything..." His voice trailed off.

"If I can't see the truth, then what's the point of looking? I'm just afraid I'll make the same mistake again." She wanted to hit her head in frustration. After the death of her fiancé, and the doubts about all she'd thought they were to each other, this questioning of herself and her abilities to recognize good and evil had been a familiar feeling. The doubts about her abilities, and what she'd missed had overwhelmed her.

"And I tell you again, Darren was one in a million. The chances of there being a second one are almost nonexistent."

"And yet it feels like…" She hesitated.

"What?" he prompted.

"What if Darren had family I didn't know about?" She bit her bottom lip gently. "What if other family members could also do what he did?"

Stefan's voice sharpened. "I thought you said he was alone in the world?"

"Sure, but what if that's just what he wanted me to think?" She groaned. "Nothing else he said was true, so why would I believe the stuff he told me about his family?"

"Shay, this guy was a man. Not a god. Not some kind of magician. You didn't fail in not seeing him for who he was. He was powerful and carefully kept things hidden from you."

"So why does it feel like I failed?" Not giving Stefan a chance to argue, she hung up the phone.

If a lasting impression of a frowning Stefan lingered in her mind, she ignored it.

Still, his voice whispered through her consciousness. *You might ignore me, but running away isn't the answer.*

IN SPITE OF the constant headache from the ongoing renovations at Chadworth School, Headmaster Robert Dander couldn't stop smiling – and not because of the school's impressive trophies he was staring at in the school's front entrance. In three weeks, he'd lost twenty-one pounds. Lisa had lost seventeen. They'd even gone dancing over the weekend, something they hadn't done for a long time. Shaking their still substantial booties and enjoying every moment.

Life was good.

The door opened behind him, and he turned to see the UPS driver hurrying in with a parcel. Robert stepped toward him.

"Do you need a signature?" Robert glanced down at the return address on the label. Another order of books. Good. The school needed them – and so much more.

"Not today." The deliveryman touched his hand to his cap and said, "Have a good day."

Robert glanced up at him. The deliveryman's eyes had darkened to a midnight black. Robert frowned. "Hey, are you all right?"

"I'm fine." Only the man's eyes had gone completely black as in no white showed…at all.

While Robert stood in shock, trying to understand, the deliveryman turned to leave. Friendly. Normal.

Except something flashed from the man's body and stabbed into Robert. He gasped and fell back a step, his hand's slamming to his chest.

Oh no, oh no, oh no. Not now. Not when he was getting better and taking care of himself. Not when he was starting to live again.

The pain sharpened, and he opened his mouth to cry for help, and the pain intensified. It felt like his heart was being ripped out of his chest. He tried to speak again and a nasty, hushed groan of pain and terror came out. A gurgle.

The deliveryman turned, frowned and took a step forward. "Sir, are you all right?"

Robert tried to answer and held out his hand. The parcel fell from his numb fingers, hitting the floor with a loud bang. Robert fell to his knees, dimly aware of Bill calling for help.

Footsteps raced down the hallway toward them.

Robert tried to speak, tried to tell them to call 911. Then the beautiful old tile of the entranceway rushed up to meet him.

A harsh whisper sounded close by, almost inside his head. But his own thoughts drowned it out. *Please not a heart attack! I'm not ready to die.*

CHAPTER 6

Monday afternoon…

THE AFTERNOON SPED by. There'd been too much damn paperwork to allow Shay to leave work early – not to mention the scheduled meetings with other staff.

She'd hoped to slip down to the Children's Hospital, one of the Foundation projects, and see how the new wing was coming along. She'd heard it was almost done. In fact, several children had already been moved in. Those kids were part of the reason she wanted to visit this afternoon. They tugged at her heartstrings, made her grateful to be able to help in some small way. Only, her schedule wasn't looking good at the moment. Maybe in an hour. She'd see.

Her phone rang. It was her favorite detective – Ronin. "Hey, surprised to hear from you so fast."

"It's not necessarily a good thing, either," he said, his voice serious.

"True enough." She waited for him to continue. When he took his time, she had an inkling she wasn't going to like what he would say next. She struggled to hide the sinking feeling in her stomach, so it didn't show in her voice. "What's up?"

"Do you have anything to do with the school on Bernard Street?"

She frowned. "Chadworth School? Yes, it's one of ours. Why?"

"The headmaster, Robert Dander, collapsed by the front door a couple hours ago. He's dead."

She gasped, her stomach bottoming out and filling with dread. "I don't understand. The headmaster is a great guy. He couldn't be more than sixty, maybe sixty-two, years old."

"He's sixty-one."

"Is it on the news?" she asked. "Normally I'd be notified of something like this." Like she had been about Westside Dental Center.

"The police are still on site. No details have been released at this time. It's the school's connection to the Foundation that has me calling.

I thought it was one of your projects."

"The old building needed upgrades to bring it up to code," she confirmed, bringing up the file on the computer. "They're due to get their second payment next week."

"And would a death like this stop the payment of that check?"

She leaned back and thought about that. "Normally not. At least not for long. We don't give the person the money; we give the project the funding. There is, of course, due diligence before we send out the money so we know how the money is going to be handled. We've been helping this school for years now. Robert wasn't the only person we've dealt with there. And they wouldn't get all the money in one lump sum anyway. It's handed out in stages."

She thought about what Ronin had said and what he hadn't said. "Was Robert murdered?" she asked, and couldn't stop her voice from showing her dismay.

"There are no signs of foul play. There were witnesses, but apparently he just keeled over where he stood. An autopsy will be performed. I'll let you know if there is anything odd."

"Okay, thanks for letting me know."

Shay hung up the phone and stared blindly at the computer monitor. She wasn't a big believer in coincidence, but what was the chance that two of the people running projects her foundation worked with, who were each set to manage a large chunk of Foundation money, would both die of heart attacks within twenty-four hours of each other?

She tried to remember the last time she'd been at the school. It had been several weeks ago. Shay took time, at least once a month, to visit each of the Foundation's pet projects. Other people could perform the checks, but she preferred to do them herself, knowing she would see more than other people might.

The last time she'd visited, the old structure had pleased her greatly. She loved knowing that the school would be able to stay open and that the graceful old lady of a building would continue to stand. Once she'd made that decision, she had no trouble convincing the others on the board about the importance of keeping the school open.

Also, as she thought back on the project and how her foundation came to be involved, she thought Bernice might have had a hand in that project coming to Shay.

Normally she would have picked up the phone and called Bernice to ask her about the school and Robert. Only now Bernice was in the morgue, ready to be buried.

Cold brushed up against her shoulders. She wrapped her arms around her chest.

Too many people connected to her were dying.

Why?

THE NEXT DAY, Shay walked up the steps to Chadworth School and opened the door. The school was busy – full of life, full of kids. The way a school should be.

Being there reassured her. That life continued. Kids still attended the school. It was still open and operating. Then again, why wouldn't it be? The death of the headmaster from natural causes was heartbreaking but not something that should stop the day-to-day operations of a project this size.

According to Ronin, nothing suspicious had been found on site. The autopsy should be done by now, but she hadn't heard the results. She'd made the trip to gauge the energy of the school.

She knew everything had energy, including the old building. Part of the reason she'd been willing to help fund the renovations was that this old building, with its tired energy, had been through so much already. She stood here and felt the contradictions you'd find in any building like this: the years of good living, the abuse and neglect, the kids' screams of joy and the fights and rage that had flared up through the decades. Still the old girl had withstood it with a grace and serenity that muted the storms going on around and through her.

With many good years early on, the energy of the building had warmed, grown and balanced itself with every additional successful year.

With time, the energy of the building had shifted slightly. The attitude of each generation of kids had affected the balance; the fight for funding affected the teachers; and the desperation of the parents added yet another element.

The building had maintained a healthy, measured calm. Shay knew its early years had to have been impressive indeed to withstand the ongoing negativity from this last decade. She saw these next years as promising a boon of new, happier and healthier energy as the renovations happened, as teachers, kids and parents realized the school was going to stay open and that children would continue to go there.

She'd come specifically to see how the death of the headmaster affected that balance. And to find out if there was some underlying negativity she had missed before.

That's what really bothered her. One death related to one of her many projects was sad...but that could be considered normal. Two deaths among her project leaders could be very sad but still be thought of as normal, considering how many people and projects she dealt with. Everyone knew, life happened. So did death.

As long as there was nothing ugly floating under the surface at either location where the deaths had occurred.

She walked into the office. The secretary was on the phone. Another worked at a computer in the back. The door to the headmaster's room was closed. Lights out.

The vice principal's door was open. Lights on.

With a smile to the busy secretary, Shay walked toward the vice principal. The Stephen Mortimer nameplate on the door matched her files. She presumed he'd be the one to step into the headmaster's shoes, but she couldn't be sure. A charity like this one had board members to satisfy.

She knocked on the open door. Stephen looked up and frowned. *Interesting.*

"Can I help you?"

"Yes, I'm Shay Lassiter of the Lassiter Foundation. I'd like to speak with you for a few moments."

Awareness shot into his gaze, but so did something else. Wariness? Fear? Or maybe just a hint of insecurity? He rose, stretched and walked around his desk to shake her hand. "Please, have a seat. I'm sorry I didn't recognize you."

"No reason why you would. Normally, I met with Robert."

"Yes." He ran his fingers through his hair, leaving it more than a little rumpled. "It's been a difficult few days. We closed the school on the day of his death, but reopened it the next, knowing that's what he'd have wanted."

"Good. I came to see how everyone is coping."

He smiled. "I think we're doing fine. Robert was a good man…but he was intense. That must have affected his health. I can't tell you how many times we warned him to relax a little and ease up on the stress in his life."

Shay nodded sympathetically. "Funny, we're all told to do that, but hearing it and then acting upon the advice, well——"

"Exactly." He added, "Robert was also extremely overweight. He had a heart condition already, so although his death is a great loss, it's not a great surprise."

Anyone overweight would be prone to such health conditions. And Robert had been obese. "Have funeral arrangements been made? I'd like to attend."

He busied himself with a stack of notes on his desk. "I spoke with his wife this morning. I believe his funeral is scheduled for next

Wednesday." He quickly wrote down the name and number of Robert's wife and handed her the note. "Here is her name and number should you want to call her. I can also send you the detailed information when I get it myself." He brought up his calendar and jotted down another note.

An obvious list maker. Shay watched him keep himself organized. His actions appeared normal, assured. No nervousness or strain evident.

She opened her inner vision and checked out his aura. Agitated. Nervous at her surprise visit. Disturbed at the unexpected workload now on his shoulders and a little angry at Robert for dying and even a bit angry at himself for feeling that way.

All normal. And this reassured her.

Finished, he looked over at her, "Do you want to see the progress on the renovations?"

She smiled. "That was going to be my next request."

The next hour was spent going over the plans, highlighting the progress and difficulties with upgrading the old school. By the time she took her leave, the kids were close to exiting their classrooms for the day. She picked up the pace. The place would be overrun with kids soon.

The dismissal bell rang as she reached her car.

While Shay drove home her mind was on the school. Everything had looked great, on the surface and beneath – not that she'd expected anything different. She didn't want to find something wrong. But so often, where money was involved, people's motivations became a little muddy.

However, so far, she'd found nothing suspicious. The headmaster's death appeared to be unrelated to the project – for that she was grateful.

She needed to check in with Stefan.

An hour later, she got him on the phone. "Now two people, both spearheading two charities that my foundation is heavily involved in, have died. Apparently of heart attacks. Both dropped dead, one at home and one at work. No signs of a struggle. No damage at the office. Nothing missing. No foul play suspected."

"But…?" he prodded.

She shrugged and shifted her cell phone to the other ear. "I don't know. I just can't quite feel comfortable about these deaths. Yet I have no reason for this uneasiness." She sighed and stared out at the water outside her window. It was a strikingly beautiful summer day with blue sky and a warm breeze off the ocean. "There is a lot of money involved, but the money has been parceled out for big renovations, salaries, upgrades. It's not like anyone is going to be able to steal the money and walk away without someone knowing. And if money isn't the motivator, what could be?"

"You're presuming foul play in both cases?" he asked.

"Maybe and maybe not. I'd feel better if I could rule it out."

"And how would you do that?" Stefan said. "You're not the police and don't have access to the their personal financial records or know the status of their health or marital situations."

She frowned. "No, but I can ask Ronin to rule those out, I suppose."

"If it's bothering you to that extent, I think you should. Ronin understands. Not everything, but he's been a big help to me over the years. Remember to listen to your instincts though. If something feels wrong, then chances are it is wrong – somehow." He coughed slightly then cleared his throat. "Energy doesn't lie; people can only deceive until you look deeper and see the truth of the energy currents. Don't go in to confirm your expectations, go in looking to find what isn't fitting together."

"Right. I know that." So what was the matter? "I think what's underlying this is the series of odd and seemingly unrelated issues. Like what I saw in Bernice's eyes at the end." Shay paused to take stock. "The black circle on David. The deaths of not one, but two prominent people involved in two of my projects."

Stefan listened and then said, "Speaking of Bernice. Dr. Maddy contacted me this morning. I'd asked her to take a look at Bernice after I spoke to you. Remember I said there was something I couldn't figure out? Anyway, she found something odd in Bernice's energy."

"Odd?" Shay said sharply? "How odd. And did she know Bernice?" Then again Bernice, and Dr. Maddy knew many people so it wasn't surprising to hear.

"A friend expressed concern about Bernice's death so she took a quick look." His voice deepened. "According to her, there was a new hook into her root chakra and the energy drained very quickly. Maddy felt it was deliberate but didn't go so far as to say Bernice was murdered."

Shay gasped in shock. "Oh no."

"She also believes the person visited Bernice in the hospital, either in astral form or by hitchhiking on another person's energy."

Silence. Shay in the process of standing up, collapsed back down on her couch. "That is so not good."

"But we can't rush to the wrong conclusion. First Bernice. Then Cummings. Now the headmaster... One of those events would be fine, two maybe, but because there are too many unusual occurrences, you're afraid they're connected and that they signal a big negative. Not everything that is 'wrong' has to be very wrong. Maybe the victim took too much of his heart medication. An accident. Maybe your personal perspective was skewed by the loss of Bernice and that affected the vision you had. If you can explain away one or two of the occurrences then the others pale in significance."

His voice changed, detaching as if called away. "I need to go. How about we meet for dinner on Saturday, and we can discuss it further?"

She smiled wryly. "Except I actually have a date."

Silence. Then Stefan's amusement rippled through his warm voice as he said, "Wow. I'm delighted to hear it. May I…?"

"You probably already knew. It's Roman, Gerard's grandson and Ronin's brother. We've emailed off and on for years, but now… He just moved here from the East Coast to take over Gerard's business until the board gets through its big power struggle."

"Oh, yes." His voice lightened, warmed. "I do remember him." An odd silence filtered through the phone.

Shay sighed. "What do you know that I don't?"

"Uhm. Maybe you should take a closer look yourself."

She leaned forward. "I did, and came up against a huge wall. So I stopped." She wrinkled her nose and sighed. "Okay, give. What did I miss?"

This time there was no mistaking the laughter in Stefan's voice when he said, "He's safe, but I think you'd better take a closer look. He certainly is."

And Stefan rang off.

KNOCK, KNOCK…

It's me again Shay. Too bad you didn't see how easy my last trick was. That was like pulling wings off a fly. An activity that had lost its appeal a long time ago. Time for change.

It was quite possible that the police would never connect the deaths to Shay. Maybe an anonymous phone call would tip them off? Send them in the right direction. Sad that they might need that.

Still, the three deaths all related to Lassiter Foundation. They should be able to make that much of a connection. To finger Shay, as a suspect, would only be a short hop away after that.

Experts said that revenge was often best served cold, but for her…after having waited a year…a little fire added to the flames would be even better.

Time to move up the agenda.

CHAPTER 7

Friday morning...

SHAY STOOD AT Bernice's gravesite, Pappy at her side. He held her arm tightly against him. Dressed in black to satisfy her grandfather's sense of proprietary, she kept her focus on him and his needs. He looked so frail, so broken.

Gerard didn't look much better. Roman stood at his side.

It was early yet, but already hundreds had arrived for the ceremony.

Long limousines and fancy cars lined the roadway, bringing even more people. The weather had cooperated, ushering sunshine and blue sky to the ceremony. Shay shifted the roses to the other hand.

Bernice had loved gold roses. The area was festooned with them, and a single gold rose lay on the ornate casket. Bernice, being who she was, had picked out her favorite funeral details long before her death. She'd also chosen to be buried in a gown that matched the roses.

The minister, another old friend of Bernice's, brought tears to everyone's eyes as he spoke of the blessing of having known her. She'd been such a major presence, a force, that no one could ignore her. No one wanted to. She'd been a light for them all.

For all her best intentions, Shay felt tears well up in her eyes. She was going to miss the old lady.

Pappy squeezed her arm. She smiled mistily at him and said, "It's a beautiful day for her."

He smiled gently and whispered, "Yes. She'd have loved it."

I am loving it, said Bernice irritably.

Shay started, her gaze widening in shock. She looked over at the familiar shimmering energy of her old friend. Bernice stood between the two old men, clear and crisp as if she were there in person – except she was present only in astral form.

You can see me, can't you? Bernice stared at Shay in delight. *How come you can, but no one else can?*

Shay rolled her eyes. Like she was going to be able to answer that question. She shrugged, motioning to the side. Then, slipping her arm free from Pappy, she excused herself for a moment as if to go and speak with someone else. And she was going to do just that, but her grandfather wouldn't understand how she'd converse with Bernice.

She walked behind the crowd and off to the side. Turning around, she came face to face with Bernice. "Oh!" Shay jumped back a step.

How come no one else can see me? Bernice complained. *I wanted to talk with Charles and Gerard again.*

"They can't see you," Shay murmured.

Obviously, Bernice snapped. *Why not though? I want them to see me, too.*

"How would I know? I doubt many people can." She hesitated, and then whispered, "Why are you here?"

I don't know. Bernice looked around. *I don't think I want to be here. But there's something…*

Shay waited for her to finish the sentence. When no more was forthcoming, she prompted, "But there's something…?"

Bernice looked worried – the edges of her form wavered, thinned, *I don't know. There's something that has to be done. But I don't know what. But something has to be stopped…*

"Something you need to say to someone, or something that you meant to do? Something you started and wanted to see finished?" Shay tried to prompt the other woman's memory.

Doubt and a tinge of fear crossed the older woman's features. *I don't remember. But there is a reason I came here. But what?*

"If we can figure out what that is and see it done, then you can leave."

Leaving would be good. I don't like this, she cried out. And disappeared.

"Wait—"

Shit. Bernice was gone.

Shay looked up to find Roman staring at her from only ten feet way.

Double shit.

ROMAN WATCHED SHAY as she stood off to the side. Though she was wearing all black, she was too dynamic to fade into the crowd. He had no idea why she'd separated herself from the group and he couldn't stop himself from checking out what she was doing.

Shay appeared to be talking to someone. Except she was alone.

Giving an excuse to his grandfather, he moved out of the crowd and slipped to the back. Shay was still several feet off to one side. He thought he heard her say something like 'wait!' but when he looked around, she was alone.

Had she been alone?

The crowd was huge. Perhaps what he heard was her talking to someone on her cell phone. That would explain the one-sided conversation. Was her cell phone in her hand?

Or was this something else altogether?

SHAY MANAGED A wry smile as Roman approached. Of course it *would* be him. *Had he heard her talking to Bernice?* Wouldn't that be perfect? First guy in a long time that interested her – okay more than interested her – and now he'd think she was nuts. Hell, she probably was. "Hi. How is Gerard doing?" she asked as he drew closer.

Roman glanced back at his grandfather who sat with his head resting on his hand. "It's a tough day for them."

"Yes. Pappy is heartbroken. He'd love to join Bernice, I think."

Roman smiled at her, the obvious warmth and the caring doing crazy things to her insides. "I'm sure grandfather has similar thoughts right now. Funerals are for the living to say good-bye. In this case, neither of the men want to do that. They'd rather have gone with her."

"What a trio."

"I have dinner reservations for Saturday." He tilted his head and studied her face. "I'll pick you up at 7:30 pm. If that works for you?"

She nodded, trying to keep her face neutral, masking the surprise and pleasure that lit her up from inside. She hadn't forgotten, but she had wondered if he might. She'd even thought he might want her to forget about it so he didn't have to follow through. *Apparently not.*

"That's perfect. Thank you. You know where I live, right?" And it was perfect when he nodded. Delight unfurled inside only to become tinged with nervousness about taking this step with this man of secrets. And the apprehension she felt should be enough to stop her from moving forward with Roman. If she'd learned her lesson, it would have. But...

"Shay! Roman!"

A call came from the center of the crowd. Gerard was waving at them to come closer. "It's Charles."

"Uh oh." Shay raced over to find Pappy, pale and shaky, leaning on

Gerard's shoulder. He looked so frail right now. Her heart squeezed with fear. "Come on Pappy, time to go home."

"There's a reception at the Foundation Center, though," her grandfather protested.

"That's nice. After you've had a rest, we'll see about stopping in. But first, home," she added, firmly.

Grumbling the whole way, Pappy allowed Shay to lead him to her Audi. They said a quick good-bye to the other two men, then Shay drove her grandfather home.

Back at Pappy's high-end apartment, she helped him sit down on the dark brown leather couch before putting on a pot of tea. He needed a few minutes to collect himself and come to terms with Bernice's burial – and *that* she could allow him. She returned to the living room after the tea had steeped. She'd found some cookies in a cupboard and put a small tray together for him.

"How are you feeling now?" She placed the tray on the coffee table. Then poured him a cup of tea.

He took it from her and settled back into the cushions, sighing heavily. "Fine. I'm fine. It's just so hard to say good-bye."

"Isn't that the truth?" she muttered as she sat down beside him and gently patted his hand.

"You know, for a moment there…" He hesitated, then forced himself to say, "For a moment, I thought I saw her. Actually saw her standing off to the side, watching us all mourn her passing." He smiled in a self-deprecating way. "Silly, wasn't it?"

He took a sip of tea.

Shay stared at him. *How interesting.* And how wonderful. She'd have to remember to tell Bernice. She'd enjoy that.

"Bernice would have enjoyed her funeral," she said warmly. It was a lie but it's what Pappy needed to hear. "It was beautiful."

"She'd have enjoyed watching us all honor her," he said with a knowing smile. "For all her faults, I loved her."

"And the loving doesn't stop with death," Shay murmured. How many times had she seen love continue beyond? It made her feel good and it broke her heart at the same time. How hard for the person left behind… Sometimes they never loved again.

How horrible that would be. *Or would it?* This way at least they'd experienced love.

"No. Love doesn't just fade away. I wish she'd been there, today."

Not knowing the best thing to say, she murmured gently, "And maybe she was. She loved you. It makes sense she'd come back to say good-bye, if she could have."

Her grandfather peered at her hopefully. His rheumy eyes filled with tears. "Do you think so?"

She put her arms around his frail body and hugged him. Pappy's heart was huge. He'd been blessed to have loved twice. First he loved her grandmother, who passed on early when his two sons were still young, and then Bernice. Losing Bernice now had to be tough. And would have triggered the memories of his first loss, and the loss of both of his sons since then. There was only his grandchildren, her brother and herself, left. And her brother had lived in Europe for last few years.

Pappy had always been a mainstay in her life. But who'd been there for him?

Bernice.

And he was such a dear man. If he needed reassurance now, she could give him that.

She knew exactly what to say. With her voice full of love for this special, hurting man, she said, "Yes. I *know* she was."

Saturday morning

ROMAN LEANED BACK from his laptop and rubbed his temple. "Grandfather, this is the third time you've mentioned my date with Shay tonight. Don't worry. I have reservations at the new seafood restaurant downtown for 8:00 pm. So everything is taken care of." The old man was driving him nuts. He'd called a dozen times since Roman drove him home from Bernice's funeral.

He understood it. Putting Bernice to rest had been a big step. Finding closure was important. Grieving would take longer. The need to connect with the living, the reaffirming of life, and the acceptance that his own death was right around the corner made his grandfather a mess right now. He'd seen it many times with victims of crime, back in his old life.

Not for first time, he rubbed the scar on his side.

"Good. Good. When is the reading of the will?" his grandfather asked.

Roman frowned, his hand stilling. "I'm not sure. Why?"

"It's just that Bernice was always very particular about her stuff. I want to make sure her estate is handled correctly."

Not their issue. Thankfully. Bernice had enough money to make even the most honorable consider ways and means of getting a piece of the pot. "That's out of our hands. The lawyers will be handling Bernice's fortune. I'm sure they have everything in order."

The grumbling on the other end of the phone made Roman smile. "Why don't you call Charles and meet him for lunch? He might know more."

Roman could almost see his grandfather perking up. "Do you think he's awake yet?"

Glancing at the clock, Roman grinned. It was almost 4:00 pm. "He was probably up from his nap an hour ago."

His grandfather hurriedly rang off.

Roman leaned back against his couch and stared across the room. He'd painted for hours last night, losing himself in his art. He'd finally put everything away around 4:00 am. No wonder he was tired. Then that's the way his art went these days. Nothing for days, then going into a painting so deeply he lost track of time.

He'd only gotten a few hours rest these last couple of nights. Add in the funeral… Dealing with Grandfather had been the hardest. Ronin would have been there, but he'd been called away on some big case.

That was life in law enforcement, the work tended to take the front seat. As Roman well knew. And of course the other issue frustrating him was about the subject matter of his painting.

His model. *Shay.*

He stood up and strode to his studio. His latest was a charcoal sketch with pastel highlights. A new look. A new technique. *Did it work?* Yeah, he actually thought it did. The charcoal played with the shadows and shapes. The paint highlighted the swells and curves.

He knew this body almost as well as his own. He needed to know Shay, the beautiful soul that called to his soul, just as well.

And damn, he wanted to check out her curves in person.

CHAPTER 8

Saturday evening…

THE DOORBELL RANG like five minutes too soon. Shay's hand slipped with the mascara wand, giving her a nice black streak across her cheek. *Shit.*

Why couldn't he be late tonight? She scrubbed her cheek clean and tried again. With that last bit in place, she stroked on her favorite lipstick and raced to the door. She'd been looking forward to tonight all week, even though she knew she shouldn't. But in this instance, logic and emotion didn't match. And right now, her heart was pounding with nervous excitement.

"Hi. Come on in. I'll be just a minute." Not giving him a chance to answer, she bolted back to her room and slipped on her heels and put in her long emerald earrings to match the skin-tight jade dress she'd bought on impulse, and had yet to wear. Feeling a little better, she did one quick turn in the mirror then walked back out to her living room.

Roman stood with casual grace in the middle of her living room, studying the painting on the wall. Her Stefan Kronos masterpiece. *Of course.* That painting never failed to attract attention.

"Do you like it?"

His gaze switched from the painting, locking on to her so suddenly it left her momentarily stunned. And feeling like an idiot.

Wearing a rueful smile, she apologized, "Sorry, I've been running behind all day.

"It's beautiful." His gaze shifted, a long, slow sweep down and then back up. So hot so sensual she could feel his gaze as a physical stroke. Viscerally. She swallowed and wondered at the intense look on his face. "Roman, are you all right?"

His gaze deepened and he smiled. *Oh God.* That heart-stoppingly slow movement had her gaze locking onto that mouth as the corners quirked. She swallowed.

"I'm more than all right." His head tilted to the side. "You look divine."

She flushed at the blatant appreciation in those dark blue eyes, as well as his words. "Thanks, but I meant the painting."

His smile deepened. "I know. It's a Stefan Kronos piece, isn't it?"

Interesting. Not many people recognized Stefan's work. "It is. I'm surprised you know it," she said lightly, snagging her shawl from the back of the couch. She threw it around her shoulders and smiled at him. Happy to be back into her coolly professional space, she said, "Shall we?"

He opened the door for Shay and waited in the hallway while she locked it behind her. "I own one of his works and have seen several of his paintings at a friend's house," he said.

She gazed at him in surprise. "Really?"

"He's incredibly talented."

"That he is," she murmured. He held the elevator door for her and pushed the button to descend to the lobby. She watched him. Everything she'd seen of him spoke of grace and strength and done with an economy of movement. He didn't fidget, glance around or hesitate. He seemed so centered. When he turned that gaze on her, like he often did without warning, it was to pin her. As if she had his focus, every tiny speck of it, during the time he stared at her. That was as unnerving as it was delightful.

In today's world, how often did one have someone's total attention? Usually cell phones went off, other people interrupted, or distractions continually interfered. She had no way to evade his gaze, and she had no wish to.

Another novel experience.

The new restaurant was a pleasant surprise. She'd planned to take Pappy for a special meal there when it opened. She gazed around, wondering at the sleight of hand that placed them at a private table for two on the rooftop under the stars. The setting was delightful.

"I assume from your expression that this is fine," he said, warm amusement lacing his voice. He held out the chair for her. Waited for her to take her seat.

"Absolutely." She smiled at him, appreciating the way that the material of his suit snugged up against his shoulders as he took his seat.

Damn. If she were in the market for an affair, this guy would definitely get top billing. Right now, though, she was guy shy, and that was enough to keep her hormones in check...

Liar. Her hormones were anything but in check. And this guy was anything but safe. Danger rippled behind those eyes. And promise. So much damn promise.

The wine steward approached, breaking her gaze. She was grateful for the distraction and stared down at the city laid out below her.

When they were alone again, she asked the one question that had kept her guessing all week. "What did Bernice say to you about me?"

He smiled. But this time it was polished, the cool, businesslike smile of a pro. She eyed him suspiciously. "She said you were perfect for me. And that you managed the Lassiter Foundation almost as well as she managed the Folgrent Foundation."

Shay gasped, then laughed. "*Almost?* How typical of Bernice."

He narrowed his gaze at her. "You didn't like her?"

"You've already asked me that." She settled back into her seat, crossing her arms over her chest. "My answer is the same. I really respected her. I even loved her, as one loves an old family friend, but I didn't appreciate how she kept Pappy on a string."

"But you understand it?"

She gave a half laugh. "I didn't say that."

"No, but it's there, hidden in your words."

"After having asked her why she'd never made a decision between the two, then yes, I guess I do. That doesn't mean I have to like it."

He winced. "I do feel for Grandfather. At the same time, he made the choice to stay on the string."

Amusement rippled through her. This man would never let himself be strung along like their respective grandparents. "Bernice said she loved them both too much to hurt the other by picking one."

His gaze widened. Then he gave a short laugh. "If that isn't Bernice all over."

KNOCK, KNOCK...

It's me again, Shay. Damn I wish you could hear me. I could tell you how foolish you are. You think you can close your doors and lock yourself deep inside. That's definitely not going to happen. I don't need open locks to give me access.

I'm like you — talented.

And you'd hate it if you knew.

I know. You'll see. I know all about what you did.

It wasn't fair.

But then you crossed the line.

That's all right. I've crossed that same line many times. In fact, I've crossed bigger and more dangerous lines. But after a few times, it doesn't matter anymore. There's no remorse. No sadness. Nothing. Just an empty space that you can fill however you'd like to fill it. It's exciting in its own way. It's different. Being alone in this vast space with the power to see inside people. To see their real motivations. That's what you pride yourself on, isn't it?

You're happy to sit inside your ivory tower and feel safe. But you're not safe. See, there's more than one type of danger.

And you'll never be safe.

Not from me.

Late Saturday night…

SHAY WALKED TO her apartment building, aware of the strong man at her side. "I really enjoyed dinner," she murmured, opening the conversation. She didn't want him to come inside. Didn't want to have to invite him in for a nightcap. But knew she would anyway. She couldn't help it. He did things to her insides, lovely hot things. Things she wasn't ready for intellectually. Things she didn't want to face. Not tonight. Maybe not this year. Or this lifetime.

Despite all that, she wanted to be with this man. And she had wanted that for a long time.

The doorman stepped out to open the glass door for her.

"Good evening, Thomas. I hope you're having a quiet evening."

He beamed as he always did when she spoke to him. "I'm having a wonderfully peaceful evening. Thank you for asking."

"Good." Roman walked to the elevator and hit the up button. Shay raised an eyebrow at Roman.

"I'll see you to your door."

She nodded gracefully. "Good night, Thomas."

"Have a good one, Miss."

She didn't need to look around to know Thomas watched their progress with a curious eye. She hadn't brought home a date in a long time.

Once inside the elevator she said, "You didn't need to see me to my door. Thomas has always looked out for me."

"I don't take a lady out for an evening and not return her home."

Simple, clean, and yet his words seemed…a bit cool. Was he upset? She peeked through her lashes at him.

Their relaxed relationship had definitely tightened, changed in the last few seconds. It had been way too long since her last date. This was awkward. She hated awkward.

"Good to know."

The elevator slowed to a stop. He held the door open for her. She walked to her apartment, searching in her bag for her keys.

Finally. She pulled them out and went to slip the key into the lock. That was when she realized the door was ajar. And froze.

"What's the matter?"

She took a deep breath. "My door is already unlocked."

ROMAN HATED SHAY'S nervous fumbling, and especially hated that her nervousness intensified the higher the elevator rose. He didn't think she was aware of it. She'd relaxed over dinner, her wariness easing before finally disappearing altogether. He'd loved watching her settle and open up.

So what made her so nervous? He'd thought they'd enjoyed dinner and that they were past the initial nervous stage. Bernice had shared a lot about her favorite goddaughter, as she called Shay. She'd told him, 'She's been hurt. Badly. Now she is wary. You'll have to work hard. But she's worth it.'

At the time, he hadn't been too worried. He'd been communicating with Shay daily and knew her, but that was before he moved back to Portland. From the instant he'd seen the first series of 'Shay' photos, he'd been interested. Time and online dialogue and painting had strengthened the bond. Whether she knew it or not. But at this moment in time they were barely friends – certainly not looking like lovers.

Roman knew he really wanted to be lovers. And so much more.

She'd been a delight all evening, full of laughter and great conversation and passion that simmered under the surface – until they got out of the car and she realized he wasn't just going to give her a casual 'good night' and walk away.

Hell, he didn't want to walk away at all.

Now, as she pulled her keys out of her purse and fitted them to the door, he realized her composure was firmly back in place – like a protective coating, keeping the world at a safe distance.

Shay's composure disappeared as she stared at her front door.

"What do you mean?" he questioned cautiously. "Did you leave it unlocked?"

Her beautiful chocolate eyes stared up at him, confusion clouding them. "I locked it before we left, didn't I?"

He had to stop and think. "You went to lock it."

"But did I?" She sighed. "Just another glitch… Goes along with my day. Sorry. I'm trying to avoid being paranoid these days."

Something about her tone of voice had him gazing at her intently. "Do you have a reason to be paranoid?"

Something moved in the back of her gaze. His senses sharpened. He narrowed his eyes at her. "Shay?"

"No, of course not." She laughed, but it sounded forced. "Nothing more than being a single female who lives alone." She pushed her door open and walked inside.

He followed her and reached out to flick on the lights. Bright light filled the living room and entranceway as she strode further into the room, her back stiff, her head turning from side to side. "Everything appears normal."

"I'll search the place to make sure."

She gave a sigh of relief. "Thank you."

If there was a little too much nervousness in her voice, he ignored it. She did live alone, and if someone had broken in, that was nothing to fool around with. He closed the front door and opened the hall closet. He searched through the long coats. "Nothing here." Systematically, he moved through the classy apartment and checked cupboards and corners. He couldn't help but admire the queen-sized bed and its thick duvet dressed in chocolate and gold. There was something especially compelling about the colors and the intimate setting. And he approved, imagined her bedding as a perfect contrast to her chestnut hair and smooth creamy skin.

Ignoring his clamoring body and the visions in his head, he checked under the bed and opened up the double closets. *Nothing.* He closed the last closet and turned to face her. "The apartment is empty."

She nodded. "Thank you."

He looked at her closer. "Shay, are you going to be okay?"

She collected herself and smiled up at him. "I am. Sorry. Thank you so much for checking. I'm sure it's nothing." Crossing her arms she walked to the front door and opened it for him.

No goodnight kiss or hug. Nothing.

An unmistakable message.

Having made sure the place was safe, he walked over and smiled. "Sleep well."

He walked out of her apartment and into the night.

Downstairs, he stopped beside Thomas. "Did Shay have any visitors tonight? When we got to her door, she found it unlocked."

Thomas's eyebrows shot up. "Oh dear. There's been no one in or out that doesn't belong."

"We'll assume then that she forgot to lock up on our way out. Thanks."

Roman walked to his car, deep in thought. He hated leaving her alone. Especially after finding the door unlocked. He'd wanted to stay and watch over her. But she wouldn't have welcomed his presence. Though he'd done a thorough search of her place, and was confident no one lurked in there, something had unnerved him. Something *had* felt off.

But what?

SHAY CLOSED HER door behind Roman and locked it. She turned back and leaned against the closed door and studied her living room. It *looked* normal.

It didn't *feel* normal.

Then she dropped her barriers to look more closely. Energy filled the room. Hers. Roman's. Yes, even Stefan's soothing energy hovered. He'd obviously checked in on her earlier.

And so had someone else…

She blinked. And checked again. Definitely traces of another presence.

Then she identified it.

Recognized something so familiar it scared the crap out of her.

Her breath caught in the back of her throat, choking off the cry ready to spring forth. *Oh God. No.* That wasn't possible. There's no way this energy could be here. Absolutely, no way. *He* was dead.

Shivers raced down her spine and her teeth started chattering. She crossed her arms across her chest. Nothing helped. Stepping forward, she snatched up her shawl from where she'd dropped it on the couch and wrapped it tightly around her.

This is not possible. Stefan, please tell me this isn't happening, she whispered. There was no comforting answer in her mind. Stefan wasn't responding.

Stefan!

Jesus. What? Can't a guy get any sleep around her, he grumbled. *What the hell is wrong?*

Because it would save time and explanation, she opened her mind so he could see her thoughts, feelings and impressions through their telepathic link.

Tell me this isn't his energy. Tell me he's dead and forever gone. Please.

Him? Stefan's voice shifted as he shook off the sleep from his mind. *No, it's not possible. It can't be Darren.*

Are you sure? My door was unlocked when I came home tonight. And it shouldn't have been.

That doesn't mean it was him.

No, but the energy was so similar to his — as if he's changed form slightly. She gave a strangled laugh, tears starting to course down her cheeks. *And yes, I know how unbelievable that sounds. Please tell me that he's dead and gone.*

Shay, he's dead. I killed him. You killed him. He can't ever hurt you again.

She sniffled. *Are you sure?*

Positive.

CHAPTER 9

Sunday morning…

WHEN SHAY OPENED her eyes the next morning, recognized her bedroom and breathed in the soothing morning light, a sense of relief washed through her. It was finally morning. And her apartment felt…normal.

It had taken an hour last night, with Stefan's help, to cleanse and secure her apartment. She still had no idea what had gone on or who her intruder was. But she'd know that energy again if she ever saw it. The cleansing process had her simply walking around and ushering out the old energy – and refilling the space with warm, loving, protective energy.

And it appeared to have worked. She had slept.

Dragging her sorry ass out of bed, Shay made her way to a hot shower. Something needed to energize her. It felt like sandpaper had been rubbed over her insides, leaving her raw – edgy. She had a crappy day ahead to go along with the night.

Another funeral. And burial at the same cemetery. This time for David Cummings. She didn't have to go, but knew she should. Besides, her consciousness prodded at her to check it out. To make sure all was well.

She stumbled through getting dressed and ate a muffin for her breakfast then headed out the door with a few minutes to spare. For a Sunday morning, there was a surprising amount of traffic. She drove up the winding road to the cemetery and parked. Walking swiftly, her head bowed against the gray skies, she joined the small, private group for the ceremony at the gravesite. David's preference as she understood it.

Staying unobtrusively in the background, she tried to look around at the other mourners. She only recognized one or two of the people, David's office staff. That wasn't unexpected. His family was at the left and a row of strangers mingled. Several appeared to be crying – also not unexpected. She looked at their energy as they stood in their own quiet spaces. Most were contained and solemn. Holding tight, their energy snug against their bodies. She'd expect that in this setting. She took a casual look to the others at her side. Again, the energies were calm, slow and contained.

No surprises here.

Several other people had joined the throng, coming up behind her. She'd stepped around, letting them come closer to the gravesite and taking her place behind them. Standing behind them gave her a better view of all assembled. Still nothing explained her intuition's insistence that had compelled her to come here or the overwhelming need to check out the energy of those around her. A thin layer of energy on the coffin remained, most likely from the workers who'd handled it.

She shifted her position for a different angle. And still nothing. Shrugging inside, she waited until the eulogy was over before slowly approaching the widow.

"I'm so sorry for your loss," she murmured gently to the weeping woman. "I worked with David for several years. He was a good man."

The widow smiled through her tears. "Thank you. I will miss him."

As Shay walked back to her car, she pondered the issue. There'd been a definite sense of loss and grief from the widow and the sister-in-law. There'd been an odd melding of their energies, but that wasn't necessarily anything important, just strange. But it had a caring to it. She hadn't seen anything that spoke of hatred, relief, or that proclaimed any ill intention – and that had been good. If there'd been foul play suggested in their energies she'd have to say something to Ronin....

Still, there'd been nothing there.

Back at her car she gave all the people a final examination as they walked slowly away from the service. Now that it was over, there was no reason for the individuals to keep quiet. At least not verbally. Their energies eased outward. One mentally sniped at another attendee's lack of decorum, thinking she was wearing a low-cut dress more appropriate for a night on the town than a funeral. Another was worried about the time away from his job and resenting that he'd have to stay later that day to make up for lost time. Another marveled at the beauty and simplicity of the grounds thinking it a beautiful spot to rest for all eternity. Shay smiled to herself – the human spirit revitalized itself very quickly. Once the sense of propriety was observed, everyone loosened up. And became their so-normal selves.

Another woman fretted about the traffic and still another was on her way to meet a secret lover, hoping her husband at her side would pick up the dry cleaning on his way to coach soccer. Only, the husband was meeting someone himself.

Shay turned back to her car and got in. So much humanity at the surface in a single gathering. For all their private lives and secretive thoughts, no one appeared to harbor any visible ill will toward the deceased.

She got in her car to head home.

ROMAN PUT THE phone back in his pocket for at least the dozenth time that morning. Only now he stood outside her apartment. "Where the hell are you, Shay?"

He'd tried both her cell phone and her home phone. No answer.

He should never have left her alone last night. Not after the unlocked door. All sorts of horrible images had filled his mind since. He'd long given up and had raced to her apartment to check it out for himself. And got no answer. There was a different doorman at the front entrance this time, and he hadn't been able to confirm if Shay had left.

All Roman could do was keep trying. He pulled out his phone and watched the time tick off. Then he hit redial.

"Hello?"

Frustrated relief washed through him, followed by quick, sharp anger. "Damn it, where the hell are you?"

There was a surprised silence at the other end.

Shit. He groaned. "Sorry. I didn't mean that quite the way it sounded, but I've been trying to get a hold of you for several hours now. After last night, when you didn't answer, I started to get very worried."

"I'm fine," she said coolly. "I was at another funeral. One of the people my foundation works with had a heart attack last week."

He ran his fingers through his hair. "Sorry again. That's a tough one. Two funerals in three days isn't fun."

"No, it isn't." She sighed. "And I have another one next week. Same thing."

"Same thing?" His voice sharpened unintentionally. "That's not good."

Her voice trembled as it crept through the phone. "No, it isn't."

"Does all this have anything to do with your apartment being unlocked last night?" An odd silence raised the hairs on the back of his neck. "Shay? Are you in danger?"

"No. No, not at all," she said quickly. "Two men had heart attacks. They ran projects my foundation funded. They were associates. There's no danger."

"Good." Relief was slow to come but when it did, it washed through him in a rush. He'd been so worried. "Good to know. You scared me."

"Sorry. I just turned on my phone. I haven't had a chance to check my messages yet."

"Well most of them will be from me."

"Then I won't need to listen to them, will I?" Her voice turned brusque, professional.

He hated that. As if she was trying to push him back. "Unless you had something specific you were calling about...?"

"I initially called to make sure you were okay after last night. Then when I couldn't get a hold of you, I started to panic. I've actually been standing outside your apartment, wondering if I should break in or not." He laughed, a short sound that made him wince as he heard it. "I was sure you'd been hurt. I've been kicking myself for not staying last night." He ran his fingers through his hair. "I guess I overreacted."

"It's all right. I'm glad you called to check on me." She paused, adding humorously, "At least if I do get murdered, it's nice to know that my body would eventually be found."

"That's not funny."

"I wasn't joking," she said, a bitter tone to her words.

He didn't know what to say to that. He didn't like her words or her tone. But how much was she not telling him? "Where are you?"

"Sitting in my car at the cemetery about to go home to rest."

"You didn't sleep last night?" He relaxed, knowing she was okay now, and happy to be talking to her. He wanted to see her. Take her out of her odd mood. Maybe coax her to share a little more. "Let's go to lunch."

Silence.

"Is that a yes?" he asked carefully. "I thought maybe the Palace Restaurant. They have a beautiful coffee bar and lunch buffet. Are you sure I can't tempt you with some food?"

"I'm tired," she said. "I wouldn't be good company."

"I'm not looking for good company." And he wasn't. He was only just beginning to realize what he was looking for. "I'm looking to spend an hour, stress free, with you. Like we did last night before we reached your place," he coaxed. "We had a wonderful evening, didn't we?"

She went quiet.

SHOULD SHE GO? Hell, no. *But did she want to?* Hell, yes.

"I'd like to meet with you again," he said promptly. "Lunch. In twenty minutes at the Palace."

And he hung up.

Shay stared down at the phone in her hand. *What the hell. What if I don't want to meet you, Roman?* Then it was too late to decline, because she'd let herself get caught up in the idea. She should have turned him down right at the beginning. Instead she'd let him assume she'd be there.

She wanted to be there. But it wasn't like she was put together for a luncheon date. She looked down at her black slacks and matching black cotton sweater. To hell with it. If he was so hot to meet her, then he could meet her as she was.

She turned on the engine and pulled out of the parking lot.

Shay?

Damn. Shay was forced to pull onto the shoulder of the road. *Stefan? What's up?*

I was going to ask you that. There's been a lot of odd energy coming off you for the last ten minutes.

She groaned. *That's one way to put it.* Quickly she explained her morning. *So I'm heading over there for lunch.*

Good. It will be good for you.

Says you.

Yes, says me. It's your time for love.

And he left, leaving her mind empty and gasping. Speaking aloud to the empty car, she said, "Damn it, Stefan. That's not fair. If you know something, tell me."

Warm laughter filled her mind.

But he stayed silent.

Irritated, yet feeling better for some odd reason, she pulled back into traffic and headed to the restaurant. *Was Stefan right? Was Roman her life partner? If so, wouldn't she know?* Of course not, not with that damn wall of his...and her luck.

Roman was standing outside the restaurant, talking on the phone, when she pulled up. He finished his call and put his phone away once he caught sight of her.

"I was afraid you weren't coming."

"A friend called. I needed to speak with him for a few minutes."

Roman smiled. "Good. Glad you're here. I have a table waiting for us in the conservatory."

She rolled her eyes at him – of course he got one of the nicest tables in the place. "Who did you have to bribe to get that table?"

He laughed. "No one. A couple was getting ready to leave when I walked in."

She didn't believe him but, what the hell, she'd enjoy a quiet lunch.

As they walked toward the door of the restaurant, Roman asked, "How was the funeral?"

She winced. "Personally, I hate funerals. Don't intend to have one after I'm gone and don't like attending them when friends and family die."

"Many people don't like them, but usually it's because of their sense of loss." He opened the front door of the restaurant for her. "Helps them to find closure."

"Not in my case," she said shortly. "I don't need them, like them, or want them."

"And you see too many people who do?"

She shot him a narrow look under her lashes. *How did he mean that?* It seemed like she was always looking for hidden meanings in everything he said. She hated that. But with her abilities, she found it instinctive to be self-protecting now.

"I've seen too many people put into the ground to find any solace in a funeral," Shay said.

The hostess motioned for them to follow.

He placed his hand on the small of her back and nudged her forward. He tilted his head toward her. "Interesting perception."

She laughed. "Not really. What about you? Are you a fan of funerals?"

He shrugged. "I see them as a necessary stage for the living and the dead."

She repeated his words. "Interesting. And what is your opinion of life after death?"

He looked startled. After studying her for a moment to make sure she was serious, he said, "I don't know that I have one. I guess I believe there is more out there than we know, but as I have no personal experience either way, I'm neutral on the issue."

It could be worse. At least he hadn't jumped down her throat or interrogated her for hours. That was good. They took their seats and ordered coffee.

"You do have an opinion, I presume?" He quirked a brow and studied her.

The curiosity in his voice made her smile. "Maybe. But you'll think

I'm crazy."

"Not at all, but now I am curious."

"I thought I saw Bernice in her room that day she died. Then again at her funeral." She hadn't meant to say anything about that.

He sat back, one eyebrow raised. "Interesting."

She leaned back and stared at him. "You say that a lot?"

A lopsided grin slid out. And damn if that smile didn't just burrow a little deeper into her psyche and make itself at home. Funny how attractive acceptance was.

And how unexpected.

"Do you see ghosts often?" His question, so casual and so calm, made her study him over her coffee mug.

She leaned forward and whispered, "You do realize how ridiculous that question is?"

"Is it? Bernice mentioned that she thought you had some weird things going on along that line."

"Bernice did? *Really?*"

He nodded.

Shay laughed. "That old sneak. Maybe she was trying to warn you away from me. Make me out to be a nutcase."

He chuckled warmly. "No, not Bernice. She loved you."

"Yes, she did." Shay's eyes got a little misty. "I miss her."

"Does that mean she won't be staying around and haunting you?"

"I wish. But that would mean she hasn't crossed over the way she should have. I wouldn't wish that fate on her."

There was an odd silence. She glanced up from her plate to find him studying her. "You're serious, aren't you?" His smile deepened. "Of course I shouldn't be too surprised. Ronin has also dropped a few tidbits about you over the last year or two."

Shay put her cup down to give him her full attention.

"And he's worked with Stefan several times." Roman watched for a response.

"Stefan is a wonderful artist." Shay smirked.

"And a skilled psychic." Roman sat back slightly as if to put some distance between them. "Apparently."

She snorted. "You said you were open to it."

"Not quite," he corrected. "I said I had no opinion either way."

She waved her fork in the air. "Splitting hairs."

"I'm open-minded about many things I'd never consider a few years back. I have a friend who is a highly acclaimed healer." He sounded like he wanted to believe her.

"Healing is good." And it was. If Roman could be open on that score, maybe he could be open to more? "Who is it?"

"Her name is Dr. Maddy from The Haven," he said.

Shay laughed in delight. "I know Dr. Maddy. She's a good friend of Stefan's. I'd like to know her better, but we're all so busy."

"If it makes you feel any better, after seeing what Dr. Maddy can do, I've had to re-examine a lot of the things I thought I knew. Am I clear on them? No. Am I open? Yes." He sighed. "How well do you know Stefan?" His deep gaze pinned her in place.

A little more at ease, she said, "Well. He's a good friend. Why?"

He shrugged, dropping his gaze. "No reason. I've heard a lot about him from Dr. Maddy."

"Ah." Shay smiled. "They are good friends. And I know Stefan helps her with her special project. She's an incredibly strong psychic."

"*Psychic?*" He looked uncomfortable again.

"That word bugs you, doesn't it?"

With a sheepish grin he admitted, "I prefer to think of Dr. Maddy as a healer."

"She is, but she's also an incredibly powerful psychic and that helps with her healing work."

TABITHA STODDARD STACKED up the files and carried them into her office at the animal sanctuary. She had a lot of catching up to do. There was never enough time to take care of things around here. She needed another assistant to just clear off the backlog. As she stared around at her small, overstuffed office, she realized she could really use a full time secretary too. Still, all was good. The new anesthesiology table had been ordered, and the plans approved on the new cat enclosure. Given the trouble they'd had getting this far, she should be delighted.

And she was. Now if only the rest of this work would clear up easily, she could get back on track.

"Tabitha!"

She looked out the window to Sue, one of the younger staff members who waved to get her attention. She opened the window. "What's up?"

"We need a signature." Sue motioned toward a large flat-deck truck backing up to the shed with a load of pet food. "Can you come?"

Right. She'd forgotten about that delivery.

If it wasn't one thing, it was twenty.

She skirted her desk and walked outside into the morning sunshine. She smiled at the gorgeous day. They really did live in God's country.

Sue walked over, a big smile on her face.

Tabitha matched it, opened her mouth to speak, and stopped.

A blast of energy shot from Sue's body at the same time something clamped down on Tabitha's heart and squeezed tight. She groaned. Then gasped. For air, for relief, for breath.

Something was terribly wrong. She'd heard about the couple of deaths connected to Shay's foundation projects, but she hadn't thought that she was in danger. And not from Sue, surely? She'd known her forever. No, the energy felt different than Sue's. Similar but not…quite…the same – and was oh so painful.

Stupid.

"Tabitha? Are you all right? *Tabitha?*"

"Shay. Contact Shay," Tabitha whispered. She had a good idea what this was. But she didn't know how or who caused it. She did the only thing she could think of doing. She sent out a psychic call for help, and she shut down, locking herself inside.

CHAPTER 10

Sunday afternoon...

SHAY WAITED FOR Roman to pay the check. She walked out into the sunshine, wanting nothing more than to go home and think about the mess her life was in. *Sigh.*

Shay?

Stefan, what's up? Instinctively she looked around but knew Stefan couldn't be beside her.

It's Tabitha.

What? Shay stepped to the side of the sidewalk beside a large flower garden. *What happened?*

She's been attacked. Psychically. She's alive. She shut her system down. I'm at the hospital now.

Shit.

Don't come. You can't help. But you need to find out how these people are being targeted. If Tabitha wakes up, she might be able to shed some light on what's happening. I've called Ronin. He needs information from you.

"On it."

"On what?" Roman stood at her side, looking at her curiously. "What's going on?"

She ran her fingers through her hair, answering even as her cell phone rang. "A friend, someone associated with my foundation has been attacked."

"What?" Roman stared at her in shock.

She held up her ringing phone. Then spoke into it. "Hello, Ronin. I guess you never get a day off, huh?"

His businesslike voice was sharp and rushed. "There is no day off for crime fighters."

Her stomach revolted as she realized why he was calling. "Stefan told me."

"About Tabitha Stoddard at Exotic Landscape?"

"Yes." Shay groaned. "She's a friend. A good one. I just saw her the other day. We were discussing the arrival of several new animals from a Canadian zoo. She applied to the Foundation for funding because she needed to build new enclosures and was hoping to expand the hospital facilities, including the purchase of a larger anesthetic table."

"How was she when you spoke to her?"

"Wonderful as always." Shay smiled through the tears gathering in the corner of her eyes. She felt overwhelmed, and appreciated the warmth of Roman's comforting arm as it slid around her shoulder. "Tabitha is…a very caring person. I know she always had the animals foremost in her mind when she made every request."

"And did you approve the money?"

"Yes. Definitely. And yes, she knew I'd approve the money. We had a great working relationship."

"This case is yet another connection to you and your foundation."

Her stomach roiled at the thought of these three people coming to an early end because of her. That Bernice could be another victim didn't bear thinking about. At least Tabatha was alive. She cleared her throat as the tears clogged her voice. "I didn't hurt them, if that's what you're suggesting. I called you about David Cumming's case because I just didn't feel good about sending the money if someone was killing to get it."

She stared blindly up at Roman. He shook his head and tightened his arm around her shoulders, tucking her up close. "Shh," he whispered against her hair.

"No. I'm not suggesting that at all," Ronin rushed to say, his voice booming above his brother's caring whisper. "Have you sent the money yet?"

"No. And I don't plan to until this is all settled." There's no way she could. "I don't want the media to connect the dots between these deaths and my projects. It would be a feeding frenzy if they were to find out."

"Yet, they are likely to anyway." His voice turned crisp. "I need access to your files for these cases."

Of course he would. "No problem. Can you come to the office on Monday, or do you want to meet me this afternoon?"

"Given that we have two deaths already and another person close to it, now would be best."

She sighed. Ronin was right. They couldn't afford to waste any more time. "I'll meet you at my office in say…half an hour?" Roman slid his hand down her back, stroking away some of the tension. She glanced up at him. He nodded and she felt better already. Not so alone.

"Sounds good."

Not to her it didn't. But she had no choice.

Someone was killing people she knew. *Because of her?* Were they targeting her, in a way?

She couldn't help wonder how many more people would die before this asshole was caught.

THE OFFICE WAS empty and cold when she walked in with Roman at her side. And it felt even colder as she realized something really wrong could be happening. The dark wooden furniture and rich burgundy carpet now looked cold and austere instead of warm and welcoming. Her family's offices were two floors up and housed the various family holdings, although her brother resided in Europe and ran the business mostly from there with Pappy heading up the North American holdings. She had the only family office on this floor.

She kind of liked the independent feel of that. Walking to the side counter, she put on a small pot of coffee. Turning, she stared around the room with new eyes. She'd always viewed this office as a sanctuary. A business sanctuary.

She'd inherited business responsibilities almost ten years ago, when she turned twenty-one, in fact. Pappy had taken her out for dinner and had presented her with the papers as a gift. Not necessarily a welcome gift, but he'd felt she was the right person to handle this aspect of the family money. The Foundation's money.

She hadn't been so sure. She'd worried about her ability to do the right thing. She'd made a lot of mistakes at the outset. Bernice had helped her and become Shay's mentor. A friend.

Her brother, ten years her senior had been a big help, but too busy for the day-to-day problems she encountered.

She enjoyed her job and all her responsibilities but especially receiving and dealing with the applications for financial help. The process gave her a clearer understanding of what all kinds of people were trying to do and why. Even better, she loved handing out money to those that fit the parameters of the Foundation's funding program.

It had been a joy to see the money go to so many good causes and playing a part to make that happen helped her feel closer to her deceased parents in some way. She hoped they would approve of her choices. There were so many other projects as well, and they were all close to her heart. She stayed in contact with the people and monitored the projects.

Often knew what was to come next for them before they understood it themselves.

"We beat my brother here." Roman grinned as if he competed regularly with his brother.

She smiled at the quiet man at her side. She'd never seen the two men in the same room. Should be interesting. "Looks like it." She walked over to unlock the wall of files behind Jordan's desk.

"Good. I want to see your system. I can run some diagnostics and see if someone has hacked into your computer system. If they haven't, and the firewalls are secure, that would narrow the pool of suspects down to only a few people that would know about your projects."

She paused and turned to face him, hope firing inside. "Can you do that?"

"It's what I do." He nodded in the direction of her office. "Let me see."

Perfect. She couldn't get to her computer fast enough. He was an Internet security specialist, and an ex-cop, and damn she was glad to have his help. The Foundation's files should be secure, but she didn't know if their security had been updated regularly to combat today's hackers. In theory, if someone wanted in, it probably wouldn't be that hard to get there. "If someone did hack in, can you find out who?"

"Maybe." He sat down and started clicking away. A look of total concentration took over his hard features. For a moment there, she could see the internal focus, the cop inside the man, the hunter pursuing his prey. Grateful not to be his target, she headed back to the main office. At the doorway, she paused and looked back. "There are two other computers out here, if that makes a difference."

His nod acknowledged her words but nothing more. Shrugging, she turned back to the outer office.

As she'd noticed when they entered, the office had a different look. A colder look. No longer bright and open but rather shadowy and dark. Could someone have been trying to get the Foundation's money? Surely there was an easier way. Like sending in an application. Her gaze went to the large filing cabinet behind Jordan's desk. She didn't keep the unaccepted applications in this office but she knew they were kept for a few years, and then discarded. The ones that were accepted went into the system and were followed up on a regular basis. These files were now mostly electronic.

From Bernice, she'd learned to keep her finger on the pulse of the Foundation's money. As she thought about it, she saw that Bernice had had a bigger influence on her life than she'd realized.

Bernice had mentored Shay and spent time reassuring her until Shay had grown into the job.

They'd often shared stories about the applications. They'd discussed the duplicates – the ones that applied to both foundations for help and the ones that didn't fit one organization but deserved consideration from the other. In fact, they had often sent files back and forth before decisions were made about funding. As Shay stared around the empty room, she wondered if there was another connection between the two foundations, one she hadn't recognized.

Had Bernice died because of that connection? God, she hoped not.

It was much easier to think that Bernice had been an old lady who'd enjoyed life to the max and had died of natural causes.

But after the black energy Dr. Maddy had seen on Bernice, Shay was no longer sure. And then she remembered Bernice's strange words at her funeral…

Could this perp be someone who'd been refused money? Someone angry enough to do something about it? That almost made sense.

A voice startled her.

"Can I come in?" Ronin stood in the doorway she'd forgotten to close. She started. The resemblance to his twin was uncanny. They weren't identical, but they were dynamite males. And very different in some essential way too.

Ronin was just as good looking, but only Roman made her heart beat faster.

"Sorry, please come in." She motioned to the coffee behind her. "Can I offer you a cup?"

"Sure." He loosened his tie and accepted the cup from her. "Are your files digital?"

"Both digital and print. We keep digital backups of most things, but all the applications arrive in paper for reviewing." She motioned to the wall behind him. "Those are all the active projects."

He sighed. "So if someone is targeting your projects, they have a lot of choices."

Ronin frowned. "I'll need all the personnel files for anyone who has access to these files – digital and paper. Then again, unless you've set up a foolproof system, any decent hacker would be able to get into your files without too much trouble. I'll talk to Roman about that."

She laughed. "He's in my office, on my computer, as we speak."

"So big brother finally made his move, huh?" Ronin grinned mischievously as he disappeared into her office.

"I heard that." Roman's deep voice rumbled toward Shay.

Heat rolled up her neck like a tsunami on an unsuspecting shore. She took a moment to breathe deeply and shoved the embarrassment down again before joining them. She leaned against the doorway and watched the two dynamos. Both tall and lean, both dark haired with a slight curl. Both had seen a lot of the world's unpleasantness and it showed in their lean, hard jaws.

As she watched them, something else hit her. "I think it's possible that Bernice's death could be related to the other three."

Both men locked gazes on her. She took a deep breath and explained what she knew about the emails. She didn't dare go into what Dr. Maddy had found. Ronin should be told, but not with Roman here.

Roman stayed quiet while she explained, then added, "There's no way to catch her killer if indeed she was murdered."

Ronin pulled out a notepad and wrote something down. "And maybe she wasn't."

Shay shrugged. "I know, but I'd hate to think that anyone shortened her life and got away with it." She winced. "She often received threatening emails and letters. It's just these last few weeks she mentioned there were some more distressing than the others."

Ronin straightened. "You never mentioned them before."

"I hadn't considered her death as anything but natural. However, now—"

"Right. Who do I contact to get a copy of this correspondence?"

Shay quickly gave him Susan Checkers' name from Folgrent Foundation. "She's Bernice's right hand. Was...Bernice's right hand." Sadness swept through her. "Normally emails and letters like these didn't bother Bernice, but something about these ones did."

"I'll follow up on those next." He made a note in his cell phone while the other two watched. "If her death is related to these others, then her death would have been the first," Roman suggested. "That's very important."

That wasn't something she wanted to think about. Because it reminded her of Bernice's last words about making a deal with the devil. A faint tremor rippled down her spine.

And she was starting to wonder if the devil wasn't their murderer.

Ronin moved toward Shay. "Let's get started. The sooner we find this asshole the better."

Turning on Jordan's computer, she pulled up the files Ronin wanted to see. Together they read over the information and compared the three cases. She printed the material he requested, and by the time they finished, he had a thick stack to take with him. They'd even opened one of the folders containing applications she'd turned down. As there were thousands, they started with the most recent of those.

"Thank you," he said, holding up the folder. "I appreciate the co-operation."

"Thank *you*," she responded. "Please find out who's killing my friends."

With a grim smile, he nodded. "I'm going to."

But likely not in time to save the next one. She pushed that thought away.

She needed Stefan's help. They had to find this guy before he killed again.

Sunday late afternoon…

HOURS LATER, FROM the safety and comfort of her own home, she checked in on Stefan.

Stefan?

She tested the door in his mind. It was closed. *Shit.* That usually meant he was painting or enjoying some private time. He didn't have a current partner, as far as she knew, but that didn't mean much. She wasn't privy to everything in his life. She generally had free access to him when she wanted. He said she was spoiled.

You are spoiled. Stefan's voice responded to her thought and rippled through her mind along with his laughter.

She laughed lightly, relieved when the connection strengthened. *So what if I am? You love me anyway, right?*

I do. Now what's the problem?

Why does there have to be a problem? Maybe I'm checking in to see how you are?

Maybe. But not this time. So…? And Tabitha is holding her own by the way.

Shay brightened. *That's good to know. I wonder if she should have security to make sure the attacker doesn't try again?*

Already done. I set up an energy field around her body and room. If anyone trips it, both Dr. Maddy and myself will know. It's better to be safe than have another murder.

She winced. *Except it's too early to say that they were murdered.*

Maybe. But three – no four – heart attacks around you in what…a week? That's not a coincidence. That's called a pattern.

I know. But who could do such a thing. And why?

Any kind of people could be responsible, as we know. And considering you control a lot of money... Stefan sighed, the sound a bare whisper breezing through her mind. She smiled.

But I okayed all the money for these places. It's not like I was being blackmailed or pressured to do that. I did it because these centers need the money to keep going. The money went where it was intended to go. If the money had been embezzled or stolen, then maybe I'd understand it, Shay clarified.

So maybe the killer is upset that you're giving the money to the center. Maybe they are trying to discredit you? The Foundation? Stefan's voice strengthened. *No, Shay. These deaths don't show you in a bad light.*

I was wondering if it was someone I'd turned down. Someone angry because they didn't get funding. And her mind had spun endlessly on the names. *I showed Ronin those files as well.*

That would make sense. As much sense as any of this does. It still doesn't put this guy's hand on the money. Neither can I see how killing these people put money in anyone's pocket.

I know, she cried out in frustration. *That's what is wrong with the money-as-motivation theory.*

What if someone doesn't like what the centers stand for? Maybe they don't think they should be charities. Or receive handouts, Stefan suggested.

There are too many possibilities. I could speculate endlessly here.

Is there another payout due soon? To a similar type of charity? Each of these centers was set to receive a payment.

Maybe. I'll have to check. I was at the office for most of the afternoon. Ronin left with information on the three charities. He's looking for anything that ties them together. She sighed. *I also told him about the nasty emails Bernice got the last couple of weeks. Ronin said he'll look into that. He needs to know about what Dr. Maddy found too. And Roman did something on my computer system. Set up better security, I think.*

Speaking of Roman...?

She didn't know what to say.

You have to let go of the fear. You can't keep refusing to test the relationship waters just because you got burnt once.

It was more than getting burnt. It was life scarring, thank you, she said lightly.

And I'm not knocking that. But Roman cares. And he's willing to go the distance.

How do you know? She almost winced as she asked the question. Stefan had ways of knowing, and she knew it. But Stefan was already speaking again.

Roman's an artist, apparently.

She remembered Roman's skill with her computer. He'd been totally focused and understood the technology like she couldn't begin to. *Roman an artist?* Interesting to think he might channel that intensity into artistic expression. She had the feeling he didn't go into anything without excelling. Eventually.

Oh, so he's an artist? That makes him all right, does it? Being an artist is on your approved list of occupations, I suppose? And how does that guarantee he's willing to go the distance?

There are other reasons. Some are better for you to find out on your own. But you do need to ask to see his studio. Look at his sketches – if only to help you understand him.

He paused. *Speaking of paintings, there is a unique art show at one of my favorite galleries. Tonight. I'd love to take you. It will be good for you. Help you escape today's problems…your sorrows.* He hesitated. *In fact, I'll pick you up at 7:00.*

Another artist, huh? She had seen artistic strength in those long fingers of Roman's as they tapped her keyboard with precise strokes. If he could turn that same dedication and focus to a canvas, she could just imagine the masterpieces he'd create.

He'd never mentioned his hobby to her, though. She'd love to get a glimpse at that intimate side of his life. What would it take to see his artwork?

CHAPTER 11

Sunday evening...

THE ART GALLERY was decked out with soft, glowing orbs hanging from the ceiling and candle sconces mounted on the walls. Hundreds of people mingled with tall fluted glasses in their hands.

A hushed appreciation – maybe awe – permeated the room.

A quartet played soft music that floated gently under the hubbub of quiet conversation. Shay loved the ambience. The atmosphere of the old stone building, the huge paned windows, and the soaring vaulted ceilings gave the impression of a long-lost era. With the women in gorgeous cocktail gowns and the men in suits or tuxedos, it made an elegant picture. She smiled.

"Are you okay?" Stefan murmured at her side. Resplendent in a classic jet-black tuxedo, he stood out in the crowd. His face wasn't as well known as some people assumed, and that was mostly due to his phobia of all media events – but he stopped women in their tracks regardless.

Shay had been surprised by his insistence that she come to this art showing, but she realized within minutes he was curious about her reaction to something. The artist in him wanted her to see this showing. To show *her* this art.

She shrugged and smiled at him. Swathed in a teal, skin-tight cocktail dress, her hair in a demure twist, she was just happy to feel glamorous and to have something other than the murders to think about.

"That's why we're here. Something to take your mind off all the problems." Stefan's pure velvet voice deepened as he stared around.

A waiter approached and held out his tray in a quiet, unobtrusive manner. The glasses glistened with golden liquid.

Shay smiled. "Thank you." She took one flute. Stefan took another. They moved off toward the first wall.

"What do you know about the artist?" she whispered.

"Not much." He stopped in front of a life-sized nude. "Except he's good."

Shay stared at the massive charcoal sketch that had been overlaid and blended with luminescent paints in jewel hues. "Wow."

"Indeed." Stefan stared at the painting.

The energy in his mind caught her attention. She studied the look on his face, her gaze going from the painting to Stefan and back again. He saw something in this artwork. Something special. She studied the painting for several long moments. The technique was stunning. The use of color as a highlight for this mix of charcoal and paint was unusual, yet it worked. It defined the artist.

There was a compelling need to stare at the painting – to get lost in the art.

"Let's keep walking." Stefan, tucked her hand against his arm, then walked to the next painting, stopping for a long look before he moved on. Shay studied the paintings. Each was more compelling than the last. All were of the same woman. Though all were nudes, all paintings of the woman were tastefully covered – in the right places. Yet the hint of what was underneath, the promise of more hidden beauty, was there. The paintings were innocent yet alluring, sexual yet classy. Blue highlights decorated all of them, adding an interesting creative touch.

"He's exceptional."

"He?" Stefan glanced at her, amusement in his gaze. "Isn't that a big assumption?"

"Is it?" She motioned to the compelling series of nine pictures, each a portion of a painting, that when fitted together showed the whole picture. "All of these are of one woman. The same model was the muse for this series. You can tell she's so much more than a model. She's the artist's passion. The other half of his soul."

Stefan stared at her, an intuitive, almost secretive knowing evident in his gaze.

"What?" she smiled. "Oh, I'm assuming that it's a he because he loves this woman. Whereas it could just as easily be a female artist who loves this woman." She shrugged. "Guilty." She stared at the bold brush depicting the well-painted form…and the undecipherable signature. "I can't explain it, but there's a male energy evident in the work."

"Energy you are seeing?"

"No. I'm not seeing. I'm not looking. I'm enjoying the show."

"Good. And in this case, you are right. It is a male artist."

She laughed. "Is there a difference between the sexes in the way an artist draws?"

"Definitely, but that doesn't mean that we can't be fooled."

They continued to stroll through the area, discussing the various poses, strokes, looks. Several times they exchanged their empty glasses for full. It occurred to Shay that this was the first calm, enjoyable evening in weeks, other than her time with Roman. "Thank you, Stefan. I'm so happy you dragged me here."

"Good." He patted her hand. "Shall we meet the artist?"

"Sure." Shay looked around. "Who is it?"

"You know him. That's one of the reasons I wanted to bring you here."

She turned to face him, surprise making her smile bright. "Really. Who is it?"

"Hello, Shay." The deep voice interrupted their conversation.

Shay looked up to see Roman standing at their side, a fluted glass in his hand. Her smile flashed. Damn, he looked good. She responded, "Hi. I'm surprised to see you here."

He laughed, a hint of mockery in his voice. "Why, don't I look like the artsy type?"

His tone of voice had her backing up slightly. "Not at all. I just didn't expect to turn around and see you standing there."

His smile turned rueful as he nodded toward Stefan. "Sorry. Introduce me to your friend."

Shay made the introductions, her gaze on Roman as she said Stefan's name. His eyes widened. His eyebrows shot up.

"Are you enjoying the show, Shay?" he asked.

She smiled warmly. "Absolutely. It's stunning work."

She smiled at him and then looked over at Stefan. It was Stefan's smile that made her wary. And that hidden laughter in his gaze. She eyed him suspiciously. *What?*

He stayed quiet, but his laughter was almost to the point of spilling over.

She glanced over at Roman.

Roman smiled at her. "Thank you. These are some of my favorite pieces. I've done several more but I believe these are my best."

Oh crap. Her gaze widened and her mouth dropped open. From the grin on Roman's face, he was enjoying her shock.

Damn Stefan for not warning her this was an art show of Roman's work.

On cue, Stefan's chuckles rolled through her mind. She shot him a dirty look and turned her attention to Roman.

"At least you know I was being honest, because I had no idea," she said, chagrin in her voice.

"I do appreciate the honesty. Not everyone is the same."

She turned to study his paintings, her mind now connecting the passion she'd seen from the artist to the model. The artist being Roman.

Oh shit. He had loved his model. Did he still care about the woman or was he over her? Could it be his ex-wife? He'd mentioned a divorce, in passing, a long time ago. Surely he didn't still carry the torch for her. Shay's mind twisted over the implications of her relationship with him. She could hardly ask him, especially here and now.

But the one thing that played over and over again... Roman, the painter, loved this woman.

So who was she? And was she still in the picture? Figuratively speaking.

ROMAN HAD BEEN deep in conversation with several clients when he glanced up and saw Shay enter the gallery. With a man. And damn if jealousy hadn't taken over. Her distinguished looking partner stayed close and was attentive the whole time. With their heads bent together, they walked the gallery, discussing his paintings.

Then he'd realized the danger. *Would she know? Did she see herself as he saw her?* In his paintings?

Having her here was incredibly personal, and invasive to his peace of mind. And it had the potential to be incredibly embarrassing, even catastrophic, if she recognized herself as his inspiration.

He hated the nervous energy that filled him. He kept up an ongoing conversation with many people as he kept a quiet watch on Shay's progress and body language. Finally, he couldn't stand it anymore. She'd tortured him enough. He had to find out.

He walked over and found out who her companion was.

Stefan. Jesus. He'd heard so much about this man. Talented artist, tortured psychic. Shay's friend. Dr. Maddy's friend. But not until now had he understood just how good a friend he was to Shay. He studied the two of them, reading the caring, friendliness, even the loving, but...not – and he breathed a quiet sigh of relief – he somehow knew Stefan was not her lover.

Just then Roman caught Stefan's gaze. Heat rose on his neck. Damn it felt like Stefan knew what he was thinking. Amusement simmered deep in Stefan's gaze and he just sat back as the scene played out. Roman shifted his gaze from the painting in front of him to the woman with the same jaw line. The same curve to her shoulder.

How could she not know?

He shifted his gaze quickly to Stefan.

And there it was. It was in the knowing look in his eyes, the knowing curve of his lips. Damn. There was no fooling the man.

Stefan knew.

WHEN THEY'D SEEN enough, she took a moment to say good-bye to the gallery hosts. Then, with Stefan at her side, she slowly did one more stroll past the paintings. Roman had returned to speak with his other guests and she was left alone to dwell on this sudden shift in her world.

A nice shift, though.

She'd gotten over the shock of discovering Roman was the artist. If she understood one thing, it was that seeing this amazing work made Roman even more attractive.

How did that work? Was it that she appreciated the man's talents? That he had a softer side? That there was an honesty to his work, to him? She already knew that from their years of correspondence. Could it be that he reminded her of Stefan? She adored Stefan. They had a bond unlike anything else she'd experienced. But the bond with Stefan wasn't a lover-like connection.

"Are you ready to go home?" Stefan asked gently.

She smiled. "Yes. Thank you for bringing me. I don't know how long it would have taken before I found out about his art another way."

"I thought this might be good for you." He nudged her toward the last painting and the large glass window. Shay stopped for one last look at the stunning woman.

"She's very beautiful."

"Yes, she is."

"There's no way he could create these...gorgeous paintings, if he didn't love her," she murmured, casting a final long look at the picture.

"No. Not likely."

"I wonder if he knows," she mused.

"I wonder." Stefan's voice was noncommittal, as if the answer was of no interest to him. And true enough, it probably wasn't.

"Maybe a better question is this: Does *she* know how he feels? It would be terrible to love someone to that extent but for them to be oblivious."

"True."

At the large window, she stopped. She could see the huge painting behind her in the reflection.

There was something familiar about the line of the woman's jaw, her neck. Shay couldn't place her. Recognition sat just outside her consciousness. Inside, she understood one thing – the woman was someone she'd met.

Somewhere.

But who?

"Ready?"

Turning back to Stefan, she smiled and nodded. On his arm, she walked out of the gallery without a backward glance.

SHAY CRAWLED INTO bed that night in a smooth, happy state. She'd enjoyed the evening. Any time spent with Stefan was special and this had been no exception.

Not to mention that their energies, when combined, always went to new heights. She'd often wondered what it would be like to have a lover that had psychic abilities like his, even if he only understood the way energy worked. And how combined energies changed, grew and melded.

It could be incredibly special.

And something she really wanted to experience in her life.

And that was not likely to happen. Not with her trust issues preventing any real connection with someone.

She pulled the bedding up to her chin and turned off the light. Peaceful, she dropped into a sound sleep.

And woke up some time later, her heart pounding, her breath rasping as it fought its way up her throat.

Shit. *Something is wrong.*

What? She hopped out of her bed and ran to her living room and felt like she was once again caught in the panic she'd felt that night, a year ago, when Darren had broken into her place.

The living room was empty. She ran to the front door. It was still locked. The bolt in place. She spun around and leaned back against the door, her body shaking with emotion.

It was just a nightmare.

Just a nightmare.

Please, let this be just a nightmare.

With a semblance of calm restored, she walked the apartment and searched, unconsciously imitating Roman's movements from the other night. As she finished, she realized what she'd done. She'd taken almost the same route that he had. Laying down another path of energy over his.

And why was that significant?

She didn't know, but patterns were just as significant in energy work as mathematics. She took a deep breath as she walked into the kitchen. A cup of tea. She needed a cup of tea. And some time to think this through. And as she walked from the kitchen to the living room and back to her bedroom, she saw the different energy field.

She came to a dead stop. And crouched low.

The energy was thin and low. Older. And covered in a soft black. Hidden in the shadows of her dark room. It was the oozing blackness of it that made her skin crawl. The only time she'd seen that same black was with Darren's energy. True, she'd seen a few things that came close – after all black was a common enough color in energy, but never did anything else have the same oozing blackness. Not before Darren, and never since.

Thank God.

She studied the pattern of the dark energy in her apartment. It centered in her living room. She twisted and bent up and down, trying to see the path, to find the person behind it. But that was impossible. There were just wisps of something there. Not enough to read. Just enough to make her nervous... *Very* nervous.

From all of this she knew one thing. Someone had been in her apartment. *Again.*

And that someone had the same energy signature as her last intruder. How? Tonight. They'd probably entered as soon as she'd left... Yet the door had been locked when she came home. And there'd been no sign of any disturbance.

Surely that meant her visitor had come in astral form. She knew she could walk through the memory of her apartment, in the time before she left for the evening and check.

Moving back to her bed, she sat down, her tea long forgotten. Closing her eyes, she turned back the clock in her head and stepped out of her body – and into the vision.

Giving herself a moment to adjust, she followed herself as she went through the preparations of getting ready for the evening. The room looked normal.

This was her space. She knew this energy. Everything was as it should be. She went through the same clothes change and then watered the plants, picked up her purse and phone, turning her head as the doorbell rang. She walked to the door. She watched herself greet Stefan and Stefan greet her. Normal.

Everything was the way it was supposed to be. So now she was sure the visitor had come in after she'd left for the gallery.

She stepped out of the vision and back into her own time in her own bedroom. She knew what she had to do, but could she do it? Now that was something else. She walked into the living room and stood over the energy wisps that littered the room.

Then she picked one and jumped inside.

CHAPTER 12

IMMEDIATELY, SHAY WAS tossed into the turbulent emotional storm. Anger was the dominant sentiment. Whoever this person was, revenge powered all his actions. There were even threads of hate spinning through the wisps.

For her.

She shuddered at the completely unexpected emotional maelstrom.

She hadn't thought this trip would bring any results at the beginning. Instead she'd been sucked in and washed away in the emotions left behind. Since it was energy, she could see the approximate time it arrived and anything that happened while the energy was active. But it didn't allow her to see the person. She could see and feel some of what the person felt, but since she was inside the energy, she saw nothing to identify the person.

Neither could she read the person's thoughts. But the emotions stormed right through her.

What could this person want? They'd come to Shay's personal space. *Why?*

She followed the energy as it walked through her apartment. It stayed to the main areas. It never ventured into the bedroom. Odd. A psychic burglar would have gone after jewelry, money, something that was easily pawned, then plan a physical trip to take advantage of the loot they'd seen.

This energy didn't travel around. It sat, as if festering. There was a faint throb to the energy. Even though it was cold and had almost dissipated, the throb was strong enough to be felt. *Double odd.* Shay looked around her apartment, hoping for something, anything to clarify the identity of her intruder.

Another odd twist. Normally she could see the energy left behind by people…for a day at least, sometimes days. If the person experienced strong emotions, it should be even longer. This person *had* been driven by strong emotions, but the force of their feelings didn't keep this particular energy warm and heavy, allowing it to stay. Instead, it was as if this person had burned up all their emotional energy, leaving little trace behind.

And what was with the cloaking layer of black energy? She'd seen something similar with Darren. She had to watch to make sure that fear didn't have her judging the energy and assume it would have the same behavior as Darren. Or having her afraid that it *was* Darren and that he'd somehow found a way back to taunt her.

No. She knew Darren was dead. It was a fact.

She'd heard horror stories from Stefan about various non-dead entities making last grabs for life through the living. If those stories didn't make one scared, then nothing would.

She didn't think that trick was within Darren's capabilities, but she didn't know for sure. Thoughts that he might return haunted her sleep and kept her nightmares alive.

Still, for all the similarities to this energy, it didn't *feel* the same as Darren's. Close. But it wasn't him. So how were they alike? She just couldn't say.

She also wasn't prepared to have entities, living or dead, walking through her apartment at will.

Tired, and knowing she'd need to rest, she added another layer of protective energy around her apartment.

Returning to reality, she recognized that her body needed to be horizontal as soon as possible. In the morning, she'd call on Stefan's expertise yet again. Something was up. If he could help her guard her space then she needed him to do that for her.

Whatever it was she needed protection from…

The two of them had put a clean, soothing protective energy around last time. She believed it would be enough.

She'd been wrong.

Monday morning…

THE NEXT MORNING Shay walked down the hallway toward her office and heard Jordan bitching to Rose about the state of her files. Shay winced. She'd left the files she'd pulled for Ronin on Jordan's desk. And Shay knew that for all her multi-colored hair and free-spirit clothing, Jordan was a neat freak. On the other hand, Ronin had needed the material, and Roman had set up some new security on her system.

The good outweighed the bad.

She opened the door with a bright smile. And kept it in place, while she pointed to the files in front of Jordan. "I'm sorry." She walked over to Jordan. "I had to pull the files at the request of the police. They didn't want to wait for Monday, and I figured that if I put them back in the wrong place you'd be even more upset, so I left them for you to file away."

Jordan glared and then blew a strand of turquoise hair out of her eyes. "I hate people going into the files. Almost as much as I hate people touching my computer." She flung her multi-colored scarf over her shoulder and sat down with a thunk.

"I know." Shay said meekly. "I'd have just given them a copy of the digital files, but they wanted to see the hardcopy stuff as well." She shrugged. "You know the paper files are more complete."

"And now messier," groused Jordan as she reorganized the contents of the top file. "Did you have to mess up the order too? They *were* chronological…"

Shay smiled at Rose, who gave a small eye roll, as Jordan slapped the file closed and then placed it in its proper spot in the huge filing system behind her.

"Glad you can keep it all straight for me." Shay walked into her office to hang up her coat, relieved that moment was over. Jordan was incredibly efficient, and normally she was even-tempered. But disturbing the files was one thing guaranteed to piss her off. Shay sat down on her big chair and put her purse away in the bottom drawer of her desk. She turned on her computer and called out, "Are there appointments this morning?"

"One." Jordan called back. "At eleven. Your ten o'clock cancelled."

Good. But she didn't say that out loud. The less pulling on her today, the better. She needed a nap already. And she also hoped to stop at the hospital and see Tabitha today.

No. Stay away from her.

Stefan? Why?

Keep her under the radar. As far as the world knows, she's in a coma. If you visit her, you'll be alerting her attacker. Because Tabatha's alive, he might see her as a loose end.

Damn. He was right but she was desperate to see for herself that Tabitha was okay.

She is, but she's staying in the ethers. Don't contact her that way either. This person understands energy. Let's not give him a reason to go after Tabitha again. I've told her what happened and that she's still in danger. Ronin also knows. She did say that a force came from Sue, her assistant at the time of the attack. She also says she's known Sue for years and it wasn't her energy that did this.

Damn. Shay knew Sue as well. She couldn't see her being involved. *So someone else is hitching a ride with people in order to attack other people?*

Possibly. They'd have to stalk the victim enough to know who and what they'd be doing and with whom, in order to pick the right opportunity.

Shay thought about that as a glimmer of something, perhaps understanding stirred in the back of her mind. She tugged it forward. *Not if this person already had anchors in the victim. And that's easily done. They just have to be able to see the person and access their chakras. If they already had those, they could just use the anchors when they wanted, and pop in and view the world from the new perspective.*

Oh shit. Realization hit her in the heart. *Like the extra eyes she'd seen in Bernice's gaze.*

Silence, while Stefan pondered that. *It would take a lot of skill.*

Would it though, Shay agreed dryly. *Think about it. Early on, they could have put hooks in to make their takeover of the unknowing individuals easier to do their will, yet again. Even better. They could even have already created a hook from the victim to the innocent bystander. Then used that as the highway for the energy to attack the victim. Even better it would look like a heart attack or rather it wouldn't look like anything hard science could figure out – and therefore investigators, medical and otherwise, would find nothing suspicious. They'd believe the person just dropped dead.*

Scary thought, Stefan murmured. *But all too possible given we have no idea the limits of energy work – for good or evil. I guess I'll need to speak with Tabitha again. In the meantime, we're all working on this case. Stay safe.*

"Here's the file on the eleven o'clock appointment." Jordan came in holding a thick folder in her right hand. In her left she had a stack of papers. "And these are the new applications for you to go over."

Shay shifted mentally. Stefan had left, and she needed to focus on today. "Good. Anything interesting?"

"A few. Then again, I always think they are all worthy, whereas you go through and see the stuff I don't." Jordan smiled, back into her normal mood now that the filing was taken care of.

"That's because you don't have to make the decisions as to who benefits the most from these grants. There's only so much money and making it stretch is a feat – and not an easy one."

"But you do it so well." Jordan laughed lightly. "So did Bernice, didn't she?"

"Yes." Shay sat back and looked over at the young, bright girl who'd quickly become a friend. Rose had too, but not with the same connection as Jordan and Shay had created. "Bernice had a talent for both sides of the business. Men handed money over without a whimper and she found worthy causes for all of it."

"Yes. That's her. I'd like to have her money to hand over."

Thinking of the grande dame, Shay nodded. "She had men eating out of her hand all her life. I don't know that she was ever caught by the same love bug as the men were, though."

Jordan raised an eyebrow. "Really? She never married?"

"She liked playing the field too much. And no, she never had any children either."

Jordan's second eyebrow shot up, to disappear under the bright strands of her hair. "Wow. Who's going to get all her money?"

Shay frowned, staring out the window. What a good question. "You know, I'm not sure. I guess that will be taken care of this week. It doesn't involve me, thank heavens."

"You have enough of your own already." Jordan walked back out. "But if they are looking for people to give it to, there is always me."

"Chances are good that all her money will go into her foundation and the board will have more to hand out. They'll need to hire someone to take over her position. That might already be in place. I've been out of the loop the last few days."

"I'm sure you have enough on your plate to deal with."

Familiar noises in the other room made Shay smile.

"I made coffee. Will you have one?" Jordan called.

"Always."

Happy to have the office back to normal and a good brew coming, Shay pulled the file toward her for her appointment that morning.

Right.

This was a soup kitchen that requested funds for two delivery vehicles and a salaried driver to deliver food to seniors and other people who couldn't make the trip on their own. Shay remembered this project, but could not remember the details. She glanced at her clock. She had an hour to get caught up.

Jordan walked in with a cup of espresso in her hand. "Are you approving this request?"

"Yes. We'll need to keep on top of their accounting to see if it's worth continuing after a year, but this isn't exactly a service many people provide. If it helps the community, I'm all for it.

"Let's hope the organizer of this charity doesn't have a heart attack like the others." Jordan returned to her desk in the outer office.

Shay swallowed. Hard. Now that wasn't a thought she wanted to dwell on. But it's not like she had a way to stop it.

Or did she?

STEFAN OPENED HIS eyes. The skylight stared back at him. Out of habit, he reached, and pinched himself. And winced. His experiences when he shifted realities were sometimes so strong and clear that occasionally he'd get lost inside them. Sometimes he couldn't tell if he was caught in a vision or had returned to reality – a sad state of affairs. Some said he was psychic; others called him a charlatan. And many labeled him just plain crazy.

He was probably a bit of each.

Stefan closed his eyes, his mind suffused with difficult memories. He always helped those that ended up on his doorstep. More often than not, they were brought there by an officer of the law. He'd worked enough with law enforcement agencies over the years to build a large network of people who called on him.

So far Shay had kept herself apart from the others and from formally working with law enforcement. She didn't think her abilities offered anything to the other psychics. She couldn't be more wrong. She could do stuff with energy he'd never dreamed possible. But she also talked about his cases as if they were only his – showing a distinct separation in her mind. Yet, if she chose, she could be an immense help to his work and the work of others.

The phone rang on cue. He rolled over and looked at it. Did he want to talk to Detective Chandler? He wracked his mind for the connection. The phone rang again. Right. Ronin.

"Hello, Detective Chandler… Ronin."

"You do realize that more people would view you in a kinder light if you didn't do that."

Stefan smiled. "Do what? And what's going on with Shay's projects?"

"See, things like that. How do you know anything is wrong?"

"Because you wouldn't have called me otherwise."

The detective laughed. "True enough. Have you spoken with her about the Foundation deaths?"

Stefan frowned. Right. *Death. Heart attacks. Charities. Tabitha.* "Yes. Almost every day."

"Good, it helps to know we're all on the same page." The detective chuckled then let his laughter die out. He cleared his throat. "I know that there isn't likely to be a connection between these deaths and what happened with Darren a year ago, but as that was my first entry into the psychic forces and the damage they can do, and now there is another weird scenario happening with Shay again – almost a year later, to the exact day...well it would be nice to know for sure there was no connection. Can you see anything linking Darren and the current cases?"

Stefan had already considered that. "Darren is dead," he said simply.

"Right." Relief washed through Ronin's voice. "I guess I just wanted to make sure. I was hearing some weird stuff with the police gossip recently. Something about dead not really being dead?"

Stefan sighed as he realized that Ronin must have heard about some of his weirder cases if he'd heard talk about dealing with the undead.

"Darren was motivated by money. People that try for the un-dead state are looking to extend their human existence," Stefan said, thoughtfully. "Usually it has nothing to do with money."

"Good. Then I can forget about Darren being involved?" Ronin asked cautiously.

"Yes. I believe so." And Stefan did believe that. He'd gotten Shay's slightly garbled message about recognizing the same energy as Darren's in her apartment, but he didn't believe she'd read it right. That asshole had been dead a long time. "Except..."

Dread filled Ronin's voice. "Except what?"

"Shay believed Darren was an orphan. I don't know if that's true."

"And if he wasn't, how does that change anything?"

"Genetically, he could have family with similar abilities."

"Right."

Stefan could hear the click of keys as Ronin worked at his keyboard. "I'm going to work that angle in my spare time. Let's not leave anything out. I've spent hours going through the files Shay gave me." He gave a short laugh. "And the nasty emails Bernice had recently received."

"Find anything?"

"Not enough. Someone was trying to blackmail Bernice, but apparently she died before she made any payments." Frustration marred his voice. "So far, there's no visible connection between the victims, outside of them being involved with projects from Shay's foundation."

"Shay's foundation. So not from Shay herself?"

There was a slight pause. "There is a difference, isn't there? I was looking at the Foundation being the connection, but it could just as easily be Shay."

"There is a lot of money involved in both scenarios."

"I wonder if someone is looking to take out the competition for the Foundation money." He gave a short laugh. "Listen to me. We don't even know for sure if these deaths are suspicious."

"Not true," Stefan corrected quietly. "They are definitively suspicious. What we don't know for sure is if foul play is involved…but at this point we have reason to believe it is." He caught Ronin up on Tabitha's message about a force coming from the delivery person but not appearing to be that person's energy, and he also shared what Dr. Maddy had seen and Shay's insights.

Just as he was finishing, his focus changed, wavered.

He hung up quickly. His sunroom disappeared into a dark clouded sky. From sunlight to darkness in an instant.

As if a storm was building.

He could only hope he'd get some warning before it broke.

ROMAN WALKING INTO the gallery for the first time since the opening night of the show. As he stared at his paintings, Shay's face as Stefan had escorted her out of the gallery flashed in his mind. Inside, his stomach had clenched in fear. *Had she figured it out?* Stefan had absolutely recognized the model in his paintings. How he'd known for sure it was Shay, was something that Roman didn't want to think about. What really bothered him was fear that Stefan might have told her.

That look in Shay's eyes… As if she'd almost recognized herself. That wasn't something he was prepared to deal with right now.

He couldn't. He didn't have the right answers for himself.

But should he tell her – before someone else did?

Why had he thought it would never come out? He might fool most of the public, but the model herself? And Stefan…

His phone rang. He glanced down and frowned. He didn't recognize the number.

"Hello?"

"She didn't recognize herself. But I did. I sure hope you have an explanation for her when she finds out."

Oh shit. Stefan.

"Not a good one, I'm afraid," Roman admitted, quietly. "I saw her confused expression as she walked out last night. As if she were on the verge of seeing the truth. I had to admit I didn't sleep well afterward."

"She hasn't put two and two together, but she will," Stefan said. "She's very astute. Right now she has something very troubling on her mind or I'm sure she would have made the connection herself."

"For some reason, I never anticipated the day she'd find out."

"It's already here. More than that, her astuteness let her see something I'm not sure that *you* see yet."

Still holding the phone to his ear, Roman looked around, glad to see he was still alone in the gallery. He walked over to the one painting that showed the line of Shay's neck and chin. "What's that?"

"The relationship between the painter and his model."

Roman frowned. "Sorry? Shay's the model. That's all."

Stefan's warm, knowing laughter filled the line. "No. It's not all. She's a lot more than a model. And I believe Shay was correct in her interpretation. Interesting times ahead."

"Whoa. I don't know what you mean." Roman walked around the room, studied the paintings, keeping a lid on his emotions. Cautiously, he protested, "True, she's been my inspiration for the last couple of years…"

"Exactly," said Stefan, "and you need to reflect on what that means." He paused as a weird sound filled the air. "Ah, I see what you aren't ready to admit." He laughed. "Shay may not see herself in those paintings yet, but she sees you very clearly as you relate to the model."

Roman stared. "What do you see? I don't understand."

"I know. But you will. I suspect Shay will have fun telling you, if you ask her." And he rang off.

"As if." There's no way he could bring the subject up with Shay. And Stefan knew that.

Damn. What had Shay seen that he hadn't?

CHAPTER 13

Late Monday morning…

SHAY STUDIED THE nervous man in front of her. It was that personality issue that caused her concern. She was used to people sitting in her office and being nervous because they wanted her support. But this guy seemed really nervous. As if something else bothered him.

But what?

She sighed. She opened the file in front of her. "Wilson, tell me about your project." And she looked him directly.

Wilson froze like a deer caught in the headlights. He opened his mouth to talk, but no words came out. He ran his fingers through his hair and then tugged at his tie. He stopped fidgeting, and his whole structure slumped. "I'm sorry. I'm just so nervous."

Using her inner eye, she studied his chakras looking for deception. Lies. Deceit.

She watched the energy circulate in his first chakra. Fear. Nervousness. Not quite panic, but a definite wish to rush away. A need to get out. The longer she watched him, the more the energy swirled, becoming a frantic vortex. So *not* healthy. She gave the rest of his chakras a glance. He was definitely centered in the heart and came from a sense of needing to be of service. A need to redeem himself.

She dropped her gaze. That part bothered her.

Redeem himself, from what? What had he done so wrong that he needed to help others in this way?

She decided to ask him. "Wilson. How did you choose this to be your calling? Or did it choose you?"

He got that deer in the headlights look again. "I…I don't know."

"You run a soup kitchen. Were you ever homeless? Were you raised in hardship?" She smiled gently at him. "I'm trying to understand why you are doing what you are doing. To see if you are going to be there in a week or a year or whether this is a fly-by-night type of thing and you'll be gone the day after I give you money."

He blinked. "You're thinking of giving me money?"

She laughed. "I think that's why you came here, isn't it?"

"Yes." He straightened, brightened. "Yes. I need money for a delivery service. There are so many people who can't come to us. We need a way to take meals to them." He leaned forward and there was the animation, the passion she'd been looking for.

Good. "Then tell me what you are looking for? A mobile kitchen or a delivery van. One with customized interiors. What?"

After that he opened up and poured the information out. She had to redirect him a couple times to make sure he answered the specific questions she needed. At the same time, she managed to satisfy her own mind that he was indeed passionate about his calling. There'd been no explanation for the issues she could see in his first chakra but she suspected it had something to do with his family life growing up.

"What about your family?" she asked gently. "Are they supportive of what you do?"

He stopped, a sadness leaching the animation from his face. "My mother passed away a couple of years ago. A system like this would have made her life much easier." He stared out the window. His first chakra oozed energy in the direction of his past. His memories. "She was bedridden for the last year. I did everything I could, but it seemed like she had deteriorated more every time I stopped by."

This was the source of the passion. Guilt and redemption – two of the biggest driving forces behind do-gooders.

But it made her feel better to know he had that type of motivation.

He'd be her next project.

She spoke with him for another hour while she finished filling out her forms. After they were done and he'd left, she sat back and smiled when Jordan asked how it went.

"It's great. He's a perfect candidate. We should be able to help him out. I'll do up the paperwork, send it out to the board, and we should be able to put this through within a week or two."

Jordan's eyebrows – was that a new ring in her eyebrow – flew up to her hairline. "Wow, that fast? You normally take weeks to months."

"But this one needs to happen sooner with the fall weather coming. He's got to get the vehicles outfitted, drivers hired and trained, and find the necessary customers – the word needs to go out soon. Once the cold weather hits, and people can't get out and about easily, they might need to double the vehicles or at least run on rotation."

"Still, this one must mean a lot to you for you to give it this kind of attention." Jordan stared at her speculatively. "Unless there's something going on here I don't know about."

Shay laughed. "Not at all. He's got good timing, that's all."

Jordan sent her a doubtful look. "Okay, if you say so." She returned to her desk, and Shay returned to hers, just as her cell phone rang.

Pappy.

"Shay, did you not get the letter?"

She frowned. "What letter?"

"About Bernice's will. They are reading it in about ten minutes, and you're supposed to be here."

"What?" She glanced at her watch. "Where's the meeting? I can leave now, but I can't get very far in ten minutes."

"We're in your building. Lawyers McIntosh, McWilliams and Malory...on the seventh floor." He sounded anxious as he added, "Can you come?"

"I'm on my way." She closed her phone, logged off her computer, snagged her purse and ran out of the door. "Rose, take my calls, please. Back in an hour or so."

She hoped.

KNOCK, KNOCK...

Can you hear me, Shay?

No, I guess not.

Too bad. I just wanted to let you know who is standing at the elevators. Your grandfather. Charles Lassiter. Standing lost and worried in the middle of the hallway.

Waiting for you, his precious granddaughter, most likely.

Not that he's going to find you. This is too good an opportunity to waste.

You'll worry, Shay...

But there's no real need, I'll take good care of him.

This time...

ROMAN DIDN'T KNOW what he was doing here in the Bernice's lawyers' office, except that as a support system for Grandfather.

He wasn't mentioned in Bernice's will. He knew that because Bernice had made it clear. Thankfully. Bernice had loads of family, even if none were close.

Still, millions of available cash brought out relatives that only dreamed of a blood connection. And the room was filling up.

He frowned. It was unusual to see so many attending this type of meeting.

"See. I said the rats would be coming to the party." Grandfather shuffled closer. "Bernice wanted everyone here so they'd know where they stood."

"Typical her." He motioned to a chair at the back row and led his grandfather to it. "We'll stay in the back."

"Good choice." Grandfather sat down. Roman stood slightly behind him and watched the proceedings.

Just when he thought everyone who was coming had arrived, Shay raced in. She stopped at the doorway, her chest heaving, her eyes surveying the crowded room. Her gaze landed on Roman, bounced off, and then zipped back. She walked toward them.

"Have you seen Pappy?" she asked in a low voice.

Roman frowned and searched the room. "No. Actually I haven't. Grandfather?"

"He was here. Saw him downstairs." A querulous tone entered his voice. "Where could he have gotten to?"

Roman leaned down. "I'll go check the men's room."

His Grandfather's face lit up. "Yes, that must be where he is."

Just then, the lawyer entered from the side door. Roman caught the look on his face as he noted the size of the group seated in front of him. He pressed a couple of buttons on his desk. Instantly a second man, dressed in a suit, but looking more like a henchman, entered and stood slightly behind the lawyer.

Interesting. They were prepared for trouble.

Shay immediately sat down beside Gerard.

Roman slipped out the back quickly and walked to the men's room. There was no sign of Pappy on the way. He pushed open the door to the men's room and walked inside.

"Charles? Are you in here?"

No answer.

Bending down, he checked the floor under the doors. No one. The room was empty. Given Pappy's and Grandfather's ages, anything could have happened.

He couldn't help but walk to the other end of the hallway and enter the stairwell and look over the railing. The stairwell was empty. No collapsed older man on the stairs. He'd take that as a good sign.

He retraced his steps to the meeting. As he entered, the group turned to look at him. He calmly took a seat beside Grandfather and, feeling the worried glances from Shay and Grandfather, he shook his head.

The lawyer continued to read from the will, his voice droning on and on.

There was rustling as several people shifted position. The audience waited, their impatience barely veiled.

Roman smiled inside.

The lawyer stopped speaking. He raised his head, took a drink of water and said, "And now I come to the bequests. To my long-time companion Grace, I leave five hundred thousand dollars."

A gasp sounded from the audience, followed by weeping from an older woman in the front row. Roman thought she might be Grace. He'd only ever seen her once. The lawyer went on to mention several other similar bequests. Then he stopped and laid the papers down on his desk and stared out at the audience.

He cleared his throat, took a deep breath, and said, "I, Bernice Folgrent, leave the rest of my estate, in its entirety, to my goddaughter, Shay Lassiter, in the hopes that she will find a good use for my life's work."

Silence.

Then outrage.

Several people jumped up and yelled. Several people burst into tears, and the lawyer was instantly besieged by nasty comments.

"This is wrong."

"There has to be a mistake."

"We'll see about that."

Grandfather gripped his hands tightly together and whispered softly, "Oh dear."

But all Roman's attention was on Shay. She slid down slightly on her seat and dropped her head back to look up at the ceiling and then she groaned.

He heard her whisper, "Oh shit."

CHAPTER 14

"BERNICE, HOW COULD you do this to me?" Shay whispered into the chaos going on around her. She sank lower in her chair, wishing she could hide. The entire room had worked itself into a frenzy.

Slowly she became aware of a gentle stroking on her hand. She let her head drop to the side and looked into Gerard's concerned gaze. Above his head, Roman gazed down at her, a half-humorous and half-worried look in his eyes.

Gerard leaned closer and whispered, "She did love you."

Shay looked deep into those warm caring eyes and understood a smidgeon of what Bernice felt when she'd looked into them. Gerard had a huge capacity for loving.

"If she did, why would she land me with the responsibility of her money?"

"Because she trusted you. She knew you would do the best you could."

Shay closed her eyes briefly. The noise still went on around her. One group had braced the lawyer around the desk, leaning over to intimidate him while they shouted their displeasure. Shay watched as the security guard struggled to keep the group back.

"Things are going to get even uglier soon. Can we slip away?"

"Absolutely." Roman stood up and helped Gerard to his feet. "Let's go before anyone figures out who you are."

"Oh Lord." Shay snagged her purse and stood up. Without a backward glance she walked to the door and slipped into the hallway. The din from inside instantly eased as the door swung shut behind her. Still shell shocked from the bomb the lawyer had dropped, Shay kept walking to the stairwell. There were a few people around, but not many. Behind her she heard Roman talking to Gerard.

"Stairs or elevators?" Roman asked.

"Elevator. At least, I will. I think you should walk down with Shay. I don't think she should be alone right now."

Shay frowned at that whispered comment. She turned around and looked at them both. "I'm all right, Gerard. A little confused. Definitely not happy, but I'll be fine."

Gerard took several small steps toward her. "I don't think you have fully thought this through. Until you have the papers signed and your own will sorted, if anything should happen to you…then any one of those people in that room could possibly inherit instead."

Shay groaned. "Seriously? I don't even get a chance to consider my way through this, and now I have consider that one of those people might try to eliminate me? Really?"

Roman took several steps forward. He pushed the button for the elevator. The door opened immediately. He motioned Shay inside. "Let's stay together. We can go to your office if you prefer, or we can go out for lunch. Somewhere private where we can sort this out."

"Lunch?" Shay spun around. "Where's Pappy? I thought he'd be here by now. We'd spoken about having lunch together earlier. Then this mess came up and I forgot about it."

"I don't know. I assumed he'd changed his mind about attending the meeting," said Gerard.

She frowned. Pulling out her cell phone, she checked for messages. None. She quickly called Pappy. No answer. "He's not answering." She gazed worriedly at the other two. "That's not like him."

Gerard pulled his cell phone out and checked. "He hasn't called me."

"He wouldn't have gone anywhere. He called me and told me to show up for the reading of the will. That's why I was running when I arrived. Before that, I hadn't even known about the meeting today."

"Maybe he's sitting in your office, waiting for you," Roman suggested. "Especially if he couldn't stand to be part of the business of Bernice's estate."

That actually made good sense. Shay punched the button for the seventh floor. The elevator came to a stop a few moments later.

"Let's go and see."

Her office was locked when she reached the main door. "Pappy wouldn't be here alone and Jordan has obviously gone for lunch." She pulled out her keys and unlocked the door. The lights were off. The main office, empty.

She walked into her inner office. "He's not here either." She spun around. The place looked normal. The energy normal. Hers, Rose's, Jordan's and that of the client who'd been here this morning. Nothing else. "Pappy hasn't been here at all today."

"So where is he?"

"Maybe he went home. To deal with his grief in private," Gerard offered.

Both Roman and Shay looked at Gerard. He shrugged and opened his hands. "Just an idea."

Shay noticed the blinking red light on her phone. She hit the voice mail button and listened to the three messages. None from Pappy. She quickly called his home number, wondering why she hadn't thought of that earlier. Nothing.

"I wonder if he's lying down…" She looked at Gerard in consideration. "I think I'll go see."

"We'll all go," Roman said. "He's normally in close contact with us. It's unusual for him not to have been at the meeting. Regardless of his personal feelings, this was another connection to Bernice. He would have wanted to have experienced that defining moment with her."

Shay closed her eyes briefly. "That is so true." She ran her fingers through her long hair. "I'm not thinking straight." She pursed her lips, hating the nerves that squeezed her gut. "Then where is he? I feel like something bad might have happened to him."

As she spoke the words, her inner sense of conviction grew stronger. "Something is wrong." She glanced at the doorway. She knew what she had to do. And what she should have done first.

"I have to go upstairs." She turned and called over her shoulder, "I'll be right back."

"I'm coming with you." Roman said at her shoulder. "Grandfather, stay here. We'll be right back."

Gerard settled into the closest chair at the reception desk. "I'll keep trying to reach him."

Shay raced out of the office with Roman close behind her. She closed the door behind her, hesitated, and then locked it. "Let's make sure we don't lose Gerard."

Roman was already at the stairwell door. "Stairs?"

"Yes." They raced up the stairs. "Pappy often takes the stairs, but I wouldn't have thought so today. He was pretty stressed."

"About the reading of the will?" Roman questioned.

"About wanting me to be there."

"So he knew? He knew what Bernice had planned?"

She paused in the act of stepping up another stair. She completed the step thoughtfully, remembering Pappy's tone of voice. "You know. He just might have. He was pretty insistent I get there."

"Would Bernice have used him to witness her will, perhaps? Or told him about what she'd done?"

"Could be either. He loved her. With no limits." She sighed heavily. *What would that be like?*

"It sounds like you don't approve."

She looked up at him in surprise. "Oh, I didn't mean that."

"No?" He didn't sound convinced.

She was quiet for a long moment. "I was wondering what it was like to be loved like that. By two guys, no less."

"Don't you already have a long string of admirers?"

She laughed. And shook her head. "So not. I'm not that femme fatale type."

With a yank, she pulled open the door to the proper floor and walked through. Behind her, she thought she heard Roman mutter, "Good."

She turned to look at him, but his face was neutral. Unreadable. A poker face.

Raised voices told her that the lawyer's office hadn't emptied yet. *Poor lawyer.* She shifted her vision to use what she called her inner eye. Energy flowed in a kaleidoscope of colors. Power fused through and around the colors, infusing the mess with an anger that was unmistakable. People were beyond angry. Some of the individual energies twisted and turned as if searching for an outlet. As if looking for a target.

She didn't dare draw attention to herself. This energy had power. Passion was like that. Anger kept senses sharp and aware. Aware in another way too, like a predator looking for its prey. That same energy allowed people to be super tuned to the whereabouts of the person they were angry with.

In this case, she was that person – the indirect object of their anger. Once they recognized who she was, she'd become the direct object of their wrath. She so didn't want that to happen.

She searched the chaos, looking for her grandfather's energy. She'd be able to identify it anywhere, but right now she was having trouble finding it in the angry crowd.

"What are you doing?"

She paused, turning to look up at Roman, and realized she'd crouched down low to search for low-hanging energy. She probably looked like an idiot.

With a slight groan, she straightened, her mind searching for a plausible answer.

Roman waited. When she didn't answer, he quirked an eyebrow at her.

She shrugged. "Just looking. For anything that might tell me where Pappy went."

"And checking out the carpet is going to do that, how?"

His tone sounded neutral, too neutral. She searched his face. Did he suspect what she'd been doing? She hoped not.

She shook her head to clear her thoughts. Then she spun around and headed into the lawyer's office. Security was assisting the last of the group out of the door, the ones that were still arguing. Shay slipped around behind them and squeezed behind the security officer to enter the room.

The lawyer was standing, staring outside, to beyond the window.

"Mr. McIntosh?"

He started. Then slowly turned around. "You're Shay Lassiter. I'm pleased to meet you." He stepped forward, his hand extended.

Shay grimaced. He looked like he'd walked through a war. "Even after today?"

He laughed. "Of course. I spent a lot of time with Bernice. She spoke highly of you."

"She was a beautiful woman." Shay felt her throat choke and tears welled up in the corner of her eyes. "And I loved her." She sniffled.

He nodded to the room behind them. "I'd hoped for a private reading, but Bernice wanted them all here, hoping that if they all heard the news up front, they'd stop hoping and pestering for something they would never get – and leave you alone."

"She would do that." Shay had to smile. "Speaking of terrible things, have you seen my grandfather, Charles Lassiter?" She studied the lawyer's face anxiously. "He called me from somewhere in the building before the reading, but when I got here, there was no sign of him." She motioned to Roman. "We've been searching for him, calling his home and cell phone, but there's no sign of him."

"Oh dear. He *was* here. I spoke to him earlier."

"When?" Roman's voice cut across sharply.

"I don't know. Maybe twenty minutes before the reading of the will." The lawyer looked down at his planner. "He was worried about you, Shay. I know he planned to call you if you were late."

"And he did. I just don't know where he went after that." She walked the room casually. There was no sign of Pappy's energy anywhere. Inside, a cold nugget of suspicion started to form. He'd been here. At least according to the lawyer...

Or had he? She turned back to face the lawyer. "Did you see Pappy in this room?"

He looked surprised at the question but answered smoothly. "No. In my office." He motioned to the door on the right. "It's through here."

Roman walked around the small austere room.

She asked, "Did he sit down?"

"Yes, he was there in the visitor's chair." The lawyer motioned to a heavy, maroon chair.

Shay moved toward the chair, then stopped and looked at the lawyer, a question on her face.

"Sure, take a look. Maybe he left something behind? Maybe his cell phone? It would explain why you haven't been able to reach him." He shrugged. "I wouldn't have heard it ringing with all the commotion going on in the other room."

Shay took out her cell and tried her grandfather's number again. Nothing.

"Maybe his cell phone battery is dead," Roman suggested.

"Good point." She gave the chair a good going over. "Nothing here." She used the opportunity to look for Pappy's energy signature. There it was. Strong and clear. Weird. It went out the other door – probably the main doorway to the office. She needed to go out there and follow his trail. With a smile directed at the lawyer, she thanked him, adding, "I'll go and check my office. He might have shown up there by now."

Roman spoke up. "Are there provisions in the will in case Shay dies before the assets are transferred?"

The lawyer raised his eyebrows so they were almost hidden under his hair. "Bernice insisted I put in a clause so the assets would go to five different charities if that were to happen."

"Good." Shay moved away from the chair and looked under it. "Make sure I know the list of charities. I'll take a look at their needs to determine the amount of money they require on an annual basis to keep them flush."

The lawyer smiled. "And that's what Bernice would have wanted."

She walked to the doorway Pappy had left by. Roman fell into step behind her. In the main reception, Shay followed the energy instinctively, taking the same route her grandfather had.

"Shay?"

Roman's voice stopped her. She turned to look at him. "What?"

"Where are you going?"

She blinked. And turned around. Pappy's energy went to the left. The main exit was on the right. Turning toward the receptionist, who was busy on the computer, she asked, "Excuse me, what's in that direction?"

The receptionist smiled. "That's McElroy's office. Did you need to make an appointment to see him?"

"I'm actually looking for Charles Lassiter. He was here close to an hour, maybe an hour and a half ago. He's gone missing and given his age..." She gave the woman a small concerned smile. "I'm worried."

"Charles was here. He saw both lawyers. But he left before the reading."

"Oh? Do you know where he went?" She held out her own cell phone, habitually checking for messages once again. "I haven't been able to locate him."

"He didn't say." She smiled. "He did say he was planning to meet a special lady for lunch."

Shay felt something go still inside of her. Surely that was *her*. Had he made other plans and forgotten to tell her? "Do you know who he was meeting?"

"No. He didn't say."

Shay didn't know what to say. Talk about being sidelined by the unexpected. Roman came up behind her. His hand landed on her shoulder and he squeezed gently. "Maybe Charles had other plans for the afternoon?"

Shay couldn't see it, but...what did she know of his private life. He'd loved Bernice...but Bernice hadn't been available... Did he have another lady friend? She'd never looked into the energy in his private life. That was...private. And came under the heading of something she'd never do to him.

"Come on. Let's go collect Grandfather. We could all use some lunch."

He led her toward the hallway and the elevator.

She was still surprised. "I'd planned to have lunch with him myself. Surely he was talking about me? I can't see him having a date."

"Why not?" Roman laughed. "And all the power to him."

"No, you don't understand. He *loved* Bernice. This is a traumatic time for him."

"And maybe he's not on a date, but enjoying the comfort of an old friend. It's *not* you obviously so let's give him some space. We'll give him another shout after lunch.

With that, she Roman led her back toward her office.

Now if only she could find some sign of her Pappy on the way back.

THEY'D BARELY LEFT the lawyer's office when Roman once again found himself wondering if Shay had psychic abilities of her own. He hadn't connected the dots until he'd seen her studying the carpet. And considered her connection to Stefan – whatever they called it. He choked on the term psychic but knew Dr. Maddy and understood some of what she did. Stefan's reputation preceded him. His skills were proven in the field.

What about Shay? Did she have similar abilities? And if so, what could she do? He'd been wracking his brain looking for a reason for her odd behavior. Even in the lawyer's office she'd gone around the room, as if following something no one else could see. But now…

"What's going on, Shay?" He turned to look at her, but she was back to studying the floor.

Roman shook his head. What would it take to have her trust him? He was a fine one to talk. And he probably should fix that. But if he confided to her it could bring up questions he had no answers for.

"Shay?"

Startled, she spun around to look at him, concern pleating her forehead. "I'm trying to figure out if Pappy came this way."

"I understand that, what I don't get is *how?* What could studying the floor tell you?" He dropped to crouch down beside her. He studied the different expressions as they crossed her face. Consternation. Dismay even. Confusion. "You can tell me, you know."

She hesitated, studying him intently. *What did she see? How deep did her insights go?* It bothered him that there was something she saw in him and his work that he hadn't seen himself. And Stefan… He'd figured it all out. Knew Shay was the model and he also had heard and understood Shay's insights into the artist's character and motivation. And until Roman had those same insights…well, he wasn't looking to share his most intimate thoughts.

Her lips quirked. "Can I?" She cast a last look on the floor then straightened in a smooth graceful movement that made him realize the superb muscle tone of her thighs. His artist's eye immediately filled in the dense quad muscle stroking up the length of her leg, the lean hollow hips, and the long, smooth expanse of skin in between. Damn. He closed his eyes.

He wanted her.

But if that wish came to fruition before he could explain his art to her and she found out…yeah, that would be a bad deal all around.

A little *too* much too explain, and a whole lot *too* late.

SHAY DIDN'T KNOW what to say. Casting another fruitless look around, she realized she was on the verge of telling him about how she could see the energy people left behind. And how she was reading that energy to try and track her grandfather, but something held her back. There was the whole trust issue again. "I don't think I can share that with you." She stared at him directly.

His brows met on the bridge of his nose. His gaze narrowed. "And why is that?"

"I don't want to deal with any criticism you might have. Especially right now. I have to stay positive – in the light." She hit the button for the elevator. She couldn't figure out why she couldn't see Pappy's energy. According to the receptionist, and Shay had no reason not to believe her, Pappy had left with the intention of meeting a special woman for lunch. If so, then his energy had to be here. And it wasn't.

She just couldn't see it. *And why was that?*

She also realized that Roman was unnaturally silent at her side. The elevator opened. She walked in. Roman followed her and stood slightly behind her. She sent the elevator down to her floor. Roman never said a word.

As the door opened, Roman spoke quietly behind her. "I'm not sure what that means, but I'm not critical, you know. I try hard to be very open minded."

She cast a surprised glance behind her. "Are you?" At his nod, she muttered lightly. "Good thing."

At her office, she unlocked the door once again.

"Finally. I was about to come and get you." Gerard sat up from his slouched position on the couch in the waiting room. "Did you find him?"

Roman said, "No. But apparently he left the lawyer's office heading for a luncheon with a special lady friend?"

Surprise lit Gerard's gaze. He was still for a moment and then he laughed and laughed. "Good for him. Sly old dog."

"That's it? That's all you can say?" Shay shook her head and motioned toward the main door. "Let's go now that *I'm* not having lunch with Pappy. I could use something to eat before my assistants bury me in work."

With Roman and Gerard discussing Pappy's life choices, she led the way to the street level. Outside, she took a deep breath and smiled as the sunshine brought out the optimist in her. The sun always seemed to keep the worries away. Still, she had no explanation for why she couldn't see Pappy's energy upstairs in the hallway or leaving the lawyer's office. She should have been able to trace him in this amount of time. Pappy was older, but his vitality was strong. His energy was normally a strong, pulsing wave.

Unbidden, Tabitha came to mind. Then Pappy's strange disappearance… Could her attacker be after Pappy? She hoped not. But was Shay missing something simple?

Such as Pappy having an innocent lunch with a lady friend? If Shay was wrong about that, was he in danger? As they didn't know who the friend was, there was no way to know. If he were in danger, Shay should have seen an indicator, something that would reveal a negative energy at work. Feel something.

Unless the negative energy was hidden…

Or an energy was hiding her Pappy?

Knock, knock…

Hey, Shay, once again, this job has proven to be too easy. I had hoped for a bigger challenge. Honestly, is this the best you can do?

Since I began this vendetta, I've watched you work. I've watched you play. And boy, you don't play much.

Do you know what I could do with all that money?

A hell of a lot more than you.

I know how to live. How to have fun.

You sit in your ivory tower and dream of better days, but you don't DO anything.

Like how pathetic is that?

CHAPTER 15

Monday, early afternoon...

SHAY WALKED BACK to her office on her own. Lunch had been a simple affair. She'd barely spoken, and Roman and Gerard had kept to general topics. She'd ignored Roman's worried looks directed her way.

Her mind was too full. She called her grandfather as she entered the elevator again. She probably should have walked up the seven flights of stairs, but she hadn't been able to stop the feeling that she'd missed something. That she should have been at the office before this. *Available for Pappy to find her.*

But he could have called her any time. In fact, she'd called him a dozen times. And still no answer. Maybe she should go to his apartment. See if he was sleeping.

At her office, Jordan bustled around, filing away documents. Rose was busy on the phone. As always, Jordan's cheerful personality made Shay feel better. Just being around the two women brightened her mood. "Any messages, Jordan?"

"The lawyers handling Bernice's estate called to set up an appointment for tomorrow for you to go over some paperwork regarding Bernice's bequest to you in the will."

"Right. I should have done that when I was there." Shay walked through to her inner office and sat down. Jordan trailed behind her.

"Should have, but they caught up with me instead, so no worries. Although..." She turned and gave Shay a curious look from the doorway. "I guess you're even wealthier now?" With a casual shrug, she called out as she walked back to her desk. "Lucky girl."

"So not," Shay muttered. She heard the other two women talking.

"You shouldn't bring stuff like that up," Rose said disapprovingly.

"Why? I'm just curious." Jordan sat down so hard, Shay could hear her chair squeak. "I didn't mean any harm."

"It's her personal life. Not office stuff."

"Whatever," Jordan said casually. "She doesn't care."

And that was that. Shay almost laughed. If only the bequest could be handled so simply. She checked her emails. Nothing important. Good enough. She walked back out. "Ladies, I'll be out of the office for the rest of the afternoon. I'll take some of these applications home tonight. Hopefully, I'll have time to go over them this evening."

"If not, then not." Rose gave her a comforting look. "You don't need to work so hard."

Jordan shook her hair, and turquoise braids flipped around her head. "You don't need to work at all. You haven't even had time to grieve for the loss of your old friend yet."

"I know. And I'm not likely to have more time anytime soon."

"All these funerals make one think, don't they?" Rose sighed and stared out the window.

Rose's statement hit Shay as she was reaching for the door. "In what way, Rose?"

Her receptionist looked up in surprise. "Oh, just about life and our lives. The parts we waste and the parts we do well with. It's like our time here is so short, and we don't understand it until it's too late."

"Now if only we could learn that lesson early in life."

With that, Shay walked out, her arms full of new applications. At the parkade level, she walked through the empty basement to her car. Unlocking the vehicle, she dumped the work in the passenger seat and hopped in.

It was just a few minutes to drive to Pappy's place…only his car wasn't parked in his spot in the parkade. She had wanted him to give up driving last year after he'd had a fender bender. It wasn't the accident so much as the stress he went through afterward. It had been days before he'd been able to drive again. Shay had suggested that it might be a good idea to give up driving, but that had made him all the more determined to get back behind the wheel. He was a good driver. But he was eighty, and his reflexes had slowed.

Regardless, Pappy hadn't appreciated the suggestion.

She hadn't repeated it.

Where could he be? He was never out of touch like this. Not this long. Unable to leave without checking his apartment, she parked in his spot and walked to his condo. On the ground floor, she let herself in with her key.

"Pappy. Pappy? Are you here?" The apartment appeared empty. She walked through, checking out the small space. Pappy definitely wasn't there. She pulled her cell phone out of her pocket and called Pappy's number. There was no answering ring in the apartment. So he hadn't left his cell at home. Unless his damn battery had died. She checked his bedroom again, but there wasn't any sign that he'd come home and laid down either. The room was spotless, as always.

She opened her inner vision and searched for any lingering energy to show he'd had a visitor.

There was nothing new. Pappy's energy hovered from early this morning, but there didn't appear to be a second energy. So he hadn't returned here with his lady friend. She locked up and walked out. At her car, she turned around and studied the area. He wasn't out walking. That didn't mean his car wasn't broken down on the side of the road or that he wasn't visiting friends.

His absence *could* be nothing.

But it didn't feel like it.

It felt like everything.

"WHAT IS GOING on between you and Shay?" Gerard walked from the building out into the sunshine ahead of Roman. He dodged around a large group that streamed passed. A horn blared and a taxi sounded its horn in response. Another typical business day in the city.

Roman laughed. "Nothing." And under his breath, he muttered, "Apparently."

"No, there is definitely something there." A teasing lilt in Gerard's tone made Roman groan.

"See, I know." His grandfather shook his finger at him. "A man knows about another man."

"And what do you know?" Roman glanced down in amusement at his grandfather. Word had it that he'd been a hell raiser in his day.

"I know you have a thing for her."

Roman shook his head. The last thing he wanted was to be grilled by his grandfather. In an effort to ward him off, he asked, "Any idea where Charles could be?"

Grandfather took the bait. "Not unless he's holed up in a hotel with that young thing he'd planned to meet for lunch?"

And was that possible? Roman would love to think by the time he hit Charles's age, he was still capable of enjoying an afternoon pleasuring a new lady. But it was hard to believe in this case. Charles had been worried about Shay. And he had a connection to Bernice and planned to attend the reading of her will; *that* he wouldn't have missed. No, it didn't make sense that he'd take off like this.

"And if he isn't with this young lady, do you have a second idea?"

Gerard shook his head and motioned around the streets. "He could be anywhere. Shopping. Resting. Doctor's appointment." Gerard shrugged. "Anywhere."

"Does he have any medical issues? Does he take any medication?"

"No, not at all. He's very healthy. I don't think he's on any medications except for his cholesterol, maybe." Gerard walked beside Roman as they returned to their vehicles at the office building where Shay worked. "I think he's healthier than I am."

"Good. As long as we don't have to be concerned with that aspect." He held the sleek Audi's door open for his grandfather.

"Not that I know of. Then again, given our age, we don't often find out what's wrong until it's too late."

Roman looked around at the busy street. What could he say to that? His grandfather was right.

As the older man buckled up his seat belt, he said to Roman, "And now that you know there's something between you and Shay, do you really want to miss out on the opportunity? I gotta tell you that even if it only lasts for a short time, it could be the romance of a lifetime." He smiled reminiscently. "And I for one, have no regrets answering that call."

With that he drove off, leaving Roman standing and staring behind him.

He didn't want to have any regrets at that age either. But he still wasn't any closer to getting to know Shay better, spending time with her, finding out what made her tick and getting her into his bed. He was even further from having her in his life on a long-term basis.

And if he failed in that endeavor, then he was afraid that he *would* have regrets.

And he didn't want that.

Shay had to stay safe. And he'd done what he could to help that along. He'd made inquiries about a new security system for her. She'd okay the installation. He'd set up his program on her computer and let it run. If there'd been any signs of a hacker, he'd find it. In the meantime, he'd ensure the security on her system was operating at peak performance to make sure no one else got in.

Damned if he was going to lose her when he'd finally found her.

Monday afternoon…

SHAY WALKED INTO her apartment several hours later, feeling disoriented and out of touch. Tension ran through her muscles. She'd checked every one of Pappy's frequent haunts. She'd returned to his place to see if he'd come home, and she had been on the phone incessantly looking for him. She'd called everyone she knew in his circle of friends. She couldn't leave it alone.

It was as if he'd just vanished.

Something had to have happened to him. And as much as she hated the thought, someone was likely to have 'happened' to cause that. He was eighty years old and that just added to the problem and her fears. His car was also missing. And that led to her next step.

She picked up her phone and called her favorite detective.

"Ronin. I'm glad I could reach you."

"Shay, what's the matter?"

"It's my grandfather." Quickly she explained.

"But it's only been what…? Four or five hours since you last spoke to him?"

She winced. "I know. It's too early to file a report as a missing person, but he's not a young man any longer. For all I know, he's had a heart attack in his car, and is parked somewhere on the street."

"What type of car is he driving?"

Relieved, she gave him the license plate number and the description of the car.

"I'll let everyone know to keep an eye out for the vehicle and I'll also give them a description of your grandfather. Now does he have any health issues? Is he a diabetic and in need of medicine at a particular time?"

Groaning at how little she knew, Shay ran through the information that she did have. "He doesn't get forgetful, at least I haven't noticed that. He's very sharp mentally. He has sustained a personal loss last week, but he's not suicidal. He doesn't have diabetes, but he has a slight heart condition and high cholesterol – nothing too bad and nothing more than anyone else his age. But I can't stress enough how unlike him this is. With evening coming, he should be home safe and sound. He also always has a nap in the afternoon. At the time he usually lies down, he wasn't at home. I know because I was there, and he wasn't."

"But he could have slept in his car. You know, just pulled off to the side of the road and laid his head back."

"It's possible," she said doubtfully, "but that's not like him."

His calm voiced suggested, "Still not out of the line of possibility."

"True. But with all the other coincidences I can't help but wonder if someone hasn't kidnapped him or worse." She hesitated. "I know it's too early to panic, but—"

"But you're worried." His voice turned businesslike. "Good enough, I'll see what I can do."

He hung up, and Shay dialed Stefan. She'd tried him several times since the reading of the will, but so far he hadn't answered telepathically. But then, when he wanted the world to go away, he was good at making that happen.

Maybe he was home now.

She waited while the phone rang and rang. Finally, just when she was about to hang up, she heard his tired voice. "Stefan?"

"Who'd you expect," he grumbled, "Santa Claus?"

She winced. "Sorry. Not a good day, huh."

"No. I'm working with the police on another case in Seattle." He sighed. "People are dropping like flies. For no reason except someone is having a damn killing fest."

"Ouch. Kinda like my life feels right now. Sorry, I know you're busy."

"Sometimes it gets pretty crazy." His tone changed, eased. "What's up, Shay?"

"It's Pappy. He's disappeared and I can't find him." Stated like that, it shook even her.

"What have you done to find him?"

Shay gave him quick description of her afternoon.

"You say he was at the lawyers', but you couldn't find Pappy's energy leaving the rooms? And he wasn't still there?"

"No. Several people said they'd seen him leave."

"Odd."

"That's why I went back up and took another look at the energy. There was nothing to show he'd gone down the elevator or the stairwell. But he wasn't still in either lawyers' offices."

"That you could see."

"True enough." She thought about that. "I don't want to sound paranoid, but is it possible for someone to have hidden Pappy's presence from me there? I can't see any other explanation. I was thinking about Tabitha's attacker, wondering if they could, through hooks, hide their energy? Maybe do the same with Pappy. And if so, why? And that makes me really worried."

"More likely they're extending the energy of the person beside them enough for them to hide behind…maybe? Like grabbing a corner of their aura and tugging it around them, as if wrapping themselves in a blanket. Such a thing would be new...again, but as you know, it's always possible to do the impossible. Of course if they can hide in someone's aura, they might be able to hide a person in their aura as well. And we won't know the extent of a person's capabilities until we see them."

Damn.

"Still," Stefan continued, "What could possibly be the purpose behind hiding their presence in your grandfather's aura? You inherited all that financial headache, he didn't."

She laughed. The first lightness of the day filled her soul. "Thank you for seeing Bernice's actions for what they are. I gather you heard me screaming earlier?"

"I didn't have a choice," he said, humor to his voice. "It's because of that I had to shut you down this afternoon. I needed to stay focused on this other problem."

"Understandable. And sorry for transmitting so loudly."

He sighed. "You want me to go looking for him, don't you?"

She hated to ask yet more of him, but.... "I'm not the tracker you are," she said apologetically. "And as I haven't been able to find him my way...I wondered if you could drop in and see where he is?"

"Okay then, while I take a look, you revisit the scene at the reading of the will. If Pappy has been kidnapped, look to the people who lost out today. Chances are they'd have the biggest reason to do something like this."

Stefan rang off, leaving Shay staring in shock at the phone. He was right.

Why hadn't she thought of that? Because she'd done her damnedest to forget that whole nightmare of being named beneficiary. How could Bernice not even mention that disaster waiting for Shay?

She crossed to her rocking chair and sat down. Now that she'd gotten hold of Stefan and he was off looking for Pappy, relaxation was easier to achieve. She took her mind back to that morning, to her grandfather's call and her dash to the meeting where the lawyers read the will. She popped into her own energy at the doorway where everyone had collected – and stopped to look around.

The room was more full than she remembered. Then again, she'd slipped into the closest vacant seat and hadn't had much chance to look around. There had to be at least two-dozen people. Most of them she didn't know at all. There were five women that she could count, maybe more. All up in the front. She recognized Grace, Bernice's assistant, and a younger woman at her side – probably Grace's daughter.

The men she hardly recognized. There was Bernice's driver on the right-hand side and a man that Shay had seen around Bernice's big house. He'd handled most of the household and gardening stuff for her. Their presence made sense. The other men...well she wasn't so sure.

With the meeting started, and from her vantage point, she walked as far forward as she could to see their faces. Then she watched as the final, shocking announcement was made. Grace only nodded, as if she'd expected the news. The same for the two men she'd recognized. Bernice might have already told them her plans. They'd been with her a long time. They were trusted friends.

People in the other rows showed shock, dismay. Some seethed with anger. But at the same time, she saw that no one recognized Shay in the back row. No one turned to point a finger at her. To them, Shay had been just a name. Not a recognizable target.

Good thing.

Still, outside of the anger and threats to contest the will in court, and any number of profanities flung at the lawyer in the front and center, she didn't see anything deceptive.

But because Pappy was missing, she looked deeper.

Hating to do it, she checked out Grace first. No subterfuge there. Grace was mourning the loss of a good friend. She was happy with the thought of all the money coming her way, and she would share that with her daughter.

Shay checked out the daughter. She'd come to support her mother. Was touched at actions and was horrified at the actions of those around her. So far...nice and normal.

Nothing untoward or suspicious.

In fact, the daughter had whispered to Grace, "Poor Shay. That's not going to be easy."

Shay checked out the men next. The first one was touched at his inheritance, but damn if he wasn't grieving the loss of a loved one. Bernice had this fifty-year-old man on the lover's string too. The second man appeared to have a longstanding friendship with Bernice, but it was not loverlike. He was also happy with the money. He'd have liked more, but that's because he wanted to go to Vegas and spend most of it.

Sighing, Shay moved to the next row. There, a bitter unfairness permeated the air.

Fucking bitch.

How dare she?

Good thing she's dead, or I'd have killed her myself. This from a distant relative that had hoped to inherit enough to avoid bankruptcy.

All these thoughts circled with the anger and disbelief. So much hatred. But in a way, the emotions were all normal. Many of these people had come expecting, hoping, for so much more. They'd been told to come, after all, so they had a right to their disappointment. And they hadn't even gotten a mention.

Typical Bernice. Do things her own way and to hell with the others.

She switched to studying the dark red, swirling anger on the left. Wow. Now these three were pissed. She studied their faces, hoping to recognize them in the future. She didn't even know them. She studied the energy that bled from their chakras. The majority bled from the first and third chakras.

Those two chakras covered money, survival, and all the basics in life. These people were also afraid. They needed the money. They had debts, big ones, borrowed from unsavory people, and fear wrapped around the hooks into their chakras. Other people's hooks. She winced at the rate of bleeding from that chakra. And the stream pulsed with fear.

How desperate were these people? Enough to come after her? Had they known ahead of time? Could they have snatched Pappy? Were they planning to hold him hostage until she paid a ransom? And she would. In a heartbeat.

She tried to take a breath, but the pain and fear made it difficult. And she knew better.

She closed her eyes and sent a bolt of white energy down her spine and deep into Mother Earth. Then she sent the energy straight up and out of her own crown chakra into the sky. Instantly her world righted itself, balanced itself. Stabilized. Her chest eased, and she could breathe again.

From her new perspective, she could study the streams that twisted and seethed throughout the room.

One man, a little further back, bled from the heart chakra. But it was his anger that caught her attention. He'd had a relationship with Bernice, and he'd felt he deserved something from her death.

Deserved. But he hadn't caused Bernice's death.

Still, it had been a few minutes now, and she didn't see anything new, just had garnered a deeper insight into the greed of mankind. What she hadn't seen, was any sign of Pappy's energy here. She could do one more thing.

She carried on into the lawyer's office where she had seen his energy right after the reading of the will. Standing in her own memory with the wisps of Pappy right in front of her, Shay couldn't resist.

She took a deep breath and jumped into her Pappy's energy. Opening her eyes, she surveyed the location. Pappy was speaking with his lawyer, not Bernice's.

The conversation moved on around her. Dimly, Shay felt the emotion running through Pappy over the discussion he was having with the lawyer. The discussion was intense, but neither man appeared upset. In fact, they seemed to be hammering out the details of something.

Pappy's business. Not hers. Always mindful of personal boundaries and ethics in a position that gave her greater awareness than she would be privy to in any other way, she tuned out of the conversation and studied the energy pouring off the lawyer. He appeared concerned, yet caring. His heart chakra was engaged, so he cared about Pappy and understood what the man wanted to do. *Good.*

She studied his chakras more closely and realized the lawyer had issues in the very root of the first chakra. She sighed as she understood what the problem was. His energy snaked forward and around Pappy, sliding out the doorway toward the receptionist, where it hooked into her first and fourth chakra. The lawyer was having an affair with her. And she was in love with him. As Shay studied the chakras involved, she realized there was no joy to be had there. She was in love, or believed herself to be, and he was only in lust. She saw that he'd had affairs with the last three women who'd sat in her chair.

Damn. And he was married. With kids.

The receptionist's energy wrapped around the lawyer's body, and there was just way too much of it sitting on the desk. It made Shay shudder, and she forcibly tried to put it out of her mind. Yet again, she found herself in a situation where she didn't really want to see this stuff – unfortunately people left traces of every action, including a hump and bump on the desk.

Her opinion of the lawyer dropped several notches. He might care about Pappy's wishes, but he sure as hell didn't take his business sense into his personal life.

Too bad. Now he had an icky look to him. She was afraid she would even have trouble shaking his hand. He wasn't her lawyer, thank heavens. She'd have a hard time if he were. She'd like to think morals and ethics were a personality trait and not a business asset, to only be used in one area of a person's life. Still, he wasn't embezzling funds – *that* she could see. Or attacking vulnerable old men.

She shuddered again and stretched as far away from Pappy's energy as she could for a better view of the rest of the office. She didn't have a very far leash in this case, but she had enough to stand at the doorway and study the other occupants.

On the other side of the room, Bernice's lawyer was on the phone. The energy drifting around the partially open doorway told Shay that he was trying to change an appointment he'd made with his wife. Good enough. All in all, the energy she saw was normal people stuff. Nothing excessive or dangerous.

Nothing more negative than she'd find in any group of normal people.

She watched as Pappy stopped to say hello to the lawyers' office receptionist. Her energy was warm and caring, same as the lawyer's. Interesting. Still Pappy was a loveable soul. Shay hadn't really expected anything else. He walked out to the hallway and pulled out his phone. She heard his phone call to her.

She could hear her own responses in a tinny, distant sort of way. She studied his actions. He appeared slightly worried about her but nothing untoward.

Up ahead, he walked down the hallway to the men's room.

She waited outside as he went in. That too was normal. She had boundaries she didn't cross. Not unless she was forced to. Going into the men's with her grandfather was one boundary she hoped she wouldn't ever be forced to cross.

Except her grandfather didn't come out of the bathroom.

Shay?

Stefan.

KNOCK, KNOCK...

Damn, Shay, there are none as blind as those that think they have perfect sight.

You, my dear, are as blind as a dead man in this case. And a dead man is what your grandfather is going to be soon.

And you won't know what happened.

I couldn't believe it when I found out that you, with all your millions, just received many more. For what? For nothing.

For that added insult, you will pay yet again.

I just have to make sure you understand that when he and all the others die, it will be because of you.

As a general rule, I don't like to kill little old men. But I will.

I have nothing personal against this dear old man. Now little old woman, that's a different story. Bernice deserved what she got. Honest. Your grandfather, however, could live out the rest of his life in peace and quiet, except that he's related to you.

You're lucky because there was something odd about him today. Something different about his energy. I let him go because I know where to find him again. Still, I made you worry, didn't I?

Slowly, unable to stop it, everyone related to you is going to disappear — one by one.

I'd prefer that you knew I was doing this, and I need to figure out how to make you really worry. I want you scared. I want you panicked. I want you to know it's you that I'm hunting. Even if you don't understand why at first…

You will by the time I'm done.

How?

Wait and see.

For now, I'll leave your grandfather alone for a little longer. And pick on someone else.

Your grandfather will still get what's coming to him, but then, so will you.

Eventually.

I'm going for maximum pain. And that means I need this to last a little while longer.

CHAPTER 16

S HAY BLINKED SEVERAL times and retuned her consciousness to her apartment.

Stefan, I'm here. With her return to the present, all her worries came flying back. She hoped Stefan had found answers that she hadn't.

What did you find out?

He's alive. But he's unconscious.

Shit. How do you know?

I could track him to his position but not to his mind. I can't see his physical location. I can't tell if he's badly hurt, either. In fact, although I can tell he's alive, I can't tell if he's injured. It's like a fog protecting him. A feminine fog.

What? What do you mean a feminine fog?

Stefan's voice, although tired, had an amused ring to it. *If I had to guess, I'd say a woman was trying to help him. Or hide him,* he added thoughtfully. *Not sure that there couldn't have been two women though. The space he is in is public. Lots of energies. Have you seen Bernice hanging around lately? This sounds like something she'd do.*

Hide him? Do you think someone has hurt him?

I'm not sure. I couldn't see clearly because of this energy. I couldn't even say that it was Bernice there, just that there was a heavy white energy blanket around him.

Would a blanket like that protect him from other people's view?

Hmmm. Maybe. Stefan's voice was slow, thoughtful. *That's possible I suppose. I found him easily enough with your energy markers. You love him and he loves you, and that means there is a strong energy exchange between you. That makes it easier to see markers. What I don't know is why you couldn't see him.*

She winced. Please do not let it be her current insecurity on reading energy. If anything happened to Pappy because of that... Then she remembered Bernice's concern words...

I suppose Bernice could be helping — or maybe hindering would be a better way to say it. She said she had to stay here for some reason. Maybe it was because Pappy was in danger? On the other hand, I don't know how much danger he could be in, so she might be helping him out more by keeping the fog there. Damn. I need to find him.

Yes, you do, Stefan said. *His life force wasn't terribly strong.*

Was he lying down? Sitting? Standing? Could you tell?

Stefan fell silent. *He's lying down, on his side, almost curled into a fetal position.*

Her thoughts turned even darker. *So he could be in any small space, and he might be injured. Did you sense a massive drain in his energy in any way?*

No. His energy is holding. He's not been shot or anything that I could tell.

Well that's good news. But not good enough. Any suggestion as to what to do now?

Slip into my energy. Track him back. His voice changed. *I have to go.*

And just like that Stefan was gone.

Shay didn't waste time thinking through the process, she closed her eyes, picked up Stefan's energy and stood in his warm glow. Damn. There'd been very few times she'd been in here, and each time there'd been a sense of wonder. So much love. So much power.

Move it. Stefan gave her a psychic prod. *Now.*

If she'd had time she'd have laughed. It's as if he were embarrassed. Then she was in his personal space. Had access to so much private information of a very private man. Good thing she held to a strong code. But she was moving swiftly, following his earlier path to her Pappy. As she didn't have to search like he had, the journey was fast.

She landed on a bench in a downtown square. Pappy's car parked in front of her and Pappy curled up on his side beside her, as if homeless and asleep. Her heart broke. He looked so lost. But also healthy and alive.

Confused and more than a little worried, she gave him a quick once over but his energy flowed, his vitals, although weaker than she'd like, were solid. He wasn't hurt. Relief washed through her.

THERE YOU ARE, Bernice complained. *Do you know how long I've been sitting here watching over him? Trying to hide him. You know what could happen to him out here like this? What took you so long?*

Shay stared at Bernice's ghost in disbelief. She'd been hiding him? Since when?

As if anticipating her question, Bernice volunteered. *I could feel something was wrong. When I thought about him, I found myself transported here. With him lying like this. Is he going to be okay?*

Shay grinned. He's going to be fine. At least she hoped so. She couldn't be happier that Pappy had Bernice for his guardian angel. *You don't know how he got here, do you?* Shay asked.

Bernice's energy shimmered. *No.*

Figures. Shay studied the area, and realized she could just see the street signs at the intersection through Bernice's 'cloak.' Damn who'd have thought she would ever be able to do that?

The sign read: Thurlow and Rasford.

Perfect. She sent that message back to Stefan, asking him to tell Ronin.

Done, came the whispered acknowledgement.

Knowing that help was coming, Shay studied Bernice. *The police are on their way, Bernice. I need you to drop your protective cloak and let him be found.*

But what if someone else finds him first? the older woman fretted. *What is going on Shay? I don't like this.*

Neither do I. But you have to leave him alone so he can get help. Inspiration struck. *Bernice, head to the hospital so you'll be there waiting for him when he comes in.*

Just then a cop car approached slowly.

Bernice shimmered in place for a moment, then she slowly disappeared.

The cop car came to a stop.

Thank heavens. Sure that Pappy was going to get the help he needed, Shay let go. And found herself sucked at sonic speed through the ethers on Stefan's golden energy highway until she was dumped back into her body on her chair.

She groaned as her physical body struggled to adjust and her consciousness took a little longer to recover in the physical confines of reality.

The phone rang as she struggled to reorient herself to the new reality.

She picked up the phone. *Ronin.* With her voice, slow and groggy, she answered, "Hello."

"We found your grandfather. Thanks to you and Stefan."

"Oh that's wonderful," she cried. "Where is he?"

"He was found on city bench just like you said and close to his parked vehicle. He seemed disoriented and confused but in good health.

He was able to talk fine, but he couldn't explain how he got where he was or what he was doing there. He's on his way to the hospital."

"Thank you so much." Shay's heart wrenched at the thought of her grandfather all alone and hurting.

"I'm hoping you have a set of keys and can move it his car?"

"I have spares. I'll take care of it." She'd have to call a cab, though that was minor. After effusive thanks, she rang off and called Gerard. His line was busy.

Not wanting to waste time, she called the cab company, grabbed her purse along with Pappy's spare keys, and headed out.

The cab dropped her off at the car. No tickets. Thank heavens for something. She hopped in, was grateful when it started, and drove the car to the hospital. Outside in the lot, she tried to call Gerard one more time. Still nothing. Roman was next.

"Shay?" his growl filled the line, sending shivers down her spine. She so had to deal with that attraction soon. "Do you have any news?"

Quickly she filled him in.

"I'll bring Grandfather."

He wouldn't listen to her assurances that she'd call after speaking with Pappy's doctor, and knowing how close the two old men were, she didn't bother arguing any further. Closing the phone, she strode inside toward the receptionist. Her grandfather was in a cubicle off the emergency room, leaning back on the white bed, staring at the ceiling. Bernice sat quietly at his side as a warm loving energy stroking Pappy's arm. Shay gave her a beaming smile as she entered.

"Oh Pappy!" She ran the last few steps and hugged him. Lying in bed, he seemed so frail and old. She couldn't think about losing him right now.

"Shay, I'm fine." He patted her back. "There, there."

She pulled back to stare down at him mistily. "Are you? What happened to you? I've spent all day searching for you." She tried to keep her voice down and in control, but failed on both accounts. Realizing she was attracting attention and disturbing others in potentially worse situations, she calmed down enough to perch on the side of his bed.

She sniffled back tears. "Are you feeling okay?" She studied his skin color. He looked fine. Maybe tired, but his color was strong. She looked deeper. His energy ran smoothly, the pulsation normal, vibrant.

Did nothing make sense anymore?

He looked embarrassed at her questions. "I don't know," he admitted. "It's like the afternoon is a blank. Just didn't happen."

"Do you remember calling me?" At his nod, she continued, "I came right to the lawyer's office, but you weren't there." Hot tears welled up again. Willing herself to calm down before she burst into tears and upset them both, she repeated helplessly, "I spent all afternoon trying to find you."

"I guess I went outside for a walk to clear my head, apparently drove off, and ended up at City Park. At least that's where the police officer found me sitting. My car was in front of me, but I was sort of napping on the bench – I guess."

"Napping?" she said cautiously, hating that he'd blanked out like that. Could he have been drugged? She'd have to wait to hear back from the doctors on his condition. "You might have been really tired if you didn't have your regular nap. Which I know you didn't have at home, because I went there and checked."

He brightened. "Did you? Well as much as I'm sorry for causing you unnecessary worry, it's nice to know you went to such lengths."

She smiled down at him. "Oh you are, are you? Well don't do it again, please. It's too hard on my heart."

"Bosh. You're a young'un. Your heart is just fine."

"And what about mine, Charles?" Gerard's shaky but surprisingly loud voice cut through the chatter.

Pappy smiled. "You didn't need to make the trip. I'm just fine."

"If you were so fine," Gerard replied testily, "then you'd know how you ended up on that damn park bench. Can't let you out of my sight without you getting into trouble. I even saved you a seat at the zoo of a will reading." Gerard shook his head. "You really missed something. Too bad Bernice couldn't have seen that chaos."

"She'd have loved it." Pappy laughed. "Nothing Bernice liked better than a good scrap. I suppose she left little bones to most people, a couple of meaty bones to a few, and a hind quarter or so to those she cared about, huh?

Gerard grinned. "Exactly. Then she threw the whole carcass at Shay here, along with the responsibility to do right."

Pappy winced. "Typical Bernice. She didn't mention anything to you before her death, Shay?"

A snort escaped her. "So not. I'd have told her what to do with her money."

Pappy grinned. "That's why she didn't. If she'd let you know ahead of time, she'd be leaving the door open to you trying to get out of the inheritance."

"Damn right I would have," Shay muttered.

"Not many people would turn down a fortune." Roman's deep

voice interrupted them.

She turned to see him standing at the end of the bed. *When had he arrived?* And damn, he looked good. She blinked and forced her gaze back to Pappy. Unfortunately, Pappy had caught her look and winked at her. Heat washed up her neck, again. She glared at him. She was so not going there with him.

Speaking of such things… "Pappy, the receptionist at the law firm said you were meeting a special lady for lunch. Who was it?"

His face went blank.

Her heart ached. This couldn't be much fun for him. She smiled down at him. "I figured it was me."

"We tried to convince her, Roman and I, that you were entitled to your flings just like any man," Gerard said a little enviously. "I hope you had a dashing afternoon."

Pappy laughed. "Damn, I hope so. Too bad I don't remember a blasted thing."

Gerard grinned. He leaned forward and whispered, "You might have to check your supply of the little blue pills to see how successful you were."

Shay rolled her eyes and caught Roman's big grin and barely hid her own smile. Men were men, no matter what age they were. And if this conversation put a smile on her grandfather's face, then she was all for it.

Monday evening…

DUE TO THE lateness of the hour, and the fact that the tests hadn't all come back, Pappy was admitted to the hospital overnight. He started to show signs of exhaustion so Shay waited for him to fall asleep. Bernice disappeared hours ago.

She was pondering the unusual amount of time she'd spent at hospitals lately when a nurse came in and nudged her arm.

Startled, she followed the nurse's movement to see Pappy was sound asleep.

"He should sleep through the night. Go and rest yourself. You look like you've had a tough day."

Standing up, Shay nodded. "I think I will. It has been tough. Tough and long."

"Go. You can't look after him if you aren't strong and healthy yourself."

With a last glance at her grandfather, Shay walked out of the hospital into the cool evening air. She had totally lost track of time. It wasn't just evening, it was pitch black outside, the dark of night. She pulled out her cell phone and realized it was past midnight. No wonder she was tired.

The thought of driving home didn't appeal, but the lure of her own bed was enough to push her forward. The streets were empty.

Her apartment was cool and dark. Not that she cared at this point – she just wanted her bed. She dumped her purse on the couch and kicked her shoes off at the front door. Walking to her bedroom, she started undressing, intent on becoming horizontal as fast as she could.

She only made it three steps inside her room when she felt it.

Something.

Off.

And damn scary. Blackness like she'd never seen before surged up in front of her. She stepped backwards. Then she turned and ran for the door.

But not fast enough.

She collapsed on the living room floor. Out cold.

STEFAN BOLTED UPRIGHT in bed. *Shay?*

He gasped, choked, his hands flailing at his chest and neck. A haze of blackness filled his room, strangling him.

He pounded his chest, trying to get oxygen into his lungs. Only to realize he had no trouble breathing.

With that he understood he was caught in a vision. Someone else's vision.

Shay's vision.

He closed his eyes, took a steadying breath, focused on Shay and jumped into her mind. Her soul stirred.

Stefan?

Yes, it's me. You're unconscious. I don't know why.

Blackness. It came out of nowhere. Surrounded me. Smothered me.

Yes, I felt it. But it's an illusion. Like a cloaking energy again. It's not smoke. It's not fire. You can breathe. You need to wake up.

She groaned. *It's hard to move.*

I'll get help.

Stefan walked throughout Shay's apartment in his astral form. He couldn't see any immediate danger, but...he didn't want to leave her alone either.

He zipped back into his body and shrugged into his skin suit, as he liked to call it. Feeling the normal, yet confining sensation of being reoriented back into the right reality, he opened his eyes. He needed to track that energy back to the source – but first things first.

Stefan opened his phone and called Roman.

"Hello." Roman growled into the phone. "You better have a damn good reason for calling."

"Shay's been attacked. You need to go her apartment. I don't have time to explain." Stefan closed the call and tossed the phone on the bed, and then lay down and jumped free again.

He slipped into predator mode…and went hunting in the ethers.

"SHAY'S BEEN ATTACKED? What the hell? Stefan. Stefan?" The dial tone rang endlessly in Roman's ear, and he knew Stefan was gone.

Shay. She was in trouble and Stefan had called Roman to deal with it. A fact that disturbed and delighted Roman. He threw back the covers and quickly dressed. Five minutes later, he was heading for Shay's apartment.

The next problem was security. How was he going to get inside the building and inside her apartment?

Luckily, the doorman recognized him, called up and buzzed him in. So Shay was talking at least. Or someone was with her who'd answered the call. With a casualness he was far from feeling, Roman strode over to the elevators and caught a ride to the twelfth floor. Once outside the right apartment, he pounded on the door. Stefan didn't say if Shay was hurt or unconscious. Roman presumed he'd have called for an ambulance if she couldn't get to the door.

The door opened in front of him.

Shay, still dressed as she'd been at the hospital, rubbing the side of her head and looking dazed, stared up at him. "Roman? What's the matter? Why are you here at this hour? I couldn't believe when the doorman called up to me." Her gaze widened. "Oh my God. Is it Pappy? Has he died?"

She grabbed his shirt with both hands and shook him – or tried to. He had close to a hundred pounds on her. He wrapped his hands around her much smaller ones and gently disentangled them, but he kept them in his grasp. "No. Pappy's fine. Let me in, please."

"Oh." She blinked owlishly at him, and then hurriedly stepped back. "Sorry. Of course. Come in." She closed the door behind him.

He ignored her for the moment, looking around to see what had caused Stefan's worry. The apartment looked as normal as he'd seen it last time. He walked further in. Nothing unusual.

He spun around and studied her. She looked like she'd come dashing out of bed with a pounding headache. Except she was still fully dressed in slacks and blouse. Just a little scattered.

"What's the matter?" she asked, confused. She walked over to her couch and sat down, pulling her knees up to her chin and staring at him. She blinked several times, as if having trouble focusing. "I don't understand what's going on."

"Neither do I." He ran his fingers through his hair and sat down on the closest easy chair. "I can only tell you that Stefan called me fifteen minutes ago and told me to get over here. He said you'd been attacked."

"*Attacked?*" She gazed at him in shock. "I did wake up a few minutes ago on my living room floor, but why would Stefan call you?"

He glared at her. "I don't know. Ask Stefan." He looked around the apartment. "I can't see anything wrong. So I don't understand… What did Stefan mean?" He spun back. "*You woke up on the living room floor?*"

She looked at him from under her lashes. What was she thinking? Was she trying to hide something? And if so, what? Groaning he leaned forward, placing his forehead on his hands. How could he get her to trust him? Damn it.

"Are you okay?" A warm hand landed softly on his. "I'm sorry Stefan worried you like this. It's late. Go home."

He snorted and glared at her. But his hand ensnared her fingers. "Stefan told me you'd been attacked. I have to trust that he didn't make that up and that means, for whatever reason, either you don't remember the danger, or you don't want me to know. Either way, that pisses me off."

She tugged her hand free. "Stefan shouldn't have called. There's nothing you can do."

"Nothing?" he snapped, jumping to his feet. "I can stop whoever attacked you from coming back and trying again. Surely that's something." His hands clenched and unclenched in frustration. "Good thing that security system is being installed in the next couple of days — it'll be tomorrow if I get my way."

"That won't help."

"Why not?" he roared.

As the last words left his mouth he watched her lower lip tremble, her eyes begin to shimmer with tears.

"Oh God. I'm so sorry." He sat down beside her and gathered her into his arms. "Why do you fight me so?"

"Because you don't believe in me. In us. Because you have walls and are keeping secrets from me." She whispered the last bit so softly he struggled to hear, even then doubting what she'd said. He leaned back slightly and stared down at her. He didn't get it. Cautiously, he asked, "Believe in you? Of course I do."

"No," she whispered from against his chest. "You don't."

"Then explain it to me, so I *can* believe." He reached down and tilted her chin up. "Make no mistake, whatever other parts you are confused about, know that I believe in you." He paused, waiting until she looked up at him, and added, "And I believe in us."

She studied him, as if trying to peer into his heart.

He let her. Something major was going on, and he needed to know what it was.

She dropped her lashes.

"Don't." He said roughly. "Don't shut me out like that."

Her gaze flew open again, this time she had a dawning realization in her hazel eyes. The colors swirled with mystery. If only he could put that on canvas.

"Are you saying…?" She tilted her head slightly, locking her gaze on his face. "Are you saying that you *care?*"

He opened his mouth to give a trite answer. And her eyes narrowed. As if she knew. He bit back the words and thought about what she'd asked. "Yes, I care."

And he left it at that.

But she wouldn't. She studied him for a little longer. "As a fellow human being, as a friend…or as something more?"

"You already know I want much more."

"Yeah?" she leaned back and stared, pinning him with a deep mysterious gaze. "How much more?"

Shit.

He felt his body freeze. While he understood something momentous was happening, he hadn't been thinking about bleeding out truths himself. Or baring *his* emotions. More like she should be the one telling the truth. Instead he'd been put on the spot. With options. And he hated this type of conversation, so full of hidden land mines.

And what should he say? It was hardly the time to tell her about his paintings. And he doubted she was ready to hear how much he really cared. Not when she'd been playing the nervous avoidance game.

He didn't want to send her running. Not now. Her life was in danger and he needed to be here. He couldn't take the chance.

SHE WATCHED ROMAN freeze mouselike, as if sensing a predator. She was no predator, but she dealt in truths. Ones he had no idea even existed. She had to know where he stood before she discussed this any further.

She had the option of watching his energy, and that reassured her like nothing else could. It swirled around her, around *them* gently. His, caressing her energy and blending with hers with loving attention. That was one truth she could count on.

That he took time to answer meant he was trying to determine the level of involvement he wanted or was willing to admit. No one had trouble saying 'friends'...unless there was something more... Perhaps neither of them had taken that path mentally.

His energy said his all was in this relationship. If she had to, she could let him off the hook and take it on faith. But – and this was a different problem – if she wanted him to commit, she had to be prepared to say the words as well.

She'd known him as an email friend for months. And he'd intrigued her then but now it was different. He'd come into her life personally with Bernice's death. Her life had been crazy since. But he'd been there every step of the way. She hadn't been exactly open and straightforward with him either.

She sighed. "That you don't answer speaks more than real words."

"Does it?" his strangled voice made her laugh.

"Yes, it does." She grinned. "I'll take it we're somewhere between friends and something more?" She looked directly at him.

"Agreed." He nodded immediately, and she laughed.

"Good. That's on both sides. Where we go from here is our choice. We appear to be at a crossroads. I can't go forward unless you believe in me. And I can't share what happened tonight unless you have an open mind. A *really* open mind." She gazed out the window for a long moment. "Like Stefan has. He is the one person who I trust over anything and everyone."

At the slight twist to his lips, she paused. "And considering that we might be heading toward the more-than-friends side of life..." Was it just yesterday that she said she wasn't going there again? Anyway, she focused on his narrowed gaze and that eerie stillness, and finished with, "Stefan and I are friends. Only friends...we've *never* been lovers. I love him like a brother and trust him with my life."

His lips untwisted into a warm smile. "Thank you for sharing that with me," he said with sincerity in his voice. "You're blessed to have that relationship with him."

She couldn't help it. She chuckled. "It comes with its own set of problems. He can read your thoughts, jump into your mind, see what you're feeling, and that's just for starters."

"So he's really…psychic?" Roman asked.

"Oh he is." She leaned back slightly, losing the hint of humor that had kept the conversation light. "And that's one of the things I need you to believe. Stefan *is*," she stressed, and then continued, "the real thing." She took a deep breath. "And so am I."

CHAPTER 17

Late Monday evening...

THERE IT WAS. The answer to that very question he'd been wondering about.

Roman turned his head, his gaze pinning her in place. She looked so normal, beautiful even though exhausted – but she also appeared to be calm. She lounged on the couch so casually after dropping a fairly important bit of information.

And indeed, her claim wasn't exactly a claim everyone would make.

"Oh." Not very intellectual but it's all he could think of to say.

She nodded her head. "Yeah." She shrugged. "It's not a term I think of when I consider my abilities. But that's what the world calls it."

"What *would* you call it?"

"I'd prefer intuitive, maybe energy specialist. I do a lot of different stuff, but most of it...only rarely." She shrugged. "As my abilities defy categorization, I try to avoid doing so myself."

"And can you do all that Stefan can?" He knew some about Stefan's telepathic abilities and mind reading from Dr. Maddy, and he wanted to ask if she could read his mind too, but at the same time, he desperately didn't want to know the answer. The humiliation, if she discovered his secret, would be too much.

"No. Not at all."

Thank heavens for that. He took a deep sigh and released the breath he'd been holding.

She laughed. "I'm not a mind reader, if that's what you're worried about."

"Then what do you *do*?" he asked curiously.

A self-deprecating smile slid off her lips. "I read energy. I can see where people are coming from, see how they use their energy, and see what they use their energy for. If they are the kind to cheat others, their energy will tell me. It they are the type to cheat on their wives, I'll usually be able to see it. And that is just for starters."

"Wow." He didn't know what to say. An interesting concept. He could see why she used the term intuitive, as much of what she saw others would intuit from body language, facial expressions, and even nuances in a voice. And he had to admit it was a relief that she couldn't read his mind.

But what *could* she see of him? He decided to ask, remembering Stefan's words on insights.

"And what do you see…with me?"

She shook her head. "I make it a policy to not delve too deeply with people I know. I use my skills to administer the foundation money as well as I can." She sighed. "It's a problem with friends. Whether it's me being afraid of reading too much into the issue or not being detached enough, I find it difficult to read my friends."

"Good. I think." But it didn't answer what he really wanted to know. And damn it, he really wanted to know. He took the plunge. "Stefan mentioned something about you having interesting insights into my artwork. Is that the type of stuff you can pick up?"

She waved her hand around. "Stefan told you that? Interesting." She shrugged. "It's not much. I just saw how much you related to your model. That she's your muse. Your passion." She hesitated. "That's why I'm surprised you're interested in me. The way I see it, you're madly in love with her."

Madly in love with her.

With his model. With Shay. She could see *that?*

He sat back on his heels. Rocked by the revelation.

His heart sighed at a sad lonely truth. Though he hadn't admitted it, he'd been in love with her for a long time. His mind filled with images he'd poured over to get everything about her, down just right. The curve of her shoulder as he painted it, the long smooth strokes making the skin glow like it was meant to. He'd tried to paint other models, women, children. He'd even tried to get into landscapes. And he hadn't managed any creative energy at all.

Was that why? He was painting the object of an unrequited love. God, that made him sound like a schoolboy. Or worse – a teenager.

"I'm sorry."

He quickly turned his head back to face her.

"I didn't mean to bring up a painful topic. It's not like I was reading energy or anything, it's just that it was obvious to me that you were obsessed with her. In a good way," she added hurriedly.

"Obsessed." *Interesting… Was he?*

Absolutely. What else could he call it? He'd given into the need to paint her two years ago then had worked up the nerve to contact her. Bad timing on his part as her fiancée had just passed away. Still, he'd stayed always there, slowly building the relationship until he could get back to Portland. Hoping she'd be ready for him. That he hadn't been able to paint anything different since that first canvas *might* be viewed as an obsession.

"That she is the other half to your heart." Shay sounded distant, hurt…insecure.

And he got it.

Oh God. And how did *that* work? He had been trying to get Shay to move forward with this relationship, and she'd assumed what, that he'd lost his heart to the model? That she was his second choice? A poor one at that?

He couldn't possibly have seen this coming. Who could?

"So, I don't want to know what happened between the two of you, but I am sorry."

"Sorry?" He felt disconnected. As if he were hearing the conversation from a long distance away.

"She's obviously unavailable to you for some reason."

He blinked. *Say what?*

She flushed. "I'm getting personal, again I'm sorry. Forget I said that."

She went to stand up, and he tugged her back down. "Please, finish what you were going to say."

Troubled, she said, "It's just that I feel like you've always admired, loved this woman from afar. The paintings are stunning. But the woman was distant. As if your love was never recognized. You never had a chance to fully experience that passion. You painted it on the canvas because you couldn't have it, have her in your life – in your heart."

He sat back. Oblivious to everything but the second truth bomb she'd just dropped. How could she possibly know all that? Especially when he hadn't seen it that clearly himself.

And even worse. How could he ever explain that she was the model? She was the one he pined for? That he loved.

And now he was certain – Shay *was* the other half of his heart.

SHAY STUDIED THE shock on his face. He really hadn't known it. How could that be? And if he hadn't known it, then he wasn't ready to move on with another relationship. And maybe that was a good thing. With the mess going on in her world, she didn't need another complication. And Roman was complicated. Even as they spoke, his energy curled up next to her. Twining into her own energy. Wanting to be close. To her.

Wanting to be with her though a part of him was unsure. Was it his own feelings causing that hesitancy or was he uncertain about his welcome?

That lack of clarity made her uneasy.

And the one truth she'd always believed was that energy never lied. But people did.

So, for whatever reason his mind might be stuck on his model, his heart and his energy from his heart, said he was ready for so much more.

Stefan had said it was time. When he'd told her, she didn't agree. She was still unsure. But Stefan trusted Roman. And if she trusted one thing for sure, it was Stefan. His judgment. His ethics. His understanding beyond what she knew. And that knowing she could trust him brought her some relief—she had to trust *someone*.

Besides, Stefan had inner knowledge about her supposed time for a relationship that he hadn't shared. And he wouldn't give her any more information at this point – suggesting free will and all that.

She mentally knocked on Stefan's mind – and found it locked against her. She sighed. Now what was he up to?

"Problems?"

"Stefan isn't answering," she said absently.

"And you know this how?" His extremely neutral tone of voice alerted her.

She turned to look at him. "Remember about that whole belief stuff? Well, I just knocked on Stefan's mind to see if he was home. I planned to ask him why the hell he contacted you when I'm fine."

He opened his mouth as if to speak, then shook his head and said, "Was he so wrong? Weren't you *not* fine a few moments ago? You said you woke up on the living floor. Surely that's not normal."

"He's rarely wrong. But that doesn't mean he's thinking the same way I am." She closed her eyes and mentally reached out for Stefan again. "He's still not there."

"I think, from what I understood, he couldn't be with you because he was going after someone."

"The black smoke. Right I remember now," she whispered as the memory of being smothered in dark nasty energy overwhelmed her. "I wonder if he can get the answers we need."

"Black smoke? If he can *what*?"

She didn't answer.

Roman leaned forward and placed a gentle hand under her chin and tilting it up so he could see her eyes. "Tell me."

Taking a deep breath, she broke the code of silence she'd kept all of her life. And she told him exactly what she knew about tonight.

He sat back and listened quietly. Not judging.

For that she was grateful.

She ventured a glance up at him. He was still studying her quietly. She dropped her gaze and sighed inwardly. What had she expected? Understanding? Acceptance?

She should be grateful his energy hadn't whipped back to wrap tightly around his body. Instead it stayed, shimmering up against her energy.

"You know how farfetched all this sounds?"

It was the thin thread of amusement in his voice that had her head coming up sharply.

"Oh yes," she said softly, a tiny smile playing at her lips. "I do. It must sound totally crazy."

He sat back, crossed his arms. "You mean what you say, but I hope you won't mind if I ask Stefan to confirm this?"

She laughed. "Ask away."

"Well, I'll have to call him."

"Don't bother. He's here now." And sure enough, Stefan's warm laughter flitted through her mind. "Go ahead and ask him. He'll answer."

Roman laughed, disbelieving. "Sure, but you'll be telling me what he said so that won't help any."

Oh boy. She grinned. "Do you really want to know the truth? Deep inside? Do you want to know if any of this woohoo stuff is real?"

"You're talking about proving it to me?"

"Yes." She laughed. "That's what I'm suggesting." She tilted her head. "So yes or no?"

He lifted his shoulders then dropped them. "Sure. Go for it."

Inside she laughed. *Go for it, Stefan. Let's make a believer of him. We could use a few more good guys.*

Her mind was instantly empty, no more Stefan. She sat back to watch.

Roman sat bolt upright, his face went slack, and if the color could be wiped off in a single stroke, that's what it looked like.

Shay laughed delightedly.

His head swiveled in her direction.

His jaw dropped, and when he could, he said, incredulously, "He's in my head?"

"Not really. But he is speaking to you telepathically."

Roman's gaze narrowed. "Stefan? Can't you appear in the living room or do something not so…private?"

Shay laughed. "It's amazing, isn't it?" She looked for Stefan's form to materialize. Her gaze switched from chair to chair, and then she realized that Stefan had sat down beside her. She switched over to look at Roman. He was looking around the room.

"Can you see him, Roman?" she asked curiously. "He's sitting beside me."

Roman studied the couch. "No. I can't."

"Too bad. It would provide the proof you seem to need."

"Or he could tell me something that no one else would know. That could be convincing proof," he challenged.

It was impossible not to chuckle. "Really? Like, do a reading?" She turned to face Stefan.

"Stefan? What about it?"

I feel like a circus show. There was a moment of silence, then Stefan sighed and said, *Sure. What the hell.*

ROMAN SETTLED BACK in his chair to see what would happen next. He couldn't believe what he'd felt so far. Then he felt that weird inner sense of connectedness again. He straightened.

Stefan's voice floated through his mind, warm and mocking. *This time and this time only I will be nice. I chose this method of providing proof for one reason only – that is to save Shay the embarrassment of finding out what I'm going to tell you. You want to know something personal that no one else would know, as proof I'm not a charlatan?*

"No. Actually I believe in you, but I'm not sure about this whole woowoo business. It's a little tough on the uninitiated."

He could see laughter flit across Shay's face. *Was she tuned in too?* He wanted to ask her a mess of questions but Stefan was speaking again.

No. She isn't 'tuned' in. Although I know why you'd be worried. You don't want Shay to know that she is your model. That you have been drawing her body, in intimate detail, for two years? Or how about this? The real reason you can't paint her face is because you can't face her? You feel that there is something deceitful in your creating her likeness without her permission. I also know why there is blue in your earlier paintings and just a skim of it in your later ones. But that revelation will have to wait a bit.

"Oh shit." Roman leaned back and closed his eyes. Now he was in really deep shit. "I'm sorry. What do I need to do to get out of this with my dignity?"

Apologize? I presume you're convinced by now.

"Yes. Sorry," he muttered. How had he gotten into this shit anyway?

By being you. Shay needs you. You need her. Why am I the only one that sees this?

Roman cast a wary glance at Shay, who appeared to be enjoying this. He wasn't. He didn't want to insult Stefan any more than he had already but...

I'm gone.

And just like that Roman's mind emptied, cooled. Stefan was gone. Thank God.

But would Stefan keep Roman's secret?

TABITHA FLOATED ON the peaceful clouds of the ethers. She walked here often, but normally she could return when she wanted to. She didn't understand what the problem was this time.

Something had happened. Something painful.

She wasn't what anyone would call soft or delicate, but even with her abilities, she felt vulnerable out there. She could hide in here. Not something she did well. Or often.

So why was she hiding now?

Danger.

She was in danger. So was someone else. *Who?* She tried to concentrate. To focus on the problem. But that was the problem with the ethers – real life problems weren't tangible parts of this reality. They felt distant. Unreal. Hard to care about.

And with that thought, Tabitha floated off again.

KNOCK, KNOCK...

Ah Shay.

You don't even know that I had your grandfather. That I led him away like a puppy on a leash. Now how wrong is that? I should have left a note in his pocket. Let you know that he'd been targeted.

Or maybe I should have just killed him outright.

But then you wouldn't have spent the day and evening worrying. Maybe I should visit him again in the hospital? No. I think I'll send you a more serious message. One of those other family members maybe.

Or a close friend.

Maybe, if they turn up dead, you'll get the message this time?

I have another targeted charity to take care of too. Isn't that new wing at the children's hospital completed now? I heard how much you love that project. Sounds like my next stop.

'Cause I'd like to up the stakes a little. And hitting the children's hospital sounds like maximum pain. Too bad you don't have any pets left to torture.

I'll have to pick off your friends instead.

And, of course, your family.

CHAPTER 18

S HAY SAT BACK on her plush leather couch and watched the expressions cross Roman's face. He was a strong man and taking a hit like this wouldn't be easy. It's not that Stefan would be harder on him than anyone else, but more than likely Roman had secrets, deep ones, ones he wouldn't appreciate anyone accessing. So far, she'd yet to see anything Stefan couldn't find out within a person's psyche.

Thank God she trusted Stefan implicitly or it would be incredibly unnerving to have him in her head. By asking for proof, Roman had opened himself up to a new reality. A scary one.

And that loss of innocence was tough for everyone…even traumatic for some.

She watched him blink several times.

Stefan? Isn't that enough?

I'm not in there anymore. He has a few new truths to deal with. That's all.

But you trust him? You didn't find anything in there that concerned you? That I should be concerned about?

He cares about you. He's confused about it, but there's no doubt he'd be devastated if something happened to you.

She didn't know what to say. It pretty well matched her impression. *I don't know that I want to fight a ghost.*

A ghost?

Yes, his model. If I'm in a relationship with him, I want him to be passionate about me. How can I know he's thinking about me and not her?

Humor threaded Stefan's voice as he answered, *I don't think that will be a problem. Trust him.*

Says you, she muttered.

He laughed. *I'm going to bed now.*

Wait, what about tonight? What did you find out about my attacker from this evening?

Nothing concrete. I'm going to do some research. Something odd is going on in the ethers. Not sure just what.

With that she had to be satisfied.

"Were you just talking to Stefan?" Roman asked in an odd voice. "Did he say anything to you?"

She understood his wariness and didn't pretend to misunderstand. "No he didn't share your secrets. He wouldn't. Stefan is all about principles and morals."

The relief on Roman's face made her laugh, but inside she didn't find much to laugh about. What concerned him so?

"You don't have to look so relieved," she said. "If he can see it, you can bet someone else can find out your secret."

He frowned. "That's the problem with secrets, isn't it? They can always come to light and hurt people."

Now she really had to wonder what he was hiding.

He sat down beside her. "If there's one thing Stefan's little demonstration showed me, it's that you two have a closeness I can't imagine. I might have dreamed of such a thing a long time ago, but to actually be able to communicate without speaking like you two do, well, that's impressive. And...I'm jealous. I'd love to have something similar," he admitted.

"Yes. It's comforting, reassuring, and also damn irritating at times. See, Stefan doesn't just get to see the stuff I want him to see, but he can see stuff I hadn't considered that anyone would ever know about." She shook her head, and continued, "No, I'm not talking about secrets, although he obviously could know about all those if he cared to look... I'm talking more about casual thoughts." She laughed. "For example I was looking in a store window at some women's clothing and I saw a pair of stilettos that I loved. At the same time I was thinking that they looked like hooker shoes. And I thought that I'd probably come off looking like a tart if I tried to wear them."

Her grin widened. "Stefan immediately laughed and added that he'd have said a high-priced call girl instead."

Roman's gaze widened. "So he's there all the time?"

"Not always, but we often leave the door open between us. I was involved in a bad scenario a while back, and I almost died." She swallowed hard. "Without Stefan, there's no way I'd have survived. Since then, that door between us is rarely closed. I don't always hear his thoughts, but every once in a while I'll hear and answer him the same as he did for me."

Roman grinned. "You are blessed to have him that close. Is this something I could learn?"

She looked surprised. "I imagine. Stefan mentors all kinds of people with various abilities. I don't know if you have any psychic gifts, but I'm sure he'd say you do even if you don't actively use them." And she'd seen for herself the power was there, sleeping.

"I'm not sure I'd want to ask Stefan for very much after tonight."

"Telepathic communication is very personal. But I like it. I never feel alone."

"And you used to?"

She thought about that. "Yes, I guess I did. Even with my fiancé, there was a sense of not being connected the same as I am with Stefan."

Just then her phone rang. She stared at it. Then at her clock. "It's two in the morning."

"I hope it's not Pappy." Then she snatched up the phone.

It wasn't. But it was the hospital. One of her relatives. A cousin, who she hadn't seen in years, had been admitted to the hospital. She'd had a note in her pocket to call Shay if anything happened to her.

Shay, after saying she'd be right down, hung up the phone slowly.

"Shay? What's wrong? Is it your grandfather?"

He had his own phone out, as if ready to call Gerard.

"No." She shook her head. "I don't get it." She explained what the hospital had said. "But I barely know this woman. I've had nothing to do with her for years."

He stood up, held out a hand to her, and said, "Then we'd better go down there and see what we can find out."

We? She eyed the hand he extended to her. It offered her more than help from the chair. The gesture seemed symbolic as it waited for her to respond.

Intrigued, yet wary, she placed her hand in his and let him help her up.

What bond had she just sealed?

Because that's what it felt like.

A bond, an agreement of some kind, that he had a place in her world.

Whether she was ready or not. Whether he loved another...or not.

STEFAN LAY IN his bed staring up at the ceiling. With Shay heading into a deep relationship, he had to admit to being slightly off-color himself. He had their privacy to respect as well as concerns about how her relationship with Roman, once it moved to the intimate level – and given what he'd seen of Roman's emotions, that wouldn't take long –

would change his relationship with Shay.

And Roman was holding a time bomb by holding onto his secret about his paintings. And once Shay made that connection…

There were going to be fireworks.

Only Stefan knew Shay had to work this out herself. With Roman.

Still he'd need to watch her because of other dangers he hadn't identified, though he'd try to keep their connecting door closed more from now on. Shay wasn't out of danger from her attacker. Indeed, with the undercurrents moving on the ethers, she was mixed up with something nasty.

He could only hope her doors were open to *him* when it all went to hell. It was dangerous for her to stay too focused on Roman. Someone could take advantage…She could make a mistake that could cost her life. Yet he understood Shay's lack of focus…

The emptiness he'd felt for so long was disappearing and an expectation was building. He too felt a special person would be entering his life soon, one he couldn't identify yet and didn't dare think about. As long as nothing sent their universal plan sideways. He'd long ago learned that it could do that in a heartbeat, when he least expected it.

And he didn't dare have something go wrong now. He'd waited too long for this vision to come to fruition.

And he'd waited too long for her.

It's going to happen. Soon.

Stefan groaned. He closed his eyes and just once, for just a quick moment, he reached out mentally and stroked the aura of the woman he loved.

The woman who didn't know he existed.

And then, he, Stefan the esteemed artist and psychic, felt a measure of doubt. Given his shadowy world, how could he ask anyone to share that with him?

Even as he basked in his recent connection to her aura, something dark slid across his consciousness. Something familiar. Something deadly that raised all his psychic hackles.

Early Tuesday morning…

THE HOSPITAL WAS quiet when they arrived. At least quiet on the outside. Brilliant lights lit the almost empty parking lot but the halls were dimmer than normal. Shay led the way to the emergency room, stopping to speak with the nurse at the desk.

"Good, I'm glad you made it. The police are waiting to speak with you." She smiled and led the way to the bed at the far right. "She's seen the doctor, and he's ordered a bunch of tests. But she's been unconscious since she was brought in."

"Who found her?" Shay asked, but the nurse had already walked away.

"We were going to ask you a few questions about that?" A police officer stood slightly off to one side. "I'm Detective Marsden. You're Shay Lassiter?"

Shay nodded. "That is correct." She walked over to stand at the end of her cousin's bed. She was almost ashamed to admit that she barely recognized her.

The woman who appeared to be in her early forties was tall, slim, with short dark hair and a hint of curl. Nothing about her cousin's appearance was familiar in Shay's mind. Really, she could have been a stranger off the street.

Shay could vaguely remember her, but that was it. How long had it been? Ten years? More? She wasn't even sure she knew the tenuous blood connection that linked them. After they lost their parents, she and her brother had clung to Pappy. Grandmother Isabella had been alive back then and Shay and her brother had grown up feeling loved and cherished.

After her grandmother's death, Shay had become even closer to her grandfather. The cousins had been there in the distance. But as Pappy hadn't been close to Grandmother's family, Shay hadn't become close to them either.

Right. Now she remembered the woman. Marie Short. Marie's grandmother was the older sister of Shay's deceased grandmother.

"You know this woman?" asked the Detective Marsden. He consulted his notebook. "Marie Short?"

She frowned at him. How did one answer that question? She didn't really know her, but she knew of her. Then she realized that Roman stood close to her side, his arm around her shoulder, to offer comfort and support should it be needed. A nice gesture, but not necessary.

"She's a distant cousin."

"Distant? How distant?"

Shay explained the relationship. "In fact, I'm not sure I've seen her in the last decade."

"Have you had any contact with her? Phone calls, emails?"

Shay shook her head. "No. Nothing." She frowned again. "I don't understand what's going on."

"This was clutched in her fist." The detective held out a small plastic bag with a scrap of ivory paper inside.

Shay reached for it and read it aloud. "If anything happens to me, call Shay Lassiter. She'll understand." She turned to stare at the unconscious woman. "I have no idea what this means." She wagged the bag in the air. "I hardly know this woman."

The detective studied her face carefully. Then he took back the evidence. "Well, if you come up with anything to explain this, please let me know."

He'd almost gotten out of sight when it hit her. She spun around and raced after him, Roman on her heels.

"Wait, Detective Marsden."

He turned around. "Did you think of something?"

"I don't know. It's just there's another odd issue going on right now, and I'm afraid that the two odd incidences make a coincidence, and I don't—"

"Believe in those," the detective finished for her. "Neither do I. So tell me what's going on."

Wincing, Shay said, "You're probably better off calling Detective Chandler." She rubbed two fingers against her temple. "But I'll give you a quick rundown." And she did, and then she checked her watch. "So much for sleep tonight."

"I suggest you head home and grab a few hours." He handed her his phone number. "I'll catch up with Detective Chandler, and if you think of anything else, call me."

She watched him walk away, slowly becoming more aware of the ever quiet Roman at her side.

"You didn't tell him about tonight?" he asked in a neutral tone.

She glanced up at him. "How can I?" she asked simply. "Look how much trouble we had convincing you?"

"Good point." Roman glanced back toward the hospital bed. "Do you want to stay with your cousin?"

"Want to? No…but I will, just for a moment." She made her way back through the quiet hall to where her cousin, Marie, slept. Taking a look at her aura, Shay studied the energy flow from the woman's chakras. Dark purple and a deep red swirled in a tempest through several of the chakras. Backing out from the chakras, she studied her cousin's aura, realizing it lay close to her cousin's body, snug, as if unable to loosen up and flow normally. Shay narrowed her eyes and looked for a cause.

It was almost as if her cousin's energy was being restrained…only there was nothing holding her there now. But there could have been earlier. But to hold that kind of grip on the aura and to have it continue long after the restraints were gone... And who or what had constrained her?

She stepped closer, and after a quick look to make sure she was alone with Roman, she reached out with both hands and stroked the surface of her cousin's aura, moving the darkness away and adding in her own, lighter energy. Then she stroked up towards Marie's head, removing the stress that had cramped her aura, easing the stiffness and the tension holding it tightly in place.

Taking her time, Shay eased the other woman's fear, a palpable emotion Shay felt the same way. She didn't know what had scared Marie so much, but something had to have made her retreat so deep inside. As she kept her auric energy in tightly, she'd also gone inside mentally.

To protect herself.

That was it. Her cousin wasn't unconscious. She was in hiding.

Shay needed Stefan's help.

Damn. She called for him. No answer. Given the time, chances were he was asleep and wouldn't appreciate being woken up. Right now, it didn't matter. They needed to bring this woman out of her self-imposed cage and find out who'd done this to her.

She called Stefan again, louder. Stronger.

Stop yelling. I'm here.

Shay explained the situation.

Stefan immediately kicked awake. *Let me take a look. See if I can find her in there.*

Good. Her energy is very low. Dangerously low. I think her consciousness is hiding.

It probably is, Stefan agreed.

And he disappeared.

STEFAN SHIFTED AND landed his consciousness beside Shay at the hospital. The disembodied world he walked made it hard for others to detect him. Even those that walked between realities like he did. Shay could see him if she'd looked but she didn't take her eyes off the unconscious woman in bed. *Shay.*

She turned toward him and grinned. "Hey," she said.

He smiled, loving her easy acceptance and lack of questions. Then he jumped into her cousin's mind. Silence enveloped him. Normally, in a quiet mind there was still a distant chatter in the background, but here there was nothing. A muted silence, like something pressing down…putting a buffer between this world and her thoughts. Like cotton wadding plugged in between her and whatever she was hiding from.

Shay had a similar sensation when she'd been attacked by Darren. She'd experienced an odd sense of not caring what happened to her. But this wasn't Darren.

He dug deeper. So odd. It's like there was nothing but emptiness. A blackness devoid of all thought. How could that be?

He wandered around, looking for a weakness, a way through the blackness to something else.

The more he pushed or tried to weasel through, the thicker it became. Cloying and stale, the denseness pressed in on him. How could *nothing* have weight? Then he understood. The black energy wasn't hers.

Someone was in her mind. Except there was no sense of a life force. The energy felt dead…or deadened, maybe. As if there was nothing vital or alive left in it. There was a distancing as if life wasn't prized enough to care about.

He spun around and realized the dark energy had been stuffed into this woman's mind. Filling it, making it seem like it was hers. Leaving no space for Marie. Almost suffocating her.

How interesting. The scientist, the student, in him was fascinated.

He'd been in other people's minds and he'd seen other energies with similar capabilities. And some with their own twisted variations. Still he hadn't quite seen *this* before.

Was this woman's mind still connected to her body or was she brain dead – and not in the sense doctors meant when they said something was dead. In this case, it appeared as if the woman's body was still alive and the brain functioning, but the consciousness had been sucked out. Shay's cousin was alive – but also dead.

He'd laugh if it wasn't so serious. This was stuff from zombie movies. He had to try and save her if he could. If not…then he needed her shell to die before someone else tried to take it over.

With his goal in mind he reached out, calling for her. *Marie?*

No answer. Not that he'd expected any. He searched the space, walking blindly forward, calling out for the woman. For a flicker of life.

Nothing.

How could he find the person who belonged here?

By tracking the person that didn't.

CHAPTER 19

S HAY STUDIED THE patterns of Marie's energy as her cousin lay unconscious. There was so little of her energy, it scared her. Not only was her aura snugged up tight, but the chakras appeared sluggish and seemed to be losing their ability to circulate energy – as if she were dying. But what had caused this?

The doctors said her cousin had no physical injuries. None that modern medicine could see, at least.

Psychic attacks chilled her to the bone. Her experience with Darren had been bad enough, but to think there could be others… The psychic conflagration in her apartment that had engulfed her ghost cat, Morris, caused a heartache she still had to deal with. The cat had been dead for a long time, but she'd so enjoyed his spirit. He'd always put a smile on her face. And she missed him dearly.

A disruption at Marie's crown chakra caught her attention. The crown chakra, the connection to the universe, or the connection to what lay beyond, held what some people referred to as a bank account of grace – goodness to draw on in need. It always fascinated her.

In Marie's case, it was empty, running on a deficit.

This was beyond odd.

And the heart chakra had a faint glow, an otherworldliness to it.

Not good.

Shay chewed nervously on her bottom lip. This felt too close to the edge. Shay opened her own heart chakra and poured energy into Marie's first chakra.

Stefan, hurry up. Shay hurried to the bedside. She reached out and caught Marie's hand. "Hold on Marie. Please, hold on."

Stefan! I think she's dying. Hurry.

Shay closed her eyes and sent warm, loving energy into the struggling heart chakra. But the energy swirled helplessly in place.

"Shay? What's the matter?" Roman came up on the other side of her, his arm wrapping around her shoulders. "The nurse said she was going to be okay."

She looked at him, sadness in her voice, "The nurse was wrong. Marie is almost gone. I don't think Stefan can even stop it."

"Stefan." Astonishment laced Roman's voice. "What's he doing here?"

"Helping me. We were trying to figure out what happened to her and how what's happened could be connected to me." She waved a hand at her cousin. "Then this…change, this lack of life presented. I can't explain it," she whispered. "I think it's too late."

STEFAN FOCUSED ON the black energy trying to absorb it into his psyche. There was a familiarity to this energy. He looked for the energy signature. But the energy was old, the signature dissipated, or he'd have seen it at the beginning.

And that damned energy still felt wrong. As if it wasn't real energy.

Shit. Stefan spun around in amazement.

It wasn't real energy in here. It was the *illusion* of energy.

With that understanding, the illusion faded from his psyche, and he could see the poor woman's mind.

Even as he watched, he saw the silver cord, barely attached at the body, start to separate.

No!

He jumped forward, frantically wrapping the cord in warm, healing energy. For several moments, he worked, calling out.

Stop. Don't leave. We can help you. It's not too late. He poured energy into her mind, into her aura, into her cord.

And all for naught.

He couldn't hold onto the cord.

It separated in his grasp. Hovered briefly and slipped free.

Stefan stood, shocked, scared, and silent, in the empty shell where Shay's cousin had once lived.

SHE PICKED UP Marie's hand and held it close to her chest.

Stefan's exhausted voice slid into her mind, tinged with frustration and overwhelmed with sadness. *Shay, I lost her.*

I know. Shay looked over at Roman, fat tears running down her cheeks. "She's gone."

He looked at her in surprise, and then moved to the other side of the bed and checked for a pulse.

His gaze, when it met hers, was black and lost.

"How? I don't understand. She doesn't have any sign of injury."

"No," Shay whispered. "She died from a psychic attack." And she knew, even as she said it, that this would be hard for Roman to take in. Hell, she was still struggling with what happened.

"Is this related to the attack on you earlier tonight? That I came racing to your apartment for?" he asked in a hard voice.

She bowed her head. "I don't know, but I'm afraid it could be."

"Does Stefan know?" Anger and fear had him striding toward her. He reached out and shook her shoulders gently. "Ask him."

With a nod, she did as he requested.

I can't be sure because I can't get a handle on the energy signature. But...I think it is.

"Stefan says, quite possibly but there's no way to be certain."

And that scared her shitless.

"Well you won't be alone again until this asshole is caught." His voice hardened. "I'll be bunking at your place for now. I may not be Stefan but at least I can watch over you. Call Stefan if you need help."

She studied him. She wasn't averse to having company until this was over. It's one thing to fight an attacker in the flesh. It was quite another to fight one you couldn't see.

And Roman had no idea how bizarre these attacks could get.

But neither did he know how to fight them either.

ONCE STEFAN WAS back in bed, he opened his eyes to stare at the ceiling. He'd seen a lot of death. He'd seen people before death, after, even during the process. He'd yet to see this sad, lingering, letting go. As if life wasn't precious enough to fight for or to believe in.

Stefan had seen suicidal people who cared more than Marie had. Often a suicidal person changed their mind when it was too late. Marie didn't seem to care either way. He didn't understand it. Had that other energy put thoughts of despair in her head, been so pervasive that Marie felt she had no choice but to let go? As if only darkness remained for her if she stayed.

Shay had experienced something similar a year ago. With Darren. He thought about that. What would be required to do that?

He couldn't fathom the answer. As someone who walked on both sides of the veil between life and death, he'd yet to see this. It bothered him. If they had a new type of predator, he needed to know.

He'd done his best, but sometimes unforeseen things…happened. Like now.

He didn't want to think that an old adversary could have survived, but what if he had?

He'd spoken with a psychic friend who'd been locked in the ice palace in her mind. She'd told him the longer she was there the more she wallowed, just didn't care.

But the energy inside this poor woman's mind had such a different feel. Like she had no thoughts whatsoever. And it had all been an illusion that disappeared when that realization took hold.

Stefan let out a sigh of relief. So it didn't sound like Darren after all. Thank heavens for that.

And this energy only seemed to dissipate because it was old. He thought about that difference for a moment longer. It appeared his attacker could mask energy. Their own, and that of others, so they hide their identity within another person. And that person could look normal to everyone, but on the inside, this psychic controlled the other person without the awareness of the other person. Sounds like another asshole who needed to be eliminated.

Oh, if only the ones that died…would stay dead."

KNOCK, KNOCK…

Yup me again. Shay, you still don't get it, do you?

I heard you went to the hospital to see your long-lost cousin. Why though? She didn't even remember you. And I asked her long and hard.

Too bad. All that and still she wasn't much help.

Of course, I'd hoped for a closer connection between the two of you. But it wasn't to be.

I guess I'll have to go back to your grandfather after all. He is all alone in the hospital…

Easy.

Maybe too easy.

I could go after some of your best friends first.

Oh, but maybe you don't have any.

Bernice is dead. That wasn't much fun either. And in no way did it have the intended impact. I wanted you devastated. She was a surrogate mother to you. You should have been hurt by her passing. Instead all you did was gain from it. Maybe you even wanted the old bag to die so you'd get her money.

And your friend Tabitha is dead, but that caused hardly a ripple in your world. Sigh.

I was hoping to toy with you. But this is damn boring.

Isn't there anyone else in your life who you care about?

God you live like a nun.

With all that money, too.

What a waste.

That's all right. I'll see what I can do about relieving you of some of that money.

Then I'll take care of you.

Tuesday morning…dawn

SHAY? CALL RONIN. *He doesn't want to wake you.*

Sleepily, Shay blinked several times, trying to sort out Stefan's whisper through her mind. And adjust to her surroundings. She was home in her own bed. But she'd only been there for a few hours. *Damn.* She glanced beside her. Alone. *Double damn.*

Focus. This is important. It's about Darren. You don't have a problem calling Ronin, do you?

No.

Now she was awake. Talk about a subject guaranteed to keep sweet dreams a long way away.

She reached for her phone. *Stefan, do you know what's going on?*

Yes. But not all of it. I asked Ronin to search out more family members of Darren's. Just in case there is someone else with the ability to do what he did.

And of course family members have the closest chance. She held the phone up to her ear, her heart pounding nervously in her chest. Darren had told her that he had no family. But then he'd lied about everything else, so…

"Shay. Glad you called." Ronin sounded too perky for this time at night.

While Shay listened, trying to shake the sleepy cobwebs from her mind, Ronin gave it to her, short and succinct. There was nothing sweet about it.

"*He had a twin?* A twin brother?" Shay shook her head, slumping back against her headboard. "Not possible."

"Not only possible, but definite, at least according to his foster care history. The brother's name is Danny."

She didn't know what to say. "Wait – did Darren even know him?"

"It's hard to say. We're looking for him right now. But there's no proof to say they'd actually hooked up."

"So it could be that the twin wasn't in contact with Darren or even know that Darren existed?"

"Absolutely. Both were in dozens of foster homes before they hit fourteen. Darren ran away several times and ended back in the system and the inevitable round of homes. His brother Danny ran away at seventeen and dropped out of sight. We're investigating the possibility that the brothers found each other...somehow...but I don't know how."

Their abilities would have drawn them together, Stefan murmured. *They wouldn't have been able to resist the pull of another like themselves.*

"But he's alive?"

"No reason to believe he isn't. Like I said, we're looking for him."

Stefan's thoughts whispered through her mind again. *Make sure he lets you know as soon as he finds out.*

"Thanks Ronin. Please keep me in the loop. Oh, and did you ever go through the personnel files I gave you?"

"First thing. They both check out, so do the staff at Folgrent Foundation. No worries there. And I'll call if I find out anything."

She hung up the phone slowly. "Damn it, Darren. When will you leave me in peace?"

Soon. Stefan murmured comfortingly in her head.

I hope so.

"Darren? Your ex-fiancé? What's going on, Shay?"

Oh shit.

Yeah, that's my call to leave. With a chuckle, Stefan disappeared.

She glanced at her doorway. And gave a start. Roman, bare-chested and looking lethal as hell, slouched against the entrance to her room, his hands shoved into jeans riding dangerous low. She swallowed. Just now realizing how little clothing she had on herself. A white cotton cami and matching boy panties.

She'd forgotten he was sleeping in her spare room.

How had the temperature in the room risen so quickly?

This man was dangerous – in so many ways.

Taking a deep breath, she tried to collect her thoughts and said, "That was Ronin. Apparently Darren had a twin brother."

Those dark eyes burned with a fire inside. "And you are thinking this twin had something to do with these attacks?"

She nodded warily, took a deep breath and explained what Darren had done. "Ronin is trying to find him now."

He'd straightened at her explanation but had let her get it out. He sauntered a few steps closer, his gaze holding hers so tightly she could barely breathe.

The room seemed hotter with his every step closer. She had a dozen reasons why she needed him to leave. Why she needed sleep tonight. Although to be honest, the night was mostly done. But now, all thoughts of sleep fled. And they were replaced with thoughts of being with him in bed.

Even as the dangers registered, her skin warmed, her nipples tightened, and she struggled to take her eyes off him.

She didn't think she was ready for this. But her body was screaming for him. It had been a year. A long, lonely year of sleeping alone, of never being held, hugged or touched with caring. Without love.

Dare she trust Roman? Dare she trust her own emotions? Her own body? She'd been so wrong before. She couldn't stand to be wrong again.

Roman sat down on the bed beside her.

"Does Darren have anything to with *this?*" His voice flowed over her like liquid heat.

She swallowed. *This?* "No, he has nothing to do with anything, including us."

"And he's gone from your heart and mind?"

"Heart, definitely. That happened a long time ago. From my mind?" She'd answer if she could think straight, but his nearness and intensity were doing things to her insides along with that blatant look that said he wanted her any way he could get her.

And damn it if she didn't want him too.

"Yes," she said simply.

"Good."

In a last-ditch effort to find some measure of control, she summoned up the courage to challenge him. "And your model? Is she an issue here?"

Her gaze locked on his lips. He smiled, a slow, long movement that made her heart race. Mentally, she could barely function at all.

"She was never an issue. She's an important part of my life. Then, so are you."

"So you aren't lovers?"

Dark secrets lit the depths of his gaze. Still, for all that she saw and all that she could sense, there wasn't anything malicious in him. Stefan would have warned her if there had been. Roman was entitled to his privacy. God knew she needed hers too.

"No. We've never been lovers."

And his energy wasn't lying. Streaks of gold slid toward her, reached for her. Waited for her. She hesitated, searching to maintain her sanity. Then she realized some of those waves of color were coming from his heart chakra. This wasn't just lust or a need to be slaked. It was obvious this was more. So much more.

He wanted *her*.

Relief blossomed inside. She smiled.

She didn't know how much she wanted him either, but maybe, just maybe, they could give it a try and find out.

ROMAN WATCHED HER awareness of him grow, and along with that, the unmistakable bloom of sexual longing in her gaze. He saw the almost imperceptible shiver whispering across her skin as she gazed at him. Good. He'd better not be the only one going crazy in this relationship. Despite the words of caution she wanted him too…yet he felt like he had to move slowly. As if any sudden move could have her changing her mind. And then she'd bolt.

With wide eyes, she stared at him. He glanced over her – enough to realize she wore only a thin cami – make that a transparent cami – and forced himself to look away.

He'd wanted her for such a long time. Too long. He didn't want just one night. He needed more.

He didn't know how much more, but if he could get her to take this step with him, they'd both find out.

Passion shimmered through his body. Lust heated his loins and fired his gaze. He tried to pull back and like a doe trembling in the headlights, she waited for his next move.

He leaned forward and gently stroked her plump lower lip. Her mouth opened, her tongue slipped out and stroked the pad on his finger. He stopped, then leaned forward and gently placed his lips against hers.

She didn't withdraw, nor did she throw her arms around him. She waited, tasting, testing the feel of him against her skin. So honest. So captivating. So sexy.

Just that bit of experimenting, that willingness to give this a try, sent shivers down his spine. God, he wanted her. He deepened the kiss.

She stiffened slightly, and then relaxed.

He withdrew slightly and she whimpered so he tugged her into his arms and kissed her as he'd been wanting to kiss her since forever.

CHAPTER 20

S HAY LOST HERSELF in his heat. It warmed her from the inside as he surrounded her with his caring.

She'd forgotten the joy of being in a relationship. For all her time with Darren, she'd never experienced this specialness, this sense of being a part of a private twosome. Or realized how much being held mattered.

Only now. Only with Roman.

Her lips parted under his assault and she couldn't think.

There was something important happening here, but somehow even finding out what that was didn't matter. At the moment, it seemed that nothing else would ever matter again – except that he never let her go.

She closed her eyes and let the tidal wave carry her off. And gave herself over to his care. She wrapped her arms around his neck and sighed sweetly. She wanted this. Wanted him.

He didn't disappoint. Holding her gently, carefully, as if she was delicate china, he deepened the kiss and held her captive in his embrace until she sagged into his arms, unable to think. Only feeling. And that was what she needed. What they both needed. To be together, just the two of them.

He lifted his head and held her close. "I've been waiting for this." He dropped tiny kisses along her cheek to her ear. "I've needed this…" He whispered into her ear, sending shivers down her spine. "For so long."

She turned her head, her hands moving to hold him so she could recapture those wandering lips with her own. She kissed him long and hard.

Pulling back slightly she said, "So have I." She smiled. "So how about a little less talk and a little more action?"

He froze, momentarily. She'd caught him off guard. He'd been gentle and caring and considerate. Worried about her. But as well as that she wanted his passionate heat and to experience his real need, to experience his passion.

And match it with her own.

A glint of lust glowed deep in his blue eyes. "Your wish is my command." And he lowered his head, taking her on a glorious ride of abandonment. Her cami disappeared under his expert actions. Her panties were tossed to one side. Before she really understood what was happening to her, she lay completely naked in front of him.

Instead of feeling embarrassed or uncomfortable, she felt sexy and desired. The blatant appreciation in his eyes raised her temperature even more, but she hated that he still had clothes on.

But she could take care of that.

She scrambled to her knees and moved his fingers away from his belt. With his hands out of the way, she quickly opened his belt and the top button of his jeans, unzipping the fly just enough to thrust her fingers inside.

"Jesus," he roared, grabbing for her hands. "Slowly. We don't want this over with before it's even begun."

She laughed.

He grinned, and raised her arms above her head and pushed her gently backwards. She stretched sinuously up, her breasts stroking against his bare chest. He groaned and lowered his weight to rest gently on her.

Heat raced across her chest as skin burned against skin.

Wanting the freedom to touch him, she twisted beneath him, trying to free her hands.

"Oh, no. Not so fast." He shifted up onto his knees. Holding both of her wrists in one hand, he awkwardly pulled off his remaining clothes.

She laughed. "It would be so much easier if you let me do that."

But he was already done. He released her hands and shifted so he straddled her lower legs, pinning her in place. Then slowly he stroked up her body. She murmured and shifted under his expert touch as he caressed her, feeding the heat building between.

She wanted, no, needed to touch him as he was touching her. She sat up in a smooth movement and wrapped her arms around him. With her face against his neck, their bodies were flush with each other's, his erection captured between them. Slowly, smoothly, she slid to one side, then just as slowly back to the other. Letting her hardened nipples stroke across his chest, she tilted her head and nipped at his chin.

He lowered his face, and she kissed the corner of his mouth, his lips, and then kissed him – hard.

He responded with deep, drugging kisses, and she reacted mindlessly, helplessly. Going where he led and happy to follow. When he pulled her up and reversed positions, she barely noticed. Except for the sheer expanse of male in front of her, available to her.

She straddled his body, her core perfectly positioned to rest on his hips. She reached down to grasp him in her hand. His groans were music to her ears as she caressed and stroked, squeezed and teased – it was his turn to thrash on the bed.

He reached up to pull her down, but she resisted. Changing her position slightly, she rose up high enough to take him inside. Slowly, very slowly, she sank down until he was fully sheathed within. She gasped and stilled, feeling the sensation of fullness. She let her body adjust while he lay shuddering in place.

She leaned over and smoothly lifted off. He opened his eyes and she sank back down. He shuddered.

She did it again, and again, settling into a smooth ride. He grasped her hips, his fingers digging into her soft flesh, and he rose up beneath her. Together they set a slow pace that quickly drove them forward. She cried out, her back arching as the tremors started deep inside and spread throughout her body.

He groaned and bucked desperately beneath her. Then he arched, the cords of his arms taut, as he held her locked in place. She sagged as he collapsed down on the bed.

Then he tugged her forward into his arms, crushing her up against his chest, his heart.

Exactly where she wanted to be.

ROMAN ROLLED OVER, tucking her up close against his side. To say she'd rocked his world would be to minimize this experience of a lifetime. He had no idea it could be like that between them.

And though she'd dominated his dreams for years the reality of her, of them like this, was so much better.

He dropped a tender kiss on the tip of her nose. His artistic eye caught, and then memorized, the tiny details. The small bump on the long, patrician nose. The full definition of her lips. Her eyes. How did he paint that stormy brown with gold flecks?

He tightened his grip on her, wishing he could slip her inside his soul and keep her there. Never to be separated.

She murmured softly.

He loosened his grip. "Sorry," he whispered against her temple.

"Sleep. You need to catch a few hours."

"Need more than a few," she answered softly. "But I'll take what I can get."

Reaching for the crumpled bedding, Roman tugged it up and over them both. Settling deeper into the center of the bed, he held her close as she drifted off to sleep.

He knew that somehow he had to share his secret. He should have done so before this. But he hadn't quite foreseen their relationship coming to this stage so quickly.

Not that he had any regrets. He'd have to hope she'd understand when the time came.

That she asked about his relationship with his model was both amusing and touching. That she might feel the fool after she found out, could be an issue.

He hoped not because finally one of his dreams had come true.

Now he had to work on making the rest happen.

He knew one thing for sure. Now that he'd gotten her this far, he was never letting her go.

Tuesday morning…

SHAY WOKE FEELING surprisingly rested, considering the late night. She went to sit up and realized Roman's arm held her in place. She smiled and tried to wiggle out from underneath.

He grumbled, his voice deep, and yet gentle in her ear. She studied his shadowed face, realizing she had nothing in the apartment that he could shave with. Too bad.

Then again, she kinda liked the shadow. Stretching up, she dropped a gentle kiss on the dimple in his chin. As he shifted in his sleep, she slipped out from under his arm and escaped to the bathroom. Once done, she grabbed a silk housecoat from behind her door and, knotting the belt, walked to the kitchen to put on coffee.

She needed a shower. Glancing at the kitchen clock, she realized the memorial service for Robert Dander was in an hour. As much as she'd come to hate funerals, she felt obligated to go. And maybe she could learn something.

Lost in her thoughts, she didn't hear Roman get up.

"Do you mind if I take a shower?"

She spun around. He stood in the doorway, bare except for softly hugging cotton boxers. Mutely, she shook her head.

He grinned, and said, "Join me?" He disappeared from view before she had a chance to answer. But not before she saw his sculpted butt disappear. She sighed. He had a really great ass.

I so didn't need to know that. Stefan's sardonic voice whispered through her mind.

She gasped, and then broke out laughing. *Sorry, Stefan.*

She gently closed the door in her mind and raced after Roman, still grinning. She couldn't get there fast enough. He'd just stepped under the hot spray when she dropped the housecoat and opened the glass door.

"Don't mind if I do," she murmured, holding up a bar of soap.

His happy gaze widened to delight when her bar of soap stroked down his front and over the hard length of him. He groaned as her fingers slipped over his shaft. "Like that, do you?" She smiled, her hand movements sensuous but teasing.

"Witch," he said thickly. In one smooth movement, he turned, lifted her, and pinned her to the wall. With his hard length poised at the heart of her, he said, "Two can play that game."

She laughed and then groaned as he slid deep inside. Hard and fast he pounded into her as the shower water pounded down on them. She cried out. Secured against the wall she couldn't move. She could only hang on as he rode her to the edge, then drove them both over.

She hung suspended against the wall, floating free in mind and spirit. Then she gently floated back to reality.

"Damn, you're good."

He laughed. "Glad you think so. Now I think we both need to finish this shower before we run out of hot water."

Tuesday, later that morning...

THE FUNERAL FOR Robert was bigger than David's. That made it easier to blend into the crowd but harder to sort through the energy of all those attending. Robert had been the headmaster of Chadworth School for over three decades. He'd interacted with the parents and students and the children of his students. It was a sign of the impact he'd left on the community to have such a crowd.

With Roman at her side – she'd been surprised at his insistence to attend – Shay tried to get an overall impression of the energy flowing through the crowd. There was a lot of it. Streams twisted and churned from person to person.

The crowd swelled as more and more people arrived.

When the memorial service was over, the crowd broke up and some moved on to the gravesite. The family was seated up close and the rest stood in a surrounding circle. Lisa Dander stood head bowed, shoulders shaking and surrounded by her loving family. And there was much love here.

There was also many other emotions. She could see the family strife, the arguments between siblings, the worry over money, and fear that there wouldn't be any inheritance coming to various members. Astonishing how much of the world revolved around who had what and how they were going to get more of what they wanted. What didn't surprise her after so long was how most of the people spent time wondering how to get what they wanted from other people.

The man on her left wanted a raise from his boss. The woman directly in front of her was hoping for a small inheritance – she wanted more, but figured she might be good to receive a little something. The two kids, forced to attend, were wanting fast food as soon as they were done, and indeed that had been the bargain struck for their good behavior here.

She almost snorted aloud. So typical. Still, nothing that she could see indicated anything untoward. If her attacker was here, she had no way to know who it was, if they were hiding or what they wanted.

Again, all for nothing.

As they retreated to the parking lot she caught it.

Just a hint.

The same energy she'd come across in Marie's mind. And from David's office. Her apartment.

How? More importantly, who? She stood on tiptoe, searching the wandering group. The energy drifted off to the left. Without a thought, she bolted in that direction.

ROMAN STARTED AS Shay bolted. He turned to see her running, not walking fast, but racing as if she were being chased. And no one was chasing her. Or even appeared to notice her. Yet in a world of slow and somber she was a darting oddity.

And hell, she was almost out of sight. He took off after her.

He couldn't see anything that would cause her wild dash. And was especially concerned because she'd taken off without saying anything to him. She was moving fast.

He picked up the pace as she went around a tree. He didn't dare lose sight of her. By the time he reached the spot where she'd disappeared, he realized he'd taken too long. She was nowhere to be found. *Damn it, Shay. Where the hell are you?*

She had to be close. He ran several feet forward, glancing from side to side. Turning around, he kept on the move, searching the way they'd come.

Shit. He stopped. Changed direction and searched again.

"Shay?"

No answer. He kept calling for her.

Damn it. He pulled out his phone and called her. The phone rang and rang. She'd probably muted the ring so as to not disturb anyone at the ceremony. He put the phone away.

Now he was getting worried. With a keen eye to the parking lot, which appeared more empty than full now, his mind raced over possibilities. Could she have gotten into a car with someone? Surely, not without him noticing. And not without telling him. Not willingly at least. And not that fast.

His mind balked at the idea she'd left without him. That wasn't her style. He frowned. She had to be here somewhere.

He retraced his steps slowly. Back at the trees where he first lost sight of her, he stopped and slowly assessed the area. She hadn't had but a minute to move away. The area was treed, but he'd have seen her if she'd still been pursuing something. So she had to be close by, out of sight.

There were only trees for cover. He walked, circling each one to make sure she wasn't lying beneath the boughs.

He didn't want to contemplate why or how she'd be in such a position.

At the next patch, just beside the first, was a low-lying spruce tree with heavy, arching branches. He pulled the branches aside, feeling like an idiot. Unable to stop himself, he searched underneath—

And caught sight of something on the other side. He hurried to the far side, lifted up the branches and found Shay lying underneath. He dropped to his knees.

He placed his fingers against her throat, and felt for a pulse. His breath whooshed out with relief when he felt the slow steady beat of her heart.

She was alive.

But what the hell happened? Anger stirred inside. She might have collapsed for some unknown reason, but she wouldn't have rolled under here on her own. More likely she caught sight of someone, ran after them, was knocked unconscious and then was dumped under the closest cover.

He did a quick check to make sure there were no obvious signs of injury before sitting back on his heels. No blood, no breaks, nothing to show she'd been attacked.

Then again, with what he'd learned from her and Stefan, attacks could happen in other ways. And those could be deadly.

He pulled out his phone and contacted Stefan.

"Stefan, I need help." He explained the situation, finishing with, "I don't know if I should move her. Do I call 911?"

"Don't move her. I'll call you right back."

Roman stared at the dead phone. What was going on? He studied Shay's prone form then leaned closer for another look. Something was shifting. He just didn't quite understand what. It was as if her form became less defined. Like he needed to put glasses on to see her better. The air fairly crackled, adding to the weird effect.

The hairs rose on the back of his neck.

Damn he wanted her awake. To know she was fine...

Then he planned to rip into her. Give her hell for taking off the way she did.

Even as he sat there, hoping no one would notice him hunched over her, she stirred.

He breathed a sigh of relief. He wanted to haul her into his arms, and at the same time, he was afraid to touch her. Something about doing so felt wrong. But damn. Should he take the risk? Would it hurt her?

It would make *him* feel much better. So would calling his brother...

Updating Ronin took only a moment. That his brother was more in tune with this stuff pissed Roman off. He hated to think all this had been going on around him and he hadn't known anything about it, for his whole life. It just made him all that more aware of how much he had to catch up on. And he would.

It also made him realize how little he really understood about security. Sure, he'd checked Shay's website completely, set up a security system that would make the computer very hard to access, and he had installers coming to tighten up security on Shay's apartment... But what good was any of that without a way to keep her safe from the dangers they couldn't see?

The damn twin was still at large, and they both hated the latest in developments.

Ronin rang off, saying, "Whatever you do, don't touch her. Apparently that's really bad for her."

Roman glared at the phone, then down at Shay. *Damn.* He'd already done that when he'd checked her over to make sure she wasn't injured. His phone rang. *Stefan this time.* Why didn't he use telepathy at moments like this? Shrugging, he answered.

"I burn through more energy using telepathy. I'm working on Shay. She should come around in a few moments. I can't have you disturbing her."

"That's why you called...?" he said. "To make sure I don't touch her?"

"You were thinking it. I'm holding you back and can't afford the energy drain. So leave us for a few moments."

"When do I know to call for help?"

Stefan's voice was hard and dry. "You'll know." And he hung up.

Roman had to be satisfied with that. He dropped the bough to hide Shay's form once again and then stood up. He checked to make sure no one was watching.

Whoever had attacked Shay had taken the time to hide her. Roman would have found her a good five minutes earlier if they hadn't. As it was, those five minutes were enough for the attacker to get away.

CHAPTER 21

S HAY WALKED ALONE in the darkness. She didn't know why she was here. She could talk and think, but nothing made any sense. She even wondered if she might be injured and lost in her consciousness. Perhaps she was in a coma.

She tried to see into her memories. Tried to remember the last thing she'd done.

Her past was blank. That bothered her.

There should be something there. People. Scenes. Sounds. Actions on her part. Things she'd done. Plans, hopes, wishes, dreams.

The complete absence of all was the worst.

She felt alone in a way she didn't recognize. Like something important, something she'd just found, was missing.

She turned around, hating the blackness. Where was the light? Where was the natural light of day? There was no change in the depth of the blackness.

She wandered around in a circle. With nothing to ground her in place, she had a hard time seeing where she was. Fearing that she was losing her mind, she sat down and pulled her knees up to her chest. With her forehead resting on her knees she rocked gently in place.

Maybe if she sat quietly and waited, someone would come.

Shay.

Her head came up. She twisted, searching through the darkness. *Hello?*

Shay? Are you there?

Yes, she shouted. *I'm over here.*

Keep talking. This energy is so thick it's hard to see through.

She laughed. *I know. That's why I stopped moving. I'm sitting in one place hoping someone will find me.*

I'm here. Stefan showed up, a big grin on his face.

She stood up and threw her arms around him.

Except he was only energy. She gasped, and then laughed for joy.

I'd forgotten. Everything. My memories were all gone. But this... Now that I see you. Hear you. I remember you. Remember this.

Good. I'd hate to have to go through an explanation. You're a little too far advanced to catch you up on your past in a matter of seconds. We don't have much time.

As long as you are here to help me escape, I'm game.

He chuckled. *There's no need for you to escape. You're home. You need to kick your visitor out.*

She straightened. *Say what?*

Remember...black energy. Your cousin Marie and the blackness inside her. The dark feeling inside? His voice darkened. *That same energy is here. I can sense it. It's a mask hiding your feelings, your memories...*

Really? Then how do I get rid of it?

First step is realization. Second step is to stop being a victim. Get angry. See the energy for what it is. An attacker. You can get free of this by reasserting who you are.

She blinked. Why was it so hard to understand what he was saying? But it was. His suggestions seemed to come from a distance. The information was out of her grasp. Even though she heard the words, they didn't compute.

They should. She wasn't stupid. According to Stefan, she was extremely capable in...whatever this stuff was. That meant something was stopping her from seeing it. Realizing it.

Something – or someone.

And that realization brought her that much closer to clarity. She was a victim here. And victim mentality was fear-based. She couldn't seat herself in fear. It made it impossible to fight back. Victims reacted. She had to act, not react.

As she went over these things, the blackness was shoved a little further back.

Now warm your inner light. Burn fiercely... brightly... from the inside. Where there is light, there can be no darkness.

Right.

Lightness. Love. Always the answer to the darkness. The negativity and the blackness that surrounded anyone. And everyone. She knew that. Somehow. And if she knew that much...

She closed her eyes, searching for the light. There was so much emptiness inside. But that couldn't be right. She wasn't empty. She was full of life and love and laughter. Sure, there would be pain inside, but she lived in the world of joy. Only she couldn't remember what she did for a living. If she did anything. She knew that she did something that helped others. Somehow.

Money. That's right. She helped others with money. The Foundation!

The darkness retreated a little more again.

And with memories of the Foundation came Bernice. Pappy. Roman. She smiled and her life came back in focus.

Memories flooded back. The blackness dissipated instantly.

Color surged at her from all areas. Noises filled her brain. Her thoughts, other people's thoughts. So much hit her all at once, she was on overload.

Easy. Stefan's voice surged through her, an anchor she could hold on to in the sea of sensation that tossed her from side to side. *Glad to have you back.*

She watched as the waves washed around her, pushing up against her legs and splashing high on her body. As with all waves, the onslaught eased, slipping back to rock gently in place and to allow her to settle into her old comfortable self.

Peace. The word meant everything to her.

Good. Now is it possible to wake up, please? Roman is beyond worried, and we're going to attract attention soon.

She studied him. *I don't understand.*

I know. That's why you need to wake up. You weren't just a victim inside. Your body was attacked as well.

She blinked. She spun around and then looked down at her body. She wasn't in her body? *Say what?*

Stefan spoke again. *You're almost there. Just not back enough. You need to come all the way home.* He sighed, reached out a hand, and squeezed her shoulder. *You're caught in your own mind. But you need to come back into your body.*

She looked down at her toes. She lifted a questioning look in his direction and raised an eyebrow. She pointed to her toes and wiggled them. "I'm in my body."

He snickered.

Both her eyebrows shot up.

He grinned and shook his head. His hand squeezed hers again, and then, as she watched him, he placed the palm of his hand on the center of her forehead. He gazed deep into her eyes and whispered, *Go home.*

She felt a shot of heat go through her forehead and down her back, circling at the base of her spine. As if she had an elastic band connecting her to something else, the elastic sprang back and pulled her through a tunnel of darkness.

There was an odd tension, as if she were connected to something else. Something she didn't understand, but it was important.

Her head snapped back, and she smacked into awareness.

She opened her eyes and groaned.

"Shay?"

She blinked and tried to turn her head. A sledgehammer pounded on the inside of her skull.

She groaned again.

"Easy. Don't try to move just yet."

She blinked, heard the voice, and recognized it, but the words didn't quite register. She pushed herself up on her forearms. And then lifted her head. Tree boughs brushed the top of her head. She tried to push up more, only to realize someone, probably Roman, had grabbed her by the arms and was lifting her free of the tree.

Hitting the vertical so fast was tough on her head. Another groan slipped free.

Roman tucked her in close to his chest and held her tight.

She slowly became aware that he was saying something over and over again. "Thank you, God. Thank you."

She must have scared him pretty well. Then again, she'd scared herself too.

Feeling stronger, her head no longer sounding the alarm of imminent destruction, she pulled back a little and said, "Let's go home."

He tugged her in closer, hugged her tight, and then released her. "If you're sure you're okay. Otherwise it's to the hospital for you."

"No hospital," she murmured. "I just need rest."

"Then you can rest at home, where I can keep an eye on you, while you explain just what the hell you were doing taking off on me like that."

She'd have laughed if she could have. But in truth, she was too damn glad to be back in his arms to be worried. She deserved to get chewed out by him. How could she explain that she thought she'd recognized the killer's energy, and that given a chance to track down the person, she'd taken it.

Had she seen who the energy was attached to? No.

And that confused her even more.

Had she been given a trail of bread crumbs to lead her into a trap? A trap she'd fallen into without a second thought. She'd been so focused on the killer, she'd even left Roman behind.

She shook her head as she realized how far from the car she'd gone. It so didn't make any sense. Why would someone try to lure her into a trap?

And why knock her out when she arrived?

Why hadn't they killed her?

ROMAN WAS SILENT as he drove the car through the traffic. He gripped the steering wheel so tightly his fingers turned white. Every turn was sharp, every braking movement hard. Shay studied his profile and watched the muscle pulse on his jaw line.

She had some explaining to do.

And she had only five minutes left in the car to come up with a plausible story. Every time she reached for an explanation, her reasoning dissolved under scrutiny. She didn't know what to tell him. Had she run after that energy of her own volition?

Yes. At least she thought so.

She'd hadn't been following a person but, rather, an energy trail.

That's the thing – she'd been alone. So who had attacked her? Had someone lain in wait for her? Directed her there? Or did someone have the ability to knock her out from a distance by psychic means?

Not nice if they had.

And if so, from how far away could they do this? She'd checked out the area before they'd left the park, but the energy had already been overlaid and dissipated with many other energy trails. She needed to go back to her memory and take another look around as she ran through the trees and away from Roman.

She straightened. It wasn't much, but it was a plan.

And she might learn something she could use to redirect Roman away from chewing her out.

Roman pulled into the parking lot, turned off the engine, and then turned to look at her. "Home."

"Good. I have something I need to do. There's a trick I can try, to figure out who attacked me."

His gaze narrowed, locking on her face. "What kind of trick?"

With a wave of her hand to the surrounding area, she said, "I can't really explain it but I need privacy and preferably peace and quiet to do this."

"Then we'd better get at it." He exited the vehicle and came around to her side to help her out. "Although you shouldn't be doing too much of anything right now."

"And being attacked is why I have to do this." She gave him a wry smile. "I don't want to give this person another chance."

He kept a supportive arm around her shoulders as they entered the lobby. She smiled at Thomas, her doorman. "Long day, and it's not even noon yet."

He smiled as he stepped to the elevator and pushed the button. "Some days are like that."

At her apartment, Roman opened the door wide, and waited for her to enter. She took two steps in and stopped. Shifting her vision, she searched the air, looking for any signs of an intruder. It appeared normal.

She took another few steps inside and collapsed on her couch.

"Everything good?"

"Yes." She sighed. "I'm fine, but could use some caffeine."

She closed her eyes and let herself relax. Her mind wandered over the mess of the last few days.

Had someone been tracking her? How would they know about the funerals? About the deaths? Perhaps they were involved. Yet, if they'd been involved, how had they known to target those people?

Her files. All that information was in her files.

But who had access? Jordan, Rose of course, and herself. Anyone who had a key to her office. Who else? The board members, maybe. But that was her brother and Pappy. They'd all approved the initial projects. And none of them took more than a passing interest in them.

And anyone who could hack into her files. But Roman had checked and said that there hadn't been any unusual access to system.

Then again, she'd attended the last two funerals; it would be expected that she'd attend the third as well. In fact, the killer had probably planned for her to be there.

Given what happened so far today, she needed to update Ronin. But if she could find out anything more solid, something that might help him put a stop to this, she needed to find it quickly.

"Caffeine?"

Startled, she looked over to see a cup of something hot being placed on the coffee table. She smiled. Before she could thank him, he bent down and kissed her hard. Heat spread through her, igniting flames she'd thought slaked. Her toes curled as she sighed against his breath. "Nice."

"Just a reminder that you're no longer alone."

Warmth filled her heart. "Thanks. I'd forgotten."

His beautiful warm eyes smiled down on her. "Don't forget again."

He lowered his head once more, warming up the hidden spots deep inside Shay. A curious sense of connection filled her heart. It felt wonderful. Comforting. Blissful. To share her good days and her bad days. And boy, did today count as one of the worst.

"I was thinking I needed to phone your brother and give him an update," said Shay.

"That's the most sensible thing you've said today. Except I called him while I waited for you to wake up." He sat down beside her and tugged her onto his lap. "Now, what were you talking about in the car?"

She snuggled close and explained her technique.

"Absolutely amazing," he murmured. "To think something like that is even possible."

"Hmm. There is so much that goes on below the surface." She sighed. "You have no idea the things I've seen. What Stefan has seen."

"It has to be difficult to know so much about everyone. To see their secrets. To know information you'd probably rather not know." He looked slightly uncomfortable.

"Absolutely. Which is why I try to block so much. It makes it easier on me." Not wanting to hold back anymore, she added, "Which is why it's important we don't have any secrets between us." She turned to look up at him. "I can find them out. I'd rather be told, up front."

He stared down at her, something immobile in his gaze. "A warning?" he asked lightly, but something had shifted in his tone. But then, to find out he couldn't hide a secret from her had to be disconcerting. At the same time, it was damn near impossible for her to not wonder about the secret he kept to himself.

She'd like to say, fine, she didn't really want to know. But she also knew it would be impossible for her to love, on that level, if she didn't have an open and completely trusting relationship. She might never know if Roman had the ability to hide his true self like Darren had, but she couldn't imagine he would. His artwork was too passionate. Too open. He gave it his all.

And then she realized it must be his artwork, his model, that he wanted to keep close to his heart.

And she could understand that. Not that she liked it, but she didn't exactly want to share her past about Darren either. So, good enough. Time to change the subject. Hopefully, when Roman was more comfortable, he'd share what he could. And that had to be enough.

At least for now.

"No, not a warning. Just letting you know some things can't be changed. I wouldn't go looking for answers." Still, she might under certain circumstances, and so she added, "Unless it was a life or death circumstance."

She grimaced at the memory. How many times had psychics been forced to cross that line and go deeper into their partner's psyche for just that reason?

"Well, I hope there'll be no life and death circumstances in our relationship." His gaze narrowed and he added slowly, "However, after today that thought is a little unnerving."

"Are you saying you'd like to back off?" Shay withdrew slightly to see his face more clearly.

He snatched her back into his arms. "No," he said forcefully. "That is not what I'm saying. I'm acknowledging that sometimes things are beyond our control."

"Oh. Good," she mumbled as she slumped against him.

"I don't have the same skills you do or that Stefan does." His voice deepened. "Is that a problem?"

"Stefan is a good friend. A great one in fact. He's also a terrific artist...and a good man." She smiled gently. "I love him. But like a friend. A brother."

He tugged her into his arms and covered her mouth with his. "I heard you the first time."

She kissed him back, and then gently retreated. "Good. Now, let me do what I need to do. Then we can put this morning behind us."

He stood up. "Am I in the way here?" He motioned to the kitchen. "I can sit further back. But I'm not leaving."

She shook her head. "Not necessary. While I'm under, just don't touch me. It will affect my energy and could snap me back too fast. And that's not good."

With that, she stretched out on the couch and closed her eyes.

Tuesday afternoon...

ROMAN STEPPED BACK, unable to leave. He'd watched her do some weird stuff lately, but he had no idea what to expect from this. She appeared to be sleeping. Except...there was an eerie stillness he didn't understand. He didn't think he'd seen anything like it before.

Her face was devoid of all expression, but there was something animated about her. No one looking at her would believe she was asleep or unconscious, yet her facial features were slack as if she were.

Whatever that meant.

He gave a quick glance around the room, realizing everything was normal looking. Needing to do something, he headed to the kitchen.

Surely, he could rustle up something for her to eat when she came back. She'd had a rough morning and needed her strength.

He opened the fridge but then heard something…off. He closed the door and tiptoed back into the living room. She was still on the couch, in the same position as when he'd left her. But if so, what had he heard? Or thought he'd heard? Feeling ridiculous, he headed back and was just about to step on the tiled kitchen floor, when he thought he heard it again.

Spinning around, he searched the room.

And saw nothing unusual.

A whiff of something passed across his nose. He turned as a faint trail of…cinnamon…passed by. Or maybe that was nutmeg? He didn't know. It was there and then gone.

He spun around and studied Shay. She was still the same. Except different. And whatever caused that difference, he didn't like it one bit.

He pulled up the armchair and sat down, keeping his gaze on her. He sensed she was in danger. He had to watch over her. Only he felt helpless. He didn't know how to handle this woohoo stuff. *Who did?*

Stefan.

He straightened. Grabbed for his phone and called Stefan.

"What's wrong?" came the question. No formalities. Stefan had gone straight to the point.

"I don't know." Roman growled. "She's lying on the couch. She said she had a way to see what happened to her this morning. And she seemed normal." Roman stopped, not knowing how to continue, what to say. "And then it changed."

"Right. What do you mean 'it'?" Stefan's voice went brisk. "In what way has she changed since you were in the room last?"

"There was no smell, then there was a cinnamon scent…or maybe nutmeg." He ran his hands through his hair. "I don't know. I can't explain it. Before she looked lifeless, now there is life, but it's not nice. Like she's scared?"

"I'll take a look." Stefan hung up.

Roman stared down at Shay, the dead phone cold in his hands. "I hoped you'd say so."

The air in the apartment chilled. Goosebumps rose on his arms. He rubbed his hands up and down his arms. He searched the room. It's not like he expected to see Stefan appear in front of him. But he hoped Stefan arrived quickly.

He shivered.

What the hell? Everything was the same except the air temperature.

He could almost see his breath. He blew out a full breath and stared in amazement. He *could* see his breath. *What was going on?* He was a plain talker, and this was not normal. He stood and walked over to the thermostat. It registered 72 degrees. A normal temperature for inside on your average sunny day.

And definitely wrong. There is no way this could be right. It had to be broken.

He turned around, wanting desperately to give Shay a good shake and wake her up. Get her the hell out of here. He wanted her at his place…where she belonged.

CHAPTER 22

S HAY STRODE CONFIDENTLY forward across the park-like setting of the cemetery. She'd had no problem finding her way. The funeral was in progress. She studied the energy as she had before. Because she was looking for a killer she had to open herself to the private dark energy of all these people, look under the surface at who they really were, to see what they didn't want anyone to see.

Horrible things. Often things that people didn't let others, even themselves, know about. Their deepest, darkest secrets were hanging like dirty laundry for her to see.

And as much as she didn't want to look, she had to. Lives depended on it.

So she did. Yet nothing triggered any alarms.

She followed her old path back toward the car with Roman at her side. She paused, caught that same whiff of energy, and stretched out, searching for the source. She thought the energy came from a cluster of people talking with heads bent together, in front of her, but when she moved toward them, they headed to their vehicles and took off. She watched as her body raced down the path toward the trees, only now she'd lost the trail. Damn it. *How could that be?* She ran to catch up to the energy before she lost it altogether.

Ahead and slightly off to the side, she thought she caught a glimpse of the same energy that she'd followed earlier. It was moving down the parking lot, parallel to the path she'd taken this morning.

That made total sense. She hadn't seen it earlier because she assumed she'd been following it. But she'd been following only one strand of that energy – as if the person had walked back and forth along the same path. That had allowed the person to keep track of her…somehow, and they'd circled around to catch her by surprise.

She ran faster. And came around the trees to find another group of people in her way. *Damn it.* Why were there so many people here? She was ready to scream. Had she been so focused this morning that she hadn't taken note of them? She whipped around the tree.

And ground to a stop just in time to watch her body fall. It appeared to be dragged under a tree bough. By itself.

She stared in shock. She couldn't see the person who was doing the dragging. She saw a weird, pinkish energy, as in her own energy distorted. As she couldn't see the other person, she had to assume they were either invisible, God she hoped not, or like Stefan had suggested, they were using her energy to hide themselves.

Maybe wrapping her aura around their body.

She stood in shock, watching. Her energy chilled, yet kept her rooted to the spot.

Only barely understanding, she studied the energy around her body, hoping her attacker would show himself. The pink vision was dispelling, the energy fraying at the edges. She concentrated, pulling more of her own energy into the vision to try and see something useful. As she stood there, desperate for anything meaningful to be revealed, she reached out a hand, and watched in horror as a hand reached toward her.

Oh God.

Stefan.

Shocked, she stared up at her best friend's face.

"Shay." His hand reached out and touched her. "Time to go home."

"No. I haven't found what I need to find."

"And you can't. Not now."

"I have to." She reached further, spreading her fingers and clutched at a wisp of the distorted energy, sucking the very essence into her space, hoping to examine it later.

He shook his head. And with an odd flick of his fingers, Shay was snapped back through time to land with a heavy groan into her body on the couch.

She opened her eyes to find Stefan, in astral form, leaning over her. "Are you okay?"

She blinked. Confused and disoriented, she murmured, "What happened?"

"That's what I'd like to know." Roman leaned over her. His energy blended with Stefan's. *What the hell?* She blinked and tried to clear her vision. Then Stefan moved. And she could see them both.

Thank God.

"Would you like to explain what the hell happened just now?" Roman carried Shay's full mug of coffee into the living room and set it down on the coffee table. "I don't understand that...but I want to."

Shay sat up in a movement reminiscent of his grandmother's before she passed away. Slow and sluggish, like every muscle had to work overtime to make her body do what she wanted it to do. Eventually Shay reached forward to accept her coffee then slumped back into the corner.

"Is it always like this?"

She looked up in surprise. "Uhm, no. Usually I recover much faster. But I was pushing the limit this time, got confused, and didn't exactly have an easy homecoming."

"Why not?"

"Stefan sent me home, actually. And that was probably a good thing. I seemed to have been frozen there – as in, locked in place and unable to move."

"There?" Roman took a deep breath. "Please, tell me – what is *there*?"

She stared at him with a hypnotic expression in her eyes that made him want to reach out, snag her up, and hold her close. Yet he'd been warned not to touch her while she did energy work and when she was recovering.

And the sharing of her experiences was all new to him. He suspected Stefan was a special friend *because* he understood her and what she went through. To do the stuff she was doing and to be alone, with no one to talk to about it, couldn't be easy.

He wanted to be one that she could talk to. Open communication was important to him. *Or was it?*

Inside, he winced as he thought about his paintings and what he kept from her.

Shay wondered if a washing machine felt as worn out after a busy wash weekend as she did after this trip. She hadn't even had a chance to sort through what happened. She'd been paralyzed on the spot. Hadn't been able to move, was barely able to think, and had been getting colder by the second.

The first attack had been on her body, but the attack while she'd been looking for more information...that attack had been on her ethereal body.

Like how freaky was that?

And if she felt like she'd entered the twilight zone, she could only imagine how Roman would feel if she told him details of her experience.

He said he wanted to know. She just wasn't sure he could handle knowing.

And she wanted to know about that energy she'd tried to grasp. She'd caught a touch of it, enough to know something about it, but she needed to be sure. She stared at her closed fist and stalled...

The phone rang, giving her a chance to put off making a decision. She dragged her cell phone out of her pocket. "Stefan? What the hell happened?"

She gave Roman a reassuring smile. "Stefan, I'm going to put you on speaker phone. Roman needs to hear this, too."

His voice filled the room. "Except I don't have an answer. I found you frozen at the scene where you were hit. There was no one around. At least not any longer. Not on any plane that I could find, but your energy was draining off too fast for me to do anything to stop it, except to break your trance and send you home."

"And how did you know to find me?"

"Thank Roman for that." Stefan paused then added heavily, "I think whoever did this was related to Darren."

She gasped. "Are you sure?"

"Yes. Look at what you're holding in your hand. Like really look. Drop all your fears, your insecurities and see what is really there. You brought home a piece of that energy. The only way you could have done that was if you had some kind of connection. Darren."

Taking a deep breath she opened her mind and switched on her inner vision and looked. There was something there, but... Grabbing onto her fears, she breathed love and light into them, releasing the fears to the ethers. Then she went deeper than she'd gone before.

And saw it. She gasped as a familiar signature shimmered in her hand. Familiar...and yet not. This signature was similar to Darren's but wasn't his. It filled her palm, quivering in place. She whispered, "It is a family member."

"It's got to be the twin," Roman said. "There is no one else."

Oh God. She bowed her head. *Damn.* "Ronin needs to know what's going on. He needs to find the twin. He has to be in this vicinity. In the city, close to me."

"Ronin does know."

"Is there nothing to be done? It's hardly safe with this person running around." Roman put his coffee down very slowly, but Shay watched the temper building on his face.

"It's all right, Roman," Shay said. "This is the first time something like this has happened. It's bizarre enough that it's not likely to happen again."

"But it could. Right?" He stared, narrow-eyed, at her. She tried for that reassuring smile again and was about to speak, but Stefan beat her to it.

"Yes. It could," Stefan said. "Any time we do energy work, there is a chance of something going wrong. The same as you could have an accident any time you get behind the wheel of your car."

Roman frowned at the cell phone in Shay's hand.

She raised it higher and smiled grimly at him. "He's right. It's very unusual for us to have a problem, but nothing is without risk. And rarely are we fighting off attackers."

He sat back and glared at her. "But this time you are. And I don't like it."

She answered tartly, "No, and I understand that. But you have to let me do this. It's what I do."

She stared him down, watching resignation and then acceptance slip into his gaze.

Stefan added, "It's what I do, too."

And that seemed to settle Roman. He stared moodily up at the ceiling.

Shay felt for him. Talk about being pushed out of his comfort zone. And she knew he didn't really understand what they were talking about. Would it help for him to have a different type of demonstration?

Stefan spoke in her head. *Go ahead if you want to.*

She grinned, watching Roman's frown deepen. *I don't think Roman is ready for another one of those displays.*

"Maybe he needs it. How else can he understand?"

Again Roman's deep blue gaze fixed on her. "Need what?" Suspicion laced his voice.

"It doesn't matter." She shrugged. "You don't need a demonstration right now, and I'm too tired for one anyway."

"What kind of demonstration? Stefan already gave me one." Roman leaned forward. "And how invasive would it be?"

"Not. And this would be what I can do." She said with a smile. "I could just walk in your footsteps today and tell you what you did."

He shook his head. "Like that would help. I was with you all day."

She laughed. "Good point. Then I'll read your energy and tell you about where you spend it."

He tilted his head. "Spend it. What does that mean?"

She leaned forward until they were eye level. "I can tell where your energy goes on a daily basis. It doesn't have to be too personal. For example..." She paused and shifted her viewing angle. "You have a close relationship with Gerard, and even though you pretend not to worry, you generally call him several times a day."

He smiled. "Of course I do. Look at his age and the personal loss he's sustained lately."

She smiled. "But you didn't have that same relationship with your grandmother or your aunts and two uncles."

"Two uncles?" he shook his head. "I believe I have only one."

She studied his energy again. "Two males and one female on that level."

"One male and one female," he corrected. "But that's all right, what else?"

Wanting to avoid an argument, but knowing he'd ask his grandfather, she studied his energy again. "You enjoy your job, but for you it's a nine to five commitment." She frowned. "Your painting is your joy. And..."

"Again, that's all superficial and has been discussed before."

"And I'm not trying to invade. Remember? However, if you want more... I can see an incident in high school that badly affected you. You lost someone you were very close to."

He straightened, a look of surprise coming over his face. "You spoke to my grandfather about that," he accused.

"No," she said gently, "I can see you dedicate a certain amount of your energy to honoring her."

"Her?" his voice was hard, stiff. "How could you know that this person is female?"

"Because you funnel soft, gentle energy in that direction. Loving energy that goes way into your past. Not to a child. Not to an animal, and yes, I can see those, too. Like your golden lab you grew up with, called Rex."

He sat back. What else could she know? Did she know about his paintings of her? Damn he should have told her himself. He didn't want her to find out this way. And yet this so wasn't the time.

Or was it?

She smirked. "Convinced?"

And the moment passed. Relieved, he smiled. "Well, I certainly am convinced you can access information in my past. How accurately, I don't know. Rex was my dog – a wonderful dog. He died when I was fourteen. I thought my world had ripped apart back then."

"But nothing compared to the loss you sustained when you were seventeen." She couldn't help but soften her voice. His pain had been real, his honoring of that special person a daily fact. One he continued to expend energy on her every day. "I can tell she's still important to you."

He said starkly, simply, "She is. She was my sister."

GODDAMN IT, SHAY. What the fuck were you doing there The walls glared back, providing no answers.

How had she been there — like that? In that form. It wasn't possible. I only went back to the area to see if you'd been found — and what did I find — you in astral form.

Try to follow me, would you? Not likely.

Not in any way. There were limitations to energy work. But there was no way Shay was anywhere close to them. It wasn't possible that she could be that good.

No way you did that on your own. It had to have been a fluke. I've tried to do something similar to shadow walking — and I failed. There's no way you're better than me. You had to have help.

There could be a few others who could do this energy work — maybe. But not Shay. Not like that. Never that bitch. Darren had explained about Shay's holier-than-thou attitude to life and money and how it pissed him off. He'd loved knowing how superior he was to her. Knowing that she had no idea how he fooled her. That his skills were strong and that knowledge gave him a sense of power.

A power that was somehow false. He'd died. Shay didn't.

And that had to be fixed. Shay couldn't be allowed to live.

Darren had planned on killing her. That he had died in her place was a wrong that had to be righted.

But how? There hadn't been enough time to kill her at the cemetery. Not with so many people around. So I went back to see if I could finish the job.

And saw Shay. On the ground where I left her…but standing up in astral form as well, now that had been…bizarre. Shay had been so clear. Easy to identify. How? What happened? There'd been another sort of energy there, too. But that wasn't recognizable either.

Another person? Part of Shay's energy, even though it looked different? It would be great to think Darren's ghost had been going after Shay, but it hadn't felt like him. No one else understood both the freedom and the sadness of living like this.

No one cared.

There had to be an outlet for this rage. Now.

Someone was going to die.

CHAPTER 23

Tuesday evening…

SHAY ENTERED THE hospital and walked to Pappy's room. Roman walked silently at her side. He'd been unapproachable since her demonstration earlier. She couldn't really blame him.

His energy didn't reach for her or slide or caress her energy any longer. No. His energy swirled as if he wore a glass jar around his body with the colorful energy inside. Yet it wasn't angry.

Whatever she'd stirred up, it had brought on a major deep-thinking session.

Her insights were obviously a very sensitive subject.

But one they'd need to broach sometime in the near future because the bond was growing, deepening between them.

He couldn't hide his feelings any more than she could avoid seeing how his energy slipped around hers and melded and blended them into one. She felt the little strokes, the little brushes of his essence constantly. Her own energy stretched eagerly, reaching for him.

Normally, his energy responded in kind. Except right now.

He was locked down, big time. She could understand. He needed to do something. He needed to be able to put a stop to this nightmare. But she didn't have any answers or any way to stop it.

They reached Pappy's door in silence. Roman stepped back to let Shay enter first. Gerard was already there. He looked up and smiled when they walked in.

"There you go, Charles. Look who finally got here."

Pappy smiled and Shay rushed over. She reached down and gently hugged him. "How are you feeling?"

She studied him intently; his face was pale and wan. "You didn't sleep well, did you?"

"I'm fine." He patted her hand. "Don't you worry."

"Well, I will regardless, so you might as well let me." She dropped a gentle kiss on his forehead. "What about the tests? Did the doctors get the results?"

He shook his head. "None that say anything. I didn't have a stroke. My heart seems fine. I just seemed to have blanked out."

Shay smiled. "I'll talk to them. See if they have any other concerns, tests they can do."

She stepped back, letting Roman in closer, and then walked into the hallway to see if she could find the doctor. Seeing no one, she headed to the nurses' station and asked about her grandfather's test results.

"Sorry. The doctor is here but hasn't gotten to your grandfather yet." The harried nurse paused her clicking on the keyboard long enough to look up and answer. "Everyone is running behind right now."

That was normal. Shay understood. "I'll wait for him then. Thanks." She turned and starting walking down the hallway. There were various carts and doors at this end of the floor. She passed a trolley full of folded laundry, and a hamper at the end of the trolley that held dirty laundry. She stopped and looked at the dirty hamper.

Something was wrong with the picture. She switched her vision on and studied the energy. A nasty black swirled up around the garments in the bin. Oozing, murderous black energy.

Oh shit. She whirled around, searching for the energy trail. The black *came* from the hallway that led toward Pappy's room. That energy hadn't been in his room earlier, and Pappy should be safe with both Roman and Gerard to keep watch. Should be...

Her heart sped up. She was almost running by the time she reached Pappy's room, only to realize the energy trail carried on past. But there was a large collection at the doorway where it must have wallowed for a moment, as if the person looked in and considered this room and then moved on.

She studied the doorway. The black had pulsed here, gathering tighter together. *In anger? In frustration?*

Then it had moved on.

That information stalled her. Shay *had* automatically surrounded her grandfather with healing, protective energy, but she hadn't done anything to the doorway.

But there was other residual energy there. Something had prevented entrance to the room. Could Stefan have...? She stepped back, opened her inner vision, and gasped.

Bernice. The doorway was outlined with the residual energy of Bernice's soul. Connected as always – to Pappy.

Her heart stalled, and then she smiled happily. The trio had a unique relationship, and no one could ever doubt the power of their bond. Now, when Pappy was in trouble, Bernice was still protecting him.

And as for that horrific energy... Shay walked slowly to the next room, where the energy entered and looped back out and turned down the hall again. She stood at the entrance and followed the trail with her eyes. The energy swelled with emotion. It tossed and roiled with the need for expression – and it had found it.

The elderly woman on the bed had half fallen to the floor. Even from where she stood, Shay understood it was too late to help her.

She studied the energy, knowing she had to go back to the nurses' station and report what she'd found. But she needed confirmation, if she could find it, evidence that this woman had died of something other than natural causes. In her heart she knew the autopsy would say she died of a heart attack. The black energy had entered the woman's body at the heart chakra and only the heart chakra. The angry entrance had slammed into that poor woman and given no quarter. From where she stood, Shay couldn't tell if the energy had drained from the woman or if she'd been given such a hard jolt that, in her weakened condition, the assault had finished her.

There was only one purpose for energy like that.

Murder.

OVER AN HOUR later, Shay headed back to Pappy's room to say goodbye. She didn't know what the normal procedure was in these cases, but as she'd initially informed a policeman who'd been standing at the nurses' center, She'd been asked to give a statement, just in case. She had no problem giving her version of the event. She really had nothing to tell.

Nothing that she could tell law enforcement.

With Roman at her side, she gave her grandfather a gentle hug and kiss goodnight. "I hope you're feeling better in the morning."

She followed Roman to the door.

Pappy called out as they were leaving, "Shay, could I speak with you for just a moment?"

She rushed back over. "What's the matter; aren't you feeling well?"

"Oh, I'm fine. I just want you to know that I spoke to my lawyer today. Made a few changes to my will."

She grinned. "That's nothing new. You do that every few months or so."

He smiled gently. "I do, but that's because I never know when my old heart is going to give out. I want to make sure everything is taken care of."

"You're not dying, and when you do go, it won't matter anymore because you'll be gone." She chuckled.

"Don't be cheeky," he chided her gently with their old joke. "I'm not going any time soon. I know that. But I do want you taken care of before then. So my question is: how is the relationship with Roman?"

She flushed and laughed lightly. "Fine."

"He's a good man."

"I know." She didn't know where he was going with this, but she knew he had something to get off his chest.

"I thought you two would be good together."

"Are you matchmaking?"

"No. I need to tell you. I gave him a picture a long time ago. A couple of years ago at least. Of you. From some family gathering. Thought maybe he'd be interested in meeting you."

She tilted her head and frowned. *Interesting.* Roman hadn't mentioned it. Then why would he? Besides, for all she knew, Pappy had sent the picture after she and Roman had started chatting anyway. "Okay...I don't know why you would have, but that's fine."

Relief washed over his face. "Good. I've been worrying over that for a long time. I should have asked you before giving it to him, but..."

"But you forgot."

"And Bernice told me not to tell you."

Bernice? Shay laughed. "Now that figures. She was trying to match the two of us at the end too."

Pappy smiled. "Maybe this is one time you should listen to your elders."

Her grin widened. "And maybe it's not."

She brushed her lips against his papery cheek, hating that such a thing had been eating away at him. He was precious to her.

And she had to protect him.

ROMAN DROVE HOME through the busy streets in a deeply contemplative mood. Finally, needing to understand, he asked, "How do you know it's the same energy?"

She gave a long, heavy sigh. "Energy is like DNA. Individual to each person. Once I see an energy signature, I can recognize the look, the feel of it again. There's a familiarity or sense of knowing that is hard to miss." She settled back. "In this case, as I not only saw it, but was touched by it, I know how this energy also feels. And the same person who attacked me at the cemetery killed that poor woman."

"And your cousin, Marie, and David, and possibly several other people? That can never be proven."

"Exactly. Look at what Stefan is up against. How can the police stop someone they can't see? How can they believe a crime was committed when there is no physical evidence?"

"There's a dead body," he countered.

She slid him a sideways look he caught from the corner of his eye. "A dead body that will show up in the autopsy as having had a heart attack – ergo, death by natural causes."

"How can so many people die of natural causes?"

"Thousands of people die every day from natural causes. And millions die every year from heart attacks. That's why an attack like this is so easy to get away with."

He couldn't argue with that, but he wanted to, damn it. How often did things like this happen in the world? With everyone oblivious, shaking their heads. "We have to do something."

She nodded, and then leaned her head back against the headrest and said, "We are."

"You and Stefan?"

"Yes."

Stefan again. "I want to help." He frowned. "What can I do?"

"I'm not sure there is anything you can do."

He drove the car around a corner. In a thoughtful voice, he said, "Can you trace this energy to a person?"

"We're trying to. Stefan picks up a thread of the energy on the ethers and then tracks it back, but he says in this case it's almost like the energy changes, morphs into something else, and then he loses it at that point. It's not a visual path in the way that you or I would think, but an inner vision, so the trail can be lost easily."

"And lost because someone is hiding?" He watched as she fumbled with her phone. "What are you doing?" he asked.

"Calling your brother." She moved it away from her head and turned on her speaker phone. "Hi Ronin, anything new?"

"Actually maybe. We've tracked the brother to Seattle, where we have a last known address. He had a girlfriend – on again, off again. Apparently, she was questioned about him today but said she hasn't seen him for a year or so."

"A year?" Shay's mind spun on the possibilities. Surely that timeframe was no coincidence?

"I'm working to track his movements from their point of departure. I'll keep you updated." He coughed. "How's my brother doing these days?"

Shay glanced over at Roman. "He's fine."

"And how are you and my brother?"

Shay coughed with obvious embarrassment. "All is well. Thanks, Ronin. Keep in touch."

Roman drove his BMW into his underground parking at home, stopping to key in the code to open the gate, then drove into his parking spot. He turned off his engine and turned to face her as she finished her call. She hopped out of the car and walked toward the elevators. Roman shook his head. Talk about determined.

He laughed, caught up and wrapped an arm around her shoulder. "I wanted to show you my place."

She raised an eyebrow. "Good. Have you got new paintings? I'd love to see them."

"Not the latest. Those are at the gallery."

He joined her at the elevator and punched in the number.

She watched, raised an eyebrow, and asked, "Penthouse?"

"I like my space." That's all he said as the elevator rose. The doors opened, and he led the way to a single door in front. He unlocked and pushed it open, letting her inside.

"Nice." She walked in, her eyes locking on the artwork covering the wall. "These are beautiful." He stood in the hallway and admired her as she wandered the large open space admiring the art.

"Some older pieces. Glad you like them."

She smiled, a look that lit her up from the inside. "It's spectacular."

"You're spectacular," he said softly. "Truly."

Her smiled warmed. She walked toward him. "Thank you." She reached up and placed a light kiss on his lips. He snatched her up and lowered his head to kiss her with the intensity he'd kept locked inside all day.

She purred in his arms. He deepened the kiss, shifting her slightly to allow better possession of her mouth. He could never get enough of this woman. She was so special. So his.

SHAY STEPPED CLOSER, wanting to be inside his mind and body. She needed this man like no other. It didn't matter that she'd said 'never again.' They were words spoken before she'd understood what was waiting for her. She'd have raced toward her future if she'd known. Roman was her future. She just needed him to be comfortable with his present, and with her.

And one perfect way to do that was right here and now.

She stepped back and smiled up at him. And her fingers went to her blue cotton shirt. She undid the buttons as he watched – a gleam lighting his eyes. His hands hurriedly unbuttoned, unhooked, and undid his clothing, tossing clothes from where he stood. Minutes later, they were both nude in the living room. Standing, staring at each other, with enough heat steaming from their bodies to make her skin glow.

He was a magnificent animal. Tall, muscled, so masculine. She didn't think he worked out but rather thought he was blessed with a natural grace and form that most men would die to have. She reached up and unclipped her long hair, shaking it free around her shoulders, then took one step closer. She reached out a finger and stroked over the lean muscles of his chest, her finger running a long, teasing stroke that ended at a nasty ragged scar over his ribs. His bullet wound. She couldn't resist; she leaned forward and dropped a kiss on the hardened center. He hissed.

"You're going to have to tell me about that sometime," she murmured.

She pulled back slightly, a smile on her face.

"Later." He opened his arms and she stepped into them.

Early Wednesday morning...

HOURS LATER, SHAY woke up refreshed and energized. Roman slumbered, face down beside her. His arm was flung across her belly. What time was it? She couldn't see a clock from her position. There was a gray light to the room, so she guessed it was probably early morning. She wiggled upright and slipped out from under him. She needed a drink and was too wired to go back to sleep.

A couple of folded t-shirts lay on Roman's dresser. She tossed one over her head, almost laughing when it came to mid-thigh on her. She gave a curious glance around.

She'd never seen his place and she wanted to take a peek. The walls in the bedroom were a light, soothing mocha with sharp white trim. His bedding, so similar to hers included a huge duvet in a rich deep chocolate with lighter stripes, now rumpled into a ball at the bottom of his massive bed.

The atmosphere was light and breezy and satisfaction oozed from the bedroom. And she smiled. She loved being with Roman, and she was seriously thinking that she might be in love with him – maybe even past thinking about it.

She walked through to the kitchen and poured herself a glass of water from the tap, loving the open spacious feeling and the bright tiles on the floor. As she sipped, she wandered around his penthouse. She'd never considered what type of home he'd have, but appreciated that this suited him perfectly.

There was a large solarium that opened up on the left that appeared to be part workroom and part sitting room. The art on the walls there, sprawled into another room that was filled with paints and easels. She wandered through the large room, loving the pictures. The half light added shadows to the images, highlighting various parts and hiding others. And there she was. That they were all the same model only reaffirmed her belief. She hoped one day Roman would share who this woman was that had grabbed his passion and held on so tightly.

And explain the relationship he had with her.

She was stunning. But his skill made her even more so. He expressed so much in so few strokes. Her profile, shoulders, everything created with minimal paint.

The blue accents on some of the pictures intrigued her.

On some of the paintings there was almost a sheen, a blue air around the central figure. Like an aura? Unusual and intriguing.

And yet the painting sitting off to the side was thick and almost three-dimensional. It held so much paint. She wouldn't have been surprised to hear that he'd carved it instead of painted it.

Fascinated. She stood back and paused. Tilted her head again. Backed up as far as she could go.

She gasped.

Inside, her heart jolted, stilled for a long moment, and then raced forward.

No. The lines were so familiar. But it couldn't be. Wasn't possible.

A soft laugh filled the air. She spun around. But she was alone. Turning back around, she caught a glimpse of something. A fragrance...cinnamon, maybe whispered through the room. *Of course it is. Do you really not know?*

She gasped. "Bernice?"

That same warm laughter.

Shay laughed too. "Aren't you supposed to be off in the light, doing things that dead people do?"

I will soon. When I know Charles is fine. Until then, I'm here. Then again, as he hasn't got long anyway, I might just stick around. Bernice laughed. *He'd like that.*

Even though Shay hated the thought of her grandfather dying, she had to smile at the thought of Bernice staying close until then. Pappy would be tickled. "I'm glad to hear he has a guardian angel. Thank you for helping him."

I love him, Bernice said simply. *How can I do any less? Now, look at the paintings. Are you really so blind?*

Shaking her head, Shay studied several paintings again.

And then she knew.

Indeed, how could she *not* have known? Tears crept into her eyes. Warm shivers rode down her spine, and her heart swelled.

Finally, Bernice said; then she disappeared, leaving Shay to face the truth.

The model was *her.*

CHAPTER 24

S HAY COULDN'T MOVE. Her mind froze long before the rest of her body, which was still trying to move forward. This wasn't possible. There's no way. Yet, no matter what she did, the fact was irrefutable. She was staring at portraits of her.

The how eluded her, and the why… Well that just blew her away. Helpless to do anything but obey her instinctive need to see more, she walked quietly forward and stared at the closest canvas directly in front of her. Unfinished, it resembled many of the others she'd seen at the gallery, but this time the face was turned coquettishly with just the jawline complete. Her jawline. Her hand instinctively lifted to touch her smooth chin that he'd captured so easily with a single stroke. She wouldn't have believed it if she wasn't seeing it.

Fascinated, she walked around the studio, stopping to shift a canvas to look at the ones hidden behind it. So many. She could see a few, discarded in a pile at the back. She reached forward to pull the canvas that had been tucked the furthest away. It was a struggle, but she finally managed to pull it into the light.

There was more of her showing than in the ones she'd recently looked at. Her face was more defined, less of a hint and more of a sketch. She looked back over at the others. He'd used less detail in those and gave more of an impression of her features. His skill had improved.

Amazing.

As she studied the paintings her mind flitted from conversation to conversation. To ones that offered uncomfortable insights about his muse, his passion. His discomfort with the many conversations. It all made so much sense.

And made her feel foolish. She'd been jealous – of herself.

She crouched down and flicked through a stack on the floor.

Studying another one, she barely heard a noise behind her. She spun around to find Roman leaning against the open doorway. His only clothing was a pair of snug boxers molding to his muscled thighs.

"Like what you see?"

She gazed at him, a tic pulsing in his cheek. Her mind so full, her heart on overload, she could hardly speak. She took a deep breath and answered honestly. "I'm not sure, to be honest."

"Oh?" He frowned, straightened and walked closer. As his gaze went to the canvas in her hand, he grimaced. "Ugh. That's an old piece."

"Why are there no other models? No landscapes or still lifes?"

She replaced the canvas in the stack before crossing the room to stand in front of him. "Is it only me that you paint?"

His whimsical smile tugged at her heart. "In a way. I've been fascinated with you for a very long time." He studied her face as if waiting for a reaction.

In truth she didn't have a reaction to give. She was too stunned. So he'd been painting her longer than they'd been communicating? Longer than he'd known her? Really? Was that possible?

When she continued to stare at him, a gentleness spread in her heart. As if sensing her acceptance, he continued. "Your Pappy gave me the original picture. Although I think Bernice sent me a couple around the same time. I thought at first that I could paint you out of my system. That if I did just one more, if I got the line of your shoulder...just right...you'd leave me in peace." His gaze roamed her face, as if memorizing the slight nuances of the real thing to compare to his artwork.

She arched a brow. "And? Did it work?"

He shook his head, a curious light coming into his eyes. "It had the reverse effect. I became obsessed. I couldn't get enough. You dominated my thoughts and my days. I couldn't wait to get home so I could paint you again, this time with the draping of a sheet, or a dress or...nothing."

She shook her head at the thought of this man, someone she hadn't even met, going through his day, eager to put her image on a canvas. It blew her away. And in a little way...it kind of creeped her out.

She studied the proud man in front of her and realized something important.

No. She wasn't creeped out and the reason it didn't creep her out...was because it was *this* man. If any other man had done this, yes. *That* would have been all wrong. But not Roman. In some way, perhaps his need to paint her every day had kept her alive in his mind – she almost understood it. To paint her had become an obsession. His passion. There'd never been any doubt about that. She knew it. Had noticed it right from the beginning.

She'd even told Stefan at the gallery.

She just hadn't understood who he was obsessed with.

Now she realized where the difficulty lay and why. And how personal this whole thing was. And why he had put up his walls. His obsession to paint her, and only her, had been his guilty secret. The reason for the distance she'd felt. And he hadn't known how she'd react.

She checked his energy now. It no longer felt invasive. The wall had been there to protect his secret and now that was out, the wall was crumbling. Not completely gone yet, though... The wall was lighter, thinner. Still there, but no longer as solid, and it was collapsing even as she watched. He'd opened up, become vulnerable. She sensed he waited...for a judgment to come. From her.

Then she remembered Pappy's confession at the hospital. Old matchmaking Pappy with Bernice as a willing accomplice. He'd given Roman pictures of her. Not nudes, just casual pictures from one of the many events in the last few years.

Roman had taken it from there.

She walked around the small room and studied the paintings. Every picture was at an angle of some sort. There were no full-on paintings of her face or a front view.

"Why are there no pictures of my face?"

"Because I couldn't get it right." He walked to a cupboard at the back of the room and pulled out several sketchbooks. He turned to face her and held out the smaller one to her. She accepted it. Turning it around, she flicked it open and walked a few feet away, engrossed in looking over all the different images. Several pages in, she glanced at the cover again, looking for a date. "When did you draw these?"

"When I first got the pictures, maybe two years ago now. I was hoping to do your face, and I tried." He motioned to the book in her hand. "But I could never get it right. Eventually I gave up."

"And why do you think you couldn't get it right?" She turned the page to see another attempt – this one looked really close.

He took a deep breath. "A couple of reasons. I didn't know you, and I was doing this without you knowing. In essence...I couldn't paint your face because I hadn't faced you about this. I felt...guilty."

Startled, she gazed up at him, her attention diverted. A man with a conscience? She didn't know what to say, so she focused on the question she needed to ask. "What is with the blue?"

Silence. Roman gave a short laugh. "I don't know what to say to that, except to say I have to add it. I don't know why." He shrugged and gave her a lopsided grin. "I gave up trying to change it a long time ago. It doesn't help that Stefan said he knew the reason for the blue...but wouldn't tell me."

She widened her eyes. If it had been a soft pink, she'd have wondered if he'd seen her aura, but blue...? "Interesting, and so typical of Stefan."

"It bothered me in the beginning, but it became one more thing to accept. Just like I used to do abstracts...but from the first time I saw a picture of you...there were no more abstracts." He shrugged helplessly.

"You've done no other type of picture since you started to work on paintings of me?"

"Well, I tried." He gave a short, self-conscious laugh. "But none of them worked. I tried for a few months to change... Only as long as I could paint you, then I could paint. But once I tried to change the subject, then I was lost. And I could do no more."

She shook her head. She handed the sketchbook back. "I don't know what to say."

"Are you...upset?"

That answer was easy. The rest *so* not. She remembered all the things she'd instinctively known about his relationship with his model. Feeling her way through, she answered slowly, "No. Not upset. Surprised. Confused. Stunned actually. And uncertain."

"Uncertain?" He jumped on that.

She winced. "I didn't mean to say that."

"But you did."

She took a deep sigh. "I'm wondering...with all this...what you really feel for *me*." At the surprised and shuttered look on his face, she rushed to explain. "Are we together now because of this?" She waved her arm around the studio. "Is this what I am to you? Your muse? Do you worry that you can't paint... Are you afraid that without me, you won't be able to paint anymore?"

Once she started, the words poured out. She hadn't realized they'd been churning inside. Or even that they'd demanded voice, until the torrent had started.

"And am I only here so you can fill in the pieces of your painting, the pieces that you haven't been able to, until now?"

The silence was absolute.

She glanced over at him nervously.

He stood as if slammed by a bullet. He barely moved. Not even a breath gusted free.

She had to finish. She had to get it all out. Then she'd leave. But she needed to know the answer first. Then she could go home and sort this out. She took a deep breath and continued.

"I guess I'm afraid that I'm only here because of your obsession. Not because I'm *me*."

HE COULDN'T BREATHE. He couldn't formulate a thought. And words strung into a comprehensive sentence seemed impossible. This is what he'd been afraid of. That she'd find out and misconstrue what she saw.

Hell, he couldn't have foreseen *this* worry of hers. It never occurred to him that she'd doubt his feelings for *her*.

But he hadn't known how to handle telling her, so he hadn't.

And that had been a mistake. If he'd only brought up the issue first.

But he'd woken up alone. And had freaked. He'd thrown on boxers and raced through the apartment searching for her. He'd been so sure she'd left to go home that when he'd found her in his studio, his first thought had been only relief because for that instant his secret was forgotten.

It had taken minutes for him to relax enough to lean against the wall and watch her. She'd been so intent, so curious, he'd quickly fallen into artist mode, watching the expressions ripple across her face. She was so expressive. He'd actually reached for a pencil and sketchbook. That's when she'd heard him.

Even now his finger itched for his pencil. To sketch that long hair as it brush over her shoulder with her every movement.

Except he wouldn't be able to hold anything. He was frozen. What he said now would decide the course of his future.

A crossroad.

What could he say?

He opened his mouth as if to speak, but no words came out.

ROMAN TRIED AGAIN, watching her as she studied him. Shay stepped toward him.

"Tell me." She narrowed her gaze, willing him to step up and speak. To tell her what she wanted him to say. What she needed to hear.

What he needed to verbalize.

That she was his model, was both stunning and gratifying, but she wanted that reaction to be about *her*, in the flesh, not her image on a canvas.

She took another step closer to him, and stood on tiptoe so she could stare into his eyes. Her gaze locked with his, probing, urging him to speak up. His eyes warmed, deepened. She offered a tiny smile in response.

His gaze burned as fire ignited deep inside. The flame dancing in his eyes, grew stronger, brighter. That intense look caused a conflagration deep inside her belly. An answering prayer of joy rolling up through her insides, carrying a song as old as time.

"Tell me," she whispered.

A tiny smile played at the corner of his mouth. He leaned closer, intent on kissing her.

She shook her head, insisting, "Tell me."

His head lowered even more.

"Tell me," she insisted, her breath brushing up gently against his lips.

He stilled. His mouth inches from hers. His warm breath played over her eyes and face. She closed her eyes, letting his closeness warm her soul and soothe her thundering heart as she waited to be released from this prison of doubt. She knew it could happen. Would happen. If he was ready.

If he meant all that his pictures said he did. If he *was* true to his passion.

Then he'd be true to her.

But she knew, first he had to be true to himself.

"Tell me."

Shay kept her eyes closed. She felt his energy surge toward her, wrapping around her, caressing her shoulders, her hips, her head. Light gentle strokes caressed and soothed even as they whispered through on a promise.

She needed to hear the words.

He needed to voice them.

"Tell me," she whispered, keeping her voice soft and delicate, yet offering him hope and a future together like none other.

He lowered his head to rest his forehead on hers. She opened her eyes to see him close his. An almost imperceptible shudder worked down his body and his shoulders lowered and relaxed. She sensed his energy sink deep into her own, blending and melding to join with hers, as one.

As calm and sure as she'd ever heard his voice, his words came as a benediction. Releasing her from her prison and giving her the strength to fly free.

She let her heart energy cross the small divide to crawl into his heart chakra and curl up inside.

So quiet, more impression than sound, he whispered, "I love you."

Wednesday, at dawn…

RONIN LOVED WORKING the night shift. Although it was closer to breakfast time, there was something magical about the city at dawn. That more crimes were committed, and there were more predators to hunt at night made his working life that much more interesting. He understood the predator mindset and he did some of his best police work at night.

His twin brother Roman often did his best work at night too. Even growing up, Roman could be found, well after bedtime, with a pencil scribbling over every square inch of his textbooks. He'd gotten hell for that many times.

Instead of art, Ronin had music in his soul. He played the trumpet and favored jazz. That both brothers had gone into law enforcement said much about who they were as men, but having a creative outlet meant they survived the rigors of the brutal world they worked in better than many others.

He had worried about his brother for years. After that bullet, Roman could have taken a desk job. Instead he'd walked away and set up his own company. And he had proved to be damn good at it. Ronin had used his services many times.

He knew that while Roman checked over Shay's site and said that there'd been nothing obviously amiss, he'd also worried that the door to the office was essentially one any two-bit burglar could break if they wanted to get inside. That just meant they couldn't narrow the field at all that way.

And Roman had gone a step further with the new security system he'd ordered for Shay's apartment *and* her office. Last Ronin heard, they were both still arguing over who would get to pay.

There were many people involved in the Foundation. Any one of them could access the information needed to identify people associated with it. But none of that explained how these people had been killed recently. He understood about the energy – well as much as any non-psychic could – but, like Stefan said, the person doing this could be anyone, anywhere and have skills they hadn't run across before.

And how scary was that?

He didn't understand Stefan's explanation about Tabitha hiding on the ethers. Like who could?

Ronin had spoken to several of Stefan's friends about other cases involving psychic criminals, trying to get a handle on how they dealt with these sorts of things, but the information wasn't helpful. Some had been enlightening in the scope of the crimes and the people who committed them, but it didn't shed light on Shay's issue right now.

His brother was playing watchdog, and Ronin knew it would take a tank to pry him away from Shay's side. Good thing; as it seemed her attacker could appear and disappear at will. He needed to brush up on his skills if criminals were taking to the ethers.

Just then his email signaled a new message. He clicked on the link and bent his head to read.

Finally. They'd found Darren's twin. He read, then reread the message. *Shit.*

He reached for the phone.

"Stefan," he began, "I found Darren's twin. He's in Seattle. In the morgue. He was a John Doe and has only been recently identified. Cause of death…as far as they can tell, heart attack. He's been there for a year."

Silence.

"Stefan?"

"I'm here." Fatigue whispered through the phone line. "I didn't see that coming."

"No one did. And if he isn't the one causing all this havoc, who the hell is?"

"I don't know, but we have to find out, and fast. There's an edge of instability here. I don't like it. In fact, I'm working at the children's hospital right now. Trying to strengthen the walls. Just in case."

"Is it working?" Ronin asked. He'd love to think something like that was doable, but he highly doubted it. He knew Shay's foundation had contributed heavily to the new wing at the hospital and that definitely made it and those who worked there, potential targets. He winced as he thought of the damage that could be done.

"I hope so. I'd planned to go home and rest, then do more tomorrow. Now I'm not so sure. It's one thing to have a villain you think you know, but it's quite another to have a nasty piece of work that is also aggressive and faceless. While we thought it was Darren's twin, I understood the potential capabilities of this person, now… Now, it's a whole new game."

Crap. Ronin hung up the phone slowly. "A whole new ballgame? Why is nothing ever easy?"

He bent over his keyboard and got to work.

ENOUGH WAS ENOUGH...

Too bad Darren was no longer here. They could play his favorite pastime. Murder. The hospital wasn't the best place for games. At least right now. It was however, the right place for real get-away-with-it murder. Everyone there was dying anyway. So who would notice one more?

And that was the pissy part of tonight. It had been too easy. The old woman hadn't even been scared. It's as if she'd waited for her maker to come. And if that didn't beat all.

The old woman had started praying as soon as the process had started. And how could she have known that her time had come? And not just praying, but almost chanting. Bizarre. There'd been nothing to it. The old woman had given up on life almost immediately. Almost grateful to end her existence.

Peaceful. As if she'd been happy to go. And damn, that wasn't the intention at all. The children's ward would have been better.

And it's not like the plan had been to take out the old woman. She'd just been the closest target to vent my anger after not being able to enter Shay's grandfather's room. The old woman had been the closest target.

But had Shay gotten the message? Not likely. It wasn't personal enough. She didn't know the old woman. She wouldn't care. She wouldn't suffer from the woman's death.

That was the whole purpose here. To make Shay suffer. To make her afraid, looking over her shoulder to see if anyone else she loved might die or when she would become the target.

There was no fun to this game if there wasn't pain caused to someone else. And fear.

Shay needed to be afraid...because she was going to get hers. And soon.

Or maybe not soon...

Maybe now...

CHAPTER 25

S TEFAN CLOSED HIS phone and closed his eyes. Damn and double damn. At what point did life get simpler? When did the number of bad guys decline? He'd thought for sure they were dealing with Darren's brother, Danny. Had to be. It made perfect sense. But he'd been dead a year. A whole year. Had died around the same time as Darren. And of a heart attack. Like Darren, like the recent victims.

A coincidence? *Not.*

Stefan knew he was missing something.

What?

There was a definite familiarity to the energy, and if it wasn't Darren's twin's, then whose was it? A parent? A child? But then it would have to be a young child. And few children hated with the degree of intensity required to kill, and kill again.

Darren hadn't been old. Twenty-eight, maybe twenty-nine and he'd died a year ago. It's possible he'd fathered a child when he was as young as sixteen, but not likely. Still it *could* mean there might be an eleven- or twelve-year-old out there with his abilities. But it was unlikely a child that age would be a killer.

It wasn't impossible for the psychic skills to develop that young, but they usually showed up at puberty. Who knows with this family? But even if they did show earlier, the pattern was they didn't develop the required strength and endurance for several more years.

More likely the killer was a sibling or a parent.

Lissa, his ghost friend, appeared in front of him. Gone was the joyous soul he'd come to appreciate. Instead a sense of gravity, of sorrow, emanated from her. She never said a word. Just sat there.

Waiting. Hoping to help, but like him, not knowing what to do.

So like her sister Alex...

Sister? Could Darren have a sister? Or another brother? Damn. He leaned forward and stared out into the dark night beyond his bedroom window. Was that it? Was there any chance there was *another* sibling? A sibling who might have lost both their siblings at the same time. Was that possible? And if so, would that be enough to cause such a reaction? To compel him to extract revenge for the deaths of his brothers? Maybe all the family he had in the world.

Thanks, Lissa.

She smiled hopefully. *I didn't help, but if you have an idea of what to do – good.*

Sometimes you don't have to do anything. Just being you, is great. He smiled at his visitor even as his mind worried on the problem.

But why focus on connections to Shay?

Unless this person believed Shay was responsible. And the only way this person could know that is if they knew what happened that night?

And understood what had gone wrong.

In that case, were they after revenge? To kill Shay. Destroy her life. Or to make her lose what was important to her?

Anyone who knew Shay, knew people were more important to her than even her projects, but Darren had always had a major problem with Shay's projects. Shay had shared how much Darren complained when he thought she cared more about them than about him. He'd been right, but that's because he must have realized Shay's heart hadn't been engaged the way Darren wanted it to be.

Stefan had been able to see that. But Shay hadn't been willing to see it.

But what about the last victim, the elderly lady in the hospital? She hadn't been associated with one of Shay's projects. Who knew why that target had been chosen? So close to Pappy but not an attack against him.

Or was the old woman a target for any number of other reasons?

If the attacker had gone after the old woman out of rage, that meant their anger was unstable. The person unbalanced. When one focused on using negative energy long term it had the effect of destabilizing the energy at the core. That could be what happened. And it would make the attacker *very* dangerous.

But now what? What or who would this person target next? Stefan had already considered the children's ward. Was there another vulnerable spot? One that held more meaning for Shay? She'd funded thousands of projects over the last decade through the Foundation. She had many friends with only a few family members to target.

More of Shay's projects? More of Shay's family? Friends?

The field was pretty open.

Stefan?

He frowned, not recognizing the voice. Lissa had left, so it wasn't her. And this voice was so faint as to be hardly distinguishable.

Stefan? Help me. Something bizarre is going on here.

He shook his head, trying to clear it and focused on the voice. *Tabitha?*

Yes! I had an ethereal visitor. When it couldn't get in my room it got pissed. Went down the hall. I followed, but they've gone into the children's ward.

"Shit." Not there. *Please not there.* He hadn't finished reinforcing the shell. It took longer than a few hours. Could take days.

Help. I need help, Stefan! Tabitha screamed.

He couldn't do this alone. He sent out a massive panicked call to anyone who could help and then he jumped free of his body.

SHAY BOLTED UPRIGHT, her mind screaming awake. A film of fear slid over her skin. She brushed hair back off her face even as she studied Roman's bedroom, looking to find what was wrong.

And found nothing. She took a deep breath and tried to reassess. At her side, Roman rolled over, snuggling closer. Her heart still pounded with fright, but the sight of the sleeping giant beside her made her smile. He slept like an infant with such peace on his face, his body open and relaxed with sexual surfeit. Just the way he should be.

So what was wrong?

The nudge came again. She sent out a questioning response.

And something exploded in her mind.

Oh God.

The hospital. Stefan was calling her to the hospital.

She jumped free to race through the ethers, her body collapsing, limp on the bed.

STEFAN TOOK A direct hit. He'd have groaned if he had a voice. Instead, he was so focused on his astral form and keeping a protective bubble over the kids on the ward, a trick that Dr. Maddy had been helping him work out, that that attack blindsided him. Again.

He was getting damn tired of this. In his world, there was always evil. Working with the police as he did, he'd seen so much, but no one could keep his guard up all the time. And tonight he'd been so far past tired, he'd let it drop.

And he just hadn't been aware of the attack early enough.

And he'd been alone. Weakened. Unprotected.

At his panicked cry, so many friends had come to help – none prepared for what they found.

Energy blasts.

Stefan, go stop the attacks. I'll protect the children. Dr. Maddy's voice filtered through his awareness. *Send Tabitha my way. She's advanced enough with energy to help.*

I'm here. Tabitha's strained voice arrived ahead of her teal energy. *Stefan, if you can, get this bastard.*

Even Lissa's energy moved frantically at his side, trying to send Stefan away.

Maddy was already protecting the children. Her powerful healing energy was a bulletproof casing around the little ones in the room. It's not as if the attacker could get through that. But they'd seen so many people capable of so many horrible things, Stefan no longer believed in certainties.

Others were there to receive the black energy, sucking it out of the ward. The person they sought appeared to have connected to the universal energy – it wasn't possible to run out of that. And right now, that was majorly bad news.

Stefan could sense the chaos on the earthly reality too, as people panicked, searching for answers to what they could only sense, but not clarify. They tried to contact him, looking for help. But he couldn't help anyone.

Stefan could only hope they were doing what they could.

Because whoever this asshole was, he had serious skills.

And serious mental issues.

This wasn't a cold, calculated act. This was murderous rage.

With the flavor of revenge.

And there was no end to this attack in sight.

Stefan needed Shay. Where the hell was she?

PANICKED, SHAY ARRIVED at Dr Maddy's hospital in astral form to see…energy… God, she didn't know what was going on…but thick turbulence filled the space. More than one person, more than one fight. At the center of it all – Stefan in a battle of wills. Only she couldn't tell with whom…or what.

The large, open communal space was dark and silent – as in the aftermath of a grenade going off. There should be noise, voices, conversation. Instead there was a complete absence of sound.

Shay spun in a slow circle, trying to sort through the impressions bombarding her. Silence. Shock. Pain and destruction. Her view was filtered through a smoky, charcoal-smelling haze. Tables were overturned, chairs tossed, toys strewn on the floor and paper floated through the air to land gently on the ground like leaves falling in the wind.

Her arrival *had* come in the aftermath of a massive blast.

An energy grenade.

She'd heard of them. Had never seen one.

And she was grateful to have missed this one too.

The energy listed and shook as the particles came together. The blast had disturbed time – making everything move in slow motion. She searched through the oddities, her instincts more useful than her eyes. She had to see through the wrongness to what was really happening.

Deep, dark colors bombarded her as wave upon wave of energy slammed into her. *Waves from the energy bomb?* Surely not?

A psychic attack? At this magnitude?

She couldn't make sense of anything. She was also too busy protecting herself. The more walls she put up, the more the waves increased. She was forced to throw walls higher and higher in an effort to keep safe. Someone incredibly powerful was blasting her. And with their continuous waves, she couldn't gain the upper hand; she couldn't find her footing in this horrific reality.

She was losing the battle.

Another wave slammed into her, lifting her off the floor. She would have dropped to the ground, but she floated in a world with no gravity – no ground.

No longer in the physical plane, the rules were different here. No physical senses, no physical touch, no Newton's laws. Nothing she could use to re-center herself.

In her mind's eye she could see the destroyed center of the room. But she could see a deep, dark black off to the left, and opposing it off to the right, a deep midnight blue. She'd landed in the middle of some kind of war.

And she had to pick a side and fast.

But who was where?

Shay, duck!

She ducked. But too slowly. The blast lifted and tossed her on her virtual butt.

Again.

There would have been a trickle of laughter, but it arrived on Stefan's panicked cry, *Another one's coming your way.*

She gasped as the blast hit at the tail end of Stefan's warning. This wave was weaker. Barely skimming over her body. Better.

Thanks for the warning, and what the hell is going on?

The ward is under attack.

She snorted. *I got that much. But who's doing this? And why?*

I don't know! I can't spare the energy to find out. I need your help. I need everyone's help. This is bad, Shay. I'm trying to protect the kids at the same time. There are too many of them for me to guard. Maddy's also protecting them now as I'm spread too thin. Help. I can't spread out any more, that's your specialty, not mine. We never got to you teaching me that trick, remember.

Damn it. What trick? What do you want me to do?

Disperse completely. Become one with the universe!

Shit. Ask for something easy why don't you?

Taking a deep nonexistent breath, Shay thinned her energy down to a misty vapor. It helped her disappear into the ether as she dealt with the waves of energy still pouring her way. *And now she was harder to target.*

Following the success of her first attempt, she thinned her energy further, and was no longer solid enough to be hit by the energy attacks. Instead, she filled the room with her very essence. She spread out to the far corners, including the ceiling. She could see other energies in the battle, and the children's energies. They were silent, still, but she could see their energies pulsing in strong healthy waves as they slept.

Nice. Dr. Maddy was full of cool tricks apparently if she could keep their consciousnesses and their bodies protected while the war raged.

Leaving the others – and God only knew who all was here – to protect the children, Shay thinned her energy even further. Within seconds she'd become little more than mist in the room, a fragrance, a mere sensation.

Surrounding her attacker. Above, behind, on her attacker – the vibrating dark purple-black ball at the side of the room.

Shay closed in on the person so bent on destruction that they didn't care who was destroyed. Anger, frustration and a horrible madness poured from this person's energy – this person, bent on maximum destruction. Emotions, thoughts, words fired from this person in an endless vent. Shay couldn't help but hear the refrain that poured through the night.

She struggled to make the words clear.

Then she heard the disembodied voice.

Hurt them all.

Make them suffer.
Make them pay.

RONIN GRABBED HIS phone and dialed Stefan.

No answer. *Damn it.* He tried again, then again. Switching tactics, he tried to call Shay. And it rang and rang. *Shit.* Someone needed to answer, damn it.

"Hello." A deep, dangerous voice growled into the phone.

Ronin reared back. "Roman? Is that you?"

"Yes. What the fuck is going on?"

With stomach churning, Ronin asked, "Why? What's the matter?"

"Shay has collapsed in bed like a coma victim, and there's a weird buzz going on in the air. I've tried calling everyone I know, and no one answers. Hell, Stefan's not answering telepathically either."

Telepathically? "Roman, can you talk that way too?" Jesus, if only. It would make life so much easier for him. The concept blew him away.

"No, but Stefan can talk to me that way. In theory that means I can learn, too. But these people have skills I'd never imagined. I want to know what the hell is going on," Roman roared.

"I'm trying to get a hold of Stefan and Shay. Wait, did you say she was in a coma?" Ronin tried, but couldn't stop his voice from rising at the end. He closed his eyes and took a calming breath. Damn this case was weird and getting weirder.

"A psychic coma or some damn thing. I can't touch her. Can only sit here and watch over her. Helpless. I fucking hate that." Roman's voice calmed somewhat. "Why are you calling?"

"Darren had another sibling. Younger by several years. Apparently she adored her brothers and they adored her." Ronin stared at the screen in front of him. "I have a photo. It's fuzzy but I thought maybe they'd recognize her. I don't know her."

"Send me the picture. Maybe I will be able to."

"Sending…" Ronin zapped the image to his brother's cell phone. "You should have it now." He waited. And waited.

"Roman? Are you there?"

"Hell. Yes," His brother snapped in fury. "And I know exactly who this is."

No.

Anger screamed through her mind, blackening her thoughts into molten rage.

How could these people do this? She'd come here for an outlet and found a fight. Well if they wanted a fight, they could have one.

There was a lot of anger to get rid of. A lot of payback to deliver. "And damn it, I refuse to be cheated. I need my vengeance. I deserve justice." The anger soared outward, blackening all thoughts into molten rage.

How could there be so many people here? And how could so many understand energy?

Until now, she'd believed her and her siblings were special. Above the others. Believed they'd been the only ones with such skills. That the world was their playground – to do with as they wished.

What a rush that had been.

She'd loved that sense of uniqueness. That sense of superiority over the rest of the world. That power to play God. And boy, had they played. Together and apart they'd done what they wanted with who they'd wanted, believing it was their right as superior beings. That no one would ever know.

How wrong could they have been?

They weren't the only ones who could do this. The only ones that played in both realities.

Disbelief fired the rage all over again and she blasted off more grenades. Barely satisfied she realized now how Shay had beaten her brothers. Not just one, but both of them.

Shay and her helper. Or many helpers. She'd known Shay couldn't have done this alone.

Then, Darren had Danny to help him. That Shay most likely had never even known about Danny's existence, hurt. Darren rarely told anyone about his twin. And he'd never tell a mark like Shay. It was private. Danny had been the other half of Darren. The two of them were identical in so many ways. But when Darren had hesitated to kill Shay, it had been Danny that had stepped in and made sure it happened.

Made sure Darren didn't change his mind.

Only something had gone wrong. She remembered their panicked cries for help as she raced toward them. Their agonized screams as they died. Both of them – at the same time. When the energy had taken one brother, it had also taken the second. Connected as always.

She'd come to their aid, entering the fight at the end – just that one instant too late. She'd seen the two energies, Shay's and this asshole's here in the children's ward. She recognized him here. He'd die tonight as well.

But there'd also been something else there at the end. Or someone else. A blue energy. Even now, she couldn't place it. It had jumped into the battle just ahead of her attempt.

And when combined with the other energies, had blown a hole through her siblings' heart chakras.

If only she'd been earlier. She could have saved her brothers. She could have killed Shay. Only she'd been too late.

Now, a year later, she would get her revenge.

Or was trying to.

No! she screamed to the ethers. You won't beat me. I am too strong. I'm stronger than my brothers ever were.

Her brothers had always said she was the strongest person they'd ever seen. Often snapped the words out in a jealous rage. She'd have grinned if she were in her physical form. Laughed out loud if she could have. She was the damn strongest. No one could beat her.

No one. And no group could either.

She closed her eyes and focused on pulling in as much energy as she could handle. She'd see this place blow, and herself with it, before she'd let these bastards win.

More. Pull more. Using techniques she'd learned a long time ago, she opened up her energy chakras and pulled at the atmosphere.

She'd show them.

CHAPTER 26

PAIN WHIPPED THROUGH Shay. Followed by heat and anger in a steady one-two punch as energy rattled through her, separating her misty form even further.

Whoever this person was, they had some serious power behind them. And they were seriously demented.

Shay struggled amongst the blasts, the energy that she was both assimilating and blending with.

Stay strong, Shay, Stefan's voice whispered through to her.

I am. I'm trying to envelop the energy. Wrap it up so it can't get any bigger.

No! Don't. It could blow you up. You have to jump inside and power it down.

I am so not able to do that.

Yes, you can. Blend with the energy, find the source, become a part of it then shut down the chakra from the inside.

That will kill the person.

An awkward silence ensued as she realized how foolish her comment was. Then Stefan's gentle voice filtered through her consciousness. *I know. But if you don't, we're all going to die. We can't keep this up.*

Damn. She shuddered. *I'm on it.*

Go quietly. Hide your tracks.

Hide her tracks? That made her pause. It meant technically no longer existing as herself, but becoming one with everything around her. She'd heard about it. Hadn't tried it yet. Supposedly it came with a dangerous hook – becoming permanently lost on the ethers. She'd have to have help to return. More help than Stefan would likely be able to provide.

Becoming one with everything, meant losing her individuality, her identity. That's where the problem lay. If she did what Stefan asked, she'd cease to exist.

Still, she had to try. If it was a one-way trip, then so be it. Better that than to have this asshole take out dozens of lives. These were her friends. And the children were innocent victims. Someone needed to stop this. To save them.

If she was the only one that could – so be it.

With a last loving regret for Roman and what they might have had together, knowing that taking the next step was the riskiest thing she'd ever done, she took a deep breath and dropped her consciousness another level.

She became one with the broken floor. One with the destroyed furniture. She became one with the very air. The very essence that made her who she was, melded and blended to become one with the black power that was filling the room. Her fragments, so tiny, so light, could attach her to the attacker and not have them know it. She'd feel familiar to the person's energy. She'd feel like she was one particle of the many.

That's because she was. She'd become *one* with everything.

And there was the danger.

If she destroyed this other person, there was a good chance she would destroy herself.

And yet there was no choice.

She separated herself further from life, from the physical reality as she knew it. With another breath of air, she slipped further away, yet again. Becoming one with the universe. One with her past.

And she became one with all.

The emotions of her attacker poured through her, filling her, hooking her, sucking her into its existence.

Memories overwhelmed her. Of children laughing. Adults crying. A barrage of images flew past, of cars. Schools. Classes. Men. Old. Young. Lovers. Haters. And then one face that made Shay gasp as hurt and betrayal threatened to swamp her.

Darren.

This person *was* connected to Darren. To the man who'd tried to kill her.

Tidbits of conversation streamed through her new awareness with emotions attached. Another face. A similar face. *Twins?* Darren and his brother. But still he was not this person she'd joined. This threat was another of Darren's sibling. A third sibling connected to the twin brothers. Another brother? No. A sister. A sister Shay had never known about. A sister that Darren had never wanted her to know about.

Because, in the end, Darren hadn't intended for Shay to survive to meet her.

But Shay had. And now, as part of everything, she understood it all. Most of all, the hate Darren's sister felt for her.

And that's why Shay had been targeted. That's why her projects had been hit. Why suspicion had been thrown on her. Why the children's hospital – her special project that even Darren had been jealous of – had been targeted. And it explained why no one had recognized the energy. As Darren had been able to hide his energy, his true person, so too had his sister hid hers.

Like Darren, his sister could mask what she was doing, keeping a completely false front in place for others to view. Yet inside, she'd been scheming and planning to destroy Shay and all Shay held dear.

To avenge her brothers' deaths by murdering innocent people…

Like Bernice. Like David. Like Robert. Like Tabitha, Marie, that elderly lady beside Pappy's room.

Shay's heart cracked, causing pain like she'd never felt before. So many victims. So many unnecessary deaths. So many families destroyed.

Stay focused. Stay in the light. Stefan's voice whispered through her essence. *We have to stop her.*

She couldn't speak. She was too full of this other person's agenda that tried to take her over. To control her. To keep her and contain her.

Careful, Stefan warned.

Shay swallowed hard. *I'm trying.*

Don't try. Do.

ROMAN RACED TO the address his brother had given him over the phone – after he identified the woman in the photo. His brother and a team met him there.

Such a small unassuming townhouse on the edge of town. Made of unassuming bricks and mortar…and filled with evil. He swore he could almost see the oozing clouds of wrongness coming off the front of the building. A couple of neighbors sat on their porches reaching for the cool night air.

The cop cars arrived with screeching brakes but no sirens. If anything, the lack of sirens sent out a stronger message that scared the hell out of those enjoying the peace and quiet of the night.

Roman motioned for the old guy sitting next to the townhouse to come down to the street level. The man scrambled in his direction. The others, realizing something was wrong, joined him. Motioning everyone to silence, the cops emptied the homes on either side of the one they needed to access.

With Ronin in the lead, they snuck up to the front door.

YES. SHAY UNDERSTOOD. She had to go inside the blackness. Beneath the memories and the emotions. She had to go deeper into the physical being. Wherever that person was. The woman wasn't here physically at the hospital. Like Stefan and Shay, she was out of her body – fighting in astral form. Now Shay had to find this person's body. Find her physical form.

And shut her down.

Struggling to keep her thoughts pure, her energy golden and warming, she allowed her own consciousness to join with her attacker's. And she sank deeper into the woman's psyche to hunt for and find the woman's silver cord. There was so much pulsing and surging energy around her that she couldn't see it. She searched the light, the dark, the nonexistent...and then she saw it. Relief washed through her. At least this person had a cord. Shay admitted to herself that she'd been worried about what specific abilities this person had and whether they truly *were* earthbound.

With the silver grey cord winking in and out of the blackness, she slid along the lit pathway, racing faster and faster, hating the panic threatening to overwhelm her. She didn't dare stop now. She couldn't fail. This was too important. Too necessary for these kids. For Stefan. And all the other souls that had come to help.

And Roman. If her attacker beat her and survived this would destroy him. They'd just found each other. To lose him now...

And just like that, she came to the end of the cord and fell into the body of Darren's sister.

And realized who this person was. With access to all her thoughts, memories, motivations. Shay stood in silence, filled with more pain than she thought possible, a greater sense of betrayal than she'd have thought there could be, and evidence of more damage than any trio of siblings had a right to inflict.

This was *Jordan.* Her assistant. With access to all of Shay's files. With inner knowledge of all of Shay's projects. With a connection to, and information about, Shay's personal life through her brother Darren.

Who had access to Bernice. To Bernice's emails. And even to the Foundation function that night.

Even though Ronin had run a check on her, she'd managed to hide who she truly was.

Jordan who was aware of her relationship with Roman. Had commented on it. Was he her next target? And then there was Pappy, Tabitha, her cousin Marie...

Her assistant knew all the pain and fear Shay had been through this last year. And all the while she'd been twisting the screw tighter and tighter. Had she been the one who sent those threatening letters to Bernice? Those horrible emails? She'd had access to all Shay's contacts as well as her computer.

And she'd been a blackmailer who went after payouts from Bernice, before she'd agree to just go away. Greedy like Darren. Wanting more and more. Only Bernice, though she'd agreed to pay, hadn't agreed to an amount. Jordan had considered her offers too low to be bothered backing down.

So this then was Bernice's deal with the devil. She'd been scared by the threats and the promise of the evil behind those letters. She'd offered to pay to make it all go away. Only her offer was too low and so Jordan had only twisted the knife harder. Demanding more and more. Why? To torment Bernice, and thus torment Shay. Jordan had known how close the two of them were.

There'd been no way out for Bernice.

Shay now knew why there'd been no stopping the emails – because money wasn't the only object of the game. Just a nice side benefit.

Vengeance had been the goal.

And Bernice had nothing to do with any of this but she was someone Shay loved. Bernice had been an innocent victim. Just like David. Like Robert… Like so many others.

For years, Bernice'd been the closest thing to a mother Shay had. Why Shay's brother hadn't been targeted too, Shay didn't know. Unless Jordan thought Shay wasn't close to him because he'd spent the bulk of the last year on various continents around the world whereas everyone else she cared about was here. Close by. Available. Visible.

Anger spiked through Shay as she realized how she'd been manipulated. How she'd been played. Not once, but twice. By Darren and now his sister. Struggling for control, she tamped down the anger slightly, not wanting to bring attention to her presence. She didn't dare risk exposure at this stage.

But she acknowledged the anger, honed it to precision accuracy. She zeroed in on the chakras and raced through Jordan's body to the heart. There she waffled, though she understood what was needed.

She knew that to use deadly force was going to take her to a place she didn't want to go. Again.

Don't use deadly force. Use love as the force. Don't direct your anger and pain at her. Instead, shine your love – for all these children and for those of us helping…indeed for the rest of all that's good and true in the world – through her heart chakra. There can only be one of two outcomes. One, the deadly blackness will dissipate under the love; or two, she won't be able to withstand the influx of energy. Remember…love conquers all.

Shay lifted her face to the light and let her love pour through. She smiled as the warmth and joy filled her. She wasn't made of anger and pain. She lived a life of love and grace. She believed in it. Chose to live her life by it. At that moment, she was in the perfect state…*of grace.*

She closed her eyes and pulled the small, vapor-sized pieces of herself toward her, glowing with love for her fellow man. For freedom to walk the path she needed to walk. She called the basic elements of her essence home.

In a wash of golden goodness.

Her energy swelled with joy. Shay's form grew as the tiny parts of her raced home. One by one, they collected to become one whole astral soul. *Hers.* All the while, she sent out strong, loving energy, healing energy, warm caring energy. Forgiving energy. She forgave Darren for his betrayal. She forgave the twin brother.

And hardest of all – she forgave Jordan.

Her heart swelled with her own joy as hurts of the last year dropped away. She released herself from the bondage of pain she'd locked herself into this last year.

Her astral form continued to grow, and her energy continued to glow. What a weight she'd carried this last year. And now, she just let it go. She felt it release, felt the emotions and memories, energy hooks, all the negative energy fall away. She let it all go.

She realized she really was thankful to Jordan for this opportunity. Shay could grow through this. And Shay could cleanse her soul.

Jordan would have to make peace in her own way on her own time.

But it wouldn't be in this lifetime.

Even as the words flew through her thoughts, the last of her astral form came home – swiftly, silently and secretively – so quickly Jordan didn't see Shay's arrival.

Until it was too late.

Shay witnessed when Jordan suddenly understood that something had changed. Something in her world had gone wrong. Shay could feel Jordan's disbelief, her anger, then her realization.

That she had a visitor. On the inside.

In a featherlight movement, Shay whispered, "Knock, knock. Guess who's here?"

"*Noooo…!*" The scream ripped from Jordan's throat in one long anguished torrent.

Distant sounds barely filtered through Shay's consciousness. Yells, pounding, splintering wood, more screaming.

Then…it all stopped…and Shay heard…nothing.

And the internal pressure, the force from too much energy contained in one confined space – burst through in an explosion.

Shay cried out as the space she was in – shattered, sending her astral form spiraling back out to the universe, in a million infinitesimal fragments.

Friday morning…

"YOU NEED TO rest," Stefan urged Roman. "You can't help her if you can't look after yourself."

Roman stared at him, knowing the pain of the last few days would never truly go away. Shay was comatose before him, still lying on his bed as she had when he'd woken up that fateful morning.

Dr. Maddy was still trying. And so was Stefan.

Shay wasn't just lost in the ethers, but her fragments were spread so thin, the pieces flung so far apart, they couldn't call her home.

"I can't sleep," he said simply. "I have to help."

What could he do? He wasn't like them. He had no psychic abilities. He couldn't track her down like they were attempting to do. Or track all the lost pieces that made up the Shay he knew and loved. Talk about a mind-boggling concept.

He shuddered and closed his eyes. "But I don't know how. Tell me what *I* can do to bring her back. I'm not like you."

Stefan's smile was tired but held real amusement. "You, more than anyone, should be able to help. You know her better physically than I do. Than anyone does." Stefan gave a short laugh. "This might not be the best time but…maybe there is none better. You are likely the only one that *can* help."

Roman shook his head, but Stefan continued to speak. "Though you aren't aware…you are a dream walker. You called it inspiration. And true, that's how you started on this journey, but one painting, one photo was never enough. You had to have more. You had to see more. You dreamed of her. Of knowing more. Of being more with her. You don't remember but in your dreams you traveled to her, so you could see her in greater detail. You walked with her in your dreams. And then you painted her."

Roman stared at him. Shock rippling through him. "*Say what?* All

I've ever done is paint pictures of her. Sure, sometimes I close my eyes to pull an image into tighter clarity, but that's all." He tried to shrug it off. The rest of what Stefan said was just too bizarre.

"And that's how you've been doing what you're doing. The first picture peaked your interest, but it can't account for the visual images you've been drawing on these last couple of years. You've been accessing the images that you have stored from walking with her in your dreams. That's how you have seen her in such clarity – in such detail. In so doing, she became a part of your psyche. A part of you. A part of your soul. It's a connection that can't be severed. You are now her safety line. Or her ground, as we call it. You are the one that can show her the way home."

There were no words. Roman could only stare, as he remembered the many tormented nights and happy mornings when he'd woken up with his thoughts full of Shay. He'd felt foolish. Like a lovestruck teenager. All the while he'd been developing a skill called dream walking? To become Shay's lifeline?

He loved that idea. Wanted to be what Shay needed. But surely Stefan was wrong? Talking about someone else? Someone with psychic abilities. Someone like Stefan.

"I think you're wrong. But I hope you aren't. *If* you're right, I still don't know how to help."

Stefan walked closer. "How, you ask?" He smiled, realization dawning on his own face. "By doing what you do best. By painting her. Your love for her is in every line. Every brushstroke. I saw it. She saw it."

Roman stared at Stefan. "She did?"

"Absolutely. She said as much at your showing that night. She understood, even then, the power of the connection you had." He smiled gently. "She just hadn't recognized the connection was to her."

"I don't understand that."

Stefan, so tired that his voice cracked, said, "There's nothing to understand. You love her. Now go paint her. All of her. You no longer need a photo of her. You know her so well. You could paint her with your eyes closed." His face lighted. "And from your expression I can see you already have done that. So do it again now. Paint every inch of her. Show her the way here. The way home. Help her to pull her energy back to become whole in her astral self. If you can do that, the shift to her body will be easy."

Roman was too scared to answer him right away. What if he couldn't do what Stefan said he could? What if he could, but he screwed it up? What if by his actions, he lost Shay forever?

He walked over to the bed to stare down at his beloved Shay. "You're crazy. It's ridiculous to say I can do any of that stuff you talked about."

"What you don't understand is that Shay is here," Stefan said. "Right now." He waved his arm around the room. "She's everywhere. But she's fragmented. She's so small she's in the very air we breathe. But she can't find her way home – or else she'd be here. You are her home. You are her other half. Now paint exactly what you see in your mind and guide her back. Ground her here."

Roman narrowed his gaze at something he couldn't quite detect in Stefan's voice. His heart sank as he thought he understood. "You don't think I *can* do this."

"I'm hoping you can." Stefan ran his fingers through his hair and down the back of his head, then admitted, "But I'm afraid that what you'll paint won't be what you're expecting." Stefan pointed to the door. "Your studio is there. Go. Close your eyes and paint Shay as you see her in your mind, right now."

With that command, Roman bolted for his studio. He picked up a blank canvas and removed the unfinished picture on his favorite easel. Not allowing himself to second-guess, he allowed himself to begin without thinking about what he'd paint.

At his paint counter, he instinctively opened red and white tubes. In a slapdash methodology he never used, he squeezed paint onto his palette and started mixing. As always, the feel of a brush in his hand calmed him. Made him feel more in control. As if what he would put on the canvas was important. Meaningful – at least it would be to him.

Nervous tension gripped his stomach. He was so afraid Stefan was wrong. Roman wanted him to be right, but... Roman was not like Stefan, or Maddy. Or Shay. Yes, Roman could paint, but his talent was nothing compared to the stuff they did...

But if there were anything he could do to help Shay...Roman would do it.

He walked back to the blank canvas and went to place a long stroke of her arm, when he realized he couldn't. His hand couldn't make the stroke. He tried again, the effort breaking a sweat out on his brow.

Stefan spoke from behind him. "Relinquish control. Let the brush tell you what to paint."

His back stiffened. Realizing Stefan could guide him, he nodded.

"Close your eyes, and let your brush speak for you."

Such an odd suggestion. But it felt right. And that was even odder still. Aware of not having painted Shay since they'd become lovers, he closed his eyes and let his hand – his brush – do as it willed. He'd been aware of every line of Shay's body for a long time and now he knew her at a physically intimate level. He dreamt of her. In that Stefan was right. Had he really travelled to see her, too? He cast his mind back. Seeing the times he stopped a painting to stare off into space. Accessing images from…somewhere.

When his arm dipped and dabbed, he was astonished, wanting to look, but he was scared to stop the magic. When his brush no longer moved, he realized someone behind him was taking a deep breath. "Well, you got that much right."

Roman opened his eyes to see he'd painted a woman's form lying on a bed. She was barely discernible in white. More like a ghosted image on the canvas.

But covering the entire form were thousands of red dots.

"What the hell is *that*?"

"That is Shay as she is now." Stefan studied the painting, and then apparently satisfied, nodded. "Now call to her in your mind. Tell her how much you love her. And need her. Call her home."

Stefan wandered the space. Spying a stack of blank canvases, he replaced the one Roman had just painted with a new, blank one. "Here. Now paint her again. We'll see if there is a change."

Thinking he was crazy, but willing to try anything if it would help, Roman closed his eyes and let his need pour forth.

Shay. Please come home to me. I love you. I need you. Don't make me live this way. Without you. I was lost until I found you, and now, you are lost to me. Please. Find me here. Come to me. Let's live our lives together. Be with me until we grow old, together. Please. Come home.

He closed his eyes and bowed his head as the litany played over and over again in his mind. He barely registered when his arm lifted and the brush started moving rapidly across the canvas. He could feel pressure inside his chest. Feel the pain of his loss and the agony of his need to have her returned to him. He'd never been much of a verbal communicator, preferring to use a canvas for his expression. And he found an odd sense of freedom in giving that expression free rein.

"Now open your eyes." Stefan's warm voice sounded at his shoulder.

Roman opened his eyes and studied the painting. The same white image lay quietly in the bed, only now it was more defined. Was it more lively than the first image?

He raced back to his first canvas and checked. He frowned. There might be a tiny change in her expression? And then again, maybe not. He returned to his canvas. The red dots had collected more closely together. In the shape of a woman's body. Not a definable solid line, but they were representative of Shay's body, as if he had used a stippling technique. Interesting. He never used that style. "But what does it mean?"

"It means she's hearing you." Stefan smacked him on his back, "Good. Now – do it again."

Obediently, Roman closed his eyes and started all over on yet another blank canvas. He explained how he'd loved her long before he'd met her. How he'd been ashamed to tell her. How he hadn't been able to explain for fear of chasing her away. And he'd do anything to keep her in his life.

Anything.

Before he really understood how much he'd done or the time that had passed, he realized a fatigue like he'd never known before had settled deep into his soul.

"Open your eyes."

Roman gazed at the more collected, but still undefined, form of a woman hovering over the slack woman in white. He checked on Shay. This time he could see the change. The stillness was gone. She wasn't back, but she no longer looked like the living dead.

"Again."

This time, Roman knew what to do. Seeing the change, knowing his efforts were working, he closed his eyes, and with determination and a hint of anger in his voice he called out to her while his arm worked at a furious pace – with a surety to it's strokes. If she was listening, then she could damn well come home.

"Shay. Get yourself back home and into my bed where you belong," he roared. "I love you. I always have. God damn it, I won't sleep with your ghost for the rest of my life. Get your beautiful ass home – now."

He could sense Stefan's surprise. Felt his bated breath as he waited to see what would happen next. Roman opened his eyes and couldn't believe the image on his canvas. "Wow."

"I'll say."

The red polka dot form had lain down over top of the white still form, injecting existence and blood into the woman on the canvas. The red became pink, giving the impression of life and a spark to her image.

He threw down the paintbrush and raced back to his bed.

And cried out in pain.

Shay didn't look any different.

His heart dropped. He'd been so sure he'd actually be able to make his paintings create truth in real life. Panic set in. Ignoring the rules he'd been told, not to touch, and with Stefan making no move to stop him, Roman dropped to her side, lowered his head and kissed her. Gently. Tenderly. Afraid to hurt her.

He pulled back, studied her for a long moment. Then spoke forcefully, lovingly, but giving no quarter. "Enough, damn it. Come home, Shay. Please."

And he dropped his head again and kissed her. Hard.

It took a few seconds to realize that the cool lips were warming beneath his, that the arms crushed against his chest were hanging on to his shirt, and that she really was responding.

He pulled back to stare into that beloved, half-lidded gaze. Tears formed in the corner of his eyes. "Shay? Oh thank God. I love you," he whispered. "Thank you for coming back."

"Thank you," she answered simply, "for showing me the way."

He dropped his forehead to rest on hers. "Good thing you came home or I'd have found a way to cross over and drag you back."

"You won't have to." She smiled, tears pooling in the corner of her eyes to slide down her face. "Just do what you did tonight. Use love and I'll always find my way back to you."

The two gazed at each other in exhaustion and hope, and then Roman lowered his head once again.

CHAPTER 27

I T WAS MUCH later, after a shower and some food, that Shay pushed her chair back and walked over to the studio to stare at the pictures Roman had created to bring her home. As she studied the last one Roman picked up his palette and quickly created a last painting of Shay at home and whole. "Just to make sure."

She laughed. But she waited willingly. She asked Stefan and Roman all the questions that burned inside. "What happened to Jordan?"

"She's dead, for starters," Stefan said, an arm around her shoulders. "I'm not sure what the coroner will say is the cause of her death though. Her heart, the actual organ, exploded inside her chest." He grimaced. "I didn't know that could happen."

"Good thing," Roman muttered, as he focused on his painting. "Saved me from having to kill her."

Shay reached a hand up and squeezed his shoulder. "I'm going to have to overhaul my hiring policies. I could have saved myself a lot of heartache if I'd known she was Darren's sister."

"You and me both," said Stefan. "But there was no indication that Darren had any family living. He was adopted. They all were and to different families. Remember? The three of them found each other somehow. Their unique abilities may have facilitated that as they became young adults." He frowned. "According to Ronin, Darren and his twin Danny appeared to have been running scams together. I don't know if Jordan was as well. That's for the police to follow up on. If they ever do."

"Not likely," she scoffed. "This is difficult for them to understand."

"Difficult for anyone who wasn't there," murmured Roman, his gaze on his canvas. "As it is, I can't imagine the explanation they gave the public for the destruction in that hospital wing and as to how the kids all survived. Some kind of explosion I believe the media said."

"They had to say something. The public doesn't want to know about people like us."

"Roman's brother is looking into Jordan's history for us." Stefan rubbed his forehead and yawned. "I think I called in everyone I knew last night. Just to keep Jordan in check."

"I hope we never find anyone that strong or that crazy again." Shay shivered, so grateful to be home whole and healthy. It had been a close call and she knew who to thank for her safe return. Hopefully she'd be given a long and healthy life to thank him.

"You and me both," Stefan said.

"Why was she so strong at the hospital? I don't understand that." Shay had puzzled over that while in a hot shower. She hadn't been able to come up with an answer.

"I think she was drawing the energy from the protective bubble Maddy and I put over the children to keep them safe. Once she recognized how strong it was, she stopped trying to damage it. Instead, she started to use it to amplify her abilities."

Shay shivered. "Smart. And nasty."

Roman wiped his hands and reached out to squeeze hers. "But she's dead. So that's no longer an issue."

"She caused so much damage. She killed Bernice. For fun, I think." Shay already explained the bits and pieces she'd found in Jordan's mind. "And the others. Poor Pappy. I'm so glad he's doing fine. I don't know if I should tell him about Bernice or not."

With a snort, Roman said, "I'd want to know my beloved was standing over me as a guardian angel until it was my time to join her."

"Good point." Shay laughed. "I'll tell him tomorrow when we take him home to his apartment."

Stefan smiled down at her. "You did good tonight, Shay. You'll have to teach me that trick."

"Not any time in the near future." She shuddered. "The trip into Jordan's mind was not pleasant. So many people. Jordan treated so many victims as toys. How wrong is that?"

"We always believe the unbelievable can't happen – until someone proves us wrong." Stefan smiled at her. "Let's hope it will be a long time before we come up against someone else like this."

Shay nodded. "I'm just hoping that is the end of their family." Shay glanced over at Stefan. "I won't sleep well until I know I'm not going to be under attack from anyone else looking for payback because I killed off their family."

"That is one of the primary issues Ronin is looking into." Stefan paused when Roman stepped back from his painting. "We will find out."

"Wow." Shay stared at the picture on the canvas.

With a self-conscious shrug, Roman said, "Not good enough for the gallery, but it certainly should do the job for tonight's mess."

"It's beautiful," Stefan said sincerely. And it was. It was also the only painting with Shay's face. She still lay in bed, the covers up tight, but there was a calm serenity to the sleeping form. So few strokes but the painting glowed with life…and love.

Roman walked to his sideboard and picked up a tube of blue paint.

She laughed. "What are you doing with that color?"

He hunched his shoulders and said almost defensively, "Damned if I know. But I have to add it."

Shay glanced over at Stefan, one eyebrow raised. The smirk on his face had her tilting her head. "Stefan?"

His gaze deepened, the smile shining from the chocolate depths. "Listen."

She frowned. "I can't hear anything."

But Stefan's grin said there was something she should be hearing.

With a start, Roman said, "I'm hearing something. Like an engine. But… *What the hell…?*"

Shay gasped. "Morris!" She spun around searching for the glowing ball. "Surely it can't be?"

Stefan laughed. "It is indeed your beloved pet. His soul scattered in the craziness of Darren's death, but he stayed with you all this time. As Roman brought you back…" Stefan nodded to the painting now sporting a ball of blue curled up on the woman's sleeping shoulder. "Roman also showed Morris the way to return in one piece. Or in as many pieces as the ghost of Morris contains."

Tears formed in Shay's eyes, to trickle down her cheeks as the truth, and the purr of her best feline friend, wrapped around her heart and hugged her close.

"So Roman saved not just one of us tonight – he saved us both." She walked over and wrapped her arms around Roman.

His arms closed tightly, holding her against his heart.

She whispered, "Thank you."

"You're both welcome," Roman said. The distant sound, like a warm, happy engine, kicked up a notch. "Although I'm not sure how to get used to a ghost cat."

Shay smiled. "No problem. After what you've been through, Morris will be easy."

"But I'm going home now." Stefan rose. "I'm way too tired to do anything but sleep for a few days." He hesitated. "I'm beyond tired actually. Must be the fallout from all those energy blasts. Hope my abilities aren't going to change over this mess."

"And mine." Shay smiled. "I don't imagine the others would be happy either."

"Happy or not, it's the life." Stefan smiled. "We will adapt, if need be."

"And speaking of those other people that stepped in and helped…" Roman said as they walked to the front door. "Thank them for me."

"Actually, I think it might be better if you two say it yourself." Stefan smiled at Shay. "Shay knows them all. Not well, but she knows them a whole lot better now than she did before. Don't forget to connect with Tabitha. She's just been released from hospital and is home now."

"And Pappy. Thank heavens." There'd been so much uncertainty, so much danger, and now it was over. Hard to believe.

Stefan reached out and gave her a hug. "I'm so glad you survived."

Tears pooled again. She sniffled them back and beamed a teary smile up at him. "Me too. Thanks for pointing Roman in the right direction and saving my life again."

His grin widened. "So we're even." He dropped a kiss on her forehead before he turned to face Roman. "Thank you for helping bring her home."

Roman smiled down at Shay, tucking her close under his arm. "And that's where she belongs."

They watched the elevator close behind Stefan. "Does it bother you that you might never have the same abilities that I do?" Shay asked, not wanting him to be envious, but showing she understood if he were.

"No. I might not like you disappearing like you have this scary tendency to do, but I'm sure I'll get used to it. Besides, I might not have *your* talents, but I have enough of my own."

"That you do." Shay realized he spoke the truth as he led her to his studio, where he'd placed the weird collection of paintings that had helped call her home. "Are you going to ever put these on display?"

"In a gallery? Oh no. Never."

"Not good enough, huh?" She laughed as she studied the weird paintings in order – from red splattered paint to the one with a hint of blue Morris.

"I don't know how I feel about so many paintings of just me," she admitted. "It's a little odd."

"Get used to it," he said cheerfully, "because now that I have you at my side, I have so much more to work with."

He tugged her into his arms and kissed her soundly.

DALE MAYER

A Psychic Visions Novel

RARE FIND

Dedication

This book is dedicated to my four children who always believed in me and my storytelling abilities.

Thank you!

Acknowledgments

Rare Find wouldn't have been possible without the support of my friends and family. Many hands helped with proofreading, editing, and beta reading to make this book come together.

I thank you all.

CHAPTER 1

Saturday early afternoon

"**I** HATE TO leave you right now," Ronin murmured against her hair. "You shouldn't be alone today, of all days."

Tabitha Stoddard tilted her head and sniffled back the tears. She managed a watery smile. "There's no quick fix for this. I just need time. I'll reminisce about my grandfather today and that will help. Go to the station and speak with your detectives. You need to deal with the phone call." She took a deep bracing breath and added, "I'm fine."

And she would be fine. It just might take awhile.

He looked at her, doubt forcing his gaze to narrow and his lips to twist. She reached up and kissed him lightly. "Go."

"I'll check in with you when I'm done."

She nodded and watched as he walked back to his truck and drove out of Exotic Landscape's parking lot. She was grateful he'd been there for her grandfather's funeral that morning. His presence had made everything so much easier.

Smiling, she turned and walked into the center. Her three-legged bull mastiff greeted her joyously. Even missing his back lower leg, he was one heck of a watch dog.

Just like Ronin who was a protector, a cop, a strong man with strong morals and ethics. A good man. A man's man. And one she'd fallen in love with.

Not that he knew it. They hadn't gotten to that stage yet. She'd planned to stay over at his place this weekend, but her grandfather's death had changed all that.

With tears burning her eyes, Tabitha stared at the picture of her standing beside her grandfather that hung behind his desk. He'd been the mainstay of her life. He'd raised her, shared his passion with her, and although there had been little softness in him, he'd been there for her every step of the way.

Unlike her father who was only there when it was convenient for him.

She snatched up yet another tissue off the desk and blew her nose. How could there still be tears? She'd done nothing but cry bucketfuls for days. Heart hurting, she wandered into his old office. He'd lived sixty-seven years and should have had another twenty to go. The doctors said it was his heart.

She didn't have a hard time believing that. As much as she loved her grandfather, she had no illusions that others would feel the same way. He'd had little heart for anyone else. He was hard. Cold. Unyielding, and unless you walked on four feet or were his granddaughter, he wouldn't give you the time of day. And that included his son and his brother, her uncle who had died when she was just a kid.

But, despite his faults, she'd loved her grandfather.

And the hole in her heart seemed too vast to ever heal.

Tripod nudged her hip with his muzzle. She reached down and laid a comforting hand on his head. He'd been by her side since she'd found him in a back alley on one of her and her grandfather's rare trips into Seattle. Her grandfather had abhorred the city and the minions that scurried around in it. She, on the other hand, had craved it while she was a teen, but after spending time at a girlfriend's place, dead center in the chaos, she'd been only too grateful to return to her wooded acres…and her animals.

She had lots of friends – of the female kind. And although she'd given it a good try, until Ronin she'd found little to commend two-legged males and risking deeper human relationships.

She admired women like her friend, Shay Lassiter. Shay combined her daily work, a partner and her psychic abilities into something that worked for her.

In Tabitha's case, she could do the work, no problem. The partner issue had so far escaped her best attempts, although she had high hopes with Ronin. That detective made her want all sorts of things in life that had eluded her. Like marriage. A family. It was fresh right now. Special. Just the thought of him made her toes wiggle and her heart sigh with happiness – and they hadn't even made it to bed yet.

Her grandfather's old desk caught her gaze – scarred, with broken drawers and bolts for handles, it was decrepit. As she stared she realized that somewhere along the way the desk had lost its leg and he'd propped it up with whatever was handy – in this case, several bricks. Typical. He'd insisted on keeping it, saying that as long as he could keep using it, it wasn't really broken – was it?

Unfortunately, the rest of his office was full of the same and most of it would need to go to the dump after she'd gone through it.

She randomly opened drawers, wondering at the collection of aged papers inside. Dennis – her mostly absent father – had already gone through the desk looking for documents he'd need to settle her grandfather's estate. He even took her grandfather's old ornate box – the one she'd seen many times over the years, but had never looked inside.

Grandfather had told her it contained private papers, hence her father taking it. He'd likely hand it over to Eric, his assistant, or his partner Germaine, instead of dealing with it himself. Tabitha was fine with that. Easier on her.

She cast a final glance around the messy room.

Her grandfather's true legacy lay outside the main buildings in the acres long ago turned into an animal reserve. And though it was expensive to run, her grandfather never shortchanged the animals' needs. He'd go without a meal rather than see his beloved pets do the same.

She'd learned that lesson well. As she stared down at the ripped jeans she'd changed into after the funeral, she realized she might have learned it a little too well. There was money, but only enough to cover the necessities. There were always more animals in need than resources at hand.

In spite of the poor relationship her grandfather had with his son, Exotic Landscape wouldn't have achieved this size or capacity without her father's donations. Guilt money. Then Shay's Foundation money had taken the place to the next level.

Sniffling, she wiped her eyes and turned too fast. Her head pounded and the room swayed around her.

Damn. When would the hurting stop?

She lost time as she sat in the office and let the pain roll.

Her phone rang. She sniffled, until call display showed it was Ronin. Her flagging energy lifted. He always did that to her.

"Hey." She walked over to the window to stare out into the late afternoon sun as she spoke into the phone. "How did it go? Are you done?"

"Yeah, it was probably a waste of time," he said humorlessly. "But I had to check it out. Sorry about having to leave."

"Not an issue," she said tiredly. "It's the job."

"It is," he agreed, "but it's still difficult when being a cop interferes with my personal life. Especially at times like this."

Traffic noises from his phone blocked out everything else for a few seconds. Abruptly, he added, "I'll still be a few hours. Do you want me to stop by afterwards?"

Her heart screamed *yes*, but…she could also use some time alone. She hated feeling so raw. Vulnerable. But grief did that to her. "I'll be fine." She rubbed her eyes again. "The next couple of days will be tough, but I will get through them."

"That doesn't mean you have to get through them alone. And those headaches are nothing to ignore," he said brusquely. "I'll stop by when I'm done here. Gotta go."

Tabitha stared down at her phone. That was the story of her life. The men all had to go – one way or the other. And yet Ronin kept coming back.

As if in response to her mood, her headache started dancing a rumba on her brain. It had to be stress as well as grief. Yeah, that was so possible. She didn't have to look far to find places where her world was off-kilter.

Besides her grandfather's death, there had been a rash of destructive incidents at Exotic Landscape. They had been irritating, costly and left her feeling as if she was under attack. She had no idea by whom. Or why. Or if any of the events were even related. They were mostly little things, like bags of dog food missing and some of the grain walking off. Break-ins at the clinic side of the main offices. Rocks through the window. Her grandfather had ignored a lot of it, but then he'd been in a whole different space this last year.

She had nothing anyone could want, and not enough of what the animals needed. She didn't need to be throwing money away fixing doors and windows and replacing stolen property.

Plus her budget had been shot with the new staff she'd been forced to hire. Not that the break-ins were the impetus behind those new hires; the real reason had been her long slow recovery in hospital after a psychic attack over a month ago. Her friend Shay had been the target. Tabitha was just a casualty. But that episode had changed her life. These incidents at the center had just helped to cement the decision to bring on more staff to ease her load.

On top of that, keeping her off balance, was the fact that nothing had been quite *right* since she'd been a victim of a psychic attack. She felt as if people looked at her differently. She could certainly not explain to her employees what had happened to her. She had a few friends that understood, but as for everyone else, she could hardly tell them she left her body and hid in the ethers to save herself from the attack, now could she?

Without warning, familiar pain slammed into her head, followed by a ripping sensation crawling through her brain. She bent over, grabbing the edge of the desk for support.

Several painful gasps later, she managed to take an easier breath. *Christ.* The attacks were getting worse. Another long moment later she managed a tiny step. When that worked, she took a second. As a test, she straightened, and when that was fine, she tossed her long braid back. Good, her head no longer felt like it was splitting in half. Whatever had been there – it was gone.

A ripple of relief slid down her spine.

Stefan Kronos, her scarily skilled psychic friend and mentor, spoke to her telepathically. *The headaches are troubling.*

And yet what am I to do, she answered just as softly, her heart warming at Stefan's caring voice inside her head. His visits were always a surprise, and always welcome. They also came from his heart. He cared and that was special. *I can hardly ask a doctor.*

He changed topic. *How are the nightmares?*

Better. Still the same nameless faceless boogie man, but the nightmares come less often. I sleep deeply once I get there, but I wake up troubled.

Hmmm. With that, he left her mind without warning. He was good at that.

Out of habit, she sent out a wide sweeping wave of healing energy throughout the building as she turned to leave. Instantly a sense of loss, of grief, bounced back at her along with a sense of finality. Energies from the staff, the animals, maybe even the building itself seemed to be adjusting to the loss of her grandfather.

It would take a long time before the energy changed to a loving reminiscence without the pain of loss.

She was reaching for her purse and keys she'd dropped on her grandfather's desk when something brutal stabbed into her head again. Her knees buckled and a scream ripped through her mind. The sound carried so much rage …and fear…and pain…

It wasn't her pain or fear.

But it felt like it was hers.

She groaned, trying not to collapse under the encroaching blanket of emotional darkness. She bent over and gasped for air.

Another bolt of pain ripped through her, forcing her to the floor. She cried out and arched her back as the next slicing pain whipped along her spine.

Then it was gone.

As in completely gone. Just like that.

She slowly sat back on her heels and clasped her arms around her ribs, gasping for air. She didn't know what the hell was happening, but Christ…it was bad.

And this had to stop. She couldn't deal with it. The pain was too much.

Tripod whined at her side. He dropped his massive head on her shoulders, his hot breath washing across her cheek.

"I'm okay, boy."

A slight film coated her skin and she shivered more from shock that anything else. Her t-shirt stuck to her and a chill walked over her back, raising the hairs on her arm. Standing was not an option. She was scared another bolt of pain would drop her. After a long moment, she slowly struggled to her feet, steadying herself against Tripod's huge body. A clammy chill and an overriding fatigue rushed though her.

She wanted a hot shower and a hot drink. The place was empty at this hour. She had night staff and security guards, but they wouldn't likely see her right now. She was so grateful that she didn't have far to walk, that her house was only five minutes through the trees.

Walking as gently as if she were recovering from a back injury, she made it down the short path without incident. After unlocking her front door, she entered her sanctuary. Tango's voice rumbled at her from the back. Her baby tiger was no longer a baby anything. In fact, he was an old man. But he was still her baby – or maybe it was the other way around as he'd adopted her decades ago. He hated it whenever she left. But it was hard to run a business with a tiger interrupting your world. She also didn't want the public in on Tango's rather dominant presence in her life. It was better to work from home much of the time.

Being scolded by a tiger was wearying but she'd miss it when his time came. He'd been depressed since her grandfather's passing. She hoped Tango stayed around for months so that she could grieve for one of the dearest males in her life, her grandfather, before having to grieve for another.

Tripod walked over to sit at the entrance to the kitchen. Almost as big as Tango physically, she'd never seen any dog, especially a three-legged one, eat like he did.

She could almost hear his voice saying, *Wouldn't have to scarf my food if you fed me more.*

She'd had Tripod since he was a pup, falling in love with him before she'd realized he'd grow bigger and heavier than her. Of course his size was a definite plus when he played with Tango. And the two old friends were inseparable.

Good thing Tango couldn't speak human. However she under-stood dog somewhat – so his message didn't go unnoticed.

Dropping her purse on the kitchen table, she smiled down at Tri-pod. She'd learned to communicate directly with some animals over the years because Tripod and Tango had insisted she learn. Not with words like people. And communication was different with each of them. With Tango, she often saw his emotions in colors while Tripod seemed more human than canine. He sent her both images and emotions although they could be hard to decipher. What wasn't hard to understand was when he told her off for being late.

Or when he was hungry.

Or when he was lonely.

She stopped and bent to hug him. He whined and then almost growled. She stared down at him. "What's the matter, boy?"

He nudged her waist. She bent and hugged him again. Waves of worry emanated from him. He missed her grandfather. She studied his energy waves. They rippled. Some higher, some tighter and still others were lackluster and almost flat. There was a buzz or a hum to them.

She'd spent years trying to decipher those waves, but she hadn't been able to figure all of them out. The buzz happened when they were communicating and she was not listening. With so many animals on the reserve talking to her, she'd been forced to learn to turn it on and off at will.

While most of the time it was a pleasant, almost comforting back-ground hum, sometimes it hit an irritating crescendo and she was forced to shut it off.

Tripod nudged her again with a whimper deep in his throat. Some-thing was wrong but Tabitha didn't know what. She did know Tripod was worried about her.

Then she felt a stab of hunger emanate from him and realized he'd switched from worry about her to worry about his food.

She smiled. Now that was normal.

"Come on, boy. Let's feed you."

By the time she was done feeding the animals in the house and herself, Tabitha was running on empty for energy. She needed a shower and a nap. Since her grandfather's death, her emotions had worn her down. She would love twelve hours of sleep and would be lucky to get four and she had no idea why sleep seemed so elusive these days. She'd tried everything but drugs. Drugs and psychic abilities were so not good together. They left her groggy and disoriented. Herbs were fine and natural and didn't mess up her system. Only she was now out of those and had to go shopping to get more.

There was so much they didn't know about energy work and the world was in desperate need of energy workers. Dr. Maddy was the best she knew, but there were others like Tabitha who had similar abilities. Tabitha's abilities and connections worked best on animals.

Some of the people she knew were seriously talented. They could all communicate telepathically with their partners, and often with other people. Unlike her. Most seemed to have mastered something she could only dream about.

Liar. Stefan Kronos's warm teasing voice rolled through her mind.

She snickered. *Except with you, and no one has said you're human.*

If not human, what am I?

His dry voice was so deadpan she had to giggle. *A god, according to most women.*

Oh, please don't get started. My feet are made of clay and I am as far away as possible from being anything heaven sent.

She gave a small tired laugh at that. *Okay, how about you're just a good friend?*

I can work with that.

Did you have a reason for being here? she asked as she headed to her bedroom. She changed out of her clothes and into a housecoat. Sometimes, it took several showers to wash away the animal odors. Tripod sat at her doorway watching intently. He always got an intense look on his face when she communicated with Stefan and this time was no exception.

He's probably listening in.

She grinned. Thank heavens for Stefan and that relationship of acceptance and understanding. *So few people would be able to understand this conversation.*

More than you think. And many more becoming aware that 'this' exists.

True. She stepped into the bathroom and groaned at her appearance. *Crap. Stefan, I look like I've been hit by a truck. You should see the circles under my eyes.*

Lack of sleep? Overwork? Stress?

All of the above, I suppose.

You've just lost your grandfather. And what else...? That knowing voice was calm and understanding. *But...*

She stilled. And asked cautiously, *What do you mean: What else?*

Do you think I don't hear you every time you cry out in pain?

She winced. *Oh, that.*

He waited, stoic and steadfast but unyielding.

It's not more blackouts, she rushed to reassure him.

Good.

I don't know what they are, she answered honestly. *Stabs of black pain. As if something was ripping into my skull. Then it stops. Comes on suddenly and stops suddenly. I can't figure out the triggers…*

He was silent for a long moment.

Psychic attacks? he asked cautiously.

I don't think so, but I don't know for sure. I can tell you that I've never felt anything like this before. She didn't add that she hoped to never experience it again. He'd know that.

Are the headaches getting worse?

The last few have been. And there have been a few more than usual. Weird ones. They come on suddenly and then just disappear. Like the pain. Then today, there's been a bizarre sense of waiting for something to happen. Then the sensation eases off again and I can almost forget about it.

When did they start?

She sighed. *A couple of weeks ago, maybe longer. But today was bad.*

Silence.

As in they happened before you spent a week in hospital and disappeared into the ethers – or after?

Tabitha hated to be reminded of that week.

And is that also when you started having trouble sleeping?

Yes, but honestly I think it's just a residual problem from being in the hospital. You know how hard it is to come back to physical reality after a long stay out of body.

Hmmm.

She winced, not sure she liked that thoughtful pause.

What are the chances that someone is trying to contact you and you aren't hearing them? Someone might have caught your signature while you were in the ethers and think you are still there.

Her gaze widened in surprise. She hadn't considered that. *Like who? And why wouldn't they be able to communicate with me? When I'm working with the animals, I'm always open.*

Again that irritating pause.

Curious, she asked, *What are you thinking?*

Just considering the information.

I'm sure I'll be fine, she said. *A good night's sleep and I'll be much better.* At least she wanted that to solve everything.

I hope so. I'll say good-bye then. But let me know if anything changes.

Stefan drifted out of her mind. Sometimes he snapped out and other times it was similar to a good-bye hug. She loved the latter.

She stepped under the hot spray of the shower and scrubbed the smell of animals off her skin. The heat washed over her in comforting waves. She bowed her head and let the day and fatigue drain away.

Then it started again.

Pain ripped through her head.

She cried out and clutched the glass doors of the shower. Agony screamed through her nerves and her knees threatened to buckle.

What was going on?

Images slammed through her, but they were woven with emotions that twisted the pictures into sensations. Pain.

Rage.

Panic.

Fear.

The rage was bad, but the fear was crippling.

Tabitha sank to her knees in the shower and could do nothing but ride out the storm. So far the attacks had never lasted long. Water sluiced down her back. The waves of agony wouldn't stop. She had no anchor to hold her safe. She had no protection from this. Her shields were up, but it didn't matter. This energy had stormed right through them and grabbed on tight.

While her mind raced to understand, she felt something so horrific she couldn't understand what was happening. It was as if someone had reached into her head and grabbed her energetic body from inside her skull…as if they were trying to rip her soul from her body.

Noooo! She screamed and tried to fight whatever demonic energy had so much power that made such a thing possible. She was caught in a struggle to stay grounded. To stay attached to her body.

She curled into a ball and tried to focus. Tried to center herself. She mentally kept her silver cord tucked up inside, but it was hard.

The pain was so strong. The sense of being yanked out of her body…intense. She felt stretched so finite she cried out in terror.

And each wave of pain and violation was stronger than the last.

There was a sense of desperation to this energy. She could feel the need of this thing pulling at her. Its panic. Its terror along with her own.

Somehow it had hooked onto her and she knew it needed her – or something she *had*.

She struggled to hold on, struggled to find the strength to be stronger than it was.

This…thing was desperate.

But then so was she.

Stefan! Help!

The next wave could be the big one. When it came, the pull was shockingly aggressive and too powerful to stand against. Her grasp slipped.

Once that bit of weakening started, she lost the advantage of being the one in possession of her body. An advantage she desperately needed.

And she started to slide.

One more tug and half of her was lifted upwards. She stared down at her bent-over body, as if she were twins joined at the hip. Her physical twin was bent over her legs, her etheric twin was sitting up. She screamed in panic and tried to lean over, tried to return to her body.

But this entity had a formidable hold. A panicked hold. And its panic had become hers.

His rage streamed through her blood.

His fear turned her emotions to icy panic.

Suddenly she was no longer alone. Stefan's powerful energy wrapped around her, supporting her, strengthening her. Keeping her safe.

Remember to love. Fear is the tool of failure. Love is the tool of success.

She struggled with his words. Struggled to grasp his meaning. And she struggled to find her center. That part of her that knew all energy was good. It was the emotions people poured into the energy that made it other than good. Her attacker was afraid. And angry. If she could help it by easing his pain…

Yes. Do it.

Her attacker gave one more tug. But Tabitha's energy had warmed and thinned, heating up more as she tried to send out the right thoughts to help her attacker. Thoughts to calm herself.

With a roar of rage and pain and loss, the link snapped.

Tabitha recoiled from the force with a final cry before she blacked out. Her last vision was that of her empty-shell of a body folded in half in the shower, the hot steamy water slowly cooling as it beat down on her back.

Then she knew no more.

CHAPTER 2

Saturday, mid-afternoon

STEFAN KRONOS BOLTED upright in his bed. His heart screamed at him to run. His body refused to move. His bedroom had disappeared into the foggy dreamscape of a different reality. Waves of energy wrapped around a tornado of emotion. A cry ripped through the air.

Stefan!

Someone was in trouble. Only it was more than trouble. A scream echoed loud enough that he clapped his hands over his ears and tried to block it – but there was no way he could. Finally the volume ebbed enough and he recognized the voice. *Tabitha.*

He'd just been talking to her. Even as he emptied his mind and called for her, he double checked the energy signature, hoping he was wrong.

Of course it was her. She'd been on his warning system for weeks now. Ever since her hospital stay. He called out to her again.

No response.

He closed his eyes and sent his consciousness to her house. Not knowing what he'd find, he didn't want to leave his body. He'd met too many strange individuals who would attempt a takeover in a heartbeat if he gave them an opening. That was the problem with being a strong psychic – he knew what existed in the shadow world.

Remembering Tabitha's earlier words about headaches and blackouts, he slipped over to her bedroom and found a pile of clothes on the floor. There was no sign of her. A weird faint roaring sound filled the air waves. From Tabitha or the house or something else?

Tripod howled at the edge of the bathroom, a loud physical mourning that poured ice into Stefan's non-existent veins. What the hell had happened here? In the background, that roaring sound grew louder and louder. If he'd had a body, the sounds and vibrations would have overwhelmed him, sending him to the floor. In this energetic form, he did the best he could and pushed clouds of energy between him and it, trying desperately to distance himself so he could think.

As the roar faded slightly, he sensed a cadence to it. It was animal. Shit. That had to be Tango. The tiger's voice was deep and raspy, as if he'd been screaming.

Stefan shuddered. Something bad had happened. He moved into the bathroom but could barely see for the steam and condensation. The shower door was closed. The rest of the bathroom empty.

Dreading what he'd find, Stefan shifted to the other side of the shower wall.

Shit.

What the hell was happening to her? He hovered over her. Her cord lay hidden protectively in the circle of her body. He could see the rise and fall of her chest as air slipped out of her body with each breath.

This was bad. Like seriously bad.

He backed up slightly and searched her etheric energy, looking for other entities in the small room, trying to get a read on what had happened. The kicked-up emotional cloud of fear and panic said she'd feared for her life. Fought for her life. His only conclusion was that she'd been attacked but won…this time.

But the cost of winning had been devastating to her.

There was no sign of an attacker. No foreign energy that he could see. Unfortunately, her aura was swollen with so much else. Grief for her grandfather, anger that he had left her, a sense of loss as she looked to her future – and then there were the animal energies. So many. Each and every one of them lived in her heart.

Her capacity for caring was huge.

And left it difficult for him to make sense of what should be there and what shouldn't. Adding to the effect, and in response to Tabitha's state, the animals had all responded with their own pain and rage.

What a mess.

And for all he knew, she was still in trouble psychically as well as physically.

Swooping lower, he could see the blue cast over her skin. If she caught hypothermia, that alone would kill her. Her body functioned at the absolute edge of survival level. Her biological system was on rapid shutdown.

Holy hell.

She was under siege from the inside.

And she needed help. Now.

❦

RONIN HAD SPENT all afternoon working and gotten nowhere. Chasing down leads on a trafficking case that had led to zero progress. Carmichael, another detective in the office, had stopped by to discuss a different case and now Ronin was way behind.

His damn desk was overloaded with his active cases and what had appeared to be a quick stop into the police station had turned out to be anything but. He stared at the stack of files in front of him. Too many files. Again. Always.

He glanced at his watch. He should be able to head out in a few minutes. For Tabitha's sake, he didn't dare stay too late. She needed him.

Now getting her to see that was a different issue altogether.

She was smart and sassy and distrustful of men…

Figures. He sure could pick them. Not that he'd had much choice. Attraction had smacked him up side the head when he'd first met her. Green-eyed leggy brunettes had never been his type. But this one… He'd had to move slowly given her trust issues. He'd made huge steps before her grandfather had passed away. He'd been there for her every day since.

If only he understood what *this* was.

He hated the pain she was in, wanted to help her, but wasn't sure how. Still he'd keep trying. He wanted what his brother Roman had. His brother was unbelievably happy. Grounded. Whatever the hell that meant. He was half of a whole, with Shay, his girlfriend, being the other half.

Ronin had heard about such relationships but hadn't really believed in the possibility. Figured they all turned sour, eventually. Ronin's marriage had as had several long-term relationships. He'd blamed his job. So had they. In truth, the job was an excuse and an escape from whatever bad relationships they had at the time.

What the hell Tabitha was to him, he didn't know.

And the relationship was so new and green it felt fresh. But was he walking down this garden path alone?

Because that would suck.

A young cop walked toward him. Geoff Tollman. After a quick glance around, he pulled a picture out of a large envelope and dropped them both on Ronin's desk.

Frowning, Ronin raised his gaze to Geoff's. "Why did you come to me?"

The young man swallowed and lowered his voice. "I didn't know who else to take it to."

That the two of them had a history played a big part in Geoff bringing the pictures to him. Ronin was pretty sure of that. The kid was his neighbor's son, and he'd helped him get into the force and through the tough years following. He'd been a troubled teen a long time ago, but he'd straightened out and become a hell of detective. They worked in the same department now. Part of the same team and that felt good.

Ronin stared down at the odd photo in front of him. "Where did you get this?"

"It was in the mail."

"Your personal mail?"

"No. Here in the office, along with the other stuff. I saw it on the pile, opened it and brought it here."

Ronin pulled out the rest of the pictures. His old buddy and co-worker, Detective Jacob Harkman, stared back at him. In the background, highlighted by gloomy lights, was an open back end of a truck. Full of cages. Nothing suspicious in itself, but…he glanced up at Geoff. "The pictures don't show anything illegal."

"I know." Geoff shrugged his shoulder. "But why send them?"

"Good question." Ronin stuffed the pictures back into the envelope and spun it in his hand. No postage. No return address. Just Geoff's first name. Spelled correctly. There wasn't anyone else in this office with that same spelling. He dropped the envelope on the side of his desk. "I'll look into it. If you get anything else, bring it to me."

"Sounds good." As Geoff sauntered toward his own desk, he called back, "It's probably nothing."

Ronin hoped Geoff was right. He'd known Jacob a long time. Being a detective took them to all kinds of places, at all kinds of hours. He studied the photos again. What the hell was Jacob up to and why had the photo been sent?

Before he had time to consider the options, his phone rang. Damn.

Pinching the bridge of his nose, he clicked his cell phone and growled, "What?"

Static whispered through his phone, but something about it was straight-out creepy.

He straightened. "Hello? Who's there?"

Help! Taaaa…!

"Hello. Who is this?"

No answer.

He snatched up a pen and jotted the number down. Then stopped. It was his number. His phone was calling his phone.

Goosebumps broke out over his skin.

Shit. He enjoyed a good horror movie the same as any other guy, but this was stepping over the creepy line. But then so had a lot of things in his life this last year – ever since he'd stepped in to help Shay after her fiancé tried to kill her.

The phone was dead in his hand. He swallowed hard and dropped it down on the desk to stare at it, his eyes narrowing at the thought. It wasn't even Halloween. So who the hell was this prankster and how did he do this?

The phone rang again.

He stared at it, loath to answer.

It rang again. He picked it up and checked the number. This call was from Stefan. But that last one…

"Hello?"

"Is this easier for you?"

He frowned. God, this man was cryptic. "What?"

"Never mind. I don't have time. I need you to send an ambulance to Tabitha's house on the Exotic Landscape property. You might need Shay's help. Tabitha is in a bad way."

"Wha—?"

Stefan rolled right over him. "Get Dr. Marsden in. He's a specialist for this kind of thing. Although this time there may not be anything he can do."

"Wait, what are you talking about?"

"Tabitha has been attacked."

And Stefan was gone.

"THERE IS A lot of money riding on this deal," the boss growled. "Fuck up and you're done."

Fez, and Roberts, his partner, nodded in unison.

This was a huge payday for them. Fez knew he had an awesome gig here. So far the work had been easy and lucrative. So good, he'd postponed his plans to move back East and start a new life. In the last five months he'd made a lot of serious money. And had spent even more.

Roberts had brought him in. He had the skills, the know how. Fez was the muscle.

And the boss? He was scary but damn powerful and a hell of businessman. He didn't take shit from anyone.

Make for a lot of fast, good deals for all of them.

Still it never did to get too comfortable. When the boss locked that gaze on him, Fez kept nodding. Obedience was paramount. He tugged at the neck of his old sweatshirt, which was stupid because the damn thing gaped halfway down his chest. Old habits died hard, especially when he was stressed.

"Are you even listening to me?"

Fez rushed to say, "Sure, boss. We'll go down to the docks now. The package has already been cleared so it should be loaded and on the road in no time."

The black, icy glare narrowed at him. Roberts stood up and headed for the door. Fez swallowed hard, stood up and muttered, "We'll take care of it now."

"You do that. And make sure that cargo is safe. It was too damn long in transit as it is. Haven't I paid enough to make this go smoothly?"

"Absolutely. No problem." Fez walked to the door. "I'll call you when the truck is loaded."

"You'll call me when you get there. Make sure you get it on the road fast. I want the truck unloaded in the warehouse tonight. Got it?"

The warning in his voice made Fez's stomach clamp down tight. He pulled out a roll of antacids from his pocket as soon as the door shut behind him. He popped two into his mouth.

Roberts snorted when he saw what he was doing. "Those damn things will kill you one of these days."

"They help. Can hardly keep any food down these days," Fez muttered, walking down the stairs beside his partner. He should go see a doc, but what the hell was he going to tell him that Fez didn't already know? And if it was bad news like cancer or something, he would just as soon not know.

He'd take keeling over on the streets to a slow painful end any day.

"Time to quit if the job is doing that to you."

"It's a good job," Fez said. "Hell, you're the one that brought me in."

"Yeah, well, you never know. I just might be the one that leaves if you don't."

Fez turned in shock. There was just something a little too serious in Roberts's tone of voice. "You wouldn't do that. Look at the money we've made."

Roberts nodded but stuffed his fists in his pockets. "And when is enough enough? I've got a bad feeling about this job." He shook his head. "A real bad feeling.

"Don't do this man. We're a team."

"Maybe not for much longer."

After that he fell silent, leaving Fez to worry in silence.

CHAPTER 3

Saturday, afternoon

TABITHA WANDERED THROUGH the gentle clouds, comforted by the familiarity of her surroundings. She didn't know why she was in the ethers again. But it was such a nice place to be. There were no worries here. No stresses. No money shortfalls to make up or difficult people to answer to. She could still mentally reach out and check on her animals – offer a hug, a stroke, or just a loving pat.

She was happy.

Like she'd been before.

That made her pause, made her consciousness kick in.

She wasn't supposed to be back here.

She'd liked it here a little too well last time. It had been hard to leave.

So why was she here now?

For…safety.

Memories flooded over her. She'd been attacked. In fact, her energy had been damn near ripped out of her body.

She shuddered and sank deeper into the protection of the shadows.

RONIN PULLED HIS truck to a ripping stop outside of Tabitha's mausoleum of a house. Surrounded by large trees with little natural light filtering through, the place had a gothic haunted-mansion vibe going on.

There was also a weird deafening silence.

He'd been this far before, but had never been invited in. Her grandfather had been the original reason; apparently she hadn't wanted to introduce the two of them, given her grandfather's health and his disposition. She'd always met Ronin outside the house or at the office.

She ran a reserve where big cats were a major part of the population…and if there was one thing he had a love-hate relationship with…it was cats. He was so not good with cats – not allergic, although that would have given him an excuse for his over-the-top reactions like a nauseous stomach, a closed up throat and headaches with shortness of breath.

And no, he hadn't gone to see a specialist. He never would.

But Tabitha didn't need to know that. At least not yet.

Now Tabitha's grandfather was gone. Would that make it easier for Tabitha to let a male into her inner world? She'd once been engaged for six months so he knew she'd opened that door once before. What would it take for her to open it again, for him?

Just how controlling had her grandfather been? Did he have something to do with her broken relationship? Had he understood she had psychic abilities? Not that she'd mentioned them to him, but he'd overheard Shay and his brother talking one night about how Tabitha was better with the animals than Shay was. He could have gotten the impression that she had abilities beyond the ordinary.

Maybe she'd gotten those abilities *from* her grandfather.

Ronin exited the truck and approached the front door. A large, imposing front facade with no welcoming porch or deck, just a single stair up to a double door. His first impression? Dark. Formidable. Dilapidated.

If her grandfather had any money, he hadn't wasted it on the house, unlike his own grandfather, Pappy, who had the golden touch when it came to big business and kept his personal place immaculate.

Ronin knocked on the huge door before reaching for the doorknob. It turned under his hand but the door did not budge. Inside a howl went up that shook him to the core. Tripod? She'd told him about the monster-sized dog, but Jesus…

The door was locked. He gave it a strong shake and saw the security system, installed by his brother, winking at him from above. He pulled out his cell phone.

"Roman, I need to get into Tabitha's house. Shut off the security system."

"Why? What's wrong?" His brother's voice sounded distracted. He was probably painting, considering it was late on a Saturday afternoon.

"She's been attacked. Stefan sent me here to help her but the house is locked up tight."

"Damn." Now his voice sharpened. "How bad was the attack?"

"I don't know. I'm trying to get in to find that out," he snapped. "The dog is howling. I can barely hear you." He paused. "Is it done?"

As he asked, he looked up at the blinking red light to find it gone. "Thanks."

"Let me know if you need a hand." There were sounds of a muted conversation. "Skip that. We're on our way."

Ronin pushed the door open and stepped inside. "I'm in."

"No wait, Shay sa—"

But he never heard the rest as something as big as a bear, crossed with a pony, raced toward him – howling.

"Jesus H. Christ!" The dog had a huge set of bared teeth. Instinctively, Ronin unsnapped the cover over his gun.

The dog came to a screeching halt, skittering forward on the wooden floor and growling so loud there should have been a half dozen dogs facing him.

In the distance, he heard his brother's voice screaming through the phone. "The dog's name is Tripod."

Because he had only three legs. Yeah, he got it. Only the damn thing looked ready to take off one of *Ronin's* legs.

"Easy, Tripod. Take it easy boy. I'm here to help."

The dog raised his head and howled again. Then it turned its head and pinned him in place with an all-too-human gaze.

Shit. He tried to remember he was a dog person. And that *most* dogs loved him.

The look in this one's gaze made him doubt that was ever going to happen.

His brother's voice reached him again. He lifted his cell phone. "Stop screaming. I'm here."

"Look, Tripod is a big baby but he knows something has happened to Tabitha."

"Understood." He ran his fingers through his hair. "But I still have to get past him to get to her."

Then his brother's next words reached through the phone and grabbed him by the throat. "Easy. If Tripod doesn't calm down, it will get bad."

Ronin stared down at his phone in disbelief. "What did you say?"

"Tripod is the guard dog. But Tango is going to be more difficult. If you can calm Tripod, then Tango will follow his lead." Roman took a deep breath. "*Maybe* it will follow his lead."

"What the hell?" Ronin muttered, keeping a wary eye on the dog as he stepped inside. She had a second one she hadn't mentioned? Why? "I don't have time for this."

"Yes. I know. But a mistake at this stage could be fatal."

At the word 'fatal,' Ronin's hand instinctively went to the gun at the small of his back.

The dog erupted into a growl that had Ronin bolting backwards. "Damn it."

"What did you do?" Roman yelled. "Ronin?"

"I reached for the gun. Apparently he didn't like that." Talk about an understatement.

"Shay's here. She says you have to put the gun away. He'll attack if you try to use it."

God! Ronin briefly closed his eyes to consider the problem, then said helplessly. "You don't understand. I have to help Tabitha."

"Ronin? This is Shay here," her worried voice came on the phone. "I do understand. But you also have to understand something else. This house, these animals are her support system. They are the guardians of Tabitha's soul, possibly in ways she doesn't even understand."

"That's just crazy." Frustration and anger hurtled through him. "Why did Stefan call me to help her? How the hell am I going to do that if I can't get in there?"

"He called you because you are part of Tabitha's support system," Shay explained, "and she needs all of us right now."

"Support system?" What the hell did that mean? Whatever. "Get me inside."

"You have to convince Tripod to let you inside."

Right. "This isn't a damn dog; this thing is the size of a young grizzly bear." In the distance he could make out vehicles but not the sound of sirens yet. "And the ambulance should be almost here. I need to do something." As he studied the dog, he added. "Maybe that's why Stefan told me to come. I can call animal welfare—"

No. Stefan's' objection ripped though Ronin's mind. *You can't. Tripod and Tango keep Tabitha grounded…connected. If you knock either into unconsciousness or, worse, kill them, we risk her losing that connection. Lose that and we could lose her.*

"Shit. This is crazy." He stared around helplessly. "So what do I do?"

Make friends with Tripod. You need to show him your energy in a calm way, Stefan continued. *The dog doesn't care so much about the gun at your back but about the shift in your energy when you reached for your gun.*

Ronin groaned and let his hand fall away. He stepped quietly forward to stand in front of the dog, then crouched slightly until he was eye level with the massive head.

"If this thing bites my head off…"

We'll bury you with all the pomp and ceremony you deserve... said Stefan drily.

"Ass," Ronin muttered half-heartedly. He'd already turned his focus on the dog.

The gaze that stared back at him was almost more than human. There was no artifice there. Only fear. And anger. Someone he loved was hurt. And that Ronin could understand. The dog wanted its owner to stand up. To have its life back to normal.

And he wanted it in a bad way.

Close your eyes and talk to him. When your eyes are open, your conscious mind interferes with what's possible. I know you calmed several irate animals over your career.

Ronin was often able to soothe a dog that had been hurt or was angry or injured. But not always. "Yeah, normally dogs respond well to me."

And animals respond to the capable, calm, almost soothing nature of your energy. But right now, you're worried and the dog is worried. So you're rubbing up against each other's fear, increasing it, instead of easing it. Tabitha talks to Tripod all the time. That's what he's looking for from you.

Shit. Tripod. I'm here to help. Ronin closed his eyes and spoke to the dog mentally. *Tabitha is in trouble and I need to get to her. She's hurting in a bad way.*

A rumble washed over him. Ronin frowned and repeated his statement. The rumble deepened. Ronin swore he could see the dog's features as clearly as he would if his eyes were open.

Only they weren't. Ronin's eyes were definitely closed.

It's a vision skill. Keep seeing the dog in your mind and stroke him in your mind. See him accept you. See him liking the attention.

Ronin struggled to follow through. He eased into the vision of the dog's face, soothing him as he spoke to him about helping him. Helping Tabitha. He reached out and felt a warming of the energy around him and the fear easing.

Then a huge tongue caught him by the chin and stroked upwards across his face.

The smell was gross, but his heart leapt. He opened his eyes to see the dog gazing into his eyes. A plea for help deep inside. "That look can't be real."

It is. Once a connection is made... Stefan's voice trailed off.

Ronin stood, gently patted the dog then squeezed between the dog and the doorway. The dog trailed behind, whining deep in his throat.

Ronin stopped to take stock. And was hit with waves of nausea and a horrible buzzing in his head. He shuddered. His whole system went into lockdown. He could hardly breathe.

Damn. A cat was here. Somewhere close by.

But Tabitha needed him. His hand at his throat, struggling to hold back the panic, he tried to study the rooms in front of him. Instead of a nice clean layout, the house appeared to be a maze. "Where is she, Tripod? Show me Tabitha."

The dog cocked his head to one side, as if understanding him, then bounded upstairs. Ronin followed, barely seeing where he was going until he dashed into a bedroom.

"Stefan said she's in the shower," he said, and felt like an idiot for talking to the dog. His chest eased slightly, making it easier to focus. He raced for the small room off to the side. Clothes lay crumpled on the floor. Otherwise, the room appeared empty.

He pulled back the shower door to find Tabitha nude, in a ball, with a bluish gray cast to her skin. Icy water beat down on her back. He turned off the water. His hands went to Tabitha's neck. He could barely find a pulse under her clammy skin.

Crap. He raced back to Tabitha's bedroom, tugging something white and pillowy off her bed. Back at the shower, he bundled it around Tabitha and scooped her up in a cocoon. As he turned toward the bedroom, a tall blonde stood in the doorway. Shay.

He didn't slow down.

"Good, you've got her." Shay was already leading the way back outside. "The ambulance is coming up the drive. Roman is waiting for them."

Ronin brushed past her, and carrying a still-wrapped Tabitha, carefully made his way down the stairs to the front door. He'd cleared the front porch when the ambulance came to a quick stop. He took his first clean deep breath. The men raced out and opened the back doors.

"She's in a bad way."

He laid his precious bundle down and stepped back as the men went to work. Before he knew it, she'd been loaded into the ambulance, one man still working on her as they ripped down the driveway.

He stood and stared down the empty road. Tripod howled, then abruptly walked over to sit beside Ronin.

Ronin stared at the huge dog who gazed solemnly back at him as if he were telling Ronin to fix this.

"WHAT THE HELL is going on?" Fez said to the empty night. They should have been here by now. That they weren't, was a huge problem. These goods had to be moved to the next destination. And fast.

Fez paced the long rows of docks. What was the hold up? He should be out of here by now. He'd called the boss once… He checked his phone again. At least his boss hadn't called back. But if Fez didn't check in with him soon, there'd be hell to pay.

Especially since Roberts had taken off to do something and hadn't come back yet. Fez glanced around. He couldn't shake the feeling that the boss was going to show up any second. The man came and went like a damn ghost.

Shit. Where the hell was his package?

Even more important, were the contents still alive?

CHAPTER 4

Saturday, late afternoon

STEFAN STOOD AT Tabitha's bedside, his medical specialist, Dr. Marsden, at his side. He studied the pale face on the white pillows. Tabitha's beauty shone in an unearthly way. Her skin appeared luminescent. He asked, "So there's nothing physically wrong with her?"

Dr. Marsden shook his head. "Nothing that is showing up on any tests. I think she's terrified…and has gone into hiding."

"Originally…" Stefan rubbed his temple and tried to marshal his thoughts. "When I heard her screaming for help, I caught scattered bits of her thoughts. She *believed* she was going to die. When I found her, she'd curled tightly around her cord as if protecting it."

The doctor nodded. "Sensible. What I can't be sure of is whether her previous attack had something to do with this one, or…if that attack left her open to this one and possibly others yet to come."

"They weren't the same attacker. I know that for sure." The words barely out of his mouth, Stefan winced. There were no sureties in this world, but as far as he knew, the woman who'd attacked Tabitha a month ago was dead. Along with her murderous brothers. "But she's spent a lot of time in the ethers leaving her body unprotected. For all we know, someone in the ethers picked up on that and was planning to take over her body."

"It's possible, but why wait until now?" Dr. Marsden walked to the end of Tabitha's bed.

"We all sleep and dream walk, and there are many other people to target. So why Tabitha? Her energy? Her abilities?"

That caught Stefan's attention. "Her abilities," he asked cautiously. "Why would her abilities make a difference?"

Dr. Marsden glanced his way. "Many people would be mentally damaged by the experience, yet Tabitha obviously has an ability to stay in the ethers."

That prodded something in Stefan's memory. The last time Tabitha had been in the ethers for a prolonged stay, she'd hidden out there until it was safe. "You think she's *choosing* to hide in the ethers?"

"Exactly. Most people, even psychics, won't do that. Can't do that. It takes a special ability to walk in the space between life and death. I've heard of that space, the In-Between."

"Hmm. Isn't that backwards? She hides there when she feels under attack…yet by leaving her body open like this, she's actually putting herself in a more vulnerable position."

Dr. Marsden laughed. "You'd have thought so, but take a closer look."

Startled, Stefan glanced back at Tabitha's long and lean frame. He shifted through the layers of energy, but it was hard because the energy was compressed, lying tight and hard against her body.

"I can barely see her aura as it is!" Stefan exclaimed.

"Exactly. It's some kind of defense system. Her energy is locked down in protective mode that stops anyone from accessing her body from the outside. Even her cord is hidden."

Stefan had never seen a case like this. Or an energy system like Tabitha's. He searched the ethers looking for her cord – the so important connection to her physical body that kept her alive…and couldn't find it.

Yet she was lying there breathing naturally. Normally, as if in a deep sleep.

"See what I mean?" The note of wonder in the doctor's voice had Stefan walking closer to study Tabitha. "Her cord is actually dispersed all around the room. If you look closely you'll see signs of it. Just not how it connects to her."

"So once again, something new." Stefan snorted at that. "Does she need anything from us?" The two men stared down at the comatose woman.

"Not from me." Dr. Marsden turned to study him, one eyebrow raised in question. "Maybe from you."

Stefan nodded his head. "Could be. I'll check." He looked around the small private room. Should he try contacting her here or from home? Here he'd have to deal with so many other interfering energies.

"Do you want to try now, while you're here?"

Stefan shook his head. "Want to? No. Should I? Yes."

Dr. Marsden turned in a slow circle to study the sparse room. "It's hardly the best place for a session, is it?"

"Depends on the number of spirit entities hanging around. Considering it's a hospital, there're likely to be more disembodied souls here than living people."

Stefan hated being in crowds to begin with, and although he was comfortable with the dead and walked the ethers as easily as Tabitha, dealing with angry, frustrated, or needy disembodied souls was not fun. If he could slip past that to the ethers, he'd be fine. But if not…

"I'll do it here. At least long enough to make sure she's fine." He spied the chair in the far corner. He pulled it up to her bedside and walked to position himself back in the corner where he sat cross-legged on the floor.

Ignoring the doctor, Stefan settled his back against the wall and took a deep breath. He released the old stale air from his lungs and consciously brought in fresh, life-giving air.

His energy shifted slowly, then faster and faster as he drew on his years of practice to make his exit from his body that much smoother.

He opened his eyes. And found himself in the In-Between. A light-colored fog filled the room that no longer existed. He swept away the fog, preferring clear openness to the muted look of clouds. Here the energy responded to thoughts and he could make it look as he wished. The practical side of him said not to bother, he wouldn't be here long enough to arrange the setting to his personal style or artistic sensibilities.

He zipped through the ethers. In his mind's eye, he focused on Tabitha's cord. On finding it healthy and happy.

And there it was. He smiled. The cord shimmered a deep lavender, almost as if it were covered by glitter paint. It was fun to see this side of her because in the physical world, she was down to earth and practical. No glitter to be found.

His journey was fast and easy as he moved through the vast space. He traveled faster and faster, navigating with his senses as he headed to her side.

Hey. Tabitha's laughter told him he'd reached her.

He grinned and opened his eyes to find her standing there smiling in front of him.

Damn. You look good.

Thanks. I'm feeling quite a bit better actually.

He studied her features, seeing what she wasn't saying out loud. She might be feeling better, but her energy didn't glow like it should. There were dark hollows, dents in her energy as if she worried and was trying to hide it. Like she'd hidden out here.

With a gentle shake of his head, he said, *No, you're not. For you, this is a safety zone. But I want to know what happened to bring you here and why you felt you needed to retreat here instead of call for help.*

The air filled with her bitter laugh. *Because I'm safe here. Only I have no idea what happened.* Quickly, she told him what she remembered.

And do you think this attack is related to all the headaches? As if someone was trying to get inside you, your consciousness? If so what's it going to take to get you back to your body?

I didn't leave my body. I'm just resting here for a bit.

And as you know from before, that little bit is likely to become a long bit.

No, she corrected. *It did last time. That doesn't mean it will this time.*

How was he to convince her to come home? *Ronin had to become friends with Tripod to get into the house.*

Really? They've never met up to now. I've held off bringing him to the house after he made a casual comment about not liking cats.

Stefan grinned, thinking Ronin had yet to meet Tango. And what fun that would be. *Is he allergic?*

No idea, she confessed, *I didn't ask him. I was too surprised at the time.*

Yet you didn't break it off? He wasn't going to let her off that easy. If Ronin was going to be her reason to come home, then he needed her mind on him now. Enough hiding.

She shrugged. *There aren't too many interesting men that can handle my abilities.*

Then you'll have to come back, won't you? Especially before the media gets wind of this. You know how they have portrayed the reserve as being in trouble recently with all the break-ins and vandalism. If the media finds out about this state your physical body is in… The center doesn't need more bad publicity or to have the donations could dry up.

Hey, that's not fair, she said. *I'm here because I was attacked.*

And Tango and Tripod? They are guarding your place and keeping your body grounded. Your absence is hard on them.

I've already been by to visit with them. She waved her hands dismissively. *They are fine.*

So much for that tactic…

Then he had it. He smiled inside. *Except that Ronin is searching your house to find anything he can about your attacker.*

He's inside the house? Right now? She went ghostly pale. *Damn. That's so not a good idea. He could be in danger. Tango knows when someone likes him or not.*

And, Stefan said gently, *Ronin is a cop who cares deeply about you. You were attacked and if, in the course of his investigation, he's attacked…*

I'm gone.

The fog swirled around Stefan, blocking her from view. By the time he cleared his vision and swept back the cotton clouds, there was no sign of her.

SHE CAME TO so suddenly, her body jerked from the harsh landing and she bolted upright, ready to run out of the room – and found herself in a private hospital room with a stern, darkly handsome doctor staring down at her. It took her a moment to recognize him. Dr. Marsden.

"*Whoa.* You're not going anywhere." Dr. Marsden reached out to stop her.

"I have to leave." She glared at him.

"Easy, Tabitha." Stefan stretched out his legs and stood up slowly. "Dr. Marsden has been looking after you."

What was Stefan doing in the corner?

"Sorry. I hate hospitals," she muttered as a poor excuse for her behavior. "And why is it you think I can't leave?"

He was wrong of course, but she didn't need to antagonize anyone further. It drained too much energy. But she really wanted to go home.

"Because you were attacked. I'd like to run some tests."

She shot him a shuttered look and shook her head. "If you know as much about this stuff as Stefan believes you do, then you understand it was a psychic attack. And that means nothing will show up on your tests."

"And you're going to do what, wait around until he tries again?" Stefan asked quietly.

Silence.

Damn. Her animals, as well as her body and her soul were vulnerable. The attack had been horrific and too damn close to being a win for the other guy to make her happy. Would he try again?

She slumped back against the headboard. "He wants my soul, not my body. At least that's what I felt during an attack. Stronger each time. And do you have any suggestions? Some magical way to keep my soul in my body and away from this thief?"

"Did you get a sense of why he wanted it?"

The two men stood at the end of her bed, their gazes intent as if they could find the answers they wanted if they could just look hard enough. Tabitha pushed back a few strands of long hair as she tried to marshal her thoughts. "I could sense he was terrified. Angry. And was looking for someone or something."

"And found you instead." Stefan walked around the side of the bed, then picked up her hand and held it tight. "*Or* was he looking specifically for you?"

"For me." She knew that deep inside. "He wanted me."

"HELLO, STEFAN. YOU used the phone this time?" Ronin grinned at the sound Stefan made on the other end. He peered through the thick wire mesh, trying to see what animal was on the other side the fenced pen. Tabitha's place was an integral part of the reserve. Anything could be on the other side of the fence.

"It saves energy. Tabitha is awake. She's afraid you'll have an argument with her cat, Tango. Apparently she left him in his cage, but she says he's wily and can get out if he has a mind to."

"Great." Horrible actually. He could already feel his heart slam against his chest. "I'm actually outside walking around the property, trying to understand the setup here." It was confusing. That there were large enclosures in the back of the house was obvious. As were the howls coming from the deep expanse.

Cats.

Why cats? He could do dogs blindfolded. This whole cat thing…not so much. At least they were all caged.

"Is she okay? Can she come home?"

"She's going to, whether anyone says so or not. The thing is she is weak, susceptible to another attack. You need to help her."

Ronin's stomach clenched. "Why me? I don't do this psychic stuff. That's your specialty. Why can't you help her? Besides, if she's that bad, she should stay in hospital for another couple of days."

"She needs both of us. And according to mainstream medicine, she's not injured. She's run down and needs to rest. That means recovering from this episode at home."

"You know she won't do it," Ronin snapped. She needed to stay safe by whatever means necessary. He understood she felt responsible for Exotic Landscape, but she had staff…good staff…and it was time for her to step back and let them carry the load.

He didn't fully understand the enormity of these attacks, but he was starting too. And that scared him. Tabitha needed protection. But how could he protect her from something he couldn't see?

He started toward the front of the house.

"No, she won't. She cares about her animals too much. And work has always been her way of escaping the rest of the world. So she's going to go home and bury herself in work – most likely paperwork at her own house."

At her house. Ronin glared at the huge monstrosity. "But she was attacked here. So how does that work?"

"Not well. I'm setting up an energetic barrier. A second security system. I'm hoping it will be enough to keep her safe. Or at least good enough to be an early warning system."

"What good will that do?"

"If she has enough warning, she'll be able to guard herself from another attack. She does have some serious skills, but last time she had no idea what was happening until it was almost too late."

"How much warning does she need?" His mind spun with the possibilities. Between Roman's security system and Stefan's psychic security system…maybe she'd be okay.

"It's only the barest of what is needed." Stefan cleared his throat, and for the first time Roman heard the fatigue running through his voice. Stefan was running on empty himself. Damn.

Abruptly, he said, "What can I do to help?"

In a hard voice, Stefan said, "Find him. Do whatever you can do to track down this asshole."

That's what he did for a living, track down perps… But how did he track down a nameless, faceless, disembodied entity?

"Search Tabitha's history. Search for any and all people connected to her who might have psychic abilities."

"Can't you see an energy signature, or whatever it's called, around her?" Isn't that what Stefan did? "Can't *you* identify him?"

"Sometimes I can. Not this time. There was nothing *normal* about this attack. She hadn't cleared away the day's energies. She was surrounded by grief and animal energies. Both completely overwhelmed her ability to notice this entity. And I can't rule out that her attacker was using animal energy to get close to her." Stefan's voice strengthened. "In fact, that's a good possibility. In which case, this person *is* working with animals."

"Fine, then that's where I'll—" There was a sharp click and his phone went dead. Stefan had hung up on him.

"Damn." Ronin stared at the house. He had work to do.

"BE CAREFUL WITH that thing. If we lose her, we've lost the biggest payday ever," Fez snarled at the forklift driver. The front lift jerked down several more feet. "Shit," Fez muttered. "We're going to kill her yet."

"Better not. I won't be happy if that happens."

The cold voice behind him sent icy shards of fear down Fez's spine. He hadn't expected his boss to show up at this moment. Then, given all the things that had gone wrong, maybe his arrival wasn't so surprising after all.

"Did Roberts come back with you?" Fez asked looking around. Roberts needed to check the delivery over. Make sure everything had survived the journey.

"No."

Fez froze at the icy dead tone.

But the boss's next words were the ones that really made his heart stop. "You know what happens to people who make me unhappy. My neck is on the line with this deal. You screw up, then I screw up. In which case you won't be looking to salvage your job because you won't care. You'll be floating down the damn river as fish food instead."

Fez nodded but kept his face turned away. Fingers of cold reached down deep inside his stomach. His boss never threatened. He promised.

Thankfully, the forklift operator unloaded the cage without any more mishaps and backed away to get the next load. They were late and time was running out. The cages had to be transferred to the new truck, which would be followed by a couple of hours of driving. Fez was taking the truck with this cargo. He sent a silent prayer to the heavens above.

Please let this job go smoothly.

Not that he expected anyone to listen to his request. They hadn't so far.

CHAPTER 5

Saturday, early evening

TABITHA PAID THE taxi before stumbling up the front steps of her house. The sun beamed beautiful farewell rays across the summer sky. Delighted to be home, she sent out a tired but happy wave of energy in greeting to both Tango and Tripod. The returning waves of deep blue and purple exuberance delighted and reassured her that all was well…or mostly well.

The front door was unlocked.

Startled, she stood in the open doorway and studied her house. She took a deep breath and mentally whistled for Tripod. Where the hell was he?

Nails skittered on the tile floors. He tore around the corner of the kitchen and raced toward her. She smiled and murmured in her head, *Gentle. I'm tired and if you knock me over I might not make it back up.*

He slowed to a skid on the tile, a deep whine coming up from inside his chest.

I'm fine, sweetie. Just seriously tired. I need to go to bed and sleep for a couple of days. "Fat chance," she muttered out loud.

"Fat chance of what?" The deep voice was an electric shock to her tired body. She stiffened as her tired gaze caught site of Ronin then she relaxed again. Strong. Capable. With his take-charge attitude. In her home.

Damn, he looked good there.

Like he belonged. Why had she been worried about having him here…?

Oh yeah, a little thing called felines…like Tango.

Her eyes filled with tears. Damn. She had to be tired to start this. She swiped at her eyes with her sleeve. He opened his arms.

And she ran forward.

His long arms wrapped around her and tucked her up close. Hidden in his embrace, she felt so protected, safe.

And dare she say it – loved?

Something she hadn't felt in a long time. She soaked up his comfort and caring until Tripod nudged her in the ribs.

She gave a small laugh and stepped back. "Hey, big guy. Let's get you some food."

With a teary smile at Ronin, she led the way back to the kitchen. She heard the front door close behind her, followed by Ronin's footsteps. In the kitchen, she stopped. There were pots simmering on the stove.

She spun around, a delighted smile on her face. "You made dinner?"

He shrugged sheepishly. "Spaghetti."

With a hand on the small of her back, he nudged her into the kitchen. A large pot in front burped. He stepped over to it and stirred the contents.

"I can't remember the last time someone cooked me a meal." Delight curled her insides. "And you've made one of my favorites."

The smile fell off his face as he studied her. Cautiously, he asked, "Really? Not your grandfather? Father? Fiancé?"

"My grandfather hated cooking. As soon as I was old enough, I took over the chore. Dennis, my father, never lived here with me."

Waving a ladle at her, he asked quietly, "And the fiancé?"

She wrinkled her nose and walked slowly toward him. "He'd never be caught in a kitchen."

"Well, I have no such issue." He shrugged those wide shoulders. "I love to cook."

Damn. She could get used to that. Her good mood restored, she said, "Perfect. 'Cause I'm starved."

"Good. 'Cause it's ready." He smiled and motioned to the table. "I wasn't sure if it was safe to leave Tripod here – nice name by the way – around the food."

"He's got great manners." She let Ronin lead her to the table and hold out her chair. "But I wouldn't trust him too far."

"That's what I thought." He quickly served up dinner under Tripod's eagle eye and carried the plates to the table. "What I don't have is a bottle of wine to go with this."

She laughed. "As much as I'd love a glass, I don't think there is a bottle in the house."

"I'll take care of that when I head out tomorrow."

Her hand dropped, her fork clattering to the plate. "Tomorrow?"

He cocked an eyebrow. "Yes. I have a few things to check on. I'll grab a bottle or two on my way home."

She flushed, and in a strangled voice, said, "Home?"

"Yep." He casually scooped up a forkful of spaghetti. "I'm not leaving you alone until this is over." And he popped the food in his mouth.

Over? She very carefully put her fork down and stared at him in shock. "Why?"

It was his turn to stare at her. "Because you were attacked?"

Cautiously, she asked, "You understand in what way I was attacked, right?"

He nodded and twisted up another fork of pasta. "Yep. Somewhat. At least what I got from what Stefan, Shay and my brother told me."

"And you think…you can help if I'm attacked again?" She didn't want to insult him, but just what was he thinking?

At the disbelief in her voice, he very carefully replaced his fork. "I know that I'm not like you and I probably can't do much to ward off a psychic attacker, but I can get help."

She stared down at her plate. "I know you believe that, but you might not even know that an attack is happening. It's not as if I'm screaming out loud."

He frowned. "Then maybe I'm going to have to sleep in the same room as you. Surely, I'd know then?"

She snorted. "Wait until you're invited."

"And how long will that take?" He grinned at her narrow-eyed look. "Hey, it was worth asking. And I've been patient."

She rolled her eyes at him. Inside, she felt the warmth uncurl in her belly. Like they'd gotten that far yet. Her grandfather's death had pushed that step back slightly. "I like sleeping alone."

Both eyebrows flew up. "And here I thought for sure you slept with Tripod." Tripod, hearing his name, gave a small yelp.

She reached out a hand. Tripod shuffled right up to her plate and sniffed. Tabitha tapped his nose to make him back up. "If you can call that sharing. Tripod is a bed hog. Besides, lots of nights I sleep with another male."

The smile slid off Ronin's face.

Good.

Then Tango roared.

"JESUS. WHAT THE hell is that?" Ronin half jumped out of his chair and leaned forward to look out the window.

"Ha. It's my cat. That's Tango."

He shot her a disbelieving look, catching the amused glitter in her light-green eyes. "There is no way a cat makes that kind of sound."

Tango roared again. This time though there was something off. Tabitha went to the living room and pushed some kind of button. Ronin followed more slowly and watched as the whole wall retracted.

What the hell kind of wall was that? And damn if she didn't have some kind of fine mesh cage behind that wall. Thank God. He was half afraid she was one of those crazy people who got so super cozy with their wild pets that they ignored common sense.

Then she pulled the wire mesh completely back.

Oh shit.

And didn't the biggest damn white tiger, with a head the size of Mount Rushmore, saunter toward her.

"Watch out," he cried as the tiger jumped. Instantly his throat clogged and his chest tightened. Christ, he could hardly breathe. He swallowed. And then swallowed again. He couldn't help the instinctive clenching of his fists. Inside, insidious emotions shifted through him. Panic. Pain. Sadness. So much worse than the last time he'd been in the house.

He took a shaky breath. This was not happening.

He was halfway to her when he realized the tiger had stopped with complete control and was on his back legs, Tabitha crushed in his embrace.

Jesus.

Ronin prided himself on being a brave soul, but he was not going that close. And he didn't care how tame the damn thing was. A wild animal was a wild animal.

Unless it's not a wild animal.

Stefan. And did one ever get used to this guy in his head?

Ronin snapped out mentally, *If you're trying to convince me that this thing is safe to be around, forget it. I have too much respect for human life to believe you.*

And in many cases you could be right. In this case however, you'd be wrong.

And why is that? Has she got some kind of special powers or something? Right about now he wished she did. He'd believe that as much as anything.

No, but they do have a special connection.

See, that's where you are wrong. All pet lovers say that about their little pooches. And he couldn't help the disgust from rolling through his voice.

He was a cop, damn it. And he'd seen more than his fair share of animals both domesticated and wild. Sometimes the domestic ones were the more dangerous.

Stefan laughed. *You'll have to see for yourself. And take a deep breath. You will survive this.*

"Promise?" Ronin muttered.

With a last laugh, Ronin's mind emptied. Damn, that was weird.

"Ronin, come and meet Tango."

"I don't think that's a good idea." Damn it, he wasn't a wuss. He took a couple of steps forward and stopped. And struggled to breathe. He so didn't want to pass out. Not here. Not with her. Not with that carnivore looking on. "I'll stick to dogs."

"Tripod is here, too."

He groaned silently and took another step into the living room.

Tango dropped to the floor and stared at Ronin, a howl starting deep in the back of his throat. The hairs raised on the back of his neck.

The look in those damn eyes…

Ronin took a deep breath and tried to stop the shakiness that was starting to vibrate his insides, making his stomach acids turn to cheese.

"Why is he howling?"

"I'm not sure. He doesn't normally do that." She reached down to place a hand on Tango's head. The howl changed. It wasn't the same tenor as the first time, but it was hardly welcoming.

Then all of a sudden, the howl cut off.

Thank you. Ronin much preferred the silence. Except now a dull roaring sound was in his head. Almost a buzz. He shook his head, trying to clear it.

Tabitha sighed heavily. "Come over here and meet Tango. He'll calm down once he meets you. And maybe you will too." She tilted her head and studied him. "And make sure that gun is safely away. Tripod hates them."

"I've already made peace with the dog." He didn't move.

"And you'll make peace with Tango, too. It's much better to meet him on equal ground. If you take one step backwards, he's got you."

"Damn." Ronin stepped forward. He could feel the heat, the intensity of that deep blue feline gaze following his every movement. Like a cat watching a mouse.

Ronin had always felt sympathy for the mouse.

For a cat, the animal was damn beautiful. The markings on its head, the eyes, the shocking white fur were something he'd never expected to see up close. And never inside a house. Not sure he wanted to hear the answer, he asked, "Do you let him out of that cage much?"

"All the time. The house is his, too."

Double damn.

When he was a couple of feet away, Ronin stopped, his gaze on the cat.

"Now what?"

She grinned. "Say hi."

He shot her a fulminating look. "Just like that."

"Well, *to* him of course."

His gaze zipped back to the waiting tiger. Did she mean it the way Stefan had said to talk to Tango? 'Cause there was no way in hell he'd be dropping to his knees and closing his eyes in front of a tiger. Talk about being a sacrificial offering. Then as if to accentuate the fact that the tiger was waiting for the appropriate response, it sat down and waited.

Taking a deep breath and feeling like an idiot, Ronin said, "Hi, Tango. Nice to meet you."

No response. Then again, what had he expected? He shook his head then winced at the heavy buzz in his ear. Under his breath, he swore again.

"That ringing inside your head… It's because he's talking to you and you're not listening."

He stared at her in disbelief. "How did you know my head is ringing?"

She snorted. "Because I can sense it. Normally I only listen to my animals but now… some things have changed and I can sense more with people too. And behind your lovely front of 'I don't like cats'…I see fear."

Heat washed up his cheeks. Damn. So what if there was fear? Hell, there was a tiger in the room. Anyone with an ounce of working brain matter would understand. Besides, it's not as if he was afraid *of* cats… He knew there was fear there, he just didn't understand what exactly frightened him.

And the last thing he wanted was her laughing at him.

With a final glance at the still gaze of the tiger locked on him, Ronin decided enough was enough for this time. He'd done well but he didn't want to push it. He turned and headed back to the kitchen, putting a little distance between him and Tango. "While you're having your fun, I'll go finish eating. Unless you're planning on feeding dinner to the two of them."

Turning his back on that damn feline was the hardest thing he'd done in a long time. And he was proud that he'd managed to do it in a calm, nonchalant manner.

Then he found the two empty plates on the table and the guilty party still licking the tomato sauce off his face.

Tripod.

ON THE ROAD at last. Only a couple of hours late. Not too bad. His boss had driven on ahead and Fez was hauling the cargo in the big rig. Roberts hadn't shown up yet. That was a pisser. Fez had called him a couple of times but Roberts hadn't answered as yet.

The highway was almost empty. In fact, the truck was almost empty too. Good. It should make the trip easier. Faster.

Most of the cages were small. Then there was the big one. What the hell was with her?

He'd always loved his job before. Enjoyed the challenge and the payoffs. It had been easy money with plenty to keep him busy.

Only something was shifting. Maybe because Roberts hadn't shown up, Fez was afraid his buddy had 'booked it' after all. That was bad news if he hadn't planned his disappearance the right way. When the boss found out he wasn't coming back to work…

He sighed. This was a good gig. It wasn't hard. Gave them lots of free time. What was there to complain about? So what if they were moving females in cages. This type of job for many people was nothing. Besides they were paid enough to squelch any kind of misgivings.

He shifted gears and took the truck into the turn.

Please keep the females asleep. They were much easier to deal with when they were quiet. Of course they'd really start screaming when they saw where they were going. There'd be no appreciation there. But at least they'd have food and water and shelter.

See, their lot wasn't so bad after all.

And if he kept telling himself that, then maybe he'd start to believe it.

CHAPTER 6

Saturday evening

THEY SERVED UP the last of the spaghetti on clean plates and ate. Tripod had been banished from the dining room this time. Afterwards, Tabitha took her coffee into the living room, Tango at her heels. The damn softie had been trying to steal her coffee for years. Tabitha never gave in, but that didn't stop the old cat from trying, or taking advantage of every opportunity that Tabitha was distracted.

As she settled in one corner of the big settee that was from her grandfather's era, she couldn't help but see the room as Ronin had to see it. Shabby, retro, well lived in. Like her grandfather, and damn if that didn't bring the tears back up again. He'd been gone almost a week. It seemed like forever.

Ronin stood awkwardly at the entrance to the living room staring at Tango. At least he didn't look like he was going to pass out anymore. She had to give him credit. He was still there. With a smile, she said, "Take a seat. I don't have much, but what I have is comfortable."

She watched with interest as Ronin chose the chair furthest away from her – and Tango. Tripod slumped to the floor in between her and Ronin. The dog was incredibly intuitive and could sense human issues easily.

The phone rang just then. She glared at the big black square relic from her grandfather's time. It continued to ring.

"Aren't you going to answer it?"

"It's Dennis, my father," she said shortly.

Ronin tilted his head. "And..."

She snatched up the receiver. "I'm fine, Dad."

"Then why did the hospital contact me at the office to say you'd been admitted?" he snapped. "I just got the message from Eric. Is it too much to offer me the courtesy of a follow up call to say you are fine?"

Of course the hospital had called him. He was her next of kin. He must have someone on the hospital board or an alert that rang some kind of alarm every time she went in. He always seemed to know. "I was admitted. I was checked over. I checked myself out." She sighed. "I'm fine. End of story."

"Tango?"

"Tango is fine. I'd passed out, someone checked up on me and called an ambulance. Not a biggie." She rolled her eyes at Ronin's raised eyebrow and turned her attention back to her father, wishing he'd hang up. She was lying and her father had a built-in lie detector. Like most fathers.

"Hmm."

She winced. "I have company right now. So maybe we can talk tomorrow?"

"Unless you're unconscious and back in the hospital," her father said grimly.

"Not likely. I'm fine. Just a little worn down."

"Isn't that why you hired more people? So this wouldn't happen?" he asked. "Are you sure you can handle that place? It doesn't sound like it to me."

Her back stiffened and she shot an angry look at Ronin. He raised an eyebrow and leaned forward. She shook her head. "Dad, I can handle the place just fine. I'm not fragile. I'm not losing it or whatever else that damn assistant of yours might have suggested." She tried to rein back the sweeping emotions and the fear over losing her grandfather's estate. "Eric is a drama queen," she said shortly. "There's nothing wrong with me or the Reserve."

"Germaine is concerned as well, and no one would call him that. Besides, look at the break-ins, vandalism and..." He took a deep breath. "And you having blackouts."

"I'm fine," she repeated, hating the dread reaching up to choke her. "Just finish handling Granddad's estate so I'm not in limbo anymore and I'll be even better." She drew a deep breath. "Look, I need to go."

"I'll stop by tomorrow. We'll go over the estate then."

As she hung up the phone, she had to wonder how she could have been so close to her grandfather and so distant with her father.

"You don't get along with him?"

Ronin's black gaze studied her. She shifted self-consciously. How did one explain a missed connection between generations? "We've never been close. He hates this place and I love it. I was close to my grandfather but he wasn't." She didn't expect him to understand, but he was smiling. "But he's a hell of a businessman and donates money to keep the place running."

"I do understand. I presume he isn't so hot on the animal thing?"

She laughed. "I swear he hates them. And he really didn't like the whole circus performer thing. But my grandfather, although retired by the time I came along, was a carny at heart."

"That must have been tough on your father when his father was still a performer. That's hardly the same as saying my father is a doctor or a lawyer. For some kids, he'd have had the best dad but for many others, he'd have been mocked day in and day out."

She had to wonder. Had her dad's life been the living hell he made it out to be?

"I imagine that as soon as he could, he got out of this place. But what I don't understand is how and why you ended up here without him?" Ronin studied her face for an answer.

"Now there's a story. My father had actually broken up with my mother before she found out she was pregnant. And she never told him. Apparently, she didn't want a child at that stage of her life. She tried motherhood out for a few months and decided it wasn't for her. She…" Tabitha sighed at all the childhood memories that had been so difficult growing up with. "She left me with my father."

As his eyes widened in shock, she laughed. "And as you can imagine, that was a bit more than he'd bargained for when he opened his door on a Sunday afternoon. He had a six-month-old child dropped in his arms and was told he'd make a better parent than the mother was."

Ronin shook his head. "Jesus."

She could just imagine Ronin thinking of his own life and what he'd do in that circumstance. "The thing is, my father hadn't planned on being a father either. Ever. He'd had so little relationship with his own dad that he figured procreation wasn't for him. So he dumped me on grandpa."

"Even though he'd had a poor relationship with his own father?" Ronin's brow lifted in surprise. "Wasn't that almost a punishment for you? He'd make you suffer as he had done?"

She smiled. "I think he was too desperate to think clearly at all. Maybe in a small way he figured grandpa owed him. I don't know and I don't care because it's the best thing he could have done. I adored my grandfather and I'd like to believe I enriched his life."

"Especially when you took to the animals the way his own son didn't."

"True."

"But your father still loves you."

Ronin stated that as a fact and she had to wonder about that. "As much as he can, I guess. I never saw a lot of him growing up. I think my father would have happily dropped me off and never set eyes on me again, but my grandfather was strong willed and he had strict rules about what my father's role in all this was."

"Sounds as if you might have gotten the best deal after all."

"I sure did." She laughed as she reached across the couch to scratch Tango's ear with her nails. "All the kids I went to school with wanted to be me."

"Goes to show you the difference a generation can make."

"Also, my father is conscious of appearances. But for me, as you can see…" She flung a hand at her old living room. "Appearances are the least of my worries."

"Not much point in tidying all the time if the animals have the run of the house. I'm sure keeping this place clean is an ongoing challenge."

She winced. "It's the hair more than anything. Mostly from Tripod. Tango stays in his enclosure much of the time. When he's in the house, he has the run of every room though."

"Including your bedroom."

Knowing it was likely the death sentence to their relationship but feeling that she couldn't short Tango either, she answered truthfully. "Sometimes he sleeps on my bed."

At Ronin's spluttering reaction, she shrugged. "Tango is good company. And if he isn't on my bed, you can bet Tripod is."

"No wonder you sleep alone." Ronin stood up. "And speaking of sleep, you're tired. And need rest. Do you have a spare room for me?"

"You don't need to stay over. I'm sure I'll be fine."

"Doesn't matter if you believe it or not. I'm staying."

There was no doubting the determined lock to the jaw or the glint in his eyes. She stood up. Let him see what he'd be sleeping in first. Then he could decide. She had several spare bedrooms but the beds weren't made up. One of the rooms didn't even have a bed in it. And the one room that was fully furnished and made up was her father's old room. She doubted Ronin would stay once he saw the accommodations.

Tango got up and walked toward Ronin. He backed up. "And getting this guy back into his cage would be much appreciated."

"If you're planning on sticking around, you need to get used to him being here. It's his home. I leave it up to him to decide where he wants to be." But she snapped her fingers, bringing Tango to her side.

"Shit."

Sighing, she stood up. "You can sleep in the spare room down this way. It was my father's old room."

"Does your father, Dennis ever stay here?"

"No," she said shortly.

Ronin fell into step behind her. Tango, as if seeming to know where they were going, led the way. Tripod brought up the rear.

At the entrance to the bedroom, Ronin stopped and stared. The far wall was large square mesh leading directly into the tiger's area.

"Crap."

WHY HIM? HE'D had enough of his ego being bashed by this damn cat thing. Ronin was not going to lose any more time on it. He hoped. "I presume the wire mesh is strong and I won't have any uninvited guests during the night." He was proud of how cool, calm and collected he managed to sound. How had Dennis liked being here with this cage?

"It's secure."

He studied the wire, walking closer to test it with his hands. It was solid. And from what he could see, there didn't appear to be any opening or hinges where the wall opened.

"I thought Dennis didn't want anything to do with the whole carny thing."

"That didn't mean he didn't want some connection to the animals. He was raised here after all. And besides, he hasn't slept in this room…" She broke off as if to consider, then shrugged. "Since… I don't remember when. Maybe thirty-five plus years."

Ronin pivoted to stare at the large room, realizing how much like the rest of the house it was. As if time had stopped. Big, old and essentially untouched in several decades.

Little had been done in the way of updating the interior or furnishings, and given where her heart lay, she'd most likely poured all the available money into the animals and their care.

And speaking of animals…

"Is this the only tiger you have right now?" He glanced around at her and saw Tango sprawled at her feet.

"Inside the house, yes. My grandfather's last tiger, Tobias, passed away a few months before he did," she paused. "In fact, I wondered if grief played a part in my grandfather's early death. Those two were so close. And up until he died, my grandfather was very healthy. He went to sleep that night and just never woke up."

"You found him?" Now that wouldn't have been fun.

She squatted and gave Tango a good belly rub. "Tango woke me up. He was howling something awful. He knew. When I heard him, I knew. There was just something different about his call. I went and checked on my grandfather and found him in bed, still curled up in his favorite sleeping position."

Ronin found it hard to believe that the damn motor coming from its throat was a purr, but it was acting like a baby house cat. "Are you and Tango that close?"

Sadness swept over her as she smiled up at him. "Yes. He came into the household when I was ten and he was just a cub. We fell in love."

"And how much longer does he have?"

"He's living on borrowed time in many ways." She sighed and straightened. "Life expectancy is anywhere from twelve to twenty years, with the white species thought to be slightly shorter than their golden counterparts."

"So he's old? How come he doesn't look it?" Then again, how would he know what an old tiger looked like? Several meters long from nose to tail with clear bright eyes and jet-black markings, he showed no recognizable signs of aging.

"He's a pampered baby." She straightened. "He's been badly affected by the passing of our tiger, Tobias, and my grandfather's deaths."

"So when did Tripod move in?" Hearing his name, Tripod nudged Ronin's hand. As mad as he'd been over the disappearance of their dinner, he couldn't help but stroke the beautiful animal's huge head. As if realizing he'd been forgiven, Tripod walked over to the bed and stretched across the bottom of it.

"He's seven now. And look… He's found your bed." She laughed. "Good thing you said you liked dogs."

Dogs were good. Much easier to deal with than this cat thing he had going on. He couldn't remember when it all started, but anyone who compared a ten-pound, fluffy domestic cat to this five hundred pound-take-your-face-off-if-you-look-at-him-sideways cat was crazy.

He might just prefer this version, but he'd rather not have anything to do with either.

Abruptly Tabitha pointed to a door off to the side and said, "There's the bathroom. I think you should have everything you need."

Then she turned to go.

"Just a question, if you do get attacked tonight, are there other animals here that I'm likely to come face to face with on my way to your room?"

She hesitated at the doorway.

He narrowed his gaze and felt his heart pound. What the hell was she hiding?

And why?

Then she laughed, a light easy laugh that made his suspicions suddenly seem foolish. "Nope, there's just the three of us here."

Dare he ask? Shit, he really needed access. And he didn't need to argue with a damn tiger when he was fighting to save her life. "And Tango? Will you lock him up in case I have to come to you?"

"He'll be in my room."

"And if he won't let me near you?" He glared at her. "Do you really want to put a cop who's going to be more concerned about saving you against a tiger that won't give him access?"

She stiffened and glared right back. "I'll be fine."

"And yet you weren't."

She walked to the doorway then paused, turned and said, "If that happens again, there won't be anything you can do about it." She was silent a long moment. "Just in case you do come across me in an odd state, try not to physically touch me."

And she walked out.

FEZ STARED INTO the back of the truck, hating the booming in his head from the noise. "She isn't calming down. Shit. She's been given so many drugs she should be fucking sleeping." She was going to hurt herself this way. God help him if that happened.

Where the hell was Roberts? He was the one who always dealt with this shit.

Fez knew nothing about this part of the job. He sure hoped the boss did. And Fez didn't need that added worry right now. He'd only stopped to check on her because he wanted to make sure she was okay. Now he wished he hadn't. What could he do? Nothing. Roberts had the stuff to knock her out. He did those jobs.

Not Fez.

Best thing would be for him to get back inside that truck and go straight to the warehouse. That might calm her down. And the others.

The look in her eye just then…. Jesus, that had scared the crap out of him.

"If you'd calm down and just sit quietly, it will go so much easier on you."

She still glared at him with that look in her eye… But she stayed quiet.

He was kind of glad about that. He'd listened to her complain enough already. Her throat had probably been screamed raw. If he was lucky, she'd lost her voice.

The guys he'd picked the shipment up from said she'd been tranq'd and would be asleep for hours. Not true.

Now he didn't know what to do. *Shit.* He closed the back of the truck, threw down the level to lock it in place, walked to the front of the truck and hopped up onto the driver's seat.

He could really only do one thing – carry on as he'd started.

CHAPTER 7

Saturday, late evening

RONIN AND TABITHA were finally sleeping under one roof. Just not the way she'd hoped. Tabitha strolled back to her own huge bed and pulled the covers back as much as she could. Tango had taken up most of the space. "Move over, boy."

Instead, he rolled toward her on his back, presenting his belly to be scratched.

"That's not quite what I meant." She smiled. "Then it seems males always interpret what I'm saying in their own way."

Tango's engine kicked in. Tabitha sat down and scratched the tiger's velvety fur. "What am I going to do when you're gone?"

It would devastate her. Losing Tobias had been difficult. She'd understood her grandfather's lingering despair months later. They'd been closer than father and son. And she was closer to Tango that she was to her own father.

Tigers had been the missing link for both generations.

Her grandfather had spent the better part of his life being a servant to the large cats. She was following in his footsteps. For the most part, she was fine with that. But she didn't want to be alone forever. Her thoughts once again returned to Ronin, sleeping so close, and yet so far away. That short distance somehow made her feel even more lonely than if she had been there, alone in the house. Knowing that they were so damn close to taking their relationship to the next level also made it difficult.

She'd been falling for him for weeks. That long slow glide of attraction that was both special and disconcerting. Sure, he had this thing about cats...but when she needed him, he'd done well with Tango. Many people would have taken one look and run.

"Just you and me, huh, boy." At least for the moment.

She slipped under the covers, shoving Tango over. Not an easy task, but he rolled back the way he'd been earlier with a contented snort.

Regardless of where Ronin slept, Tabitha had to admit she did feel better having Ronin staying there. It felt right. With that thought, she turned off her lamp and slid lower under the covers.

IT WAS THE middle of the night when she woke. Her heart pounded in her chest with a ferocity that had her panicked and searching the corners of her bedroom. She'd also woken alone. Tango had slipped out of her room sometime in the night. She glanced at her clock. It was 2:34 am. She'd managed less than three hours.

A shadow crossed her nervous system, accentuating the feeling of wrongness.

Then she understood. Shit.

Someone was out hunting… She was the prey.

Again.

Taking a deep breath, she sank energy lines down her legs, through the heels of her feet and deep into the ground. She had to be grounded. She desperately wanted to jump ship and hide in the ethers, but she didn't dare leave her body alone and unprotected. Not if she was the prize. Well, she wasn't going to make it easy on whoever was doing this. Not this time.

Knowing it was foolish, but unable to resist the instinctive move, she scrambled out of bed and raced to the spot behind her bedroom door. She understood it was a psychic attack, but that didn't mean her attacker wasn't here physically as well.

Except that neither Tango nor Tripod had raised the alarm. And they would have if there was a stranger in the house.

"Tabitha?" The male whisper slipped into the room, so soft it was almost silent.

Ronin? How did he know?

"Yes," she whispered.

"Are you okay?" His voice deepened as he moved closer.

She didn't know what to say. That his interruption when she'd just acknowledged that her attacker could be here physically was disconcerting. She was certain it wasn't him. There was no way. She'd have known Ronin's energy anywhere. That didn't mean someone couldn't be using him to attack her though. Stranger things had happened. And she'd let him inside the house.

A basic rule. Another of her grandfather's rules broken this last week.

But anyone who could do what this guy had almost done last time, most likely didn't need to be inside her home. He could be outside prowling the grounds. He could be miles away.

Trusting her instincts, she peered around the door. Ronin stood there in his jeans, bare chested, his gun in his hand.

Shit.

Why wasn't Tripod having a fit over the gun?

"Are you okay?" he repeated.

She took a deep breath and brushed a long strand of hair back off her face. "Yes. I think so. I just woke up a few minutes ago." She motioned to the firearm. "What are you doing here – and with that?"

He glanced around her room as if still searching for something wrong, then glanced down at the gun in his hands. "Tripod sounded the alarm."

She stared at him, then at the massive dog that strolled into her room, looking unconcerned. "Really? And what alarm was that?"

The frown as he glanced down at the dog sitting quietly, calmly at his side, was telling. "He woke me up, started whining and wouldn't quit until I followed him here."

"Interesting," she murmured. Since when had Tripod taken to a stranger like that? Normally he'd have barked until he lost his voice. Or called to her telepathically. She eyed the dog suspiciously, asking mentally, *What are you up to?*

He stared back with an innocent look on his canine face.

But she knew him. And he'd done what he'd done for a reason. The end result was he'd brought Ronin to her rescue. To her bedroom.

And she *had* woken up with that sense she was being hunted. Maybe Tripod had brought Ronin here in response to her own fears…

"I had a bad dream. That's all." She managed a natural smile. "Tripod must have picked up on it."

"What kind of a bad dream?" His voice hardened. "And don't lie to me."

She could just imagine him in an interview room. He was a good cop. And suspicion wove through his voice. He needed an explanation. She likened him to a bulldog, not willing to let go of something he wanted.

She gave in with grace. "I had the feeling I was being hunted."

His gaze narrowed. "As in an intruder, a nightmare or a psychic attack?"

She winced. "A nightmare – I hope – but…there's no way to tell at this point."

"Do you still feel that way?" He glanced around the inside of her room, those sharp eyes peering into corners looking for hiding places. Then he spun around to check in the direction of the hallway and other rooms behind him.

She shook her head. "No. The air is lighter now. The sensation is gone."

He studied her.

She stared back calmly.

"Good. Then try to get a little more sleep." And he walked around the side of the bed, placed his weapon on the night table and lay down on top of the covers. He closed his eyes.

"Uhmmmm?" She stared at him in shock. "What are you doing?"

"Going to bed. I suggest you do the same. If anyone is going to hunt you, they'll have to go through me," he muttered before a yawn took him. He rolled onto his side and looked ready to fall asleep.

She didn't know if she was outraged or honored. That he'd want to protect her went along with his cop image, but she didn't want him here in her room if it was just professional…

Wait. Of course she did. She didn't want to be attacked, but at the same time she wanted it to be more than for just a professional reason on his part. She hesitated then asked, "What if I don't want you sleeping here?"

"Too bad. Besides, I've wanted to sleep here for a while. Now's my chance."

She gasped at the smirk in his voice. She'd been wanting the same thing, but not like this.

She didn't know what to do. What to say.

He rolled over, grabbed the corner of her bedding and pulled it back so she could get in. "Come on, sweetheart, get over it. Get some sleep. You need sleep, time to heal."

She crawled into bed, her movements stiff and hesitant. "And who says I'm going to get over it?"

"I'm telling you to." He yawned again then added in a sleepy voice, "And do it fast."

She'd have gasped in outrage but he appeared to be asleep already. Damn, how could he do that? She never fell asleep so easily. She pulled the covers up to her neck, rolled over and closed her eyes. And couldn't sleep.

Frustrated, she tossed and turned.

"What *is* your problem?" he asked. "Do you want Tango here, instead of me? Well too bad."

"Ha!" She sat up again taking umbrage at his tone. "What is your problem with cats anyway? You seemed to handle Tango just fine tonight."

"Because I stayed the hell away." He chuckled softly. "Besides, I like some cats – I like you, kitten."

"Oh no, you don't." She glared at him, but inside her heart was softening. He'd always been able to do that to her. Make her go gooey inside with that deep-throated chuckle and the soft sexy tones. "This is important. I thought we had something special going on here. But cats are a huge part of my life."

The laughter fell from his face. He propped himself up on one arm so he could look at her. His bare chest gleamed in the moonlight. She swallowed, wishing she hadn't noticed. But now that she had, she couldn't think of anything else but that huge expanse of muscled body displayed in front of her. With effort, she tore her gaze away and focused on his face.

"As far as I'm concerned – I'm in," he said suddenly. And damn if those eyes of his didn't deepen and pull her into a mental embrace.

She sighed happily. "Okay then." And fell silent, not knowing where to go next.

His lips quirked in a small intimate way that sent her heart racing. She leaned back against the headboard and tugged the covers up to her waist. He reached out a hand and gently smoothed out the wrinkles of the top blanket. A heavy sigh escaped and he said in a troubled voice, "I don't really understand why, but something happens when I see cats." He stared out the window. "I don't know how to explain it. I'm not allergic, but my chest doesn't seem to understand that. It locks down and I can't breathe. At the same time, it's emotional overload. It's how I imagine a panic attack would feel. I get headaches and a lot of times there's a horrific buzzing in my head."

Now that was a different story. And one that gave her hope. "So it's not that you don't like them, but you don't like the way you react to them?"

He shrugged. "Something like that. I can handle it, but it's not exactly comfortable. And given a choice of never being in the same room with one, I wouldn't be."

"And yet you were in the same room with Tango."

"It's not as if you gave me much choice." His face twisted into a mock grin. "Besides, I didn't want to look a fool in my lady's presence. Not exactly manly."

His lady? Her insides wiggled. Maybe. Maybe this was something they could work around. And his reaction to felines, such a strong reaction pointed to several options. An undiagnosed allergy, or her favorite theory – a traumatic event in his history. Even if he didn't remember the event, his body might. And that was something that could be worked on. She'd have to mention it to Stefan.

"Do you remember when this started?"

He groaned and flopped down on his back beside her. "You know there are a lot more fun things I'd like to be doing in the middle of the night while lying on a huge bed with a beautiful woman at my side instead of talking about my problems, right?"

Tabitha grinned. *What the hell...* "And if I still want to talk about this?"

He snorted, glanced at the watch on his wrist and said, "Then get over it. You have 30 seconds, 29, 28, 27..."

She reached for her pillow and hit him over the head.

He laughed, snatched the pillow and tossed it. Then he tugged her free of the bedding before flipping her over. He quickly tossed his leg over hers, trapping her beneath him.

She was too surprised to move. Damn, he moved fast and sooo smoothly.

Then he lowered his head.

She gave in happily as his warm lips moved gently on hers. Questing, seeking, asking.

This is not where she thought the night would end up. Yet maybe she should have. Is this what she wanted? Hell yes. Was it the right time? Maybe not. But she didn't think that mattered anymore.

He lowered his head again. This kiss was no longer as gentle. It sought answers, asked permission, all while offering a taste of what was to come.

She swiftly fell under his spell. She wrapped her arms around his back and pulled him close, deepening the kiss. He resisted, keeping himself ever so slightly up and away, his lips still on hers but not devouring. He lifted his head and looked at her. "Are you sure?"

She blinked at him. Then smiled. "Yes."

His lips quirked. "In that case..."

The touch of his lips this time was sure, confident, knowing. She sighed happily and slid deeper into his embrace. She wanted him. She wanted it all.

He slid his lips across her skin, leaving a wake of heat and coolness behind. He traced the shape of her ear then dropped tiny kisses down her neck to her collarbone. Tabitha arched her back, giving him better access. He threaded his fingers through her long hair. She twisted gently beneath his gentle caress, her fingers stroking his wide shoulders and back.

He trailed his lips up her throat to reclaim her lips. His lips plundered and caressed and teased, and she was a willing victim. She shifted restlessly.

"Easy," he murmured.

"I don't want easy," she whispered hoarsely, digging her nails into his back.

He reacted swiftly, grabbing her hands and pulling them over her head where he held her gently. She didn't try to get away. Instead she twisted, dragging her lace cami across his bare chest. He bent his head and took the silk-covered nipple into his mouth and suckled. She gasped and arched even more.

"God, I love the sounds you make like this," he whispered.

She hadn't even been aware of making those tiny cries. She tugged her hands free and slipped them down inside his jeans to curve over his muscled buttocks. And dug in her claws.

He roared and bounced off the bed. In a smooth motion, he stripped the jeans off and kicked them to the side. His boxers joined them right after. She kneeled on the bed, watching him. He stood before her, tall and proud and ready. She reached out with both hands.

"Oh not. Not yet." He nodded at her clothing. "Your turn."

With a big bold smile, she crossed her arms and pulled her cami up and off. She tossed it beside his clothes. In a smooth muscled movement, she bounced to her feet, and with a snap, she dropped her panties to the bed where she kicked them in the direction of her bra.

She dropped onto the bed where he waited for her.

He reached out to stroke her smooth, silky skin from hips to ribs then down again, looking, learning, memorizing. A gentle gasp escaped as his touch sparked a trail of embers in its wake. In a surprise move, he pulled her into a loving hug and held her close.

She snuggled deeper, cuddling his erection.

He nudged her chin up to where he could see her face and took a long look. The heat in his gaze brought heat to her cheeks. He whispered, "You are seriously beautiful, you know that?"

"Thank you." She stretched up to clasp his face on both sides and kiss him, gently at first then with more enthusiasm. His heated hands slid around to her back and down to cup her cheeks before he pulled her tight against him. Rolling over, he settled between her legs. She lifted one foot and stroked the back of his calf, smiling up at him.

Dark hair, devilish blue eyes, a wicked smile…and he thought she was beautiful. What more could she ask for?

Then he dropped his head and kissed her. Oh right, he was also a dynamite kisser. He deepened the kiss and she was lost. When he lifted his head, she whimpered, raising her head to find him again. He dropped light caressing kisses on her cheeks, her eyes, her throat. She twisted restlessly beneath him. Sliding her hands over his back and shoulders, she tugged him down for another deep kiss. A gentle kiss. A loving kiss. A kiss full of promise. And found she wanted so much more.

She burned. Everywhere. Her hands had a life of their own, sparking a matching response from him. Skin slid against skin, embers flared to life as every inch of his smooth skin was stroked, squeezed and caressed.

And kissed.

Oh God, his kisses…nectar to a starving woman. She hadn't realized how much she needed this. This touching. This closeness. This connection to him.

He slid to one side, his fingers doing crazy things to her hormones as they stroked down between her legs. She gasped then moaned, her legs shifting restlessly under his clever touch. He leaned over and slipped his tongue between her lips, smoothing across her tongue. His fingers stroked her in tandem to his devilish tongue. She shivered.

She tried to touch him, pull him closer, but he shifted out of reach. "I can't let you," he whispered. "I'm too close to the edge."

Widening her legs, she hooked one leg around his and toppled him where she wanted him.

And he landed perfectly. The tip of his erection sat just inside her but no further.

It was too much and so not enough. She groaned in frustration.

He laughed, raised up on his hands and plunged all the way to her center.

Arching, she cried out with pleasure. *"Yes."*

And then he pulled back and paused.

She groaned. Tugging his mouth back to hers, she murmured against his lips, "Tease."

"Witch," he countered before his mouth closed over hers.

Then neither could talk as his hips drove him into her over and over again, setting up a tempo she matched with every beat. Tension twisted inside, turning tighter, taking her higher. Until she couldn't take any more.

"I can't…" she cried.

"You can. Take it. Take me. More…"

He shifted slightly, hooking an arm under her thigh and plunging deep, grinding against her center – and that move sent her flying. She cried out, her head arching back into the pillow, her body still braced to take him as he thrust harder and harder.

He arched his back and shuddered, pulsing deep inside her.

A long groan escaped as he collapsed beside her.

She giggled, wrapped her arms around him then snuggled close.

He opened one eye. "You should not have enough energy to laugh after that."

"Except I feel great!" She curled into a ball, her legs layered between his and her arms around his waist. Nose to nose, she smiled deeply at his satiated glow and then she closed her eyes.

And fell asleep.

SHE CAME AWAKE a second time, her heart pounding as she gasped for breath. This time was worse. She could hardly breathe. Her chest constricted in panic.

What was going on?

She bolted from the bed and stood beside her bathroom door, only realizing at the last minute that Ronin had been sleeping soundly beside her. Ronin came awake like the big cats he said he had trouble with. Instantly. He searched the room, his gaze zipping back to her. "Tabitha?"

How could she explain? She wrung her hands as she paced.

"Something is out there." She didn't know how else to explain it. "It's hunting me."

He reached her in seconds. His strong arms wrapped around her, tucking her in close. And in that moment she knew she was no longer alone.

Thank heavens. This was damn spooky stuff.

She glanced around. The bedroom door was open. And there was no sign of Tripod. She walked to the open mesh and saw Tango stretched out on one of the many cushions, completely relaxed.

Tripod…? Surely he'd have sounded an alarm if there was danger. Yet he hadn't.

She'd met too many people with weird psychic abilities. Did someone have the ability to affect her animals? She hoped not. She desperately needed them exactly as they were – for herself.

Ronin peered over her shoulder to search the enclosure. Then he walked to her bedroom window and pulled her curtain back to search the yard out front. "How bad was it?"

"It wasn't outside. And neither is it likely to be visible to the human eye." She stood with her arms wrapped around her chest and answered his original question. "Bad, but not incapacitating."

In shock, Ronin spun around. "Has it ever been as bad as this last time?"

She gave a dry laugh. "How easily you forget. You found me in the shower unconscious the last time, remember? My instinct is to run and hide in the ethers, but I'm trying not to leave my body open to an attacker. I can protect it under most circumstances, but we don't know just what someone might be able to do in this field. And Stefan is afraid that my body might be exactly what this person is after."

"Your body?" He reached up and pinched the bridge of his nose as he searched her face. "Really?"

With the sensation fading, she could afford to smile. A little one. "Yes. Some people are dead. Their souls don't want to cross over. Their souls are, in fact, trapped here and are looking for a way to live again. They only need a physical body. And some are trying to stay here forever."

Ronin's breath rushed out. He shook his head as if trying to deny her words. "And they can just slide back into a life, into another body again?"

"If they can take control of the body, then they can take over and live again." She nodded. "Yes. It's odd and shocking and crazy but it's…true. Ask Stefan. He's seen cases like this. Hard to forget."

Ronin shook his head. "Wow. Every time I get close to these freaky 'woo woo' cases, I have to wonder how any of this could happen while the rest of the world is completely oblivious."

"They are *mostly* oblivious," she corrected, "but at the same time, there are more and more people waking up to the psychic potential within themselves."

"And therefore to the potential for these horrific attacks," Ronin said.

"Of course, but also the potential for skills and healing beyond anything most people can imagine."

"Dr. Maddy, for instance." He smiled. "Now she is something."

Tabitha laughed. "Isn't she though? And she's not alone in what she can do." She walked toward him. "There are people who can see through solids, hear a pitch lower and higher than most animals. Some people can appear as one thing while being something different altogether." She shook her head and studied the emotions sliding across his face…shock, disbelief, curiosity. He'd been exposed to some of this mess through the other friends in their circle, but this was a bit much for anyone. "It's a whole different world once you see below the surface."

She walked closer and almost reached his side when she felt it again.

The hunter. Searching for his prey.

"Shit," she whispered. "He's back."

"Who?" Ronin immediately stepped to her side. "And where?" He turned around in circle, his eyes searching for the predator.

She shuddered as her spine froze. Inside, she felt as if a spotlight shone down on her. "He's found me."

"Hide," Ronin ordered, his gun once again in his hand as he stepped protectively in front of her. He searched the area. "Where is he?"

"Everywhere," she whispered. "He's everywhere."

Ronin spared her a single look. "And so how do I find him?"

"I don't know." She spun around. "He's not showing an energy signature." Knowing Ronin wouldn't understand but not having time to explain, she studied the air in the room. But there were no strange energies.

Then another wave reached for her, over her. This time it was so strong. Even as she stood in place, the emotions hit her.

Fear.

Panic.

Hatred.

She cried out as she dropped to her knees.

Ronin dropped beside her, wrapping an arm around her shoulder. "What is it? What can I do to help?"

"It's him." She screamed and slapped her hands to the sides of her head as the same claw-like sensation dropped inside her skull.

She struggled to set a bolt of energy, her ground, deep through her house, deep into the earth beneath her – as strong and as deep as she could manage. And just like last time, it was almost impossible to hold on. She struggled against the fear, knowing that fear was the most debilitating. Her fear. Ronin's fear. Her attacker's fear.

The combined energies were enough to kill them both. Maybe all three of them. Oh God, had she put Ronin in danger too?

"Tabitha?"

"I'm trying…"

She bent over, trying to shut out the roaring buzz that was increasing by the second, she whispered over and over again, "Stay centered. Stay grounded. Stay balanced."

She had to survive this.

Don't fight.

She didn't know where that thought came from, but she realized she was going about this the wrong way. She was trying to fight off the attack. When she should be giving in to it, then detaching from it.

Observing it.

She straightened slowly, hearing Ronin cry out in the background. "Tabitha? What are you doing?"

"I'm going to try something," she whispered, her voice barely audible. "Don't touch me while I'm doing it."

And she sank within herself, emotionally, physically and psychically. She slipped into her own energy, feeling her way through the heat of her body to the heat of her soul and grounding herself inside.

Another wave of emotion whipped at her, closing in on her soul. It grabbed on and gave her energy a good shake.

She lost her center of balance, scrambled to get it back, then lost it again. Panic swept through her, crying out to her, calling, pleading, begging, for something…someone…to help.

She gasped.

They wanted help.

A scream of anger blasted through her mind. And the pain in her side near her belly region made her want to cry out at the top of her lungs. Something else pricked her side. She barely felt it with everything else that hurt. After a moment, the pain eased.

Only to be replaced by a rage that wouldn't quit.

She felt it at the DNA level.

Then it got worse. That same hand reached deeper into her psyche, deeper into her soul, latched on…and yanked.

Just like last time, she was pulled up through the top of her head.

She screamed as her body collapsed to the floor while from her waist up, she was lifted up and free of her body.

No! She was desperate to stay.

Ground. Ground. Struggling against her own panic, she poured energy deep inside her body and through it to the ground below. She could do this.

As if enraged at being thwarted, she was given a second hard yank… and she was pulled higher up.

There was so much rage behind the energy assault, she could hardly deal with it. Emotions swamped her as she was bombarded by colors and emotions. The pain was so extreme that she was buffeted on all sides even as she shuddered deep inside. She couldn't get a coherent thought to stay long enough to understand it.

And then it was buried under the pain of the next wave.

There was so much fear, it crippled her. She had no time to adapt. To accept. To detach. She couldn't adjust. She wasn't used to this level of panic or this pain. And she definitely wasn't used to the overwhelming sensation of captivity. Imprisonment. Death.

Another heavy yank and she was pulled higher until her knees were now at her waist. She screamed her own scream, a sound of horror and inevitableness. He was too strong.

Too desperate.

And he grabbed hold harder and ripped one more time.

And pulled her loose.

The last thing she saw was her body folded in half on the floor, with Ronin hovering helplessly at her side, his arms wrapped protectively around her. He was trying to save her – but he was trying to save the wrong part of her.

Then she knew no more.

HELPLESS, RONIN COULD only watch as Tabitha slumped to the floor. She'd been in the same position for a few minutes already, but this last change was shocking. As if she'd been suspended by some kind of string that had been cut, and her lifeless body collapsed to the floor.

He checked for a pulse.

And couldn't find one.

His heart ripped open. Dear God. What was going on?

How could this be?

It was not possible.

Instantly Tango started roaring, the sound loud enough and haunting enough to raise the hairs on the nape of Ronin's neck. Tripod appeared at Tabitha's side and sat on his haunches. He tilted his head back and howled, the sound slicing through the atmosphere with shocking clarity.

Tabitha was in trouble.

Big trouble.

This was so bad. Tabitha wasn't just out cold… She appeared to have moved out permanently. That couldn't be.

She'd be dead if that was the case. And maybe she wasn't dead yet, but she was most definitely dying.

"Stefan? Where the hell are you?" he yelled to the empty room. He pulled out his cell phone to dial when a tired cranky voice answered him – in his head.

Does no one sleep anymore?

"It's Tabitha," Ronin said starkly. "She's gone. This time it looks really bad."

Stefan never said a word. The air around Ronin warmed, moved. Like, what the hell? Ronin hovered protectively over Tabitha as he caught movement out of the corner of his eye.

"Jesus. What is that?"

What? Stefan asked.

"Movement. I swear I can see something moving off to one side but it's not there when I turn my head. As if it's not really there."

It's me. Close your eyes, realize I'm here in spirit form, then open your eyes again.

Ronin followed the instructions even as his mind said he was crazy. When he reopened his eyes he saw a deep blue cloud at Tabitha's side. "Jesus." His mind balked and as it did – the cloud disappeared. "Hey, where did it go?" He spun around. "Where did you go?"

I didn't go anywhere. Your belief system kicked in and changed your perception. Work on it later. We have to help Tabitha now.

"And how do I do that?"

She needs to go back to the hospital. Get Dr. Marsden. Have him meet us there.

"That I can do." Ronin called for an ambulance. "Can anyone else help her?"

Yes. I'm calling them. You calm the animals while I help Tabitha. Stefan, in a somber voice, added, *this time, I don't know if I can save her.*

"HOW BAD IS she?"

Fez pulled on his gaping neckline and tried to school his face to project a confident smile. His boss narrowed his gaze on him.

Rushing into speech, Fez said, "She's had a rough trip, no doubt about it. But I'm sure she'll pull out of it." *Like hell.* He prayed she didn't do anything major like try to escape or die on his watch. Counting on Roberts to handle this stuff before had been way easier. He didn't like being responsible. Especially when it wasn't his job.

"Is she eating and drinking?" His voice, so cold and clipped, cut off Fez's hopes instantly.

"Not when I left. If Roberts would show up, he could fix her." The boss's gaze turned flat, dead looking. Ah shit.

"Roberts won't be back. You'll have to handle it."

No. No. Where was his partner? What the hell had happened here? And Fez didn't know how to do Roberts's job. Shit. Shit. This was not good. Could Roberts have booked it like he'd suggested he might? Or had the boss 'taken care' of him.

Shit. He shouldn't have mentioned his missing partner. But now he was starting to worry about his own skin. Especially if he was expected to look after the cargo without Roberts. He didn't show his concerns – instead smiled brightly. "I'm sure she is drinking and eating now."

"I'm not. Go back and watch over her." That gaze became lethal. "Or else…"

Oh crap. "I came to get my pay—" Fez, perspiring heavily, wiped his brow with his sleeve.

"You'll get paid when I get paid and that will be when she's delivered safe and sound," the boss said flatly. "If anything stops me from getting my money, you can be damn sure you won't be getting yours either."

And that nervous feeling since Roberts went missing deepened to much more. Somehow this gig had gone south and this job was bad news. And he wanted no part of it. Well, no further part in it.

He hadn't gotten this far in life by being stupid. He knew when to listen to that gut instinct. Too bad his instincts hadn't kicked in earlier. He could have left with Roberts.

His partner must have some money stashed to have pulled off his disappearing act. Fez wished he'd asked more questions because Fez was broke. He needed this payday.

And pushing for money right now just might be the stupidest thing he'd ever done.

Better he did as he was told and keep this female alive. At least long enough for the sale to go through.

Then the boss could eat his dust.

CHAPTER 8

Sunday, wee hours of the morning

HUNGER. FEAR. PANIC.

Emotions rolled through Tabitha as she was buffeted from side to side by her experience. She beat back at the pain and struggled to retain consciousness.

It was all too impossible.

But at least she was still alive.

Or was she?

Could she have died?

And was this....death?

No. At least not any form she'd understood death could take.

Another sound of rage rippled through her. She shuddered but the agony was at a visceral level. She couldn't escape. This agony had become hers. Not her attacker's.

Something was happening to her.

To her body. To her soul. To something that was an inherent part of her.

She couldn't move away from either the attacker's or her emotions, but she didn't feel a physical pain. It was there, but in the distance as if it was a cloud away. A cloud? Listen to her. She was talking as if she were dead. And that so couldn't be.

Why couldn't it be? her conscious mocked. *What's so special about you that death wouldn't find you? He found your grandfather and so many of your friends.*

I'm not ready, she whispered. Too damn bad. And something tugged at her. That same grabbing sensation. As if someone needed her. Or wanted something from her.

She tried to identify it, but blacked out before she could identify it.

THE SMELL HIT Tabitha first when she stirred back to consciousness. Rank, old and stale. Cigar smoke. Animal odors. Feces. Of many kinds. Fear. The dominant smell was…blood.

Instinctively, Tabitha wrinkled up her nose.

Memories flooded her. She'd been attacked again. Hadn't she?

She'd only surfaced a few minutes ago. But surfaced to what? Where was she? And if she could move her nose, was she here physically? She desperately wanted to stretch. Her body felt cramped, imprisoned in some way. It was a horrific feeling, but she didn't know if the sensations were physical sensations or psychic ones.

How was she to tell?

The stench was horrific – and that was physical. But her house didn't stink and that meant she wasn't at home. Her hopes fell. And if she wasn't at home, then where the hell was she?

She tried to assess her surroundings but she couldn't open her eyes. She felt heavy. As if her body was too big to move. As if whatever had happened to her was so bad she shouldn't look.

Beneath the sensations ran a thin river of anger. A molten lava river ready to burst into flame at the right moment. Her tense muscles sang in readiness.

Tension? Muscles? What the hell was going on? The last thing she remembered was being ripped from her body while Ronin was at her side. *Ronin?* Where was he? Had that been a bad dream? Or was *this* the bad dream? She knew it was impossible to sort through realities if she didn't ground herself in one of them. She'd tried to ground herself in her house.

But she either hadn't been – or had ground had moved.

And that terrified her. She hadn't realized that was a possibility.

In the distance, she heard sounds of a door opening. Her muscles came to life. Waiting…

Maybe she was at home? No. She couldn't be. She had to remember that. And if she wasn't at home, she wasn't in her own body, and therefore the muscles she could move as if her own – weren't hers.

Talk about a mind bender.

She had to consider that this was a possession – one where she had somehow possessed someone else. How could she have been forced to do that against her will?

She'd never heard of it happening to anyone else without their effort. Of course not. That would be too easy.

And that idea of possession was obviously not the whole answer because in order for her to possess someone else, they'd have to be here too.

They'd have to be sharing the same body.

And that just creeped her out. How could anyone drag a soul out of its body and into their own? And even if they could – why would they? That just didn't make any sense.

Especially when she didn't want this.

She'd never considered possession in the sense of wanting to possess another soul. She'd heard Stefan talk about other cases where possession had happened. Where someone else stepped in and took over a person's body…regardless of the original owner.

Is what she was going through the same sensation of what a person trying to possess another felt like? Did they want to feel strong young muscles tightening beneath them instead of their current existence?

Or was this something else again? Damn, but she wished she could see. Something. Anything. But her eyelids wouldn't open. Why? Then it hit her. Because they weren't her eyelids?

Yet.

A door slammed shut. She heard a muffled sound that was oddly close. Her body shifted, tightened. Apprehension rippled through her. Nausea climbed her throat. But was it hers or her host's?

Separating host from visitor would be impossible if she couldn't detach. Tabitha tried to shut out the many conflicting sensations and just listen. And footsteps were striding across a hard floor toward her. Steel-toed boots on concrete maybe? At least a work boot. Heavy. So it was likely a male approaching, one with a slightly uneven gait. So she definitely wasn't at home. She could think of many other places that she'd been in this last year that might sound like this.

She could sense her body – or the body she was in – tightening, as anger and panic built. The footsteps strode closer still. Her body quivered. Then a sharp clatter sounded. She jumped back. It was close. So damn close. And it wouldn't quit. As if this person walked with a pipe dragging along the side of a cage and made sure to bang on every pipe in the metal cage. *Clack. Clack. Clack.*

Cage? Hell. Was this person, now her, a prisoner?

And the footsteps would then belong to her captor. *Asshole.*

She shuddered and felt an answering ripple from all around her. So weird. Yet in a strange way, almost comforting. She and her host were connected. Their emotions and reactions connected. It was hard to be disturbed by this as she could sense the other person's reaction to her every emotion.

It meant she was not alone in this body. Only there was also some sort of disconnect between them.

The sounds grew and grew and changed tone as if someone raked a pipe along several different cages. Her stomach cramped with every step taken. If he was trying to psyche her out, he was succeeding.

She wanted to hide. To back into the furthest corner where he couldn't find her. But somehow she thought she might already be as far back as she could go. It was hard to tell.

She could sense the panic rising inside. Not her panic. Yet it was her panic. She was terrified. Only she didn't know of what. And that made it worse.

"There you are. How are you doing now, my beauty?"

Tabitha frowned. Was he talking about her? Damn. She wished she could see. Was she blind? That would certainly add to the horror.

"Still won't eat or drink, huh? Well, we can't have that. You're worth far too much money for me to have you be stubborn to the point of hurting yourself."

She wanted to hide away from the silky insidious evilness in his voice. She wanted to. But nothing she did made the muscles react. Not to her commands. Or to her fears. She really was living inside someone else's body.

His words finally penetrated her beleaguered mind. Just what did money have to with this?

Then the possibilities pummelled her brain. White slave trader. Sex trader. Kidnapping. Extortion. Blackmail.

Her mind spun with the horrible possibilities. This poor person. The emotions ripped through her in waves of pain and loss and revulsion.

"So are you going to have a better day today?" The voice that spoke was really close. A horrible voice. And that was when she realized there was a solid dark blanket or some kind of covering over her prison.

"Yah need to. We have some more traveling to do. Just a short trip from here. And you need to be in good shape when we arrive." There was a metal click. "Then you're his problem."

The voice got closer, encroaching on her space, pushing against her boundaries. She backed up to the corner of her cage. The cover over her prison was pulled to one side and she heard a small pop. She fell back and there was a stinging sensation in her shoulder.

She bounded to her feet, opened her mouth to scream... but... instead...out of her mouth came a horrific...roar.

Stefan couldn't explain the compulsion to come to Tabitha's house. Tabitha herself was in the hospital in critical care. Dr. Marsden, who'd seen so much, had been shocked at her condition, telling Stefan over the phone, "I have no idea what is keeping her alive."

And that's why he was here.

To find answers.

Stefan, Tabitha's friend and mentor, exited his car and climbed the stairs to Tabitha's front door. She'd invested no money in outward appearances and had put everything into the animals and their protection. She'd had a decent security system, but Roman was boosting it for her. Then yesterday Stefan had beefed it up yet again. Apparently that hadn't been enough either. The contents of her house were precious in more ways than one. The energies of its inhabitants were special.

He closed his eyes and waited for the energy of the house to calm. It automatically picked up the pace of its movements with the arrival of any stranger – person, animal, or thing. As Stefan stood there, the energy would eventually recognize him and his attachment to the house's energy.

He let his energy soften, soothe and expand. Using an adaptation of a technique he'd learned from Shay, he thinned one layer of his aura to spread like a blanket of comfort over the interior energy of the house. Within seconds, the house energy calmed and the two energies did a dance of recognition before assimilating into one.

He smiled as the door in front of him opened on its own.

He stepped through to the front hall.

Tripod waited a good ten feet in, his long tail sweeping a wide arc on the floor, a full throated whine wailing from his throat. Hearing Tango in the background, his voice just starting to pick up full strength, Stefan sent out a wave of comforting soothing energy to the tiger. And a greeting. He'd met the big cat many times on an energy level. It was inevitable when he spoke with Tabitha telepathically. Tango's energy was all over her. This would be the first time he met the huge cat on a physical plane.

Stefan walked forward and bent over to give the big guard dog a scratch behind his ears. Waves of grief and anger poured from the big animal. "Sorry, Tripod. I'm here to help. We're doing everything we can. You keep her in your thoughts and I will too. Together we'll keep her grounded so she can find her way home." At least he hoped.

The dog whimpered. Stefan understood. He could sense the dog's distress. And the dog's confusion. "You probably haven't been fed either, have you?"

He checked out the dog's energy. There was a thread of hunger but it was suppressed under the distress. Even if he set food out for the animal, chances were good the dog wouldn't eat.

He walked into the kitchen and found dry kibble. He poured several cups into the dog dish. Tripod could eat when he wanted to. If he wanted to.

Sue, from the center, could also deal with that problem. She had pitched in last time Tabitha had been incapable.

Sending out a second wave of soothing energy to Tango, Stefan strode calmly to the back enclosure. It spread from floor to ceiling at the back of the house and was connected to a larger outside enclosure to give the tiger more roaming space. Stefan stood and waited.

Tango's roar reached him before he saw the elderly white tiger. Did Tabitha even know how old this guy was?

Tabitha was in her late twenties and this guy had been in her life since she was little. Tango's father, Tobias, had been with her grandfather for decades before her. And Tobias's mother before that – probably given another name starting with T as well. Stefan remembered Tabitha mentioning something about it being a convention her grandfather had used after his wife, Tansy had passed away.

She'd been the impetus for this house and enclosure having been as crazy about tigers as her husband. Stefan also understood Tango had been here all his life. He was also born with a minor defect in his leg – if Stefan remembered correctly.

The massive animal sauntered toward Stefan. The cage wall was the only thing between them. He knew Tabitha spent most of the time with Tango. In fact, her bedroom had some kind of doorway as well. The large cat had never known freedom in the sense of being wild.

And times had changed. There were large reserves around the world that were dedicated to taking care of animals like Tango. Exotic Landscape covered acres of land – and yet it was never enough. The property value of a piece this size within commuting distance to Portland was astronomical. And Tabitha couldn't care less about its monetary value. The property value to her was all about the amount of space she could give to each animal.

Tango? How are you?

The roar of pain rippled through Stefan's mind. Tango was afraid. For Tabitha.

There was so much information rolling off the big animal yet it appeared to be emotional in nature. Stefan couldn't see if Tango actually understood what had happened. He'd know Tabitha wasn't here though. And that was enough to throw both animals out of their comfort zone. All animals were intuitive, but beloved pets even more so.

Stefan had no idea what would happen to Tango if Tabitha didn't survive. Her father was alive but had as little to do with the place as possible. And from what Stefan understood from Tabitha, Dennis wouldn't keep it running if anything happened to her.

Tango was too old to move to another reserve. He was past his twilight years. And his energy said he was close to going. Tabitha had broken down in tears more than once over the thought of losing her feline companion.

The old tiger didn't appear to be in any actual physical pain. But then, Tabitha was a strong healer, with animals her focus. It made sense for her old friend to live so long and be so healthy if she'd dedicated a certain portion of her healing energy to that purpose.

He could see an odd thread of energy heading from Tango to Tabitha's bedroom. Then maybe that was to be expected. Maybe the big guy was searching for her, too.

Animals had such interesting abilities that no one, especially humans, understood. Stefan hoped they would eventually understand all. But like humans, some animals appeared to be so much more capable on an energy level than other animals. Reassured that Tabitha's animal family was fine, he made his way to the bedroom easily by following the trail of turbulent energy through the house. He stopped just inside to see if there was any foreign energy. He didn't think she'd been physically attacked, but he was here to make sure.

The room was essentially clean of energies. Ronin, Shay, Tabitha, Tripod. Tango.

Keeping his energy close and tight, he checked out the bathroom where she'd been attacked the first time. The same energies hovered, but there was an extra one.

Dark and faint and at ceiling level only.

What was happening here? Another truth filtered forward.

That ceiling-level energy belonged to an animal.

RONIN STOOD AT Tabitha's bedside at the hospital and cursed under his breath. Talk about a panicked trip – again – to arrive back at the same damn room she'd just left. He couldn't help but think she needed to stay here awhile this time.

He already hated this woo woo stuff. That was fine and dandy when it was other people and he could do his cop stuff to help out, but this time it was more personal. Way more personal. And they belonged together, damn it.

He felt so helpless. And so lost.

He loved her and yet he hadn't been able to protect her.

Surely, there had to be something he could do. He'd been working on breaking the vandalism side of the case but when no one saw anything, no one heard anything and no one was admitting to knowing anything…he could only hope his brother's new security system would turn the tide. Ronin felt the break-ins and damage had to be an inside job, but after running through all the new hires, he'd come up with zilch.

Tired, he ran a hand down his face. He'd been here all night. And now he had to go to work.

"Tabitha, where the hell are you?" He stood up and whispered, "Please come home soon."

Ignoring the curious look from the nurse who was walking past the open doorway, he strode out to start his day.

And stopped at the hospital room door. *What was that.*

He thought he heard a sound of some kind.

He spun around and stared narrow-eyed at Tabitha. There was no change showing on her face. He walked closer to make sure. No. She looked the same.

Then what had he heard?

Feeling like an idiot, he leaned in until his ear was almost touching her pale lips.

Then he heard it again.

He straightened. No way. It couldn't be.

But…unable to help himself, he leaned over again. And there it was.

He shook his head in disbelief as he collapsed at her bedside. Numb, he leaned over for a third time. And heard nothing. He sat back up and stared at her slack features.

Damn. He could have sworn he'd heard what sounded like a terrified roar.

FEZ LISTENED TO the telephone conversation going on in front of him. He desperately needed sleep. And that wasn't going to happen any time soon. In fact, not until the sale went through.

His boss sat at his desk, his hand clenching and unclenching. He'd already snapped the pencil in his hand. From the shouting going on the other end of the phone, the buyer was even more pissed.

He'd sent a representative to come and see the product.

The buyer's voice screamed through the phone. "Who the hell do you think you're talking to? I ain't giving you shit if I don't like the product. Do I look stupid? I ordered a healthy, whole female for breeding, not an old sick one."

The yelling had Fez sinking deeper into his seat. Oh shit. He wished he'd just called in an update instead of showing up in person. And he really wanted to find out about Roberts. He'd seen something in the river behind the warehouse this morning. Looked like a floater – someone he couldn't identify but his gut said he didn't need to…because he already knew.

He wanted to ask the boss, but hadn't found the courage.

He was pretty damn sure it was a man caught up in the log. When he'd made his way closer it had come unstuck and floated further down.

But he was damn sure it was his old partner.

Had that been the boss's handiwork? Fez hadn't been part of it and he didn't know if the boss would do his own dirty work. There was a new guy at the warehouse. An older scrawny guy named Keeper. Why the boss had hired him, Fez didn't know. Hell he wasn't big enough to do any work.

The boss shifted in his old wooden office chair, glaring at the phone. He shook his head, ready to blast back when the angry voice snapped again, "And I want her now. Don't you dare try to pull a fast one on me. I'll fucking take you out if you try to stiff me. I paid a hefty deposit. Give me the healthy female I ordered or give me my fucking money back, with interest."

"Do you know what we had to go through to get her in the first place?" the boss said in a hard voice.

Fez really didn't want to be here.

"I don't give a damn. My order was very clear," the disembodied voice snorted. "From what my man saw, this damn thing is almost dead, for crying out loud. Deliver what I paid for or else—"

"She's just stressed. She needs to settle into her new home and adapt to her surroundings. She'll pick up in no time. We've seen it before."

"Then you can hang onto her until she's healthy again. If she doesn't pick up, then sell her somewhere else. Or sell her in pieces for all I care. The Chinese are always happy to buy them in that form."

"We can't keep her. You know that." The boss clenched his fist around the stapler, his knuckles growing white. "We bring them in specifically for the client. You don't want it, that's your problem. No refunds. Read the fine print in the contract."

"Like hell. I want my money back if she's not delivered in good health and on time." There was a sharp click as the buyer hung up.

The boss glared at Fez. "You heard him. I'm in the supply and demand business. If I don't come up with the goods, then I'm screwed. And if I'm screwed then you're screwed. So make sure she looks good and is delivered on time."

He smiled in a dark cold twist of his lips and added, "Do you understand?"

Then he made a dark slashing movement across his throat to cement his message. Chills rippled down Fez's throat and he swallowed. He turned and walked out of the boss's office silently and for the first time he understood the phrase 'quaking in your boots.'

And now he knew. There was no question in his mind. Roberts was dead.

Fez was going to be next. Maybe not today. Maybe not tomorrow. But if the boss had taken Roberts out because he'd found out Roberts was planning on skipping town...then Fez had better watch his every step.

He had a measly hundred bucks in his pocket and knew he'd never see another dime from the boss until this job was done. The hundred might get him a bus ticket, but only to the next damn state. Not far enough to avoid the long reach of the boss if he came after Fez.

He considered his options as he walked to the truck. His boss's truck. If he stole that, the boss would never stop looking for him. After a few moments, he realized there were no good answers. But the easiest way to get away alive was to get his full pay by completing this job.

And that meant making sure this deal went down. His stomach acids gurgled, making him slap his pockets for the open packet of stomach aids. Damn. Where had he put them? He slapped his back pocket. There.

He yanked the roll out and opened it, popping two into his mouth.

At least one part of him would feel better soon.

To make the rest of him feel better, he needed money. And for that to happen, they had to get the female to eat and drink. And maybe find a nutritional booster of some kind. Anything to have her looking strong and healthy long enough to complete the deal.

He needed that damn payday.

So he could escape while he still had the chance.

CHAPTER 9

Sunday morning

T ABITHA CHOKED, TWISTING frantically as she tried to control the noise, but the roaring continued…out of her mouth…or rather her soul and whatever mouth she was physically attached to. So loud it would have hurt her ears – if they'd been her own.

Then the sound cut off. And her shoulder started to throb. She swayed in place, struggling to stay upright, then stumbled and collapsed on her side. What was that? Had she been shot? There wasn't much pain. But she didn't feel well.

Or right.

Something was off. A half laugh choked free. She was captive in another's body. What was normal about that? No, her host felt off. Drugged. And given the sluggish sensation that felt like it was rippling through her veins – the host was unconscious.

It would help so much if she could see. Why the hell couldn't she?

Then as if just by asking the question, clarification came. She had to accept the body of whatever person she was in and see through *their* eyes.

So far she'd been fighting her host. Fighting against understanding it.

She should have been doing the reverse of that. In the beginning, her panic was understandable, but her awareness was here now. And she was late in figuring out what was happening.

The simple rule of energy. Become one with the energy. Be that energy. Be one.

Instead of fighting, she had to become one with it. Then she could use the host to show her what was going on. She'd done similar things before. Essentially reading the energy of any animal was a similar process. She had to change her energy to blend with theirs, become one with theirs, and then they were essentially one with her it would make sense she could then see their energy.

She would *be* their energy. She wasn't a separate observer, although she knew people whose abilities ran in that direction. In her case, she had to join with them in order to get the clearest vision of what was going on.

Closing her inner eye, she sank deeper into the unique and frightening experience. That overriding fear made this horrific experience difficult to accept. She took a deep breath and searched for a ground. She was alive spiritually, so therefore she was attached to something.

Tango? Tripod? Her body? Although the latter was in doubt. But she had to believe it was there for her. That her friends were protecting her.

Mentally she reached for Tango. And hit a blockage. Someone else kept crossing her path, interfering, calling to her.

She called to Tripod.

And found the same thing.

Therefore, she had to ascertain what interfered first. Connect with it, then move it to one side.

Stilling, she quieted her mind and waited.

There.

Another energy whistled through her mind, requesting a response. A connection. She'd never had such a thing happen before. Never knew it could invite her like that. Who was this entity? And why was it connecting to her?

A whisper of a sound. A cat's cry, muted, but crying out in pain…and fear.

Tango?

No. Not Tango. A different energy. A feline energy though. Another cat.

A big cat. But not Tango.

Then she understood. Although she had no idea how this came about, she thought she understood where she was.

Inside a large cat. Potentially a tiger. Potentially one that might be connected to Tango and through him – to her. If such a thing was possible.

And its spirit was calling to her.

She'd always understood her animals were equal to humans in many ways. She'd seen their interactions, their caring, their intelligence. She hadn't given them credit for being capable of energy work though. Or that they could have energy abilities like this.

And perhaps she was giving this one too much credit.

Maybe this animal hadn't consciously cried out to her. It was just crying out emotionally. In need. To whoever would listen.

That meant to her. Relief washed through her as she understood.

Thank God.

Then she sensed something else. A lighter energy, softer. Younger. Somewhere close by? Were there other felines in this room? She could hear slight movements, rustling around, but nothing like the screaming and pain she'd heard from her host.

Tabitha hated the pain that rippled through her system. It was cloudy, confusing. There was no cub here. But she could see in her memories – the tiger's memories – cubs. In days gone by.

The tiger was old. Sick. And maybe dying. But there was something else… She couldn't quite grasp it.

Something had triggered her need to communicate. Something had sent her crying out.

Tabitha thought of all the problems inherent in moving a large cat like this one, especially if she'd been caught in the wild. She'd have been tranq'd right from the beginning. Somewhere along the line she'd have woken up and found herself captive in a foreign world. With foreign smells, sounds.

When she'd woken up, the tiger would have screamed with rage…and panic.

And had somehow snagged on Tabitha's energy and dragged her here. Into the cage with her. Why? How? She didn't know. But the female cat had. And now Tabitha was caught inside. With it.

And what could she do about it now?

Soothing the animal was paramount. Maybe then she could get the cat to relinquish its hold on her.

Tabitha also needed to check out her host's body. See if there was anything she could do for her. To heal her as much as she could and to find a way to escape. But having a tiger run loose in whatever part of the world they were in was a whole different story than being free in the wild. She knew that's where the tiger desperately wanted to return, but Tabitha had no idea if they were in India or the U.S.A. For all she knew the tiger had been captured in China.

She could physically be anywhere in the world. Energy traveled across the world in a heartbeat. That she'd connected as strongly as she had *should* mean the location was close by her home. But nothing about this scenario was normal so she couldn't bank on that.

Just as important, she needed to check in with her own body and keep it alive – if possible.

The same questing energy that she'd sensed earlier pulsed again.

Tabitha opened up her mind to the soft wave of it and sent out a probe to the energy. There was a hesitation, fear, but also a request for reassurance.

There was another feline. A young feline.

Very young.

Her heart ached as she understood this animal's panic. She sent out waves of calming energy, healing energy. Energy to ease the animal's fear. She'd dealt a lot with similar issues over the years as animals were brought into the reserve. Some had to be tranq'd for the trip; others were completely accepting.

She gentled her own energy more, aligning hers to the young male's, adding soothing thoughts and above all else, caring, compassion and empathy. She loved all animals and when one was in pain, she lived it with them.

She sensed this link of energy was another reason she'd locked on Tabitha. And if it was a feline, as she suspected… maybe it understood Tabitha had a soft spot for those, too.

She searched out the cat's energy pathways and stroked along the meridians, trying to figure out if it was physically hurt. The shoulder pain she'd noticed first appeared to be where she'd been shot by a tranq dart – probably on initial capture. The site was sore, puffy, but not serious.

Pain drew her to the back right leg – the older tiger's back leg. There was something wrong there. An old injury perhaps? If she could open her eyes she could take a closer look, but that meant the cooperation of the feline.

She sent warm healing energy to the spot. Tabitha *could* heal at this level. Instantly there was a lessening of the tension in the space they shared. As if the cat knew, understood and responded to her energy. Maybe it didn't know Tabitha was there, but the energies were blending naturally now. That would also help the animal to calm down. Having a foreign energy inside the cat's body would not be comfortable or easy on either of them. Especially if the energies couldn't find a way to exist together peacefully.

Animals normally responded quickly to treatments. At least the cat appeared to be willing to accept her initial attempts.

Still emanating even, calming waves, Tabitha tried to get a better idea of what was wrong in the cat's world.

And getting her vision back would be major.

She sent out her energy in the direction of the cat's head. And into the skull and eyes. There was some resistance, but she thinned her energy to the density of the cat's energy and became one with it, helping it become comfortable with her energy as she became comfortable with its energy. She settled in. With a sigh of acceptance, of knowing, she sank deeper into the experience.

Then the cat opened her eyes.

To bars.

Rusted bars of a small cage. Only big enough for the cat to stand, take a few steps and turn around. A plywood floor. An attached water dish was perched halfway down the inside of the cage. It was full. The cat was thirsty. But she was too scared to drink.

Tabitha didn't blame her.

There was darkness all around. A cover of some kind surrounded the bulk of the cage, but one end was open.

She stared at the large paws crossed in front of her. A dirty gray paw with slight stripes. She was sharing space with a tiger with some variant coloring. There were many white Bengal tigers…but her coloring wasn't quite right.

There was gray and a lot of it, but that could be dirt. Or it could be something else. A thread of excitement wove through her consciousness. There was an extinct species of blue tiger, the Maltese tiger. Some scientists believed it never existed in the first place. Rumor said their slate gray fur shone blue in some light. There were also black tigers, but then this tiger's fur was too light for that. If she could see more of its body, she might know for sure. She'd never expected to see a blue tiger in her lifetime.

The tiger was slowly adjusting to its latest drug dose. Whoever these captors were, they were more concerned about the animal staying quiet and not hurting itself than having it actually eat and drink to stay strong and healthy.

It was obvious this tiger had been hunted and taken from the wild. There was no sense of comfort or familiarity with cages or humans. There was no understanding of the confinement or the lighting. The water dish was new. Images of creeks and ponds flashed through her mind. The cat was desperate for water.

But it was more desperate for its freedom.

She moved back and forth as the big cat struggled to its feet and staggered throughout the small space. It roared in anger, a weak defiant sound echoing through the large space.

And that brought up another issue. If the tiger couldn't be controlled, it would most likely be killed. Or kept so confined, it wouldn't survive anyway.

Unless it was destined for a zoo. No. That wouldn't be. Not this way. If the animal was being imported through the proper channels there'd be vets, trainers, people to look after the tiger, to see to its comfort. All efforts would be made to reduce the animal's distress – and not through the overuse of tranquilizers.

Of course, it may be for a zoo in a third world country where the restrictions were lax and the paperwork wouldn't be looked at very closely if at all – for a price.

This was likely a black market deal.

As the thoughts took her to other animals in her world, Tabitha lost her focus. And couldn't see anymore.

She closed her own eyes and breathed into the big cat that surrounded her and reconnected with it.

Then opened her eyes once again.

The room appeared in shades of beige and shadows. Cat eyes. Cat vision. It was likely to be dark in this room. Shadowy. Her human vision would have seen one thing and interpreted it with her human eyes, but her cat's vision was different altogether.

And maybe that explained the color of her fur. Maybe dirty white fur looked like slate gray when viewed from a cat's eyes.

Then she was distracted again as the big head swung from side to side as if looking for an opening, a way out. She studied the change in view as the head swung. The large warehouse was full of empty cages. There were double doors up ahead, but she didn't think the cat understood them to be an exit…as in maybe it didn't understand the concept of doors. But then her mind, or rather its mind, was groggy and dominated by confusion.

Tabitha struggled to stay connected and yet separate. To keep in tune with the tiger but also to allow Tabitha to think on her own. Not an easy thing to do. But she had to keep clarity of her own thoughts and actions. Somehow she had to stay separated from her host so she could do something for both of them.

What she really needed was to find out their location. In what city was the animal being kept? The man had spoken English. Guttural and slang, but English nonetheless. That might help narrow the country down. The man had said something about more traveling to come.

Meaning they could be anywhere in the world – including the U.S. And as helpful as it would be, she didn't want to believe the tiger was in – or destined – for the U.S. Money drove the markets and poachers were in the supply-and-demand market. That meant global markets in today's world. So the tiger could be destined to be shipped anywhere.

She figured if she could free the tiger, the big cat would release her. She could be dreaming, but that was her goal. A hope – and she needed something to hang onto right now.

On top of that, she wasn't sure how her own physical existence was doing. How could she check? Would her attempt to return to her body trigger the tiger's strong emotions so she would be yanked back?

How could she let the tiger know what she needed to do? And that she wouldn't desert her. She wanted to help the tiger.

A roar ripped through her head. Of rejection. Of loneliness. And fear.

She tried to calm the tiger down again, but this time the tiger wouldn't let her. She was too agitated.

Pulling back, Tabitha eased her own feelings down inside the tiger's ballooning emotions – so the big cat would feel Tabitha's emotions.

She wanted out. The tiger wanted out too. They both wanted their freedom.

How did she argue or try to show logic to a panicked animal? How could she prove she was trustworthy? That her word could be counted on when she was pretty sure tigers understood instinct and action, response in the present. Not promises of future acts.

Especially when she couldn't guarantee that she could come back. Thinking through energy laws, she realized she could always find a trail back here. She'd use anchors to make the travel easier and faster.

But she had to go deeper to place them. Deeper into the tiger's psyche to make sure they stayed in place.

Only deeper was more dangerous. For both of them.

But that recourse was likely the only answer.

As she tried to descend to where she needed to go, emotions pummeled at her and images filled her. Images of the tiger's old life, the trees, tall grass. The wind. Racing across a field. Basking under the sun. Freezing in the snow.

Still caught in the tiger's memories, there was a sudden pain in her shoulder and hip. Loud noises followed. Confused and hurting, the large cat had stumbled in a daze of pain. She struggled to escape. To hide. Only she could hardly move. The tiger's body burned. She wanted it to stop. She could hardly breathe. Or run.

The tiger hadn't gone down easy. And they'd shot her again. Only the cat had reacted badly to the drugs and she was sick. Tabitha saw the sweating as a separate issue now. Not caused by a sense of panic, but more by drugs. The cat's body had reacted. Swelling. She found it hard to breathe. And she was so thirsty. She was already old. And now with the drugs…she was in a bad way.

The poachers didn't seem to know about her distress – or maybe they didn't care. But a dead tiger wasn't worth much. In the Chinese medicine industry it was, but if capturing her was for that, they could have shot her dead up in the mountains. That would have been much easier. And much faster.

The drug reaction explained the debilitating weakness, the fever and confusion. In fact, Tabitha would swear the big female was dying. And that made her own heart ache.

But there was still something else in there. Tabitha went deeper.

And found the other feline energy she had sensed earlier.

What she understood at a primitive level made her want to rage against these men. And made her want them to pay.

And made her want to help the tiger in a big way.

Because, and against all odds – the old female tiger was pregnant and carried one cub.

Had the poachers known? No. That would have changed the deal entirely.

Tabitha had to help.

But how?

As she considered the almost full-term cub, she realized the energy of the cub was distinct, separate – and yet at the same time it was one with the mother.

That made sense, as all energy was connected.

Parts of other people's energy gravitated naturally to a person they connected with in some way. In her case, it was the energy of people she'd been closest to through her life and those that stayed close to her…some of their energy stuck to her. So therefore Tabitha should be able to find some of those energy fragments and follow them home. She'd already found Stefan's signature, but it was so faint that it wasn't usable, as if it couldn't quite reach her.

Instead of an energy line, it was more a sensation of him being there, searching for her. Or maybe that was wishful thinking.

But there was no denying Tango's energy. Whether it was the feline connection or something else, Tango's signature was strong and loving in Tabitha's heart.

She sent warm loving energy to Tango. He'd be lost if she died. In fact, his energy vibrated at a tense level that said he was already nervous and heading into seriously scared territory. And the color had deepened to a dark blue instead of the lake-blue it normally vibrated with.

She smiled. Maybe she did know what to do.

Sending out a wide green band of healing energy, followed by a gently loving band in lavender, Tabitha surrounded the caged female tiger with energy that would make her feel good. Make her calm. Not afraid. Not alone. Letting Tabitha slip away. At least long enough to check on family and…her body.

Next, Tabitha carefully wrapped her own loving essence around Tango's energy. Added layers and layers of loving, healthy energy like wisps of colored cotton candy until the entire thing was thick and solid looking. Then she blew a breath into the center, making a hollow, and sank into it. Became one with it. She shifted deeper and deeper, feeding the energy trail as she slipped along the pathway, following it back and back and back hoping to find the reality she recognized. Faster she flew as energy warmed, reconnecting to the animal that had shared so much of Tabitha's life.

He'd been there for her after a trying day at school; he'd cleaned her face on the day she'd graduated; he'd been ecstatic over the arrival of Tripod. A kindred soul, in so many ways. A playmate for Tango when she was gone from the house.

Tango had been there listening to her spout off joyfully when she'd gotten engaged, and he'd been there listening to her tears after she'd been jilted. He'd been there for her every step of the way.

She knew him as well as she knew herself. As she thought all this, she fell into Tango's space.

His energy kicked into overdrive. If he could have twisted his lithe body around her, he would have. Instead she was the one wrapped around him. Inside him. Outside him. She was him.

He jumped and spun and howled. And his roar was deafening.

His joy…her joy. Both brought tears to her eyes, if she'd had eyes…or tears.

She cried out his name repeatedly. She couldn't seem to stop. The sense of safety and being home overwhelmed her. Such a relief. Such a feeling of joy. It was finally over…

Only not quite. Reality intruded. She was in Tango's body now. Not her own. Still, she'd managed to leave the other tiger – mostly.

Tango, I need help.

The purr increased to deafening proportions. He'd always understood her moods. And she his.

I need to get to my body.

She stopped and thought about what she'd said, what she was doing. This was stupid. Tango couldn't go to her body. He was trapped inside his own massive physicality. She needed a way to get from here to her body.

Then she heard footsteps. And a voice.

Tango? Are you all right?

Stefan!

STEFAN WANDERED THROUGH Tabitha's living room looking, seeking something that had to be there, but not sure what. The house was old and empty, but there was a disturbance in the atmosphere that went beyond the lack of furniture. Part of the house had felt empty on his first pass – as if Tabitha had disappeared completely.

Tango had lain despondent in a corner of the large enclosure. Not eating or drinking. Tripod was acting the same. Just like any well-loved pet would, given the absence of their beloved owner.

Stefan wandered back through the house again. He'd learned a long time ago to not ignore his instincts. That prodding voice that said to keep looking. He was here because he was supposed to be here. If he was lucky, he'd understand the reason why. Soon.

He wandered over to Tango's cage once again. He searched for a change. Something to understand this nudge inside him to keep searching.

Just then Tango came racing through the pen into the main area where the caged wall was all that separated him from Stefan.

But he looked different. Happy. Energized.

Stefan narrowed his gaze and studied the tiger. It was almost delirious. Rolling on the ground, rubbing his back on the floor, all four legs in the air as he tossed his head with abandon. It was a joy to see.

The cat looked…ecstatic. *And how could that be?*

"What do you know that I don't, Tango?" Stefan murmured, studying the big cat's aura. Sure enough, the color had shifted, brightened. Was now surrounded by a lavender sheen.

Tabitha?

Surely that was her energy mixed into the big cat's energy. *Could it be?*

He stepped close enough to press his face against the heavy gauge divider.

"Tango?" he called out. "Come here, boy."

Tango jumped to his feet and bounded to Stefan, rubbing his side along the cage. It was if he understood Stefan. Or someone connected to

Tango understood and brought the big cat close. *What were the chances?*

Tabitha? Is that you? Stefan asked telepathically. *Are you with Tango?*

Yes!

FEZ WALKED CALMLY into the warehouse. At least on the outside he hoped he appeared confident and in control. At least someone needed to be. Keeper was there waiting for him. "How is she doing?"

"Not eating, but maybe had water."

Fez brightened up. "Water is good."

"And the bleeding stopped."

Fez closed his eyes briefly then said in an ominous voice, "What bleeding?"

"From the original poachers. They shot her with tranq darts, but one site seemed to close over, only she gnawed on it and ripped it open. But it's stopped again."

"That's a good sign." At least he hoped it was. "We need her to eat." He lifted the blanket slightly and the rank odor of meat gone off filled his nostrils. "No wonder she's not eating. What is this crap?"

"I'm hardly going to put good stuff in there to go bad. When she's hungry enough, she'll start eating. Then I will get her fresh stuff." Keeper spat on the old wood floor and walked away as if the conversation was over.

But it wasn't. Not by a long shot. Fez didn't know where the boss had found this guy but he wasn't worth the pennies he was paying him.

Fez grabbed him by the shoulder and spun him around. "She gets the best. And she gets it now. You aren't paying for her food. We are. Now go and clean that shit out of there and bring her fresh meat."

"You ain't the fucking bos—"

Fez punched him in the nose. "I'm the boss when the boss isn't here. I'm following his orders and you will follow my orders. Now get to it. And give her fresh water too."

When Keeper shot him a resentful look, Fez smiled cruelly and said, in a soft voice, words that echoed the boss, "And do it now – or else."

CHAPTER 10

Sunday noon

AT THE SIGHT of Stefan, a wave of sadness washed through Tabitha. Hers or Tango's? She didn't know or care. There could also be vestiges of the other tiger's energy floating through her energy space. And that tiger also had homesickness as a major issue.

The poor thing.

What thing? asked Stefan accurately, reading her mind.

She quickly explained who the other tiger was and what had happened to her, then tried to explain what had happened that Tabitha had ended up inside of the tiger.

There was a long shocked pause from Stefan. *Tabitha...are you sure...that's what happened?*

Doesn't make any sense, does it?

Not only doesn't it make sense, it requires a level of unprecedented power to do something like that.

But it also explains how and why I was hooked and grabbed. Think about it. The most logical way the tiger found me was through Tango. I already have a strong open connection to Tango. She nodded to herself as she realized something else. *I used to connect to Tango while I floated in the ethers. If this other tiger could connect to the ethers, theoretically it's possible she'd connected to Tango. It was just an easy step to me.*

And that would explain how there were no strange human energies here, Stefan added thoughtfully. *I saw the animal energy but couldn't see whether it was from other animals you'd worked with. I never thought your attacker would be a tiger.*

She laughed. *And yet look where I am right now.*

But you also have Tripod and any other number of animals in your life.

But not as close and as loving as Tango. Or in as much distress. Tripod would be a very close second, but Tango has been in my life so much longer.

So you're thinking that the tigers are connected? By love? By circum-

stance?

Unless we want to contemplate that psychic tigers exist.

She heard Stefan's whoosh as he exhaled. *Yeah, a bit of a mind bender, isn't it?*

Definitely.

We have some incidents involving animals to draw on, but nothing like this. Stefan paused then added, *I can't say it's a comforting thought to consider that any animal at any given moment can reach out and yank their beloved owner into their own psyche when they hit a bad spot in life.*

Probably not any animal. Special ones, yes. Consider this possibility too. An animal in the wild looking for anyone to help them – and they grab a hold of those of us open enough to be accessible. She felt his shudder. This mind-link thing with Stefan was so intimate at times she could sense his very movements.

As I can with yours, but since you are inside your tiger…yeah, that's more than what I was expecting to find when I arrived at your door today. He gave a half laugh. *And it feels weird on my end so I can't imagine how you are feeling.*

Just why did you come here now? she asked. *That you'd be here when I arrived…*

Remember there are no such things as coincidences. When you are in tune with the universe, you will always be in the right place at the right time. You just might not always like the lesson to be learned by the experience you get to go through.

She snorted. *Like getting yanked out of my body? What the hell, Stefan? I figured out how to come back to Tango by building on our bond, but how the hell do I get back to my own body?*

There was only a long silence in her head as Stefan contemplated her through the cage. *You should have gone back naturally on your own.*

Yeah, but I tried that – it didn't work.

I have no idea then. You've already defied psychic laws as we know them because it shouldn't be theoretically possible to live without the cord attached. How to reattach a severed cord has always been considered impossible. Not that yours is detached. I don't know what it is.

If it were, in theory I'd be dead. And I'd have disappeared to the ever-after long before now.

What's the chance you are still attached but stretched so thin no one can see it? He gave a small laugh. *Or could it be masked, hidden in some way? Not that many could see it normally anyway.*

I don't think so. Could she have hidden it instinctively, something so natural and fast that Tabitha hadn't been aware as the process happened?

Could... Tango? Stefan asked cautiously.

Tango? Tabitha wanted to laugh. It was ridiculous to think of an animal doing something like that. But was it? Look at what the female tiger had done. She wanted to shake off the concept of her animals having any kind of ability. To harm her or help her. *Such a foreign concept.*

But is it a wrong one?

I don't know, she whispered. *It's been so hard to deal with this as it is. To try to understand that an animal had that level of competence...*

I think we're giving the animals too much credit. Whatever they're doing would be out of pure instinct. He walked across the room, his head bent in thought. *You could have helped this tiger without severing the cord, so why do it this way? And if the cord is still attached, why hide it?*

I have no idea.

That's what we need to understand. There has to be a reason. Find that reason and we'll understand more about what's going on.

She understood that, but it wasn't helping her get back into her body.

What about the other tiger, does she know that you've left? Stefan asked.

Yeah, that's the thing, I'm not sure I'm totally gone. She took a deep breath. *I feel splintered into many little bits and pieces.*

Have you split your energy? Stefan asked curiously. *I've been trying to do something similar but it takes a lot of energy to maintain.*

I don't know, Stefan, she cried. *I just tried to build a stronger bonding energy with Tango so I could travel here, but I can still feel the older female.*

The other tiger is an older female? Older than Tango?

Maybe a little. I don't know. Why?

Could she be related?

No, I don't think so, she answered slowly then remembered the odd coloring, *I'm not so sure they are the same variant. She's got an odd tint to her fur.*

More likely she panicked and sent out a cry for help on the ethers. Stefan paused again. *Tango would likely be open and responsive and like you said, through him, she found you.*

Stefan studied Tango as if trying to see her face, at least that's what she thought he was staring at. In truth, through Tango's eyes, Stefan looked odd. Gray, yet distinct.

Stefan asked, *Has Tango ever done this before?*

Not like this. I've connected with other tigers – Tobias being one ex-

ample – but I haven't noticed other tigers connecting to me. At least I don't think they have. She shrugged mentally. *But maybe it was natural for them and felt natural to me so I never noticed.* It was starting to sound like she'd been unaware of a lot happening lately. Had her life disintegrated so much that she'd been this far off balance?

So what's different now? Stefan asked.

There was a long pause as they both thought about it. Tango lay down on the floor and rolled on his back, happy and content. Tabitha laughed. *He's so not bothered.*

Have you done this with him before?

Sure, she said.

He paused. *Sure what?*

Yes, I've been communicating with him since forever, and there is no closer communication than telepathy. But because he doesn't use the same language, I found it easier to hop into his energy and spend time with him that way.

The shock coming through the airwaves made her pause and ask, *Why?*

It's very unusual. You know that, right?

What is?

The jumping in and out of other people's psyche.

Well, I'm not jumping into anyone. Only animals. And Tango was open to the idea at the beginning and now we both love our time together. It's a wonderful feeling. She shrugged. *We played our version of hide'n go seek too. I'd disappear and he'd come find me.*

Sure, he said humorously. *But that just makes the situation all that more unique. Have you done this jumping in and out with other animals?*

Yes, if they were doing poorly and I couldn't figure out why. I can enter their energy systems and check out their bodies. Dr. Maddy does a similar thing.

Similar, yes. But she doesn't jump into other people's minds and take possession.

Shocked, she jumped back, affronted. *I'm not taking possession. Holy crap. That would be just wrong.*

He stood in front of her, his head tilted to the side. *So what is it then?*

I'm not making Tango do anything. I'm a visitor. Spending time with him. He can't come to me so I go to him. I don't make him sit up, roll over, or roar. She hated that feeling of justifying her actions. She'd never do anything to hurt Tango. *I'm here like you and I speak telepathically with Tango in a similar way.*

I'm not accusing you of going too far or of doing anything wrong. What I'm trying to understand is the ease with which you do it. He shook his head. *I can slip into people's minds and speak with them, show them images, give them information – but I've never tried to persuade them to do anything. Because to me, it is morally and ethically wrong.*

Me too. She let her breath out on a long sigh. *Sorry. I didn't mean to snap at you. I hadn't considered that what I was doing was wrong. Tango and I are so close that it never occurred to me that I wasn't welcome.*

Given the complete look of happiness on that overgrown tabby cat, I'd say you were very welcome.

Mollified, she said, *I hope so. I'd never do anything to hurt him.*

And that bond between you is obvious. It's also probably why this other tiger, once she caught scent of your connection, had no trouble yanking you into her space. You were already used to it.

No. That's where you're wrong. Tango never yanks me.

Stefan laughed. *But if you look at the times you're in his space, I'm sure you'll see a recognition of what you're doing on his level. Whether he ever initiated the contact or just put out the suggestion and you responded by jumping in, this other tiger did no less. When you didn't respond initially, she reacted with a stronger message.*

True. And... She thought about the number of times she felt compelled to be with Tango after her grandfather had died. Had that been at her instigation or his? *I never thought of our bond in that way,* she admitted. *But now that I take a closer look, I guess that's reasonable.*

The real trick is to figure out how to break the connection. As far as we know, if you are in the person when that person dies, then you are likely to die too.

Especially considering that we're not sure how I'm still alive at the moment.

Stefan took a huge gusting breath and added gently, *If you are still alive.*

STEFAN WAITED A long moment. From the shocked silence and then a weird blankness in his mind, Stefan understood Tabitha had withdrawn. How far back, he didn't know. He pinched the bridge of his nose and sent her a warm hug. He had no idea what to say to help her deal with her situation. He could only hope time would help. He just didn't know how much time she had.

Nothing was ever what it seemed, and most people lived out their lives never understanding this other layer of existence going on around them. An underground society was probably a better way to look at it. Maybe it was just as well. Those that were aware were often too overwhelmed by the circumstances their intimate knowledge brought them.

As if the ones with awareness were forced to step up and deal with things others had no inkling of.

He turned around to survey the room. It was colder than when he'd first arrived. He glanced back at Tango and found him asleep.

Hosting a second being in your aura had to be draining – a hell of a sleep aid.

Still, as long as Tango wasn't being hurt by the visits, who was he to judge? And as he studied the old cat, he realized Tango was likely enjoying an extended life because of the way Tabitha'd handled him physically and psychically. Tabitha would have taken care of even the tiniest ailments her beloved pet might have experienced. Even pushing off the discomfort that old age often brought.

So Tango might have the best deal after all.

Was she doing the same for the ailing old female she'd joined, too? If so, they might have a little more time to find a way to help Tabitha there as well. Once that female died… Stefan shook his head. He didn't want to imagine the consequences of that connection to Tabitha being severed.

They had to find the host tiger and help her. Maybe then Tabitha could be released.

And he knew just who to ask for help in finding that tiger.

RONIN?

Ronin bolted to his feet, accidentally kicking the hospital chair backwards. The question came out of the blue and was so sharp and clear it couldn't be anyone other than Stefan. Damn that guy anyway.

Sorry. I just thought you'd like to know that I spoke with Tabitha.

Ronin walked to Tabitha's side. He'd stopped at the hospital on his way to the office, wishing to hell he knew how to help her.

"How can you speak with her?" he said, casting a glance around to make sure he was alone. "I'm staring down at her unconscious body and there is no way in hell she's awake or even conscious."

She's inside Tango.

"She's *what?*" he asked incredulously. He studied the pale, waxen features of the woman in front of him. So not possible.

And yet, apparently it is. Because I'm at her house and talking to her.

There was only so much woo woo stuff any normal guy could stand, but being a cop who'd recently had that whole believe-it-when-I-see-it thing going on, he was still adapting.

Staring at Tabitha and wishing to hell she was berating him again for his attitude on cats was a whole different thing than understanding she was inside that damn tiger.

Except…that's where she was. At least part of her.

Ronin pounced. "A part of her? What part?"

He stared down at the main part, her body, that hadn't moved since he'd arrived.

Part of her consciousness. So I know this is going to be tough, but we need your help as soon as possible. Here's why.

Stefan gave as clear and as concise an explanation as possible – and left Ronin completely confused. He struggled to sort through the bizarre concepts. "So let me get this straight. There is most likely an old tiger captive in a cage, most likely hunted down by poachers, most likely getting ready to be sold to yet another person, in some country somewhere in the world, that I'm supposed to track down."

I guess that sounds a little bizarre when you put it that way, Stefan said.

"You think?" Ronin snapped. "And how do you expect me to help here at all?"

Um yeah, Tabitha says they are in a warehouse with lots of cages.

"Oh, that's great. Does she have any idea what country she is in? Do you know how many countries could have an English-speaking captor?" He paced the small room. "A little more information would help, you know."

That would be too easy, Stefan said, his voice all business. *What I can tell you is that if that sick tiger dies while connected to Tabitha, well…I wouldn't give a penny for her chances of surviving this trip.*

And he was gone.

Shit.

THE TIGER DIDN'T look so good. Fez winced. She'd slumped into the far corner. And didn't move – even when prodded. They needed a vet in here and fast.

But who'd pay for it? His boss should. They'd hoped to make this deal happen faster than this. He didn't understand what was taking so long. None of them had time for this. Especially not this female tiger.

He glanced at the haunch of fresh meat lying untouched beside the water. So not good. At least the asshole, Keeper, had done what he was told.

He studied the tiger's still form. There was still blood on her flank. Maybe there was something else going on. He wouldn't trust those damn poachers to not have shot her with real bullets. Hell, she could be riddled with buckshot and no one would know. It's not as if she'd received the care she needed from the beginning.

It was all too possible they'd left it too late now.

There wasn't much in the world that made him feel so low and like such a loser as what he was doing with this female cat. Going into it, he'd looked at all these jobs as easy money. He'd only been working for the boss for five months and it was four months too long. At least now that he'd seen that thing in the river. And understood he himself was living on borrowed time. This job could be the catalyst for his own deep swim.

The tiger was caged. But he was starting to see bars in his own world. How could he get out of this mess? There was nothing nice about seeing a floater.

All Fez could think about now was getting the hell out of here – with no holes in his damn skin.

Go back East. Find a job where he could hold up his head. Instead of this. The animal was tearing his heart out.

Who'd have thought he still had one?

CHAPTER 11

Sunday early afternoon

TABITHA BURROWED DEEPER into a ball. She didn't give a damn whether she was hiding from her problems. The ethers had always been her comfort zone. Her escape from the painful reality of her physical existence. Okay, so it wasn't the same type of escape as for other people. But she'd dare anyone not to do the same, given the shock she'd just been given.

Was Stefan right?

Was she dead?

God, she hoped not.

If she'd had a body, she'd be shivering uncontrollably. As it was, she felt shivers sliding up and down her nonexistent spine. How did that work? Surely that meant she was still connected to her body. Surely...

She desperately wanted to see her body. Could she? When she'd been alive and doing out-of-body experiences, she could. But then she'd been attached by her cord. What was she now?

Even if her cord was hidden or spread thin, it should still function the same.

She closed her eyes and thought herself to her body.

When she opened her eyes, it was to see her slim frame lying under the hospital sheets, machines moving noisily at her side. She looked like she was comatose but according to Stefan, the machines were there to keep her alive, to keep her breathing in case that all stopped. She shuddered. She so didn't want to die.

If they unplugged that machine, she would. She knew it.

And that so couldn't happen.

A weird clacking sound caught her attention.

Ronin. Typing furiously away on the laptop on his knees, his phone open in his hand. Sitting vigilant at her bedside.

God, she missed him.

Tears came to her eyes. Or it felt like they did. Suspiciously, she reached up to her astral cheeks but there was no wetness there. Duh. She leaned over her body and damn if there wasn't a sheen of moisture in the corner of her eyes.

She *was* still connected! Hadn't she just proven that?

Somehow.

If that was true, she had to trust the process and that she'd find a way back into herself soon. As soon as she could help the tiger.

There was such a sense of connection to Ronin. Watching him there by her side, she fell in love a little more. Knowing he was sitting and watching over her gave her an insight into his feelings she hadn't seen before. How could she resist that?

She slipped behind him, and unbeknownst to him, she kissed his cheek.

Ronin straightened, almost dropping both the laptop and phone in the process.

Whoa.

Had he felt her?

Ronin searched the room, his gaze dark and narrow. Then he put a hand to his cheek.

She gasped.

He spun around.

She stared into his dark eyes.

And Ronin stared back.

She swallowed. Then whispered, *Ronin, can you see me?*

He cocked his head to one side, as if listening intently, and his eyes lost their focus.

Such a reaction could only mean he was hearing something, maybe even seeing something but didn't know what or how. And being analytical, he might be struggling to understand instead of going with his heart.

Ronin?

His gaze narrowed, then suddenly he spun around and stared at her body prone in the bed. He carefully placed his laptop on the floor and pocketed his cell phone then walked to her bedside. He stared down in confusion, then his gaze caught on her face. He reached down to touch a tear.

"Tabitha, is that you?"

Yes!

But he couldn't hear her.

"Stefan? Is that you?" Ronin asked.

No, Stefan said, *it's Tabitha trying to talk to you.*

Tabitha could hear Stefan speaking in a three-way communication system that she imagined could only work with psychics. But she could hear Ronin, could see him lift his head and speak out loud to the empty room accusingly, "Damn it. I thought I heard something. Why can't I hear her clearly?"

He pointed to Tabitha's body. "And why is she crying?"

Tabitha was mortified. It was one thing to react honestly with true emotion while believing herself alone; it was quite another to have someone else explaining it to a third party. Then her sense of humor popped up. At least there was a translator. She should be grateful for small mercies.

I am a lot of things, but not a small anything, Stefan said with a light smile.

"Huh?" Ronin asked, turning around. "You people are making me crazy."

Then tune in, damn it, and save all of us this trouble, Tabitha muttered. *And fast.*

He can only learn and believe and grow at his pace. Not yours or mine.

His twin is psychic. That Ronin can even sense me means he has the basis for so much more – so why isn't he learning?

He can. Stefan answered imperturbably, *but consider that Roman had no idea what he was doing until it was brought to his attention and didn't believe it until he was forced to use his skills to help you.*

So why is Ronin so blockheaded? she grumbled. *Hit him over the head or something.*

Is that a serious suggestion? His grin slipped through in his voice. *Even if I wanted to do it, I'm not exactly close enough physically to carry out that request.*

"Carry what out? What the hell is going on?" Ronin snapped. "I feel as if I'm only get half a conversation."

You are. Tabitha is the other half. She was talking to you and she wants you to wake up your psychic senses so she can contact you directly. I believe she mentioned how a solid blow to the head might help.

Ronin spun around. "What?"

Tabitha laughed, but it was a hollow sound in her heart. Of all the things she missed, not being able to talk, touch, and love Ronin topped the list. She could talk to Tango and Tripod, and Stefan was always there for her whether she was dead or alive.

Thanks.

It is comforting, she insisted. *No matter what happens, I know that you are there.*

Yes, but if you die, the best thing for you is to go onward, not stay here because you can communicate with me. He sighed and added, *and I suggest you try to contact Ronin as soon as possible.*

I did. You saw the results.

No. I heard the aftermath. He heard you. He just doesn't know what he heard.

Damn it. He's so frustrating.

Stefan laughed out loud. *That's only true because you care.*

Oh, I care. Then there's the fact that he doesn't like cats. That does slow the development of a relationship with me, for sure.

Stefan stilled then he started to laugh. And laugh some more.

It's not that funny, she muttered.

Yes, it i-is. Stefan came to a stuttering stop. *How can you let something like that stop you?*

It's hardly a small issue, she gasped. *Look at where I am at the moment.*

He smiled, and humor still threaded his voice. *True. But does he have a reason for not liking cats?*

We spoke about it briefly. He actually gets a physical reaction. Shortness of breath, his face flushes. She tried to remember what else he'd said.

Could be several explanations. Allergies. A trauma he was in associated with a cat. Even a reaction to an event so long ago he doesn't remember.

That's what I thought. But there's been no time to get deeper into the issue.

Well, maybe you should make time. And with that, Stefan slipped away.

Time. She had nothing on her hands but time. It would be a good time to focus on Ronin's story. But she had no way to communicate with Ronin. She'd only ever been able to communicate with Stefan and her animals on an energy level.

RONIN HAD ALREADY started researching the people close to Tabitha after the first attack, and that research hadn't borne any fruit yet. Nothing that connected to what was happening at Exotic or to Tabitha herself personally. He'd left a couple of messages with his buddy Jacob, but hadn't heard back from him yet. Jacob had a long history in undercover work and was often involved in setting up sting operations. Some of them had gotten him into trouble with Internal Affairs. He was involved in something heavy right now. The office rumor mill had supplied that information. Something very hush hush.

Still, that wasn't helping solve the incidents at the reserve. The break-ins. The vandalism. The thefts in the medical side of the building. An inside job perhaps. That said someone close to the reserve. Close to her.

Her grandfather's only relative besides Tabitha and her father was a brother who'd died when Tabitha was a child. Ronin had started searches on her close friends, and most of them were psychics, lending weight to their involvement if he were to connect the two problems involving Tabitha – only there was no proof they were connected.

He'd also reviewed the information from Stefan. That the attack came from a tiger was beyond anything he'd ever heard. It blew him away. How could he reconcile what he knew to what he was learning?

In a way, he couldn't. He had to take it on faith…something he'd done a lot of since he'd met Stefan and his group of friends.

But considering that a tiger would attack anything vulnerable if it had the opportunity, maybe it wasn't all that impossible. He hadn't understood that such an attack could cross such great distances. Surely it would be more reasonable to look closer to home first.

This stuff and his inability to understand all of it – so he could resolve the case – was making him crazy.

Once again, he couldn't bring any of his cohorts in on the problem with a full explanation. But he could ask a few questions and get some idea of whether smuggling endangered species into the country was also a local problem.

If he made the assumption that the tiger could connect with Tabitha because it was close, he needed to narrow his search down to smuggling rings in the U.S. Apparently psychics connected better to events that were closer, geographically, so Tabitha connecting to the tiger made sense that way as well. There were no guarantees, but he had to find a way to narrow this problem somehow.

And if he was narrowing it down even more within those same parameters, he'd start with the West Coast. It was the closest destination for many shady import and export companies looking to tap the U.S. market, particularly those from India and China.

He suddenly remembered those pictures Geoff had handed him. The two detectives he worked closely with, Geoff and Carmichael, both with some experience in animal smuggling, had offered to go through animal smuggling cases. He picked up the phone and called Geoff.

"Geoff, have you got any leads on the animal smuggling?" If only he knew what kind of tiger Tabitha had connected with, he could narrow the field slightly.

"Not much, except it is big business. The animals are flown in, shipped over in containers, driven to their destinations. You name it and people are trying it. Of course much depends on the species. Just last month there was a case of a guy's suitcase completely stuffed with snakes from South America. Like who does that?"

"Crazy," Ronin said. "What about bigger animals? Tigers, lions, that kind of thing?"

"There's always a black market for those. You can buy them locally to some extent, but people always want something not easily obtainable. Transporting them is another problem. Just think of the logistics involved in bringing over big cats. Can you imagine the howling going on in there? You'd have to keep them drugged up the whole time. And cats are fussy. They don't do well in transport. Just ask my wife. Every time she takes Fluffy into the vet, it takes days to regain her trust." Geoff laughed. "Like you'd know. You hate those damn things, don't you? Why are you asking?"

Ronin smiled. "I guess a lot of you guys know about my cat thing, huh?"

"Hell, yeah. So what gives?" Geoff wheezed on the other end of the phone.

"Just a line I'm tugging on a different case. Searching for a smuggled tiger. Wondering what the black market in trading live big cats looks like."

"Like always — it looks like money. Good money. Just don't get caught." He laughed. "Like you know, anything illegal will pay off big if you have someone willing to pay — if the stakes are high enough."

Ronin thanked him and hung up. Now, if only he could connect with Jacob. That detective knew everyone and anyone. He'd worked the docks for years. Several years ago, he'd been part of a huge sting that stopped a large human-trafficking ring. Since then, Jacob had kept a pretty close eye on everything going on. He could be a big help. And those pictures Geoff had dropped off were just as likely to be from that big sting. Why someone would try and get Jacob in trouble could also be due to any number of undercover jobs. If anyone recognized Jacob in these pictures, they could easily assume he was a dirty cop.

With this reasonable explanation, the tension in his shoulders relaxed. Someone was seeing exactly what they were supposed to see if Jacob was undercover. He was supposed to look like he was involved in shady deals. When Ronin got a moment, he'd explain go over that with Geoff.

First, he called Jacob again, and this time he actually got through. He explained his problem.

A long whistle sounded through the phone. "Animal trafficking is big. But a tiger is usually by special order. They are available domestically so the order would be for something unique. Think about it; it's not exactly something you could keep in the basement until the market improves. There are some companies that do special orders of that thing, but they've been skirting the law for so long we've had a hell of a time trying to pin anything on them."

"Names, please."

"I might be able to come up with a couple." He listed off several that Ronin didn't recognize. "Keep in mind, this is a supply-demand chain thing. They don't bring in a product on spec and even if you could catch the supplier, you'd have a hard time connecting it to the buyer."

"What's the chance of seizing the animal?"

"If you're lucky, it's possible. It would be easier with a tiger than, say, a monkey or something even smaller – like snakes. Huge market trafficking snakes."

"Why?" Ronin shook his head. "I just can't see that many people wanting dangerous snakes."

"People will always want what they can't have. And will go to great lengths to get it." He coughed and cleared his throat. "I presume you have a reason for asking about this tiger thing?"

"Yeah, a big one. And time is an issue. Keep an eye out, will you? Let me know if you hear any whispers anywhere along the road."

A second long whistle slipped through the phone. "Will do. Just think a fully grown tiger can jump...what...thirteen to sixteen feet with prey in its mouth."

"I'm expecting it to have been drugged and kept in a cage the whole time." Taking a chance, he added, "And I'm looking for a more or less old warehouse in a deserted part of town."

"It would have to be. Transport and delivery would have to happen fast to avoid detection, so an empty warehouse makes sense. I'll think about those, and write up a few possible leads I can think up to off hand." Ronin could hear him scratching down some notes. "I can check on a few around here." Silence again. "Another angle to pull on is the documentation required to pass it off to the authorities, too."

Ronin responded drily, "In this day and age, anyone can get the required documents for anything." He rubbed the bridge of his nose. "Send me an email with names of people who do that kind of forged paperwork too if you have them. I'll add them to my list and follow up."

"I'll let you know if I find anything." Jacob hung up.

Ronin's brain circled and ran with possibilities. Leaning back, he stared at the now-unresponsive woman who had become so important in his world. "Damn it, Tabitha, I wish you could at least figure out where you are physically located at least."

STEFAN HAD RUN out of ideas on how to find the tiger with such a dominant energy that it could suck Tabitha into its own space.

He'd dumped it on Ronin and hoped the detective could do his thing.

Animals were not up his alley.

They were Tabitha's thing.

Or at least, until now, they hadn't been his thing. He wasn't sure he had the luxury of excluding them any longer. He'd never had pets. He did know that because of his different energy, most animals reacted to him, one way or another.

Sometimes positively and sometimes negatively.

He was sure that Tango and Tripod accepted him because Tabitha was so well blended with his energy. The animals would sense that. But that didn't mean this strange tiger would be as accepting.

Should he try to connect? He sensed a blockage down that path, but that didn't mean connecting was impossible...

Or would he end up in the same condition as Tabitha? If so, how would that help anyone? Could he walk the ethers, a theoretical halfway point, and call Tabitha? Would she hear him? Would she be able to use him as a guide to bring her home?

Still, if she had anything to add that would help them locate the tiger, then maybe...

He stared around at his open living room where the sun shone so innocently in through the myriad of stained glass panes and had to wonder.

Nothing lost, nothing gained.

Except your soul, snapped a testy voice – a testy astral voice.

Stefan glanced over. *Lissa.* Of course it would be her. Stefan had many ghosts in his life, but none as persistent or as caring as this one. She was the deceased sister of another good friend and since a terribly nasty case he'd helped resolve, she'd been a regular in his life. She claimed it was because he needed someone to watch over him.

And you do.

He laughed. Young and full of life, Lissa was the antithesis of most ghosts. *What could you possibly do if something does go wrong? he asked her.*

Marshal the troops, Lissa said with a laugh. She'd started calling his group of friends a team or a troop, as if they were psychic crime fighters.

That was a joke.

No joke. You can't defy fate. If it's going to happen…

So not.

She laughed. *Look at what you're trying to do now.*

Tabitha needs help.

There is always someone in your world that needs help. There always will be.

He frowned. Even though he knew that, he liked to maintain the fantasy that he had a choice in this regard.

You made that choice a long time ago.

He glared at his wispy visitor. *And I can change it too.*

You can try! She laughed and started to fade away.

Wait, Stefan called out. *Do you have any idea how to find this tiger?*

Tiger? She brightened. *There's a tiger involved? Awesome.*

Her response reminded him that she was still a teenager. *There could be all kinds of animals involved.*

Then why not use another animal to track it?

As quickly as she appeared, she disappeared.

Stefan stared after her in shock. 'Out of the mouth of babes…'

So simple.

When hunting humans, they used humans.

When hunting animals, maybe they should use animals?

He wasn't much of an animal lover, he knew many who were, such as Kali, another psychic friend, and her search and rescue dog. Or Shay and her ghost cat Morris. Stefan still didn't understand how that worked.

Maybe Tango could go after the tiger. Stefan had been considering that, but it wasn't something he could do easily.

And if he couldn't – who could?

KEEPER WALKED OVER, a worried frown on his face. Fez shook his head and said in exasperation, "Now what?"

"The tiger is acting funny."

Fez hunched his shoulders. No, not again. He said ominously,

"What do you mean by funny?"

"I mean she's acting funny…" He shrugged. "Weird like."

Fez rolled his eyes. "Is she eating? Drinking? Is she hurting herself in any way?"

"No. She's lying down relaxed and calm. Almost asleep. If I didn't know better, I'd have said she'd been tranq'd with a different kind of drug. She seems almost content. Happy. But we didn't give her anything."

"That's supposed to be a good thing – right?" At the other man's shrug, Fez added, "Keep an eye on her. Just in case."

The other man sauntered back to the cages. Fez didn't know what to think about the tiger's condition. Maybe the tiger had finally calmed down enough, after she'd had several good meals and water. Maybe she'd finally decided that everything was going to be okay.

Then he remembered the look in the big cat's eye. He tugged at his collar again and swallowed hard.

Yeah, that wasn't likely.

The last time he'd looked into her eyes, he'd seen into the heart of her. She might look relaxed and calm, but there was no way he'd trust that look. She'd had a look in her eyes that he'd never forget.

She had murder on her mind.

And he was the prime candidate.

CHAPTER 12

Sunday mid afternoon

TABITHA STUDIED RONIN as he worked. How long had he been sitting there? Shoulders back and sitting straight in his chair, his fingers clicking away on the keyboard. Every once in awhile he'd frown, then shift and carry on. A man on a mission.

How, when she could only communicate via cats, could she communicate with Ronin?

She could use Stefan, and that worked – somewhat. It didn't stop this gnawing need to be held in his arms and be told it would all be okay. There was only so much she'd share through Stefan.

She glanced over at her body and shuddered. So close and yet so far. Then she frowned. But was it?

If she could communicate through Tango, why couldn't she get back into her body the same way? With all the times she'd traveled into his space and home, she'd damn near created an energy highway.

Why the hell hadn't she thought of that? She'd been so focused on reaching Tango, she'd forgotten to use him to extend her travels. Excited, she closed her eyes and thought her way back into Tango.

He slept heavily, as if he hadn't had a good sleep in forever. And he probably hadn't – at least for several nights.

With a slight release of her nonexistent breath, she sank back into his mind. And smiled. He was racing across open fields in joy. Not chasing anything, just stretching out and using his muscles like they used to work when he was younger. He'd gotten old on her.

Very old.

She'd done all she could but had yet to find a way to stop death from taking those she loved. And she'd tried.

With a wiggle, she realigned her energies with his, gave him a mental hug as she always did, and then traveled back the way she'd always gone before – when her life had been normal. Only always before her actions had been instinctive. There'd been no doubts. No questioning of how. She'd taken one road in and the same road out. Without thinking about it.

Only now she couldn't do that.

Energy wasn't a highway, in that it had no definite directions of travel. Energy floated all around and crossed dimensions and time. To find the same pathway back would be almost impossible. She should be able to close her eyes and think herself back home, but having tried that, she knew it wasn't working. Something was stopping her.

Most likely the connections to the tigers.

Maybe they were keeping her contained? Could she use them to get home instead? She was at the origin. Tango. So what if she could get Tango to find her? She could travel with him back into her body.

God, how bizarre.

Was it even possible? It was because she'd experienced Tango in her space already, but how could she get Tango to actually do the traveling? Prodding a sleeping tiger was never a good idea.

She almost laughed.

Then sighed. He was sleeping so soundly.

She grinned. How about directing his dreams? She whispered gently into his mind, *Tango, come to me. Tango, please come. I need you.*

Tango's paws jerked, but outside of a slight shimmer, his energy remained still and quiet. She didn't want to scare him or have him thinking she was desperately in trouble. That could backfire in a big way.

She smoothed his energy as she planted images of how she'd seen her body the last time in the hospital. Then she placed overlaid images of the two of them playing, of walking through his acres of space. Together.

You'd like that again, wouldn't you, boy?

His feet jerked and his legs shifted as if he were already running. *Just go and get me. Tell me it's time to get out and play our game.* She kept murmuring the same suggestions over and over again. Tango slept on, completely oblivious. *Damn it, Tango. Why won't you come to me?*

She sat back, and if she'd had arms and knees she'd have crossed them over each other. Instead she sat in a whirly ball of energy. Unsure of how and where to go.

As she pondered her quandary, she almost missed seeing the solution. Some of Tango's beautiful dark blue energy lifted and drifted lazily away. Other strands had been doing the same thing with every thought and every action he took in his dreams. But this strand of energy seemed to have purpose and was thick enough to be out there and do something useful.

It shimmered as all healthy energy did, but… She studied it. What was different about it?

Then she got it. There was another energy intermingled with Tango's. A warm chocolate mixed and twisted in a caring way. It was Tripod's energy. Surprised and charmed, she watched as Tango's energy went out in search of Tripod sleeping soundly on the other side of his caged enclosure.

It dipped over Tripod, stroked along his back, and appeared to nuzzle up against the side of his head.

She'd never seen this before. If she'd ever wondered about the relationship between the two of them, this blew her earlier understanding away. They were *that* close.

As she watched the gently caring energy smooth over Tango's canine brother, she realized that she knew so very little about animal energy work. She'd never been in a situation where she'd have even looked for something like this. And usually not looking, in energy work, meant not seeing. The mind would be completely overwhelmed if ninety percent of the energy activity wasn't filtered out.

Tripod never moved except for a huge, gusting breath coming from his chest. He seemed to sink deeper into sleep. Happy and content.

"Tango, how lovely to see you checking up on him."

Then the energy picked up and skirted the huge dog's body and headed out into the hallway. Curious, not letting him know she was riding there because then he might change his actions, she followed just behind him. As they'd been so close for so long, her energy would also appear as his energy. That was the nature of loving energy.

The energy slipped out into the hallway and down the long corridor to her bedroom.

She smiled with delight when she realized Tango was coming to check up on her.

Tango's energy swirl lifted to cover the top of the bed. It settled down on top.

She waited. And waited.

Damn it. She'd hoped he would realize that she wasn't really there.

After a few moments, the energy became restless and slunk over the surface of the bed and around to the other side. It paused, lifted, then hesitated in the air for a moment before circling around up above, almost creating a tornado. She could see the energy spread until the ceiling was completely covered. She had no idea what Tango was doing, unless he was still looking for her.

Then it hit her. Tango had found her as she was right now – hiding behind him.

Clever boy, she whispered. There's no fooling you, is there. Tango's energy seemed to nuzzle up against hers. She kept her field of energy tight and thin. Unwelcoming. She didn't want him to receive the same comfort he'd expect if he actually found her. She wanted him to run to her body looking for the same thing.

Just like that, the energy zipped off.

Pulling her with it.

Tango had no hesitation in his direction. Guided by instinct, he was searching the ethers for her, following the instinctive need to find her. His energy raced forward.

Then he came to a stop. At her bedside.

Tango's energy nuzzled her body in a warm loving way. Blending with her energy, sinking into it just as he'd so many times before.

Smiling, she closed her spiritual eyes, cried out a happy welcome, and sank into Tango as he sank into her space.

She was home.

RONIN LOOKED UP from his laptop. He'd only been here for a half hour. He'd been running around all morning. Had ended up in some of the seediest areas in town looking for smuggled animals, checking out names and locations Jacob had sent him, feeling like a fool because he didn't even know if the tiger was here in the U.S.

But he had to do something. And of course there was always his job. He had cases stacked up. Not the least were the break-ins at Exotic Landscape. But he hadn't been able to resist checking on her again.

He walked over to the bed. She looked...better? He bent over. Yes, her cheeks were rosy and she was breathing easier.

How and when and why hadn't someone contacted him? He spun around, wanting to race out and yell at the overworked staff...but at the same time he didn't want to leave her side.

As he turned back, she opened her eyes and stared straight at him. Her lips twitched in a tiny smile. "Hey."

"Hey." He grinned, his heart pounding inside his chest. "There you are. It is damn good to see you."

"Same," she whispered. Her eyes drifted closed. "I still feel a little rough."

"Nothing like going for a trip on the wild side."

She winced. "Now that was bad."

"Then again, when you crashed, as you did, after our lovemaking session… That was bad too. At least for me." He tried to make it humorous, but as her gaze widened in shock he realized he'd failed.

"It had nothing to do with you," she gasped. "You did not do this."

"I know that much." He picked her hand up and brought it to his lips. "But maybe if we hadn't been so passionate, you'd have gotten more rest. Been less susceptible. Stronger."

He hadn't allowed himself to focus on the possibility, but it had eaten away at him. Just below the surface.

"No." She shifted her head from one side of the pillow to the other. "Besides, I'm fine. And while I've been in the ethers I might have figured this out. But I'm not sure."

"I hope so." He gripped her hand. "This has been incredibly difficult."

"Ya think?"

He laughed, mostly out of relief. "What did you figure out? See anyone?"

"Yes," she said in surprise. "I heard them. They speak English. I saw a couple of faces, but no, I didn't recognize anyone. And honestly, I didn't get a clear view." She explained what little she'd heard about the buyer and about the tiger's pregnancy and her overall health, ending with the fact that they were afraid the deal would go south. Tabitha wrinkled up her face. "I guess that doesn't help much, does it?"

"Everything helps, but descriptions would be better…" He raised a brow in question then he leaned over and kissed her. Hard.

"Definitely, but I might know a faster way." She smiled. "Stef—" And then she cried out, her back arching high up on the bed.

He reached out. "Tabitha, honey…what's wrong?"

"It's happening aga—"

Her body went rigid, her face froze.

"Jesus. Don't fight it. Do what you did last time and come back."

"Help me," she gasped painfully. "Better yet – help her."

She twisted from one side to the other, tugging at the sheets and covers. Her face scrunched up in a horrible rictus and she collapsed backwards on the bed.

Then her face went slack. Her mouth fell open.

Someone came running in behind him.

"What's going on—oh Jesus. *Move. Move!*"

Ronin stepped back out of the way as the team checked her over.

He knew what had happened, but how could he tell the medical staff?

He had to find that damn tiger. Maybe then Stefan could find a way to separate Tabitha from her – and fast.

CHAPTER 13

Sunday late afternoon

PAIN RIPPED THROUGH Tabitha's mind as if she'd been stabbed. She understood what was happening, but not why. Psychic pain was amplified by one's lack of understanding. But once that awareness was there, the pain should have been almost eliminated, instead it was almost worse. Of course…

She immediately shut off her mind. It was her consciousness that was struggling. As she stopped trying to control it, the pain eased and the journey sped up until she was there.

Back inside the tiger.

Screaming in rage.

Tabitha adjusted more quickly this time and her eyes were open. The tiger had been so calm before. So what the hell happened to change that?

As if in slow motion, she watched two men struggle to subdue the tiger.

"You should have gotten here earlier, Timothy." One of the men puffed with effort. "She's been sleeping comfortably all morning."

"Until we approached," the stranger said. "The tranq should have taken effect already. At least I'm looking for a better reaction than this. She should be calmer. I just need to make sure she doesn't have an infection and that the wound is clean."

Tabitha could feel the tiger's pain. A collar had somehow been placed on her neck while Tabitha had been gone, and she'd been tethered down. A type of muzzle stopped her jaws from opening. She heaved up on her back legs.

"Jesus, Timothy, did you get a blood sample yet?" the first man panted. "I'd like to get out of here in one piece."

Then she realized she could see the men's faces – barely. Tabitha desperately tried to study the men's features. If she could only ID them… She was pretty sure she'd seen one man before. The Timothy guy might be a vet, which meant he had a license and there'd be paperwork to help them track him.

Unfortunately, the tiger was in full-blown panic now and was going to get herself knocked out again.

Timothy groaned. "Shit. You said this would be easy."

"Well, if you'd arrived when you said you were going to, it would have been."

The tiger's emotions swamped Tabitha so she sent out wave upon wave of soothing, calming energy. She needed the tiger awake and calm so Tabitha could see the damn men, but because of the shape the female tiger was in, if she sent out too much calming energy she was liable to put the tiger to sleep.

The tiger finally stilled. Tabitha could feel her chest still heaving, but the soothing energy she'd sent to the tiger had stopped her struggles and that was what was important.

"Jesus. Finally," Timothy said.

"At least she won't hurt herself this way. Hurry the hell up, will you."

"Okay, got it." Timothy shifted. Tabitha could feel a hand on her haunch, assessing her injury. The tiger's old injury. The new guy had to be a vet, and that would be a good thing.

One of the men stepped back.

"Weird coloring. Must be something wrong with her." The first man turned his back on them and walked away. Tabitha tried to find something memorable about him to tell Ronin, but what did one say about a tall, skinny, homeless-looking bum who wore clothes pulled from a garbage can? He looked as if he hadn't seen a toothbrush or hairbrush in years – the same as every other homeless guy she'd ever seen.

His buddy, whom she'd heard and seen before, was better dressed but still he didn't look dressed up in his rough jeans and denim jacket. He was bald and more round than tall and made a great comedy counterpart to the first man – only nothing they were doing was funny to her. He walked with a gimpy leg. Not bad, just off in the stride. She filed that information away.

The vet was young. Had to be a student or a young graduate. Italian looking. She struggled to see the details.

Only she couldn't control where the big cat looked. The tiger made that determination and now that she lay quiet, Tabitha could only see in one direction.

And she couldn't get a decent look at any of their faces.

The tiger's anger stayed inside, riding just below the surface, letting Tabitha know that if any one of them let down their guard and she had an opening, they'd be dinner.

And speaking of dinner… She had to persuade her host to eat and drink again. The tiger, in the family way, needed more than she was taking in. Tabitha could feel the thirst in her mind. The tiger didn't know what a watering bowl was and the idiots had made sure it was small and hard to reach. Best if they'd left her a large open tub of it. Still, it was water and she needed it. And there was food – if not for herself, for the babe growing inside her belly.

She'd protect her cub and herself by any means possible. And that cub…

Tabitha couldn't believe how intimate the sense of love – the bonding – that raced through her as part of the tiger's experience.

It was so special. So loving. Tabitha hadn't experienced anything like it. Her connection with Tango was the closest thing she had to compare this to. But Tango was her friend. He wasn't her baby, no matter that she treated him that way.

If that's what all mothers felt during their pregnancies, especially at full term, maybe she should consider having a family. That level of connection would be hard to experience any other way.

She wanted to know what it was like to care for someone so much that she'd do anything for them. Even die.

She felt privileged to be here, living the experience inside the majestic cat; privileged to be part of their bond, even for only a few hours.

And it would be only a few hours if she didn't get this tiger to drink again. She closed her eyes and filled the tiger's mind with images of water and creeks and lakes and ponds. Then showed them pouring that water into the water dish at the side of the cage. Then she repeated that visualizing process, over and over again.

Several long minutes passed before the suggestion showed any effect. The tiger finally lurched to her feet once again and inspected the foreign dish. She dipped her nose into the water then started to lap it up.

Relieved, Tabitha waited until the tiger's thirst was quenched. She realized the bald man had stayed to watch her.

"There's a good girl. Fez isn't going to hurt you. I'm doing my best to keep you safe." He took a step closer and pointed out the chunk of raw meat at the side and said, "Now how about a nice bite of roast?"

Only Tabitha had lost track of what he was saying. Her mind had caught on the one word in there of interest. Fez? So Timothy and Fez, possibly someone called Keeper, but she wasn't sure about that last one. Besides, any names these guys used probably changed depending on the situation.

But at least she had something tangible. She needed to tell Ronin. Somehow.

RONIN SLAMMED THE door on his truck and walked across the Exotic Landscapes parking lot. He worked a case until he got to the bottom of it – until he had someone to pin to the wall. In this case, he felt like he was running around in circles. He'd probed into the black market buying and selling of endangered animals and hadn't gotten anywhere. He'd also been working the break-ins at Exotic Landscape – and so far, nothing. They might not have anything to do with the current problem, but still they were part of the file.

He'd just finished saying he needed more information, more avenues to pursue, when he received a call from Sue at Exotic Landscape.

How did another incident – cut fences to the lynx pens this time – have anything to do with this? And damn it, why did this case have to involve more cats?

A dumpling-shaped, middle-aged woman walked out the front door to meet him. Tabitha had told him about Wendy, but he'd yet to meet her. He'd met Sue and several of the security guards but not this new manager. Considering the problems in Tabitha's life, he wondered what kind of a background check Tabitha had done on the new hires.

As much as she needed more staff, she didn't need to add the wrong people to her roster.

He held out his hand to her and smiled briefly. "I'm Detective Chandler."

And had to wonder at her speculative look.

She rushed to say, "I'm so glad you're here. We just found this a couple of hours ago." As she explained, she walked in the direction of the double front gates of the enclosure. "The side of the pen has been damaged. It appears that the person was trying to release or to steal the two female lynx."

Either case likely pointed to neighbourhood kids playing a prank or something more serious. He asked, "The females are unharmed?"

"Yes. They are in this pen only a short time while adapting to their new surroundings. They've been checked by medical, but we've waiting for Tabitha to get back before the surgeries were done."

"Surgeries?"

"Most of the animals are neutered after they arrive – if they haven't been already." She motioned in a wide arm sweep. "It makes the animals easier to deal with and generally stops people wanting them for breeding purposes. We list that on the website hoping it will stop the inquiries."

"What kind of inquiries?"

She shrugged. "I haven't been here for long. We ask for donations or virtual adoptions for the care of the animals. Many ask for visitation rights, home visits, and even more want to purchase the animals. Sometimes for breeding purposes."

He frowned. "And that's not allowed?"

"No. No they stay here their entire lives. Not at all. This is their home forever. They get all they need here and have room to roam in a decent space created for them. No cages unless they have medical needs that are being addressed. Each animal is safe and secure from the public."

Ronin had to smile. She was a walking billboard in support of Exotic Landscape. Maybe Tabitha had made a great hire. Except many of these incidents could have been carried out as an inside job. He studied Wendy but she didn't look strong enough to cut the fence. That didn't mean she wasn't in partnership with someone else who wanted the animals though. She could have found a buyer for them…

The B&Es could have been an inside job, too. He'd taken a close look at all the staff already.

"Of course. These break-ins will slow down donations. Nothing like bad press to make those dry up."

He shot her a sidelong look. As they came around the corner, he switched his gaze to the pen. There was a big patch showing where the gaping hole had been.

Damn. Whoever had done this meant for the animals to go free. But why these ones in particular? Why not any number of her pens? Or was that just for convenience? These pens were closest to the road. Had they run out of time? Or… He spun around searching for cameras. They were still there and that meant there could be a record of what had happened. He could hope.

The question was – why had they done this and did they plan to do more?

He glanced around. Wendy had disappeared. But then the offices weren't normally open today. Still, he wanted to see the security feed.

Could he find someone here who knew how to access them? Tabitha had new hires, but the security system was even newer.

He dialed his brother – and got no answer. Damn it. He vaguely remembered there being some shindig of Shay's he'd planned to attend.

Checking his watch, he realized he could check the feed on Monday when the usual security people were here.

His phone rang. Stepping outside, he answered Jacob's call.

"Ronin, I've got someone willing to talk," Jacob said. "Six o'clock tomorrow morning, at Land's End."

"HEY, FEZ."

"What?" Fez turned from the back of the truck where he was unloading the day's shipment. Most of the food was raw meat for the big cat. The last of the other animals he'd transported had been picked up yesterday.

"I think you should come and see her," Keeper said from behind him. "She doesn't look right."

Not again. Jesus, Keeper was simple. He was repeating the same phrase over and over again. "I'll be there in a minute."

He finished storing the meat, wiped the sweat off his face and turned back into the warehouse. The black cloth was covering the tiger cage. He lifted a corner and tried to peer inside.

And came face to face with the tiger's eyes. Her massive jaws opened up. *Rawrrrr!*

"Jesus Christ." He bounced backwards, almost tripping over his own feet as he raced to put distance between himself and the tiger.

The other man was laughing like crazy, bent over and slapping his thighs.

"Oh, my God. You look so funny." Keeper howled again and pointed a finger at him. "You damn near shit your pants."

Damn near felt like it too. But he wasn't going to say that to this asshole. "Did you do that on purpose?"

"Do what? Hell, I just told you to come here because she doesn't look right. I didn't say go lift the corner of the cloth where she's lying and scaring the shit out of her."

Fez barely stilled the impulse to beat Keeper's head in. Asshole. "Well, she looks damn normal to me."

"Well, she isn't." The other man sobered up instantly. "Not at all. She's abnormally calm. I just don't know how that can be."

"Well, maybe you should just be thankful that she is," he snapped. "Besides, that's what you said last time."

"No. She's *too,* content. I think someone is slipping her drugs. It's the only explanation. I know I didn't do it. I don't think it's you, so who the hell is drugging her?" He looked around the warehouse as if seeing it for the first time. "And does that mean the boss is doing something that doesn't include us? Or is someone else involved, maybe one of the delivery guys?" He lowered his voice. "The security here is pretty lax. I know we were counting on no one knowing what we really had…but what if someone finds out?"

"And what good would drugging the tiger do? Sure, it keeps her calm but that would benefit us and no one else." Fez had to think about that. In this lowlife location, their movements could have been tracked. It wouldn't have taken much for a curious someone to figure out what they held captive.

"Unless it also makes her more docile around the guy who drugged her, too," Keeper said. "In which case, it would be easier to steal her."

"And there is someone else who knows she's here. The young kid you brought in. Timothy. Maybe he slipped her something we don't know about?"

Keeper gasped. "No way. He's just a kid. Besides, why would he? No one knows about the tiger. He wouldn't tell, so there's no point in giving her an extra shot."

Looking around as if afraid someone would overhear, he added, "Besides he said the blood tests came back positive. The old girl is pregnant."

"What?" Fez couldn't believe it. But it was damn good news. That meant the boss would be happy. The buyer would be happy. And the damn deal could go through. Then Fez could get his damn money. "Now that is very good news."

"Maybe and maybe not. Someone could be trying to scoop their sale." Keeper nodded wisely.

As if he knew anything. But Fez did know there'd been trouble with the boss and the buyer. But that's 'cause the tiger had been ailing.

But a pregnant ailing tiger was a helluva bonus.

And Fez took that one step further. What if the buyer really wanted the tiger but decided to not bother paying? With the pissing contest going on between the boss and the buyer, the buyer could do that out of spite.

In this business, lots of people just took what they wanted. Especially if they didn't like doing deals with certain people. Especially if they felt they were being screwed in the first place. If the buyer found out about the pregnancy, there was no guessing what he might do.

To Keeper, he said, "We need to boost security around this place.

We can't take the risk something will go wrong."

"You mean something else going wrong, right?" Keeper groaned. "There is no way to increase security. Short of camping here overnight."

Fez just stared at him, waiting.

"No way." Keeper shook his head. "You can stay overnight if you want. I'm going home for a decent meal and a beer."

"Sure," Fez said mildly, "then get your ass back here for the first watch. I'll relieve you at 2:00am."

The other man groaned. "You aren't serious?"

"Return in *four* hours or don't bother returning at all." Keeper needed the money just as much as he did. The man stared at him, stomped his feet a few times, his mouth working, then stormed out to the other room.

Fez watched Keeper leave. He'd be back. He turned to stare at the cloth-covered cage. "Looks like it's just you and me, girl."

A deep howl started from the far end. There was no way she'd be able to get out. Just the fact that she'd reacted this way though…

"Shit." He gave into the fear and backed up several paces then turned and ran to the far side of the warehouse. As the door closed on his heels, he swore he could almost hear the damn feline laughing.

STEFAN OPENED HIS eyes, though sleep still clouded his mind. The bedroom swam and twisted in front of him. The air swirled in black clouds, taking him somewhere…else.

He had no idea where he was or where he was going.

The clouds cleared. Blue sky and sunshine shone above him. He floated in the clouds above a generic countryside. He zoomed in faster and faster, seeing the land come rushing up toward him. He zipped down to follow a blue ribbon slashing across the land.

Closer and closer he went. Faster and faster he flew, swooping lower and lower until he was skimming across the water. He hadn't recognized any landmarks while flying down, and now at water level there were no buildings that he could see. Faster and faster, the wind whipped past so hard it brought tears to his eyes.

And then he stopped and hovered in place to study the surroundings. He didn't have a time frame either. Was this the past, present or the future?

He was still traveling forward, but almost in a slow gliding motion. He was coming up to a town. Not a town. A city. *Portland.*

With the tears flooding his eyes, he could barely see. And then he came to a sudden stop. A dirty river. Derelict buildings. And empty streets.

But it was the body floating in the water that caught his attention.

A man.

Dead.

But the dead man was important.

Even so, Stefan could feel his energy zapping his system. He had to travel home soon. If he could just get a closer look at the man's face…

Pulling on the last of his reserves, he dove lower until he was lying parallel above the body and gazing straight into the dead staring eyes.

Stefan hit the end of his rope. He was sucked back in time and space through the wind and the clouds and the sky – back through a long black tunnel – and slammed back into his body that still lay on his bed.

CHAPTER 14

Sunday early evening

TABITHA CURLED INTO a tight ball of energy. She had no idea what to do or how to do it. She could go back to Tango and potentially back to her body – unless she'd died the last time.

Only the connection to the tiger went both ways, and now she was attached to her existence here and fearful for her life – and the tiger's life. How could Tabitha leave her alone?

She'd heard the men's discussion about drugs. Were they talking about the effects of her calming energy on the tiger or had someone else entered the warehouse and attempted to drug the tiger? She didn't feel anything new, but Tabitha had felt a wash of wrongness in the tiger's body since she arrived. The body felt different from Tango's, but then he was tame, happy, and healthy. Trinity – Tabitha had named the tiger following her grandfather's naming scheme of all pets starting with T's (and, damn, she hadn't wanted to ask about her own name) – was wild, hurting, and on death's doorstep.

Trinity was tired. Hurting. Scared. Almost to the point of giving up.

Tabitha rocked back and forth in her virtual space, wishing to see a way forward. The tiger was a victim here. But then so was Tabitha. She hated that feeling. And her awareness was so much stronger because the tiger's feelings were bleeding into Tabitha's emotions, amplifying them, making Trinity's feelings Tabitha's. This amplification connected her to the tiger in a big way – they were both victims.

Her mind stalled.

Victim. That's what she felt like. That's what she'd become. That's what she was.

Because she'd slipped into the victim mentality.

She was letting the circumstances dictate what she could do. She was reacting…not acting. She was letting the situation get the best of her. Instead of doing something constructive about it.

That had to stop.

Trinity slowly eased her legs down to stretch out in front of her while Tabitha's mind wrapped, shifted, and reformed the new reality of the situation. There was no way in hell she was going down as a victim.

Not in this lifetime. Unless her life was already over. But she couldn't go there. She didn't dare. She had to figure out how to take back control. And that started at the emotional level. Then the mental, and finally she knew she could manifest intent in her physical life.

She took a deep breath and released it. Then took another. As she started to feel better, she realized that her energy was uncurling, stretching away from her, relaxing too. Her energy was changing as her mental shift grabbed hold. She smiled as the tension slipped down her spine and into the ground, opening her consciousness.

Fear had sunk so deep inside Tabitha, she hadn't recognized it when it crept up and took hold. But it was there, almost rank with its stench.

She shone a little light on her fears, letting them breathe, letting them swell before releasing it to the ether.

As she released all that in front of her, she could see them. See what she'd held deep inside, hidden even from herself. Things that were clogging her soul. Things that were holding her back from the next step. The hurts were all there too.

Tobias's death.

Her grandfather's death.

Tango's impending death.

Tripod's eventual death.

Her uncertainties over Exotic Landscape.

So many regrets. So many fears. And along with those, so many fears of what was to come. So many hurts she'd hidden from herself. So many losses and wishes and dreams. She was like a water slide, with all these memories and dreams and thoughts gushing from her out of this big pipe – as if the process was releasing everything that had held her back. It was what she needed to do to lighten her soul and let it breathe again.

Let her soul live. And stretch. And thrive.

And act.

She waited, feeling the power surging through her. She didn't need to be confined in here. She could go anywhere. Any time. Including to her body.

It was fear not reality that had held her back.

Now she knew what to do.

She needed to go to the source. And that meant the tiger's source.

Tabitha pushed gently into Trinity's memories, easing into it, one gentle pulse at a time. She had the names Fez and Timothy, now she needed the faces. Tiger vision was different and she'd seen the general outline of the men, but not their features with any clarity.

She wished she could transmit the images to Stefan. He'd be the one to translate them to paper. But there was no guarantee she could.

Damn it, where was Ronin? She needed him. In so many ways. More than she'd understood before. She sent out another gentle pulse into the old tiger's memories and watched as the curtains of the big cat's mind opened slightly. Tabitha was taking a dangerous chance doing this. She didn't want to open the memories too wide or deep. If Trinity had many traumatic instances in her life, reliving them could bring back the same shock and stressors as she'd experienced in the wild. In fact, given the state Trinity was already in, any number of these could kill her.

And most likely Tabitha along with her.

Taking a mental step back, she approached the next layer of energy with love, sending out warm caring thoughts to tamp down the fear. She wanted the memories to be like an old black and white movie. Something distant and hard to relate to.

Not something that would cause Tabitha's heart to race or her adrenaline to kick in.

Trinity lay at one end of the cage. She'd responded well to Tabitha's suppression energy and that had calmed her aggression, eased her fears, and worked to save her from feeling pain. It was easier on them all this way. But dangerous too, especially if the men assumed it was safe to approach the tiger – if that were to happen, Trinity's instincts would override Tabitha's work and, given the opportunity, she'd attack her captors.

Tabitha knew Trinity would never be happy in captivity. She could live on a reserve to the end of her days, but the caregivers would never be able to let down their guard. Tabitha also knew she might be able to do some energy work to help Trinity adapt; she certainly helped the animals on her reserve that way. Anything that helped the animals live a healthier and happier life worked for her.

Humans could learn a lot from them. So could she.

As that thought crossed her mind, the layers of Trinity's memories pulled back and she watched a stream of disjointed images ripple past at super speed. She tried to slow them down but nothing she did worked.

The film raced by in a never-ending stream of hunting, feeding, mating, birthing. Then the film started to crackle as if it was breaking. It got deeper, darker, and more sinister. A loud pop sounded so close that Tabitha could feel the sting as something bit into her hip. She gasped and could feel the burn and shock and terror Trinity experienced during her capture as if it were today. Trinity had survived a lot in her life, she was old for a wild tiger, but she hadn't been expecting to run from a gun. She hadn't even seen that coming.

When she'd woken up, Trinity had been caged.

Tabitha watched the rest of the bad-quality film, searching for something usable. From inside the darkness, she could hear sounds in a distance and understood the animal had been kept sedated. She had no idea for how long. To Trinity, with the fear and rage rippling through her, it seemed endless. She'd been kept drugged for far too long. Tabitha understood the need from the poacher's point of view, but for the tiger…it was an endless myriad of pain and fear.

Tabitha had to wonder where Trinity came from. Not that it mattered, but someone had obviously gone to a lot of trouble. The fur on the tiger's paw was a dirty gray and black. Tabitha hadn't had a clear view of the rest of her body. She could be a white Bengal. White tigers were rare in the wild. They were legal to own and breed in many parts of the U.S. but the color came with its own set of problems. White tigers, with their distinctive recessive gene, were so inbred that the breed had multiple problems.

But what if this wasn't a white tiger? What if she was a rarer variation? What if that slate gray on her front leg and paw were the same all over? What if she really was a famed Maltese tiger?

There'd been reports since forever of blue tigers, but confirmed sightings were few and far between and none in the last several decades. Then there was a rare black tiger species – although her coloring didn't go that far.

But if she was any one of these rare breeds, she should have been treated much better. The world would want to know that one of the species had been found in its natural habitat and it would be protected – as were all extinct and endangered animals. And the penalties for smuggling it would be stiff.

From the memories she'd accessed, she knew this tiger had been captured in the wild.

If it was the breed she suspected, it was one of the last of its kind.

That made Trinity even more special. It made her…a rare find.

❦

"A FLOATER?"

Stefan's tired voice sounded flat, disembodied. Ronin had observed the famed psychic on just enough calls to realize he'd probably just climbed out of another vision.

It was late on a Sunday. He should be back at the hospital, not still at the office, but he'd needed to check in. There'd been a surprising number of people here. He tried to focus on Stefan's conversation.

"Do you have a location?" Ronin asked.

"Portland, but nothing more detailed."

But a city was good. If the floater was related to Tabitha's problems. "Does this guy have something to do with the tiger?"

"I'm hoping so." This time there was a thread of humor in Stefan's voice. "It could be another case though."

Ronin paused to digest that. So, a body somewhere in Portland… he thought, but could they count on that, considering he didn't get a good look. And maybe or maybe not related to Tabitha's predicament. Couldn't these psychics make it easy for once? "Have you any idea how little help this is?" he asked in frustration.

"No. And I don't want to know. Thanks." Now his voice was sounding positively cheerful. "I just pass over the information. It's your problem now."

Ronin pinched the bridge of his nose and took a mental step back. Since meeting these people, he'd learned that nothing ever fit together in a straight line…at least not until they solved a case. Then the puzzle pieces fell nicely into place. But the path getting there was beyond twisted. The stuff they found out in the pursuit of their answers made him realize a long time ago that most people lived their nice happy lives blind to everything around them. When it came to the area of psychics, there was a whole other world just under the surface.

"Please tell me you have something more."

"Check your email."

And he hung up.

Ronin groaned. He'd turned off the notifications on his phone a long time ago, hating to be always attached to the damn thing. He walked back to his desk and opened his laptop.

The email program took a moment to load before he saw Stefan's email. With an attachment. He opened the attachment and was reminded, Stefan was an *artist!*

The scanned black and white pencil sketch might as well have been a photograph. The lines around the man's face were so well blended, the shading so realistic that if he hadn't understood Stefan's talent, he'd have assumed he'd taken a picture of the dead floater.

Behind the first sketch was a second one, of the surrounding buildings.

Bringing them both up on the big monitor beside him, Ronin studied the images. He sent them to the printer and waited.

He'd pick them up in a minute. The old rundown buildings along the edge of the river were interesting. The buildings had no identifying names or numbers. He had no clue where the buildings were located, but he thought some of his buddies might.

Ronin knew a couple of techs that might be able to help. He whipped up a few emails and sent them off with a note saying he was on his way over to talk to them. But first, the printer.

The big printer was in the outer office. Beside the coffee. Several of his buddies were standing around and talking when he entered the room.

He searched for the printouts. The one of the river was there, but not the floater. Crap. He'd have to go back and reprint it.

"Hey Ronin, is this yours?" Brent held up the floater's image. "Where the hell did you get that?"

"A contact." He deliberately kept Stefan's name out of the discussion. "Quite the sketch, isn't it?"

"This is a sketch?" one of the men asked.

"Looks like a photograph."

"Of a dead guy."

"Yeah. He had to have been there to have seen it in this kind of detail." The paper was passed from hand to hand as they studied the artistry.

"Anyone recognize the dead guy?" Ronin asked. He glanced up at their faces, and damn if there wasn't a shadow crossing Geoff's face. "Geoff? Do you?"

He shrugged his shoulders. "Damn if I know. The guy's face is all distorted."

"Yeah, he's a floater."

"We've had a few of those come in the last month. None around this guy's age that I know of though."

Brent said, "How can you tell what age?" Brent peered more closely. "Guy could be anywhere from twenty to sixty."

"The water is never nice to flesh, but this guy doesn't look like he was in all that long. I've seen worse."

With that announcement, several of the guys grabbed their coffees and headed back to their desks. Brent handed the picture back to

Ronin. "Good luck."

Ronin watched him walk away. He would check on the recent floaters from the morgue and check with the lab techs to see if they could help improve the image.

Ten minutes later, he knew that wasn't going to work.

"Sorry, but the guy's features are too distorted," said the lab tech. "We can set up a facial recognition scan and run it through the database looking for someone, but it's a long shot."

"Run it anyway. Besides, I have a second problem for you. Is there any way to figure out this location?" He handed over the second picture.

They fell into a discussion about the minor landmarks in the picture. Finally the lab tech shook his head. "Sorry, Ronin, but there's not much to go on here. No skyline. No physical landmarks. It's just a few old buildings."

"Yeah, that's what I was afraid of." Ronin picked up the picture and walked out.

What was the chance that Stefan could return to the same place and find some landmarks this time? Possibly keep his eyes open, for heaven's sake.

4:30 am

THE WAREHOUSE WAS steeped in darkness. And silence.

The darkness was a bit too dense to see much. Fez wanted to open a window, maybe turn on a light. Something.

Tonight this place was giving him the creeps. He'd come in and relieved the idiot, Keeper, about a half hour ago. Keeper had been asleep when Fez arrived. Now, alone at 4:30 in the morning, Fez wished he'd left Keeper asleep and just stayed here to keep watch over the tiger.

He'd never been afraid of the dark before. Neither had he been afraid of being alone.

Tonight, he had to admit to both.

He was tired and chilled with a powerful need to constantly look around. He just needed a good night's sleep. Keeper had slept through his shift – lucky bugger. Sleeping wasn't exactly the best way to stand guard, but it sure as hell helped pass the time.

Happy with his decision, he curled up in a far corner of the warehouse where he had a good view of the front entrance and the tiger's cage and closed his eyes.

Every sound was amplified in the dark. Somewhere in the far side of the warehouse he heard the scurrying of little feet. Probably rats. The damn place was infested with them. The dampness from the river brought them in. At least it was dry in here. And a few rats didn't bother him.

It's not as if there were any animal control or health inspectors that came around this corner of the world, and if they did stop in, there was always money to grease the wheels to make them go away.

He struggled to get comfortable, shifting his fat bottom on the cement floor, wishing there was at least a chair to sit on. He leaned back against the wall and closed his eyes.

Then opened them. *What was that?* He caught his breath as he heard something over by the tiger's cage. *Voices.*

Quietly Fez regained his feet and tiptoed toward the cage, his head cocked in the direction of the sound. He stopped and waited breathlessly. Then he took another step and thought he heard it again. He took several more steps toward the tiger's cage and waited. The warehouse seemed alive with weird sounds. Air whistled from the blowing wind. Timber creaked with age. And he swore there were sounds of people moving.

What the hell was going on? He hopped to his feet and walked over to the tiger, peering into the cage. The tiger lay sleeping on her side. Calm. Quiet. Peaceful.

He turned around to face the empty warehouse. Shadows seemed to shift even as he watched. Now he knew his imagination was working overtime, and that pissed him off as much as it scared him.

Seeing nothing to justify the sounds, he slowly retraced his steps back to his spot. Then he heard something that sent shivers down his spine. Breathing. As in human breathing. As in a person. So loud he imagined the hairs on the back of his neck lifting.

He willed himself to turn and see who it was. Wishing he had a gun, he spun around.

The blow came out of nowhere. It smashed into the side of his head.

And he dropped like the heavy weight he was – to the ground.

CHAPTER 15

Monday early morning

NOW THAT SHE had some inkling that Trinity had come from the wild with this coloring, she suspected Trinity to be a Maltese tiger. Tabitha dredged through her memory for all the information she could find about them. And there was damn little. Maltese tigers hadn't been seen in decades in the wild. She knew of none in captivity, but that didn't mean there weren't any. It was an endangered species and the whole world would celebrate if they knew Trinity existed.

If they knew.

Which, considering Trinity was being smuggled, they weren't likely to ever learn. And she was old. By any medical standards, being pregnant at her age was rare. Not that Mother Nature cared what humans deduced. She was forever throwing up new and wondrous things. But did the smugglers truly understand what they had?

Understanding the problem and the precious cargo helped, but not enough. So what if there were buyers and sellers and good guys and bad guys out there? If she couldn't see any to identify them or find a way for others to find her, none of that mattered. Somehow she had to get Ronin the information she'd found. But what was that? Just a name. And a vague face.

She needed more.

She wondered if she could create enough energy disturbances to upset the asshole standing guard. She'd learned his name was Fez and she'd managed to stretch her energy out enough to raise the hairs on the back of the guy's neck. But he'd gone back to sitting down. She'd been trying to get a good look at his face, but there were so many shadows she couldn't see it clearly enough. She'd tried, but unfortunately didn't have a photographic memory.

But Stefan did. She'd been trying to tell Ronin the details earlier but she'd been yanked away before she could say anything. Now maybe she had a better idea.

She closed her eyes and sent out a strong message. *Stefan. Stefan? Stefan!*

Taking a chance, she told her subconscious to transmit the images to Stefan. They could be the answer to saving Trinity. And for good measure, she told herself to send anything else that might be useful.

What the hell? Where are you and why? Stefan's voice growled in her head. Faint and odd sounding but still identifiable. The diction was off, but it was clear enough to hear.

I need you to see some images. Pictures I can see but can't remember.

Silence.

Not sure that will work.

You can often connect in such a way that you just see into my mind and save me from trying to explain. Why can't you do that now?

Because you aren't here in front of me. You're in someone else's mind.

Damn it. I've seen one of the men that's holding the tiger. His name is Fez. I can see his and Timothy's face, but I'm no artist.

You know every step away from the original blurs the details. You'll have to try and grab the details.

He was right, but she didn't like it. *Suggestions?*

Clear your mind and use the energy. Try to remember and come home. I'll tell Ronin.

Crap.

Stefan disappeared and the fog moved in again.

She needed another look. She stared through the tiger's eyes out at the warehouse. It drained a lot of her energy to do this but the rewards could be worth it.

She closed her eyes and stretched a bit of her energy away from the tiger's cage toward where she'd sensed the asshole the last time.

The idiot appeared to be sleeping. She stretched out a little more, trying to get a look at his face, but there was something wrong. There was blood around his head. Lots of it.

He'd been attacked.

And she hadn't heard it.

That terrified her. Had she been so focused on contacting Stefan that she'd missed it? Or had the attackers been so quiet, she'd not have heard them?

The shock zapped her back to the tiger where she curled up into a ball. A new fear took over, blending with that of the tiger's. Who the hell had hurt Fez? Were they still here?

In the background, she heard a door rattle.

RONIN HAD WALKED a lot of seedy streets in his time, but these slums were pretty bad. He'd already seen several drug deals go down. Life here was a whole new world. The hookers strolled the sidewalks, looking ready to call it a night. Businesses thrived down here, but at this hour of the morning it appeared only the underbelly was alive. During the day, it teemed with people from all walks of life. Many were visiting. When this was your life, escape was damn near an impossibility – so many never did.

He walked around the corner to find Land's End Cafe. From the outside it had that tired, worn down look – the same as so many of the other local businesses. Open twenty-four hours, there were likely more cockroaches eating at the restaurant than clients. Still, he ordered two coffees and watched the grizzled waiter pour them. As he accepted the steaming cups from him, he was surprised to see the rich color. He wasn't sure what he'd expected. He'd taken his chances on the coffee here – it could've been anything from sludge to a tea-looking brew.

The diner was empty, but the traffic outside was steady. From a table in the corner, he watched the world walk by. His eye caught on an old couple holding hands. His smile warmed. He'd planned on having a wife and a family to grow old together. The growing old together was what he was looking at. The comfortable reassurance that they knew each other inside and out. That their love had been the light they'd walked with for every day of their lives.

He had to admit, he wanted some of that for himself – with Tabitha.

But that girl seemed to thrive on trouble. He didn't feel in sync with her world. As much as he wanted to be, that didn't guarantee he'd find his place in it. And he hadn't been able to help her. Yet.

"Ronin?"

Ronin glanced up. A scraggly looking man in oversized pants and jacket, with a full and unkempt beard and an old flattened hat stood in front of him. Just a middle-aged man down on his luck. Nice disguise, except the man's eyes were clear and direct. And faintly familiar.

Ronin nodded and motioned to the seat across from him and the waiting cup of coffee. "Take a seat."

"Thanks." The man sat in the chair.

Trying not to stare, Ronin studied the coffee swirling in his mug. "What do you know?"

The man took a sip of his hot drink first. "There's some talk about a rare cat. Doing poorly."

Now they were talking. Ronin leaned forward. "Where?" he asked in low undertones. He didn't know if it was a rare cat Tabitha had hooked up with, but that made sense. He should have asked her. The various states had different laws regarding owning and breeding large cats, but he'd also learned that anything was available for the right price.

The other man shrugged. "Can't be sure."

"What *can* you be sure of?"

"It's rare. It's hurting, and there is some in-fighting going on between buyer and seller." The older man inhaled the caffeine fumes, then lifted his cup and took another sip, then sighed happily.

"Names?" Was he an informant or an undercover cop? That Ronin couldn't tell said much for his disguise.

The other man took his time then shook his head. "That I can't do." He put down the empty cup and stood up. "Thanks for helping an old man out. Appreciate it."

He shuffled past Ronin and went out the door.

With a snort, Ronin stood, pissed at not having more. As he turned to leave, he saw a crumpled piece of paper on the table. He could've sworn it hadn't been there before. He snatched it up and raced out the front door so he could see which direction the old man had gone.

There was no sign of him. He'd disappeared.

Ronin glanced down at the paper in his hand. He smoothed it out. And found what appeared to be a phone number scribbled across the sheet.

STEFAN WOKE FROM a deep sleep, silently, stealthily. Alert. As if he was under attack – or preparing to attack. Only there was no sign of anything. Or anyone. He shifted his vision to search the energy in the room. It all appeared normal. His guards were still in place. The house remained safe. His security system untouched.

So where was the danger?

Faint images of a collapsed man filled his mind. He sorted through the images, trying to figure out who the man was. And why was Stefan receiving the images?

He grabbed his pencil and sketchbook and went to work. The picture came together relatively quickly.

After a few moments, he closed his eyes to bring the image up again. And caught that same scent of wrongness he'd felt on waking.

He sent out a probe, searching the ether for what had disturbed him. Nothing. He lay quiet for a few moments, listening. Nothing obvious, but still…something was wrong. He couldn't identify it. But that didn't mean it wasn't there.

Tabitha? He wished he knew for certain. Too often he dealt with multiple cases at once. There could be any number of things wrong. Restless, he set the sketchbook aside and stepped out onto his deck as the early morning light was cresting the horizon.

He took a deep breath of the crisp air. There was still a bite in the cool morning, but not enough to ease the rising temperature of worry. If only he could figure out what was wrong. He stared across the property. He was far enough out of town that he was often visited by wildlife. No animals moved.

He cocked his head to the side, turned to glance back into his bedroom, then walked through to his front door. He threw it open. Then stared. There was the merest whisper through the large bushes in front of him. He shifted his vision to search for energy. Blues and greens swirled in the early morning dawn. He used colors to help his plants grow. Those not native to the country utilized the energy to adapt. The colors helped stabilize, helped them to adjust. In part, that was why they'd done so well here.

Tabitha's face rose from the colors, letting him know he was between realities. She opened her mouth, but the words flew from his lips. "My grandfather's box."

FEZ SAT QUIETLY in the corner of the warehouse. His head was killing him – and his boss looked like he wanted to finish the job. When he'd first arrived, he'd had a genial smile on his face that made Fez's blood run cold.

Now he was talking to the buyer. Only Fez didn't understand the conversation. And yeah, that might be from the knock on his noggin. He reached up a tentative hand to touch the wound. Blood was still dripping down the side of his neck.

He needed medical attention but had no money. He was also damn sure the boss would toss him in the river rather than help him. The longer he listened, the more he realized the boss was dousing his chances of ever getting away.

"No," the boss said into the phone, "I'm sorry to say, she's definitely not improving. I don't think she's even going to make a week. I should be able to refund this transaction by the weekend."

This time Fez couldn't hear the buyer's half of the conversation, but the glint in the boss's eye said he wasn't backing down. None of this made any sense. He groaned and leaned back to rest his head.

For whatever reason, the boss wanted to back out of this tiger deal. And that was seriously bad news.

His boss continued. "No. There's no option at this point. I'll make the arrangements."

When he hung up the phone and stared at Fez, Fez said querulously, "We did everything we could to make this deal happen. Now you cancelled it?"

The boss snorted. "Damn right I did. She's pregnant. That changes everything. There is no way in hell I'm going to sell short the best deal of my life." He smiled, a cold, hard smile. "She's worth so much more now."

Fez didn't know what to say and couldn't think straight either. Money…he needed money. "But…my paycheck?"

"Oh you'll get paid. No worries there." His boss pulled out a small notepad and dropped it on the floor in front of Fez. "We're going to run a private auction – contact a few more people. Some high-end collectors."

"I need money now," Fez protested. "And this buyer… What about when he finds out?"

The boss opened his wallet and pulled out some bills. He threw them at Fez. "This will tide you over for a week. It won't be longer than that and you'll get your full pay."

Fez leaned forward, shuddered at the pain, and picked up the money. "And the buyer?"

"This buyer can go to hell," the boss said calmly. "Once I give him the money back, he's got nothing to do with this anymore. If he wants her after that, he can bid in the auction. If he asks, I'll tell him she's made a miraculous recovery and is pregnant to boot." He smiled. A twitch of his lips that made Fez's heart quake with dread.

"And if he doesn't like it, too damn bad." The cold smile turned to ice. "I have solutions for assholes like him too."

CHAPTER 16

Monday morning

TABITHA HAD TO get home again. It was early, she'd heard something out in the warehouse a while ago, but it had calmed down.

In fact, outside of trying to grab something useful for Ronin to help her and the tiger, she'd had no real reason for staying as long as she had. Except to provide comfort. Trinity was calm and peaceful when Tabitha was there beside her.

But once she left her, Trinity's energy would thin and she'd feel the fear and panic that much stronger – even with Tabitha's suppression energy.

Tabitha understood Trinity was sick. In a way that was beyond healing. Heartsick. And maybe soul-sick. There was only so much she could do to make Trinity's remaining time as easy as possible. Given the situation, that wasn't much. If they could get her to the reserve, she'd do better but any measure would be only temporary. As for the cub inside…

If it could survive this nastiness, then there could be a decent life for it. Tabitha already felt the same warm maternal feelings the tiger did, as if the cub were her own. It would be brutal if something happened to it, but she also knew the dangers of getting this attached. The cub most likely wouldn't be able to stay with her, although it could live at Exotic Landscape quite nicely. She'd have to fight for it. Better these assholes had left her in the wild.

Tabitha sent a warm, loving energy jolt to the tiger's energy chakra and then to the baby. She poured protective energy around them both as she backed up and away before finally turning and sweeping into the ether to find Tango.

As her energy had never left Tango's, he only gave her a surprised greeting as if to say, 'What is your problem, I was sleeping here?'

She laughed with joy at the familiar surroundings and gave the big cat a warm hug. His energy rolled through her, around her, warming her and bringing tears to her eyes. She felt so sorry for all the lonely people in the world who never had a chance to connect on this level. She'd been truly blessed. Her father was one of those who'd never connected, and as such had missed out on one of life's truly great experiences.

She shifted back to check on Tripod, who barked a warm greeting, before she dashed back to her physical body. This time she slid back inside effortlessly.

She opened her eyes. And saw she was back in the hospital.

This trip had been much easier on her body and on her soul. Her room was empty. She had no idea where Ronin was, but he couldn't be expected to stay here forever. Knowing that, she wanted to return to her house. Even connected as she was and knowing that the tiger could pull her back at any time, Tabitha would be better off at home. She could only hope that the protective healing energy she'd left behind had the power to keep Trinity calm for a day or two at least. That would hopefully free Tabitha long enough to sort out her life here. She did not want to get tugged backwards like she'd been twice, but that appeared to be the only thing the tiger knew to do to make herself feel better.

And Tabitha would have done the same thing under the same circumstances.

She threw back her covers and gently sat up, letting her legs swing over the side. The room swam in front of her. She clasped a hand to her face and shuddered. Then groaned. "I feel like I'm going to puke."

"Oh dear." Footsteps raced to her side. "Let's get you back into bed."

Strong arms reached around from behind Tabitha and helped her shuffle backwards to lie down again. "Now, let me raise you up a little bit and see how that feels."

The nurse pressed a button and the top half of the bed rose slightly. Then a little more. As it moved up again, Tabitha protested, "That's good." Not quite what she meant to say, but the nurse appeared to understand and lowered the bed slightly.

Tabitha took a deep breath, grateful when her stomach and the room behaved. With a small smile, she whispered, "Thanks. I guess I wasn't really feeling as good as I thought I was."

"You just need a day or two to recover."

Tabitha gave a broken laugh. "That much time I don't have. I have an hour or two at the most."

"I don't think there is going to be a doctor here for several hours."

The nurse patted her hand. "Just rest." She walked out.

Tabitha let her head roll to the side. She wouldn't let something like the lack of a doctor stop her. She'd leave the minute that she could stand and walk that far.

You should wait until you're strong enough, Stefan announced in exasperation.

She smiled tiredly. *That would be sensible, but just think...you wouldn't recognize me then.*

No, but I'd be totally okay with you trying the sensible route once in a while. Especially if it would keep you safe.

"Well, I'm not strong enough to walk across the room yet."

Good thing. You also need to speak with Ronin.

She bolted upright – only to cry out as her head started pounding. When the pain eased, she threw back her covers for a second time. Dizzy or not, she did need to speak with Ronin. *I'll call him. I have a name and a twist in this psycho situation.*

Good. And I have another piece of art. I sent it to him a few moments ago.

"Do I get to see it?"

You need to. Confirm if it's your Fez character.

She gasped. *You did it.*

Maybe. Not sure it's a decent likeness. Had no idea cats saw in that perspective. Grays and blacks.

I know. But her night vision has been a blessing in the dark.

Tabitha...

She froze at the warning tone in Stefan's voice. *What? What do you know?*

I saw you early this morning. You were trying to say something about your grandfather's box.

She straightened, her mind racing. *My father has it. There were documents in it. I thought he'd need it to handle the estate. Then this nightmare with the tiger started and it slipped my mind.*

It's important. Find out what's in it. Having said what he needed to, Stefan slipped away.

She searched the room for her cell phone and found it on the little portable table.

She dialed Ronin and got his voice mail. Rather than leave a message, she redialed. Again, there was no answer.

Calling the Center, she caught up on work with Wendy and learned about the sabotaged fence.

That was majorly bad for a lot of reasons, but the biggest was that normally that type of disturbance on the reserve was something her psychic radar should have picked up on, on an energetic level. The mess with Trinity was screwing her energy radar around. If she'd overlooked that incident, what else might she have missed?

At least the lynx hadn't run from the pens, which meant the protective energy she used to calm the animals had worked – partially at least. *Please let the new security system have caught this person on camera.* She pressed Roman's number on her phone to see what he knew.

"Tabitha," he said. "Sorry to hear you're in the hospital."

"Me too. I'm on my way out of this damn place. Never to return, if I can help it." She went on to explain about the vandalism and the location and asked about the cameras in that area. The damaged pens were on the side of the center but reached back into the trees.

"Do you have someone else who can check the feeds while you are in the hospital?" He paused. "I'll check mine here, and I can send it to Ronin. If there isn't a feed, I'll run by this afternoon and make sure all the cameras are working."

She frowned. "I'm on my way there so will check it out first thing. This has to stop. I seem to be plagued with problems on all sides."

"Maybe it's all the same problem."

"Maybe." Distracted, Tabitha hadn't realized she'd made it to the cupboard and pulled out a large paper bag with her belongings in it. She dressed quickly.

With a last glance around the empty room, she slipped out the door and down the hallway to the exit. Like hell she was sticking around. She had to pay the bill, but she could call them from home.

Outside, weak but gaining strength with every breath of fresh air, Tabitha searched the parking lot for a cab.

Only to have a truck pull up in front of her.

Ronin.

With a stern look, he asked, "Going somewhere?"

RONIN STUDIED TABITHA. She looked terrible.

He didn't know if he should show her the pictures he'd printed off right now or later.

Stefan had sent him a new one. He'd passed it around the office but no one recognized the guy's face. A black and gray sketch of a man's head and shoulders showed. The man could have been sleeping except for what appeared to be a pool of blood at the top of his skull. If he wasn't dead, he wasn't in good shape either. His pudgy cheeks sagged and his eyes were closed, adding to the corpselike look.

According to the email, this was one of Trinity's guards. He thought about the next part of the email. Then he'd been thinking about that part a lot. Stefan had said, 'Tabitha saw the image through the tiger's eyes and I could see this variation through my connection to her.'

How was that possible?

Tabitha slumped in the corner, her eyes closed. He wanted to bring her up to date on all he'd been doing to try to find the tiger. But would telling her he still had no solid leads depress her more?

He'd tracked the phone number the homeless man had left behind down to someone who dealt in the black market, and he was hunting him now. There'd been no answer at the end of the phone, and given that this guy dealt in what he dealt in, maybe that was normal. He wouldn't have recognized Ronin's number.

Ronin had been on his way to the office when he decided to swing by the hospital. He'd just had the feeling that he should go…

Damn good thing he did.

Because she looked like walking death. He cast another glance at her slumped in the corner of the truck and wondered if he should just turn around and take her back to the hospital.

STEFAN STOOD IN his studio staring at his blank canvas.

He'd tried a lot of odd and original stuff lately. That was the one thing about psychic abilities – there really was no level of comfort, of knowing the capability of your skills because they were forever changing. Forever growing. He'd done things in this last month that he'd never considered possible – stuff he'd never considered doing before. His abilities never put a judgement on such things. He could only try something when the idea struck him and often, new things didn't work the first time. If he gave it a rest and tried again a few days or weeks later, sometimes it did work. It was as if his first attempt was more a notice to his abilities, telling them that this was something he wanted to be able to do. Informing his skills and abilities that the next time he tried this he wanted it to work. So the ability had to evolve the new maneuver. And yes, Stefan had no illusions of how people would react if he tried to talk to them about this.

Thankfully his group of like-minded friends was growing. As were the crazy situations.

Look at this Tabitha nightmare. A tiger had actually psychically grabbed her with enough desperation that Tabitha had been helpless to resist. In fact, that had been the first time Stefan had any understanding of the power of an animal's will. His friend Sam, who lived just out of town, could help see the injuries sustained by an animal by connecting to the animal and seeing the damage. Tabitha connected to an animal on their energy level and worked her magic from there. That was the same method that Alex, another friend, used with plants. He himself did something similar with his garden but with a few other tricks thrown in.

Still, this was the first time he had seen an animal as the instigator in a psychic trauma. The connection was less Tabitha's energy work and more about her very intimate connection to Tango. He'd sensed yet another energy in her house, too. Although it appeared to belong and also appeared to be animal in nature, he couldn't help but wonder if that new energy wasn't connected to all this as well.

Or was it simply the new tiger's energy brought back to the house with Tabitha? Why and how? He had no idea.

He stared at his canvas and wondered what that idiom 'we're all connected' really meant. He'd been trying to paint from the images Tabitha sent, but could he connect to Tabitha and the tiger so he could see the man through the tiger's eyes and capture his face? If he could, this would be much more accurate.

How differently did a tiger see from a human? He knew there were differences but was not sure how that would all translate to his brain. To his own psychically artistic brain.

He picked up a paintbrush, surprised to realize he really wanted to know the answer to that question.

"DID YOU SEE it?"

Timothy had barely entered the fancy office when the man sitting behind an ornate desk jumped on him verbally. Add that hard stare and cold tone, and Timothy wished his damn tuition wasn't so hard to come by. It was obvious, this guy would slice his throat if he didn't like his answers. It was barely morning by the world's standards and Timothy hadn't gone to bed yet. This guy looked as he'd been up for hours already.

Then again, he ran his business like a captain ran his ship. Tight. Timothy had been approached by a middleman. Someone who'd found out that he'd checked the tiger over. Now he was reporting to the buyer. At least he hoped that's who was glaring at him. And if he'd realized who that boss was prior to this, he'd have walked away. As it was, he wanted to get the hell out now.

But as always – he needed the money.

"Yeah. I did." Timothy nodded. "The tiger didn't look bad at all. I don't know where the rumors came from, but the female was lying in a corner of the cage sleeping soundly when we arrived."

Silence. Timothy stood straight, knowing that to shift or show any uncertainty would possibly cause him more problems than this was worth.

"So there was nothing wrong with her?" The man leaned over the desk and gave him another hard look. As if lying to him would mean the end of Timothy.

Timothy had no wish to lie, but he didn't have much to add either.

"I didn't say that." Timothy shrugged. "I ain't no vet, just a pre-medical student, but she looked to be okay. There's an injury on her hip that could use a bit of attention, and a shot of antibiotics would probably help there. She had the remains of a good-sized bone in there covered in chew marks. So she's eating and I presume drinking after all this time." He held his hands out, palms up. "Honestly, she looked fine to me considering…"

He hesitated.

The man raised that snake gaze and held him captive. In a soft dangerous voice, he asked, "What is it?"

Timothy shrugged. "The blood tests said the tiger was pregnant."

The other man's gaze widened in surprise then settled with a satisfied look. "Is she now? That's very good to know." The man gazed out the window at the tiny rays of morning light creeping in. He absently said without turning around, "Could you identify the species?"

"Only that it was unlike anything I'd seen before. She was gray." The younger man didn't care and didn't want anything more to do with this. The tiger was alive and well and as far as he could tell, she didn't even appear to be under any stress. He figured he should tell this guy everything. He might get a bonus. "They are probably giving her something to keep her calm."

"Do you think so?" The boss's gaze sharpened and he nodded slowly. "Smart. She won't hurt herself by fighting this way."

"So we're good?" Timothy asked, backing toward the door. He just wanted to get the hell out of here.

The boss nodded. "For the moment. When we do the snatch, we'll need you to check her over." He pulled an envelope out of his pocket and handed it over. "I'll give you a call tonight or tomorrow. This needs to happen fast."

Timothy accepted the envelope. "No problem. I'm in class all week." Careful to keep the casual look on his face, he turned and walked out, choosing the stairs over the elevator.

He'd thought the warehouse where the tiger was kept was rundown and cold. Spoke of back room deals and shady clients. Bookie style. This guy and his rich-ass office probably owned this whole building. Well, what did he care? He carefully tucked the envelope beside the first one in his jacket pocket. Playing both sides might get him killed, but everyone had to make a living. Some of them did a better job at it than others.

Like him.

CHAPTER 17

Monday noon

BY THE TIME Ronin drove up to Tabitha's house, she was almost wishing she'd stayed in the hospital. Her energy had long since flagged. She watched the driveway appear and hoped Ronin knew to slow down. She wasn't antisocial, but she didn't appreciate uninvited visitors in her personal space and so hadn't made any improvements to the private driveway. It badly needed gravel. She ran a tight ship at the reserve and the animals never suffered, but to compensate, she barely kept back enough to live on. She took home the same salary as the other employees.

"Looks like you have company."

She straightened. "Oh hell," she murmured. "It's my father." That's the last thing she needed.

She ignored Ronin's sharp look as he parked beside her father's BMW. "Is that a problem?"

"Not always."

He hopped out and walked around to open her door. "He has keys?"

"Yes." She didn't add anything more. She didn't have the energy to spare. Ronin opened the front door. *Where was Tripod?*

She called out, "Dad?"

"In the back."

She walked through to the living room, wanting nothing more than to head to bed. Even the hospital bed sounded good right now.

Her father was sitting with Tango at his feet.

She felt Ronin come to a halt beside her. Right, the damn cat thing. "Dad, Ronin. Ronin, this is Dennis, my dad."

The two men nodded at each other. She watched her father's cool eyes assess Ronin. "Ronin is a detective." Perversely, she watched her father's eyebrows shoot up.

"You need a detective?"

She sighed. "Why are you here, Dad?"

"You collapsed again," he snapped, as if that were reason enough. And maybe that would be okay if they had a normal father-daughter relationship. But theirs was anything but normal.

"Wow, your intel is as sharp as ever."

"No need to be snippy." He frowned. "You know I only want what's best for you, right?"

"Sure." She walked over and bent down at Tango's side. He opened one eye and his big engine kicked in. She glanced around. "Where's Tripod?"

"I let him out back."

On cue, Tripod started barking like mad from Tango's room.

"Tripod!"

He arrived just as she finished speaking. He howled and jumped for joy.

Knowing she shouldn't encourage his bad behavior but unable to resist, she patted her shoulders and opened her arms wide.

He planted his front paws on her shoulders and proceeded to clean her face. She laughed until tears rolled.

"I do wish you wouldn't encourage him," her father said in exasperation.

Maybe that's why she'd done it. So it would piss him off. The older she got, the less grownup she appeared to be. With a last hug, she pushed Tripod down. As soon as she did, Tango jumped up and took Tripod's place.

Only Tango draped his forearms around the back of her neck and rubbed his head against her.

Tears welled up again. These last few days had been difficult. So close to the tiger and unable to hug her physically. Tango understood. She could feel the waves of empathy – sorrow even – roll off him. She hugged him hard and burrowed into his thick fur. Emotion hit her hard in waves of unending sadness. The old ailing female, her unborn cub, her grandfather and…Tobias, her grandfather's tiger that died six months ago.

She'd loved that old tiger. At the memory of her old friend, the tears started to pour. She tried to stifle the sound but knew her shoulders were shaking. No amount of control could still the shakiness. She just didn't have anything more inside.

A strong hand wrapped around her waist. Ronin – and he'd come this close to a cat. But she could see her father in front of her…and she didn't miss the look of disgust on his face.

She'd battled that look all her life. With her grandfather alive to run interference, she'd managed to ignore it as much as possible. These days, everything seemed to bug her.

Then she realized there was an unnatural stillness in the arms wrapped around her. Bone and pliant muscles had turned stiff, unyielding… A silent quest for dominance had suddenly reared its head.

"Easy, Tango."

Tango's eyes glittered. *Shit.*

"Ronin, back up slightly."

She sensed the unwillingness in him. What a time for Ronin to decide to face his fear.

"Tango?"

And felt his neck ripple and cord as he opened his mouth, a roar ripping from deep below.

After a long nerve-wracking moment, Ronin stepped back. But only a bit.

Still in the way of male animal, it might be enough. She sent warm loving energy to Tango. If she had to, she could drop him in an instant. Energy worked both ways, to heal and to hurt. Or in Tango's case, to discipline. When he was young, she'd been forced to overwhelm him to the point he couldn't move a time or two until he understood. She hadn't had to do it since.

Then everyone was off kilter and over protective right now. Between her father's energy and Ronin's energy, her own scattered space…everyone was acting out. "Tango…" She sent a strong mental warning to him. He howled. She scolded him. "Leave him alone; he's a friend."

He whined. Then he cocked his head and looked down at her like a petulant child denied a toy.

He dropped down and padded back to his pen to sulk. "Thanks, Tango."

Her father stood and watched as Tango headed through the flip panel to the outdoors. "That animal is dangerous," her father snapped. "He's going to kill someone one day."

"And yet you let him into the house to sit with you." She so didn't need this right now. Her emotions were too raw.

"He knows me." Her father turned to glare at Ronin. "He obviously doesn't know or like you. Since when do you try to challenge a tiger? If it wasn't for her, you'd have had your hands full."

Tabitha closed her eyes as her father started showing his testosterone.

Abruptly she turned and headed to the kitchen, Tripod at her heels.

She put on a pot of coffee, wondering if she was going to have to feed the men too. If so, too damn bad. She stared into her empty fridge, wondering if fuzzy blue cheese, eggs and wilted peppers would work as an omelet. Even the concept sounded bad. She slammed the door, stole a cup of coffee from the pot and turned to lean back against the counter. Closing her eyes, she let the steam bathe her tired eyes.

"Bedtime?" Ronin asked gently.

She laughed, a broken sound that came off harsh and cold. It wasn't his fault. And it wasn't fair to take it out on him. She pulled on her flagging energy and said, "It's too early, as much as I'd like to. I have to go to the office and touch base. Your brother might be coming by to check the cameras. And I need to assess the cut fence and go over the security feed."

"Isn't that why you have hired help?"

"Oh, that's funny." She took a sip of her coffee, loving the heat as it slipped down her throat. "New complex security system and new staff don't work well without training. And I haven't had time to complete that aspect. Soon." Very soon, she added to herself.

Ronin poured a cup of coffee for himself. "Do we offer your father a cup?"

"He doesn't drink coffee." And she didn't say anything more.

He studied her face. "Food? You haven't eaten."

She took another sip of coffee. "There isn't much of anything here to eat." And damn if that didn't bring tears to her eyes.

He put his cup down and then removed hers from her hands and placed it on the counter beside her. He tugged her into his arms and just held her.

She nestled in close, just wanting to hide away until she felt better. Until she was strong enough to handle the shit flying through her world. After a moment, she cleared her throat and looked up at him.

"Thanks."

He nodded and stepped back. He reached inside his coat pocket and pulled out several large pieces of paper folded many times over. "This probably isn't a good time to ask, but I'm not sure waiting is any better. I need to know... Do you recognize any of these?"

She took the first one from him and frowned at the image of a bloated dead man. "No."

He handed her another one. This time it was a series of derelict buildings backing up to a creek.

Again she shook her head and handed it back. "No. Not at all."

"And this is the third picture."

"That's Fez!" she said, "after he'd been attacked."

"Good. How about this last one?"

Another man lying down on the ground as if asleep.

She frowned and turned the paper slightly. "No, I don't think so."

"Damn." Ronin took the paper back and held it up to see it better.

"That's Bruce Tappet." Her father's voice spoke from behind her. "What the hell does that lowlife black market dealer have to do with my daughter?"

Bruce Tappet. Interesting. That was the name registered to the phone number he'd been given.

RONIN CHECKED HIS watch as he walked into the station. He'd told Tabitha she had two hours before he'd return to make sure she knocked it off for the day. He'd used up twenty minutes just getting to work. Plus he needed to shop if he hoped to get dinner tonight.

"About time you got here. Figured you'd gone on vacation or something." The laughing comment came from the left side of the hallway as soon as Ronin walked into the office.

He smiled good-naturedly at Carmichael. "Not likely." At his desk, he logged on to his computer and checked his emails. Nothing useful. He set up a search on the name of Fez and Bruce Tappet. There were no hits on Fez, but Tappet had a long record. Small stuff though. There was an address on record so Ronin wrote it down then he sent an email to the coroner, attaching the picture. A moment later he picked up the phone to call her personally. "Dr. Candace?"

"Well, well. So how's my favorite detective?"

"Looking to see if you can recognize a couple of faces. I just sent the sketches by email." He paused as he heard her click on the keyboard. "I'm thinking one might be your floater."

"Sketches? I presume your artist knew them personally then?"

Ronin laughed, but it was without humor. "If you knew Stefan, you wouldn't ask that."

"Stefan Kronos?" She clicked on several keys. "In that case, I'll take a look. That man is something else."

Not knowing if she was talking about Stefan's psychic skills, art skills or his good looks, he stayed quiet.

"Wow. Damn, he's good."

"Do you recognize any of them?"

"The last one is lying on my table right now."

"That man has been tentatively ID'd as Bruce Tappet." Ronin's heart sank. He'd been hoping the guy wasn't dead. Hard to get answers from a corpse.

"Nothing tentative about it. His fingerprints are a match. According to Detective Carmichael Woodrow he's got a long rap sheet."

"When did you get him and do you have a cause of death?"

"Not yet." She gave a rasping cough. "I'll send you both copies of my report when I'm done."

As he put down the phone, Ronin had to wonder what his old friend's interest in Tappet was. He decided to find out. Carmichael's desk was empty. After giving the office a quick look over, Ronin opened his phone and called him. "Where are you?"

"Just leaving the parking lot. Why? What's up?"

"Bruce Tappet."

"Yeah, he met his maker a few days ago." Carmichael snorted. "His lifestyle finally caught up with him."

"Murdered?"

"Most likely. Waiting on the ME report. Why the interest?"

"He links to a smuggling deal I'm working on."

"Really." Carmichael snorted. "Well, he was the man for it. That man had his hands in damn near everything."

"So I've heard. What do you know about his dealings with rare animals?"

"Not much. Was he into that crap too? Then again, it's hardly a surprise." Carmichael added. "Anything anyone wanted, he could usually get. At least that's the word."

That was no help. "Okay. Good to know. Anyone handling his case? I wanted to check out his address, hoping for a lead." Ronin opened his notebook and double checked the address he had listed.

"I can take another look at the evidence." Carmichael coughed. "Let me know what you find. It's a mess. I figure some junkie tossed it first. The techs didn't find anything obvious so far. Then not all the tests are back yet."

"Will do." Ronin pulled the car keys from his pocket and headed to the parking lot. Finding the address where Tappet had lived was no problem. Ten minutes later, he was there.

Leaving his truck somewhere safe was the issue. The area was run down and poor. Old Bruce hadn't been doing all that well if this was his place. He double checked the number on the apartment building and walked to the ground-level corner apartment. The crime scene techs had been there and gone, so it should be empty. But in this neighborhood, there was no way to know for sure. He rapped on the door several times. Hard. There was no answer. He knocked again. When there was still no answer, he reached for the knob and gave it a twist. The door opened. Cautiously, he kicked it open with his foot and unbuckled his gun, calling out, "Hello. Anyone home?"

No answer. He entered slowly to find that he wasn't the first person to check out the apartment. Tossed was right. The single couch had been dumped on its back and the upholstery had been slashed. The cushions had received the same treatment. Newspapers and takeout-food containers were strewn across the floor. The coffee table and small kitchen table and chairs were tossed randomly across the floor. The single bedroom apartment was small and dirty, the smell so rank the odor leached into the walls. It had been in this condition for a while.

Ronin walked into the bedroom and it was in a similar state. Someone had gone through everything here very carefully. Had they been looking for something or were they just pissed that Bruce didn't have what they wanted?

Either way, there wasn't much left. There was no desk or laptop, tablet, or cell phone that he could find. He moved the mattress and kicked through much of what lay on the floor. The closet was full of dirty laundry and boxes and bags. But so much had been dumped in a heap. He picked through it, hoping for something useful. If Bruce had been smuggling tigers, there'd have been records somewhere.

But Ronin was too late.

He gave the room as close a go over as he could but found nothing. He shouldn't be surprised. If it had been important, the man would have kept it well hidden. Or…Tappet still had it on him when he died.

Ronin grabbed his phone and called Dr. Candace. "Did Bruce Tappet have a notebook on his person when he was brought in?"

"I have no idea. Let me look."

Ronin could hear sounds of her rustling with something in the background. "There was nothing in the clothing and nothing listed on his file."

Damn. "All right. Thanks for looking."

He hung up. With a last glance around, Ronin left the room.

As he closed the door behind him he realized he had just enough time to pick up some groceries and get back to Exotic Landscape on time.

He hadn't even made it to the car when his phone rang. Dr. Candace.

"It was in his boot."

CHAPTER 18

Monday afternoon

THE ANIMAL SMELLS hit her first. Acrid, wet woolliness and yeah, fear swamped her as she walked inside the office of her beloved reserve for the first time in days. She'd taken the long way around to say hi to many of the animals. Now inside, she could hear sounds from the medical rooms in the back. It was surgery day. She should have been in there taking care of business. The will was there but her strength was not. Still, she walked to the door and peered inside. Her new vet, Zane, was treating an injury on a dog.

"There you are." Sue's voice broke her concentration. Tabitha turned and was engulfed in a warm hug. Tears collected in the corners of her eyes.

"I'm glad to be back," Tabitha admitted, "even if it's only on a part-time basis for a day or two."

"You should be in bed." Sue led her to her office and pushed her gently into her seat. "I've been coming into the office to help out, so the workload shouldn't be that bad. Please don't overdo it. I'm going to grab you a cup of coffee." And she raced away.

Tabitha logged into her computer and settled in to get a few hours of paperwork done. She doubted Ronin would be late, so she set aside some work to take home.

First she needed to see the security feed. Bringing it up, she forwarded it to the right day and time. She watched in shock as the male dressed all in black walked to the lynx pen and cut the wires. There was something off about the figure. She didn't do people readings the same as she did animals and that was too bad right now. He carried himself like a young man with a spring in his step and he didn't appear to require much effort on his part to nip the wires. That interested her as that was heavy gauge steel. It shouldn't have been that easy. She wanted to groan at the ease with which he destroyed the barrier.

Interesting that he walked away without attempting to touch the animals. They were hidden in the back of the pen. She leaned forward. *There.* The man jerked around as if he heard something. Then he raced away. Interrupted most likely. She had security guards. Chances were good one was on his rounds at that hour. She needed to show this to Ronin.

Had this man acted alone? Or had there been another man waiting by the vehicle, or worse, causing damage to another pen? She clicked through the different camera feeds looking – but no…there was no one else. She slumped back.

The man had just cut a chunk of fence then disappeared. If he'd intended to steal the animals, that would be a different story altogether. She'd have to wonder if he was connected to Trinity's smuggling. Speaking of which, she didn't have all that long before she'd have to go back and check on Trinity to reinforce the energy keeping her calm.

Sue came in with her coffee. Tabitha asked, "Did you watch the feed?"

Sue nodded. "Yes. I'm presuming it's someone still trying to make trouble for the Center."

Her mind puzzled over the video feed. There was some-thing…almost familiar about the person she'd viewed. But she wasn't sure what it was about him that tweaked her memory.

As she mulled over the problem of who this man was, she buried herself in work. The door opened.

Ronin.

"Ready to go?"

Surprised to realize it had been more than three hours since he'd dropped her off, she nodded and stood up stiffly. "Take a look at this first."

"Your dad said not to be late." He sat down to watch the feed.

She paused. "He's still there? Maybe that's a good thing. I need to ask him about a box he took from my father's desk. Stefan said it was important.

That caught his attention. He raised his eyebrows. "In that case we need to know what's inside that box. Your father had an overnight bag in the front hall. I'm thinking he's planning on sticking around for a few days."

He returned his attention to studying the feed. "Damn little useful here. I'll call Roman see if he hasn't anything clear enough to print a couple of images off for me." He stood up. "Let's go. Your father is cooking."

She shook her head at that. *Why would he stick around?* It had been years since she'd slept under the same roof as her father. Unless it had something to do with Grandpa's death? And the future of the place. Had her grandfather changed the paperwork? Would she lose the Center? Her heart squeezed tight. Her grandpa wouldn't have pulled a fast one on her. Surely not. He'd loved her. This was her place. But it had also been his. Worried, she hardly noticed when Ronin parked the truck in front of her house and hopped out.

She followed slowly, her mind worrying about her future and her animals.

Her stomach, now devoid of food, cramped tight, and a shakiness worked its way up her legs. Hating the fearful thoughts overwhelming her common sense, she entered the house to find wonderful smells coming from the kitchen. She had no idea when she'd last eaten, but the smells highlighted how empty she was.

She took a deep breath and walked into the kitchen. Tripod greeted her as always, his comforting yelps of welcome and his soothing, caring energy so happy to see her. She crouched down and hugged him. The love so freely given helped ease the rawness inside. After his boisterous greeting, she straightened and walked over to her father, who appeared to be making chilli. In spite of her worries, her stomach growled.

"Dad, why are you still here?" She hadn't meant it to sound like an accusation but it slipped out that way. There'd been a lot of that in their relationship. Accusations and miscommunication. With her grandfather gone, her father had lost the chance to mend fences with him. But for everything else it meant a whole new day.

Especially for her and her father.

His back stiffened, the only indication that he'd heard her. "The chilli is almost done. Start setting the table, please."

With a look at his blank face, she slowly complied, hating the sense of impending doom.

"Can I help?" Ronin asked. He stepped in front of her, taking the plates from her hands. "I'll put these down. Maybe you could get the rest of the stuff."

She nodded and rushed to the sideboard for the cutlery. She didn't know what was wrong, but something was bothering her father. She wanted to ask him but the words wouldn't come out.

Tripod was underfoot and she accidentally kicked him. He yelped and bounded out of the way. She stopped and leaned her head back. *Damn. Sorry, Tripod.* She sent him soft, loving, apologetic energy. *I didn't mean to hurt you.* His response as always was generous and accepting. He whimpered from the side.

She bent and hugged him. "Sorry baby." Tripod and Tango, like all animals, were sensitive to moods and tension, and she'd been the one he was responding to. To her fear, her emotional pit and her energy blocks. The animal in him could do no less than respond. He leaned into her hug, almost knocking her over. She laughed. He woofed and wagged his tail happily.

Feeling better, she stood up and turned around. The table was set and her father had already served dinner.

Ronin held her chair for her – a nice gesture.

She opened her mouth to ask her father about the estate when he said, "Your grandfather's will is a bit convoluted."

Her appetite drained away as he spoke.

"It shouldn't be," she said. "I saw it a couple of months ago." She paused, remembering Stefan's message. "I gave you a box from Grandpa's desk. Full of his papers. Have you been through it yet?"

"No. I took a brief look but it didn't appear to be legal documents, so I left it for later."

"I need to see it," she said abruptly, her gaze sliding to Ronin.

His gaze widened in understanding. "It would be good if we could see that box tonight, if possible. It might have a connection to the break-ins going on at the center."

"Connected to the break-ins?" Her father stared at her, open-mouthed, then adding, "Tonight?"

Tabitha nodded. "As soon as possible. There could be something in there regarding the will, too. Maybe it will have the information you need to help out with the estate stuff."

"That would be good." Her father nodded. "He had some bequests for people, but not much in the way of contact information for them."

"And you can't find them?" Ronin asked as he lifted a spoonful of chilli to his mouth.

"Not so far."

"Like who?" Tabitha asked.

"Jumbo. Now a last name would help, for a start."

Tabitha laughed. "That's so Grandpa. I have Jumbo's contact information. If he's still alive." She shrugged. "I haven't seen him in a couple of years."

Her father frowned. "And Chester."

"Chester is another old carny buddy, but I'm pretty sure he died of cancer last summer."

"That's what I mean. How am I supposed to find these people?" her father complained.

"Is that why you're here?" she asked. "To find out about his friends?"

Her father's face lowered and he played with his food. So obviously not. She put her spoon down and looked at him. "What's wrong? Is there something in the will that I'm not going to like?"

His eyes opened wide in shock. "No. Not at all. The house is yours. Exotic Landscape is yours. There's a little cash but…" He looked at her apologetically. "Not much."

She snorted. "That's nothing new." She smirked. Inside she smiled with relief. The place *was* hers. Thank God. "Grandpa never had much."

Leaning back, she closed her eyes briefly. The panic started to un-knot, the band around her chest loosening, and she opened her eyes. "Thanks, I needed to hear that."

With a shake of his head, he smiled reassuringly. "Sorry, I should have made that clear right from the beginning. He had more than you think. I've been trying to get him to invest for years. We'll need to talk about what you want to do with it, but you aren't destitute."

Removing her hand from her heart, she sighed happily. "I have a roof over my head and the animals are safe, so we're good."

"This house needs some work," he said. "A new paint job inside and out. New furniture. I bet the plumbing needs to be updated."

She snorted. "As you said, there isn't much money." She swallowed her mouthful. "Besides, I'm not ready to make changes."

"Don't wait too long. I know you loved him, but it's time to make this space yours and not just live in his house."

She tilted her head. Interesting choice of words. "Is that what you felt, Dad? That it was never your home? That is was always his?"

"It *was* always his house. I didn't live here long enough to change that."

His words rang true, but there was something more going on here. But what? She knew little about her father's friends, his likes, his dislikes. Except for his business associates like Eric and Germaine. She'd heard a lot about those two. Then her father had a talent for business. He was good at making money, but not at relating to her.

Or she to him.

"You never really felt at home with him," she said intuitively. "The house had nothing to do with it."

His face set and he refused to meet her eyes.

"Why was that? What was so wrong between you two? I get that you don't like animals in the same way as I do, but there's got to be something else there. Something that drove a wedge between you two."

He gave a mocking laugh. "Everything was black and white with him. Right or wrong. His way or the highway." He stabbed the contents of his bowl viciously. "I chose the highway."

Tabitha stared, shocked. She knew the two hadn't been close but hadn't realized the level of animosity. It saddened her. Her grandfather had been everything to her. Her father almost nothing. *Why was that?*

"Was it me?" If it was, that would make her feel worse, but she'd rather know now. She'd lost her grandfather. She didn't want to lose her father as well.

"What?" He shook his head. "No. Not at all." For the first time since they sat down, he smiled at her warmly. "He was very happy to have you."

"Well, whatever your problem with grandpa was, it's over. He's gone." And damn if she didn't feel the tears collecting in the corner of her eyes again. She sniffled them back. "It's time to make peace with whatever it is and move on."

"That's what I'm hoping to do here and now," her father said without looking up.

She looked at him in surprise, her full spoon halted in midair. "*With me?* What do I have to do with it?"

She glanced over a Ronin who sat eating quietly across from her. He listened but stayed out of the conversation. That was probably wise. She turned her attention back to her father.

"In a way, everything." He put his spoon down and dabbed his mouth clean. Then he put the napkin down. Tabitha slowly put her spoon back and waited Whatever this was, it was big. And difficult.

She studied him closely for a long moment. Unable to handle the suspense much longer, she asked, "What's wrong, Dad?"

He took a deep breath, raised his eyes to stare at her and said, "The real reason my father and I never got along…" He gave a short laugh. "We had a huge fight about it. Once he knew the truth…well…I think he honestly hated me." He stopped, glanced at Ronin, then back at her. "I told him…"

She prodded. "Told him what?"

With his gaze locked on her face, he said, "I told him I was gay."

AS BOMBSHELLS WENT, this one was big. Like over the top, completely re-evaluate your life type of big. Ronin kept quiet, but he watched the shock dawn on Tabitha's face. Only it didn't appear to be as big a shock as he might have expected. *Had she known? Had she any inkling?*

He couldn't imagine hearing that himself. From a close friend, sure. Even a sibling. But from a parent? Wow. Having no parents himself, he didn't have an understanding of how that relationship would work.

Both Tabitha and Ronin had been raised by their grandfathers. But for different reasons.

The silence at the table grew and he realized that perhaps he should leave. Give them privacy. No one said anything to him. In fact, they were oblivious to his presence, but he felt as if he was in the way. He polished off his chilli and damn, it had been good. He realized he had a perfect excuse.

He stood up and said into the shocked silence, "You cooked, so I'll do the dishes. Tabitha, eat up."

"Don't worry about it, Ronin. I'll do them," Tabitha said, her eyes never leaving her father's face.

He walked over to her side and nudged her plate closer. "No, you won't. One, you should be in bed, and two, you have more important things to work on right now."

Ronin walked to her father's side and collected his empty plate. "Thank you. It was excellent, by the way." Loaded with dishes and silverware, Ronin headed to the kitchen.

Whew. There were some times when people really should be alone.

This was that time for them. And he'd be happy to clean up. He'd seen the kitchen earlier, enough to know that Dennis was a decent cook and cleaned as he went, so whatever washing up that was left would be minimal.

Maybe by the time he was done, they'd have worked through their differences, and they could put their heads together to solve at least some of the problems facing them.

In fact, he wanted action. Not this damn waiting for something to happen. He'd found many leads, but there was nothing concrete. His mind went back to the mess at Tappet's house.

What had the person been looking for? The coroner had the book she'd found in Tappet's boot, but it was in code. She'd sent it to the lab. It would be analyzed, and if there was time, someone would try to decipher the code. All she'd added was that she'd seen a lot of WC listed. That meant nothing to anyone he'd asked. He'd already requested to have the pages scanned and sent to him. With any luck, they would be waiting for him when he logged onto his email.

That wasn't all. This was a busy and frustrating day. He'd already run Fez's name through the databases and come up with nothing.

So far the search for a Timothy, vet or pre-med student, was resulting in a huge list. He needed something to narrow it down. There were just too many to contact personally.

There were so many elements at play. The tiger on the black market connected to Tabitha. The break-ins at Exotic Landscape. The man on the video cameras. If he'd been wanting to release the lynx, why hadn't he taken them?

If he hadn't wanted them, then why did he bother to cut the pen open?

"Maybe he put something into the pen?" he murmured to himself. Considering that idea, Ronin thought about all the things that could have been slipped into the pen without showing up on the surveillance camera. And dismissed the idea. The staff had searched the pens for the animals, and would have noticed anything majorly different.

He checked the time then called his brother.

"How's Tabitha doing?" Roman asked.

"She can't keep this up. Hell, she was slim before but now she's one step away from being gaunt."

"I can imagine." Through the phone, Ronin could hear his brother sigh. "Okay brother, what do you need?"

"Did you get the security system checked out on Exotic Landscape?"

"I did. There are some uncompleted sections, but that's all part of the new office expansion happening in the back of the building."

Had he heard anything about that? Ronin wasn't sure. "I don't think she wanted everything monitored. She's operating this as a reserve, not a zoo."

"Except she needs to bring in donations to keep the place running, and live web cams bring an audience. That brings in money." Roman continued. "But they also bring in the bottom feeders. These camera feeds clearly show where the animals are located."

Ronin ran his fingers through his hair. "There is decent security, strong fences and as much as most people might want to keep these animals, to go and stealing them is a much bigger step than most of the general public is willing to take."

"And that other level of the world already has suppliers for these animals." Roman's voice deepened. "I'm getting the feeling that the two incidents aren't related."

"So do I. And that just pisses me off. I'm not making any headway on finding Fez or figuring out how Tappet was connected to Tabitha's tiger."

"Black market specialist, Bruce Tappet? What's going on with him?"

Ronin brought his brother up to speed.

"So someone offed Bruce. No surprise there. He was working for Colby."

Ronin's gaze widened. "Winston Colby? Jesus, I forgot about him."

"You don't want to do that. Turn your back on that guy and you'll get you head cut off."

That's when he remembered Tappet's code book and the multiple WC entries.

CHAPTER 19

Monday late afternoon

TABITHA STARED AT her father, shocked, confused…and yes…she felt betrayed. How long had he kept this bottled up inside? Telling her years ago would have helped them both?

She'd been very close to her grandfather, but she'd turned to him because she had no one else. In her heart, she'd wanted her father. But he hadn't wanted her. That had been her belief.

With his disclosure, she felt her whole childhood being flipped. Her surety disintegrating.

He sat across from her, staring at her steadily. Those soft gray eyes willing to accept whatever judgement she'd placed on him.

What he must have gone through.

Her grandfather hadn't been an easy man. In fact he'd been damn hard. Unyielding. And no way in hell would he have accepted his son's sexual orientation.

But times had changed. At least for other people. For her grandfather, his best days had been while he was in the circus. He'd loved the life. Loved the people. When he left the circus community, he'd changed. Or maybe it had happened after Tabitha's grandmother passed away. In recent years the animals were the only things he'd continued to love and he'd forever reminisced about the good old days.

If her father had grown up in today's world, he'd likely have found acceptance amongst his peers. Forty years ago, the phenomenon hadn't quite started.

"I'm sorry."

His gaze widened. That was obviously not what he'd expected to hear.

Then again, it was not what she'd expected to say.

She took a deep breath and clarified. "I'm sorry that grandfather felt so threatened that he couldn't accept the truth. I'm sorry you felt so threatened you couldn't share the truth with me. And…I'm sorry for me."

Then she added in a soft voice, "I spent a lot of my childhood wondering what was wrong with me that you didn't care enough to be around. What was wrong with me that I was so unlovable? I turned to animals, like Grandpa, because they loved me back. Unlike you."

A horrified sound ripped from his mouth. He leaned forward and covered Tabitha's hands with his and said, "There's nothing wrong with you. You're perfect. You always have been."

"And yet Grandfather raised me. You were never here," she accused, pain rising to the surface. "Ever."

"I couldn't." So concise, so clean, so cold.

She sat back and closed her eyes. "Tell me."

In a halting voice, this man who ran million-dollar corporations shared how hard it was when he told his father. How he'd been kicked out. How he'd been forced to leave the animals he'd loved and never come back. How he'd tried to be straight. How he'd wanted to be normal. And for a little while, he succeeded. With her mother…

"Then your mother and I broke up. She left and I tried to go out with other girls." He traced the wood grain in the tabletop. "I drank a lot. Experimented with anything and everything. I'm not proud of what I did, but I was hurting, and I did everything that would dull the pain and make me forget what I was." He took a deep breath. "And finally I realized I was lying to myself. I was never going to be normal. And my sexual orientation was never going to be 'normal' as per my father's standards."

He turned to look back at her. "When your mother arrived with you, the long and short of it is she came to me with a three-month-old baby and said that you were my responsibility."

"She walked out of your life and my life that day, and I knew I was no more equipped to raise you than she was. I was a mess," he admitted. "And my lifestyle was not safe for a baby."

He settled back in his chair to stare out the window moodily. He let out a broken laugh, but there was no humor in it. "Can you imagine? And my life back then…I was living in a house with four other party animals. There was booze and girls and guys and drugs everywhere." He turned to glance over at her. "I planned to get my life together, but it would take time and I knew here was the one place where you'd be safe. Where you'd have someone to love you. And where I could still be in your life. So here you are." He waved an arm around the room. "And the place still looks the same today as it did back then."

Tabitha had let him talk uninterrupted. She didn't know what to say or what to think. So much of her history needed to be rewritten. She had no problems with her father's sexuality. His explanation made sense and answered a lot of questions.

But not all of them. "Why didn't you take me home with you later when you started sorting your life out?" She tried to keep the hurt out, but a lifetime of holding it all in was hard and now that the dam was breaking, she needed to hear the answers.

"That was your grandfather. He said I was unfit to raise you and now that you were under his care, you'd stay here. I could visit, but I'd never again have custody." He traced a knot in the wooden table, his face twisting with old memories. "Unfortunately, my uncle, your grandfather's brother, was there at the time. He'd been a major part of our lives when I was growing up. But at that time, they were having some kind of major disagreement. Maybe he wouldn't have been such a hardass then if his brother wasn't around all the time feeding him venom. The thing is, once your grandfather set down rules, he never would reverse them." He shrugged as if shaking off the memories. As if he didn't care.

And she'd bet he'd cared a lot back then.

She didn't want to think about the legalities involved. Her grandfather had been a very interesting person. She had no memories of his brother. As far as she knew, he'd died when she was little. Her grandfather hadn't always been easy to live with, but there'd been one thing she'd never doubted. He'd loved her.

Maybe he'd needed her as much as she'd needed him. And maybe he'd felt as guilty over his son as his son felt over his own daughter.

Her grandfather had often spoken of his life in the circus, but never of his life with his son or any extended family. She'd had no idea if her father traveled with him or stayed elsewhere. Or had he come along later? She dredged through her memory banks, trying to figure out what she knew about her grandmother, and realized she was coming up blank. Just bits and pieces from her grandfather's stories.

"You aren't saying much."

Startled, she pulled herself back to the conversation. And him. She studied the uncertainty in his gaze, the tension around his mouth. This had to be hard for him. And liberating. For that she was glad. But she could do so much more. "For the record...I don't have a problem with you being gay. I want you to be happy." She smiled tentatively. "I just want you to be in my life."

His gaze warmed as she spoke. He tilted his head. "You can't possibly think I don't love you?"

She snorted. "As much as you're capable of, maybe. But from my perspective, there hasn't been very much of your love thrown my way. If you'd told me this a long time ago, it would have been much easier for both of us." She sighed. "I could have told you a long time ago that it didn't matter to me. That I loved you as you were."

"I couldn't," he admitted softly. "That was a promise I was forced to give my father. To never tell you. To never poison you with my twisted, perverted lifestyle."

"Ouch," she murmured. "He was very strong in what he believed was right and wrong."

"His version of it."

"And is that why you are finally telling me? He's dead and gone and can't judge you anymore?"

"I no longer need his permission." He smiled. "But I made a promise to him and I couldn't break it while he lived."

"That had to have been difficult," she murmured.

"The hardest thing was he wouldn't let you stay with me when you were younger because you might be influenced by me and my 'sordid' lifestyle."

She shook her head, her heart sad. "He missed out on so much."

"And so did I." Her father's voice thickened suspiciously. "And I have to ask: Has this happened too late?"

There was sheen to his eyes and she felt the answering moisture in her own eyes. God, what he had been through. What she'd been through. Because of a judgmental old man who couldn't handle his own fears. She'd loved her grandpa and that would never change, but he'd done his son wrong. She strongly believed there was plenty of love to go around. It was so sad that these two strong men hadn't believed in themselves or in each other.

And it was well past time for this to be cleared up. And laid to rest.

There was an uprising of emotion. A welling of pain bubbling up and over...to dissipate under the gift of acceptance. An ache from an old wound she'd barely recognized, having lived with it so long...began to ease.

And a freedom she hadn't recognized before as having been denied...opening.

She smiled. "Hello, Dad. Welcome to our new life together."

She reached out a hand.

He stood up, grabbed her hand and pulled her into his arms.

She burrowed in close, reveling in such a simple thing she'd missed all her life – her father's hug.

LATER THAT NIGHT Tabitha curled up in Ronin's arms. At Ronin's quiet insistence, her dad had left to get Grandfather's box. He had keys and when he returned would let himself back in, so they'd gone to bed.

To enjoy each other. She hoped. Her mind couldn't stop tossing and turning on her father's words. His life. Her life. How one thing had impacted so many? So not fair.

"You're thinking too loud," Ronin murmured. "Go to sleep. You need rest."

She turned her smile to his shoulder and kissed his hard muscled skin. "Not my fault," she murmured. "My mind's got a lot to work on."

Looking into his deep brown eyes, she shifted enough to let her hand glide down his hips and then up between their entwined legs. "But maybe I can think of something else."

Fire smoldered as he shifted restlessly under her touch. He slid his hand up her smooth long lean body, stopping to explore her ribs, before sliding higher to cup her breasts. Stoking the fire within, soothing, caring, promising. Finally he reached to tilt her chin up and lowered his mouth. He brushed her lips once, twice. Then followed with a deep melting kiss that left her wanting so much more.

He rolled onto his back, pulling her gently on top.

Smiling, she sat up, gently guided him into her. "Nice." She sighed. When she began to move, it was gentle. Easy. She loved that about Ronin, the big strong, take-charge cop had the ability to lie back and let her – take charge. It took a strong man to surrender. It took trust. And she hoped – love.

Needing more, he tugged her down for a long drugging kiss. She sighed, a low thrumming sound as pleasure slid through her. All thoughts left her mind. There were no more questions. No doubts. No insecurities. There was just now. Just him. Just them.

She surrendered to it. To him. To the moment. And let herself ride. Head back, eyes closed, she let the heat set the pace. When need pulsed through her, demanding action, she leaned over and framed his face, wanting to see the dark depths of his eyes.

And found them full of love. Her system overloaded with joy.

She cried out, arching her back.

His hands clenched her hips, holding her in place as he drove up inside her…once, twice. He twisted beneath her and shuddered with his own release.

God she loved that. Knowing she'd brought him this, that she accepted what he'd so freely offered... She leaned over and kissed him gently, before sliding down to lie beside him.

"So good," he murmured, lazy satisfaction in his voice. He tugged her up against him, his fingers drawing slow circles on her shoulders.

"Mmmm." She nuzzled his shoulder, happy and calm for the first time in... Since...? She had no idea since when.

Peaceful silence stretched between them. She yawned sleepily. Tired, but not tired enough to sleep, she wanted to enjoy the moment. The closeness.

"That was a good thing you did tonight," he said quietly, "for your father.

What? For a moment there, she'd wondered what he was talking about. She twisted her head so she could see his face. "I didn't do anything."

"And that makes it even more special."

She stared up at him, puzzled.

"Your acceptance. Not many people would have given it so quickly or so easily."

She smiled and nestled closer. "It was awkward but it explains so much. I truly am happy for him. To live one life but desperately want another for yourself... That would be hard."

"Sounds like his early life was tough."

"His teen years," she correctly gently. "As a child, he'd have been fine. My grandfather loved him. It would have started once he understood he was different."

His heart beat a steady tempo under her ear, his body heat was warm and cozy. She yawned. "I desperately need a good night's sleep."

"Then sleep."

"I will, but..." She winced, knowing he'd have a hard time with this. "But I need to check on Trinity. Reinforce her energy so she stays calm."

He'd stiffened at her initial words, his arm tightening around her.

"Is that safe?"

"Yes," she answered honestly. "We have to find her. This connection I have with her... It could be very dangerous if she dies and I'm still in her heart line."

"Heart line?"

"A bond that could take me with her," she added softly.

"Then I'd better get back to work."

He started to rise.

She pushed him back. "You need rest too."

"I need to find this tiger. I have several leads, but nothing concrete."

"I'll go reinforce the tiger's energy. You get some sleep. Then I'll sleep and you work."

At that suggestion, he lay back down. She hoped he'd sleep – they both needed it, but she had things she had to do. She'd left it too long. The feeling came over her suddenly. That inner knowing that she'd cut her time short. Possibly too short.

Shuddering, she closed her eyes and opened her inner vision. She knew the pathway now. She jumped free and raced to Tango. He slept soundly. His energy rippled and shifted like quicksand, absorbing her into his own. The acceptance warmed her heart all the way to her soul. She grounded herself mentally and emotionally before returning to the energy highway that would lead back to her aging female tiger. Tabitha closed the gap faster and faster, and then slowed down as she reached Trinity. She dropped into the huge cat.

She sighed and stretched, feeling so feline and graceful inside. That she was truly one with a tiger was a wondrous thing. It produced a feeling like no other. She opened her eyes and smiled.

The tiger lay calm and peaceful in a corner of the cage. Her stomach gurgled loudly. "At least you've eaten, milady," Tabitha murmured gently, easing the energy to the meridian relating to the stomach region. The noises eased. The tiger stretched out with a contented sigh. Tabitha loved the feel of the power in the long legs, the big toes that stretched, then curled gently.

Such a different body. Such a different experience. Murmuring softly, she stroked and soothed, reinforced and calmed the tiger's meridians along with her aura. The tiger was doing so well.

In the background, she heard noises. There'd been something earlier, but it was low key so she hadn't recognized it. Now the noise level had risen. Men. Arguing.

And coming closer.

Tabitha poured out soothing energy for her sake as well as for the tiger's. She didn't recognize the voices. *No. Wait.* One of the men was Fez. So he was fine after all. Too bad. She'd have liked him to suffer for his part in this.

"I want to move her because of the change in plans. I didn't go to all this trouble to lose her at this stage." A cold chilling voice slipped through the air. Hushed but authoritative...

Tabitha knew she'd have no trouble recognizing it again. She tried to search through the darkness. Trinity's vision was excellent at night time, but the cover on the cage was absolute. Almost. She managed to coax Trinity to stand up and walk over to stare out between the slight parting of the covering. She could hear Fez talking. "Maybe beef up the security?"

"You are the security. Why would I add more than you and Keeper?"

"Because we can't always be together. Because they know we're here. And because I was attacked."

"You're the idiot who allowed someone to sneak up on you." The boss snorted. "Maybe you're the problem."

Silence.

Tabitha grinned to herself. A falling out among thieves.

"If you'd seen your attacker, at least we'd have some idea of who was after her. The question is why?" This last bit was added thoughtfully.

Tabitha watched as Fez walked into view. He winced involuntarily with every step he took. It was obvious he needed to lie down. Or go see a doctor, at least. His head was covered in dried blood.

"You're thinking the buyer might have been checking her out on his own?" Fez shrugged. "Why? Because he probably didn't believe your story."

There was an uncomfortable emptiness in the air. Tabitha could only hope these two would do or say something that would help her out.

"No one," the boss said in a silky voice — a spider to a fly, "is going to screw this up."

Tabitha held her breath. Now that man scared the crap out of her.

"No one will," Fez stepped into her line of vision again. He was holding his head. "I don't feel good."

"A bashing over the head will do that." As if making a sudden decision, the boss said, "Stay here."

Clip. Clip. Clip. "I'll be back in a few minutes." And a door shut. Quietly. Too quietly.

Tabitha wondered if Fez knew his days were numbered. She didn't think anyone screwed up twice with this boss.

And apparently getting hit over the head was akin to screwing up.

RONIN SWORE HE could tell when she left her body. And didn't that stretch his sense of reality? What part of her had she left? And what part of her had left? These were questions that he couldn't answer, but they reverberated in his mind. Her body, still draped over his, had become…boneless. It was weird because it was more than as if she were asleep. It's as if she had died except her chest still rose and fell in a relaxed manner. Her color looked normal; her breathing sounded normal; but she didn't *feel* normal.

He wanted to get up and go to work. Sleep was the furthest thing from his mind now.

Tabitha needed to get back fast. That something could go wrong and he'd never know… He didn't want to dwell on that.

He couldn't believe what he'd seen and done these last few days. But there was one person who could possibly help him deal with his cat problem. If he would.

Reaching out gently so as to not disturb Tabitha, he snagged up his phone and called Stefan.

"Hey, I'm hoping you can help me." He stopped, not really sure how to start. Should he even ask? At least Stefan might be able to give him answers no one else could. And he needed to deal with this fast – if he could. He tried again. "I have a little problem."

"Really?" Stefan murmured, humor in his voice. "I'm not a counselor."

"Damn. Not that kind of problem," he growled. "Another problem. A problem from my past. At least Tabitha suggested it might be from there…if such a thing is possible."

"What type of problem?"

"Cats. I get a weird reaction when I'm around cats…" He winced, took a deep breath and explained what happened when he came close to them. He groaned. "Most of the time it's no big deal, but around Tabitha…" He gave a bitter laugh. "And if I tell myself that often enough, I might believe it."

"And what do you want from me?" Stefan asked.

"I wondered…" Ronin paused and stared moodily at the ceiling of Tabitha's bedroom. "If you can see inside my mind…my history, my energy… Is there anything in there that would explain this?"

"Interesting problem." Stefan's voice grew distant, thick in an odd way. Ronin wasn't sure what to make of it.

"What does that mean?" he joked. Even admitting there was a problem was hard.

But necessary.

Whoa. Stefan was in his head again. Ronin stared nonplussed at the phone in his hand. Should he just hang up?

Give me a moment, murmured the whisper in his ear.

"Yeah, sure. Take your time." Yet…he couldn't help but hold his breath. It was such a weird feeling. He could sense Stefan's progress through his mind. Like a cat creeping up on a mouse to trap it. A shudder rippled down his spine.

Thanks. Can't say I've ever been called a cat before.

Ronin winced. Shit. "Sorry, but having you move around in my head, it's a similar feeling to a spider on my arm. Raises the hairs on the back of my neck too."

Hmmm. Interesting.

"What? What's interesting?" he asked cautiously. "As in the stuff about the cats is interesting or something else?" He waited, but no more was forthcoming. "Stefan? Is something wrong?"

No, there isn't. At least not the way you are suddenly concerned. You don't have a cancer eating away at your physical body, but a kind of fear has been eating away at your psyche. Interesting. You play music, huh?

Ronin frowned. "Yeah. Both my brother and I do. How did you know that?"

I can see it in your energy. It's how you soothe your soul. And… He gasped. A gasp so loud that Ronin sat up, accidentally shifting Tabitha's position beside him. "What?"

Then Stefan chuckled. It started as a simple light laugh and transformed into a full-on belly laugh. The waves of laughter rolled through Ronin's mind. It was contagious. He grinned. "Well, I'm not sure what you're doing in there, but I'm thinking it can't be all bad."

Oh, it's not bad at all, Stefan gasped when he could finally talk. *In fact, it's bloody perfect. And it confirms that just like your brother and regardless of how you feel about it — you are psychic. And the reason you are terrified of cats…is you're being haunted by one!*

FEZ WATCHED THE boss walk away. For several moments, it had appeared there were two men standing, his vision had been so blurry. It had been all he could do to speak clearly. He knew he wasn't thinking clearly or he'd have disappeared already.

Damn. He took several shaky steps to sit down on a nearby crate. If his days were numbered before, now he figured he could count his life in hours if that tiger died. If he could just hold on for a week.

He shuddered. This was not how he'd planned to get the hell out of here.

He stared at the cage and its contents. What had seemed like a simple transport job had gone sour. Why? Why couldn't she just be handed off to the buyer? Greed, of course. All because the tiger was pregnant. So a bigger payday. It was one thing to sell her for that price when she was old and ailing, but now… Yeah, the boss had gotten greedy.

Determined to take a closer look, he stood up slowly, bracing himself on the wall, and made his way to the cage.

He pulled back the drape and let light into the cage. A growl started, but it came out without any heat.

"Have you given up, girl?" Fez said painfully. "I don't blame you. I'm almost there myself."

He tried to study her, but she kept wavering in and out of focus. He swore he saw a woman in the cage with her.

He leaned closer and blinked several times.

CHAPTER 20

Monday evening

TABITHA STARED INTO the injured man's eyes. Could Fez see her? No. Not possible. She gave herself a good shake. There was no way. But of course there was a way. So often psychic powers lay dormant for decades until some trauma woke them up. She didn't know what the reason could be in this guy's case, but it sure seemed as if he was seeing her inside Trinity.

His next words proved it.

"Hey, lady. Are you all right?"

What a question. Was she all right? *No.* But how could she make him understand that?

And could he hear her? If he could see her…

"No. I'm not all right, you asshole," she finally said in exasperation. He reared back and slapped a hand over his mouth.

She wanted to do the same. *Holy shit.* He could hear her. Stunned, she stared back into his shocked eyes.

Fez swung his head in a slow bullish manner. "No. No. This can't be so. I musta had a bigger knock on my noggin' than I thought."

"Oh, you heard me all right. What's the matter, have you never seen a woman trapped inside a tiger before?"

He backed up in a panic, shaking his head like a crazy man. She could see the whites of his eyes as they darted from side to side, searching for an exit. He swallowed heavily before opening his mouth. No sound came out.

He shuddered. A visible movement rippled down his body.

She knew how he felt.

At the same time, she recognized the gift. If he could see and hear her, he could help them.

If he didn't run screaming from her, never to return.

"Hey, what city are we in?"

His mouth worked. "Portland."

She brightened. First piece of good news she'd heard in a long time.

"Where in Portland?"

"The Olde Riverside Shipyard area."

"Do you have an address?" she prodded.

Of course her luck ran out. His phone rang and he fumbled, trying to pull it out. "Yeah." He turned his back on the cage and ran his hand over the back of his head. "Yeah. Yeah. I'm fine. Just a conker of a headache."

He moved further out of hearing distance. Tabitha watched, her ear tuned in. She realized she was separating mentally from the tiger in an effort to hear better. Feline hearing was incredibly acute. She pulled back inside and mentally spread her energy outward, connecting, blending and becoming one with the tiger, pouring energy into the tiger's hearing. She listened in on Fez's phone call.

She heard little bits about a buyer, moving, vets.

And nothing else.

Suddenly she heard the phone click closed and the sound of Fez muttering, "Shit, shit. Shit."

"What's the matter? What happened?"

Fez's spine stiffened at the same time his neck almost disappeared into his hunched shoulders. "I don't need this. I just wanted to get paid and get the hell out of here."

"And I can help."

She was taking a chance, but it's not as if she had anything to lose. And from the sound of it, neither did he.

He walked closer.

"I have got to be concussed if I'm seeing you. There's no way you're for real."

She laughed. "Hey, this isn't the way I expected to spend my last couple of days either. But I need help and you need help. Between us, we can do this."

He looked toward the front door. "Do what? I'm so screwed here..."

"And I'm what? Do you think being caught inside a tiger is fun?"

He frowned. "You're inside the tiger. You're not the soul of the tiger?"

That question surprised her. But then again, for anyone not into the psychic stuff, maybe that was as reasonable an explanation as anything.

"No. I'm psychic. The tiger, in her panic caused by you assholes, reached out and nabbed me. Now I'm connected to her. She's dying and I need to help her in order to escape." She knew that would sound crazy to him, but there wasn't a better way to say it.

He just stared. Then laughed, but that turned to a groan quickly. He held his head in his hands. "Don't do that. It hurts."

That wasn't good. She needed his help. "You should get that injury looked at."

"Ha. I got no money, and if I leave here and the boss finds out, I'm dead."

"Let me help. Tell me where we are so I can get someone here to help the tiger. We'll pay you so you can move away and start over again."

He stared at her.

"Hurry. Before someone comes. What can it hurt? You get to live, I get to live, and the tiger… Well, she'll be able to live out the rest of her life in a better place than this."

"He'll kill me if he finds out. There's no place I could hide without having to look over my shoulder for the rest of my life."

"My friend is a cop. He'll help us."

Fez laughed, a grainy coarse sound of despair.

"No, he won't. He'll get killed just like the rest of us."

"Why?" Tabitha didn't understand.

But it was bad. Fez's face twisted with despair. "Because the boss is a cop, too."

RONIN COULDN'T PROCESS Stefan's words. He'd had one cat in his lifetime. Mr. Boots, a tuxedo cat he'd lost when he was nine. It had to be the death of Mr. Boots that had brought this on.

"Haunted?" That was unbelievable.

Not in the sense many people would interpret that word. Stefan said. But he'd refused to elaborate any further.

So much for clarity. He'd left with a disturbing final comment. *You'll find out the details soon, I'm sure.*

What? And how?

He wasn't sure he wanted to find out anymore. Not now that the memories were flooding back. Losing his beloved pet had devastated him. His parents had tried to comfort him, Roman had tried to share his beloved dog at the time – and that had helped some. But watching Mr. Boots get squished under the tires of that damn car… Yeah, that was something he hadn't forgotten – or gotten over apparently. At least according to Stefan.

Ronin could understand now that it had been pointed out to him.

Especially now that his chest tightened and his throat constricted just thinking about it. The same reaction he had whenever he saw a cat.

He'd been having the reaction to the loss of Mr. Boots over and over again.

God, the mind was a tricky bugger. It was scary to think that Mr. Boots had been sitting in his psyche this entire time. Then he remembered what Stefan had said about the cat haunting him. Did that mean Mr. Boots was still here?

The death of his pet had been his first experience with death, and he'd learned a harsh lesson that day.

He'd been learning to play the piano around the same time. It had been his way of dealing with the pain. He still played. A lot. Usually to calm down or to reconnect with the better things in life. His brother had learned to play at the same time. And Roman had also excelled at art.

Ronin couldn't draw a straight line. And he'd tried, oh how he'd tried.

Being twins, there'd been a certain competitiveness between them. One that had grown over time. They'd fought like little bastards when they were small, had even grown up with different groups of friends. The loss of their parents had pulled them together.

He had no idea what to think. Or who to talk to. *A ghost cat.* And yet why did that sound familiar? Hadn't Shay had a similar experience? It wasn't too late to call, and he needed to know. Moments later, he had Shay on the phone. She listened for a moment then chuckled.

"No, Ronin, not a similar experience – that experience. Morris is with me still."

"Explain," he said tersely.

With a laugh, she said, "Morris was around me but in a free floating energy. During my return to my body through Roman's painting, he painted Morris and through that process pulled Morris back to his original ghost form. As he still is today."

Silence. He shook his head. "I had no idea. Sure, I'd heard a little about this, but I didn't really understand. *Who could?*"

"I know. I wasn't sure if Roman would have told you about the blue in his paintings or not."

"So in a way, he was picking up Morris's presence as well."

"That's because at the time he was painting me, Roman was actually walking in his dreams to visit me. Morris was always around, but spread far and wide. Roman sensed a presence around me and painted blue, representing this presence, into every painting. He didn't realize it was Morris."

"You do understand how far from normal you're sounding right now?"

A light tinkling laugh swept through the phone. "You don't sound much better nowadays, do you?" she teased.

"I know," he grumbled.

"Maybe you should talk to Mr. Boots the same way you talked to Tripod when Tabitha was hurt. Let Mr. Boots show you the way." And she hung up.

He snorted. *Like hell.*

CHAPTER 21

Tuesday, just before dawn

TABITHA'S MIND REFUSED to function. The litany of prayer reverberated in her head. *Please God, let it not be. Please God, don't let a bad cop be involved.*

How could she save this tiger if those who were supposed to help were the ones doing the hurting?

And if Ronin tried to investigate, wouldn't that put him in danger? A bad cop would do what was necessary to keep his activities secret. If cornered, he'd have nothing left to lose by killing another cop.

Her heart pounded inside her chest as the implications grew.

She had to tell Ronin. Before he walked into something he wasn't prepared for.

She needed to leave Trinity again to tell Ronin, but she had to get Fez to help her, too. Help them all.

"You could call my friend."

He stared at her, a bit of fire starting to come back to his eyes. "Call a cop? Are you kidding? I'd get murdered over something like that."

"Apparently you're likely to get killed over this anyway," she reminded him. "Or have you forgotten that?"

He shook his head. "I'm not a snitch."

She groaned softly. "Remember that part about being dead? How much of it didn't you understand?"

She knew prodding him wasn't the best idea, but she was out of time. And so was Trinity. She needed antibiotics and maybe surgery. She was fading badly. If it wasn't for the energy Tabitha was pouring into her...she'd look so much worse If she died...

Well, this whole mess would get really bad for everyone. Her. Fez. Ronin. The reserve. All the animals in her care.

"No," Fez said. "Big difference getting killed on the job or turning snitch."

She stared at him. "Really? This is a job to you? A job worth dying over?"

"I'm good. I ain't gonna die." But he kept glancing nervously at the front door and tugging on the completely destroyed front of his sweatshirt.

His fear was palpable. But it was his fear, not Trinity's, and not hers. He had some reason to be afraid. Something he knew that made him afraid.

"Has anyone else died on this job?"

He jumped back. *"Whaat?"* A shudder swept through his frame, taking the last bit of color from his ruddy complexion.

Bulls-eye. And she remembered Stefan's sketch of the floater.

"Did your partner die? Did your boss take him out back and shoot him? Or was it your predecessor? Are you replacing a man they deep-sixed in the river?"

That did it.

He bolted for the front door and ran outside. She did not hear a sound from him, but his silent scream of terror echoed on the energy waves around her.

Shit.

RONIN WALKED BACK into the bedroom and checked on Tabitha. She was still in a comatose state. He hated to leave her, but he had to find the asshole who was hunting tigers.

Tabitha's father, Dennis, walked up to him as he stood by the doorway.

"It's early. What's going on?"

Ronin didn't have a clue what to say. Did Tabitha's father have any idea what his daughter could do? Or had she gotten her skills from her father?

Dennis frowned at Ronin, who was still working out what to say. He looked past him toward the still form on the bed.

If Ronin hadn't shifted to cast yet another glance at Tabitha, he'd have missed it.

A look of horror and…recognition on Dennis's face.

Then he turned a bleak look toward Ronin and said, "It's gotten worse, hasn't it?"

Oh boy. "Worse?" he asked cautiously.

"Don't play games." Dennis snapped. "You couldn't be in her life and not know she goes off into these weird catatonic episodes."

"So she did this as a child?"

"My father told me about them. He laughed. Said he'd seen it before. Said his brother used to get them too. Said I should ignore them." Dennis shrugged. "I was so out of my element at the time, I did try to ignore them. He said she was getting better years ago." His face hardened. "But that was obviously just another lie."

And there was that bitterness again.

Genetics. What were the chances that Tabitha's great-uncle or grandfather had been psychic and hadn't shared that information with her? *Or had one of them?* He glanced back at the bed. They hadn't discussed her grandfather much. It seemed as if the old man had held a lot back from his son, and vise versa. That had to have been tough. Dennis would have grown up feeling as if he was always on the outside.

Which would have made for a difficult life.

And would have created an angry man.

As he stared at the clouds blistering Dennis's face, he had to wonder what extent an angry man would go to, to get his revenge on his father.

That made him ask, "How did your father die?"

Dennis's eyebrows shot up. "Damned if I know. Poisoned by his own personality for all I care. I assumed it was old age. I got a report from the medical examiner, but I can't say I read it."

He didn't say it, but Ronin got the impression that Dennis might have danced for joy on the old man's grave.

Definitely no love lost there.

But as Ronin watched the worry shadow Dennis's face as he studied his daughter, he realized the man loved her. He might have done something to hurt his old man, but he'd never have done anything to hurt Tabitha.

"Let's go take a look at that box."

TABITHA RETURNED FROM this trip shaky and feeling, shocky. Trinity was fading. Her unborn cub was suffering, Fez was panicking and this situation was sliding into the sewer fast.

She slammed back into her body so quickly, it hurt, damn it. But there'd been no time to slow down. Or inclination. She needed to contact Ronin immediately.

The hard landing forced a groan from her lips. She wanted to hop up and run from her bed, but her body moved similar to molasses on a frosty day. Getting this flesh-and-blood cage to do anything was almost impossible. *Shit.* She should have slowed down for the re-entry. Damn. She knew better.

"Rnnn?" The garbled message slipped from her numb lips. She tried again. "Ronin." Better, much better. Only it was barely a whisper.

"Tabitha? Are you okay?"

She couldn't open her eyes yet, but her mouth worked, trying to answer him.

Her father asked, "What's wrong with her?"

She groaned, a sound this time that would have been better kept silent. *But her father? Really?* She so didn't have time for this. He knew nothing of her abilities and this night's weirdness went way beyond that level of basic comprehension.

Finally, she could open her eyes. She was lying in bed with both men looking at her.

First things first.

"Trinity is in the Olde Riverside Shipyard area of Portland. Fez is alive, but he has a bad head injury. The floater Stefan found might be his old partner…or predecessor. I can't be sure."

"Finally!" Ronin narrowed his eyes as he grabbed for his phone. He opened his mouth to say something else. She didn't give him a chance to speak. "And his boss is a cop. You're dealing with a bad cop, Ronin."

"And how do you know that?" he demanded. "Did you see him?"

"Fez told me."

She struggled to sit upright. Her bones were rubber and her muscles had a mind of their own with no interest in obeying her commands. "I mean Fez saw me. As in he *saw* me."

She shot a warning glance her father's way.

And realized he'd caught it. Not understood it, but…

"What the hell is going on here?"

She'd have laughed then, only her nerves decided to come back to life right that moment and sent liquid fire up her veins. She cried out as all her biological systems came alive. Finally.

Or you could do things the right way and not cause all of us to panic. Stefan's voice rippled through her mind.

She'd have laughed if she could, but everything hurt too much. "Right. I could do that too."

Ronin stared down at her and she realized she'd spoken out loud instead of inside her head where Stefan was. "Sorry," she said apologetically, "I was thinking of a conversation with Stefan from before."

From the sudden widening of Ronin's eyes, she knew he'd understood.

Her father was also here and getting more upset and impatient. Not good.

"Dad, there's lots to explain, I just don't know how to explain all this, or even if this is a good time."

"You explain. I have phone calls to make and a search of the Olde Riverside Shipyard area to organize." Ronin stepped outside the bedroom.

"Are you having more blackouts?" her father asked. "Talking to imaginary friends again? Seeing things that aren't there?"

She swung her legs to the floor and stared up at him. "Did I have problems like that as a kid?"

He glared at her. "All the time!"

She shrugged. "Then chances are I am having lots more of them. Because they aren't bad things, Dad. I'm psychic. That means I see things you don't. Talk to people you can't. Among other things." She waved a lofty hand in his direction. "And it's way too late for you to try to do anything about it."

She looked over at her father, wondering how to get rid of him so she could talk to Ronin openly.

"Oh, I know that expression," he said. "Forget it. I've been cut out of your life way too long. I'm in now and I'm staying."

She raised an eyebrow and wondered if he'd still want in once he understood. She decided to give him a chance. He hadn't been there for her until now, but perhaps, as he claimed, that hadn't been entirely his fault. This was way out of normal, but she'd really love to be honest, to have no secrets from him. He'd shared his history and orientation and now she wanted to share hers.

Or rather, she wanted a relationship with her father, one where she didn't need to keep a part of herself separate from him. The actual sharing part wasn't something she was too keen to do at the moment.

She pushed herself upright, happy to see her legs were working again. She walked the short distance to stand in front of her father. "There are lots of things you don't know about me. About what I can do. I'm happy to include you, but…" She narrowed her eyes at him. "I don't want to hear any talk about getting help of any kind. No doctors, no shrinks, no carny witch doctors."

He gasped at the last one. "Did he used to threaten you with those, too?"

She smiled. "He might have tried when I was younger, but not once I was old enough to understand."

"Understand what? I really don't know what you're talking about. When you say you're psychic, surely you're not talking about carny palm readers or crystal ball readers?"

She sighed. His history could really impinge on his ability to understand. "No, Dad. I'm not." She watched some of lines on his face smooth out, then added, "What I do is much more than that."

He paled. "What do you mean?"

Well, it was now or never. With a long look at him, she said, "I'll give you the short and fast version. You can ask questions later."

In as clear and concise an accounting as she could – considering that time had become a huge element – she explained her abilities and what was currently going on in her world.

Her father kept looking toward the hallway as if searching for Ronin to get confirmation, then back to Tabitha. He had to have felt as if he'd fallen down a rabbit hole, lost forever in someone's horrific fantasy.

She fell silent, studying him to see how he was taking it.

He stared at her but never made a sound. She gave him a moment to process, as he didn't appear ready to ask questions.

She twisted as Ronin returned, saying, "I tried to get Fez to help get me and Trinity out. He's terrified of getting killed though. He's got some weird sense of honor that getting killed on the job is okay but being a snitch isn't. Even if it saves his life."

Ronin nodded. "Not the first time I've heard of that." His phone rang again and he left to answer it.

DENNIS STARED AT the daughter he'd never gotten to know, and wondered how she could be so different from him. Not for the first time, he wondered if she really was his daughter.

Now if only he could find something solid in her story to latch on to. *Psychic. Yanked by a tiger out of her body? Floating in the energy highway?*

He shook his head. Did he even want to know more?

And how much of this could be laid at his father's feet and all that carny bullshit?

"Wondering if you can walk out of my life as fast as you walked back in?" she asked him. No – she challenged him. As if to say, *Hey old man. If this is too much for you…*

But he'd faced tougher foes than her across many a boardroom. "Is that what you're wondering?"

"What? Wondering if you're ready to disappear or are you wondering if I am?"

The words she flung at him reminded him of how gracefully she'd taken his news. Was it because the younger generation had been raised in a more open era? Or was it just her? His daughter.

"Look, Dad," she said defensively, "I know this isn't your thing. Feel free to leave."

He laughed. "That is not going to happen. Do you really think I'm going to walk out after it took so much to walk in?" But now she looked as insecure as he'd felt when he'd arrived.

"Oh, Father, the problems you created." He didn't realize he'd said it out loud until Tabitha's gaze narrowed. He smiled. "I did love him. But I buried it under all the hate."

She tilted her head and studied him. Then with gentle sarcasm, came back with, "I really do love you too. I just forgot under all that hate."

He blanched and took a shaky breath. "Jesus. You don't pull your punches, do you?"

She looked away as if in shame, bright flags of color on her cheeks.

"That was a little harsh," she admitted. "Grandpa loved me. But he wasn't you. I never had a father to show up during parent-teacher meetings, or to see me in a concert, to watch as I graduated." She shrugged. "Those things didn't mean anything to Grandpa."

"I know. I never had them either."

Her gaze flew up to meet his, seeing the truth in them.

"Sorry," she said.

"Sorry," he responded gently.

She gave him a sad smile. "He missed out on so much."

"So did we."

"And yet here we are."

Standing across from each other. Both closer than they'd ever been before, but not to where either would like them to be just yet. Too much had happened. Or rather not happened.

Now it was just awkward.

But they'd come so far already. It didn't have to stop at this point.

"I'd like you to meet Eric, my live-in partner."

Her eyebrows flew up at the mention of his assistant whom she'd spoken to many times but had never met. Dennis hadn't been able to take that step – until now.

"Okay," she said. "Better make it quick in case I'm not here next weekend."

Shock slammed into him, making his heart pound deep inside.

"What? You were really serious about this tiger stuff?"

"Very," she said, her voice thinning. "If Tabitha dies, there's a good chance I will too. For all I'm standing and looking normal to you, my heart chakra, my cord, is connected to her."

"And if you survive this time? We all die eventually. What happens when her time comes? You said she wasn't in good health to begin with. So what happens then?"

Soberly, she stared at him. "I don't know."

CHAPTER 22

Tuesday at dawn

TABITHA LEFT HER father to stew on her words and headed out to find Ronin. It was still the middle of the night for many people. There was so little he could do right now.

Only she couldn't find him. In the kitchen, she turned around slowly, wondering if he'd really left. Wouldn't he have said something first? Wouldn't she have heard him close the door or something? Hear his truck start up at least?

Her father came in behind her. For the first time, she realized he was fully dressed. "Did you not go to bed?"

He waved in the direction of the living room. "I was working."

She glanced at the clock. "So late?"

He hesitated. "I couldn't sleep."

Him too. She certainly had enough nights like that herself. Especially lately.

"Did Ronin drive away?"

"No. I didn't hear any vehicles."

"Neither did I." She frowned and walked out the back door. The stars were bright in the sky, adding to the glow of a waxing moon. Another couple of nights and the moon would be full.

She studied the long pathway into the trees. Tripod barked at her. He stood at the end of the glow of light from her backdoor and stared at her. "Did he go down there, honey?"

Tripod barked again. She glanced down at her slippers and robe, wondering when she'd put that much on. Tripod barked again.

She started down the path toward him.

"Tabitha? Where are you going?" her father called from inside the house.

"Tripod is upset. I'm going to check it out."

"Wait a sec!" her father said. "Let me grab my shoes. I'm going with you."

She could hear a mad scramble behind her.

"You shouldn't be walking around out here on your own."

"Really? And who else is going to check out the place? It's mine, remember?"

His exasperation wove through his voice. "Yeah, I do know. I hate that you live out here all alone."

"That's not going to change."

"It was one thing when your grandfather lived here, but now that you're alone…"

"What, you think I can't handle it?" she asked incredulously. "Dad, I've run this reserve on my own for well over a decade. Grandpa couldn't get around much anymore. Not for a long time. Living here alone is no hardship."

Tripod barked louder from somewhere in the trees. Tabitha raced after him. Then she heard sounds of someone running off. She raced off after them. If there'd been someone on the grounds…

RONIN SWORE AS his fourth attempt to raise anyone on the phone failed. It was five in the morning. This night was done for him.

He heard barking then a shout. He spun around. *Damn.* He'd automatically come out the front door of Tabitha's house instead of out back door where that damn cat was.

He wasn't ready to face that yet. And neither had he shared Stefan's insights with Tabitha.

He heard Dennis shout. Ronin raced back inside and out through the back door. "Tabitha?" he roared, "Damn it. Where are you?"

"Back here!"

Her shout came from the path heading toward the office of Exotic Landscape.

He reached her side in seconds, almost knocking Dennis over in the process. "What the hell is going on?"

"Someone was here." She held her hand to her chest and gasped for breath. "Jesus, I almost caught him."

"Are you crazy?" He caught her by her shoulders. "You actually went after the intruder?"

"Of course I did. This is my home. My place. My animals. I will do everything I can to keep them safe," she snapped.

He gave her a good shake. "Oh, of all the dumb-ass stunts."

She gasped and opened her mouth to blast him when he tugged her forward and kissed her. Hard.

She was still spluttering when he set her back. A snicker had him turning to see Dennis trying to hold back his laughter.

"Love is a many splendored thing," Dennis murmured.

"Ha. Tell your daughter that."

This time Dennis guffawed. "As if that will help."

"Hey, guys. I'm right here." She stuck her face in Ronin's face. "And what was that comment all about?"

He sighed, tugged her forward and led her back to her house. "Stay here with your father while I go and check out the place."

Once back in the circle of the outside patio lights, he gave her a gentle push and sent her back toward the house. "I'll be back in a few minutes."

"I'll come with you," Dennis offered.

Ronin nodded toward Tabitha. "I'd rather you stayed with her. She's might bolt."

Dennis sighed and followed Tabitha inside.

With a backward glance, Ronin headed down the path to the office of Exotic Landscape.

"IF HE THINKS for one minute that I'm going to stay home like a 'good little woman,' he's sorely mistaken," she muttered to herself as she stormed into her house and up to her room. Her movements were sharp and jerky but efficient as she stripped off her nightclothes and changed into jeans and a t-shirt. This night was over, and the thought of more sleep had become a distant dream.

Some asshole was messing with her place. With her animals.

She reached for her phone and called security. The phone rang and rang.

"Crap." She pocketed her phone and went in search of her shoes.

"Where are you going?" her father asked, standing in front of the doorway. From the wide stance and crossed arms, she deduced he had thoughts about stopping her.

"My security men aren't answering. I have to make sure they haven't been knocked out, that they're awake and on the job."

He frowned. "Isn't that a job for the police?"

"Ah, the police is here, remember?"

"I don't think he wants you out there."

"No, he doesn't. But those are my men. One of them should have answered. Neither did. That could mean trouble."

Her phone rang just then. She pulled it out and checked the number. "It's Ronin."

She answered it. "What's up?"

"I've called for paramedics. Your security guard has been knocked out."

Her gaze flew up to meet her father's somber look. "I'm on my way. There should be a second guard there. Neither answered their phones."

"I'm on it." She could hear the sounds of doors opening and closing. *Was he inside the center?*

"Where is the guard?" she said sharply. "I'll come look after him."

"He's outside the back door of the clinic."

"Have you checked inside? We were wondering because of the earlier break-ins if maybe junkies were after the drugs there."

"Do you keep many?" Ronin sounded distracted.

"Hell no. But the junkies might not know or care."

"Right. Bring your father."

"Will do. Be there in five." She put away her phone and slipped into her shoes. "He wants you to come with me. One of my guards has been attacked. Ronin has called for the paramedics, but I need to go and see what I can do."

Her father was already pulling the door open and said, "Does this happen often?"

"First time. Some other problems started a few months ago." Outside, she led the way back along the path to the office.

"Was your grandfather worried about anything?" Dennis asked. "Did the break-ins upset him?"

"Yes. He'd gone very quiet these last few months. As if something bugged him, but he never talked about it."

"No autopsy was done – did that bother you?"

"No." She shrugged. "I didn't see the sense. He was old, his health failing." From the pathway, she could see the lights were on inside the center. She frowned and picked up the pace.

She entered the front door and found the lights on throughout the building. She walked through the office, her heart sinking as she took in the mess. The desk drawers had been pulled out and dumped, the chairs had been overturned, the pictures tossed.

Damn. What about the animals that just had surgery over the last couple days? They shouldn't be disturbed. She hurried through to the clinic side and found the animals untouched. They were nervous, stressed and hurting from their various procedures, but as far as she could see, their energies were solid. No additional injuries or damage.

Immediately, she poured waves of calm energy over the pens and animals, stretching it out, letting it float to the far corners of the reserve.

It's okay. Everything is fine. Relax.

As she turned her attention to the rest of the center, she heard Ronin call her.

She raced to the surgery to find Thomas, her long-time security guard, stretched out on the table.

"What on earth…?"

"My thoughts exactly." He motioned to the door at the far end of the room. "This is the second guard. The first one is outside."

She studied the man's face. There was no apparent injury, but he was definitely out cold. As if sleeping. Or drugged. Her heart sank.

She pulled his sleeve back to see a red injection site. She closed her eyes. "Ah hell. He's been drugged."

RONIN LEFT TABITHA and her father at the center and did a quick look around. He was pretty sure that the intruder was gone, but this was no longer a simple case of mischief. Now two guards had been attacked, which said something about the seriousness of the intruder's intentions.

He headed for the security system, wondering if the intruders knew about the upgrades. He knew his brother's company received a copy of the feed. Had they received an alert of an intruder?

His phone rang, and he knew it was Roman before he picked it up. This happened sometimes, as if Roman could hear his thoughts.

"Are you at Exotic?" Roman asked.

"Yeah," Ronin said. "Two guards were attacked and we disturbed an intruder heading for Tabitha's house."

"Professional job?"

"Quite possibly. The guards were knocked out with drugs. The offices have been tossed." Ronin stared out into the early morning light. Inside, his stomach knotted. "What the hell is going on?"

"There were no alarms set off on our end."

"Well, that answers that. The system's new; it has to be an inside job." Ronin paused. "Who installed it?"

Roman's tone turned thin and hard. "I'll be checking into that. You check on her the staff at Exotic?"

Ronin snorted. "Working on it. She doubled her staff after her extended hospital stay. She had to. She's still not back to full strength. At this rate, Exotic will need a new owner, too."

Silence.

"Is that a possibility?" Roman asked seriously, "because that's motive right there."

Ronin thought about it. "It's possible," he answered slowly. "There's no one else in her life at the moment except her father. And those that work at the center."

"Who inherited everything when the grandfather passed away recently?"

Running a hand across his forehead, Ronin told himself to think. To see this for what it likely was – a money grab. Trust his business-minded brother to cut through the distraction and get to the root of the problem.

"Tabitha did, supposedly. Is there any money in this place? It's run by donations and the sweat off Tabitha's back."

"And a large amount of donation money from Shay's Lassiter Foundation."

So true. "I'll look into the inheritance issue and who the beneficiaries were and who stands to benefit if Tabitha can't."

"Although, I doubt anyone could make the tiger do what the caged tiger's done to Tabitha," Roman said, "that doesn't mean the intruder you disturbed tonight wasn't after something else."

"Shit." Ronin hung up the phone.

While he worked his way back to the offices he heard the sounds of the ambulance in the distance. He pulled out his phone again and keyed in Tabitha's number. "Hey, I'm on my way back. I didn't see anything, but that doesn't mean he's not arou—"

Ronin's head screamed in agony. He dropped his phone, both hands going to his head as he fell to his knees.

"Jesus. Tough bugger, aren't you?"

A second blow dropped Ronin face first into the dirt.

Then he knew no more.

CHAPTER 23

Tuesday early morning

TABITHA SCREAMED, "RONIN. Ronin!"

No answer. She stared at her father in shock. "He stopped talking mid-sentence. I heard another voice. Something about *Jesus, a tough bugger, aren't you.*"

Her father stiffened an odd look coming over his face. He shook his head. But his voice was calm – maybe too calm. "That could be anything. Try him again."

Already opening her phone, she sent her father a suspicious look. Hating that because she didn't truly *know* her father, his words were sending off internal alarms. Wondering if she could trust him.

She walked to the far side of the surgical room where she could look out the window and keep an eye on the still-unconscious guard and her father.

There was no response to the call. She knew there wouldn't be. Something had happened to Ronin. Talk about being in an ugly spot. What could she do? *Roman.* She called him on her phone.

"What?" growled Roman.

"I think something has happened to your brother," she answered quickly, "but I can't check because I'm standing guard over the other two men who've been attacked. The ambulance is just coming up the road."

"I was just speaking with him. He was fine." Now Roman was all business. "What's happened."

She quickly explained.

"Stay inside. Don't let anyone in or out, do you hear me?"

"I hear you, but I can't do that. One guard is on the ground outside and I have to deal with the paramedics. After that I can go look for Roni—"

"No. I'm on my way and I'll call for backup. You stay put." He paused for a second. "Are you alone?"

"No, my father is here." She turned to stare at her father... only to realize he'd left. "Shit."

"What?"

"My father was just here." She walked into the other room looking for him, loathe to leave the guard alone. "But he's disappeared."

She swallowed. "Maybe he went out to direct the paramedics. Just get here fast."

"Already in the car."

He hung up, and she walked to the window. Sure enough, there was her father, directing the ambulance. She heard him yell, "They are over there. One outside, the other in."

He pointed to where Tabitha and the guards were.

As the paramedics ran inside, Dennis bolted in the other direction. She lost sight of him as she raced to her patients. What was he up too? Then she didn't have a chance to worry.

Thankfully, the paramedics were in and out in minutes. The injured men were safely on the way to the hospital. She'd wanted them to wait for her to find Ronin, afraid he might need their services more than her guards, but they only had room for two. They'd promised to come back, if needed.

She shuddered.

By then, it might be too late.

She locked the front door and raced out the back. Tripod's panicked bark pulled her up short. She sent a hard wave of soothing energy his way. Immediately, she was slammed with his panicked response and pictures from his mind.

Ronin on the ground. Blood in the dirt. The smell bothered Tripod, Ronin's limp body bothering him. She could see even as she ran to his side that Tripod was nudging Ronin's body and whimpering. She soothed Tripod's energy, and forced her body to move faster.

Tripod, easy boy. Take it easy.

The dog whined deep in the back of his throat. He calmed, knowing she was close, but it still wasn't enough.

She took a quick glance around, but there was no sign of animal or human energy that she could see. Stefan would say that the only thing stopping her from seeing other people's auras as well as she did animals was that she did not *want* to see them.

Humans had layers that were less than nice to see, and the more they tried to hide the layers, the more the deception showed in the disruption to their energy. Who'd want to know that level of information about their fellow man?

Up ahead, she could see Tripod standing guard over a crumpled form.

She knelt beside Ronin and checked for a pulse. His color was paler than normal but his pulse was still strong. He looked fine. Except he was out cold. She started to key in Roman's number again but heard his shout before she finished. She yelled, "Over here!"

Tripod barked as Roman's footsteps came closer. "Easy Tripod. He's a friend."

"How is he?" Roman asked, dropping to his brother's side. He immediately started to check his brother over.

"He's out cold but I can't see any injuries."

As Roman ran gentle fingers over his head, Ronin groaned.

"Easy, Ronin. You've been knocked on the side of your head."

Ronin's eyelids fluttered open. "What the hell happened?" he said, but the words came out more as a snarl.

Tabitha smiled. "I was hoping you could tell me that. We were talking on the phone and all of a sudden you stopped – mid-sentence."

His stared at her, a distant look in his eye before everything suddenly seemed to snap into focus.

"I was talking to you and then…nothing." He grabbed hold of his brother's shoulder and pulled himself into a sitting position. He reached a tentative hand to the back of his head. "Ouch… Did you see anything?"

Tabitha shook her head. "No. But I heard another voice saying 'Jesus, tough bugger aren't you' right before we got disconnected. That's when I called Roman. The paramedics left with my injured guards and I followed Tripod here."

He looked at her then shook his head. "Thanks, Tripod. Glad you found me." He reached out a hand. "Help me up." With Roman's assistance Ronin stood. He took two steps in the direction of the offices and stopped.

Tabitha watched him reach an arm out wondering what it would cost him to ask for help?

"Not as much as you might think," he muttered when she put an arm around his ribs.

"I didn't say anything." She stared at him carefully as they walked slowly back to the office. "And you need to get that injury checked."

"Right." *So not going to happen.*

"What?" She stopped in outrage. "Yes, it is going to happen. Injuries like yours kill people."

Stop reading my mind.

"I'm not reading your mind. Now stop arguing. You're getting checked out."

Roman laughed. "You two sound like an old married couple."

Tabitha snorted. "As if that would happen."

Ronin murmured. "Sure it could." *If he could deal with his cat shit and she could deal with him.*

Tabitha stopped. "That works for me."

What was going on? Was he speaking telepathically or was she just tuning into his thoughts. And how did that work? She heard him think, *How much further? My head is killing me.*

"Not much," she answered. "Just a few more minutes."

He leaned heavily on her shoulder.

Roman spoke quietly behind her, "Do you want me to take him?"

No, she doesn't. I'm fine. Or I will be as soon as I can sit down.

Tabitha shook her head. "He said he's fine."

There was no doubt now. Somehow Ronin had suddenly started talking telepathically to Tabitha in his head. At first he assumed he was speaking out loud. *Damn.*

She couldn't stop her instinctive call to Stefan for help. This was definitely his specialty not hers.

She motioned to the open back door as they approached. Roman rushed forward and opened the door wide. Ronin grabbed the doorframe and pulled himself past the doorway. He stumbled into her office and collapsed into the visitor's chair. "I just need a minute."

Roman snorted. "You'll need more than a minute."

"I'll be fine. A drink of water would be good."

Tabitha rushed to get it, as she returned she heard Ronin say, "Dennis, Tabitha's father brought over a box of papers he'd taken from her grandfather's office last night. We were thinking there might be something in there to explain the current situation."

As Tabitha watched and worried, Ronin closed his eyes as a wave of pain crossed his face. After a moment, he added, "A few hours ago, while we waited for Tabitha to return from..." He shrugged as if the right word failed to appear. "Whatever she was doing, we took a look inside."

She gasped. "Really? You didn't tell me. What was in there?"

"We haven't had a chance to sort out everything as many of the papers are really old. But there was a bundle of hate mail that went way back. No name or identification on any of them and each was signed, 'You know who I am.'" He straightened, tentatively at first then with more confidence. "The last one was particularly nasty."

She narrowed her gaze. "Then what are you not saying?"

Roman reached out and grabbed her hand. "Tabitha? Where's your father?"

DENNIS HAD NO idea where Ronin could be, but he had a horrible feeling he understood how Ronin came to be attacked. And God damn him if he was responsible…

Surely not. Damned well better not. But that voice on the phone…and the language…

He knew this acreage well after years of being involved, even if only on a periphery level. He'd supplied much of the money that had gone into building this place. It was his way to ease his guilt for ignoring his daughter and for letting his father dominate him. Damnation. He should have done something about reconnecting with her a long time ago. Now with his father's death, the bonds that had held him back had suddenly dissolved, setting him free.

He'd built himself a life without his daughter and his father. A decent life. At least he'd thought so. But that voice he'd heard through Tabitha's phone – God, it sounded like someone he knew. And knew all too well.

He barreled down the back path heading to the large feed barn.

Please let him be wrong.

Please. Now that he'd lost his father and regained his daughter, he didn't want to lose another person in his life. *Please, let me be wrong.*

He whipped along the pathway searching for the back gate. He was probably too late. But he could hope…

The morning light shone clear. There were a few animals stirring, but as he ran past he could see them shy away from him. Probably just as well. If he found what he was afraid he would find, he might just do some violence himself.

TABITHA STARED. THEN she spun around to stare out the open door. "He directed the paramedics then took off to the back of the reserve. I figured he was looking for Ronin. But I haven't seen him since. *Shit.*"

She ran to the back door.

"Tabitha, wait. Don't go out there alone."

She stopped at the doorway. "Then someone come with me. He

could be lying injured anywhere. I'm not leaving him out there alone." She spun around to look at Roman. "You said you'd call for backup. Where are they?"

Ronin said gently, "He called a couple of my guys. Figured as they'd been handling the break-ins, it made sense to get them in on this. They are on the way."

She threw up her hands. "Fine, I don't care who you bring in. Just, please, let's figure this out and stop it."

"We don't know who is involved and how far this goes." Roman added, "Or how long this has been going on."

That stopped her in her tracks. "What are you talking about?"

"You said your grandfather went real quiet the last few months before he died. How do you know that something nasty wasn't going on? Maybe he was being blackmailed? Or threatened?"

"My grandfather? This has something to do with my grandfather?" She hated the rising panic in her voice. She stared at them. "Or are you suggesting he might have had something to do with this nightmare? Because there's no way he'd be involved with anything illegal."

They just stared at her. Her stomach roiled at the thought. "No. No. Oh no." She walked backwards several steps, shaking her head. "I'm not going to stand here and listen to something so ridiculous. I'm going to find my father."

She turned and dashed outside, but after several feet, she stopped and bent over, breathing hard. Desperately trying to make sense of this. Of what they were saying. Of what they weren't saying.

She wanted to throw up. But at the same time, she wanted to rant and scream at them.

And that just brought her father back to mind. He was the one she needed to ask some of these questions. He might have the answers.

Or he might not. She didn't know him enough to tell. What she had learned – the important things about him – had come these last few days. After her grandfather's death.

Each new calamity sent her body reeling and her mind grappling for a solid ground to stand on. And none of what was going on right now seemed related to the bigger issue in her life. Trinity.

Or was it?

Or rather, how was it not? What were the chances that Trinity and the problems at the reserve were *not* related?

Zero to none, she'd say. She was also assuming the problems at Exotic Landscape had something to do with black market animals – when it might have no connection at all.

Or was someone trying to make her look incompetent? Make her look as if she couldn't handle the responsibility?

And there was only person who'd benefit from that. Her father. The reserve and everything to do with it would belong to him.

Her heart squeezed tight, clogging up her blood flow and sending pain radiating outward. She took a deep shuddering breath as she forced herself to contemplate such a betrayal. It couldn't be. Her father didn't want Exotic. He'd never wanted it.

No, there had to be another explanation.

She turned slowly to face the brothers who were standing beside her now. Ronin looked better, but his color was still off. Then again, she was sure hers was way off too.

"We can't answer these questions until we find my father." She ran her fingers through her hair. "I need help to do that."

"We're here."

She shook her head. "Ronin, you can stay here until the staff arrive." She glanced down at her watch. "Which should be in the next half hour. Explain about the guards and that the reserve is locked down to the public today. Wendy might have to field calls if the media finds out." She glanced at Roman, who stared back at her steadily. "Will you come with me? Help me search for my father?"

"Like hell," Ronin snapped. "I'm going with you. He can stay here."

Roman turned to glare at him. "You're not one hundred percent and you're needed here. You can be the hero next time."

Ronin stood firm, glaring at his brother. Then he shook his head like an angry grizzly bear. "I'm doing fine. I'm going with her."

"Damn it." Roman glared at his brother, then as if realizing there'd be no reasoning with Ronin, he said, "Then tell me where you're going. I'll be following as soon as I can."

A few minutes later, she led the way through the maze of pathways. As she walked, she dialed her father yet again. Still no answer.

"What do you think happened to him?" asked Ronin.

A shudder of denial whispered through her. "I hate to say that I hope he's lying unconscious somewhere, but that is preferable to finding out he had something to do with this mess."

Ronin stayed quiet after that. She was no fool and she hadn't had a relationship with her father. But she'd hoped – and after yesterday's revelation – she'd believed, if only for an hour, that they had a basis for one.

And that made his possible betrayal that much worse.

DENNIS'S PANIC INCREASED with every step. He had to be wrong. He'd spent many hours bitching about this place. About the money he was constantly forking over, first blackmailed into it by his own father to help with Tabitha's care and then by his guilt. He'd thought he would be free after his father's death, but instead the bonds holding him here had been reinforced. He didn't object to helping out the reserve. It was all tax deductible and he could use that. He made money. A lot of it. But he'd also invested much of it into his father's pet project.

He hadn't thought it was an issue. But now little things came back to haunt him.

Comments that meant nothing at the time, but in the greater scheme of what he knew now he had to wonder about. To question. If he was right, his whole life was about to be brutalized by yet another betrayal. He'd thought he'd been through the worst and now he knew there was a possibility everything he'd been through so far was a prelude to this.

"Dennis? Is that you?"

Dennis spun around to see Germaine, his long-term friend, business partner and the financial head of his company, standing in front of him. A big smile on his face.

With a big gun in his hand.

CHAPTER 24

Tuesday morning

TABITHA SENT A wave of questing energy out to her animals. Surely one of them was bothered by something. If there was anything going on, intruders or other predators, the animals always sounded the alarm. Except she'd already sent out a layer of suppression energy to calm them all down. Crap.

She would have to do a systematic search for her father. There were acres of land here. If her father was around, he could be just about anywhere.

Then she heard panic in the lions' corner. Something was wrong. She bolted in their direction, calling back, "Over here."

"Did you hear something?" Ronin called behind her.

"The animals in this left corner are disturbed by intruders. They've gone into hiding but I can sense their panic…and fear."

She veered left, then right, her feet flying over the gravel path.

Just as she was about to turn the last corner, her shoulder was grabbed from behind. "Wha—?"

A hand slapped over her mouth. Ronin whispered against her ear. "*Shhh.* There are voices up ahead."

She stiffened. She'd been listening for the animals, not for people.

"Let's see if we can hear what they are saying."

She craned an ear, closing her eyes to hear better. The sounds were muffled.

Her father's voice. "What's going on here, Germaine? And what's with the gun?"

Tabitha shot a horrified look at Ronin, then watched with equal shock as he unclipped a weapon of his own.

She didn't have time to adjust when she heard the response.

"What's to figure out? God, you're slow. A brilliant money man for sure, but your instincts are just about non-existent when it comes to people."

Her father's pained voice answered, "Obviously, when I trusted you all these years. Maybe you could explain. What are you even doing here?"

A coarse laugh disrupted the serene air around them.

"This place is a gold mine. See, getting my hands on it is a bit of a problem."

"A big problem, I'd say. You won't get it by killing me. Even if you do, it's still not going to be yours by killing my daughter."

"Ah, but I like to think long term and killing your father was just the first step."

Tabitha gasped in shock. Her grandfather had been murdered? And she hadn't known?

Ronin squeezed her arm in warning. She stared at him in pain as she listened to her father scream in outrage. "You killed the old man? Why, for God's sake? What did he ever do to you?"

"He wasn't…shall we say…cooperative."

Dennis spoke, his voice vibrating in anger, "So you killed him? Over this place. Why? It's a money sink. That's what it is. I pour thousands into it every month."

Germaine said, "And that's why I had help doing this. There is someone who doesn't appreciate all the money being funnelled in this direction. He seems to feel it could be better spent on him."

Tabitha strained to hear her father's shocked whisper, "Please, no."

That coarse laugh again. But Tabitha was already vibrating with outrage. Her poor grandfather, and although she didn't understand who the accomplice was, it was someone else close to her father.

More betrayal.

"Of course it's true. You should know that power, sex and money are really the only motivators in the world. And we have them all here." The disgust in Germaine's voice confused Tabitha.

"I would have never done this. But then you brought that pretty boy into your life. A second wind, a midlife crisis. A fucking joke is what it is."

"My relationship? That's what this is all about?"

"No. But that's what cut the bonds of loyalty for me. We were best friends. Until you decided to come out of the closet. I kinda knew all along but I just didn't want to confirm it. The status quo was working, so why mess it up? Then you started with the pretty boy. What is he, fifteen to twenty years your junior? And now that you are openly gay, people started looking at me. We'd been such close friends for so long, they assumed we must have been lovers. That you'd taint me and my family with your perversion was disgusting. It wasn't so bad in the beginning until you and pretty boy started living together a couple of years ago. I wouldn't have done anything about it, although I was trying to figure out how to get out of the company without losing everything. If I'd known before this recession, I could have cut and run. It was really bad timing when stocks plummeted. We're barely back on our feet as it is."

"And this makes sense, how? Why?"

"God, you're dense. See, I want the whole company." Germaine laughed. "And once I realized what you *could* control, if you so chose, well, then I wanted that too."

"Could control?"

Tabitha's thoughts mirrored her father's question.

"Your father always made the provision that you were to look after Exotic Landscape if your daughter Tabitha was incapable. After being in a coma several times in the last month, the break-ins and the vandalism problems, it's obvious that she isn't mentally or physically stable, and that means she isn't capable of managing Exotic Landscape. So this property should fall nicely into your hands."

"Hell," her father said in disgust, "I don't want it. I don't want anything to do with it."

"Too bad, because the paperwork has already been taken care of. After your pretty boy, Eric, got a hold of your father's will, a handmade one... He really didn't trust anyone...did he?"

"*Paperwork?* Eric?"

Tabitha was too angry to speak. This was all about taking Exotic Landscape? It wasn't even her grandfather's property. It was hers. She'd made sure of that a while ago. At least she thought she had.

"No, that's not true," Dennis protested. "We have the official will."

"Well, hand-written ones are official too. Not when written under duress of course, but as we've already filed this one, giving Eric the right to manage it and you the ownership of the property, it's all good."

Ronin's arms were the only thing keeping Tabitha from racing into the middle of the mess and decking the asshole flat to the ground.

"And how is that going to help?" Her father's bewildered voice made Tabitha hurt. He didn't understand because he didn't want to see the level of betrayal in his world. She couldn't blame him. She didn't even know these assholes, and look at how she felt.

"Then, as you've been living common-law with pretty boy for several years, he stands to inherit everything."

"No, my daughter does," Dennis protested.

"And that was the final straw that brought pretty boy to me in the first place." Germaine laughed. "He found out you made out a will that left everything to your daughter and not to your lover."

"He's in my will. I left him a half million dollars." Her father's voice cracked in shock.

"And no one wants half a million when you give millions to a daughter you can't even stand. A daughter you hate."

Even after everything, that statement hurt.

"I have *never* hated my daughter," Dennis said. "I hated my *father*." He groaned. A sound so full of despair, Tabitha hurt for him too.

"What do we do?" she whispered.

But Ronin didn't have a chance to answer.

"I don't think that's going to be a decision you will have to make," said a rich voice from behind her. "No, don't bother turning around."

She stiffened.

"Shit." Ronin swore under his breath.

"Don't turn around, just keep moving forward and join your father." There was a rustling beside her. She caught the new arrival sliding Ronin's gun out of its holder. Damn.

"Who are you?" Tabitha asked as she walked ahead of Ronin.

Her father came into view. "No," he cried out. "Leave her alone."

The asshole Germaine asked, "Dennis, what part about the inheritance didn't you understand?"

Tabitha groaned. "The dead part, of course."

She was shoved toward her father. She stepped over to his side. "Hey, Dad. You really shouldn't have taken off like that."

"I didn't want to. But I thought I heard *his* voice through your phone talking to Ronin before he was knocked out."

"And you did." Germaine smiled. "And now we have the whole family here, including the security specialist. Except you really don't want to assume that those in an office know nothing about security themselves. It's so easy to fix things with inside people."

Security specialist? He was assuming that Ronin was Roman. Good. Then he couldn't know that Roman would be on his way in minutes. To delay their plans, in order to give Roman more time, she said, "You haven't fixed anything. I had the deed transferred into my name before he died."

"Ah, yes. You certainly filled out the paperwork and left it with your father to take care of. Of course, he gave it to Eric to handle. Only he made sure the papers were never sent off. But then…you haven't been capable of handling things around here in a while." And he smiled, a nasty smile that made her cringe. She looked at the second man also holding a gun. He was maybe in his mid to late thirties. "Dad, who is the second asshole?"

He glared at the younger man. "Eric, my assistant. Also known as pretty boy, apparently."

She gasped. "Your partner – the one you live with? The one you wanted me to meet?"

"Not this way." He sighed, a sadness on his face that broke her heart. "Not at all now."

"Sorry, Dennis. But if you think I'm going to wait around while you rekindle a relationship with her…" Eric shook his head, long black curls flying around his attractive head.

"Dad, we're going to have to talk." She snorted. "Pretty boy is all about glitz and short-term gain. He's not going to go the distance."

Eric gasped. "That is not true. I've been there for him all these years. Where the hell have you been?"

She didn't have much to say to that. But he looked like a disgruntled boy who'd been denied his toys. "Somehow I doubt my father has treated you badly." She sensed Ronin's shift from one foot to the other. She took several steps forward. "My father's a very generous man."

"Generous is not the same as having it all yourself. My looks aren't going to last forever. I decided I didn't want to wait for him. I'm still young. I don't want to tie myself down. But I need money to live as I want to. And between the two of you, there is a hell of a lot of it."

"See, I don't get that." And she didn't. She spent everything trying to pull enough pennies together to keep the reserve functioning.

Eric smiled. "Your father never told you, huh? Your grandfather left you a nice little trust fund. And then there's the value of all this land. So close to town. It's worth thirty million, easy. And as the manager of the reserve is incompetent, your father will be forced to shut the doors or hand the reins over to another manager while the animals can be moved elsewhere. It'll be easy to sell them off to private investors. The land will be sold to recoup costs and pay off the massive debts."

She gasped in anger. "I don't have any debts."

"Well, as there's no more money coming your way from Dennis." The gun wavered toward her father. "You will start accumulating them now."

"No." She shook her head. "There's no way you can do this."

"And, about your office manager?" Eric laughed. "Wendy is my sister. I'm sure this will turn out just the way I want it to."

Tabitha couldn't even begin to think of the type of damage that Wendy could have done while Tabitha had been out of commission. Wendy had been referred to her by one of her regular suppliers. *Had they known? Were they in on it?* It could take months to sort out the damage. Just the thought of losing Exotic Landscape to this slime in some land grab made her physically ill.

"She's going to heave."

She bent over, gasping. Ronin gently rubbed her back. Dying now would likely kill Trinity as well. She couldn't let that happen.

"Easy, honey."

"What are we going to do with them? We can't just shoot them," Eric whined. "That would leave all kinds of unanswered questions and evidence we don't want."

"She's got lions here. Tigers. All manner of animals that are looking for fresh meat. And Wendy will make sure they aren't found for a long time."

Tabitha froze. Ronin growled. For him, this would be a nightmare come true but inside, Tabitha's heart leapt with joy. Now this would be the first positive break as far as she was concerned.

Eric smiled. "Perfect."

"The early morning feeding time is soon. The cats will be hungry and they should finish them off quickly. We need them to kill them before anyone comes."

"Or we can shoot them to draw the animals. The scent of blood will speed up the process."

The men were busy talking, but Ronin had a strong grip on Tabitha's arm.

"Don't worry. They'll never touch us."

Her father snorted. "They'll take us down in minutes and go after the soft tissue first."

She sighed. The men in her life had so little idea of her world. "No, they won't," she reassured the two men in her life.

"Put them in with the lions." Germaine motioned to the gates behind them. "Wendy said lately the lions have been more aggressive than any of the others."

Ronin's grip tightened.

She winced but didn't bother trying to reassure him. She was more afraid of the bullets.

"The lions are one path over. Get moving."

RONIN TENSED LOOKING for a break. He'd take a bullet over a lion any day. But it sounded as if he might be getting both.

The two men motioned him toward the other two. He'd easily take on one guy. Two on most days. But two men with guns was asking for a death sentence. Or he could trust Tabitha. She appeared to be unconcerned.

That's because I am.

He quaked at the thought of her reading his mind. There were a lot of things in life he could handle, but he wasn't so sure that was one of them.

And I didn't read your mind. You're speaking telepathically.

He snorted. "You're crazy."

Dennis turned to look at them.

Eric said, "Hey, no talking."

Ronin shrugged. They were standing in front of the lions' pen. Tabitha walked up to the computerized lock and entered the passcode.

She opened the door and motioned her father and Ronin inside. As they stepped past her, she whispered. "Run for the trees on the left."

"And you?" Ronin asked as she stepped inside. "I'm staying right behind you."

Her father bolted. With one last look at the two men holding guns on them, she zigzagged for the trees herself, Ronin beside her.

Shots fired behind her, but they were either shooting into the air or they were lousy shots. Either way they reached the trees safely.

Her father was already there, looking around anxiously. "We have to get out of here," he cried, "before the lions find us."

"They already have." Tabitha spun around. "Nothing happens in their space without them knowing about it."

"Shit." Dennis spun around, terrified.

"Calm down. It's your fear that will set them off. Stay calm and let me handle them." He nodded and she turned to face Ronin, making sure he understood. She saw his face. "Are you hit?"

"Yeah, but it's just a scratch. I'll be fine." He lifted his arm to show her a long red streak under the tear in his shirt.

It looked raw but wasn't bad. It would sting for a while but wouldn't slow them down. Still, it had to hurt. She gave him a quick kiss. "Sorry."

He shrugged philosophically. "It could have been so much worse."

"Yeah." She gave a short hard laugh. "They could have done some target practice."

Dennis backed away from him. "No way that's nothing. That's

fresh blood. That's a dinner bell to a lion." He kept backing up. "Nothing personal, Ronin, but Jesus."

Tabitha sighed. "Stop backing up, Dad. If you get too far away from me, I can't protect you."

He stopped in his tracks. "You? Protect me? How?"

"Because the lions are already here."

Her father jumped back toward her. "Where?" he snapped.

She hated to answer him. "Nisha is above you."

She watched sympathetically as the color completely drained from the faces of the two men beside her. Poor Ronin. He'd done well so far but this… yeah, this would push the strongest of men into full-on panic. And yet he was holding on better than her father.

Her father's reaction wasn't one she'd seen him have before. But it would also explain some of the reasons why her grandfather despised him. Her grandfather would consider his obvious fear to be a weakness. Moneymaking hadn't been important to her grandfather. Animals were. If her father couldn't stand to be around the animals, then he'd be nothing in her grandfather's eyes…although her dad appeared to handle Tango and Tripod just fine. Then again, he'd met them many times. They knew him – unlike the ones out here.

She called up to the tree and the lioness watching them with interest. "Nisha, do you want to come down and meet these two men?"

At the same time, she sent Nisha a warm loving greeting to boost the continuous wave she'd been blasting out since entering the compound. There was another female in here and one big old male. Captain was old and cranky. Salba was the second female, and she was young and hyper. Tabitha expected she was racing toward them right now. Nisha was the dominant female, the hunter of the pack. The one to keep an eye on. Automatically, Tabitha did a quick scan of Nisha's energy. She looked good. Happy and calm.

But hungry.

She glanced at her watch. Feeding time. Not that the lions would be a problem. They had a great relationship. But all animal trainers knew that any animal could be dangerous.

Nisha stood up and stretched, then jumped lightly to the ground.

She walked over to Tabitha first and jumped up, placing her big paws on Tabitha's shoulders in her usual greeting, then she rubbed her face against Tabitha's head.

"Hey, baby. How are you today?" Tabitha murmured, giving the loving tabby a big hug before stepping to the side so she'd jump down. "Nisha, this is Ronin and my father."

At Nisha's head shake and snort, Tabitha laughed. "She's not impressed."

"You know," Ronin said, "that's understandable. I'd be happy to leave anytime. How about now?"

"I'd have preferred leaving ten minutes ago." Her father went to take several steps backwards.

"Don't move, Dad," she cautioned. "All animals know how to sense fear in others."

He took a shuddering breath and nodded quickly.

"Same for you, Ronin." Tabitha could feel a bright energy racing toward her. "Here's Salba. That means Captain won't be far behind."

"Oh shit. You mean there are more of them?" her father groaned softly.

"Only three here. They get along famously."

"Uh uh."

She laughed at the stiff nod from Ronin. "Hey," she said gently, "you're holding up really well."

Beads of sweat formed on his forehead and he gave a short laugh. "Like hell. But I'm still standing."

Just then, a light brown streak came flying toward him. Ronin's eyes became wide and he opened his mouth to scream. And caught it at the last second.

"Stop, Salba." The lioness roared lightly and wrapped itself around Tabitha's legs. Tabitha laughed and bent over to hug her. "Good girl." The lioness gave her a rambunctious greeting then twined her long lithe body around the men's stiff legs.

Neither moved. Neither bent to touch her. Neither breathed.

She grinned. "Doing good, guys. But there's one more."

"Hello, Captain." And she sent out a wide loving wave of cool soothing energy toward the big old male that strode toward them, his nose lifted, checking out the air. Picking up the scent of the males. The scent of the blood.

Easy, boy. We're just here to visit. All is well. She tweaked his aura, laying down a light suppression energy wave on his system. He roared, but it was a happy one. He walked up and rubbed his huge head against her ribs.

She smiled and gave the big teddy bear a scratch under his chin.

"Hey, big guy. Life is treating you pretty good, isn't it?"

He started to purr. His big diesel engine rippled outward across the countryside. Tabitha laughed and looked up at Ronin. He was staring at her in bemusement.

"He's not dangerous?"

"Oh, in the right circumstances, he's very dangerous. But with me…? No." She shook her head. "As he doesn't know you two, I laid a layer of energy to keep his hunting instincts suppressed."

"Thanks, I think."

Ronin glanced over in the direction of the road. "Nothing personal, but any chance we can get the hell out of here now?"

"WHERE THE HELL is Dennis and the others?" Germaine scanned the pen. Rocks, brush, trees. And no sign of the rest of them. "And why is there no screaming? Yelling? Hell, the damn lions should be roaring…shouldn't they?"

The two men stared at each other.

"I'm more worried about them getting away," Eric said. "There's no way they can be allowed to live at this point. We have to make sure they can't tell anyone."

Germaine groaned. "We can't go in there. We should have shot them dead and then thrown their bodies over the damn fence."

A cold hard voice spoke from behind. "A little too late for that."

Eric stiffened. "Shit."

"Don't say a fucking word," warned Germaine.

"Hey, I'm not going down for this," Eric cried. "I haven't done anything."

"Don't. Just don't. Keep your mouth shut," Germaine snapped. "They don't know anything."

"I wouldn't say that exactly. Hands out of your pockets and turn around slowly."

They turned slowly. Eric gasped. "We put you in the lions' pen!"

Roman smiled a little grimly. "Actually, you put my twin brother in there. But he's fine. No thanks to you. At least one of you, if not both of you, is a lousy shot. Not that it matters. There are cops coming up behind me."

The two men looked at each other. Then bolted into the closest field. The fence wasn't high enough to slow them down.

They heard shouting behind them, but neither of them slowed enough to make the words out. Big mistake.

Coming from the side and ripping forward at an incredible speed in their direction was another cat.

"Oh shit. That's a fucking tiger."

CHAPTER 25

Tuesday 8 am

TABITHA HEARD THE shouting. "Sounds as if help has arrived." She scanned the paths to see which would take them to the new arrivals. "The sounds are coming from over there."

"And what's over there?"

She sighed. "Tigers."

"Dangerous?"

"Remember the part about all wild animals in captivity still being wild creatures in the right circumstances?"

Then a horrific scream made her pull in her shoulders. She lay down on the gravel in front of the astonished men and jumped free of her body. In spirit form, she raced down the path toward the chaos. She could hear Boran, a big male. He was running, chasing prey, his blood pumping with the hunt.

Shit.

She slammed into him. He never faltered. Up ahead, Eric peeled across the ground at a breakneck speed. He saw the fence in front of him and flew up as high as he could go. She watched as he made it almost to the top before Boran jumped and clawed at him.

The male cat caught him by the foot. Eric screamed again and scampered up higher. Boran couldn't go any higher.

He was pissed. The man struggled at the top of the fence but it didn't have a bar to support him. He had to get over or climb back down again. He chose over.

She watched and wondered what she should do. She'd have loved to seen Boran eat him for breakfast, but that was hardly fair. Plus it might make Boran sick.

She gave Boran several good loving strokes of sympathy as he paced below the prey. *Sorry, buddy.*

Sighing, she slipped back to her body. She groaned at the harsh landing but managed to sit up fast and face the other two. "Eric is sitting at the top of the fence between the tigers."

"Between the tigers?"

"Yeah, there are two females on the other side. And Tango's pen joins in at the far end."

"He goes out with the other tigers?"

"Of course," she said. "Socializing with other tigers is important to his well being."

"Can we leave now, please?" Her father's voice quivered. "As much as I hate what Eric has done, I don't want to see him as tiger bait."

"Too late," said Ronin cheerfully. He went to take a step forward when Nisha twined around his legs. "Is it safe to leave?"

"Yes, but they are happy with the company." She bent to scratch the sides and belly of the biggest lion in her family. Captain sucked it up.

"Amazing."

She studied Ronin's face, a fat grin on her own. "You do realize you're barely reacting?"

ONCE BACK ON the path and feeling as if he'd been given a second chance at life, Ronin turned to see his brother approaching.

Roman called out, "Hey, you survived the lions?"

"Yeah, can't say I'm as bothered anymore." Ronin slapped Roman on the shoulder. "Amazing what a little hands-on experience will do for a guy."

The two brothers grinned. "If you're ready," Tabitha said, "let's get Eric down and you guys can take him away. My place is a mess and I have a lot of animals looking for food."

"Yeah, I presume you've picked up Germaine already?" Ronin asked.

"No. We think he's hiding in the one of the pens. We're looking for him now."

"Not the smartest place to hide."

"And yet you're fine."

Ronin motioned to Tabitha, who'd entered the pen where Eric hung, suspended, just out of the cat's reach. "She's the reason. I can't say for sure how these guys would act without her, but in there with her, the damn things were pussycats." Ronin shook his head. "I had no idea such a thing was possible."

"Like that?" Roman pointed out Tabitha's progress toward the tiger.

In the distance, Tabitha called, "Boran, come here, boy."

And the damn tiger barreled toward her, his big body jumping and twisting with joy.

"Jesus."

Roman stood beside his brother, watching as Boran knocked her to the ground, lay on top of her and proceeded to clean her face with long slow licks.

Eric chose that moment to sneak down the fence and bolt for the gate. Roman let him out and Ronin cuffed him. Dennis left with the police and their prisoner. Germaine had been picked up on the other side.

"Tabitha, we got Eric." Ronin called out.

She waved a hand in the air but didn't appear to be in any hurry. After a moment, she stood up and walked to a gate on the far side. From where the men stood, Ronin could see that Tango and a large golden-colored tiger were pacing on the far side. She pinned in the code at the gate and walked through to Tango.

"Boran isn't too happy to be left behind."

Ronin watched the golden tiger pace and whine at the closed gate. "Neither is the golden one," Ronin said. "She's magic with them."

"It's an energy thing."

"Can you see it? The energy stuff?" Roman asked.

"No," Ronin said, "but weird stuff is definitely happening."

"Like?" His brother slid him a long sideways look.

"I can't say exactly. It happened after the knock to my head." He shrugged. "I'll ask Stefan about it."

"It seems he's always around."

A contemplative silence fell between them.

Roman nudged him. "Is she the right one?"

Ronin didn't have to guess at his brother's meaning. "Hell, yes."

With a grin, Roman asked, "Does she know?"

"She should. It seems as if she knows everything else." Ronin laughed. "It's an odd feeling."

"You'll get used to it."

TABITHA BENT AND gave Tango a big hug. "It's been a long day, hasn't it, big guy?"

He rubbed himself all over her, hard enough to make her stumble against the fence. Boran's cold nose poked at her from the other side.

Feeling better about life than she had in a long time, she reached through and scratched his nose. "We got the guys. Somehow, we'll fix the rest of this mess."

She had to. That so many people had been involved in the damn conspiracy scared her. She'd been so unaware. It had happened under her nose and she never knew. Then her father had also been totally taken in. That had to be tough for him.

Her poor grandfather. She had avoided going through his papers, not being in great shape herself. She'd been happy to leave everything to the others. The pain had been too sharp for her to delve in any deeper until she could handle it better. Now, there was no choice. She needed to find out if anything else had gone wrong and to make sure her house was in order.

She'd spent her life helping these animals. She would make sure they were taken care of.

She glanced through the fence to see Ronin standing on the path with his brother, watching her. She waved at him. She had a mess to clean up, but with Ronin at her side and her father back in her life, she was confident she could handle it.

She opened the gate to return to Ronin's side through Boran's pen when her knees buckled.

She cried out. "Ronin!"

"Tabitha, what wrong?" Ronin cried.

The cries inside and outside overwhelmed what little clarity she had left. A roar, loud and panicked, ripped through her mind. Ripped into her body and soul.

Trinity was in trouble.

With all the chaos here, she'd forgotten about Trinity. And her own fate that was so connected to the captive tiger.

Now it was too late.

"It's Trinity!" she screamed. Through the long distance of energetic time, she heard the sound of gunshots.

Her body jerked. Once. Twice.

She looked down at her body.

Blood welled from her side, with more coming from her left hip.

"Noooo!" she screamed. *Stefan, help.*

And she collapsed.

RONIN RACED TO the fence. "Tabitha? Tabitha!"

No answer. Roman was at his side, studying the locks. "I can open this gate," he said, "but I do not know what to do about the tiger."

Ronin stared through the fence at Boran. The Bengal tiger roared fury. The gate was open between Tango and Boran, but they were more concerned with Tabitha, who'd fallen face first on the ground. They circled her, nudged her. Tabitha never moved.

"What do we do about him?"

Just then Boran roared at the top of his lungs. Then Tango answered.

"Ah shit," Ronin cried. "There's no way we can get in there."

"What about the other staff?"

"Which ones?" Ronin searched for Sue. "The ones that double crossed her to steal the damn place or the ones that worked here before that?"

"We need Stefan." Ronin was already keying in his number.

Roman looked at him quickly. "Can't you call him telepathically?"

"No idea." Ronin lifted the ringing phone to his ear. "Can you?"

"Sometimes." Roman stared back at Tabitha and the milling tigers. "I expect he's already over there with her."

"Well, he's not answering his phone."

I'm busy. Stefan's exasperated voice slipped through Ronin's head. *I can only help one of you at a time, and right now that's Tabitha.*

"What can I do to help?" Ronin rolled his eyes at his brother as he put away his phone.

Get in there and keep her safe.

"And the tigers?"

Remember that personal problem about cats you asked me to look into?

Damn, he didn't want to go in there. He'd survived because Tabitha had taken care of the lions. Now it was his turn to take care of her…and he could barely function.

You have to. Someone has to keep her safe.

STEFAN LEFT RONIN to make a decision about the cats. He had bigger issues. Tabitha had disappeared quickly. She'd had no warning. That meant the layers of calming energy she'd left surrounding Trinity had been cut through by something major. Something drastic. And there were injuries showing on Tabitha's body. Which meant, as he assumed it had something to do with the tiger, that Trinity had been the one injured.

That was no good. They had to separate Tabitha from Trinity before the tiger died. Yet Tabitha would give everything to keep that tiger alive. She invested herself a hundred percent in her animals. If she failed in this case, it could kill her too.

As he looked down at her prone body, he realized she might already be past the point of saving. Except…he could see her cord, faint and thin…and that was a first. He zipped down the path. Flying as fast as he could travel, he whipped through the ethers, desperate to keep an eye on the tricky cord as it wove in and out of the clouds. He'd never been able to see it before. He could only assume that whatever method she'd been using to return to her body had helped to strengthen it.

Animal energy surrounded it, protecting it. Tango's. Tripod's. And another one's… He'd sensed the same extra energy inside Tabitha's house – Tobias! Stefan smiled in wonder as he searched through the rest. There was a lot of Ronin's energy, but as if it wasn't sure – as if he wanted to help out but did not know how. Stefan couldn't waste any time offering suggestions.

This was it. He knew it in his heart. This was the last chance to find the tiger and save Tabitha.

Just then he saw the cord lead into a warehouse.

And could see the address.

TABITHA SLAMMED BACK into Trinity's sinewy body. And screamed. Her body twisted in agony. So much heat. So much panic. Her leg refused to work and blood dripped steadily onto the floor of the cage. And her mind was so afraid that she couldn't function. It sent her emotions immediately back into victim status.

She opened her eyes, adjusting to Trinity's sight.

Instantly, she slammed her eyes closed and opened her hearing.

"Well, she's dead. See what price you can get for her now." Footsteps strode away, angry, clipped.

"Damn it. The boss is going to get you for this," Fez blustered to the stranger's retreating form.

She re-opened her eyes as she lay down a mess of healing energy, trying to keep Tabitha alive. Trying to stop her from bleeding to death. They had to hang on. Ronin would save them.

Somehow.

She poured healing energy into the wound, into Tabitha's aging heart. She needed her to keep the faith. To keep trying. Once an animal gave up, it was almost impossible to bring them back.

The smell of blood, of fear, of death, surrounded her.

Stefan, I could really use some help.

No answer.

Crap. *Ronin, where are you?*

RONIN STARED AT the gate Roman had managed to open. He took one step forward when Stefan spoke.

3346 Calder St.

And just as fast, Stefan was gone. Ronin quickly relayed the message to Roman then took a deep breath. "You go to that end and help her there. Save the tiger."

"I'm on it. I'll take a few men from here." Roman turned away then stopped and looked back at Ronin. "What about you?"

Ronin smiled grimly. "It's time to face my past." And he turned to walk into Boran's pen.

The tiger raced toward him, his roar deafening…and freaking scary. The huge cat was going to defend Tabitha, and as far as he was concerned, Ronin was an intruder.

When Ronin approached cautiously, he heard Stefan say, *Talk to him. He's an animal. He's a feline. You have an affinity for them or else your pet wouldn't have been there in the back of your psyche all this time.*

"Haunting me, I believe you said. How is that having an affinity?"

Oh, it is. You loved him and that love is what attracts him. He needs it as much as everyone else.

"Except he's dead."

Energy never dies. Remember that rule of physics.

"And that applies now – how and why?"

Because he can help you deal with Boran.

"What?" And then he had no time to ask any more questions. Boran was on him.

Never show fear.

Ronin snorted. He took a deep breath, closed his eyes against the rush of tiger teeth.

And waited.

Nothing.

He peeked under his lashes to see Boran sniffing around his legs.

With a second deep breath, he murmured, "Hey, Boran. Let's help Tabitha, okay?" He took several steps toward Tabitha.

Boran roared again, but he seemed confused. He milled around Ronin's legs and got in the way but didn't attack. In truth, he seemed not to know what to do with Ronin.

Ronin took another step forward and Boran swatted at him. Not in anger or hunger. It was playful. Maybe. Ronin didn't want to count on that. And if the next swat was any worse, Boran would draw blood. "Boran, we have to help Tabitha. She's in a bad way."

He took another step. Boran roared. Ronin felt his throat close up. *Shit. Shit.* No time for a panic attack. Feeling like an absolute idiot but willing to try anything, he murmured, "Mr. Boots, if you're here, please tell Boran I mean Tabitha no harm."

There was a weird whooshing energy, as if a bird darted past so close to his face that he could feel the movement of the air.

Boran whined.

"It's not a good time for any of us, is it?" Ronin offered.

He had no idea if Mr. Boots was here or if he'd spoken to Boran — if he even could be, for that matter. However, Boran walked back over to Tabitha. He glanced up at Ronin as if to say, *What's taking you so long?*

Stiffening his spine and expecting to feel claws raking his side open at any moment, Ronin dropped to his knees beside Tabitha. He knew one shouldn't touch a psychic when they were deep in a session. But he had many times and so had the animals… Surely that didn't apply in Tabitha's case? She wasn't even in her body, was she?

He lifted the corner of her shirt and sucked in his breath. Bullet holes. One on the hip and one on the top of her thigh on the opposite side. Blood was slowly dripping from the wound and sliding down to pool in her flat belly.

There was no smell of gunpowder, but the blood was real.

Except there had been no shots fired. There'd been no gunfire, but the gunshot wounds were unmistakable. The smell of fresh blood was something he would never forget. The small entrance wound was clean and too damn real to ignore. He ripped off his shirt and used it to staunch the flow of blood. That it was sluggish and dark scared him. He was afraid the worst of the bleeding would be internal. He slipped a hand underneath but found no exit hole. Shit. That was so not good. He reached for his phone to call for a paramedic.

And heard Stefan's voice. *They can't help her.*

"Then who can?" he called out, grateful he was alone in the field. "There has to be someone or something that can."

Dr. Maddy. But I can't reach her.

"Where is she? We have to find her."

No. The problem is the tiger is dying. Tabitha appears to be showing the same injuries as the tiger. You need to find the tiger and try to save it.

"Roman is on his way, but what can I do from here? I can hardly leave her. Not bleeding and in the middle of two damn tigers."

Both tigers are essentially her pets.

"Yes, but she said something about laying down a level of suppression energy to keep the aggression levels of the animals down. If she's out like this, what happens to that? Will these animals turn on her?"

Interesting, murmured Stefan. *That's very clever of her. The energy stays for a long time and these animals know her.*

"Animals in captivity attack their owners and trainers all the time."

This is a very different situation.

Ronin stared down at Tabitha. Sue, one of the workers from the reserve, called out to him. "Is she okay? Have you called for an ambulance?"

Ronin shouted back, "Yes." Although it was a lie. He'd yet to call anyone. He looked down at Boran, now lying beside Tabitha.

"Do you think you can move Boran to another pen?"

Sue snorted. "If he's not hurting anything, then maybe he's better in there with you. He's very protective of Tabitha. If we try to move him he's likely to be difficult."

Ronin blew out his breath hard. *Shit.* He could feel the sweat dripping down his back, but at the same time there was this voice inside saying these reactions were what he'd expect to see. Because these were the reactions he'd always had to cats. That didn't make them real.

"So, assess," he said aloud to himself. "You're in here with two tigers. Two tigers that appear to be uninterested in your presence. You made it across the field to Tabitha. You managed to speak with Boran and now you are squatting between the two of them. Not only that, your stomach isn't attempting to empty itself. All in all, this is major progress."

Maybe Stefan was right.

I usually am.

"And always irritating," Ronin said absently as he stroked Tabitha's arms. "Are you sure there's nothing I can do from here?"

There's always something you can do. You can fill her with love, cover her with adoration and make her want to come home to you. She's using her animals to ground herself. And in a weird way, she uses lots of them. As if she doesn't believe that one will be enough. Or if one betrays her – dies, so to speak – then she'll have backup.

"Yes, that would be Tabitha," Ronin added thoughtfully. "Her grandfather. Her mother. Her father."

Exactly. Dennis was right. Her grandfather had no time or energy for humans. If you walked on four legs he'd bend over backwards to help, but in his world the two-legged animals were the ones you couldn't trust. He'd made sure she learned that.

"And he treated Tabitha that way?" Ronin asked incredulously.

Her less than the others, but his distrust encompassed everyone else. She lived with that prejudice. Was raised with it. Breathed it on a daily basis. And don't forget she was her father's daughter. Her grandfather could never reconcile himself with the parts of her father that she inherited.

"She said they were close."

He's the closest role model she had to formulate her values. There was her father, but he left. She had a fiancé and he bolted. All of this reinforcing her grandfather's views. Leaving her with only one lesson — that animals were the ones you could trust. But animals die too — and at a much younger age than humans. So she made sure she had many so that there were always some of them around to love her.

"Wow. She's really messed up because of her childhood."

And yet she's still strong, relatively sane and a good person. And most of that she learned through her relationships with animals. She learned to work with energy to help them. She could use it to help people, but she doesn't really believe they deserve it.

"Ouch. That's a little harsh, isn't it?"

Not for energy work. Look at yourself and how your relationship with animals was impacted by the death of your pet.

"That just means I was a neurotic kid who never quite grew up."

No. You're missing the other life event that happened at the time. I'd hoped you'd make the connection but...

"Now what are you talking about?"

You spent days weeping over your cat. And you blamed your father. He was the driver of the vehicle that killed Mr. Boots, wasn't he?

Ronin winced. He'd deliberately buried that fact. "Thanks for that reminder."

And do you remember what came afterward?

"No. I obviously don't want to either."

Yet it's time. You can't sit on these time bombs forever.

Ronin stared down at Tabitha. "So tell me then. We're out of time."

You told your father how much you hated him. That he was a killer and you were going to spend the rest of your life making him pay. Making killer's pay...

Horrible images flooded Ronin's mind. Him screaming at his father, who stood staring down at the still body of Mr. Boots. His mother trying to shush him. He sat back on his heels and realized this was the reason he became a cop. He wanted to make sure that others paid for what they'd done wrong.

"How can such a small incident be the driving force, a passion for a specific career?"

Because at the time, it wasn't a small incident. Your father, accident or not, had taken someone you loved.

"All my life, I was driven to be a cop..." he murmured.

And then in a nasty karmic twist, both your parents were killed and you lost them too.

Jesus.

Think about why you don't do art like your brother does.

"Because I suck at it," Ronin snorted. "Like that's hard to work out."

Because you were drawing on the sidewalk when Mr. Boots got hit.

CHAPTER 26

Tuesday mid-morning

LASSITUDE OVERTOOK TABITHA. The blood loss made her weak. And angry. With the added injuries, Trinity was likely to die. And the baby with her. Tabitha poured love and healing and caring into Trinity, trying to help her to deal with the shock, the pain and the blood loss. Trinity's heart was pumping steadily, which meant blood continued to leak from the double bullet holes. But neither were in vital spots. Neither would kill Trinity if she'd arrived in time.

Unless Trinity gave up. Damn, she needed Ronin to find them. Where was he?

And she couldn't shake the nagging suspicion that she might need to have Trinity close to her body to save her. How that would work, she didn't know. But Trinity was injured and Tabitha could help heal her. It would be much easier if she was physically there to help her. But her body was with Boran and her spirit was here with Trinity.

Stefan, I need to have my body here.

That's a little hard to do.

I know. But I think it's the only way.

I'll tell Ronin.

"YOU WANT ME to what?" Ronin sat back on his heels in shock.

Take her to Trinity.

Ronin gave a broken cry. "Isn't that going to cause more damage?"

Roman is almost at The Olde Riverside Shipyard. I'll direct you when you get closer. Grab her and go. There was a pause, then Stefan shouted, *Now!*

Shit.

Ronin hopped to his feet. His sudden action caused both tigers to rise, growling in the back of their throats.

"I don't have time for this. I have to take her somewhere and I have to take her now."

He bent down and scooped Tabitha up. Her head lolled to one side. He tried to shift her weight so he could carry her comfortably and he needed to move fast.

Boran growled.

"Damn it, you have to let me take her. Mr. Boots, tell him, for Christ's sake."

And damned if Boran didn't narrow his gaze as if he was listening to someone. The fur on the back on his spine relaxed. Not having time to waste. Ronin called back, "Thanks, Boran...and Mr. Boots." He hadn't said anything to Tango. He cast a long glance back to Tabitha's pet and said, "You know I'm helping her – right?" He kept walking forward, and damn if he didn't catch a glimpse of something... someone... inside Tango. He stopped and stared. The image disappeared. He shook his head and all but ran to the gate where Sue waited to unlock it.

"How is she?" Sue asked.

"Not good. I'm taking her to get help. I don't have time to explain. Make sure the cats are okay, please."

"They're fine. Tabitha has always been able to connect in an unearthly way with her felines."

Ronin groaned. "You don't know the half of it."

Holding Tabitha tightly, his muscles straining, he raced to his truck then struggled to get Tabitha on the front seat and buckled up safely before anyone saw what he was doing. No one would agree to him taking an injured woman into town and to a deserted warehouse.

Christ, Ronin hoped he was doing the right thing.

ROMAN CHECKED THE area. He had only three other cops here. Geoff and Carmichael were here with him and there was more spread out to cover the back of the place. Inside, the warehouse was silent. And that was unusual in itself. Either they'd been found out, or the place was deserted. According to Stefan, the tiger was here.

Somewhere. According to Tabitha, there were two men looking after her.

Apparently Ronin was on his way. With an unconscious Tabitha. This shit was freaky. He struggled to understand Ronin's decision to bring her here and not take her directly to the hospital. Perhaps she wasn't badly injured.

She is, Stefan said. *This needs to happen.*

Roman leaned up against the wall, his gun out and ready. Thankfully Ronin's men were here. He wouldn't want to deal with this without any backup.

As it was, they could be shorthanded, depending on what they found inside. Carmichael and Geoff were in front of him framing the front door. Carmichael pushed it open.

The door moved silently.

Immediately a nasty smell leaked outward.

"Oh gross," Carmichael whispered.

Roman leaned forward to see inside. The place appeared to be a huge open cavern. But it looked as if he might be in the right place. There were cages of all sizes stacked along one side and several big cages down at the far end. The smell was rank. Was anyone hosing this place down?

Down the way, they heard someone talking.

"See, I don't know if you are really in there or not, but to believe I'm talking to a lady in a tiger… That makes me crazy."

Roman almost laughed. He was definitely in the right place.

"What the hell is he talking about?" asked Carmichael in a harsh whisper.

Geoff shrugged.

Roman shook his head. There was no way to explain. And this job did make people crazy. Jesus, could this guy actually see Tabitha?

"Hell, it doesn't matter. You're not a cop anymore, Roman. Stay here with Geoff. I'll scope it out and come back."

And Carmichael disappeared inside.

TABITHA'S STRENGTH WAS waning. Trinity sucked up everything Tabitha threw at her to keep her calm and to help ease her pain. She didn't have a lot of energy left to heal the bullet holes. And the less energy Tabitha had to heal, the more agitated Trinity became and the harder it became for Tabitha to work.

And then there was Fez.

He was on guard duty. He didn't have a gun, so Tabitha was still unclear about who shot Trinity.

And then she didn't have time to wonder as Trinity growled and tried to bite her injury. Tabitha was exhausting herself trying to stop Trinity from doing more harm.

"See, if you're in there, then that's my beliefs about life and death blown right out of the water. I don't know what to do with that. I want to help you, but there's a part of me that thinks you are my meal ticket out of here. You're incredibly rare and if I find the right buyer for you... Wow, I could make a fortune. But I got to convince them you are in there. So how do I do that?"

The damn idiot didn't seem to realize that soon there was only going to be a dead carcass to sell. "You realize I'm dying in here. That you shot me and now I will not survive without medical attention."

His face lit up. "There you are! And how do you know about medical attention. Is that something animals think about?"

Oh Lord. He thought she was the animal. "Why did you shoot me?"

"Oh hey, that wasn't me. That was the buyer when he realized he'd been double crossed. And if he couldn't have you, he figured no one would." He leaned in close. "Although I'm thinking he's got a vet here right now. He could have killed the tiger but instead placed those shots so she wasn't really badly hurt by them."

Wasn't really hurt? Jesus. Maybe Fez should get shot in the same damn places and then he could decide what hurt. With great difficulty, she reined in her emotions.

"Where did he go?" She was sorry she missed seeing the asshole shooter. He's the one she really wanted. Anyone who put orders for these animals were just as culpable in her mind. She wanted to nail his ass.

"They heard something outside and disappeared." He looked around as if afraid they'd snuck up on him. "Between you and me, my boss won't tolerate this. He'll take care of that asshole – permanently."

"Take care of them?" she asked cautiously. "Like kill them?"

"Oh yeah, he'll kill them. He's killed a lot of people."

Tabitha paused her energy work long enough to study Fez's face. Because he thought she was a tiger and wouldn't be able to tell anyone, he appeared to be treating her as a confidante.

"What's your boss's name?"

"Ha. He insists I call him 'boss.' He doesn't like real names to be used." Morosely, he added, "But everyone knows my name. If anyone goes down for this, it's going to be me."

"Unless you help me."

"What can I do? I'm no vet."

"No, but men are looking for me. They are coming to help me."

He looked around fearfully. "Here?"

"I hope so," she muttered, pushing more healing energy into the injury. She had almost stopped the bleeding, but the damn bullet was still in Trinity and that was a lot harder to deal with.

Trinity would pull through if Tabitha could get her out of here. Captivity, particularly in bad situations like this, did something to the psyche of an animal. They fought it and fought it and fought it then they gave up. That was dangerous. Animals had been known to lie down and die even when nothing was physically wrong. In this case, Trinity was hurting and injured and needed to keep her spirits up.

To that end, Tabitha gently pushed a little more energy into her heart chakra. Brightening and softening, bringing light into all her dark places.

"When?" Fez cleared his throat, reminding Tabitha he was still there. She hadn't exactly forgotten, but she was struggling to keep her focus as it was. Her connection to Trinity was draining her life force at the same time as Trinity's. So the dying Trinity was trying to be saved by the dying Tabitha. She'd have laughed at that mind-bend if she could have. Instead, she just wanted to cry.

Fez cleared his throat.

She struggled to answer. It all seemed so pointless. But Tabitha knew that was Trinity's energy expressing Trinity's thoughts…her negativity. Tabitha pushed them back, fighting the depression with love. It took several minutes for the despair to leave and for her to remember that Ronin and Stefan were fighting for them. And they had friends who were coming to help.

Damn right. Stefan's voice rippled through her mind.

Oh God, Stefan. This is so hard.

Her feelings are dominating. It's a difficult thing to fight the onset of negative emotions of another soul at the same time you are absorbing her feelings.

And how, she murmured in her mind. Just his presence was light, healing, soulful. She immediately felt soothed, blessed.

And could see where she'd gotten sucked into confusion again. She had to think without her body and the experience of the physical – to be one of pure energy, pure love. To distance herself from the injured body, the pain. She could feel her spirits rising yet again. Healing energy poured into her, through her and into Trinity.

The cycle continued, each lap stronger, more powerful, more energetic. Trinity started to heal even as Tabitha watched. Trinity grabbed the energy and used it herself. Intuitively, her body knew and understood what to do. Tabitha watched as torn muscles struggled to push out the bullet, struggled to stitch the muscles together, to fill the flesh behind it. It would take time, but Trinity had turned a corner. Trinity's earthly experience wasn't over yet. Shaky but gaining strength by the minute, Trinity stood up. And roared.

Fez screamed. "Holy shit."

Footsteps sounded behind him. Fez turned and Tabitha watched as his face became respectful. "Sorry bos—"

The boss stepped back with a smile and yelled, "Police, hands up."

Fez stared in confusion.

"Put the gun down and get your hands up." When Fez stood in shock, his hands automatically going up, the boss yelled, "Now!"

Fez's arms shot straight up.

The boss brought out a second gun and fired. Then fired his police issue gun sending a second popping sound echoing throughout the vast warehouse.

Stunned, Tabitha watched Fez collapse, a red stain spreading across his chest. The boss had just shot an unarmed man. *What just happened?*

Stay quiet. Stefan whispered. *The balance of power just shifted.*

Ya think, she murmured. She stared out of the cage at the boss. Casually dressed, he held a gun as if he was used to handling one. He walked over to Fez and said in a low voice, "Fucking idiot. Do you think I was going to let you ruin things for me? Hell, I wasn't even planning to pay you."

He looked around, then carefully placed the second gun in the downed man's hand, giving the appearance the man had been armed and dangerous. Then he called out behind him, "All clear."

ROMAN HEARD THE call and came in through the back. He'd been peering through a grimy window and had seen the man go down. Until he walked closer, he hadn't seen a gun in the slain man's hand.

Then he saw the tiger and everything else went out of his mind. Jesus, she was big. Even hurt and in pain, she was a majestic animal. He walked closer to the cage slowly, trying not to set the animal off.

How could he tell if it was Tabitha?

"Tabitha?" he whispered.

The tiger turned those huge unblinking eyes on him. But there was no sign of Tabitha in them.

"Do you know this animal?" Carmichael asked.

"Maybe." Roman studied the tiger. "And maybe not." He motioned to the rest of the warehouse. "You should probably check to make sure no one else is in here."

Carmichael nodded. "Search is in progress. Although I doubt anyone is still here. I thought you were looking for a woman or something. And the tiger. But wasn't this op to find a woman?"

"Sorta." Roman walked around the tiger's cage, hoping the cop would take off and leave him alone to figure out the Tabitha-tiger thing.

He heard the other cops as they searched the area. Keeping his back to the tiger and a wary eye on the men, he called his brother on his cell phone.

"I'm pulling up outside," Ronin said. "Did you find her?"

"I think so. But there's a problem…"

CHAPTER 27

Tuesday late morning

TABITHA WATCHED THE events unfold around her. She had been able to help too, by slipping a fine strand of energy out of the cage and down to Fez. He lay still, but there wasn't a massive pool of blood.

She'd never worked on a human. Hadn't planned on doing so either, but when the need was upon her, she'd found herself wondering what a guy like Fez would do with a second chance. Besides, he'd be a perfect informant against the cop that shot him.

Unable to help herself, she slipped another stroke of energy over his body. He wasn't dead and heat pumped off his chest. She slipped her energy into the injury and down into the pool of sluggish blood pumping from the torn veins and damaged muscle. The bullet had gone in high and had gotten lodged in the shoulder blade. Therapy was going to be a bitch.

Still, if she could, she'd see to it that he stayed alive long enough to make it there. He'd do jail time unless he could cut a deal. She lifted her gaze. And stopped.

Roman.

Yes. She was saved.

He stared at her. There was no recognition in his gaze. He narrowed his gaze as if trying to see inside Trinity.

Roman? Can you see me?

No answer. No sign he was aware of her in any way. Though Fez could see her, obviously Roman couldn't.

Roman walked up behind the cage and pulled out his phone.

Please let him be calling Ronin.

RONIN WALKED SILENTLY into the vast warehouse, his gaze quickly scanning the room. He headed for the cage at the far end and tried to avoid jostling Tabitha.

"Jesus, is she dead?" Carmichael said, standing in front of him, a complete look of shock on his face at the sight of him carrying the unconscious Tabitha. "What the hell happened, Ronin? What's wrong with her? And why is she here and not at the hospital?"

"You wouldn't believe it even if I could explain." Ronin said as he laid Tabitha down on the dirty floor parallel to the cage. He straightened and turned to stare into it. A lean, mean wild looking gray – or was that blue? – furred tiger stared at him, with haunting light-green eyes. Tabitha's eyes. "Jesus. Tabitha? Are you in there?"

"Hey, Ronin. Talk to me. What is going on?" Carmichael stood over Tabitha, a worried look on his face. "And what does this have to do with Tabitha Stoddard? She's hurt bad, man. Like, really bad."

No, she wasn't, but he wasn't going to be able to explain the problem to Carmichael. Not to mention it would put everyone at risk.

"Ronin?" Roman walked over, his worried gaze on Tabitha. "How's she doing, brother?"

"The same."

"The same as what?" demanded Carmichael.

"She's somehow connected to the tiger," Ronin said shortly. What was he supposed to say?

"Connected?" Suspicion threaded through Carmichael's voice. "How?"

"Yeah, it's a little hard to explain. But she sees what it sees. Hears what it hears and is in fact," he took a deep breath, knowing how bizarre this was going to sound, "inside its body. I don't get it myself."

"What? That's crazy." Carmichael's face was a study of shock, disbelief and mockery. Slowly, uneasy suspicion filtered across his face.

"And yet it's the truth." Ronin didn't know what to do with her now. "Any time, Tabitha. If there is something else you need from me, now would be a good time to let me know."

"Did Stefan tell you what to do when you got her here?" Roman asked, standing beside his brother. "These are hardly sterile conditions."

"No." Ronin glanced up. "As always, his orders come with no explanation and of course he's not here now."

Yes, I am. And I'm monitoring the situation.

"Monitoring?"

Roman looked at him, one eyebrow raised. Ronin rolled his eyes and mouthed Stefan.

His brother gave him a hard half laugh. He knew that weird sensation of speaking out loud in answer to a conversation in his head.

"So now what?" Ronin said quietly.

The energy is…off. As if she's waiting for someone to do something.

"Hey, Ronin, you're really starting to scare me," Carmichael said. "You're talking about crazy stuff here. It's like you're in your own world and talking to no one."

"We found this guy skulking around outside." A cop pushed another man in front of them. Ronin gave him a quick perusal and recognized him as the man who'd exchanged a phone number for his cup of coffee. So he'd been involved in this mess, too.

The cop nudged the informant another few steps forward, saying. "Says his name is Keeper. And he doesn't know anything. Of course."

Typical.

Ronin turned his attention back to Carmichael.

"Actually, I am talking to someone you just can't hear." Ronin understood. He walked over to the tiger's cage and studied the big padlock. He could pick the lock if needed.

Tabitha says the key is in Fez's pocket, Stefan murmured.

Ronin walked over to the downed man and checked for a pulse. "Roman, make sure the paramedics are coming for this guy. He's still alive."

"Alive?" Carmichael spoke up. "No way. I checked."

"Well, he is." Ronin rummaged for the key and found it in Fez's right pocket. He straightened and held the key up. "Glad to see this."

But Carmichael was staring from Fez to Ronin, a calculating look on his face. Then he said, "You know Fez?"

Ronin spun on Carmichael. "Do you?"

Red washed over Carmichael's face. He blustered, "Not really."

Ronin glared at his long-time friend and co-worker while he asked his brother. "Roman, did you make the call?"

Silence.

Ronin turned to see a stranger had somehow entered from the warehouse behind the tiger's cage, and was now holding a gun on his brother. Anger lined Roman's face as he said, "Sorry, Ronin."

Shit.

Ronin took a deep breath and said, "Who the hell are you?"

"The owner of the tiger."

Ronin felt Carmichael start, as if that was news to him.

"Really? And you of course have papers saying so."

"I can produce any and all paper anyone wants," the stranger said smoothly. "Of course."

"And who did you buy the tiger from?"

The man laughed. "From the asshole holding a gun on you, of course."

Ronin turned slowly to see Carmichael standing behind him, with his police-issue revolver pointed at Ronin's chest. He wondered where Geoff and the other cop were. They should be holding Keeper in place behind him somewhere, but…

He stared into the eyes of the betrayer. "Black market animals? Where's the money in that?"

Carmichael shrugged. "I 'procure' things for people. This was the first time for a tiger." He smiled at Ronin. "And I wouldn't worry about the other two helping you out. Isn't that right, Geoff."

Geoff laughed. "True enough."

Ronin slid a gaze to his younger friend, to find him holding a gun on Keeper and the poor cop. "Both of you? You're both in on it?"

"I tried to warn you," Geoff said. "With the damn pictures."

"How is that warning me? The pictures were of Jacob not Carmichael?" Ronin couldn't believe what he was seeing. His mind raced for ideas.

And fast, please, whispered Stefan.

"Yeah, they used to be partners, remember."

Then Ronin got it. "You were hoping to have Jacob blamed if something went wrong."

"Something always goes wrong." Geoff called back, a humorous note in his voice. "Figured I'd start laying the groundwork."

"Kid's got balls," said Carmichael. "We had a good thing going for a few years. Then we heard about Jacob and some hush-hush undercover stuff. Figured we'd need to spread the suspicion a little." He chuckled. "He was a perfect patsy. Besides, he has been in trouble with Internal Affairs a couple of times. Figured they'd look real hard this time."

Carmichael glared at the stranger. "And it's not your tiger, it's mine. That deal is off. I gave you your money back."

The stranger laughed. "Like hell she's yours. You are nobody. Just one more bad cop. Big deal. There are dozens just like you. But this tiger…" He waved the gun in Trinity's direction. "I shot her." He laughed. "But look at her now. She's not only alive and well, she's stronger than ever."

The stranger's too shiny smile made Ronin stiffen. He'd seen many similar men. Guys without a conscience. Ones that would do whatever they wanted with no concern for others.

Then the stranger added, "And that makes her worth a bloody

fortune. Add in the cub…"

Not good.

"Who are you?" Ronin took a few cautious steps toward Tabitha, who lay as still as ever on the floor.

The man chuckled and then laughed. "Oh, that's rich. Winston Colby, at your service. You're trying to protect someone I'm trying to destroy. An excellent parting shot to someone else who died a week ago. But now…now everything's perfect."

Roman frowned at Ronin, a warning look his eyes.

Colby? This was the black market dealer cops had been trying to bring down for years? Ronin was confused. "I'm sorry, *what*? I'm trying to protect the tiger and Tabitha here. Who are you trying to destroy – Carmichael?"

"Not him," he corrected. "Her."

Ronin struggled to understand. "Tabitha? What has she done to you?"

"Everything. Absolutely everything." His face twisted in hate, which made Ronin take several more quick steps to stand over her protectively.

The stranger laughed. "That won't help her. I'll tell you why – she's taken everything that should have been mine. My animals, my reserve, my house…my fucking place!" He glared at Tabitha, fury shining in his gaze. "My grandfather started that place with her grandfather. They were brothers, partners. Until her grandfather cheated mine out of his half."

TABITHA WANTED TO hide. There was no where to go. Her grandfather and his brother started Exotic? She had a cousin? *This man?*

She paced the cage, the pain of betrayal firing up a horrible inner knowing that there had to be something wrong with her for all the men in her life to treat her so badly.

Trinity roared.

Shit. She shuddered, desperate to shut down the emotional pain shattering her world…before it affected Trinity and made everything worse.

Her cousin continued to speak. "My grandfather left me a letter telling me all about his cheating bastard of a brother and how he'd tricked him out of his portion of the property. My dad told me to forget about it, that there was nothing we could do." Winston laughed. "But he was wrong." He motioned the gun toward Tabitha. "I kept tabs on the family, especially Tabitha. Watched her grow up with animals that should have been mine. I sent her grandfather letters every year once I was established. Telling him about the animals I dealt in. The money I was making. And that one day…one day I'd get what was coming to me."

He shook his head. "Then the bastard up and died. I already had this tiger on order once I heard about its existence. I was going to show the old bastard what I had."

He smiled. "But this… This is even better."

Tabitha listened in horror.

"WHY THE HELL is she crying?" Winston snapped motioning to Tabitha's still form.

Ronin looked down. Sure enough, there were tears streaming down Tabitha's face. No change in her expression but for the eerie tears sliding slowly and steadily down her pale skin.

"She's crying because she didn't know. About her grandfather's actions. About her uncle or you. About the hate, distrust and fear that has tainted her family." Ronin lifted his head to stare at Winston.

Winston stared at him, his gaze narrow with suspicion, emotions flickering rapidly across his face. "How do you know that?"

Ronin kept his gaze and voice steady as he answered. "Because I know her."

That made Winston laugh. "Too damn bad. See, I heard you earlier. I figure I can have the tiger and I can have her captive inside. And isn't that some freaky shit? Is she psychic? Because that's just going to piss me off more."

"Well, if she is, then maybe you are, too," Ronin suggested. Stefan had said the same thing to him about Roman.

"Then having her as my pet tiger while I figure it out is even better." Winston peered into the cage where the tiger paced back and forth, its big head moving from side to side. "She's really in there, huh?"

He laughed, turned and shot Tabitha in the back leg.

Trinity roared, her back leg going out from under her. She twisted and snarled.

Carmichael gasped. "Holy shit. Is that for real?" He took a step closer to Tabitha staring in shock at the new wound on Tabitha's leg.

At the same time Tabitha began to bleed, blood also slipped down Trinity's fur and an eerie sound came from the back of her throat. She locked her gaze on Winston as if waiting for her chance.

Ronin dropped to Tabitha's side and clamped his hand over her wound. "You'd shoot your cousin while she's helpless? What kind of man are you?"

And immediately realized his mistake.

Winston went berserk. "I'm the man in control. And I'll fucking shoot her as many times as I want to." He fired again and the shot ricocheted off the cage. Tabitha's body jerked as the bullet grazed her arm this time. Trinity's front leg buckled. And she howled, the sounds sending ice down Ronin's back.

A gun went off, but it whistled past Ronin from behind and hit Tabitha's cousin in the shoulder. Winston screamed.

Everyone scattered for cover.

Shit. The game shifted – again. Who had fired that shot?

"Roman." He threw the key to his brother while shots fired behind them. Ronin grabbed Tabitha's arms and dragged her back around the edge of the cage to safety.

He searched the warehouse, but there was no sign of anyone else. Ronin watched as his brother raced to the cage and undid the padlock. He pulled open the bars and backed away.

Trinity jumped awkwardly. She was in obvious pain but did her best to hobble over to Tabitha.

He tried to keep Tabitha covered with his body, his own gun out in case. This was critical timing. He'd seen Winston slip around the corner of another cage. Who knew where the others had disappeared to? The poor unsuspecting cop that had been caught up in this trouble would have called for backup if he could.

But who'd shot Winston? And why did he have such poor aim?

Winston screamed from the far side, hidden in the darkness. "Stop or I'll shoot her. I'll kill my fucking cousin *and* the damn tiger. See if I care if they both die."

"Damn it, Roman," Ronin whispered. "Who shot Winston?"

"I didn't see." Roman stared down at Tabitha. "She's really connected to the tiger, isn't she?"

"Yes. And I don't know how to separate them. At this rate, she could die no matter what we do."

"What the hell?" Roman backed up slightly.

Trinity was glowing. Blue lights surrounded her large body giving her an eerie shimmering look.

"Holy crap." Geoff approached Tabitha slowly. "This is too damn bizarre."

Hearing something, Geoff spun and crouched, his gun pointed out in front of him. A gun fired. Geoff dropped in place, screaming and holding his knee to his chest.

Winston shouted, "Shut the hell up or I'll put one through your heart."

Instantly, Geoff's voice dropped to agonized sobs.

The sound of yet a different gun cocking resounded in the huge warehouse. And a strange voice said, hard, determined and very cold, "You won't be shooting anyone again. Now get those hands up."

Ronin peered out from behind the cage. "Holy shit."

Keeper, the informant he'd met, was pushing Winston toward Ronin. Keeper called out, "Ronin, you there?"

And then Ronin understood. "Hey, Jacob. Nice disguise."

Carmichael stepped out from behind the tiger's cage and walked forward, a gun in his hand. "Keeper?"

New cops poured into the place, all with guns trained on Carmichael and Winston. Geoff continued to sob from the floor in the middle.

"Drop the gun Carmichael," Keeper said. "This is over."

"What the heck?" cried out a voice from the crowd. "What is happening to *her?*"

Everyone turned to watch the tiger. Trinity stood, weak and bleeding, with a deep vibrating blue glow surrounded her. A clearly visible, luminescent light surrounded her for all to see.

And her gaze was on Carmichael. That same unholy howl from deep in the back of her throat filled the warehouse.

Carmichael backed up, his gun pointed at her. In a trembling voice, he screamed, "What the hell is she?"

"It doesn't matter to you," Keeper said, his voice hard. "Now drop the fucking gun."

Carmichael squeezed the trigger.

Trinity's body jerked once, then twice.

In a split second, Keeper dropped Carmichael where he stood.

Ronin raced forward, arms out protectively, screaming at the other cops, "Don't shoot the tiger."

Not that it mattered, Trinity had crumpled to the ground. Cops quickly raced to secure Winston.

"Jesus, Ronin," Jacob asked. "What the hell is going on here?"

Ronin shushed everyone and walked quietly, slowly toward Trinity. She lay on her side, howls and whimpers sliding out of her mouth.

"Take it easy, Trinity," Ronin soothed. "Please calm down."

Trinity struggled to her feet, her head hanging. Then gathering her strength, but obviously hurt, she staggered backwards a step before limping to Tabitha's side. Ronin whispered, "Oh Jesus. Please, sweetheart, stop. Let us help you."

Trinity collapsed beside Tabitha. Close but not touching.

Someone in the growing crowd around them asked in a prayer-like whisper, "What is happening to the woman?"

In a bizarre movement, Trinity's spirit shifted to appear to be Tabitha's spirit. Then it switched to have Tabitha's spirit change places to be Trinity's spirit. Then they switched places.

And again.

Then again.

As if some kind of electrical short was happening. The two bright-blue lights kept switching from one body to the other.

"Christ." Whispers, swear words and prayers erupted from the observers. No one had ever seen anything like this. Not even Ronin.

"Jesus," Ronin cried out. "Stop this. Stefan, help."

You're the one that's going to have to help.

"Me?"

You. You have to reach out. One hand to Tabitha and the other to Trinity. You need to ground them both. The problem is Tabitha uses her animals as a ground. Since she's connected to Trinity, Trinity used her as a ground as well. It caused an electrical loop that has shorted. You have to complete the circuit.

Ronin reached out a hand to both Tabitha and Trinity.

Roman pulled his brother's hand back. "Are you sure?" he asked urgently. "This looks incredibly dangerous."

"No choice." And there wasn't. He had to do this. Ronin closed his eyes. Reached out both hands again and….

…closed the circle.

Instantly, a thousand pins and needles pricked his hands. As if an electrical current was hitting him – but not traveling through him.

In his mind, he said, *Tabitha, I have no idea what to do but if you do, please use me as you need to. I don't want to see you in pain any longer. Let me help you.*

No, I don't want to bring you into this, Tabitha cried. *You won't survive. Let me go.*

No, Ronin whispered, *I don't accept that.*

He refused to back off. Closing his eyes, he realized there was one other element he might be able to bring into play. *Mr. Boots. If you're there. If there is anything you can do. If there is anything I can do. Please help.* Then he sent his plea out wider. *If there is any other animal out there that can help…please… Tabitha needs us.*

And with that plea, a weird buzz filled his mind. His hands tingled, his spine straightened and he threw his head back as energy surged through him. And the last of his doubts crumbled. Acceptance that there might be something to Mr. Boots followed. And that there might be something to Stefan's words about his fears, about Tabitha's skills and this crazy-ass mess they were in right now.

He took a deep breath, desperate to save Tabitha. And as he thought it, his energy went outwards to heal her. Loving energy poured from his heart into hers.

And suddenly it was as if he'd stepped into a new world. A world of no sound. A world with no visuals. A foggy world. And he moved toward a voice calling his name. "Ronin?"

He turned. There Tabitha was, standing in front of him, a huge loving smile on her face.

"You're dead?" he asked starkly, his heart ready to cry.

"No," she rushed to reassure him, "I'm not. Not at all. Look." She pointed to the side, and there was Trinity resting peacefully on her back on the ground. Except there was no ground.

"She's okay now?"

"We're in the ethers. My favorite place to retreat."

Ethers? Him? No way. Still, Ronin looked around at the bizarre world. "We're not dead?"

"No." She laughed, her face beaming with love. "We're fine."

"How do we go back?"

"As soon as you think about it, we'll go back. But there's someone who wants to say good-bye." Her voice softened. "It's past his time to go."

He looked at her in surprise. "Who?"

And then he held a wiggling black and white tuxedo cat in his arms. *Mr. Boots.* Damn. He buried his face in his beloved cat's fur, tears coming to his eyes. Christ, he felt eight years old again, his heart stuffed full with emotion. "Does he *have* to leave?"

"No. He might stay if you can see and recognize him. He's been there for you all these years. I believe he's ready to go, but what he does now…" She shrugged.

A familiar voice cut in. "Hey, Ronin, you in there?"

And pain slapped across his face hard.

"That means it's time to leave." Tabitha laughed.

Then she disappeared. He blinked then blinked again to find Roman in front of him, his hand ready to slap him again.

"I'm here," Ronin croaked.

"Good thing," his brother said worriedly. "You've been out a long time."

Ronin shook his head, struggling to shake off the fog. He twisted to look at Tabitha. To find her still lying in front of him – only this time her eyes open and she smiled at him.

Oh thank God. Swallowing hard, he held out his hand and said, "Hey."

"Hey yourself." She reached up a hand to clasp his. "Thanks."

He snorted. "I didn't do anything."

She smiled and said with a knowing look, "Trinity and I both thank you."

That's when he realized Trinity lay beside him, her big head on his legs...alive. "Whoa."

Tabitha laughed. "Yeah, welcome to my world."

"Jesus."

Roman laughed. "Well, whatever you did brother, it worked."

Tabitha sat up. "That it did."

CHAPTER 28

One month later

TABITHA OPENED THE cage wall and let both Tango and TJ into the living room. TJ tripped over his big paws in his eagerness to get to Tango. Tripod dropped his big nose and sniffed the cub hard enough to tumble TJ over on his back and keep him beside his mother. The cub yelped several times as Tripod licked his belly before letting him back on his feet.

The cub, TJ, turned around and waddled to where Trinity was resting. She'd survived against all odds, at least for a little longer. But as Tabitha had said to Ronin earlier that day, "Where there's a will, there's a way. And there is not always an explanation for miracles. You have to live with a little faith."

Well, Ronin figured he lived with a lot of faith these days. He watched little TJ get sidetracked by Ronin's scent and tumbled over toward him. His fat roly-poly body was shiny with a healthy gloss. And damn if there wasn't a slight slate gray-blue tinge to his fur.

Ronin scratched the cub under the chin then sent him back to his mother.

Trinity's engine started to rumble before he got halfway. He yelped at her then charged and barreled into her front paws. She grabbed him, flipped him over and proceeded to clean him.

"It all looks so normal, doesn't it?" he asked Tabitha as she walked back toward him. "Even Tango is okay with the new additions."

"Tango has taken to the two newcomers better than anyone could have expected," she murmured. "Then again, I explained to him what we've all been through."

Ronin grinned. "Like he'd understand that."

"You might be surprised."

He snorted. "I don't even understand everything, so how could he?"

"It's likely we'll never understand all the details," she said softly.

"And you know something? I think I'm okay with that."

"Considering you gained and lost a cousin on the same day—"

"And learned more than I wanted to about my grandfather."

He sighed. "I didn't do well with betrayal either." In fact, the department was completing a full investigation to see what else Carmichael and Geoff had been involved in. Both were in jail and would do many years. Fez had survived and was yapping pretty loud. The DA's office had cut him a deal to roll over on the others and he'd do his time back East. He'd promised to be a different man from now on. Something about having seen a vision. The DA thought he was nuts, but as long as he held up in cross-examination during the trial, they didn't care.

Ronin understood that Fez's vision had been seeing Tabitha inside Trinity. If Tabitha had helped yet another person to have a better life, then it was all good.

Tabitha wrapped her arms around his waist and looked up at him, a loving smile on her face. He was never going to get tired of that look. He bent down and dropped a kiss on her forehead.

"And through it all, I found you," she said.

"I was always here," he protested. "Always."

"But a little reserved, a little on the sidelines. Interested but not involved."

"Yeah, that sure changed." He grinned. "I'm all in now." He'd even seen vestiges of other cats that had lived here before. Tobias for one. Ronin now realized Tobias's ghost was one of the energies he'd sensed early on, adding to his haunted feeling.

"And that's the way it should be."

"You're sure Mr. Boots is gone, huh?" He asked yet again.

Tabitha was healing, Trinity was healing, and he himself was healing. But damn it, it bugged the hell out of him that Mr. Boots had been there – waiting for him all his life – and he hadn't known. Now that he understood that, he thought it was unfair Mr. Boots was gone.

And then he heard it.

A tiny, faint meow.

Tabitha raised her head from his shoulder and laughed delightedly. She whispered in his mind, *Remember, energy never disappears. It only changes form.*

There on the floor was a black and white ball of energy beside TJ. Beside, around, over and on top of the sleeping cub.

Then the meow came again. The black and white energy shifted, a long ghostly paw stretching out over the cub before sinking back down to curl up and sleep.

"Mr. Boots!"

EPILOGUE

S EVERAL WEEKS LATER, a laughing group entered the large theater. Tonight was a special session with the Portland Symphony Orchestra featuring a series of visiting musicians. Stefan held the door open for several women, all special friends in his life. Dr. Maddy dropped a kiss on his cheek as she entered with her partner, Drew, at her side. This was the first time he'd had so many of his friends in one place.

Shay linked arms with Stefan. He smiled down at her. Stefan had always been reclusive, and he still had trouble understanding how his life had suddenly become so full.

You love it. Tabitha stood in front of him, and Ronin, tall and strong, stood relaxed at her side.

Ha, says who?

Tabitha laughed, mysteriously. *Your time will come.*

He rolled his eyes and followed the group to their seats.

The lights dimmed almost immediately. He settled back to listen.

He needed this relaxing time. They all did. There'd been so much pain and panic in all of their lives, it was important to take time to enjoy the good things about life when they could. And tonight was one of those times.

Stefan didn't have a musical bone in his body. But he adored listening to all different kinds of music. It called to him in the same way colors sent him running to his canvases. The urge to create surged through him as the notes swelled and filled the theatre. The house was packed tonight, and he could easily see why.

He closed his eyes and leaned his head back, letting the powerful notes roll over him.

When the song changed, he didn't bother opening his eyes; he just waited, suspended in joy and peace.

The delicate, haunting sounds of a harp filled the air, rolling in waves across his skin. Goosebumps rose and he shivered both in joy and fascination. Who could create such beauty? Who had such power, such talent?

Beside him, he heard Tabitha gasp. Then Ronin made a comment, followed by several others who murmured in delight.

Stefan frowned, but he opened his eyes to see what they were reacting to.

Colors floated on the ethers, wide lazy bands and narrow bouncing waves. One color, then several other colors danced and played throughout the theater. Filling it with life, with joy, with happiness.

He leaned forward, amazed. It was stunning.

Dr. Maddy murmured, "It's the harpist."

Stefan followed the ribbons of colored energy back to the source and turned to study the musician. And froze. He didn't need to see the details of her face. He knew them. He didn't need to see her energy; he knew it well.

It was *her*. His beloved. The other half of himself.

And a perfect stranger.

Shay, ever perceptive, said, "I believe Tabitha mentioned that now it was *your* time – your time for love."

This concludes Books 4-6 of Psychic Visions.

Read the first Chapter of Eyes to the Soul: Psychic Visions, Book 7

SNEAK PEEK FROM PSYCHIC VISIONS: EYES TO THE SOUL (BOOK #7) CHAPTER 1

L ET ME SEE.

No. Celina Wilton shook her head, then immediately stopped. He couldn't see her. And no movement was going to stop the voice in her head. The cruel, cunning voice of a predator. One who'd found his prey. And like most predators, he loved to torment his victim.

It was unthinkable. She – a ghost-whisperer of today – herself now haunted in the very worst of ways.

Let me see.

No. She refused to give him what he wanted.

I won't go away. You know that.

And I won't let you see. No matter how long it takes.

Soft, mocking laughter filled Celina's head. She trembled. Who was this evil soul? Why was he doing this? She'd asked, but he hadn't yet answered. He had something else on his mind. Plans. She desperately wanted to know what they were, but didn't dare give him the satisfaction.

It will take forever…and I have more time than you.

Not if I have anything to say about this. But did she?

She hoped so. But she hadn't found a way to change the situation yet. She needed someone to help her. Only there wasn't anyone in this world that could. She'd been caught in a web of her own making, thinking she knew what she was doing – until this evil found her. And taught her a major lesson – that she really knew nothing. That being able to see a ghost or two did not make her a pro. That she was an innocent in a world she thought was safe and easy, only to find predators lurking in the shadows. It was a sign of her own naiveté that she hadn't known predators *could* exist in this ghost world.

She wished she could turn back time to when she'd seen her first ghost and ignore him. If only she'd treated him as the fantasy figure her friends had all said he'd been.

Except then she'd have missed communicating with Caslo, her childhood friend. Her dead best friend.

She felt so alone.

Like she'd always been alone.

Right now she was surrounded by people as the orchestra broke up for the last practice before the new show opened. Chairs were shuffled back and cases opened, voices raised in laughter.

Celina waited for the noise to die down.

"Celina, are you coming out for a drink?" Jacob Coburn, friend extraordinaire, asked from beside her.

"I was thinking that an evening at home would be better. I could use a good night's sleep before the big performance." She reached for her purse behind her chair and double checked the clasp, her hands sound and sure. She'd been living without her eyesight for so long that this was normal. Natural. She stopped just short of thinking *comfortable*. There was nothing comfy about this.

There also wasn't anything natural about people's responses to finding out she was blind, the pity in their voices.

She was blind. Not deaf, regardless of the often hushed whispers, nor dumb, even though many friends instinctively jumped up to answer for her. Being used to others' behavior didn't make it easier.

And Celina hated being called disabled or *worse* – differently abled. That was not her. Would never be her. Her condition was a stumbling block on the pathway of life and for – her – a handicap. She was handicapped regardless of politically correct terms. Besides, she wasn't *completely* blind.

She could see shadows sometimes, but not always and only if she strained her eyes.

"Come on. One drink won't make a difference, surely." He hesitated then added, "Besides, I want you to meet a friend of mine. He's planning on joining us."

She paused, closing her violin case before choosing her words carefully. "Where are you going?"

"To Chico's."

She stilled. Why there? It had to be a coincidence. They couldn't know. She didn't dare tell them. Their sympathy would be more than she could stand.

"I'll drive you home afterwards. Just one drink to celebrate all of our hard work," he said in a coaxing tone.

She could hear the smile in his voice. Jacob knew her too well. Knew how to get her cooperation.

"Opening night is tomorrow, and after that we won't have a chance for weeks," he said. "We've got this. But it took tons of effort – team effort – and the team wants to celebrate…"

"And I'm part of the team," she finished for him. There was no arguing the logic. And one drink wouldn't hurt her. In fact, it might just ease her tension for the coming night. Then again, all nights were tough these days. But why Chico's? Any place but there.

As if hearing her thoughts Jacob added, "Chico is putting on a special deal for us. He's expecting us."

Crap. Of course he was. That old man was generous to a fault.

"Fine. One drink," she said, giving in with a gentle smile.

Bruce walked past, clanging metal to metal. "A big drink then, if it's only one." More metal clanged, letting her know he was busy collecting the music stands to carry off to one side. Bruce played the drums and could have played with the best rock bands in the world, but the classics had stolen his heart.

"I'll be done here in a moment. Mind if I catch a ride with you two?" Bruce asked, his voice fading slightly as he walked away. "I'll take a cab home afterward."

"Sure thing," Jacob said to Bruce, and to Celina, "I'll go lock up your harp."

"Thanks." Chico's? Well if she had to… she could do this, like she'd done so much before. With a deep breath, she put on her sweater, grabbed her purse, walking stick and stood. Bruce snagged the chair as she left it. "Don't sit back down. There's no chair any longer."

"As always." She smiled. "You're always stealing the chair out from under me."

"I wait for you to stand," he protested, but the smile in his voice was that of a young boy playing tricks. Still his words reminded her that he was always careful to tell her when he took her chair.

"You do. Barely," she teased.

"Complain, complain, complain. Good thing you're so beautiful, with alabaster skin, that jet black hair. And those eyes…" He gave an exaggerated swooning sigh then added, "Not to mention having a voice like an angel, otherwise we might not put up with you." Bruce walked back toward her, his shoes echoing in the almost empty hall. He laughed. "Who am I kidding? With just one of those qualities we'd still be hanging around like smitten puppies."

Celina snickered. "As if. You all have the women sniffing around you now. There's a different woman in your bed every night. Just because I'm blind doesn't mean I can't see."

"How the hell you do that I don't know." Jacob protested, his voice moving closer to them. At her side again, he added, "Besides, *I* don't have a different woman in my bed."

Celina leaned closer and whispered, "That's because it's a different guy instead."

Jacob gasped, an embarrassed pause filling the air. He whispered in a shocked voice, "How the hell would you know?"

"The different men's aftershave that clings to you. Men usually stick to one kind. And you're often surrounded by different ones."

"Damn, really?" His voice full of chagrin as he said, "I shower every day."

"Yeah. Those goodbye kisses must be dynamite."

Jacob's lusty laughter rolled through the almost empty music hall. "Oh, they are – they are."

"Besides," she added because she couldn't resist. "Your voice also deepens when you're around an attractive male."

"Oh no." Bashfulness colored his voice. "I had no idea."

"Most people wouldn't notice," she reassured him. "But my senses are sharper than most people's."

"Ugh," Jacob grumbled. "Still, it's a little unnerving to consider anyone being able to notice such mannerisms."

A heavier footstep walked toward them. Jacob leaned closer and whispered, "You won't tell anyone, will you?"

"I haven't yet." She reached out a hand and patted his shoulder, hitting him somewhere around the collarbone. "The world is a little more accepting now…"

"But the music world is very small. And not that accepting."

"I won't say anything," she promised. "Of course, my silence might require a drink to seal it."

"Blackmailing me, are you?" His voice was overly hearty as Bruce walked over.

"What's she blackmailing you for?" Bruce asked. "Maybe I can get in on this deal."

Celina's laugh tinkled freely across the spacious room. "Go find your own deal to make. This one is mine." With that she walked toward the exit.

"Wait for us," Jacob called out, the clipped sound of his footsteps echoing as he raced to catch up.

She put out a hand to grab the large square handle on the big double doors when Jacob said, "I've got it." The heavy door whooshed open. Cooler air hit her in the face as she walked through the small entrance room to the exit. She waited, a small smile on her face, for Jacob to open the exterior door for her.

The fresh air rushed to greet her. She tilted her face slightly into the breeze, loving the wash of coolness. Portland street sounds and smells greeted her. Gasoline. Car engines, people joking and laughing. The hum of an everyday evening.

She tilted her head, straining her senses, searching for something, anything other than what was on the surface. A habit she couldn't break since her accident.

And found nothing. Thank heavens. She had no idea what she'd do if she ever did – it hadn't happened yet.

"Are you all right?"

She started, then relaxed. "I'm fine. It looks like a beautiful night out."

"It is, but how you could know that I'll never understand."

With a smirk his way she stepped out into the night.

THE BAR WAS hopping. Celina didn't need to get any closer than the curb to hear the music flowing out of the pub in front of her. Lights flashed and bounded behind her eyelids as she faced the building. "Surely they don't have an old disco ball in there, do they?" She laughed as the colors flashed her way again.

Jacob approached from the right, his steps tired, heavier on the weaker left leg, his laughter bright regardless of his obvious fatigue. Excited. Almost too excited. She tucked that away inside.

"They do indeed. This place hops all the time. Come on, let's go find the others." Jacob grasped her elbow gently and tugged her toward the noise. She couldn't explain the instinct to pull back. Jacob's touch? Or the destination? She'd been to many a pub over the years and several of those same ones since her accident and subsequent eye surgery.

At this time of night the pub was loud, as in it was possibly too much of a good thing. She'd prefer a glass of white wine in the corner by a fireplace listening to live music. This felt like tequila shots being egged on by everyone in the room.

She sighed inwardly. She only had to stay for one drink, and hers wouldn't be a shot of anything. She'd have a Baileys and coffee if she could. Although caffeine wasn't the best thing at this time of night either.

"Just one drink, then I'll take you home." Jacob said quietly from her side, as if understanding her reticence.

"And I'm going to hold you to that," she muttered as Bruce opened the door and she was hit by the full blast of music and people spilling into the entranceway. Jacob tightened his grip on her arm and half-led, half-dragged her forward through the ruckus.

"Celina's here!"

A cry went up to her left as Jacob nudged her into the large group.

The fun was infectious, loud – and, as it included her, irresistible. She was grabbed and hugged, her cheeks bussed as people talked to her, over her and around her.

She recognized most of the people by their voices, some by their hugs and others that just felt the need to keep a hand on her.

That was another thing she didn't understand. Once she became blind, so many people seemed to feel that her ability to recognize them would be enhanced by physical contact – at least she assumed that was the cause. They were right, but not in any way that they'd understand. With her eyes closed and her sight gone, she couldn't see the bright colors that filled the pub. They were still there, she knew – she'd seen enough of them over the last several decades – and to a certain extent she still saw a pale ghost of them now.

The bright colors were one of the things she missed most about not being able to see. The vibrant, moving ribbons of sound – especially when she played. They used to fill her eyes with tears; then she realized that she was the only one who could see them. It was such a disappointment to have lost the brilliance of those colors with the loss of her eyesight. That she could see them at all now was wonderful, but... it wasn't the same. She'd thought of herself as both a musician and an artist, controlling the colors as they danced to the notes she played. She made artistic creations in the air while her music was art for the ears.

It hadn't taken her long to accept that the visual art was a gift even if she was the only one who could see it – and was still a gift in faded form.

And with so few gifts in her life, she'd been happy to have what little there were. Although she'd had a few low spots in her life, she'd also been blessed.

She needed to remember that.

"What took you guys so long?" Cindy asked beside her. Cindy played a wicked trombone and couldn't sing a note, much to her chagrin.

"Just cleaning up behind you," Bruce teased. "Everyone raced out so fast no one took the time to clean up."

"Ah, well. What would we do without you?" Cindy moved something that tinkled – ice in a tall glass – past Celina. "Here, the first drink is on me as thanks!"

Jacob laughed. "Well, in that case…" He took a long drink. Celina could hear him swallowing. He was that close to her.

"Celina, what will you have?"

She started at Cindy's question, the word *nothing* on the tip of her tongue. Bruce spoke up before she could and said, "She'd like a glass of white wine."

"I do, do I? Maybe I want something else," she said. The instant spark of anger felt odd inside. She didn't want to be here and really didn't want people answering questions for her – even if they were decent answers.

What was wrong with her today? She shouldn't be so waspish. He was only trying to make it easy on her. Like everyone tried to make everything easy on her. There was just no making this…easy.

I can make it easy. Just let me see.

No. Never.

I can do it without you, but it would be more fun with you.

No. Killing people is not fun.

Oh, it so is.

That dry dusty chuckle reverberated inside her head. She trembled.

Especially when no one knows who I am, the nasty voice whispered. *Or what I can do.*

I don't even know what you can do. I don't want to know, she cried silently in her mind. How had her life come to this?

That's easy. You wanted me here You wanted to have your eyesight back – so I stepped in to help you.

No. No. She shook her head.

Oh yes. See, you still don't believe me. Or understand why. That's funny. I'm so going to enjoy your reaction when you do find out about me. He laughed. *Maybe a little proof is needed.*

What? No. She shook her head, not caring if other people stared at her strangely. She knew she'd become odd this last year, but who could blame her? She'd lost her fiancé a year ago from an aneurysm. She'd been involved in a serious car accident three weeks later. And it had been bad enough she'd ended up with several busted ribs and a head injury, with her eyesight compromised by the trauma that even surgery hadn't been able to fix. Then to top it all off, she had somehow collected a vengeful ghost. One who wanted her to believe he could do so much.

She was being haunted. If such a thing were possible.

No proof. Please, she whispered in her head. *I believe you.*

No. I don't think you do. So give me a moment. I've been planning something like this for a while. It's the perfect time. This way you'll know for sure.

The weird blackness left her mind. Thank heavens. She needed help. Someone who could understand what she was going through. But it wasn't exactly something she could go to a doctor for. And a psychologist would have a heyday inside her head. Weren't there enough people in there already?

Bruce lifted his glass beside her, the ice smaller, softer, clinking softly along the glass. "Another. I want a couple of tequila shooters," he cried. His suggestions brought on screams for shooters.

Celina sank back into the booth beside Jacob. She wanted to leave. She didn't know what kind of proof this evil thing inside of her was going to offer, but she wanted no part of it.

"Are you okay, Celina? You look ill."

"I'm not feeling well. Please, I know I haven't finished my wine." In fact, she hadn't touched it. "But I'd really like to go home."

Cheers broke out beside her. Instinctively she turned. "What are they doing now?" she asked.

"Just tequila shots." The tone of his voice sounded slightly odd. She stilled, her mind racing to turn the suspicions and fear squeezing her chest into something calming. She had to get out of here. Now. Urgency had her lurching to her feet. She struggled to find the entrance to the pub. She stumbled into one person and bounced off another. "Sorry," she said. "Sorry, I'm sorry. I'm just trying to get some fresh air."

"Celina, wait."

But she couldn't. An inner drive propelled her forward to the entranceway, only she was jostled from one side to the other with no room for her walking stick. And the entranceway was no longer where it should have been. She hit a wall. Hands out, she scrambled back as far as she could down that wall.

Under all the loud music and laughing a roar built. No one appeared to notice. She tilted her head, listening as the sound rapidly grew.

In the background, as if in a movie on slow motion, she heard the first screams. Then more.

Then the sound of a huge roar. A crash. Panicked cries. Glass shattering, sprinkling down on everything and everyone.

Finally silence. The horrible, deafening silence.

Celina waited, shock, fear, terror holding her locked in place. She couldn't see. She could only hear. She bowed her head. Fatalistically, she turned ever so slowly to stare blindly at the blank chaos in front of her. She could only imagine the scene.

A woman screamed. And screamed. A man groaned. Then another one off to the side started to cry.

"Help me," a woman whispered close to Celina. "Please help me."

Celina reached out a hand in her general direction and was jerked forward as the woman clutched at her and tried to pull. "I'm here. But I don't know what happened."

"I don't know." The woman started to sob. "Help me, please. I'm hurt."

Instinctively Celina crouched at the injured woman's side, patting her hand gently. There wasn't much she could say, but she knew comforting sounds were coming from her mouth.

People moved slowly amidst the cries of pain and the weeping. Something dreadful had happened but she had no idea what could have taken place.

A man in front and off to the left of her said, "A large truck drove into the front of the pub. He's halfway inside the damn room. He's hit dozens and probably killed half of those."

Oh no. Her heart seized as she turned to face the chaos. "Jacob? Bruce? Are you okay?"

There was no answer.

"Jacob!" she screamed. "Where are you?"

She couldn't hear any response over the building noise as people cried out for help and still others wept for their friends and family.

She tried to control her panic. *Oh God. No. Please, not my friends.*

She didn't dare try to find them in the mess. She gazed in the direction of the injured woman, her hand gently patting her on the shoulder. She'd never felt so helpless. How had this just happened? And why? And did the predator have anything to do with it? Her heart pounded in her chest and she could barely breathe. And that's when she heard something else.

Silence – from the woman whose hand she held. Silence, where moments before there'd been raspy breath. Silence, where moments before there'd been broken weeping. Celina stroked up the woman's arm to her throat and pressed two fingers against her sticky skin.

And bowed her head. The woman was dead.

No, her heart screamed in denial. This couldn't be happening. They'd just come for a fun hour of celebration. Not this life-changing disaster.

She'd already survived one of those. She wouldn't wish anything like that on anyone. And never twice.

Underneath her sorrow and budding grief, she heard that hateful laugh inside her head.

What do you think? Was that enough proof?

She froze. *Oh God. No!*

Oh yes. Do you believe me now?

Books 7–9 are available now!

To find out more visit Dale Mayer's website.

https://geni.us/dmpv7-9

Simon Says...: Kate Morgan
(Book #1)

Welcome to a new thriller series from *USA Today* **Best-Selling Author Dale Mayer. Set in Vancouver, BC, the team of Detective Kate Morgan and Simon St. Laurant, an unwilling psychic, marries all the elements of Dale's work that you've come to love, plus so much more.**

Detective Kate Morgan, newly promoted to the Vancouver PD Homicide Department, stands for the victims in her world. She was once a victim herself, just as her mother had been a victim, and then her brother—an unsolved missing child's case—was yet another victim. She can't stand those who take advantage of others, and the worst ones are those who prey on the hopes of desperate people to line their own pockets.

So, when she finds a connection between more than a half-dozen cold cases to a current case, where a child's life hangs in the balance, Kate would make a deal with the devil himself to find the culprit and to save the child.

Simon St. Laurant's grandmother had the Sight and had warned him that, once he used it, he could never walk away. Until now, her caution had made it easy to avoid that first step. But, when nightmares of his own past are triggered, Simon can't stand back and watch child after child be abused. Not without offering his help to those chasing the monsters.

Even if it means dealing with the cranky and critical Detective Kate Morgan …

Find Simon Says… Hide here!
To find out more visit Dale Mayer's website.
https://geni.us/DMSSHideUniversal

Author's Note

Thank you for reading Psychic Visions, Books 4-6! If you enjoyed the book, please take a moment and leave a short review.

Dear reader,

I love to hear from readers, and you can contact me at my website: www.dalemayer.com or at my Facebook author page. To be informed of new releases and special offers, sign up for my newsletter or follow me on BookBub. And if you are interested in joining Dale Mayer's Reader Group, here is the Facebook sign up page. http://geni.us/DaleMayerFBGroup

Cheers,
Dale Mayer

About the Author

Dale Mayer is a *USA Today* best-selling author, best known for her SEALs military romances, her Psychic Visions series, and her Lovely Lethal Garden cozy series. Her contemporary romances are raw and full of passion and emotion (Broken But ... Mending, Hathaway House series). Her thrillers will keep you guessing (Kate Morgan, By Death series), and her romantic comedies will keep you giggling (*It's a Dog's Life*, a stand-alone novella; and the Broken Protocols series, starring Charming Marvin, the cat).

Dale honors the stories that come to her—and some of them are crazy, break all the rules and cross multiple genres!

To go with her fiction, she also writes nonfiction in many different fields, with books available on résumé writing, companion gardening, and the US mortgage system. All her books are available in print and ebook format.

Connect with Dale Mayer Online

Dale's Website – www.dalemayer.com
Twitter – @DaleMayer
Facebook Page – geni.us/DaleMayerFBFanPage
Facebook Group – geni.us/DaleMayerFBGroup
BookBub – geni.us/DaleMayerBookbub
Instagram – geni.us/DaleMayerInstagram
Goodreads – geni.us/DaleMayerGoodreads
Newsletter – geni.us/DaleNews

Also by Dale Mayer

Published Adult Books:

Shadow Recon
Magnus, Book 1

Bullard's Battle
Ryland's Reach, Book 1
Cain's Cross, Book 2
Eton's Escape, Book 3
Garret's Gambit, Book 4
Kano's Keep, Book 5
Fallon's Flaw, Book 6
Quinn's Quest, Book 7
Bullard's Beauty, Book 8
Bullard's Best, Book 9
Bullard's Battle, Books 1–2
Bullard's Battle, Books 3–4
Bullard's Battle, Books 5–6
Bullard's Battle, Books 7–8

Terkel's Team
Damon's Deal, Book 1
Wade's War, Book 2
Gage's Goal, Book 3
Calum's Contact, Book 4
Rick's Road, Book 5

Kate Morgan

Simon Says… Hide, Book 1
Simon Says… Jump, Book 2
Simon Says… Ride, Book 3
Simon Says… Scream, Book 4
Simon Says… Run, Book 5

Hathaway House

Aaron, Book 1
Brock, Book 2
Cole, Book 3
Denton, Book 4
Elliot, Book 5
Finn, Book 6
Gregory, Book 7
Heath, Book 8
Iain, Book 9
Jaden, Book 10
Keith, Book 11
Lance, Book 12
Melissa, Book 13
Nash, Book 14
Owen, Book 15
Percy, Book 16
Quinton, Book 17
Hathaway House, Books 1–3
Hathaway House, Books 4–6
Hathaway House, Books 7–9

The K9 Files

Ethan, Book 1
Pierce, Book 2
Zane, Book 3
Blaze, Book 4
Lucas, Book 5

Parker, Book 6

Carter, Book 7

Weston, Book 8

Greyson, Book 9

Rowan, Book 10

Caleb, Book 11

Kurt, Book 12

Tucker, Book 13

Harley, Book 14

Kyron, Book 15

Jenner, Book 16

The K9 Files, Books 1–2

The K9 Files, Books 3–4

The K9 Files, Books 5–6

The K9 Files, Books 7–8

The K9 Files, Books 9–10

The K9 Files, Books 11–12

Lovely Lethal Gardens

Arsenic in the Azaleas, Book 1

Bones in the Begonias, Book 2

Corpse in the Carnations, Book 3

Daggers in the Dahlias, Book 4

Evidence in the Echinacea, Book 5

Footprints in the Ferns, Book 6

Gun in the Gardenias, Book 7

Handcuffs in the Heather, Book 8

Ice Pick in the Ivy, Book 9

Jewels in the Juniper, Book 10

Killer in the Kiwis, Book 11

Lifeless in the Lilies, Book 12

Murder in the Marigolds, Book 13

Nabbed in the Nasturtiums, Book 14

Offed in the Orchids, Book 15

Poison in the Pansies, Book 16

Quarry in the Quince, Book 17
Revenge in the Roses, Book 18
Lovely Lethal Gardens, Books 1–2
Lovely Lethal Gardens, Books 3–4
Lovely Lethal Gardens, Books 5–6
Lovely Lethal Gardens, Books 7–8
Lovely Lethal Gardens, Books 9–10

Psychic Vision Series

Tuesday's Child
Hide 'n Go Seek
Maddy's Floor
Garden of Sorrow
Knock Knock...
Rare Find
Eyes to the Soul
Now You See Her
Shattered
Into the Abyss
Seeds of Malice
Eye of the Falcon
Itsy-Bitsy Spider
Unmasked
Deep Beneath
From the Ashes
Stroke of Death
Ice Maiden
Snap, Crackle...
What If...
Talking Bones
Psychic Visions Books 1–3
Psychic Visions Books 4–6
Psychic Visions Books 7–9

Heroes for Hire

SEALs of Steel

Badger: SEALs of Steel, Book 1
Erick: SEALs of Steel, Book 2
Cade: SEALs of Steel, Book 3
Talon: SEALs of Steel, Book 4
Laszlo: SEALs of Steel, Book 5
Geir: SEALs of Steel, Book 6
Jager: SEALs of Steel, Book 7
The Final Reveal: SEALs of Steel, Book 8
SEALs of Steel, Books 1–4
SEALs of Steel, Books 5–8
SEALs of Steel, Books 1–8

The Mavericks

Kerrick, Book 1
Griffin, Book 2
Jax, Book 3
Beau, Book 4
Asher, Book 5
Ryker, Book 6
Miles, Book 7
Nico, Book 8
Keane, Book 9
Lennox, Book 10
Gavin, Book 11
Shane, Book 12
Diesel, Book 13
Jerricho, Book 14
Killian, Book 15
Hatch, Book 16
Corbin, Book 17
The Mavericks, Books 1–2
The Mavericks, Books 3–4
The Mavericks, Books 5–6
The Mavericks, Books 7–8

The Mavericks, Books 9–10
The Mavericks, Books 11–12

Collections
Dare to Be You…
Dare to Love…
Dare to be Strong…
RomanceX3

Standalone Novellas

It's a Dog's Life
Riana's Revenge
Second Chances

Published Young Adult Books:

Family Blood Ties Series

Vampire in Denial
Vampire in Distress
Vampire in Design
Vampire in Deceit
Vampire in Defiance
Vampire in Conflict
Vampire in Chaos
Vampire in Crisis
Vampire in Control
Vampire in Charge
Family Blood Ties Set 1–3
Family Blood Ties Set 1–5
Family Blood Ties Set 4–6
Family Blood Ties Set 7–9
Sian's Solution, A Family Blood Ties Series Prequel Novelette

Design series

Dangerous Designs

Deadly Designs
Darkest Designs
Design Series Trilogy

Standalone
In Cassie's Corner
Gem Stone (a Gemma Stone Mystery)
Time Thieves

Published Non-Fiction Books:

Career Essentials
Career Essentials: The Résumé
Career Essentials: The Cover Letter
Career Essentials: The Interview
Career Essentials: 3 in 1